THE MAMMOTH BOOK OF
LEGAL THRILLERS

Also available

The Mammoth Book of Ancient Wisdom
The Mammoth Book of Arthurian Legends
The Mammoth Book of Battles
The Mammoth Book of Best New Horror 2000
The Mammoth Book of Best New Science Fiction 13
The Mammoth Book of Bridge
The Mammoth Book of British Kings & Queens
The Mammoth Book of Cats
The Mammoth Book of Chess
The Mammoth Book of Comic Fantasy
The Mammoth Book of Dogs
The Mammoth Book of Erotica
The Mammoth Book of Gay Erotica
The Mammoth Book of Haunted House Stories
The Mammoth Book of Heroic and Outrageous Women
The Mammoth Book of Historical Detectives
The Mammoth Book of Historical Erotica
The Mammoth Book of Historical Whodunnits
The Mammoth Book of How It Happened
The Mammoth Book of International Erotica
The Mammoth Book of Jack the Ripper
The Mammoth Book of Jokes
The Mammoth Book of Lesbian Erotica
The Mammoth Book of Lesbian Short Stories
The Mammoth Book of Locked-Room Mysteries and Impossible Crimes
The Mammoth Book of Men O'War
The Mammoth Book of Murder
The Mammoth Book of New Erotica
The Mammoth Book of New Sherlock Holmes Adventures
The Mammoth Book of Nostradamus and Other Prophets
The Mammoth Book of Oddballs and Eccentrics
The Mammoth Book of Private Lives
The Mammoth Book of Seriously Comic Fantasy
The Mammoth Book of Sex, Drugs & Rock 'n' Roll
The Mammoth Book of Short Erotic Novels
The Mammoth Book of Sports & Games
The Mammoth Book of Sword and Honour
The Mammoth Book of Tasteless Lists
The Mammoth Book of the Third Reich at War
The Mammoth Book of True War Stories
The Mammoth Book of 20th Century Ghost Stories
The Mammoth Book of Unsolved Crimes
The Mammoth Book of War Diaries and Letters
The Mammoth Book of the Western
The Mammoth Book of the World's Greatest Chess Games

THE MAMMOTH BOOK OF
LEGAL THRILLERS

Edited by Michael Hemmingson

ROBINSON
London

Constable Publishers
3 The Lanchesters
162 Fulham Palace Road
London W6 9ER
www.constablerobinson.com

First published in the UK by Robinson,
an imprint of Constable & Robinson Ltd 2001

Collection and editorial material
copyright © Michael Hemmingson 2001

A copy of the British Library Cataloguing in
Publication Data is available from the British Library.

ISBN 1–84119–266–X

Printed and bound in the EU

Contents

ACKNOWLEDGMENTS

"Night of Silken Snow" by Francis M. Nevins, Jr, first appeared in *Ellery Queen's Mystery Magazine,* copyright © 1994 by Francis M. Nevins, Jr. Reprinted by permission of the author.

"Veil's Visit" by Joe R. Lansdale and Andrew Vachss, first appeared in *Veil's Visit* (Subterranean Press), copyright © 1999 by Joe R. Lansdale and Andrew Vachss. Reprinted by permission of the authors.

"Oh, Brother" by Mark Leyner, first appeared in *Tooth Imprints on a Corndog,* copyright © 1995 by Mark Leyner. Reprinted by permission of Harmony Books.

"Reasonable Doubts" by Michael A. Black, first appeared in *Detective Mystery Stories,* copyright © 1999 by Michael A. Black. Reprinted by permission of the author.

"The Tender Offer" by Louis Auchincloss, copyright © 1955 by Louis Auchincloss. Reprinted by permission of the author.

"Pleading Guilty" by Scott Turow, from *Pleading Guilty,* copyright © 1993 by Scott Turow. Reprinted by permission of Farrar, Straus, and Giroux.

"The Case for the Defence" Graham Greene, from *Collected Stories,* copyright © 1967 by Graham Greene. Reprinted by permission of Penguin Publishing.

"A Great Dance" by John F. Dobbyn, first appeared in *Ellery Queen's Mystery Magazine,* copyright © 1998 by John F. Dobbyn. Reprinted by permission of the author.

"The Partner" by John Grisham, from *The Partner,* copyright © 1997 by John Grisham. Reprinted by permission of Random House.

"Triumph of Justice" by Irwin Shaw, from *Five Decades,* copyright © 1978 by Irwin Shaw. Reprinted by permission of Bantam Doubleday Dell.

"Dogs and Fleas" by John Lutz, copyright © 1997 by John Lutz. Reprinted by permission of the author.

"Speedball" by Brian Hodge, copyright © 2001 by Brian Hodge. Printed by permission of the author.

"The Pardon" by James Grippando, from *The Pardon,* copyright © 1994 by James Grippando. Reprinted by permission of the author.

"Best in the Business" by Tom Sweeney, copyright © 2001 by Tom Sweeney. Printed by permission of the author.

"Bail Hearing" by Morris Hershman, first appeared in *Mike Shayne's Mystery Magazine,* copyright © 1981 by Morris Hershman. Reprinted by permission of the author.

"Thicker than Water" by Henry Slesar, copyright © 2001 by Henry Slesar. Printed by permission of the author.

"When Randolph Woke Up" by Kevin L. Donihe, copyright © 2001 by Kevin L. Donihe. Printed by permission of the author.

"The Case of the Crying Swallow" by Erle Stanley Gardner, copyright © 1997 by the Estate of Erle Stanley Gardner. Reprinted by permission of the Estate of Erle Stanley Gardner.

"Waiting for Alaina" by O'Neil De Noux, copyright © 2001 by O'Neil De Noux. Printed by permission of the author.

"Hard Getaway" by Robert J. Hoyden, copyright © 2001 by Robert J. Hoyden. Printed by permission of the author.

"The New Lawyer" by Mike Wiecek, copyright © 2001 by Mike Wiecek. Printed by permission of the author.

"White Russian" by Michael Hemmingson, copyright © 2001 by Michael Hemmingson. Printed by permission of the author.

"The Formula" by Marc Lodge, from *Alfred Hitchcock's Mystery Magazine,* copyright © 1994 by Marc Lodge. Reprinted by permission of the author.

"Unreasonable Doubt" by K.L. Jones, copyright © 2001 by K.L. Jones. Printed by permission of the author.

"A Murder Coming" by James Powell, copyright © 1972 by James Powell. Reprinted by permission of the author.

"The Adventure of the Nefarious Nephew" by Michael Mallory, copyright © 1999 by Michael Mallory. Printed by permission of the author.

"Prayer Denied" by Jeremy Russell, copyright © 2001 by Jeremy Russell. Printed by permission of the author.

INTRODUCTION

There's been a long-standing pop culture intrigue with the courtroom drama – both true and fictional. From classics such as *Twelve Angry Men* to the implausible cases of Perry Mason, to the more recent mega-bestseller status of novels by Grisham and Turow, to the world's watching of live broadcasts of the O.J. Simpson and Lorena Bobbit trials . . . We sit on the edge of our seats waiting for the next trick question by an attorney, the next twist in the case due to new evidence or crafty legalese, and finally: the verdict.

We wait hungrily for the verdict. Remember how on edge you felt when you went to see movies like *Absence of Malice, And Justice for All, The Rainmaker,* and *A Civil Action*?

The people who populate the judicial arena fascinate us – the lawyers, of course, and the judges, jurors and witnesses.

What is it about the courtroom that's so enthralling? And fiction set in the legal world?

I believe it is because that in the courtroom, the shape of a person's life – future – hangs in balance. A person is accused of a crime, is being sued or is suing, is caught up in divorce or custody proceedings, and what happens in the courtroom will change their lives for better or worse. The three components of the legal process – the judge, the attorneys/solicitors, and the jury – hold a great deal of power in this rendering.

We human beings pride ourselves on the civility of the modern court – we bring society's problems into a public forum for resolution, rather than resorting to the task of taking the law into our own hands, where the innocent could be wrongly punished . . .

We're fascinated by those who stand before the court, their futures in jeopardy, because we know that at any time, we could be the ones in court ourselves. One day we will stand before judgment. We know the power a jury or judge's decision can have. We know the power a good lawyer can wield – sometimes the guilty go free, when they have a good lawyer . . .

That's power.

And pop culture loves power.

We also love lawyers, despite all the bad lawyer jokes. Take a look at many of our hit TV shows – a good percentage of them have to do with lawyers and the law.

Law schools around the world are packed with people pursuing degrees, hoping to pass the necessary exams so they can practise in court. They want money, or they want to change the world.

The stories inside inside this volume are about people who wish to make money in the legal world, and lots of it; and people who want to change the world, to bring murderers to justice or to make life easier for other human beings.

Many of the stories have a murder involved somewhere, because much of today's legal thrillers are still centred around the all-encompassing mystery genre.

But not all of these stories are murder mysteries, and not all of them are contemporary. Some are set in the past, one is set in the future.

One is about a lawsuit filed against Satan.

The stories come from the United States, United Kingdom, and New Zealand.

The stories come from all kinds of people, too – there's the Big Names, of course, but there are stories written by real, practising lawyers and professors of law, who know their stuff; and in one , a real process server writing about a process server (important people in the judicial world, since they make sure the right papers get to the right people).

There are writers in here who are seen quite a bit in the pages of *Alfred Hitchcock's* and *Ellery Queen's,* who have legal thriller novels published, who publish mainly in the small press, and who are new names. Like many of the Mammoth anthologies, it's a mixed bag.

It's a really good mix, though.

Michael Hemmingson
San Diego, California, 2000

NIGHT OF SILKEN SNOW

Francis M. Nevins, Jr

He sat most of the night in the high-rise suite's bay window, watching soft feathery snow slide down from the black sky and coat the sleeping city in white, trying to ease his anguish with the cool detached thinking of a lawyer. From one perspective, he told himself, the person responsible for all but the first crime was the President of the United States. Or at any rate, whichever political correctness guru had told the President he had to be perceived as reading more books by women: whoever had dreamed up the notion that at the end of the President's evening jog he should casually drop in at a Washington bookshop that just happened to be open late, and should purchase and then offhandedly recommend to the reporters surrounding him a novel, almost any novel, with a female byline.

The presidential pick had been *Slumber Party*, by an unsung author named Margaret Crane. Within a week she was sung to the rafters, within two weeks her book was on every bestseller list, and by month's end her agent had signed a three-million-dollar movie deal with the hottest young director in Hollywood. Ten days after the deal was closed, her husband left her and filed for divorce, and for his equitable share of the windfall. That was the crucial link in the chain of events that hadn't yet ended but had left Loren Mensing sitting alone in a night of silken snow, trying to ease his anguish.

That fall semester he was teaching an evening section twice a week. On those days he would walk the three miles from his condo to school, and after class let out at 9:50 p.m. he would treat himself first to a few drinks at the Legal Eagle tavern a block from the University Law Centre and then at closing time to a cab home. The bar was all but empty on that raw fall night and he was nursing another bourbon-and-decaf at a corner table with an enlarged still of Gregory Peck from *To Kill a Mockingbird* framed on the wall behind him at right angles to a framed enlargement of John Barrymore from *Counsellor at Law*. He didn't see her until she was standing over him and him and then he didn't recognize her.

'Was I that forgettable?' she asked in the cool sophisticated tone of the female lead in a romantic comedy film from the thirties. Without waiting for an invitation, she dropped into the chair beside him. Loren struggled to keep befuddlement out of his face as he studied her. Tall, late thirties, curly ash-blond hair, no makeup, wearing designer jeans under her overcoat . . . She ordered a double Maker's Mark straight up from the exhausted barmaid hovering over her and then Loren remembered.

Five, no six years ago, a bitter cold night in the first week of January. Airports all over the Northeast and Midwest shut down by snow and ice storms. Loren's flight back from the annual meeting of the Association of American Law Schools, along with dozens of other flights from countless starting points and with countless destinations, had been diverted to Chicago. Hundreds of numbed and frustrated travellers were packed like freight in airport vans and hauled through snow-choked access roads to whatever hotels and motels the airlines had made arrangements with. He was standing straddle-legged in the rear of the van when a skid on an ice patch sent her sprawling into him and they helped each other up and began talking. Later they shared a drink in the bar of their motel – Maker's Mark straight up, on her recommendation – and when they decided they were too wired for sleep they went for a post midnight swim in the heated basement pool. Thanks to the late hour and the fact that most of their fellow strandees either hadn't had swimwear in their luggage or hadn't been travelling with just a carry-on bag, they had the pool to themselves. The motel was built on a hillside and two of the basement walls were sheets of glass. They could float warm and relaxed in the pool and gaze out at huge soft snowflakes sifting down to the silenced earth. After a while the woman had ducked underwater and the next thing Loren saw was her teal-blue maillot flying in an arc to the lip of the pool. Then she streaked away to the deep end and began swimming laps past him, keeping her distance at first as if to test him, then stroking closer and closer until she slithered up into his arms and clung to him in a sort of erotic desperation. It was the first time he had made love in water. The rest of the night they had spent in his room. 'Just first names,' she had said. 'I want this to stay magical.' What name had she given him? He thought she had called herself Peggy. When he woke at seven in the morning he was alone and his nametag from the law-school conference wasn't in his jacket where he thought he'd put it at the meeting's end. She wasn't on the airport van that shuttled him back to O'Hare an hour later. He never saw her again. Sometimes he wondered if he'd dreamed her.

'The security guard at the law school told me I might find you here after class,' she said, and took a healthy sip of her bourbon as if she needed it for courage. 'Loren – Professor Mensing –' she tried to hold back a giggle but it slipped out '– it's crazy, we've been lovers but I don't know what to call you – I think I need your help.'

'I guess we're beyond just first names then?'

She looked puzzled for a moment before her face cleared. 'You mean how did I find out who you were? Well, your picture does get in the papers now and then even in Missouri. And when the media began focusing on me a few months ago I thought of you and – but you *don't* know anything about me except my first name, do you?' She took another sip of Maker's Mark, this time a dainty one. 'I am Marnie Crane,' she told him.

If Loren had been drinking any of his own laced coffee he would have spluttered it all over himself. The *Slumber Party* woman, propelled to celebrity status by presidential decree! Weren't Peggy and Marnie both diminutives for Margaret? 'You don't look much like your picture in *Newsweek*,' he said. 'In the flesh you're much prettier.' Then he caught the implication of his words and felt his ears burn.

'It's lousy,' she said without missing a beat. 'I hate every photograph of myself I've ever seen and I almost never let anyone shoot me. The professional job on the dust jacket of my book isn't too bad.'

'Haven't seen the book,' Loren said. 'Sorry. Ahhh – you live out on the edge of St Louis County, right? I did read in *Newsweek* about your husband moving out and filing for divorce and a half interest in your copyright. Is that litigation what brought you here?'

'Partly curiosity about you but mostly that,' she admitted. 'I would like you to represent me.'

'I'm not licensed to practice in Missouri . . .'

'Along with my attorney there,' she went on. 'From what I've read about you, I'm hoping you'll come up with a strategy my regular lawyer wouldn't have thought of in a thousand years. I can pay you very well to try.'

'The law school pays me reasonably well to teach.'

Her soft brown eyes seemed to glow with shadowed light. 'The fee needn't be just in cash,' she whispered.

At midnight, when the bar closed, they cabbed downtown to the high-rise hotel where under an assumed name she had taken a suite on the executive floor. They sat in flanking tan leather armchairs in the empty lounge reserved for that floor's tenants and looked out at the phantom glow from the night lights of the city as he listened to the rest of her story.

A woman in her early thirties, attractive, living for years in an emotional shell after a short, disastrous marriage to an abusive drunk when she was twenty. Beneficiary of a share in a trust fund created under the will of a distant cousin's widow whose husband had been the founder of the Crane Chemical empire. Blessed with a guarantee of forty to fifty thousand dollars of unearned income for the rest of her life, Margaret Crane had lived quietly in a modest frame house on a hill overlooking one of the westernmost suburbs of St Louis County, reading, gardening, keeping a diary, tinkering off and on with various drafts of the novel she had dreamed of writing since her days as a literature major under Stanley Elkin and Howard Nemerov at Washington University. She had driven into St Louis one Sunday afternoon for a jazz recital and happened to meet a man, tall, thin, prematurely gray, soft-spoken, gentle, and eaten alive by barely acknowledged loneliness, as she herself was. His name was John Burke and he was a graduate of the University of Missouri Law School but had discovered he had a minimal aptitude for legal practice and was eking out a modest living as a municipal bond broker. 'The first movie we saw together was a revival of *Marnie*, the Hitchcock picture. That's what he started calling me. He said I reminded him of Tippi Hedren.' After a few weeks she had felt herself falling in love again. Terrified at the prospect of making another wrong choice, she ran. That was six winters ago, when the blizzard had grounded her plane at O'Hare and chance had thrust her against Loren in the van trundling stranded travellers to motels.

'Did you put me in your diary?' Loren asked.

Her eyes misted with bittersweet memory. 'Half a page,' she said. 'And I have tiny handwriting.'

Sometime during her three months on the run from herself she made a decision. Margaret Crane and John Burke were married by a judge in the St Louis County Courthouse one morning late in February. 'It was a terribly windy day. The license blew out of Jack's hand as we were running across the plaza from the clerk's office to the courtrooms and we had to chase after it.' There were no witnesses, no bridesmaid or best man, just the two of them. Jack had given up his apartment in midtown St Louis, moved into her house, and encouraged her to resume serious work on her novel. 'He did the cooking several nights a week so I'd have more time to write.' Eventually she was satisfied with *Slumber Party* and the manuscript was submitted to one publisher after another. After a year and a half a small house offered her a contract. When it was published, it attracted the same attention and readership as almost every other first novel: next to none. Until the evening of that carefully orchestrated visit to a Washington bookshop at the end of the presidential jog followed within a few short weeks by heaps of fame and money.

'That was when Jack changed,' she said. 'It was – as if the man I knew and loved had crumbled to dust and a stranger had taken his place. He blew up at me day after day for no reason. Twice he slapped me. I swear I never asked for any of that money and attention but Jack bitterly resented me for getting it out of the blue while he had to keep slogging away as a bond salesman. And then I suppose he started thinking about his situation like a lawyer.'

'That's when he moved out and sued for a divorce?'

'We call it dissolution in Missouri. He filed for divorce and for a judgment that he owns half the copyright in *Slumber Party* and the other novel I wrote while the first one was making the rounds. It's called *Women's Places*. It won't be out for a few months yet and already there are movie offers in six figures.'

'Is his lawyer any good?'

'He's representing himself,' she said.

'That's usually a bad mistake. You know the old saying, a lawyer who represents himself has a fool for a client?'

'Jack is no fool,' she told him. 'I'm afraid this is a very simple case. He doesn't need to cut someone else in on what he can squeeze out of me.'

'What makes you so sure he's entitled to a half interest? I don't remember Missouri as being a community property state.'

'The courts in Missouri do what most states do nowadays in divorce cases. They practice what's called equitable distribution of marital assets. Practically speaking, it's almost the same as community property. Thank heaven he can't take any of my trust fund!'

'Okay,' Loren asked, leaning forward, 'so how can I possibly help you?'

In the nightglow she pressed her lips together until they were a thin pencil line of flesh slightly darker than her face. 'I don't know,' she admitted after a long hesitation. 'Moral support? Maybe investigating Jack's life before we met, finding some dirt I could use to make him drop his financial claim?'

'That's a job for a private detective,' Loren said. 'I'm sure your lawyer's thought of that already . . . Wait a minute, here's a thought. Suppose you claim you'd written most of *Slumber Party* before you married him? Wouldn't that take the copyright out of the category of marital assets and make it like your trust fund, something he can't reach?'

She chewed on her lower lip in concentration. 'I'm afraid it wouldn't help much. All but a few scenes of the final draft were written after our honeymoon. I discarded most of what I'd done when I was single.'

'Could he prove that?'

'I hate to admit it, but yes he could, very easily, by subpoenaing my diary. I kept detailed notes on how the script was going.'

'Damn.' Loren stifled a yawn, realized that he was more than half asleep, and glanced at his wristwatch. 'Peggy . . . Marnie . . .'

'I guess I still think of myself as Marnie,' she said.

'It's way past my bedtime. Why don't I grab a cab home and we can talk more about your problem in a day or two, after I've had time to give it some more thought? Are you staying in town that long?'

'Maybe a lot longer.' She hesitated, her eyes squinting in concentration. 'I'm – well, just a little afraid to go home.'

'For heaven's sake, why?'

'Suppose – just suppose something should happen to me while I'm still legally married. The income from my trust fund would shift to other Cranes I've never even met, but Jack would wind up with half of everything else.'

'You mean your will leaves half your estate to him?'

'It used to leave him everything. After we were married we made wills in each other's favour. When he walked out and started divorce proceedings I hired my own lawyer and he told me to tear up my will right away and I did.'

'You made a new will?'

'I don't have any family to leave my property to, and I'm afraid I've never had a favourite charity. But my lawyer said if I died without a will before the divorce became final, Jack would take everything by intestate succession, but if I died and had a will he could claim against it and be entitled to half. I figured he'd be tempted less if I had a will, so I made a new one that cuts Jack out and leaves everything to whatever distant relatives would get my estate under the laws of intestate succession. It was the only way I could think of to handle the situation.' She paused, just long enough so that Loren stopped concentrating on the legal issue

and focused on her. 'I don't think it's worked,' she said then.
'I – believe someone's been following me the last few days.'

'Jack?'

'No, a man much younger than Jack, a stranger. Or maybe my
overheated imagination,' she added with a low, nervous giggle.

Loren stood up from the leather chair and strode to the glass-
paneled lounge door as if he half expected to see an assassin with a
gun on the other side. 'I'm taking you to your room now,' he told
her. 'And you're going to put on the deadbolt before I go
downstairs. I'll call you in the morning.' He looked at his wrist
watch. 'Late.'

'That would be nice,' she said. He was grateful that nothing in
her voice invited him to do more, because at that hour he was too
exhausted either to love or protect her properly. With the barrier
of her suite door between them, they softly wished each other
good night a few minutes later.

He called a cab from a pay phone in the lobby and was waiting at
the corner for a glowing roof light to appear on the night-
cloaked street when a man came out of the shadow of the bar
diagonally across from the hotel and trotted in Loren's direction. A young man of bantamweight build, dressed in contemporary grunge: reversed baseball cap, dark warmup jacket, and
sweatpants. Untrimmed moustache blending into half a week's
whiskers. His face made him seem near thirty, but probably he
was closer to twenty. 'Yo,' he said. 'Four Eyes. Clark Kent. You
with the glasses.' His voice was weak and hoarse and he kept
clearing his throat as if something were wrong with his larynx.
Loren felt knots form in his stomach but made himself face the
youth.

'Next time I even think you and her are together, you both get a
slice cut out of each eyeball. Clear?' Grunge kept his hands buried
in his sweatpants pockets. Loren prayed he wasn't carrying a
knife there, hoped against hope for a patrol car to glide along one
of the cross streets. Nothing moved in any direction. It was as if
they were the last creatures alive in the city. Loren swallowed
fear.

'You wondering why I care, stud?' Loren was silent, fighting the urge to vomit in the gutter. 'It's 'cause the slut's my mother,' Grunge flung at him. He made a gesture of obscene contempt and turned his back so that Loren could see the St Louis Cardinals logo on his cap as he jogged away into the shadows.

When the cab drew up a minute later, Loren asked the driver to circle the block, but by then the youth had melted back into the empty night.

The first thing he did after deadbolting himself into his own condo was to reach for the phone and wake up an old friend, a retired detective captain who now headed a private security agency. Ten minutes of conversation and it was agreed: the agency's best available operative would be in the hotel lobby first thing in the morning with instructions to call Marnie Crane's suite, explain Loren's arrangement, and offer protection. The next thing Loren did was try to get some sleep. He failed. Too many turbulent memories whirled through him.

When he reached his office a little before noon the next day, he found three pink message slips thrust under his door, all from her number at the hotel. She picked up on the first ring and he told of his encounter with Grunge in the deserted street. 'Now we know who's been following you,' he finished. 'Now you see why I arranged for a bodyguard.'

'Loren, I . . .' She seemed unable to speak for several seconds. 'I appreciate your concern but – whoever that young man is, he can't be my son.' She heard the question in Loren's puzzled silence and answered it without being asked. 'I have never had a child or been pregnant,' she told him. 'I've been sterile all my life.'

Loren had never studied or offered a course in copyright law, but five years earlier a faculty colleague who, among other subjects, taught intellectual property had had to undergo bypass surgery in mid-semester, and Loren had wound up taking over that class for a month. After Marnie had flown home without incident and an agency in St Louis County had assumed the security function, he remembered his old lecture notes and spent two days poring through them for a legal point he had scrawled down at the time but never pursued. When he found it again, he put in a week's worth of evenings on research. Then he made two long-distance calls, first to Marnie and later to the lawyer handling her divorce, a superannuated solo practitioner named Kurzweil whose phone voice was a senile cackle. That evening, but this time at a decent hour, he again called his friend the retired captain and hired the agency for a research job beyond his own capacity. His free time during the rest of the semester he devoted to writing a brief for the St Louis County Circuit Court. An hour after his final class of the term, he caught a flight to Lambert International Airport, where Marnie and Kurzweil were waiting near the luggage carousels. The divorce lawyer's hair was the colour of dirty snow and his face was wrinkled like a crumpled map. Loren rented a Camry and followed them to the Ritz-Carlton, a luxury hotel in the county seat of Clayton. They sat over an elegant high tea and conferred, with Loren lecturing more than he would have in class.

Halfway across the room a short, balding, triple-chinned man of perhaps forty was loudly sipping tea, wolfing petits fours, and carefully not looking at Loren's table. Loren remembered seeing the man in the tearoom when he and Marnie and Kurzweil had entered. *Her local bodyguard*, he had thought. *Out of his element here like a fat carp in champagne.*

When the conference broke up and he was alone in his suite on the top floor he phoned the manager of the St Louis agency, who laughed at Loren's question uproariously.

'Wrong church, wrong pew,' he spluttered between guffaws. 'You didn't come close to spotting our security, Professor. Remember seeing a bland middle-aged couple, quiet as mice, sitting in the lobby as you went into the tearoom?' Loren was silent. 'Didn't think you would. Those were our guys. Married couple, twenty years apiece in the Secret Service before they went private. They followed you in from the airport and beat you into the hotel while you were parking. I just got off the phone with them before you called.'

'They never came into the tearoom, just hung out in the lobby?'

'They came in ten minutes behind you,' the manager said.

'Had their eyes on you every second. You just never made them. That's why they're detectives and you're not.'

'Did they notice the fat guy?'

'Not only notice him, they think they can ID him. Woman sneaked a snap of him with a midget camera in her compact. We'll check around and let you know in a day or so.'

Another stalker in Marnie's life, Loren thought, and remembered that he'd better ask about the first one, the bandit-moustached youth who had claimed to be Marnie's son.

'Missed him too, hah?' The agency manager knew Loren was paying his bill but couldn't seem to keep his contempt for an amateur out of his voice. 'Kid was out at the airport when you flew in. He stayed fifty, sixty yards away from you and the woman and the lawyer, but he was there. Followed you into Clayton in a dark-gray '92 Nissan Sentra but didn't go into the hotel. Our couple spotted him but stuck to the script and stayed with your party. We have no idea where he went, but we got his license number. Give us a day. Any other way we can serve you, Professor?'

Loren said nothing for more than a minute, the phone handset pressed to his ear, eyes squeezed shut as he thought furiously. 'Just one more thing,' he said then, very softly. 'How are your contacts with the police out here?'

'Hell of a lot better than P.I.s in storybooks or else we wouldn't be in business,' the manager said. 'Why do you care?'

'Because I want you to get hold of whatever doctor they use when they need to get more details from a witness,' Loren told him, 'and arrange for the person to hypnotize me.'

On a chilly Thursday morning he stood at a lectern in the Kniep Courtroom of St Louis University's School of Law with a clamorous potpourri of students and media people at his back, a handful of curious professors in the jury box off to one side, and a copy of his brief before him. The judge hearing his motion had seen the potential importance of the issue Loren had raised and, being both an alumnus of the law school and a member of its adjunct faculty, had arranged for the oral argument to be held in its moot court facility, where interested students and professors as well as the press could attend. Marnie Crane, in a long-skirted midnight-blue ensemble and her hair pinned back in a business-like French twist, sat at the polished counsel table to Loren's left with little Kurzweil nervously twisting his ancient fingers beside her. At an identical table to Loren's right sat gray-thatched Jack Burke, alone and frowning. The judge rapped his gavel three times and the courtroom buzzing died.

'Your honour,' Loren began, 'as you know, I've been admitted to the Missouri bar *pro hac vice* for purposes of arguing this motion. It's unusual for a state court to have to decide an issue of federal copyright law and especially one that so few lawyers are aware of, but this is the court's duty today. Section two-oh-one(e) of the Copyright Act of nineteen seventy-six is as clear as legislative drafting can ever be.'

Judge Dumbleton peered over the bench at Loren through huge-lensed trifocals and spoke into the portable micro-phone set up for him. 'Perhaps for the benefit of those in the audience who have not read your brief, Professor, you should summarize the section.' Even with the mike his voice was close to inaudible. Kurzweil had told Loren over high tea that behind the judge's back the courthouse crowd called him Mumbleton.

'With pleasure, sir.' Loren turned a page of his brief. 'The section provides that if an author hasn't voluntarily transferred his or her rights, then "no action by any governmental body or other official or organization purporting to seize, expropriate, transfer, or exercise rights of ownership with respect to the copyright, or any of the exclusive rights under a copyright, shall be given effect under this title." The only exception to this rule is in bankruptcy cases. We contend that the plain meaning of two-oh-one(e) is to preclude state courts from dividing up an author's copyright interests as matrimonial property in a divorce action.'

'Why would Congress have wanted to deprive state courts of this power?' Loren had to strain to make out the question.

'I'm not sure the result was consciously intended. As my brief indicates, section two-oh-one(e) was first proposed in nineteen seventy-three when the Soviet Union joined the

Universal Copyright Convention. There was fear in certain quarters that the Soviet government would pass internal legislation nationalizing the copyrights of dissidents like Solzhenitsyn and then be able to sue in the courts of other countries, including the United States, and have the publication of dissidents' works enjoined. Section two-oh-one(e) was designed to thwart any such ploy.'

'Professor, your brief does not explain why this section of the copyright act was broadened to cover expropriations by our own federal or state governments.'

'The legislative history makes it clear that it wasn't broadened inadvertently,' Loren replied. 'But no one involved in the process seems to have realized that they were creating a link between copyright and divorce law that hadn't existed before. Nevertheless, the language of the provision is clear and the principle is squarely in line with several other changes in the nineteen seventy-six Copyright Act that expand authors' rights.'

'The court is bothered,' Judge Dumbleton remarked, 'by the way 201(e) discriminates against women.' His glance flitted about the courtroom as if in search of approving nods from media feminists. 'Does it not deny married women their equitable share of the copyrightable works created during their marriage?'

'It discriminates against women only if you assume that all or most authors are men,' Loren said. 'A glance at the counsel table to my left will show the court that the author in this case is not. A few minutes with the card catalog of this university's library or any library in America will show the court that vast numbers of authors are women. Section two-oh-one(e) treats men and women exactly alike. It protects the author spouse from involuntary transfer of copyrights regardless of which sex the author happens to be.'

'Thank you, Professor Mensing. The court will now hear opposing counsel.'

Loren took the empty chair beside Marnie at the counsel table as Jack Burke in his pin-striped lawyer suit rose with brief in hand and replaced Loren at the lectern. 'May it please the court,' he began in a fine rich baritone. 'As the court knows, I am a member of the Missouri bar, representing myself in this matter. I am by no means an expert on copyright law.'

'Nor is anyone in this room,' Dumbleton said. 'Unless of course the fellow who teaches it at the school is present.' The audience tittered and giggled as courtroom spectators will when a feeble joke is cracked by a judge on the bench. 'Proceed, counsel.'

'Your Honour, the only reported decision raising the two-oh-one(e) issue is *In re Marriage of Worth*, decided by the California Court of Appeals in nineteen eighty-seven. The court in that case flatly rejected Professor Mensing's thesis and ruled, first, that copyrights were community property under California law and, second, that that law was not preempted by section two-oh-one(e) of the Copyright Act.'

'Missouri of course is not a community property state,' the judge interrupted.

'For purposes of this issue, there is no significant distinction between community property states and those that practice equitable division of matrimonial assets upon divorce. Furthermore, at least one of the two leading law review articles on the subject contends that the very act of an author's getting married should be treated as implied consent to judicial division of copyright interests if the marriage is dissolved. If there's implied consent, there's no involuntary transfer, and therefore no two-oh-one(e) issue.'

'The other leading article, the one cited in Professor Mensing's brief, I believe contends just the opposite?'

'Indeed, your honour. But . . .' Loren had prepared thoroughly and none of Burke's arguments surprised him. The active part of his mind began to wander. After a while he realized that both what Burke said and how he said it were disturbing him profoundly. Marnie slipped her hand into Loren's beneath the counsel table and he could feel her tremble as if something in that packed courtroom beneath its oval of harsh light was terrifying her.

'Thank you for an excellent presentation.' Judge Dumbleton cut Burke off after what seemed to Loren like hours. 'The court will take the matter under advisement. And,' he said to the dozens of students beginning to stir in their seats, 'thank you all for coming. I look forward to your practicing before me in a few years if I'm still alive then.' The room exploded in another round of titters as Dumbleton pounded his gavel, rose, and meandered offstage through a private exit. Three university security guards moved along the centre aisle gently herding students and reporters out of the chamber.

'We're going to lose,' Marnie whispered to her lawyers as the courtroom emptied. Loren felt an uneasy pang. Where was the agency bodyguard who was supposed to be watching her? The three of them and Burke were alone in the room now. 'That judge has decided against us already, I can feel it.'

'*I* think our argument went very well indeed,' Kurzweil croaked as if half the credit for it were his.

'No.' She twisted in her chair to face Loren. 'We have to settle now. Maybe he'll take a quarter or a third of the copyrights if we . . .' Burke nodded curtly to his estranged wife and her legal team and strode past his adversaries' table and up the carpeted aisle. 'Jack, wait!' She snatched her purse from the floor and trotted in his wake with Loren and Kurzweil half a dozen steps behind her.

'She's gone crazy,' the older attorney panted as they passed through the narrow vestibule to the main corridor of the law school. 'This is no time to . . .' Loren didn't wait for him to finish but crossed the reception area to where several women students were congregated with disappointment on their faces and copies of *Slumber Party* clutched in their hands. 'She went in there, Professor.' One of the women pointed to the entrance door of the law library across the corridor. 'She was a few feet behind her husband and then another man went in a few seconds after her.'

The bodyguard, Loren thought. *Good*.

'Wiry little guy with a thick moustache,' another student chimed in. 'Needs a shave.'

Loren's heart dropped. He whirled and raced into the library and through the turnstile with his eyes darting everywhere for Marnie and Burke and then he saw them huddled together halfway down a narrow aisle flanked by high orange-painted steel shelves, and he ran toward them frantically waving his arms. 'Get out!' he roared. 'He's in here somewhere. Both of you, out now!' Marnie's mouth opened in the birth of a gasp of fright. He seized her arm and hustled her along the aisle with a befuddled Burke in their rear, and the three of them stormed out of the library into the main corridor where Loren hunted wildly for some sign of the bodyguard but saw only a few knots of students and Kurzweil. 'Will you kindly tell me what . . .' Burke began.

That was the moment when all hell broke loose. The whiskered youth stepped out of the library behind them and drew a semi-automatic pistol from his jacket and dropped to a combat crouch screaming 'Slut!' and 'You damned whore!' again and again as he aimed at Marnie and Burke, who stood paralyzed six inches apart. The pistol made a coughing sound and there was stereophonic screaming from the panicked students in the reception area. Loren dived for Marnie and knocked her to the floor as the pistol coughed and Burke tumbled on top of him. For an endless moment he thought he'd taken a bullet himself and then he knew the blood oozing down him was Burke's. 'You okay?' he panted. Marnie was ghost-faced and silent, but didn't seem to be bleeding. Loren crawled erect as university security guards surrounded him. 'George is chasing him down Lindell Boulevard,' one man said. 'He's Marine Reserve and a Gulf War vet, he'll catch the bastard. Cops are on the way.'

A tall young black guard looked up from where he knelt with a hand on Burke's carotid artery. 'This one's gone,' he said. 'Lady seems okay.'

'Oh Jack,' Marnie said softly and shuddered beyond control. 'Oh God.' Loren struggled to her and held her close as the wailing of sirens came nearer.

'Two of them.' The axe-faced detective lieutenant pulled his earlobe and frowned at Loren across a desktop littered with food wrappings, Styrofoam cups, and official paper. 'A tag team.'

It was midafternoon. The temperature had dropped twenty degrees, and forecasters were predicting snow. Kurzweil had vanished long ago, Marnie was in her own suite at the Ritz-

Carlton under police guard and sedation, and Loren still sat on the edge of the splintery chair in the lieutenant's cubicle, trying to absorb and align what they now knew.

The first thing they'd learned was why the agency bodyguard had vanished. Sitting in the courtroom audience, he'd spotted the other hit man, the balding fat one, who in turn had sensed he'd been recognized and made a hasty exit. The bodyguard had taken a fool's chance, leaving Loren and Marnie unprotected while he tried without success to catch the fat man. 'Which gave Tubby's sidekick the opening to take the lady out,' the lieutenant concluded. 'Only his aim was off.'

By then they had recovered the semi-automatic which the young gunman had tossed down a Lindell Boulevard sewer in his flight from Fearless George, and a usable print had told the police who he was. As luck would have it, the shooter might easily have served with George in the desert. 'Seven years in the infantry,' the lieutenant had summarized for Loren after scanning the report. 'Won all sorts of marksmanship medals, got terminated in the defense cutbacks, chose killing civilians for his new career. He's been a suspect in a few hits for hire around St Louis, but this is the first time he's left real evidence behind.'

'And he thought Marnie Crane was his *mother*?' Loren marveled.

'Ahhh, that was a load of bull. His mother lives here in town and he visits her every week. We have her place under surveillance now in case he tries to hide with her.'

Thanks to the surreptitious photo Loren's private agency pair had snapped in the Ritz tearoom, the fat one's identity was known too: he was a professional with murder warrants out for him in three states. Loren could hardly believe he hadn't noticed either hit man in the courtroom, but the place had been packed, his back had been to the audience, and his mind on the oral argument. He sat beside the chaotic desk and dredged deep into himself, trying to sort it all out while the lieutenant chewed dry bagels, slurped rancid coffee, fielded phone calls, shuffled papers, and behaved in general as if he were alone in the cubicle. When Loren raised his head and cleared his throat, the lieutenant looked at him without interest. Then he went back to his paperwork, while Loren wrestled the temptation to open the floodgates and tell the whole story.

He sat in the dark bay window of his hotel suite and watched the silken snow sift down through the deep night and coat the city and thought back to another snow-cloaked night almost six years ago. 'That was a beautiful night,' he said. The woman in the matching club chair at an angle to his seemed herself again, the shock and sedation worn away, but the carafe of wine they'd ordered with their late supper had not erased the tautness at the corners of her eyes and mouth. 'I remember that night as if it were yesterday.' He paused then. 'Do you?'

'I'll never forget it,' she replied soft as the snow.

'Tell me what you remember.' He reached for her hand and took it between his own.

'Well – I fell against you in that airport bus and we had a few drinks in the motel lounge, Maker's Mark straight up. Later we went down to the pool for a swim and we could see the snow falling all around us through the glass walls.'

'Tell me something you didn't put in your diary later,' Loren said.

The request shook her for a moment, then her teeth began to play with her lower lip. 'Darling, how could you possibly know what I did or didn't put in my diary?' Behind the note of forced gaiety Loren heard fear.

'Because I drove to your house late this afternoon while you were sedated,' he said, 'and broke in and searched till I found it. I don't have it with me now.' He reached into the breast pocket of his blazer. 'But I made a photocopy of the half page about us. Tell me something that's not on it.'

The fear was crawling into her eyes now and she took short breaths through her mouth as if there weren't enough air in the room. 'My God, Loren! I know you saved my life this morning but . . .breaking into my house . . .'

'So you owe me,' he told her. 'I saved your life and your copyrights too. Come on, just one detail.'

She swallowed, licked dry lips, tried to concentrate. 'You – told me you were a law professor,' she began.

'No, I didn't. All we exchanged were first names. You said you wanted the night to be magical, remember? You knew nothing about me till you read a write-up in the paper a few years later.'

'Oh, of course!' She tried to smile at him, but the acid of fear made it ghastly. 'I'm sorry, the shock of seeing Jack murdered right in front of me has messed up my memory.'

'Let's try again. What color was your bikini?' he demanded. 'The one you wore in the pool that night?'

'I – why it was, was blue. Loren, why in the name of . . .?'

'It wasn't a bikini.' Loren said it as if he were in court, crossexamining a hostile witness. 'It was a maillot. Whose room did we make love in, yours or mine? What did the note say that you left on the pillow?' She sat in shrunken silence as Loren stood and loomed over her. 'Come on, one little detail! I had myself hypnotized the other day so hundreds of details came back but I could remember so much of it before. Such a magical night and it's a blank?'

'There was an ice storm, both our planes were grounded in Chicago . . .' she began in a dull, trancelike, hopeless voice.

'You're not Margaret Crane,' Loren said. 'You look something like her, probably you're related, but you're not Marnie. She went back to St Louis County and married Burke and he brought you into the picture. You got good at forging her signature and you learned to look as much like her as possible. She was a loner, there weren't many people you had to fool. The two of you killed her and disposed of the body and settled back to enjoy fifty thousand a year in trust income. Everything went fine until the President made a bestseller out of that novel she'd sold before she was murdered. Suddenly money was pouring down on the two of you like that snow. Burke got greedy. Dumped you and sued for a half interest in the copyright. You couldn't blow the whistle on him without convicting yourself.

'Then you remembered that half page in the real Marnie's diary. You knew who I was and what I did from that news article, and you came to me. For legal advice, but mainly to involve me in your next murder plan. That kid who stopped me on the street, threatened to kill us both, claimed to be your son – he was your hit man. You were setting the stage so when the right moment came you'd go over next to Burke in some public place and the gunman would pop out of nowhere and scream names at you and seem to fire at you but hit Burke. Leaving his lawsuit moot and the copyrights all yours. The shooter was a top marksman in the military but you were still taking a big risk. I'm not surprised you needed sedation.'

She sat stunned and spent in the club chair, her eyes focused on the shifting snow and seeing nothing.

'You made some mistakes,' Loren said. 'Your biggest was telling me Burke was a failure as a lawyer. I heard him in court today and it was perfectly plain to me and Judge Dumbleton that he was an excellent lawyer. But I sensed something wrong from the first time you approached me. I'm a middle-aged academic. There aren't . . .' He had to stop for a few moments. 'There aren't many magical nights in my life. I remembered Marnie vividly. I always will. Something about you was subtly different. I didn't understand how you were using me until the shooter came out of the library screaming at you. I tried to knock both you and Burke to the floor but . . . Not that either of you were worth saving . . .'

She shuddered uncontrollably like someone in an epileptic fit. Then she relaxed as if a crisis had passed, stood with her arm on the back of the club chair, and smiled at him almost fondly. 'You win,' she said. 'I confess. It all happened just the way you figured it out.' For a moment Loren almost believed she looked stronger because she was sharing the bloody truth. 'Now just what do you think you can do about it?' she demanded. 'I didn't live with Burke for three years without learning some law. You are my attorney. Whatever I tell you is a confidential communication. You have an ethical obligation never to repeat it to a soul.'

He'd expected that and had spent most of the long drive back from his break-in rehearsing his answer. 'The hell I do,' he told her. 'As far as I'm concerned my only obligation is to Marnie Crane. The real one. I don't owe you a damn thing. But let's just suppose you're right, let's suppose it's unethical for me to go to the police. What's my punishment? Will I lose my license to practice law in Missouri? I don't have one, remember? I was admitted temporarily just to argue your motion.' She tore at him with her eyes but stayed silent and unmoving. 'But if it meant I could never appear in court anywhere again it would be worth it to put you away,' he said. 'Do you think I'd let you get away with murdering . . .' He stopped. He'd exposed too much of himself already. 'Get out,' he said.

She stayed where she was like the stone image of a woman. A lamp across the room etched her reflection into the dark glass of the bay window. 'You're – going to tell the police?'

'Maybe I have already and they're waiting for you in the corridor. Maybe I'll wait awhile, see if the second hit man gets lucky.'

Her eyes widened with uncertainty, and he wanted to sing.

'You never saw him, but there was a fat bald fellow in the tearoom downstairs when we went in the other day. He was also in court with us this morning and would have killed you if the bodyguard hadn't spotted him and scared him off. He's still out there waiting for another crack at you.' When he saw the surge of naked fear on her face he felt the savage pleasure a rapist feels. 'If he was in the tearoom ahead of us, he must have known exactly where we were going. Only three people knew that: you, me, and Kurzweil. Remember how you told me Kurzweil had you make a will leaving all your estate to whoever your, I mean the real Marnie's, intestate successors might be? Well, either he knew who they are, or found out, and made a deal with one or more of them for a piece of all your property, the house, the copyrights, everything. And then he hired the fat man. A professional killer.'

He waited and let the terror eat into her before he went on. 'I phoned Judge Dumbleton's chambers late this afternoon and learned something that confirmed my hunch. It wasn't the judge's own idea to hold the oral argument at the law school, it was Kurzweil's suggestion. The fat man couldn't have shot you in the County Courthouse because everyone has to pass through a metal detector at the entrance doors. Law schools don't use them. That made you a sitting duck.'

'Oh my God,' she kept mumbling. 'My God, what can I do?'

'That,' Loren said in a voice of chilled steel, 'is your problem. Maybe you'll be safe from him in a cell if you confess. Now get out.'

When she was gone he deadbolted himself into the suite and went to the bay window and sat looking out at the night city, reliving that other night of silken snow when the chain of events began.

'I wish I could have known you better,' he said quietly into the empty darkness. 'I wish I could have saved you.'

VEIL'S VISIT

Joe R. Lansdale & Andrew Vachss

1

Leonard eyed Veil for a long hard moment, said, 'If you're a lawyer, then I can shit a perfectly round turd through a hoop at twenty paces. Blindfolded.'

'I am a lawyer,' Veil said. 'But I'll let your accomplishments speak for themselves.'

Veil was average height, dark hair touched with grey, one good eye. The other one roamed a little. He had a beard that could have been used as a Brillo pad, and he was dressed in an expensive suit and shiny shoes, a fancy wristwatch and ring. He was the only guy I'd ever seen with the kind of presence Leonard has. Scary.

'You still don't look like any kind of lawyer to me,' Leonard said.

'He means that as a compliment,' I said to Veil. 'Leonard doesn't think real highly of your brethren at the bar.'

'Oh, you're a bigot?' Veil asked pleasantly, looking directly at Leonard with his one good eye. A very icy eye indeed – I remembered it well.

'The fuck you talking about? Lawyers are all right. They got their purpose. You never know when you might want one of them to weigh down a rock at the bottom of a lake.' Leonard's tone had shifted from mildly inquisitive to that of a man who might like to perform a live dissection.

'You think all lawyers are alike, right? But if I said all blacks are alike, you'd think you know something about *me*, right?'

'I knew you were coming to that,' Leonard said.

'Well,' I said. 'I think this is really going well. What about you boys?'

Veil and Leonard may not have bonded as well as I had hoped, but they certainly had some things in common. In a way, they were both assholes. I, of course, exist on a higher plane.

'You wearing an Armani suit, must have set you back a thousand dollars –' Leonard said.

'You know a joint where I can get suits like this for a lousy one grand, I'll stop there on my way back and pick up a couple dozen,' Veil said.

'Yeah, fine,' Leonard said. 'Gold Rolex, diamond ring . . . How much all *that* set you back?'

'It was a gift,' Veil said.

'Sure,' Leonard said. 'You know what you look like?'

'What's that?'

'You look like Central Casting for a mob movie.'

'And you look like a candidate for a chain gang. Which is kind of why I'm here.'

'You gonna defend me? How you gonna do that? I may not know exactly what you are, but I can bet the farm on this – you ain't no *Texas* lawyer. Hell, you ain't no Texan, period.'

'No problem. I can just go *pro hac vice.*'

'I hope that isn't some kind of sexual act,' Leonard said. 'Especially if it involves me and you.'

'It just means I get admitted to the bar for one case. For the specific litigation. I'll need local counsel to handle the pleadings, of course . . .'

'Do I look like a goddamned pleader to you? And you best not say yes.'

' "Pleadings" just means the papers,' Veil said, his voice a model of patience. 'Motions, applications . . . stuff like that. You wanted to cop a plea to this, Hap wouldn't need me. I don't do that kind of thing. And by the way, I'm doing this for Hap, not you.'

'What is it makes you so special to Hap?' Leonard asked, studying Veil's face carefully. 'What is it that you *do* do?'

'Fight,' Veil said.

'Yeah,' I said. 'He *can* do that.'

'Yeah, so can you and me, but that and a rubber will get us a jack off without mess.' Leonard sighed. He said to Veil, 'You know what my problem is?'

'Besides attitude, sure. Says so right on the indictment. You burned down a crackhouse. For at least the . . . what was it, fourth? time. That's first degree arson, malicious destruction of property, attempted murder –'

'I didn't –'

'What? Know anyone was home when you firebombed the dump? Doesn't matter – the charge is still valid.'

'Yeah, well they can valid *this*,' Leonard said, making a gesture appropriate to his speech.

'You're looking at a flat dime down in Huntsville,' Veil told him. 'That a good enough summary of your "problem?" '

'No, it ain't close,' Leonard said. 'Here's my problem. You come in here wearing a few thousand bucks of fancy stuff, tell me you're a fighter, but your face looks like you lost a lot more fights than you won. You don't know jack about Texas law, but you're gonna work a local jury. And that's *still* not my big problem. You know what my big problem is?'

'I figure you're going to tell me sometime before visiting hours are over,' Veil said.

'My problem is this. Why the hell should I trust you?'

'I trust him,' I said.

'I know, brother. And I trust you. What I don't trust, on the other hand, is your judgment. The two ain't necessarily the same thing.'

'Try this, then,' Veil told him. 'Homicide. A murder. And nobody's said a word about it. For almost twenty years.'

'You telling me you and Hap –?'

'I'm telling you there was a homicide. No statute of limitations on that, right? It's still unsolved. And nobody's talking.'

'I don't know. Me and Hap been tight a long time. He'd tell me something like that. I mean, he dropped the rock on someone, I'd know.' Leonard turned to me. 'Wouldn't I?'

I didn't say anything. Veil was doing the talking.

Veil leaned in close, dropping his voice. 'It wasn't Hap who did it. But Hap knows all about it. And you if keep your mouth shut long enough, you will too. Then you can decide who to trust. Deal?'

Leonard gave Veil a long, deep look. 'Deal,' he finally said, leaning back, waiting to hear the story.

Veil turned and looked at me, and I knew that was my cue to tell it.

2

'It was back in my semi-hippie days,' I said to Leonard. 'Remember when I was all about peace and love?'

'The only "piece" I ever knew you to be about was a piece of ass,' Leonard said kindly. 'I always thought you had that long hair so's it could help you get into fights.'

'Just tell him the fucking story,' Veil said. 'Okay? I've got work to do, and I can't do it without Leonard. You two keep screwing around and the guard's going to roll on back here and —'

'It was in this house on the coast,' I said. 'In Oregon. I was living with some folks.'

'Some of those folks being women, of course.'

'Yeah. I was experimenting with different ways of life. I told you about it. Anyway, I hadn't been there long. This house, it wasn't like it was a commune or nothing, but people just . . . came and went, understand? So, one day, this guy comes strolling up. Nice-looking guy. Photographer, he said he was. All loaded down with equipment in his van. He was a travelling man, just working his way around the country. Taking pictures for this book he was doing. He fit in pretty good. You know, he looked the part. Long hair, but a little neater than the rest of us. Suave manner. Took pictures a lot. Nobody really cared. He did his share of the work, kicked in a few bucks for grub. No big deal. I was a little suspicious at first. We always got photographers wanting to "document" us, you know? Mostly wanted pictures of the girls. Especially Sunflower — she had this thing about clothes being "inhibiting" and all. In other words she was quick to shuck drawers and throw the hair triangle around. But this guy was real peaceful, real calm. I remember one of the guys there said this one had a calm presence. Like the eye of a hurricane.'

'This is motherfucking fascinating and all,' Leonard said, 'but considering my particular situation, I wonder if you couldn't, you know, get to the point?'

Seeing as how Leonard never read that part of the Good Book that talked about patience being a virtue, I sped it up a bit. 'I was out in the back yard one night,' I said. 'Meditating.'

'Masturbating, you mean,' Leonard said.

'I was just getting to that stage with the martial arts and I didn't want any of the damn marijuana smoke getting in my eyes. I guess I was more conservative about that sort of thing than I realized. It made me nervous just being around it. So I needed some privacy. I wasn't doing the classic meditation thing. Just being alone with my thoughts, trying to find my centre.'

'Which you never have,' Leonard said.

'I'm sitting there, thinking about whatever it was I was thinking about –'

'Pussy,' Leonard said.

'And I open my eyes and there he is. Veil.'

'That'd be some scary shit,' Leonard said.

'Looked about the same he does now.'

'Yeah? Was he wearing that Armani suit?'

'Matter a fact, he wasn't,' I said. 'He looked like everyone else did around there then. Only difference was the pistol.'

'I can see how that got your attention,' Leonard said.

'It was dark. And I'm no modern firearms expert. But it wasn't the stuff I grew up with, hunting rifles, shotguns and revolvers. This was a seriously big-ass gun, I can tell you that. I couldn't tell if he was pointing it at me or not. Finally I decided he was just kind of . . . holding it. I asked him, politely, I might add, if there was anything I could do for him, short of volunteering to be shot, and he said, yeah, matter of fact, there was. What he wanted was some information about this photographer guy.

'Now hippie types weren't all that different from cons back then, at least when it came to giving out information to the cops. Cops had a way of thinking you had long hair you had to be something from Mars out to destroy Mom, apple pie and the American way.'

'Does that mean Texas too?' Leonard asked.

'I believe it did, yes.'

'Well, I can see their point. And the apple pie part.'

'I could tell this guy was no cop. And he wasn't asking me for evidence-type stuff anyway. Just when the guy had showed up, stuff like that.'

Leonard yawned. Sometimes he can be a very crude individual. Veil looked like he always does. Calm.

'Anyway, I started to say I didn't know the guy, then . . . I don't know. There was something about his manner that made me trust him.'

'Thank you,' Veil said. I wasn't sure if he was being sarcastic or not.

I nodded. 'I told him the truth. It wasn't any big deal. Like I said, he wasn't asking anything weird, but I was a little worried. I mean, you know, the gun and all. Then I got stupid and –'

'Oh, *that's* when it happened?' Leonard asked. 'That's like the moment it set in?'

I maintained patience – which is what Leonard is always complaining he has to do with *me* – and went on like he hadn't said a word: '– asked him how come he wanted to know all about this guy, and maybe I ought not to be saying anything, and how he ought to take his pistol and go on. I didn't want any trouble, and no one at the place did either.

'So Veil asks the big question. Where is the guy right now? I told him he was out somewhere. Or maybe gone, for all I knew. That's the way things were then. People came and went like cats and you didn't tend to get uptight about it. It was the times.'

'Groovy,' Leonard said.

'We talk for a while, but, truth was, I didn't *know* anything about the guy, so I really got nothing to say of importance. But, you know, I'm thinking it isn't everyday you see a guy looks like Veil walking around with a gun almost the size of my dick.'

'Jesus,' Leonard said. 'Can't ever get away from your dick.'

'No, it tends to stay with me.'

'How about staying with the story,' Veil said, still calm but with an edge to his voice now.

'So I ask Veil, it's okay with him, I'm going back in the house and get some sleep, and like maybe could he put the gun up 'cause it's making me nervous. I know I mentioned that gun several times. I'm trying to kind of glide out of there because I figure a guy with a gun has more on his mind than just small talk. I thought he might even be a druggie, though he didn't look like one. Veil here, he says no problem. But I see he's not going anywhere so I don't move. Somehow, the idea of getting my back to that gun doesn't appeal to me, and we're kind of close, and I'm thinking he gets a little closer I got a small chance of taking the gun away from him. Anyway, we both stick. Studying each other, I think. Neither of us going anywhere.'

'Neither the fuck am I,' Leonard said. 'Matter of fact, I think moss is starting to grow on the north side of my ass.'

'All right, partner,' I told him, 'here's the finale. I decide to not go in the house, just sit out there with Veil. We talk a bit about this and that, anything but guns, and we're quiet a bit. Gets to be real late, I don't know, maybe four in the morning, and we both hear a motor. Something pulling into the driveway. Then we hear a car door close. Another minute or so, the front door to the house closes too. Veil, without a word to me, gets up and walks around to the drive. I follow him. Even then I think I'm some kind of mediator. That whatever's going on, maybe I can fix it. I was hell for fixing people's problems then.'

'You're still hell for that,' Leonard said.

'Sure enough, there's the guy's van. I'm starting to finally snap that Veil hasn't just showed up for an assassination. He's investigating, and, well, I don't know how, but I'm just sort of falling in with him. In spite of his sweet personality, there's something about me and him that clicked.'

'I adore a love story,' Leonard said.

'So anyway, I wasn't exactly shocked when Veil put the pistol away, stuck a little flashlight in his teeth, worked the locks on the guy's van like he had a key. We both climbed in, being real quiet. In the back, under a pile of equipment, we found the . . . pictures.'

'Guy was a blackmailer?' Leonard asked, a little interested now.

'They were pictures of kids,' I told him. Quiet, so's he'd know what kind of pictures I meant.

Leonard's face changed. I knew then he was thinking about what kind of pictures they were and not liking having to think about it.

'I'd never seen anything like that before, and didn't know that sort of thing existed. Oh, I guess, in theory, but not in reality. And the times then, lot of folks were thinking free love and sex was okay for anyone, grownups, kids. People who didn't really know anything about life and what this sort of thing was all about, but one look at those pictures and I was educated, and it was an education I didn't want. I've never got over it.

'So he,' I said, nodding my head over at Veil, 'asks me, where does the guy with the van sleep? Where inside the house, I mean. I tried to explain to him what a crash pad was. I couldn't be sure where he was, or even who he might be with, you understand? Anyway, Veil just looks at me, says it would be a real mess if they found this guy in the house. A mess for us, you know? So he asks me, how about if I go inside, tell the guy it looks like someone tried to break into his van?

'I won't kid you. I hesitated. Not because I felt any sympathy for that sonofabitch, but because it's not my nature to walk someone off a plank. I was trying to sort of think my way out of it when Veil here told me to take a look at the pictures again. A good look.'

'The guy's toast,' Leonard said. 'Fucker like that, he's toast. I know you, Hap. He's toast.'

I nodded at Leonard. 'Yeah,' I said. 'I went inside. Brought the guy out with me. He opens the door to the van, climbs in the front seat. And there's Veil, in the passenger seat. Veil and that pistol. I went back in the house, watched from the window. I heard the van start up, saw it pull out. I never saw the photographer again. And to tell you the truth, I've never lost a minute's sleep over it. I don't know what that says about me, but I haven't felt a moment of regret.'

'It says you have good character,' Veil said.

'What I want to know,' Leonard said looking at Veil, 'is what did you do with the body?'

Veil didn't say anything.

Leonard tried again. 'You was a hit man? Is that what Hap here's trying to tell me?'

'It was a long time ago,' Veil told him. 'It doesn't matter, does it? What matters is: You want to talk to me now?'

3

The judge looked like nothing so much as a turkey buzzard: tiny
head on a long, wrinkled neck and cold little eyes. Everybody
stood up when he entered the courtroom. Lester Rommerly – the
local lawyer I went and hired like Veil told me – he told the judge
that Veil would be representing Leonard. The judge looked down
at Veil.

'Where are you admitted to practice, sir?'

'In New York State, your honour. And in the Federal District
Courts of New York, New Jersey, Rhode Island, Pennsylvania,
Illinois, Michigan, California, and Massachusetts.'

'Get around a bit, do you?'

'On occasion,' Veil replied.

'Well sir, you can represent this defendant here. Nothing
against the law about that, as you apparently know. I can't help
wondering, I must say, how you managed to find yourself way
down here.'

Veil didn't say anything. And it was obvious after a minute that
he wasn't going to. He and the judge just kind of watched each
other.

Then the trial started.

The first few witnesses were all government. The fire department guy testified about 'the presence of an accelerant' being the
tip-off that this was arson, not some accidental fire. Veil got up
slowly, started to walk over to the witness box, then stopped. His
voice was low, but it carried right through the courtroom.

'Officer, you have any experience with alcoholics?'

'Objection!' the DA shouted.

'Sustained,' the judge said, not even looking at Veil.

'Officer,' Veil went on like nothing had happened, 'you have
any experience with dope fiends?'

'Objection!' the DA was on his feet, red-faced.

'Counsel, you are to desist from this line of questioning,' the
judge said. 'The witness is a fireman, not a psychologist.'

'Oh, excuse me, your honour,' Veil said sweetly. 'I misphrased my inquiry. Let me try again: Officer,' he said, turning his attention back to the witness, 'by "accelerant," you mean something like gasoline or kerosene, isn't that correct?'

'Yes,' the witness said, cautious in spite of Veil's mild tone.

'Hmmm,' Veil said. 'Be pretty stupid to keep a can of gasoline right in the house, wouldn't it?'

'Your honour . . .' the DA pleaded.

'Well, I believe he can answer that one,' the judge said.

'Yeah, it would,' the fire marshall said. 'But some folks keep kerosene inside. You know, for heating and all.'

'*Thank* you, officer,' Veil said, like the witness had just given him this great gift. 'And it'd be even stupider to smoke cigarettes in the same house where you kept gasoline . . . or kerosene, wouldn't it?'

'Well, *sure*. I mean, if –'

'Objection!' the DA yelled. 'There is no evidence to show that anyone was smoking cigarettes in the house!'

'Ah, my apologies,' Veil said, bowing slightly. 'Please consider the question withdrawn. Officer: Be pretty stupid to smoke *crack* in a house with gasoline or kerosene in it, right?'

'Your honour!' the DA cut in. 'This is nothing but trickery. This man is trying to tell the jury there was gasoline in the house. And this officer has clearly testified that –'

'– That there *was* either gasoline or kerosene in the house at the time the fire started,' Veil interrupted.

'Not in a damn *can*,' the DA said again.

'Your honour,' Veil said, his voice the soul of reasonableness, 'the witness testified that he found a charred can of gasoline in the house. Now it was his expert *opinion* that someone had poured gasoline all over the floor and the walls and then dropped a match. I am merely inquiring if there couldn't be some *other* way the fire had started.'

The judge, obviously irritated, said, 'Then why don't you just ask him that?'

'Well, judge, I kind of was doing that. I mean, if one of the crackheads living there had maybe fallen asleep after he got high, you know, nodded out the way they do . . . and the crack pipe fell to the ground, and there was a can of kerosene lying around and –'

'That is *enough*!' the judge cut in. 'You are well aware, sir, that when the fire trucks arrived, the house was empty.'

'But the trucks weren't there when the fire *started*, judge. Maybe the dope fiend felt the flames and ran for his life. I don't know. I wasn't there. And I thought the jury –'

'The jury will *disregard* your entire line of questioning, sir. And unless you have *another* line of questioning for this witness, he is excused.'

Veil bowed.

4

At the lunch break, I asked him, 'What the hell are you doing? Leonard already *told* the police it was him who burned down the crackhouse.'

'Sure. You just said the magic word: crackhouse. I want to make sure the jury hears that enough times, that's all.'

'You think they're gonna let him off just because –?'

'We're just getting started,' Veil told me.

5

'Now officer, prior to placing the defendant under arrest, did you issue the appropriate Miranda warnings?' the DA asked the sheriff's deputy.

'Yes sir, I did.'

'And did the defendant agree to speak with you?'

'Well . . . he didn't exactly "agree." I mean, this ain't the first time for old Leonard there. We knowed it was him, living right across the road and all. So when we went over there to arrest him, he was just sitting on the porch.'

'But he *did* tell you that he was responsible for the arson, isn't that correct, Officer?'

'Oh yeah. Leonard said he burned it down. Said he'd do it again if those – well, I don't want to use the language he used here – he'd just burn it down again.'

'No further questions,' the DA said, turning away in triumph.

'Did the defendant resist arrest?' Veil asked on cross-examination.

'Not at all,' the deputy said. 'Matter of fact, you could see he was waiting on us.'

'But if he *wanted* to resist arrest, he could have, couldn't he?'

'I don't get your meaning,' the deputy said.

'The man means I could kick your ass without breaking a sweat,' Leonard volunteered from the defendant's table.

The judge pounded his gavel a few times. Leonard shrugged, like he'd just been trying to be helpful.

'Deputy, were you familiar with the location of the fire? You had been there before? In your professional capacity, I mean.' Veil asked him.

'Sure enough,' the deputy answered.

'Fair to say the place was a crackhouse?' Veil asked.

'No question about that. We probably made a couple of dozen arrests there during the past year alone.'

'You made any *since* the house burned down?'

'You mean . . . at that same address? Of course not.'

'Thank you, officer,' Veil said.

6

'Doctor, you were on duty on the night of the thirteenth, is that correct?'

'That is correct,' the doctor said, eyeing Veil like a man waiting for the doctor to grease up and begin his proctology exam.

'And your specialty is Emergency Medicine, is that also correct?'

'It is.'

'And when you say "on duty," you mean you're in the ER, right?'

'Yes sir.'

'In fact, you're in *charge* of the ER, aren't you?'

'I am the physician in charge, if that is what you're asking me, sir. I have nothing to do with administration, so . . .'

'I understand,' Veil said in a voice sweet as a preacher explaining scripture. 'Now, doctor, have you ever treated patients with burns?'

'Of course,' the doctor snapped at him.

'And those range, don't they? I mean, from first degree to third degree burns. Which are the worst?'

'Third degree.'

'Hmmm . . . I wonder if that's where they got the term, "Give him the third degree" . . .?'

'Your Honour . . .' the DA protested again.

'Mr Veil, where are you going with this?' the judge asked.

'To the heart of the truth, your honour. And if you'll permit me . . .'

The judge waved a disgusted hand in Veil's direction. Veil kind of waved back. The big diamond glinted on his hand, catching the sun's rays through the high courthouse windows. 'Doctor, you treat anybody with third degree burns the night of the thirteenth?'

'I did not.'

'Second degree burns?'

'No.'

'Even *first* degree burns?'

'You know quite well I did not, sir. This isn't the first time you have asked me these questions.'

'Sure, *I* know the answers. But you're telling the jury, doctor, not me. Now you've seen the photographs of the house that was burnt to the ground. Could anyone have been *inside* that house and *not* been burned?'

'I don't see how,' the doctor snapped. 'But that doesn't mean –'

'Let's let the jury decide what it means,' Veil cut him off. 'Am I right, judge?'

The judge knew when he was being jerked off, but, having told Veil those exact same words a couple of dozen times during the trial already, he was smart enough to keep his lipless mouth shut.

'All right, doctor. Now we're coming to the heart of your testimony. See, the reason we have *expert* testimony is that experts, well, they know stuff the average person doesn't. And they get to explain it to us so we can understand things that happen.'

'Your honour, he's making a speech!' the DA complained, for maybe the two hundredth time.

But Veil rolled on like he hadn't heard a word. 'Doctor, can you explain what causes the plague?'

One of the elderly ladies on the jury gasped when Veil said 'the plague,' but the doctor went right on: 'Well, actually, it is caused by fleas which are the primary carriers.'

'Fleas? And here all along I thought it was carried by rats,' Veil replied, turning to the jury as if embracing them all in his viewpoint.

'Yes, fleas,' the doctor said. 'They are, in fact, fleas especially common to rodents, but *wild* rodents – prairie dogs, chipmunks, and the like.'

'Not squirrels?'

'Only *ground* squirrels,' the doctor answered.

'So, in other words, you mean varmints, right, doctor?'

'I do.'

'The kind of varmints folks go shooting just for sport?'

'Well, some do. But mostly it's farmers who kill them. And that's not for sport – that's to protect their crops,' the doctor said, self-righteously, looking to the jury for support.

'Uh, isn't it true, doctor, that if you kill *enough* varmints, the fleas just jump over to rats?'

'Well, that's true . . .'

'That's what happened a long time ago, wasn't it, Doctor? The Black Death in Europe – that was bubonic plague, right? Caused by rats with these fleas you talked about? And it killed, what? Twenty-five *million* people?'

'Yes. That's true. But today, we have certain antibiotics that can –'

'Sure. But plague is still a danger, isn't it? I mean, if it got loose, it could still kill a whole bunch of innocent folks, right?'

'Yes, that is true.'

'Doctor, just a couple of more questions and we'll be done. Before there was these special antibiotics, how did folks deal with rat infestation? You know, to protect themselves against plague? What would they do if there was a bunch of these rats in a house?'

'Burn it down,' the doctor said. 'Fire is the only –'

'Objection! Relevancy!' the DA shouted.

'Approach the bench,' the judge roared.

Veil didn't move. 'Judge, is he saying that crack *isn't* a plague? Because it's my belief – and I know others share it – that the Lord is testing us with this new plague. It's killing our children, your honour. And it's sweeping across the –'

'That is *enough*!' the judge shrieked at Veil. 'One more word from you, sir, and you will be joining your client in jail tonight.'

'You want me to defend Leonard using sign language?' Veil asked.

A number of folks laughed.

The judge cracked his gavel a few times and, when he was done, they took Veil out in handcuffs.

7

When I went to visit that night, I was able to talk to both of them. Someone had brought a chess board and pieces in and they were playing. 'You're crazy,' I told Veil.

'Like a fuckin' fox,' Leonard said. 'My man here is right on the money. I mean, he *gets* it. Check.'

'You moved a piece off the board,' Veil said:

'Did not.'

'Yeah, you did.'

'Damn,' Leonard said pulling the piece out from between his legs and returning it to the board. 'For a man with one eye you see a lot. Still check though.'

I shook my head. 'Sure. Veil gets it. You, you're gonna get life by the time he's done,' I said.

'Everything'll be fine,' Veil said, studying the chess board. 'We can always go to Plan B.'

'And what's Plan B?' I asked him.

He and Leonard exchanged looks.

8

'The defense of *what?*' the judge yelled at Veil the next morning.

'The defense of necessity, your honour. It's right here, in Texas law. In fact, the case of *Texas v. Whitehouse* is directly on point. A man was charged with stealing water from his neighbour by constructing a siphon-system. And he did it, all right. But it was during a drought, and if he hadn't done it, his cattle would've starved. So he had to *pay* for the water he took, and that was fair, but he didn't have to go to prison.'

'And it is your position that your client *had* to burn down the crack . . . I mean, the occupied dwelling across the street from his house to prevent the spread of disease?'

'Exactly, your honour. Like the bubonic plague.'

'Well, you're not going to argue that nonsense in *my* court. Go ahead and take your appeal. By the time the court even hears it, your client'll have been locked down for a good seven–eight years. That'll hold him.'

9

Veil faced the jury, his face grim and set. He walked back and forth in front of them for a few minutes, as if getting the feel of the ground. Then he spun around and looked them in the eyes, one by one.

'You think the police can protect you from the plague? From the invasion? No, I'm not talking about aliens, or UFOs, or AIDs, now – I'm talking crack. And it's here, folks. Right here. You think it can't happen in your town? You think it's only Dallas and Houston where they grow those sort of folks? Take a look around. Even in this little town, you all lock your doors at night now, don't you? And you've had shootings right at the high school, haven't you? You see the churches as full as they used to be? No you don't. Because things are *changing*, people. The plague is coming, just like the Good Book says. Only it's not locusts, it's that crack cocaine. It's a plague, all right. And it's carried by rats, just like always. And, like we learned, there isn't but one way to turn that tide. Fire!

'Now I'm not saying my client set that fire. In fact, I'm asking you to find that he did *not* set that fire. I'm asking you to turn this good citizen, this man who cared about his community, loose. So he can be with you. That's where he belongs. He stood with you . . . now it's time for you to stand with him.'

Veil sat down, exhausted like he'd just gone ten rounds with a rough opponent. But, the way they do trials, it's always the prosecutor who gets to throw the last punch.

And that chubby little bastard of a DA gave it his best shot, going on and on about how two wrongs don't make a right. But you could see him slip a few times. He'd make this snide reference to Leonard being black, or being gay, or just being . . . Leonard, I guess, and, of course that part is kind of understandable. But, exactly like Veil predicted, every time he did it, there was at least one member of the jury who didn't like it. Sure, it's easy to play on people's prejudices – and we got no shortage of *those* down this way, I know – but if there wasn't more good folks than bad, well, the Klan would've been running the state a long time ago.

The judge told the jury what the law was, and told them to go out there and come back when they were done. Everybody got up to go to lunch, but Veil didn't move. He motioned me over.

'This is going to be over with real quick, Hap,' he said. 'One way or the other.'

'What if it's the other?'

'Plan B,' he said, his face flat as a piece of slate.

10

The jury was out about an hour. The foreman stood up and said 'Not Guilty' about two dozen times – once for every crime they had charged Leonard with.

I was hugging Leonard when Veil tapped me on the shoulder. 'Leonard,' he said, 'you need to go over there and thank those jury people. One at a time. *Sincere*, you understand?'

'What for?' Leonard asked.

'Because this is going to happen again,' Veil said. 'And maybe next time, one of the rats'll get burned.'

Knowing Leonard, I couldn't argue with that. He walked over to the jury and I turned around to say something to Veil. But he was gone.

OH, BROTHER

Mark Leyner

Aaron and Joshua Zeichner are twin brothers charged with first-degree murder in the artillery, grenade, and sub-machine gun killings of their parents, Sam and Adele. Aaron and Joshua, twenty-three years old, are being defended by the impassioned, histrionic, tactically virtuosic attorney Susannah Levine. Levine has argued that her clients, who admit to the killings, were induced by irrational fears into believing, mistakenly but honestly, that their parents were about to kill them. Mounting a defense that featured a cavalcade of expert witnesses and culminated in the riveting and lurid testimony of the brothers themselves, Levine has methodically constructed the theory that even though they were not at the moment of the killing under direct threat, the Zeichner twins killed their father and mother out of fear for their own lives. Levine has implored the jury to apply the concept of 'imperfect self-defense' and render a verdict of voluntary manslaughter – a verdict that would save the twins from the electric chair and might result in prison terms of only several years.

But here all similarities to the Los Angeles trial of Erik and Lyle Menendez end.

Unlike the Menendez boys and their attorney, Leslie Abramson, who claim that a history of abuse made the brothers fear that their parents were about to kill them, Levine and the Zeichner twins maintain that, conversely, it was a history of loving, exemplary parenting that drove the boys to kill their mom and dad in self-defense.

It's unfortunate that the Menendez trial – set amid the wealth, privilege, and glitter of Beverly Hills, showcased by daily coverage on Court TV, decocted for the rabble each morning in indignant tabloid bold and expatiated upon by an all-star squad of belletrists wringing Racinian drama from the ergonomic keyboards of their Power-Books – has all but eclipsed the Zeichner case. Trent Oaks – where Sam and Adele Zeichner were slaughtered in a twenty-minute barrage of howitzer shells, rocket-propelled grenades, and expanding 9-mm Luger combat rounds as they sat in their den working on Aaron's University of Pennsylvania application essay – is no Beverly Hills. It's a rather unremarkable middle-to upper-class suburb whose shopping mall and high school soccer team are its main sources of pride and distinction.

No cable channels, no tabloids, no Dominick Dunnes have found their way to the modest, stucco, Tudor-style Trent Oaks County Administration Building. In fact, the gallery is often empty except for family members, a prospective witness or two, and me. (I'm covering the Zeichner trial for the German magazine *Der Gummiknüppel*.) The disparity in media attention is particularly regrettable because the Zeichner case provides an even more illuminating anatomy of the 'imperfect self-defense' theory – and its implications for our society – than does the Menendez trial.

Here we have no abusive miserable childhoods, no tyrannical father, no disturbed mother. We have, to the contrary, a pampered Edenic youth. We have Sam Zeichner, a father who undergoes rotator-cuff surgery just so he can pitch batting practice to his eight-year-old son, Aaron, an uncoordinated, astigmatic child dying to make his local Little League team. Sam Zeichner, a father who spends a month of weeknights and weekends sculpting a topographical battlefield map of Waterloo out of marzipan for little Joshua, a Napoleonic War buff with a bulimic craving for molded almond paste. And we have Adele Zeichner – vivacious, gregarious, resourceful, indulgent Adele Zeichner – who, determined to give her children every possible advantage, commuted to work with Walkman earphones splayed against her pregnant belly so that Aaron and Joshua could listen – in utero – to Telly Savalas reading Pindar's Epinician Odes in ancient Greek. Adele Zeichner, racking her brain each and every morning to come up with a new sandwich for her boys to take to school. From Fluffernutters and clotted cream on date-nut bread to shaved Kobe beef on crustless challah and tripe with melted Stilton on focaccia – in twelve years of public education the Zeichner twins never found the same sandwich in their lunch boxes. (A logistics expert testifying for the defense estimated that Adele Zeichner prepared more than 1,920 unique sandwiches for her boys.)

Photographs of the boys' bedroom reveal children who wanted for nothing: there were large-screen televisions, CD-ROM computers, cellular phones, vintage Coke machines, souvlaki rotisseries, etc. Birthdays were celebrated with Hammacher Schlemmer catalogue binges, backstage passes for Def Leppard, Super Bowl box seats on the fifty-yard line, treks through the Ecuadorean rain forest. How many kids do you know who received blowguns, curare-tipped darts, and a three-layer manioc birthday cake from hallucinogen-addled Jivaro headhunters for their tenth birthday?

But this wasn't simply a case of parents obliviously lavishing material objects on their children. There was nurturing and understanding and support at every juncture of their upbringing. There were special tutors if the boys had trouble with algebra, sports psychologists when they faltered in gym class. When the time came for those inevitable adolescent experiments, be it Satanism or transvestism, Mom and Dad were right there to facilitate these difficult rites of passage – Sam rummaging through his cartons of college books for a volume of Aleister Crowley, Adele loaning Josh a velvet-piped, silk chiffon Carolina Herrera for a cruise through the mall. Never was a hand raised in anger, never was a sarcastic or deprecating remark directed at those boys. Often neighbours would notice lights in the master bedroom burning deep into the night as Sam and Adele sat and listened patiently to their sons' teenage tribulations, determined to treat them respectfully, without carping or condescension.

And with each caring gesture, Aaron and Joshua grew increasingly certain that their parents were going to kill them. The more sympathetic and generous Sam and Adele were, the more fearful their sons became that their parents were about to snap. Or so Susannah Levine would have us believe.

As argued by their attorney, and according to their own sworn testimony, the Zeichner twins had become inculcated by television with the belief that normal parents are confrontational, contemptuous, and abusive. Consequently, they perceived their parents' gentle and empathic behavior as 'bizarre,' 'frightening,' and, ultimately, 'a grave threat.'

Addressing the jury in her opening remarks, and frequently punctuating the idea by banging her head against a stanchion near the jury box, Levine asked: 'How many made-for-television movies, how many celebrity confessions, how many episodes of "60 Minutes" and "48 Hours" and "20/20" and "Prime Time Live" and "Eye to Eye with Connie Chung" did these boys have to watch before they became convinced that normal parenting is abusive, that the relationship between a parent and a child is violently adversarial – and that their parents, Sam and Adele Zeichner, were *not normal,* that something was terribly, terribly odd about the way their parents were treating them? In Aaron and Joshua's minds, their parents were either consciously dissimulating – in other words, perpetrating some sort of evil ruse to lull the boys into a false sense of security – or they were unconsciously repressing their inner desires to kill their children. To Aaron and Joshua, each new gift and each successive gesture of compassion brought them one step closer to what they called "the breaking point." '

Under direct examination, Joshua discussed the time he and his brother first realized their parents were spinning dangerously out of control.

> LEVINE: Was there a time when you and Aaron were *not* scared of your parents?
>
> JOSHUA: When we were very young, we thought that the way our parents behaved was normal. We just figured that's how every family was – until we became aware of how other parents treated their kids.
>
> LEVINE: You became aware of this from watching television?
>
> JOSHUA: From TV and from other kids.

LEVINE: Was there one incident in particular – a dinner?

JOSHUA: Yeah. I'd been bugging Mom for a week or so to make lobster in black bean sauce, which was one of my favourite things. So this one day Mom decided to make it for me and she told me to invite a friend. And as soon as she came home from work that afternoon, she started cooking. And it's a pretty involved meal because she makes all these side dishes and everything so it was taking a really long time and me and Aaron and our friend Sean, who was eating over, we got really hungry, so we went to Wendy's and we just stuffed ourselves. And then when we got home, we saw that Mom had set this beautiful table and she looked really tired but she was sort of beaming because she knew how much I loved what she'd made. Anyway, we all sat down, and me and Aaron and Sean couldn't eat a single bite we were so stuffed. And we had to tell my parents that we'd just gone out to Wendy's because we hadn't felt like waiting.

LEVINE: And what did your parents say?

JOSHUA: They said they understood that sometimes when you're very hungry, your stomach gets the better of you, and Mom said don't worry about missing out on the meal, that she'd make lobster in black bean sauce sandwiches for us to take to school tomorrow. And they said it was silly for us just to sit there at the table – why didn't we go off and play and have a good time.

LEVINE: When you were all off by yourself that night, do you remember what your friend said?

JOSHUA: He said that our parents were really, really weird. He said that if he'd done what we'd done his parents would have beaten him within an inch of his life. He was just astonished and I think appalled at how our parents reacted.

LEVINE: Do you remember how you and Aaron felt that night?

JOSHUA: Very, very scared.

LEVINE: Joshua, I want to leap ahead now from this first night of fear to your final, culminating night of fear. On the night after your high school graduation, did your parents present you and Aaron with graduation gifts?

JOSHUA: Yes. Our parents gave each of us a brand-new Infiniti J30.

LEVINE: And do you remember how you felt that night?

JOSHUA: We were absolutely *terrified*. We felt that this was the final straw. And we knew that unless we did something first we were goners.

LEVINE: When you say 'the final straw' and 'goners,' what do you mean?

JOSHUA: That they were going to kill us.

LEVINE: And by 'doing something first,' what did you mean?

JOSHUA: A preemptive strike.

The 'preemptive strike' that Joshua Zeichner referred to in his testimony will certainly go down in history as one of the most brutal assaults in the annals of parricide.

The boys positioned a 105-mm howitzer on a small hill several blocks from the Zeichner residence. Using infrared and night-scope equipment, they launched a fusillade of artillery rounds on their home. Scores of spent brass casings found by police offer grim testimony to the relentless salvos. Following the howitzer barrage, the twins drove one of the new Infiniti J30s back to the house. From the trunk of the car, they removed a Soviet-made RPG – an infantry-held, antitank, rocket grenade launcher – a Heckler & Koch MP5SD3 9-mm submachine gun and a Glock twenty-round 9-mm semi-automatic pistol. Aaron, wearing IL-7 Mini-Laser IR illuminator goggles attached to a Kevlar infantry ballistic helmet, knelt on the front lawn and fired a dozen of the cone-shaped, armour-piercing, rocket-propelled grenades into the den where his parents had been working. The boys then clambered through the den window and raked the room with 9-mm sub-machine gun fire.

Aaron offered details of the assault when he testified under direct examination:

LEVINE: Do you know what your parents were doing in the den?

AARON: They were writing Josh's essay for Penn.

LEVINE: Why were they writing it? Why hadn't Josh written his own essay?

AARON: Josh had just thrown together this really awful essay. You couldn't even call it an 'essay,' it was just this piece of garbage he scrawled down in two minutes and he showed it to our parents and they said, 'Dear, why don't you work on this a little more and see if you can refine some of the interesting thoughts you sketched out here' or something like that. And it was due the next day. But Josh didn't want to work on it that night.

LEVINE: Can you recall why not?

AARON: I think because 'Baywatch' was on – that was one of our favourite shows.

LEVINE: So when your parents asked Josh to rewrite his essay and Josh said no because it conflicted with your plans to view 'Baywatch,' how did your parents react?

AARON: They said something like 'Josh, you've been under a lot of stress lately, why don't you enjoy your program with your brother and we'll write the essay for you.'

LEVINE: How did that make you feel?

AARON: Absolutely terrified. We were sure at that point that our parents were planning to kill us.

LEVINE: Can you explain to the court why you thought that?

AARON: We just thought it was like the final stage in their whole passive-aggressive approach to us – this whole being-so-super-nice-to-us thing had to flip into the really hostile thing sooner or later, and we decided that night that it was going to happen.

LEVINE: How many artillery shells hit the section of the house where your parents were working?

AARON: I think we got three or four direct hits.

LEVINE: Then you two went in?

AARON: No. First I fired a couple of the grenades into the den.

LEVINE: You were the first to enter the den?

AARON: Yes.

LEVINE: Was your father alive?

AARON: No.

LEVINE: And your mom?

AARON: She was alive – barely.

LEVINE: Aaron, how many rounds does a Heckler and Koch 9-mm submachine gun magazine hold?

AARON: Thirty-two.

LEVINE: And how many magazines did you and your brother fire?

AARON: I think we went through about eight clips.

LEVINE: And then what happened?

AARON: We ran out of ammunition – and Mom was still alive. So we decided to go to the store and buy more, but we didn't have any money.

LEVINE: What did you do then?

AARON: I asked Mom for money.

LEVINE: And what did she say?

AARON: She said to get her wallet out of her pocketbook and take what we needed.

LEVINE: And when you returned home with fresh ammunition, what was your mother doing? Was she trying to get out of the room?

AARON: No, she was trying to finish the essay.

LEVINE: Your honour, I have no further questions for the witness at this time.

Susannah Levine is one of several controversial defense lawyers, both lauded and vilified by their colleagues, who bring the full weight of their notoriety to bear on every case they try.

National Association of Defense Attorneys President Blair Potters, introducing Levine at a recent NADA junket in Cozumel, Mexico, said: 'Imagine a Mayan architect-priestess who transforms a rank, uninhabitable tract of jungle into an intricate maze of aqueducts, sluices, and sewers whose mathematical and astrological symbology is only apprehensible when viewed from an airplane, and you'll have some idea of the scope of Susannah Levine's accomplishment in constructing cogent, elegant defenses out of the tangled mental landscapes of her clients.'

Of all Levine's courtroom maneuvers and pyrotechnics, none provokes as much debate and invective as her zealous advocacy of the imperfect self-defense theory – the theory that a person, although not actually under attack, but who *believes* that he or she *will* be killed, can claim self-defense as a mitigating and even exculpatory motive in the commission of a homicide.

Walter M. Elkin, a former prosecutor and now a law professor at F.I.T. in New York, has written a series of oped pieces denouncing the theory as 'nihilistic,' and criticizing Levine for what he calls 'pernicious and self-serving evangelism.'

'If we allow people to murder each other as a result of perceived threats of hypothetical menace, our communities will quickly disintegrate into atomized, internecine war zones,' Elkin said. 'We will become a nation of 250 million belligerent tribes of one.'

Levine is unapologetic. 'My responsibility is to defend my clients to the very best of my ability. If I'm shrill or monomaniacal, it's because I care so deeply about them – they're decent people who've been caught in the undertow of a paradoxical culture, and they're thrashing in the dark to stay alive.

'The Cold War didn't end, it devolved from the geostrategic to the interpersonal. Imperfect self-defense is just a legal byproduct of the preemptive first-strike doctrine that now governs our behavior on the streets and in our bedrooms. We need to move toward an interpersonal version of MAD – mutually assured destruction. If each of us is sufficiently armed and booby-trapped to ensure massive reciprocal damage to everyone else, we might be deterred from murdering one another. There will be a kind of pandemic stalemate, and then you won't need people like me ranting in courtrooms, banging our heads, and spitting up in the name of justice.'

On completion of the Zeichner case, Levine is off to Minneapolis, where she's defending a young woman who, believing that her parents thought she was going to kill them, deduced that they were going to preemptively kill her, so she killed them first – in other words, preempting an erroneously anticipated preemption.

'This should be a wild one,' Levine enthused. 'We're dealing with infinitely reflecting mirror images of fear – Chinese boxes of paranoia within boxes of paranoia.'

Late one afternoon – the Zeichner case had just gone to the jury – I watched Levine toss her briefcase into a factory-fresh, jade-green Infiniti J30 parked in front of the Trent Oaks Country Administration Building. She saw me scrutinizing the car.

'It's my retainer,' she shrugged.

'Is that Aaron's or Joshua's?' I asked.

'Aaron's. I actually like Josh's better – it's red – but they impounded it as evidence.'

I laughed.

'Seriously,' she said, 'if you ever kill your parents . . .' She handed me her card.

'Listen, my parents were pretty wonderful,' I said, 'but they were no Sam and Adele Zeichner!'

She shook her head ominously. 'They were probably much better than even you know. You probably don't even remember the *really* good things they did to you. It could take years of therapy before it all comes out.'

She revved the engine and vanished in a plume of exhaust.

The streets were empty thanks to the draconian provisions of a newly enacted curfew that prohibited armed teenagers from congregating in public after 3 p.m. The crepuscular sky was a pousse-café of azure, rose, and vermillion.

I popped a cassette into my Walkman, and listened as Telly Savalas intoned Pindar's twelfth Olympian ode:

Hai ge men andrôn
poll' anô, ta d' au katô
pseudê metamônia tamnoisai kulindont' elpides

'Men's hopes, in endless undulation, soar and plummet, borne on falsehoods, that heave and tumble, in the wind.'

REASONABLE DOUBTS

Michael A. Black

Everything in the conference room had an expensive look to it, from the leather chairs to the thick bronze-coloured carpeting underfoot. I sat with my hands folded on the highly polished mahogany table, trying not to seem out of place in my J.C. Penney sport coat and slacks. Mr Mason Gilbert sat at the head of the table, looking like some feudal lord, as his secretary read off the firm's agenda for that day. When she paused, Mr Gilbert rotated his head and smiled. He was a massive man, close to three-hundred pounds, but still very regal-looking. His suit was obviously hand-tailored, and his gray beard impeccably trimmed. When he spoke, his voice had a resonance perfected by many oratories in the courtroom.

'Thank you, Stella,' he said. He took a deep breath and shifted his huge body forward, placing his forearms on the table. 'As you all know this firm has been recently engaged to represent Dr Todd H. Gooding in a murder trial. Since we are the second firm to accept this case, and now must play catch-up to someone else's inefficiency, I expect that all of you will give this matter your utmost attention.' He looked around at the twelve of us seated around the table.

'I want Ms Buckley to be my secondary on this,' Mr Gilbert continued, nodding at Mary Buckley, the petite brunette sitting across from me. 'Additionally, I am proud to announce that we have Mr Mark Shields with us. Mark's a recent graduate of Northwestern Law School. He's going to be going an internship here, until the results of the bar exam come out this summer, after which I'm sure we'll be considering him as a future junior partner.' Mr Gilbert smiled benignly at me. I nodded a quick acknowledgment to the sets of probing eyes, and felt myself blush.

'Mark, why don't you assist Ms Buckley on the Gooding case,' Mr Gilbert continued. 'Janice, our regular secretarial assistant is off on maternity leave, and I'm sure your youth and vigour will be an asset.'

'Thank you, sir,' I said, glancing across the table at Mary, who eyed me carefully.

'With that, I suggest we adjourn for today,' Mr Gilbert said. 'Mary, if you and Mark would stay for a moment.'

The others filed quietly out of the room. Mary stood and smoothed her skirt. She was small, and delicately built, with refined, pretty features. Her dark hair was attractively styled and she wore no jewelry except a gold serpentine chain around her neck.

'How's your father, Mark?' Mr Gilbert asked, gathering up his legal pad as he rose.

'He's well, sir,' I said. 'And thrilled that I was accepted here to do my internship.' I smiled. 'He still hasn't forgotten how much you helped him and the union.'

Mason Gilbert smiled broadly, as if recalling with relish the memory of the lawsuit several years ago. He'd won a large settlement in a wrongful death suit when my father and several other ironworkers sued a major corporation on a safety issue.

'He's a fine man,' Mr Gilbert said. 'And I'm looking forward to working with with you, Mark. However,' he canted his head back, 'in order to be a good lawyer, you have to look the part. Ms Buckley, after you pick up the Gooding file from Shelby and Associates, take Mr Shields over to Neimann Marcus and pick out a new wardrobe. Put it on the corporate account.'

'Yes, sir,' Mary said. I followed her into the hall and began admiring the series of framed photographs showing Mr Gilbert with virtually every important political figure in the Chicago area in the last three decades. Mary started to speak, then noticed that I was lagging behind her. She glanced at me obliquely and said, 'Come on, Rookie. We don't have time to dawdle while I break you in.'

At the store Mary picked out light pastel shirts and power ties, while I stood and looked in the mirror as a tailor adjusted the length of my trousers and inseam. After making sure that all the shirts would be tapered as well, she marched me over to Florshiem and picked out four pairs of Oxfords, two black and two brown.

'Leave the loafers for your social times,' she said, handing the clerk the corporate credit card.

'Speaking of social times,' I said tentatively. 'How about a drink after work?' She looked to be about my age. Maybe a few years older. Her dark eyes swept over me momentarily before she answered.

'I don't think that would be a very good idea,' she said.

'Oh? Why not?' I tried to smile ingratiatingly, even though I felt crushed. 'Just a little get acquainted, show-me-what-to-look-for type of thing.'

'For one thing, you barely look old enough to drink,' she said. 'And for another, we have work to do. You can begin by looking over this.' She handed me the Gooding file we'd acquired from Shelby and Associates. 'Then get acquainted with the copy machine while you make duplicates of everything in the file. One for me, and one for you. Then later, between drinks by yourself, you can go over it and tell me tomorrow what you think are the weak points in the prosecution's case.'

'I guess that means you're too busy tonight, eh?' I said.

'I'll need the file back by quitting time,' she said, glancing at her watch. 'I have to catch the five-fifteen train home.'

That night in my small apartment near the law school I glanced through the file while pondering my good fortune. To be accepted for my internship at such a prestigious law firm, and then to be working with Mr Mason Gilbert himself on such a high profile case . . . It was almost too good to be true. I decided to buckle down, since Mary seemed all business, and go over the file.

After several hours I knew all the police reports and discovery items backward and forward. Basically, Dr James Gooding had been arrested and charged with the murder of his ex-wife, Laura Gooding, neé Pearson. She'd kept her husband's name because of their two children, a boy of six and a girl of ten. They were presently staying with Laura's sister in Indiana. Laura had been thirty-eight, blonde, and extremely pretty. She and Dr Gooding, a well-known surgeon, had been married for twelve years, and had been divorced for eighteen months. The split had not been on friendly terms, with Mrs receiving a hefty settlement, custody of the children, and a large monthly alimony payment. Additionally, she'd also retained their swank townhouse in Winnetka. On October 12th, after dropping the kids off for school, Laura Gooding had gone to the grocery store and then returned home. She'd been stabbed six times in the chest with a sharp-edged instrument, which had not been recovered at the crime scene. Her body had been found just inside the bedroom door.

Her ex-husband had been questioned by the police at his home shortly after the body was discovered that afternoon. Dr Gooding, who usually played golf on Wednesdays, said that he had been downtown most of that morning attending to various personal matters, among them dropping off his BMW for a service. He could think of no one who could verify this offhand, but did state that he had called his answering service several times during the day. This was verified by the investigating officers, through the micro unit detail sheets of Dr Gooding's cellular phone. Admitting no definitive alibi for the time of the murder, estimated to be around ten o'clock, Dr Gooding declined to accompany the officers down to the station for an interview, and stated that he wanted to confer with his attorney. The attorney, Henry Shelby, who had handled Gooding's divorce, advised him not to make any statements concerning the matter. Gooding did, however, allow the police to take several items of his clothing.

I made a star in the margin next to the part about them confiscating the clothes and scribbled no warrant/possible motion to suppress.

Preliminary tests subsequently indicated that the stain on Dr Gooding's shirt was blood of the same type as his ex-wife's. And a button of the same kind as that of the confiscated shirt was recovered at the crime scene. One of the extra buttons on the left shirt-cuff had been pulled off. Dr Gooding became a prime suspect. Adding fuel to the fire was a recent request that had been filed by Laura Gooding's attorney requesting an increase in the monthly child support payments so that the Gooding's daughter could enter an exclusive private school. There had been allegations of abuse during the marriage, and the police had responded to domestic disturbances at the household on several occasions, especially during the last few months at visitation pick-ups and drop-offs. Two weeks before she was murdered, Laurie had obtained an Order of Protection against her ex-husband.

When he was pulled in for questioning, James Gooding had denied killing Laura and also declined to make any further statements on the advice of his attorney. The police, however, found two neighbourhood youths who remembered seeing a dark-haired man with a long nose driving a red Pontiac Firebird in the area of the townhouse around ten-thirty the morning of the murder. One of them even recalled a portion of the car's vanity plate: SALLY . . . Gooding's receptionist later admitted that he had borrowed her car that day. It just happened to be a red Firebird with the vanity plate SALLY4TH.

I wrote, *Possibly coached by police?* in the margin.

The case seemed totally circumstantial at this point. The motions to suppress had already been exhausted by the previous firm, but it was winnable for sure, for someone like Mr Mason Gilbert. I wrote down three pages of notes on different strategies for each of the weak points I'd noted. By the time I looked at the clock it was close to one. I stretched, then closed the file, thinking that I'd better get some sleep if I wanted to seem sharp for the morning strategy session with Mr Gilbert.

'Since we did not have the advantage of being in on this from the start,' Mr Gilbert said, 'I requested a week's continuance before beginning the trial. We're really at a disadvantage that Todd waited so long before hiring us. This case might have been won at the preliminary hearing.' he glanced over the scribbling on his yellow legal pad. 'We're definitely going to need John Flood on this one, Stella.'

His secretary made a quick nod.

John Flood was an almost legendary private detective who had a long history of working with Mr Gilbert. One of the framed photos in the hallway showed Flood, Mr Gilbert, and Tyrone Port, a black gang member whom they'd cleared of shooting a Chicago Policeman over a decade ago. I'd done a paper on the case for a project in school. Flood had tirelessly searched some of the worst areas in the city to find the missing witnesses who corroborated Port's claim that he was smoking pot in a drug house far from the scene when the policeman was murdered.

'Mary,' Mr Gilbert continued. 'Did you file that discovery motion on the DNA that they're sure to introduce? Their RFLP tests should have been in last week.'

'Yes, sir,' Mary said. 'They were served this afternoon.'

'Good,' Mr Gilbert said, smiling. 'Now get busy preparing an attack on any weak points in their presentation. And consult our list for a DNA expert we can use to dispute them. We've used Dr Kilmer in the past. See if he's available.'

Mary nodded, scribbling furiously on her legal pad.

I seemed to be the odd man out.

'Shouldn't we wait to see if the DNA evidence clears him?' I said spontaneously. No one else spoke. Mr Gilbert, who had seemed to ignore my comment entirely, continued to peruse his notes. He raised his eyebrows slightly, then cleared his throat and said, 'We were fortunate to draw Judge Foxworth for this trial. Besides being a woman, Judge Conlan is much too pro-prosecution. Especially if any type of domestic violence is alluded to.' He looked up. 'That's another area where we'd better be prepared, Mary.' She made some more quick notations, then surreptitiously glanced at her watch when Mr Gilbert looked back to his pad. 'Make sure you tell John to address that aspect in the customary manner.'

Mary said, 'Yes, sir.'

'Well, I guess that about does it for today,' Mr Gilbert said. He flipped the legal pad on the table and heaved a sigh. The rest of us stood and began to file quietly out of the room when Mr Gilbert called to me.

'Mr Shields,' he said. I stopped and turned.

'Yes, sir?'

'Nice suit,' he said, and smiled slightly.

In the hallway I caught up to Mary, who was rushing to her office, cradling her legal pad to her chest like a schoolgirl.

'Some briefing,' I said, following her through the door. I wanted to ask her if I sounded like a total idiot in there, but she seemed too preoccupied. She grabbed her purse and began slipping on her coat as I spoke. Glancing up at me as she was putting her notes and a couple of books in her briefcase, she asked abruptly, 'What time is it?'

'Five-ten,' I said, after checking my watch.

'Oh, damn,' she muttered and brushed past me, pausing at the door to snap off the light.

'You in a hurry or something?' I asked.

'Yes, I'll miss my train,' she said, glancing at her watch again. 'It's already too late. I'll never make it now.' She turned and started back to the office. After dropping her briefcase onto one of the chairs she angrily flipped on the light, then picked up the phone. Sensing that it was a private call, I waited in the hall, but heard her telling someone named Mrs Marcos that she was going to be late. I heard more muted conversation and gathered that this wasn't sitting well with Mrs Marcos, whoever she was. Mary slammed down the phone and bustled out of the office again. This time I had my briefcase and fell into step beside her.

'Problems?' I asked, as we pushed through the door and headed for the elevators.

She seemed to consider this for a moment, then a small pair of parallel wrinkles appeared in the space between her eyebrows.

'I have to pick my daughter up from the day-care centre by six-thirty, or they charge me for an extra day,' she said.

I remembered her saying yesterday that she had to catch the five-fifteen, and it was already past that now.

'Well, how far do you have to go?' I asked.

She reached out and punched the down button before she answered.

'Wilmette,' she said, looking up at the elevator indicator lights.

'That's not really that far, is it?' I said. She frowned in my direction, and I quickly added, 'I mean, I could get you there before six. We could take my car.'

'You drove?' she said.

I nodded and she seemed to consider this for a moment before saying, 'Okay, Rookie, you're on. Get me there before six-thirty, and dinner's on me.'

The street was cluttered with people as we pushed through the revolving doors onto the sidewalk. Mary pushed on ahead of me toward the parking garage. At the entrance a homeless guy was hawking *Street Smart,* a local tabloid that partially funded the homeless shelters. Mary went by the man without slowing, and glanced back at me angrily when she turned and noticed that I'd stopped to give the man a dollar for one of the papers.

'How far is your car?' she asked impatiently.

'Will you relax? I told you I'll get you there in time.'

'Right,' she said. 'You know I'm in a hurry, and you stop to buy a paper from some bum.'

'Just trying to help the poor guy out,' I said. 'Maybe he can earn enough for a good meal, or something.'

'Oh, right,' she said. 'Try a half-pint of wine.'

'Well, the paper's hysterical,' I said. 'Ever read it?'

'No,' she said, walking so briskly that I found myself quickening my own steps just to keep up with her. 'I have enough to worry about going over my case files.'

Mary's mood seemed to improve once we drove out of the parking garage and hit Lake Shore Drive. The traffic was pretty heavy, as usual, but I was extremely adept at zipping around in my little sports car. We managed to get to the outskirts of the city quickly, after which the traffic thinned considerably. It was six-twenty-four when I pulled up in front of the day-care centre. Mary came out a few minutes later with a small girl of about five, who had bright brown eyes and a cute smile that matched her mother's.

She gave me directions on how to get to the train station, where we got her car. After strapping Laurel in the car seat, Mary walked over to my driver's side window.

'Thanks, Rookie,' she said. 'I owe you. If you want, you can follow me to my place and I'll fix you that dinner.'

'Sounds good,' I said, thinking that I really wished she would stop calling me rookie.

Mary lived on the second floor of a nice-looking townhouse. After going up the stairs and unlocking the dead-bolt, she opened the door and Laurel ran inside. The rooms were all nicely carpeted and spacious. The kitchen was off to one side and the living room floor had several toys and dolls strewn about. Mary ushered me into the study, plopped her note pad onto the table, and told me to start looking up everything I could about DNA in the book she gave me. I did while she cooked in the kitchen.

For dinner we had salad and tuna casserole, with ice cream for dessert. I'd had better, but the company was so pleasant that I thoroughly enjoyed myself. After dinner Mary put Laurel to bed and then joined me in the study, sitting across from me at the finely polished wooden table.

'This was one of the few nice things that I managed to salvage in my divorce,' she said, running her hand over the shiny surface, smiling wistfully.

I didn't know what to say, so I just smiled too.

'Anyway, let me see what you've got so far,' she said, becoming all business again.

'First, let me ask a question,' I said.

She canted her head and looked at me.

'Did I sound like a real idiot today or what?' I said.

That brought a smile.

'You sounded like a rookie, Rookie,' she said. 'That's why I'm gonna break you in, and make you a top-of-the-line defense attorney.'

'Is that what you were, before you went to work for Mr Gilbert?' I asked.

'No,' she said. 'I worked for the State's Attorney's Office.'

'You were a prosecutor?' I asked.

'Yes,' she said. 'That's how I met Mason. I was prosecuting one of his clients. He offered me a job with his firm after the trial was over.'

'He must have been pretty impressed,' I said. 'Did you win?'

She looked at me for a few seconds before she answered, then said, 'Actually, I lost, but I must have impressed him.'

*   *   *

The next day I was saddled with paperwork as soon as I walked in the door. Mary gave me several briefs to prepare, regarding revised witness lists and evidence. I finished these and was walking down the carpeted hallway towards Mary's office when I almost literally bumped into Mr Gilbert and another man.

'Mark,' Mr Gilbert said with a broad smile. 'This is my good friend and associate, John Flood.'

Flood, who had a thick crop of wavy reddish hair, to match his complexion, extended his hand and I shook it. He muttered that he was glad to meet me, then shifted his body to put his overcoat on. I caught a glance of the butt of a revolver sticking out of a small holster on his belt. Two thick rubber bands had been wrapped around the grips. Flood saw me looking at it and grinned.

'It makes it easier to hold,' he said. His voice was deep and resonant.

I just nodded. Mr Gilbert and he shook hands. Flood said he'd be in touch.

I watched the big detective stride down the corridor, and suddenly felt Mr Gilbert's hand on my shoulder.

'Mark, one thing you should learn is the value of having a man like John Flood on your side.'

At the end of the day I felt exhausted. Perhaps it was because all day long someone would hand me a bunch of notes on a legal pad and tell me to retype them to make sense. Paralegal work for sure, but I figured that the experience would be invaluable. Here I was actually working a case, and a big, high-profile case at that. The notes were all disjointed, and I had a hard time putting everything together. Or maybe it was just that I wasn't grasping the overall strategy. The big picture, as Mr Gilbert called it. I went in to check if Mary wanted a ride home after work, thinking that I could perhaps steer things into a date of sorts. After all, it was Friday night. But when I knocked at the door she looked up in surprise. Paul Sorakas, one of the firm's junior partners, was sitting on the edge of her desk, his head lolling back causally, and the vestiges of a fading smile on his lips. His chin jutted out when he saw me.

'I just wondered if you needed a ride, or anything,' I managed to say.

'Oh, thanks, Mark, but Paul's taking me out tonight,' she said.

I could hear Sorakas mutter something as I turned and left, and Mary shushed him. I collected my things, and decided to head down to an old haunt of mine on Rush Street. The place turned out to be packed, even though it was still relatively early, but I managed to belly-up to the bar and ordered a tall cool one. The bartender brought my beer, and I drank half of it before turning around to survey the room. The college-crowd was filtering in and a haze of cigarette smoke hung in the air like a wispy fog. Several sets of cute girls wiggled by and smiled. I let my gaze trail after them, then suddenly caught a glimpse of someone familiar. Near the front of the room, sitting in a booth with a long-haired kid in his late twenties, was John Flood. I watched the big private eye as he spoke, showing something to the long-haired guy. Then more people passed in front of me. I felt someone touch my shoulder.

'Got a light?' a girl asked, a cigarette between her fingers.

'Sure,' I said, and dug into my pocket for my lighter. Even though I didn't smoke, I always carried one for such occasions. I reached over and lit her square. She thanked me, but turned away before I could even offer to buy her a drink. I shrugged, and looked back toward the booth when the crowd thinned again, but both Flood and the long-haired guy had disappeared.

I didn't get a chance to meet Dr Todd Gooding face-to-face until later the next week, if you could call it a meeting. He was a rather large man, much bigger than he'd looked on TV, and his face, with its angular bone structure and long nose, looked almost like a human caricature. He seemed very preoccupied, which I suppose was normal under the circumstances, as he passed me in the long hallway. Gooding smiled weakly as he walked by. I knew that he'd posted one-hundred-thousand dollars bond to stay free pending the trial.

Jury selection was scheduled for Thursday and Friday, and opening arguments were to begin the following Monday. Mr

Gilbert had me running to this office for optimum-juror psychological profiles. The company was feeding data into its computer system to give up information on the best type of juror to select, depending on which of several strategies Mr Gilbert selected. The psychological profiles included everything from educational levels to religious affiliation. I was pretty impressed with the lengths that Mr Gilbert seemed to be going to research even the most abstract aspects of the case.

'Sometimes a case can be won or lost before the trial even starts,' Mary said. 'That's why Mason gets the high fees that he does. He wins.'

'I guess he does,' I said.

'We've got to file an amended witness list, too,' she said. 'John Flood's found someone who can corroborate Todd's claim that he was downtown the morning of the murder.'

'Oh, really,' I said. 'Who?'

'Some street artist,' she said. 'He draws quick thumbnail sketches of people, then sells them, like those old-time street photographers. He saw Todd in the park reading the paper, and drew a picture of him.'

I raised my eyebrows. 'That's certainly good news. How'd Mr Flood find him?'

'I guess just by being out there beating the bushes,' she said. 'He's bringing him by at eleven, so if you want to sit in on the interview . . .

'You bet,' I said.

At eleven Mary stopped by the law library where I was busily going over more prospective juror profiles. 'He's here,' she said. I stood and stretched, glad to be dealing with a real, flesh-and-blood witness instead of a bunch of computer printouts. Grabbing my legal pad, I followed her down the hallway to one of the conference rooms. Flood sat at one end of a long wooden table. Mary sat down across from him. I stared at the other person at the table. He was the same guy that I'd seen Flood talking to in the bar last Friday, except that the kid's hair had been pulled back into a pony tail.

'Mark, this is Harry Norridge,' Mary said. She introduced me as her assistant. 'He's the witness I mentioned.' Norridge smiled and nodded to me as I sat down. 'Show him the picture, Harry,' she said. Norridge reached down and picked up a beat-up leather portfolio. He started speaking in a high-pitched, almost effemi-nate-sounding voice as he undid the straps, and took out a spiral-rimmed sketch book.

'I noticed him right off because of his distinctive facial struc-ture,' Norridge said. 'I didn't put it together that it was him until I saw his picture.' He nodded his head at Flood, and unfolded the sketch pad. I glanced down at the drawing. It was Todd Gooding all right. The resemblance was unmistakable.

'And you're sure you saw him on the morning of October 12th?' Mary asked, scribbling notes.

'Yes, of course,' Norridge said. 'See, I always put the date on the lower right hand corner of my drawings.' He pointed to the paper, on which was written: 10/12. I lifted the pages below it and saw 4/27 and 4/28, yesterday and today's dates, written on each.

The strategy session that afternoon was substantially more up-beat. But Mr Gilbert cautioned us about over-confidence.

'Remember we still have that DNA to contend with,' he said solemnly. 'And we'll have to attack the credibility of the officers conducting the investigation.'

'What tactic are we using for the DNA?' Marty asked.

Mr Gilbert seemed to consider this for a moment, then said, 'I've got John looking into some avenues on that. Hopefully he'll be able to turn up some sort of evidence that Laura Gooding used cocaine quite frequently. Snorted it. Therefore, a sudden nose-bleed wouldn't be all that unusual, so it could have gotten on the shirt previously.'

'Would the post show that?' Mary asked.

'The toxicology reports came back negative,' Mr Gilbert said. 'But we have to build a case that she was an occasional user. Then the length of time a bloodstain containing her DNA could have been on Todd's shirt will be open to question.'

Mary nodded, taking notes.

I'd been paging through her file on the case as they spoke. I stopped at a picture of Laura Gooding, her pretty blonde face staring with tired ecstasy into the camera lens as someone had snapped the photo. Paperclipped to the page was a note from Mr Gilbert to John Flood. *We need evidence of drug usage – Find some ex-boyfriends. Especially one-nighters. We've got to trash her.*

This suddenly bothered me. Made me realize all at once that the victim in this case had been a real, breathing, vibrant woman, whose life had been prematurely snuffed out in brutal fashion. Quite different, I realized, from the abstractions I'd argued about so passionately in law school.

The next week passed quickly, with jury selection and motions being filed. Our opponents were a male/female team of prosecutors, each with lots of trial experience. I was in and out of the courtroom, mostly running errands, but they usually saved a seat for me behind the defense table. Every night Mary gave me a stack of briefs to proofread, and I once again found myself burning the midnight oil. Mr Gilbert's opening statement was brilliant, and as the trial started he never seemed to miss a beat in the cross-examinations. He made the police look like overzealous bunglers. It wasn't until the state started to present the DNA evidence, proving that it was indeed Laura Gooding's blood on the shirt, that it seemed like we had an insurmountable obstacle to overcome. But Mr Gilbert seemed completely at ease as he attacked that also.

'Dr Brighton,' he said, stepping up toward the witness chair as he cross-examined the state's forensic expert. 'You couldn't really be sure of exactly when that stain was made on my client's shirt, could you?'

Brighton considered this, then said, 'No, I could not.'

'So then it's possible that the blood stain could have been there for a few days prior to the murder, isn't that right?' Mr Gilbert said.

'Yes, I suppose.' Brighton's reply was tentative.

'Possibly even longer than that?' Mr Gilbert said, pausing to catch the eyes of a few of the jurors.

'Yes, possibly,' Brighton said.

'Were any other tests done to determine if there were any drugs in the blood sample found on Dr Gooding's shirt?'

Brighton, a heavyset man in his late fifties with thick glasses, was obviously more than just a little intimidated by Mr Mason Gilbert.

'I'm not sure what you mean,' he said. He spoke with reticence, almost a quiver in his voice.

Mr Gilbert smiled patiently, then stepped forward. His large figure seemed to loom in front of the witness stand.

'Let me rephrase that. Was the blood sample, to your knowledge, tested for the presence of any street drugs?'

Brighton swallowed nervously, then replied in the negative.

'Then, it's possible that traces of some drug, cocaine for instance, may have been in that sample, isn't that correct?'

The prosecution objected, saying that the question called for a conclusion on the part of the witness, but the judge overruled.

'I have no way of knowing that,' Brighton said, unsure as to what Mr Gilbert was getting at.

'But it is possible then, is it not?' Mr Gilbert asked, his stentorian voice making the question seem more like a statement.

'Yes, I suppose it is,' Brighton answered. 'But without further testing –'

'Nothing further,' Mr Gilbert said, cutting him off. He smiled reassuringly at Dr Gooding as he walked back to our table.

The state needed one more day to finish up its case. In the redirect, they re-emphasized the certainty of the DNA evidence indicating that the blood on the shirt was Laura Gooding's. When they'd finished, Dr Gooding looked ashen. He leaned over and whispered something to Mr Gilbert, who nodded and gave him a encouraging little pat on the arm. But in the closing argument the state would once again wave the bloody shirt for the jury to see, and review the summation of their witnesses. Judge Foxworth admonished the jury not to discuss the case or form any opinions about it, but as I drove Mary to pick up her daughter at the end of the day, I kept seeing the picture of Laura Gooding in my mind's eye. I was beginning to have reasonable doubts about our client's innocence.

'Do you think he did it?' I asked, as we pulled up in front of the day care centre.

'What?' she said, looking at me sternly.

'Gooding,' I said. 'Do you think he killed her? Are we just putting up a smoke screen?'

'We're doing our job,' Mary said. She half-opened the car door, then paused to look at me. 'The state presents its side, then we present ours. You'd better get with it.'

I blew out a slow breath.

'I suppose so,' I said. 'But I just can't get that image of Laura Gooding out of my mind . . .

Mary paused, and then sighed. She said, 'Look, Mark, you have to learn to disassociate yourself from certain aspects of the case.' She smiled, then said she'd be right back.

As she went inside I grabbed that old *Street Smart*, paper that I'd bought from that homeless man the first time I'd driven her here. Figuring it would take my mind off things, I began paging through it. The ad seemed to jump out at me: Street Artist – Caricatures while you wait. The phone number after it looked strangely familiar. I reached in back for my briefcase and snapped it open. After paging through my files on witness information I found the one for Harry Norridge's beeper. The numbers were the same.

The next morning when I got to court I still couldn't get Laura Gooding's face out of my mind. Her sister and mother had both taken seats behind the prosecutors every day, and I couldn't look at either of them. The prosecution began to call its final group of witnesses, including the detective who had initially interviewed the good doctor and taken the bloody shirt as evidence. It was clear now that we would have to put Gooding on the stand to offer a counter explanation of how the blood had gotten on his clothing – something that Mr Gilbert had said that he didn't want to do, if at all possible.

Just as the prosecution closed, Dr Gooding whispered to Mr Gilbert that he was feeling ill. A brief recess was called, during which Gooding went to the washroom with a nosebleed. When he'd finished putting compresses on his face, Mr Gilbert smiled and said that he wanted to convince the jury that Laura was the one with the nose-candy problems.

I swallowed hard as I looked at Gooding's light blue shirt. It was splattered with crimson spots. A double set of buttons adorned each cuff.

'We definitely don't want the jury to see you looking like that, Todd,' Mr Gilbert said. He turned to me. 'Mark, I'm going in to speak to Judge Foxworth and request an extended recess. Would you go over to one of the department stores and get Todd a new shirt.' He patted me on the shoulder.

'Yes, sir,' I said. Gooding gave me his shirt size, and I left immediately.

When I got back, I found out that we'd adjourned for lunch. I went looking for Dr Gooding in our conference room, and ran into John Flood instead.

'I've got the new shirt,' I said.

Flood looked at me quizzically. He was holding a large white paper bag, apparently from one of the street vendors in front of the courthouse.

'For Dr Gooding,' I said. 'Have you seen him?'

'What? No,' he said. He abruptly got up and walked out of the conference room. I checked the rest of the rooms along the back corridor, and went down by the judge's chambers. Through the glass window next to the closed door, I saw Mr Gilbert leaning over a desk as Judge Foxworth sat smoking a cigar, his robe hanging on a clothes rack behind him. They appeared to be deep in conversation, so I didn't want to bother them. I checked along the rest of the corridors, then saw Mr Gilbert walking toward me.

'I have the shirt,' I said.

He smiled broadly.

'Good, Mark. Good.' He seemed to regard me closely for a few seconds, then said, 'I'll give it to him.'

I handed it to him and he left, hurrying down the hall. I ambled through the empty courtroom toward the main hallway again. It wasn't too crowded, and I decided to hit the washroom before going down to try to grab a quick bite to eat. I pushed open the door and went to the sink, turning on the tap and cupping some cool water to splash on my face. As I leaned down I caught a glimpse of someone's shoes in the adjacent stall. They were shiny black patent-leather shoes. The kind that uniformed cops wear. I wet my face, and reached for some paper towels to dry off. The toilet next to me flushed, and when the door opened, Henry Peppers, Judge Foxworth's personal bailiff, walked out holding a large white paper bag.

His eyes widened momentarily when he saw me, then he grinned.

'Oh, you're with Mr Gilbert,' he said, smiling and holding up the bag. 'Got to get the judge his coffee and rolls,' he said. He shuffled out of the washroom. I continued to dry my face. A second toilet flushed, and John Flood came out. He looked at me and licked his lips as he came up to the sink and rinsed off his hands.

'You find him?' he asked.

I nodded.

He grunted, crumpled two paper towels in his big fist, and went out. I dropped my towels in the waste can and then walked over to the stalls. Each one was clean and empty.

When we reconvened that afternoon, Judge Foxworth had Henry call the court to order. Then the judge called both sets of attorneys into his chambers. When they came out a few minutes later, the state's attorneys looked crestfallen. Mr Gilbert walked over and patted Gooding gently on the shoulder, then turned and lowered his considerable bulk into his chair. Deep in my gut, I knew what was coming next.

'Ladies and gentlemen of the jury,' Judge Foxworth said, smiling. 'I thank you for your service, but I am releasing you all at this time. After hearing the evidence thus far, I have to conclude that the state has failed to prove its case beyond a reasonable doubt. Too many questions have arisen in my mind to justify allowing these proceedings to continue any longer. I am therefore declaring a directed verdict of not guilty.'

Smiling broadly Gooding turned and embraced Mr Gilbert. At first I thought he was crying, but then I realized that he was softly chuckling. Mary smiled and reached over to squeeze his arm. I watched the jury rise and begin to filter out, then glanced over to the prosecution. Both state's attorneys were leaning over talking to Laura Gooding's mother and sister.

'I know he did it,' her sister was saying, the tears running ceaselessly down her face. 'I know he did it.' She enunciated every word. I quickly looked away.

It wasn't until later that day, back at the firm, that I had time to assemble my nerve and go in to see Mr Gilbert. Winning the big case had imbued a sort of party atmosphere throughout the place, and most of the staff was taking off early. I waited until the big man was alone in his office before rapping gently on the door.

'Mark,' Gilbert said. 'Come in, come in. I just realized that I never paid you for buying that shirt today.' He reached into the back pocket of his pants and removed his wallet.

'Mr Gilbert', I said, my voice cracking.

'Yes?'

'I'm a little bit disturbed by what happened, sir,' I managed to say.

He continued to paw through his billfold, seeming to ignore my comment, then withdrew a twenty.

'Will this cover it?' he asked, holding the bill toward me.

'No, sir, I'm afraid it won't,' I said. I handed him the envelope that I'd been carrying.

'And what is this?' he asked. The space between his eyebrows wrinkled.

'It's a letter of resignation,' I said.

He looked at me curiously, then set the letter down on his desk.

'Hardly necessary, since you were never an official member of this firm,' he said, then smiled. 'But, Mark, the strain of handling a high profile case, especially a murder case, puts everyone through an emotional wringer. It's over now. Take a few days off to think things over.' He went back to his papers, as if I'd been perfunctorily dismissed.

I stared down at him, saying nothing.

Finally, he looked up and said, 'I take it that something more is bothering you?'

'Yes, sir, there is.'

'And what, pray tell, might that be?'

'I know what happened today,' I said. 'What really happened.'

He raised an eyebrow querulously. 'Suppose you elaborate on that.'

'Gooding was guilty,' I said.

He smiled slightly. 'Mark, Mark, Mark, you must learn, if you intend to stay in this business, that you can't be concerned with petty emotions.'

'What about the truth?' I said.

'It isn't about truth,' he shot back, his voice still steady and deep. 'Nor is it about guilt or innocence. It's about representing your client to the best of your ability.'

'And winning,' I said.

'Yes, and winning,' he said. He continued to stare at me, then added, his voice a low, rusty shadow of his rich courtroom baritone, 'You've got a lot to learn about these things.'

'You paid off the judge, didn't you?' I said. 'Flood used the white paper bag to make the drop to Henry, the bailiff, in the washroom.'

Gilbert licked his lips, then canted his head as he drew in a laborious breath.

'Mr Shields, I don't have the slightest idea what you're talking about,' he said, his voice rising again to its lawyer-like resonance. 'But, I should caution you that making spurious and unsubstantial allegations will not sit well with any aspirations you may still harbour regarding a career as an attorney in this city.'

He met my stare with an imperious one of his own. I noticed that his gray beard had been carefully trimmed to a point, so that the bottom of it obscured the dollop of his double chin.

'I believed in you,' I said. 'My father believed in you.'

'And I believe that I did very well for him and his union, too,' Mr Gilbert said. He began shuffling though his papers.

'I looked up to you. Like you were some kind of hero, or something.' My voice cracked as I spoke.

With a disgusted sigh, he glanced up from his desk and said, 'It isn't about being a hero, either. Now if you have no more prattle, you may leave. 'He looked at me for a moment as he grasped my letter, dropped it in the wastebasket, then said, 'Good-bye, Mr Shields.'

I turned to go, but paused at the door. As if truly seeing him for the first time, I said, 'Hello, Mr Gilbert.'

I had placed my briefcase in the hallway and the rest of the firm's happy party-goers were gingerly stepping around it. Mary caught a glimpse of me leaving and called out my name. I shook my head and pushed out the door into the hallway. In its emptiness I could hear only the scuffing of my own shoes along the marble tiles. Then the skittering sound of high-heeled pumps came tapping along behind me, followed by Mary's voice.

'Mark, wait. Where are you going?'

She'd caught up to me just as I pressed the down button for the elevator.

'Out of here,' I said.

'But why? What's wrong?'

'Gooding did it,' I said disgustedly. 'And we got him off. Not even legally, either.'

She canted her head and looked at me, then said, 'Remember what I told you about having to disassociate yourself?' She walked over to me and put her hand softly on my arm.

'Maybe you can, but not me,' I said. 'I just can't get Laura Gooding's face out of my mind.'

'Well, think it over,' she said. 'Don't make any rash decisions.'

'I already have,' I said. 'He threw my letter of resignation in the trash.'

She closed her eyes and squeezed my arm gently. After a moment she opened them and smiled. A single tear wound its way down her cheek. For me or for innocence lost? I wondered.

'So what are you going to do now?' she asked.

'Wait for the results of the bar exam,' I said, after blowing out a slow breath. 'Then apply at the State's Attorney's Office, I guess.' The elevator doors popped open, and I stepped inside. 'Who knows, maybe I'll do better on that side of the table.' I grinned. 'At least I'll be able to look at myself in the mirror.'

'Well, when you do,' she said, smiling at me from the hallway, 'at least you'll see one of the best-dressed rookie prosecutors in the city.'

She stood momentarily framed in the portal then wiped off her cheek. 'Bye, Mark,' she said. I nodded. Moments later, the elevator doors slowly slid closed, then locked together.

THE TENDER OFFER

Louis Auchincloss

Valerian Shaw, a member of the flourishing midtown Manhattan corporate law firm of Treanor, Saunders, Arkdale, Rosen & Shaw, had long assumed that, by the time he should have reached the age of sixty-four, he would have achieved a modicum of emotional and financial security. Although, like most of his heavily taxed generation, he had scanty savings, he had figured that his ultimate pension should be adequate to keep him comfortably as a widower in his small apartment on Riverside Drive where, surrounded by his books and collection of New York iconography, he would be able peaceably to pursue to the grave his hobby of metropolitan history.

But in his sixty-fourth year, with only three to go before his mandatory retirement, a strange thing happened. He began to lose his professional nerve. Valerian found himself now uncomfortably conscious of a widening discrepancy between the pace of his working efforts and that of his partners and associates. The image that seemed to stick in his mind was of them all engaged in a forced march across the slushy bog of the endless legal technicalities of the seventies, a quagmire of statutes and regulations and judicial opinions, and of himself sticking in the slime, falling behind the resolutely progressing backs of the others. He began at last to be afraid that he would not be able to pull his weight in the firm until the retirement age.

And then, as if to justify this gloomy foreboding, the basket in which for thirty years he had toted most of his legal eggs burst its bottom and dropped its cargo on the street. Standard Bank & Trust Company, the small but reliable depository of the fortunes of some of New York's oldest families for which he had so long laboured, first as an associate and then as a partner, on whose board of directors he had conscientiously served, and all of whose principal officers he had come to regard as his particular friends, was merged, taken over, consumed, raped, by First National Merchants' Loan. The new amalgamate ('Thank you very much, old Val!') would be quite adequately represented in the future by Lockridge, Kelly, First National's old-time, hard-nosed legal experts, who had designed the plan that had resulted in Standard's sudden siege and quick, fluttering surrender.

Valerian at first tried desperately to persuade himself that the blow was not a fatal one to his position in the firm. Might another bank not seek a general retainer? Might his friends at Standard not yet gain control of the amalgamate? And surely he had other clients. Was the vault not full of wills? The partners were very kind. But it was a matter not of months but of weeks, and very few of them, before the computer began remorselessly to show the steady increase of unbilled time and the widening discrepancy between the overhead of Valerian's little department and the revenues that it engendered. He could not fool himself that he would long escape that 'soul-searching' interview with the senior partner.

Cecil Treanor and Valerian had been classmates at Andover, Yale and Harvard Law, but Cecil was not a man to be too much counted on, even by so old an acquaintance. He had a convenient way of packing noble ends with rather less noble means in the same box without any seeming awareness of the least impropriety or even inconsistency. At Yale, for example, he had written a series of controversial columns for the *News* attacking the powerful senior societies, only to end by accepting the bid of Skull and Bones. At law school he had composed a brilliant note for the *Review* on legal restraints to anti-Semitism, and had then joined a club in Boston that excluded Jews. Years later, as president of the New York State Bar Association, he had thunderously preached the gospel of *pro bono publico* while keeping his own clerks so busy they hadn't a minute left for the needy. And always these compromises, if such they were, seemed to be effected without any interrupting cough in that emphatic tone, without the interposition of a single cloud over that beaming countenance. Sometimes of late Valerian had begun to feel that that beam was more like a hard electric light.

That Cecil should come to Valerian's office for the soul-searching talk was in itself indicative of its importance, but his tone was milder than Valerian had expected.

'We've never been just a "money firm," and we're never, at least while I'm around, going to be one. We measure a partner's contribution by many factors other than the fees he brings in. In your case, Val, there are qualities of experience and wisdom and compassion and integrity – yes, sir, good old-fashioned integrity – that are indispensable to a firm like ours. Some of our younger partners don't know the value of those things, but they'll learn.'

'It's good of you to say that, Cecil.'

'Nonsense! You and I go back together to the flood. One doesn't forget that. But, as Hamlet said to Horatio, "something too much of this". What I came in to suggest, now that you have a little more time on your hands, is that maybe you could help me out a bit.'

'In what?' Val was instantly alert.

'Well, how about giving me a hand on a new piece of business?' Cecil paused here to assume a graver look. 'My client Zolex is casting a hungry eye in the direction of Pilgrim Publishers.'

'Pilgrim! But that's one of the finest houses in the book business! What does Zolex know about literature?'

'Oh, Zolex knows a bit about everything. Don't forget they acquired the Heller chain last year. Department stores sell books, don't they?'

'I suppose they do.' Val saw the sudden gleam in his partner's eye and knew that he must be careful. 'Simeon Andrews in Pilgrim is an old friend of mine.'

'I'm aware of that.' Cecil was watching him carefully now. 'I thought that might come in handy. You've always taken an interest in publishing, have you not?'

'Oh, nothing special.' Val began to feel very nervous. 'Not enough to be any real help to you. Frankly, Cecil, I don't see myself working on a corporate takeover. Even the vocabulary gets me down. Terms like "bear hug" and "blitzkrieg" and "shark repellent"!'

But there was no answering smile from Cecil. 'I use those terms, Val. They are merely technical. Are you suggesting there is anything illegal about the acquisition by Zolex of a controlling share of Pilgrim's common stock?'

'Oh, no, of course not.'

'Are you suggesting, then, that I am violating any of the canons of ethics by advising Zolex how most expeditiously to acquire that stock within the law?'

'No, no, you're perfectly ethical. I guess it's the huggermugger of the whole thing that sticks in my craw. The way we go about it. First checking the files to see if we have ever had any legal connection with the target company. And then the stealthy lining up of stockholders and the secret approaches. And finally – *bang* – the unleashing of the tender offer, like a Pearl Harbour attack!'

'Of course, if it's all so distasteful to you, you needn't have anything to do with it. I can see I'm wasting your time.'

'No, please, Cecil, of course I'll do it! I'm just shooting my big mouth off. You know how I am.'

Cecil nodded briskly to accept his partner's collapse. It had been wholly anticipated. He then proceeded to a more delicate matter: a proposed fifty percent reduction in Valerian's share of the firm's profits. This was accompanied by what was known jocularly among the partners as the 'old fart' formula: 'We old farts have to keep moving over to make room for the younger men!'

But Val knew perfectly well that only one old fart would be taking the cut.

Nothing had added more to Valerian's malaise in the firm than Cecil's development of a large department, highly trained and specialized, to be dedicated to the art of corporate acquisitions. When the practice of company raiding on a large scale had begun Cecil had denounced it as dirty business, and had loftily told his partners at a firm lunch that they should act only as defenders in such cases. The 'snide art,' he stoutly maintained, of preparing and launching a surprise attack against some unsuspecting company, whose officers, about to be stripped of their livelihood, might like as not be numbered among one's closest friends, ill fitted gentlemen supposedly devoted to the pursuit of justice and the reverence of law. But when Cecil's own corporate clients had begun to look to other firms for just this service, he had performed more than a volte-face. He had made his firm the first in the field! Like Philippe-Égalité in the French Revolution, he wore the lilies of France on his liberty cap with perfect aplomb. History to Cecil, Valerian sometimes mused, must have seemed like a fancy-dress ball. Was there any reason that Justice Holmes and Al Capone should not have had a friendly drink together?

Valerian was somewhat relieved to discover that his role in the preparation of Zolex's project was confined to a study of all the material on Pilgrim Publishers that the firm had been able, with the necessary discretion, to lay its hands on. He did not quite see what value this would have in a proxy fight, but Cecil assured him that he needed someone at hand with the overall picture in mind. He suspected that the senior partner might be making up work for him, but even if this were so, why should he complain? He only hoped that he would not have to be present at any meeting, once the matter became public, with his old friend Simeon Andrews.

Ordinarily he lunched with the editor of Pilgrim every couple of weeks, but now he discontinued the practice, and at his club in the Pan Am Building he frequented the buffet, knowing that his friend was apt to lunch in the main dining room. But one day at noon, crossing the lobby, he felt a firm pull on his sleeve and turned to confront the countenance that he had been avoiding.

'Where have you been hiding, Val?' Simeon demanded. 'I've been looking out for you all week.'

'I've been having a sandwich sent in to my office. I'm keeping pretty busy these days, Sim.'

'Too busy for a little business talk? Too busy for a proposition I want to put to you? How about the regular dining room? I hate just to eat and run.'

Valerian submissively followed his friend to the latter's regularly reserved table in a corner of the green-walled room hung with Audubon prints. Simeon's table was directly under a print that depicted two red-tailed hawks fighting in the air over a bleeding rabbit clutched by one. Valerian, unpleasantly reminded

of the impending fate of Pilgrim, shuddered. Was it possible that
Simeon had got wind of the raid?

But Simeon seemed wholly absorbed in gravely applying a
piece of lemon peel to the rim of his pre-iced martini glass. Bald,
wide-eyed, he was as still, except for his moving fingers, as some
great bird of prey on a bare limb. Valerian had always associated
this stillness with his friend's reputation for being able to pick the
best as well as the most popular books without even reading them.
His secret, Simeon used to boast, was that if his eyes were
sometimes closed, his mind was always open. Nothing was too
refined, too esoteric, too vulgar, or too pornographic for his
consideration.

'Do you remember, Val, that you once mentioned to me that it
would be a great idea if some house were to publish the un-
expurgated diaries of Philip Hone and George Templeton Strong
in a joint edition?'

'Why, yes,' Valerian replied, astonished at his friend's memory. 'Allan Nevins published only half of each of them. And
Strong really begins where Hone leaves off. Put together, they'd
make a week-by-week, almost a day-by-day account of life in
New York from eighteen twenty-five to eighteen seventy-five.'

'Precisely. Well, that idea of yours stuck in my mind. That's
how a good publisher operates. Those fifty years represent the
transition of New York from a minor seaport to a great metro-
polis. By eighteen seventy-six the job was pretty well done. Fifth
Avenue boasted as many chateaux as the Loire Valley, and all the
great cultural institutions had been founded or at least planned.'

'And do you know something else, Sim? I've read the manu-
scripts of those diaries in the New York Historical Society. The
unpublished parts are just as good as the published. Nevins
simply had to cut because his editors wouldn't give him the
space he needed. But imagine, if he'd had an editor with your
vision!'

Simeon sipped his drink complacently. 'Well, I've been looking into it. It seems to me perfectly feasible. I don't say it would
be a great money-maker, but any publishing house that's worth
its salt should be willing to stick its neck out from time to time.
We owe it to the public. We owe it to history!'

'Oh, Sim, that's wonderful!'

'*If* we decide to go ahead with it, would you consider serving on some kind of advisory board? On questions of how much explanatory text we need and how many footnotes? We wouldn't be able to pay you much, but then, it shouldn't take too much of your time.'

'Pay me! I'd pay *you* for the privilege! My God, man, this project has been my dream of dreams!'

Simeon smiled, pleased at such a display of enthusiasm, although probably considering it a bit on the naive side. But Valerian didn't care. He ordered a second martini, although he knew it would make him tiddly in the middle of the day. He began to calculate how many volumes would be needed – not too many, not more than ten. His mind was already a gallery of possible illustrations. His second cocktail came, and he swallowed it in a couple of minutes. He started to run off to his friend the names of possible editors . . .

And then, when Simeon had suddenly sprung up from the table to buttonhole a former mayor whose memoirs he had his eye on, a terrible thought came to Valerian. The radiant dome of his new fantasy was shattered.

Zolex!

Was it conceivable that a massive corporate conglomerate, controlled by men concerned with profit alone, would countenance such a project? Of course not! The mere suggestion might cost its proponent his job.

Valerian deliberately reached over now to pick up Simeon's half-finished cocktail, and finished it for him. His heart was beating rapidly, and the big crowded room blurred before his eyes. Through his mind throbbed the slow, marching melody of the old hymn: 'Once to-o ev-er-y man a-a-and na-a-tion, comes the-e-e mo-o-ment to-o decide.' Simeon came back to the table.

'Sorry, old boy, but I had to have a word with Tom. He's given me an option on his autobio. Of course, he can't write a word of English. Seen any good ghosts lately?'

'Simeon!' Valerian exclaimed sharply and then abruptly paused. His friend eyed him curiously.

'What is it, Val?'

Valerian seemed to be looking at the editor from the other side of a deep crevice. Could he jump it? Would he stumble? He lowered his eyes to the tablecloth as with an audible gasp he took the mental leap. But he fell! He fell and fell!

'Val, are you feeling all right?'

Valerian looked up, dazed, from the bottom of his pit. 'I'm all right, Sim,' he said in a flat voice. 'I want to tell you something about a client of ours.'

Simeon's big watery eyes stared as he listened to Valerian's tale in absolute silence. But when the latter had finished, and the editor responded, his tone was curiously emotionless. He shook his head.

'Well, I'll be damned. It seems we live in a new age of piracy. Thanks for the tip, old boy.'

'Of course, you realize I've put my professional life in your hands.'

Simeon gave him a shrewd look. 'Of course, I do,' he said softly. 'But never fear. I shall be discreet. And now, I think, everything points to a very good lunch.'

Valerian reflected that it was indicative of the strength of the man that he could even think of lunch at such a moment! He tried to quell the rising surge of panic in his stomach by telling himself that he had only done his duty as a friend. And as a citizen. And as a student of New York history.

Valerian soon heard at the office that somebody besides Zolex scouts was picking up Pilgrim stock, but this was not an unusual development. No matter how secret a raider's precautions, there were always nostrils keen enough to pick up the scent of impending war. What disturbed him was that the lawyers working on the matter did not seem more disturbed. The general expectation that Pilgrim would go down with only a few bubbles continued unabated.

On the Sunday afternoon before the filing of the tender offer Valerian took a long walk with his frayed and shaggy poodle in Central Park. As he circled the reservoir and let his eyes rest on the southern skyline, his mood was one of static resignation. It seemed to him now that his little gesture was merely symbolic of his own uselessness and futility in the modern world. There was no law but that of the market, no right but that of the strong. The irresistible and unresisted materialism of the day was a flooding river that had penetrated every fissure and cranny of his world, inundating poor and rich, unions and management, the most popular entertainment and the greatest art. He visualized, tossing on its raging surface, the torn pages of the diaries of Philip Hone and George Templeton Strong.

On Monday he did not go to the office until the afternoon. He had no function in the filing of the tender offer or in the subsequent call on the target. Was it his imagination that the receptionist's greeting was saucy?

'Mr Treanor wants to see you immediately, Mr Shaw. He said for you to go right in the moment you arrived.'

Valerian, his overcoat on his arm, his heart pounding, entered the office of the senior partner. Cecil jumped up at once, without greeting him, and strode to the window where he stood with his back to his visitor.

'How did things go at Pilgrim, Cecil?'

Very well, no thanks to you,' the bitter voice came back to Valerian. 'In fact, I've never seen a smoother takeover. They capitulated at once. It was positively friendly! Your friend, Simeon Andrews, played his cards with the greatest astuteness. He sold his own stock for ten million plus an agreement that he would be chairman of the board of Zolex-Pilgrim for three years! It seems to be a question of who took over whom!'

Valerian felt his panic ebb away as he stood silently contemplating the wide, tweeded back of his former friend and about-to-be former partner. He took in the surprising fact that he was not surprised. There was something almost comforting in the flatness, the totality of his desolation.

'Andrews had another condition,' the voice continued. 'If we are to continue as counsel to Zolex-Pilgrim, the price will be your resignation from this firm. He informed me all about your indiscretion. He had already flared the Zolex project, so you told him nothing he didn't know, but he says he cannot afford to be represented by a firm with such a leak. Of course, I had to agree with him. I told him that you would cease to be a member of the firm as of today. I assured him that, if you refused to resign, we would dissolve the firm and re-form without you.'

'That won't be necessary, Cecil. I resign. As of this moment.'

Cecil whirled around. 'How could you do it, Val?' There was actually some feeling in his voice now. 'How could you do it to me? After all I've done for you? Looking after you and inventing things for you to do? And saving your stupid neck from our ravenous younger partners?'

'There's no point talking about it.'

'Of course, I'll have to tell the firm about it. I'm afraid there can be no idea now of a regular pension. But if you will let me negotiate the matter for you, I'll see that you get something. We don't want you to starve, after all. I'll put it to the partners as a kind of aberration on your part. Perhaps even that you've had a small stroke.'

'Any way you want it, Cecil. I leave that entirely to you.'

'But, Val, how *could* you?' Cecil's voice now rose to a wail. 'How could you betray a client? How could you violate the most sacred of the canons of ethics? What are the younger men to think of us? When I tell them at firm meetings what the ideals of Treanor, Saunders mean to me, to clients, to the bar, to the public? Won't they simply laugh at me?'

'I guess they may, Cecil,' Valerian replied wearily as he turned now to the door. 'I guess they really may. Why don't you just tell them you've gotten rid of a rotten egg?'

FROM "PLEADING GUILTY"

Scott Turow

Monday, January 23

MY ASSIGNMENT

The Management Oversight Committee of our firm, known among the partnership simply as 'the Committee,' meets each Monday at 3:00 p.m. Over coffee and chocolate brioche, these three hotshots, the heads of the firm's litigation, transactional, and regulatory departments, decide what's what at Gage & Griswell for another week. Not bad guys really, able lawyers, heady business types looking out for the greatest good for the greatest number at G&G, but since I came here eighteen years ago the Committee and their austere powers, freely delegated under the partnership agreement, have tended to scare me silly. I'm forty-nine, a former copper on the street, a big man with a brave front and a good Irish routine, but in the last few years I've heard many discouraging words from these three. My points have been cut, my office moved to something smaller, my hours and billing described as far too low. Arriving this afternoon, I steadied myself, as ever, for the worst.

'Mack,' said Martin Gold, our managing partner, 'Mack, we need your help. Something serious.' He's a sizable man, Martin, a wrestler at the U. three decades ago, a middleweight with a chest broad as the map of America. He has a dark, shrewd face, a little like those Mongol warriors of Genghis Khan's, and the venerable look of somebody who's mixed it up with life. He is, no question, the best lawyer I know.

The other two, Carl Pagnucci and Wash Thale, were eating at the walnut conference table, an antique of Continental origin

with the big heavy look of a cuckoo clock. Martin invited me to
share the brioche, but I took only coffee. With these guys, I
needed to be quick.

'This isn't about you,' said Carl, making a stark appraisal of my
apprehensions.

'Who?' I asked.

'Bert,' said Martin.

For going on two weeks, my partner Bert Kamin has not
appeared at the office. No mail from him, no calls. In the case of
your average baseline human being who has worked at Gage &
Griswell during my time, say anyone from Leotis Griswell to
the Polish gal who cleans the cans, this would be cause for
concern. Not so clearly Bert. Bert is a kind of temperamental
adolescent, big and brooding, who enjoys the combat of the
courtroom. You need a lawyer who will cross-examine opposing
party's CEO and claw out his intestines in the fashion of certain
large cats, Bert's your guy. On the other hand, if you want
someone who will come to work, fill out his time sheets, or treat
his secretary as if he recollected that slavery is dead, then you
might think about somebody else. After a month or two on trial,
Bert is liable to take an absolute powder. Once he turned up at
the fantasy camp run by the Trappers, our major league baseball
team. Another time he was gambling in Monte Carlo. With his
dark moods, scowls, and hallway tantrums, his macho stunts and
episodic schedule, Bert has survived at Gage & Griswell largely
through the sufferance of Martin, who is a champion of toler-
ance and seems to enjoy the odd ducks like Bert. Or, for that
matter, me.

'Why don't you talk to those thugs down at the steam bath
where he likes to hang out? Maybe they know where he is.' I
meant the Russian Bath. Unmarried, Bert is apt to follow the
Kindle County sporting teams around the country on weekends,
laying heavy bets and passing time in sports bars or places like the
Bath where people talk about the players with an intimacy they
don't presume with their relations. 'He'll show up,' I added, 'he
always does.'

Pagnucci said simply, 'Not this time.'

'This is very sensitive,' Wash Thale told me. 'Very sensitive.'

Wash tends to state the obvious in a grave, portentous manner, the self-commissioned voice of wisdom.

'Take a look.' Martin shot a brown expandable folder across the glimmer of the table. A test, I feared at once, and felt a bolt of anxiety quicken my thorax, but inside all I found were eighteen checks. They were drawn on what we call the 397 Settlement Account, an escrow administered by G&G which contains $288 million scheduled to be paid out shortly to various plaintiffs in settlement of a massive air crash case brought against TransNational Air. TN, the world's biggest airline and travel concern, is G&G's largest client. We stand up for TN in court; we help TN buy and deal and borrow. With its worldwide hotels and resorts, its national catering business, its golf courses, airport parking lots, and rent-a-car subsidiaries, TN lays claim to some part of the time of almost every lawyer around here. We live with the company like family in the same home, tenanted on four floors of the TN Needle, just below the world corporate headquarters.

The checks inside the folder had all been signed by Bert, in his flourishing maniac hand, each one cut to something called Litiplex Ltd., in an amount of several hundred thousand dollars. On the memo lines of the drafts Bert had written 'Litigation Support.' Document analyses, computer models, expert witnesses – the engineers run amok in air crash cases.

'What's Litiplex?' I asked.

Martin, to my amazement, rifled a finger as if I'd said something adroit.

'Not incorporated or authorized to do business in any of the fifty states,' he said. 'Not in any state's Assumed Names registry. Carl checked.'

Nodding, Carl added like an omen, 'Myself.'

Carl Pagnucci – born Carlo – is forty-two, the youngest of three, and stingy with words, a lawyer's lawyer who holds his own speech in the same kind of suspicion with which Woody Hayes viewed the forward pass. He is a pale little guy with a mustache like one of those round brushes that comes with your electric shaver. In his perfect suits, sombre and tasteful, with a flash of gold from his cuff links, he reveals nothing.

Assessing the news that Bert, my screwball colleague, had

written millions of dollars of checks to a company that didn't exist, I felt some peculiar impulse to defend him, my own long-time alliance with the wayward.

'Maybe somebody asked him to do it,' I said.

'That's where *we* started,' Wash replied. He'd taken his stout figure back to the brioche. This had come up initially, Wash said, when Glyndora Gaines, our staff supervisor in Accounting, noticed these large disbursements with no backup.

'Glyndora's searched three times for any paper trail,' Wash told me. 'Invoices. Sign-off memo from Jake.' Under our procedures, Bert was allowed to write checks on the 397 account only after receiving written approval from Jake Eiger, a former partner in this firm, who is now the General Counsel at TN.

'And?'

'There is none. We've even had Glyndora make inquiries upstairs with her counterparts at TN, the folks who handle the accounting on 397. Nothing to alarm them. You understand. "We had some stray correspondence for this Litiplex. Blah, blah, blah." Martin tried the same approach with one or two of the plaintiffs' lawyers in the hope they knew something we didn't. There's nothing,' he said, 'not a scrap. Nobody's ever heard the name.' Wash is more shifty than smart, but looking at him – his liver spots and wattles, his discreet twitches and the little bit of mouse gray hair he insists on pasting across his scalp – I detected the feckless expression he has when he is sincere. 'Not to mention,' he added, 'the endorsement.'

I'd missed that. Now I took note on the back of each check of the bilingual green block stamp of the International Bank of Finance in Pico Luan. Pico, a tiny Central American nation, a hangnail on the toe of the Yucatán, is a pristine haven of fugitive dollars and absolute bank secrecy. There were no signatures on the checks' backs, but what I took for the account number was inscribed on each beneath the stamp. A straight deposit.

'We tried calling the bank,' said Martin. 'I explained to the General Manager that we were merely trying to confirm that Robert Kamin had rights of deposit and withdrawal on account 476642. I received a very genial lecture on the bank secrecy laws in Pico in reply. Quite a clever fellow, this one. With that beautiful accent. Just the piece of work you'd expect in that business. Like trying to grab hold of smoke. I asked if he was familiar with Mr Kamin's name. Not a word I could quote, but I thought he was saying yes. God knows, he didn't say no.'

'And what's the total?' I thumbed the checks.

'Over five and a half million,' said Carl, who was always quickest with figures. 'Five point six and some change actually.'

With that, we were all briefly silent, awed by the gravity of the number and the daring of the feat. My partners writhed in further anguish, but on closer inspection of myself I found I was vibrating like a bell that had been struck. What a notion! Grabbing all that dough and hieing out for parts unknown. The wealth, the freedom, the chance to start anew! I wasn't sure if I was more shocked or thrilled.

'Has anybody talked to Jake?' That seemed like the next logical step to me, tell the client they'd been had.

'God, no,' said Wash. 'There's going to be hell to pay with TN. A partner in the firm lies to them, embezzles, steals. That's just the kind of thing that Krzysinski has been waiting for to leverage Jake. We will be dead. Dead,' he said.

There was a lot that was beyond me going on among the three of them – the Big Three, as they are called behind their backs – but I now thought I could see why I was here. Through most of my career at G&G I have been viewed as Jake Eiger's proxy. We grew up in the same neighbourhood and Jake was also a third or fourth cousin of my former wife. Jake was the person responsible for bringing me to the firm when he left to become Senior Division Counsel of TransNational Air. That is a long tradition at Gage & Griswell. For over four decades now, our former partners have dominated the law department at TN, becoming rich on stock options and remembering their old colleagues with the opportunity for lavish billing. Jake, however, has been under pressure from Tad Krzysinski, TN's new CEO, to spread TN's legal business around, and Jake, unsure of his own ground with Krzysinski, has given troubling signs that he will respond. In fact, in my case he seems to have responded some time ago, although I can't tell you if that's because I divorced his cousin, used to drink my lunch, or remain afflicted by something you might politely call 'malaise.'

'We wanted your advice, Mack, on what we should do,' said Martin. 'Before we went any further.' He eyed me levelly beneath his furry brows. Behind him, out the broad windows of the thirty-seventh story of the TN Needle, Kindle County stretched – the shoebox shapes of Center City and, beyond that, upraised brick smokestack arms. On the west bank of the river, suburban wealth spread beneath the canopy of older trees. All of it was forlornly sullied by the dingy light of winter.

'Call the FBI,' I offered. 'I'll give you a name.' You'd expect a former city cop to recommend his own department, but I left some enemies on the Force. Reading my partners' looks, you could see that I'd missed their mood anyway. Law enforcement was not on the agenda.

Wash finally said it: 'Premature.'

I admitted that I didn't see the alternatives.

'This is a business,' said Carl, a credo from which all further premises devolved. Carl worships what he calls the market with an ardour which in former centuries was reserved for religion. He has a robust securities practice, making the markets work, and a jet-lagged life, zooming back here to Kindle County at least twice a week from D.C., where he heads our Washington office.

'What we were thinking,' said Wash, who laid his elderly hands daintily on the dark table, 'some of us, anyway, is what if we could find Bert. Reason with him.' Wash swallowed. 'Get him to give the money back.'

I stared.

'Perhaps he's had second thoughts,' Wash insisted. 'Something like this – he's impulsive. He's been running now, hiding. He might like another chance.'

'Wash,' I said, 'he has five and a half million reasons to say no. And a little problem about going to jail.'

'Not if we don't tell,' said Wash. He swallowed again. His sallow face was wan with hope above his bow tie.

'You wouldn't tell TN?'

'If they didn't ask, no. And why should they? Really, if this works out, what is there to tell them? There was *almost* a problem? No, no,' said Wash, 'I don't believe that's required.'

'And what would you do with Bert? Just kiss and make up?'

Pagnucci answered. 'It's a negotiation,' he said simply, a deal maker who believes that willing parties always find a way.

I pondered, slowly recognizing how artfully this could be engineered. The usual false faces of the workplace, only more so. They'd let Bert come back here and say it was all a bad dream. Or withdraw from the practice for a while and pay him – severance, purchase of equity, call it what you'd like. A person feeling either frightened or remorseful might find these offers attractive. But I wasn't sure Bert would see this as much of a deal. In fact, for three smart guys they seemed to have little idea of what had happened. They'd been flipped the bird and were still acting as if it was sign language for the deaf.

Wash had gotten out his pipe, one of his many props, and was waving it around.

'Either we find some way to solve this problem – privately – or the doors here will be shut in a year. Six months. That's my firm prediction.' Wash's sense of peril no doubt was greatest for himself, since he had been the billing partner for TN for nearly three decades, his only client worth mentioning and the linchpin of what would otherwise have been a career as mediocre as mine. He has been an *ex officio* member of TN's board for twenty-two years now and is so closely attuned to the vibrations of the company that he can tell you when someone on TN's 'Executive Level,' seven floors above, has broken wind.

'I still don't understand how you think you'll find Bert.'

Pagnucci touched the checks. I didn't understand at first. He was tapping the endorsement.

'Pico?'

'Have you ever been down there?'

I'd first been to Pico when I was assigned to Financial Crimes more than twenty years ago – sky of blue, round and perfect as a cereal bowl above the Mayan Mountains; vast beaches long and lovely as a suntanned flank. Most of the folks around here are down there often. TN was one of the first to despoil the coast, erecting three spectacular resorts. But I hadn't taken the trip in years. I told Carl that.

'You think that's where Bert is?'

'That's where his money is,' Pagnucci said.

'No, sir. That's where it went. Where it is now is anybody's guess. The beauty of bank secrecy is that it ends the trail. You can send the money anywhere from Pico. It could be back here, frankly. If it was in the right municipal bonds, he wouldn't even have to pay taxes.'

'Right, ' Pagnucci quickly said. He took this setback, like most things, in silence, but his precise, mannerly good looks clouded with vexation.

'And who's going to do the looking?' I asked. 'I don't know many private investigators I'd trust with this one.'

'No, no,' said Wash. 'No one outside the family. We weren't thinking of a private investigator.' He was looking somewhat hopefully at me. I actually laughed when I finally got it.

'Wash, I know more about writing traffic tickets than how to find Bert. Call Missing Persons.'

'He trusts you, Mack,' Wash told me. 'You're his friend.'

'Bert has no friends.'

'He'd respect your opinion. Especially about his prospects of escaping without prosecution. Bert's childish. We all know that. And peculiar. With a familiar face, he'd consider this in a new light.'

Anybody who's survived for more than two decades in a law firm or a police department knows better than to say no to the boss. Around here it's team play – yes, sir, and salute smartly. No way I could refuse. But there was a reason I was going to law school at night while I was on the street. I was never one of these lamebrains who thought cop work was glamorous. Kicking doors in, running down dark alleys – that stuff tended to terrify me, especially afterwards when I got to thinking about what I'd done.

'I have a hearing Wednesday,' I said. This took them all back for a moment. No one, apparently, had considered the prospect that I might be working. 'Bar Admissions and Discipline still wants to punch Toots Nuccio's ticket.'

There was a moment's byplay as Wash proposed alternatives – a continuance, perhaps, or allowing another G&G lawyer to handle the case; there were, after all, 130 attorneys here. Martin, the head of litigation, eventually suggested I find another partner to join me at the hearing, someone who could take over down the road if need be. Even with that settled, I was still resisting.

'Guys, this doesn't make sense. I'm never going to find Bert. And you'll only make them angrier at TN once they realize we waited to tell them.'

'Not so,' said Wash. 'Not so. We needed time to gather facts so that we could advise them. You'll prepare a report, Mack,' he said, 'something we can hand them. Dictate it as you go along. After all, this is a significant matter. Something that can badly embarrass them, as well as us. They'll understand. We'll say you'll take no more than two weeks.' He looked to Martin and Carl for verification.

I repeated that there was no place to look.

'Why don't you ask those thugs down at the steam bath where he likes to hang out?' Pagnucci asked. Talking to Carl is often even less satisfying than his silence. He is stubbornly, subtly, but inalterably contrary. Pagnucci regards agreement as a failure of his solemn obligation to exercise critical intelligence. there is always a probing question, a sly jest, a suggested alternative, always a way for him to put an ax to your tree. The guy is more than half a foot shorter than me and makes me feel no bigger than a flea.

'Mack, you would be the saviour of this firm,' said Wash. 'Imagine if it did work out. Our gratitude would be' – Wash waved – 'unspeakable.'

It all looked perfect from their side. I'm a burnt-out case. No big clients. Gun-shy about trials since I stopped drinking. A fucked-up wreck with the chance to secure my position. And all of this coming up at the most opportune time. The firm was in its annual hysteria with the approaching conclusion of our fiscal year on January 31. All the partners were busy choking overdue fees out of our clients and positioning themselves for February 2, a week and a half from now, when the profits would be divided.

I considered Wash, wondering how I ever ended up working for anybody in a bow tie.

'I say the same thing to you I've said to Martin and Carl,' Wash told me. 'It's ours, this place, our lives as lawyers are here. What do we lose if we take a couple of weeks trying to save it?'

With that, the three were silent. If nothing else, I had their attention. In high school I used to play baseball. I'm big – six three – and never a lightweight. I have good eyehand, I could hit the ball a long way, but I'm slow, what people call lumbering when they're trying to be polite, and the coaches had to find someplace to play me, which turned out to be the outfield. I've never been the guy you'd want on your team. If I wasn't batting, I wasn't really in the game. Three hundred feet away from home plate you can forget. The wind comes up; you smell the grass, the perfume from some girl in the stands. A wrapper kicks across the field, followed by a ghost of dust. You check the sun, falling, even with all the yelling to keep you awake, into a kind of trance state, a piece of meditation or dreams. And then, somehow, you feel the eyes of everybody in the park suddenly shifted toward you – the pitcher looking back, the batter, the people in the stands, somebody some place has yelled your name. It's all coming to you, this dark circle hoving through the sky, changing size, just the way you've seen it at night when you're asleep. I had that feeling now, of having been betrayed by my dreams.

Fear, as usual, was my only real excuse.

'Listen, guys. This was carefully planned. By Mr Litiplex or Kamin or whoever. Bert's three sheets to the wind with his sails nowhere in sight. And even if I do find him, by some miracle, what do you think happens when he opens the door and sees that he's been tracked down by one of his partners, who undoubtedly is going to speak to him about going to prison? What do you think he'll do?'

'He'll talk to you, Mack.'

'He'll shoot me, Wash. If he's got any sense.'

Bereft of a response, Wash looked on with limpid blue eyes and a guttering soul – an aging white man. Martin, a step ahead as ever, smiled in his subtle way because he knew I'd agreed.

Pagnucci as usual said nothing.

THE CASE FOR THE DEFENCE

Graham Greene

It was the strangest murder trial I ever attended. They named it
the Peckham murder in the headlines, though Northwood Street,
where the old woman was found battered to death, was not
strictly speaking in Peckham. This was not one of those cases
of circumstantial evidence in which you feel the jurymen's
anxiety – because mistakes *have* been made – like domes of
silence muting the court. No, this murderer was all but found
with the body; no one present when the Crown counsel outlined
his case believed that the man in the dock stood any chance at all.

He was a heavy stout man with bulging bloodshot eyes. All his
muscles seemed to be in his thighs. Yes, an ugly customer, one
you wouldn't forget in a hurry – and that was an important point
because the Crown proposed to call four witnesses who hadn't
forgotten him, who had seen him hurrying away from the little
red villa in Northwood Street. The clock had just struck two in
the morning.

Mrs Salmon in 15 Northwood Street had been unable to sleep;
she heard a door click shut and thought it was her own gate. So
she went to the window and saw Adams (that was his name) on
the steps of Mrs Parker's house. He had just come out and he was
wearing gloves. He had a hammer in his hand and she saw him
drop it into the laurel bushes by the front gate. But before he
moved away, he had looked up – at her window. The fatal instinct
that tells a man when he is watched exposed him in the light of a
street-lamp to her gaze – his eyes suffused with horrifying and
brutal fear, like an animal's when you raise a whip. I talked
afterwards to Mrs Salmon, who naturally after the astonishing

verdict went in fear herself. As I imagine did all the witnesses –
Henry MacDougall, who had been driving home from Benfleet
late and nearly ran Adams down at the corner of Northwood
Street. Adams was walking in the middle of the road looking
dazed. And old Mr Wheeler, who lived next door to Mrs Parker,
at No. 12, and was wakened by a noise – like a chair falling –
through the thin-as-paper villa wall, and got up and looked out of
the window, just as Mrs Salmon had done, saw Adams's back
and, as he turned, those bulging eyes. In Laurel Avenue he had
been seen by yet another witness – his luck was badly out; he
might as well have committed the crime in broad daylight.

'I understand', counsel said, 'that the defence proposes to
plead mistaken identity. Adams's wife will tell you that he was
with her at two in the morning on February 14, but after you have
heard the witnesses for the Crown and examined carefully the
features of the prisoner, I do not think you will be prepared to
admit the possibility of a mistake.'

It was all over, you would have said, but the hanging.

After the formal evidence had been given by the policeman
who had found the body and the surgeon who examined it, Mrs
Salmon was called. She was the ideal witness, with her slight
Scotch accent and her expression of honesty, care and kindness.

The counsel for the Crown brought the story gently out. She
spoke very firmly. There was no malice in her, and no sense of
importance at standing there in the Central Criminal Court with
a judge in scarlet hanging on her words and the reporters writing
them down. Yes, she said, and then she had gone downstairs and
rung up the police station.

'And do you see the man here in court?'

She looked straight at the big man in the dock, who stared hard
at her with his pekingese eyes without emotion.

'Yes,' she said, 'there he is.'

'You are quite certain?'

She said simply, 'I couldn't be mistaken, sir.'

It was all easy as that.

'Thank you, Mrs Salmon.'

Counsel for the defence rose to cross-examine. If you had
reported as many murder trials as I have, you would have known

beforehand what line he would take. And I was right, up to a point.

'Now, Mrs Salmon, you must remember that a man's life may depend on your evidence.'

'I do remember it, sir.'

'Is your eyesight good?'

'I have never had to wear spectacles, sir.'

'You are a woman of fifty-five?'

'Fifty-six, sir.'

'And the man you saw was on the other side of the road?'

'Yes, sir.'

'And it was two o'clock in the morning. You must have remarkable eyes, Mrs Salmon?'

'No, sir. There was moonlight, and when the man looked up, he had the lamplight on his face.'

'And you have no doubt whatever that the man you saw is the prisoner?'

I couldn't make out what he was at. He couldn't have expected any other answer than the one he got.

'None whatever, sir. It isn't a face one forgets.'

Counsel took a look round the court for a moment. Then he said, 'Do you mind, Mrs Salmon, examining again the people in court? No, not the prisoner. Stand up, please, Mr Adams,' and there at the back of the court with thick stout body and muscular legs and a pair of bulging eyes, was the exact image of the man in the dock. He was even dressed the same – tight blue suit and striped tie.

'Now think very carefully, Mrs Salmon. Can you still swear that the man you saw drop the hammer in Mrs Parker's garden was the prisoner – and not this man, who is his twin brother?'

Of course she couldn't. She looked from one to the other and didn't say a word.

There the big brute sat in the dock with his legs crossed, and there he stood too at the back of the court and they both stared at Mrs Salmon. She shook her head.

What we saw then was the end of the case. There wasn't a witness prepared to swear that it was the prisoner he'd seen. And the brother? He had his alibi, too; he was with his wife.

And so the man was acquitted for lack of evidence. But whether – if he did the murder and not his brother – he was punished or not, I don't know. That extraordinary day had an extraordinary end. I followed Mrs Salmon out of court and we got wedged in the crowd who were waiting, of course, for the twins. The police tried to drive the crowd away, but all they could do was keep the road-way clear for traffic. I learned later that they tried to get the twins to leave by a back way, but they wouldn't. One of them – no one knew which – said, 'I've been acquitted, haven't I?' and they walked bang out of the front entrance. Then it happened. I don't know how, though I was only six feet away. The crowd moved and somehow one of the twins got pushed on to the road right in front of a bus.

He gave a squeal like a rabbit and that was all; he was dead, his skull smashed just as Mrs Parker's had been. Divine vengeance? I wish I knew. There was the other Adams getting on his feet from beside the body and looking straight over at Mrs Salmon. He was crying, but whether he was the murderer or the innocent man nobody will ever be able to tell. But if you were Mrs Salmon, could you sleep at night?

A GREAT DANCE

John F. Dobbyn

I hadn't seen Jake Barnes for more than a hand shake in three – I guess four years. It stunned me to think of that, because I truly loved the old man. It was just lack of time. There wasn't a day I wasn't on trial in one court and on call in two others.

That sounds like an excuse – especially to me. But now it was catch-up time.

I knew Jake was leaving at ten. That meant crosstown through Boston traffic in twenty minutes. I slipped a ten between two fingers and held it through the slot in the glass to the front seat of the cab.

'And a dollar for every light you make – green or red.'

I felt the ten slip through my fingers. An East Boston accent punctuated the grinding of the gear shift.

'Start counting.'

Red and green traffic lights whipped by until they began to resemble a string of Christmas lights. For some reason, it brought me back to Christmas break of my third year of law school. I was young, pumped, and dumb enough to call blind for an interview with the lion of the criminal defense bar, James Patrick Barnes.

He gave me exactly ninety seconds. I took the first ten to introduce myself. In the second ten, he scanned my résumé with a remarkable lack of fascination. That left time for one question: 'Why do you want to defend a lot of guilty people, kid?'

'Everyone deserves a defense, sir. The constitution . . .'

He skidded the résumé across the desk. 'Does this look like a cocktail party?'

'No, sir.'

'Then let's skip what you tell your relatives around the punch bowl. Why do you want to defend guilty people?'

For the first time in an interview, I thought someone wanted the raw truth. 'Because I like a good fight, sir.'

The old buzzard slammed the desk. I grabbed the chair to keep from bolting.

'Get out of here, kid. This is a law office. I'm in court in ten minutes.'

I was at the door when I heard him bark, 'Be back in this office when you get a law degree. I'll give you a fight.'

And fight we did, for five years, but always on the same side. We tried everything that could come into a criminal court. We won some that were losers, and lost some that deserved losing, but never without the best scrap a client had the right to expect.

The years rolled by like pages of a calendar in a windstorm. Within four years, my name was on the door as a junior partner, and I found myself more and more frequently pushed out onto a limb. The only thing that kept my ulcer in check was the invisible view of Jake holding the safety net below me.

The biggest hurrah of those five years was our defense of Frank Boyle, head of the New England teamsters. He'd been set up on a murder charge by powerfully connected enemies. It was front-page fodder for the five weeks of trial. It was also a case in which Jake forced me to take the leading role. We finally won it on a jury verdict after three days of deliberation.

I came into the office the next day with a bottle of champagne. I took one look at the door panel, and the floor nearly dropped out from under me. My name was off the door. I stepped into my office and found everything personal in cartons on the floor. There was not a trace of the personal bullets I had sweat over that desk. For the first time, I walked into Jake's office without knocking. I didn't even get the question out.

'You're fired, kid. You're looking for a job.'

I guess I just stood there with the champagne bottle hanging inappropriately from my hand.

'You can take your things or send for them.'

There was a hollowness in his voice that baffled me as much as what he was saying. 'Close the door on your way out, kid.'

He had his back to me. I heard him say in a hoarse voice,

'Before you go, you've got a call to return in your office.'

I closed the door and somehow drifted back to my phone. I called up the message. It was from the senior partner of the top civil litigation firm in Boston. I could only tune in every third word, but the substance of it was an offer of a junior partnership with a price tag too outrageously large to comprehend.

I went back through Jake's door for the second time without knocking.

'I don't want it, Jake.'

He looked up with what looked like slightly swollen eyes.

'I know, but you better want it, kid. You're out of a job.'

'That's my decision.'

He stood up and shook his head. His eyes came up to meet mine.

'There is no decision. I knew you'd balk, but we both know it's the right move. I've brought you as far as I can. Go the distance, kid. Don't let me down.'

I tried to argue, but nothing came out. He held out his hand. I had all I could do to take it without dissolving. I felt every gift a father could give to a son in that handshake. I think he felt it, too.

I was nearly out the door when he caught me with that powerful voice.

'Kid!'

I turned around.

'It was a great dance, wasn't it?'

A heartfelt nod was all I could get out.

In the next six years, I plowed twenty-six hours a day into the civil litigation that came across my desk in geometrically expanding complexity and dollars-at-stake. I saw less and less of Jake, not through lack of love, but lack of time. It was nearly six years to the day that I went to McDonough's Funeral Home for the wake of his wife, Mary. I knew they were close, but I never realized how close until I saw what two years of Mary's decline under cancer had done to him. The old dark-blue serge hung on him like a hand-me-down from a man twice his size. The bright light was misted in those blue eyes that had pierced like laser beams.

We hugged, and I sorely regretted the time apart.

The next day I was back in the mesh of my own cases, and before I knew it, it was another year before I gave serious thought to my friend and adopted father. It hit hard when I heard the buzz around the lawyers' bars that the old Viking had been brought down by drink.

A slight taste for the grape seems endemic to trial lawyers, but it's also a breed that has a clear sense of when one of its close circle of warriors has slipped over the edge.

I dropped by the office, but Jake was out. One thing led to another, and it was three months later when I read in the *Globe* that the mayor's son had been charged with vehicular homicide. He'd apparently left a party in South Boston under the influence. Someone was killed by a hit-and-run two blocks from the party at about the same time. An anonymous tip put the D.A. onto the mayor's son.

What really caught my eye was that Mayor Connoly had retained Jake Barnes to defend his son. I shouldn't have been surprised. Jake and the mayor had been close friends from childhood through their law-school days at Harvard. It was just the rumours about Jake's drinking. Then I thought, if I were in trouble, whom would I call – sober or otherwise? There was only one.

I had to be in Suffolk Superior Court on an important motion that morning. By the time I was out of the hearing, I ran into a cluster of trial lawyers who seemed delighted over some news that indicated that Jake still had the old mustard. Apparently the killing took place at two in the morning. They had young Mike Connoly in custody by four-thirty. The D.A., Mack Hensler, was at the station house to personally read him his Miranda warnings and take his confession.

I could visualize Hensler at the arraignment that morning presenting the confession like a newfound original of the Magna Carta. Without a doubt, his hunger to unseat and eventually replace his old rival, Mayor Tom Connoly, was in a feeding frenzy after that confession. What the lawyers were laughing about was that apparently Jake Barnes strode into court with a motion to exclude, quash, kill, and otherwise dispose of the confession on the grounds that young Connoly had been in no mental state to validly waive his Miranda right to remain silent. Hensler had hanged himself on his own rope. He had so effectively proven that Connoly was intoxicated at two a.m. that Jake was able to convince the court that he would not have been sober by four-thirty when the confession was signed. The confession was excluded as evidence, and the D.A. was left with only circumstantial evidence to try to hang Connoly.

That did it. I had to see Jake. I was thrilled just walking into our old offices. I was more thrilled to see Jake pacing like a tiger behind his desk with a phone to his ear. He threw me a grin and waved me into a chair. He jotted something on the legal pad in front of him and said something about meeting in twenty-five minutes before he hung up.

'You heard.'

He looked ten years younger than the last time I'd seen him.

'Good news travels, Jake.'

He just smiled back at me, and a lot of understanding passed between us. He smacked the back of his chair the way he used to.

'I'd love to chat, son, but this is my day.'

He scooped his hat off the rack.

'Where're you going, Jake?'

He leaned over close.

'Witness. A real gift.' He nodded back at the phone. 'It seems that one Carlo Peruzzo was at that same party last night.'

'And . . .?'

'Peruzzo lives out in Winthrop, close to young Connoly. He says he rode home with Connoly. Peruzzo drove Connoly's car because Connoly was somewhat in the bag. All of which means that at the time the D.A. says the homicide occurred in South Boston, Master Connoly was in the Sumner Tunnel under Boston Harbour.'

He was at the door by the time I was on my feet. He turned for a quick, sad smile that said we've got a lot to talk about.

'Come back, will you, son?'

I was choked again. I was also determined. 'I'll be here, Jake.'

The trial date for Mike Connoly came up fast. I sat in the spectators' section behind Jake the day he put the witness,

Peruzzo, on the stand. Jake led him through the preliminaries, and then gave him his head. Peruzzo looked from one juror to the other as he told of an uneventful ride to Winthrop with young Connoly. By the time Peruzzo left Connoly, it was an hour after the homicide took place according to the D.A.'s own time-table.

The judge took the morning recess before cross-examination by the D.A. When the court reassembled, the D.A. was in a flurry of consultation with his associates at prosecution table. He finally asked to approach the bench with defense counsel. I couldn't tell what was going on, but it clearly had everyone in high-C.

The judge finally sent the jury out for lunch and led both counsel back into chambers at quick march. I knew this could go on for hours, and I was due at an injunction hearing in another courtroom. Whatever it was, I knew Jake could handle it.

I got home that night in time to flip on the eleven o'clock news. I stood there frozen with chills, topcoat still on, listening to what had happened in the courtroom after the conference in the judge's chambers. According to the news account, the D.A. took Jake's witness, Peruzzo, on cross-examination and waltzed him through a complete recanting of his story. The way he told it this time, the defense had hired him to commit perjury. The whole alibi was a fraud. The final plunge of the dagger was in Jake's back. Peruzzo implicated the mayor and named Jake as the payoff man.

The judge ordered a transcript of Peruzzo's testimony to be sent to the bar disciplinary board to begin disbarment proceedings against Jake.

There was no redirect examination. Jake Barnes collapsed in the courtroom. He was rushed to the Massachusetts General Hospital with a coronary.

I got there as fast as I could, but I couldn't see him until the next morning, and then it was brief. I took his hand beside the bed.

'What happened, Jake?'

The eyes flickered.

'Don't believe everything you read in the papers, kid.'

'I know you were set up. Who did it?'

He mumbled something like 'Blindsided.' Then the drugs took him back to wherever.

I called my office from the hospital and told my secretary, Julie, to put everything and everyone on hold until further notice. She said it couldn't be done. I said it could if I'd been hit by a truck. She agreed. I told her I had been. At least, it felt that way.

I was at the lock-up in twenty minutes, waiting for a guard to bring young Connoly to the lawyers' interviewing room. The cold steel and linoleum were a far cry from the plush floors and flocked walls I'd done business in since leaving Jake's good company. I wondered why it felt so good to be back.

Mike Connoly was quick enough to accept my offer to pick up the reins of his case. He was over twenty-one, but I suggested a call to his dad for his approval. He got it, and we were in business.

Beyond that, Mike was relatively useless. He remembered being at the party. He remembered seeing Peruzzo there, although he had never met him previously. He had only one drink, but the next thing he actually remembered was waking up in the lockup the following morning. The one thing he was dead sure about was having nothing to do with bribing an alibi witness.

I was on the street in fifteen minutes, walking a shortcut to the courthouse to file my appearance as counsel for the defense. The judge was good enough to set up a quick phone conference with the D.A., Hensler, to work out a schedule for continuing the trial. I pleaded for two weeks and got one week, which is what I wanted in the first place.

By the time I grabbed a quick, stand-up hot dog from a pushcart on Washington Street and checked in with my office, there was a message to get in touch with Frank Boylan. I wasn't surprised. Frank was the third of the trio of inseparables who'd grown up, in the old days, in the Irish barrio of Charlestown. The other two were Jake and the Right Honorable Mayor Connoly. They had all climbed out of the tenements of Charlestown, frequently by pulling on each other's bootstraps, and the bonds between them had never slackened.

Frank Boylan's office on Tremont Street proved the adage that a cluttered office is a sign of an organized mind. Frank was round, bald, sixty, and you can find at least one of him in every pub in Dublin. In fact, at his diminutive height, it would have been easier to find him in a pub than behind the rambling mounds of files on his desk. His secretary was on break, so I walked in.

'Mr. Boylan. You in there?'

'Boyyo! You got my message. How's himself?'

'Holding, last time I saw him.' I followed the voice till I caught sight of him behind the desk. I'd have sat, but I would have lost sight of him altogether.

'He's a fighter. You know that even better than I do, Jimmy.'

It seemed funny to be actually called by my name by one of Jake's generation.

'I got something for you, Jimmy. Peruzzo came to see me this morning out of the blue. I hadn't seen him since I represented him a few years ago. He wants me to represent him on the perjury charge.'

I don't know why that came as a shock. The breadbasket of Frank's practice had for many years been the string of probability technicians, social consultants, and financial facilitators (book makers, prostitutes, and loan sharks, respectively) under the dominion of Don Angelo Capelli, with headquarters in the North End and a territory that ranged throughout New England. Being non-Italian, Frank Boylan was up against a glass ceiling, as they say, in terms of the level of mobster he was allowed to represent, but the practice was lucrative and dependable. In fact, it promised to pick up. The mayoral election was three weeks away, and His Honor, Tom Connoly, had promised a full strike at all levels of the mafia in what he hoped would be his next term as mayor.

'Did you take the case?'

He stood up, which didn't make much difference in his elevation. The lines on that map of Ireland he wore for a face spelled pure stress.

'You don't understand, Jimmy. I'd cut off my arm for Jake. But Peruzzo's connected all the way up to . . .' He nodded toward the North End of Boston. 'I can't say no. I know where a lot of bodies are buried, so to speak, from the practice. Besides, and this has got to be between us. This never came from me. They're jumpy as cats at the top. There's a split between the big shot and his number two man that could break into a shooting war any day. If I do something that calls into question my loyalty . . .'

I thought of Jake, and what he'd do if things were reversed and Boylan needed his loyalty. I suddenly felt the need of fresh air. Boylan caught me at the door.

'Listen, Jimmy. This could help Jake.'

I waited.

'If the big man, you know who I mean, has to go to war, has to . . . shed some blood on the streets of Boston to preserve the family kingdom, he could run afoul of the mayor's promise to come down on the mob if they so much as jaywalk. Tom means it, and they know it. The election's in three weeks. If they could do something to discredit Tom just before the election, they'd have open streets if his opponent gets in. Do you take my meaning, Jimmy?'

'Are you saying the mayor's opponent is in the pocket of Angelo Capelli?'

He shrugged his shoulders until his neck disappeared. I scanned the beads of sweat that covered his forehead clear back to the nape of his neck. He was a piece of work, this Irish minor-league *consigliere*. But he sowed the seed.

I was nearly out the door when I decided to call in an owed favour.

'I'm going to talk to Peruzzo. Where do I find him?'

There was a hesitation, but the look on my face stirred enough guilt to get it out of him.

'He lives in Winthrop.'

He handed me a scribbled address.

'Jimmy, just go light on where you got it, right?'

I just smiled. 'It'll be our little secret.'

I needed a quick handle on the case, and the office of Matt Hensler, the D.A., was a short, brisk, head-clearing walk from Boylan's office.

He was happy to inform me that he had blood samples from the right, dented fender of young Connolly's car that matched the blood type of the victim. He also had a witness who saw the red

Eagle Talon swerve down D Street in a blue-collar section of
Southie and clip the elderly deceased under a streetlight as he
stepped off the curb at two a.m. There was no direct identification of Mike as the driver, but Peruzzo's little flip-flop as a
perjured alibi witness was probably enough to fill that square.

One bit of gold I dug out of our chat was the name of the
victim. Lewis Resnick had been seventy years old at the time of
his demise. He apparently left his apartment on D Street after
midnight that Saturday night to cross the street to a 7-Eleven for
the Sunday paper, as was his weekly habit. He barely made it off
the curb. He had lived alone and had no known family. Another
dead end.

I asked Hensler why he thought Peruzzo changed his story in
mid trial.

'Cold feet,' was Hensler's explanation. With typical modesty,
he said, 'When he realized I was going to pick him apart on cross-
examination, he knew he'd be facing life as a three-time loser. He
just quit while there was still time to make a deal.'

Jake had always taught me to keep an open mind on the facts right
up to the time the jury comes in. That was an option I couldn't
afford with six and a half days left before trial. I decided to take a
basic assumption as indisputable and go from there.

Assumption: Jake wouldn't bribe a witness to keep his grand
mother out of the electric chair. That meant Peruzzo was lying
about the perjury and his doing so opened a floodgate of questions. What brought a midlevel member of the Capelli mob into
this business in the first place? It was straining coincidence to
believe that Peruzzo met Connoly at that party by chance, given
the bizarre string of events that followed. Peruzzo knew he'd be
facing cross-examination when he took the stand, which made his
about-face look the more contrived from the beginning. And if
the whole sequence of events did follow a script from the outset,
including the hit-and-run death of Mr Resnick, who wrote the
script?

Jake once said, 'When a hunch is the sum total of your options,
ride the hunch like it was proven fact, and see who blinks.'

If Mr Resnick's departure from this earth was part of a

deliberate plan, my first move in playing catch-up ball was to find out who Mr Resnick was in life. My years with a high-stakes litigation firm had put me in touch with a select breed of private investigator who can do more than track errant husbands.

I reached Steve Casey at his club in Wellesley. The location suggests expensive, which is true. He is also worth every dime he charges, and more. I laid out my needs, and the fact that I had to have the information by ten that evening. Any other investigator would have laughed. Steve just raised the rates.

I hung by the phone through the evening until Steve called about nine-thirty. It seems that the deceased was, in Steve's words, a gnome who lived in a row-house in Southie for the better part of his life. Nothing seemed to distinguish him from a hundred other elderly gentlemen chewing a cigar on the front stoop on any summer's evening.

My heart was sinking at the thought of another dead end, when Steve earned his fee.

'On the other hand, Jimmy, would it brighten your youthful countenance to know that in his will he bequeathed the controlling stock in a chain of dry-cleaners, four restaurants, a string of auto dealerships, and about six other random businesses around this Bay State?'

'Steven, my youthful countenance will grin from ear to ear if you can tell me who's named in the will.'

'One legatee. Try Francis Augustus Angelino.'

'Could we be talking Frankie Angelino?'

'We are indeed. Are you grinning, James?'

I sucked in one deep breath and went for the gold.

'Are we talking the inconspicuous, apparently unconnected son-in-law of Don Angelo Capelli?'

'The same. Are you grinning now, James? You should grin now, because tomorrow you'll get my bill.'

'Let's face one disaster at a time. I hear some tumblers clicking into place here. Tell me if this scans. We know all of the families are pouring dirty money into legitimate businesses. I assume the Capelli family is no exception. They need a parking lot for the ownership of the straight businesses, some clean name that would obscure the fact that your friendly dry cleaner is the mob. They pick your gnome, Mr Resnick, and put all the legitimate stock in his name. Their insurance policy in case he dies of natural or other causes is Resnick's will. Does that work?'

'Superbly, James.'

'Then if Don Angelo's second-in-command is getting frisky, Mr Resnick becomes an important pawn in the game. Whoever owns Resnick owns a sizeable empire.'

'So it would seem.'

'You're very agreeable, Steve. Let's see if I can get some mileage out of your expensive findings.'

It was midnight when Carlo Peruzzo climbed the steps to his Winthrop duplex. I was sitting in the dark at the far end of the porch. I let him get the key in the lock before breaking the silence.

'Carlo!'

The shock spun him against the wall, and his right hand instinctively went for the inside of his coat. When it came up with nothing, I knew he was unarmed. I started to breathe again.

His first words that weren't curses amounted to an inquiry as to my identity.

'I'm the one who can keep you alive, maybe even through the end of the month. Sit down.'

His instinct was to come for me. I kept it calm and controlled. My trump card was that he couldn't see me in the dark. For all he knew, I was leveling a howitzer at the knot in his tie.

'Sit right where you are, Carlo. In the light.'

I could see him squinting into the darkness for the glint of a gun barrel. He was off balance, and I deperately wanted him to stay that way.

'When you sit, I talk. These could be the last words you'll hear.' He had no idea of what I meant by that. I wasn't sure either, but he sat.

It was like having a personal audience with the Pope, in one sense only. You may get one chance in a lifetime. After that, it's all 'I shoulda said . . .'

'Relax, Carlo. You look tense. I'm sort of on your side.'

'Yeah? Why do I need you?' I'm leaving out some of the more colourful words.

'To stay alive. Let's discuss a recent murder on D Street in South Boston.'

If I shook him, it was imperceptible.

'Yeah? Who got whacked?' He said it the way you'd ask who was pitching for the Red Sox tonight.

'Lewis Resnick.'

That didn't exactly knock his socks off either.

'Oh yeah. That guy in Southie. Maybe you ain't heard. The mayor's kid is going down for that one.'

It was clearly time to take my best shot before the momentum swung completely to his side. I was relying partly on fact and partly on guesswork to fill in the missing pieces – but the guess work was prepped by years of tutelage at Jake's elbow.

'This is going to be a brief conversation, Carlo. Just so you know where I'm coming from, I'm going to share a little family business. Resnick was a straw man for the Don. The family put an impressive amount of cash into stock in Resnick's name. The insurance policy against Resnick's getting frisky with the stock was a will leaving it all to someone the Don could trust.'

The supercilious smirk had dropped off. I had his attention. My guess was that when Carlo was sent to dispatch Resnick, he was told no more than necessary. My hunch was apparently on key. He knew this wasn't street gossip. I had to have this from high up inside the family. I kept it in low key.

'Things got shaky, Carlo. The Don is looking at a civil war with one of his capos. You have ears. I'm sure you know who I mean. The Don probably didn't share this with you, but he was afraid Resnick was going into the camp of the opposition. That's when you got the call to kill two birds – Resnick and the mayor's chance of relection. You drug the kid at the party, then whack Resnick with Connoly's car on the way to Winthrop. You insure Connoly's conviction with that recanted alibi and lay the bribery on the mayor. To that extent, we found you reliable. Then you went sour.'

He was stone silent. He just looked at me with eyes that showed something between fear and panic.

'Before he died, Resnick made a second will. He left everything to another gnome who's in the pocket of the Don's aforesaid treasonous capo. You know why he did that, Carlo?'

He was now clearly over his head, which was hanging forward with his mouth slightly open.

'He did it because someone tipped him off that he was going to be whacked. Who could that have been, Carlo?'

The second-will business was, I'm afraid, a total lie. But the sweat that was now staining his collar told me to press the advantage.

'More to the point, Carlo, who do you suppose the Don believes tipped him off – you and the Don being the only ones who knew about your mission?'

Now Carlo really wondered who I was and what I was there for. I could read the panic in his face. He started to get up.

'Sit down, Carlo. I'm still speaking. You'll know when I'm through.'

He sank back like a man who expected death at any moment.

'Why did you do it, Carlo? Why did you tip off Resnick?'

The floodgates opened.

'I never did. I never told him nothin'. The Don has to believe that. I've got to talk to him.'

'You're talking to me now, Carlo. I'm the one you have to convince. Why didn't you follow the plan?'

'I did! I did everything the Don told me.'

Sweat pasted his hair to his forehead. He started rubbing his palms on his knees. I kept my voice low and calm.

'Not everything, Carlo.'

He was in open panic. He seemed oblivious to the fact that we were on an open porch.

'What do you mean? I did Resnick with the kid's car.'

'We're satisfied with that. That's not everything.'

He was on his feet starting forward.

'Stay in the light, Carlo.' He froze on the spot and lowered his voice.

'I called in the tip to the police. Like the Don said, I gave the kid a phony alibi. Then I flipped on the alibi. Nobody told me nothin' different.'

He had just taken young Connoly off the hot seat. I was

halfway there. I was as sweaty as Carlo when I made the plunge for the touchdown, but I couldn't let it show in my voice.

'The Don was displeased that you laid the bribery on the attorney, Barnes. That wasn't part of the plan. That could be trouble for the Don.'

The river flowed. 'I thought it would make it more believable if I said the lawyer set it up. So what? What does the Don care about an old lawyer? It worked.'

That wasn't all that worked. My heart was pounding so hard I hoped it wasn't drowning out Carlo's voice on the recording machine I had strapped to my chest. I had all I could do to keep my voice from breaking.

'You've said your piece, Carlo. I want you to stand up now and go in the house. You'll be hearing shortly.'

I didn't say from whom. I'm sure Carlo thought I meant the Don. Actually, I meant the district attorney. In any event, he went into the house, and I slipped off the back end of the dark porch.

I made two copies of the tape recording in the car on my way back to the city. I dropped off one copy with the midnight-oil burners in the district attorney's office, together with a promise to testify as to its authenticity. More important from my point of view, I was in time to get the second copy to the City Editor of the *Boston Globe* in time for the morning edition.

The cabbie swung to the curb and skidded to a stop. He flipped down the flag and proudly barked, 'Thirty-two.' I knew he was announcing the number of traffic light he'd made. I also knew that half of them were red. I hate to reward crime, but I paid him double the offer, since I could see that we had gotten there before Jake left.

I scrambled up the steps. I had the morning edition of the *Boston Globe* under my arm. The lead story across the top of page one was Jerry McCann's, telling of newfound evidence connecting the killing of Resnick to the mob, exonerating young Connoly and the mayor, and, most important, clearing Jake's name of bribery and perjury.

I walked into the room just as they were saying the last decade of the Rosary. I waited while the standing-room crowd left for the church. Tom McDonough, the funeral director, gave me a few moments alone with Jake.

There was so much I hadn't said, and now I didn't know if he could hear me.

I tucked the *Globe* under his arm. It seemed to rest there as if he were taking it with him.

I said an *Ave* for the greatest soul I'd come close to on this earth, and I started to leave. I thought I heard a voice, but maybe I was just recalling something Jake said to me a long time ago. This time I could answer him.

'You bet, Jake. It was a great dance.'

FROM "THE PARTNER"

John Grisham

The law firm Patrick worked for before he died filed for bankruptcy protection a year after his funeral. After his death, the firm's letterhead properly included him: Patrick S. Lanigan, 1954–1992. He was listed up in the right-hand corner, just above the paralegals. Then the rumours got started and wouldn't stop. Before long, everyone believed he had taken the money and disappeared. After three months, no one on the Gulf Coast believed he was dead. His name came off the letterhead as the debts piled up.

The four remaining partners were still together, attached unwillingly at the hip by the bondage of bankruptcy. Their names had been joined on the mortgages and the bank notes, back when they were rolling and on the verge of serious wealth. They had been joint defendants in several unwinnable lawsuits; thus the bankruptcy. Since Patrick's departure, they had tried every possible way to divorce one another, but nothing would work. Two were raging alcoholics who drank at the office behind locked doors, but never together. The other two were in recovery, still teetering on the brink of sobriety.

He took their money. Their millions. Money they had already spent long before it arrived, as only lawyers can do. Money for their richly renovated office building in downtown Biloxi. Money for new homes, yachts, condos in the Caribbean. The money was on the way, approved, the papers signed, orders entered; they could see it, smell it, almost touch it when their dead partner snatched it at the last possible second.

He was dead. They buried him on February 11, 1992. They had consoled the widow and put his rotten name on their handsome letterhead. Yet six weeks later, he somehow stole their money.

They had brawled over who was to blame. Charles Bogan, the firm's senior partner and its iron hand, had insisted the money be wired from its source into a new account offshore, and this made sense after some discussion. It was ninety million bucks, a third of which the firm would keep, and it would be impossible to hide that kind of money in Biloxi, population fifty thousand. Someone at the bank would talk. Soon everyone would know. All four vowed secrecy, even as they made plans to display as much of their new wealth as possible. There had even been talk of a firm jet, a six-seater.

So Bogan took his share of the blame. At forty-nine, he was the oldest of the four, and, at the moment, the most stable. He was also responsible for hiring Patrick nine years earlier, and for this he had received no small amount of grief.

Doug Vitrano, the litigator, had made the fateful decision to recommend Patrick as the fifth partner. The other three had agreed, and when Lanigan was added to the firm name, he had access to virtually every file in the office. Bogan, Rapley, Vitrano, Havarac, and Lanigan, Attorneys and Counselors-at-Law. A large ad in the yellow pages claimed 'Specialists in Offshore Injuries.' Specialists or not, like most firms they would take almost anything if the fees were lucrative. Lots of secretaries and paralegals. Big overhead, and the strongest political connections on the Coast.

They were all in their mid to late forties. Havarac had been raised by his father on a shrimp boat. His hands were still proudly calloused, and he dreamed of choking Patrick until his neck snapped. Rapley was severely depressed and seldom left his home, where he wrote briefs in a dark office in the attic.

TRIUMPH OF JUSTICE

Irwin Shaw

Mike Pilato purposefully threw open the door of Victor's shack. Above him the sign that said, 'Lunch, Truckmen Welcome,' shook a little, and the pale shadows its red bulbs threw in the twilight waved over the State Road.

'Victor,' Mike said, in Italian.

Victor was leaning on the counter, reading Walter Winchell in a spread-out newspaper. He smiled amiably. 'Mike,' he said, 'I am so glad to see you.'

Mike slammed the door. 'Three hundred dollars, Victor,' he said, standing five feet tall, round and solid as a pumpkin against the door. 'You owe me three hundred dollars, Victor, and I am here tonight to collect.'

Victor shrugged slightly and closed the paper on Walter Winchell.

'As I've been telling you for the past six months,' he said, 'business is bad. Business is terrible. I work and I work and at the end . . .' He shrugged again. 'Barely enough to feed myself.'

Mike's cheeks, farmer-brown, and wrinkled deeply by wind and sun, grew dark with blood. 'Victor, you are lying in my face,' he said slowly, his voice desperately even. 'For six months, each time it comes time to collect the rent you tell me, "Business is bad." What do I say? "All right, Victor, don't worry, I know how it is."

'Frankly, Mike,' Victor said sadly, 'there has been no improvement this month.'

Mike's face grew darker than ever. He pulled harshly at the ends of his iron-gray mustache, his great hands tense and swollen with anger, repressed but terrible. 'For six months, Victor,' Mike said, 'I believed you. Now I no longer believe you.'

'Mike,' Victor said reproachfully.

'My friends, my relatives,' Mike said, 'they prove it to me. Your business is wonderful, ten cars an hour stop at your door; you sell cigarettes to every farmer between here and Chicago; on your slot machine alone . . .' Mike waved a short thick arm at the machine standing invitingly against a wall, its wheels stopped at two cherries and a lemon. Mike swallowed hard, stood breathing heavily, his deep chest rising and falling sharply against his sheepskin coat. 'Three hundred dollars!' he shouted. 'Six months at fifty dollars! I built this shack with my own hands for you, Victor. I didn't know what kind of a man you were. You were an Italian, I trusted you! Three hundred dollars or get out tomorrow! Finish! That's my last word.'

Victor smoothed his newspaper down delicately on the counter, his hands making a dry brushing sound in the empty lunchroom. 'You misunderstand,' he said gently.

'I misunderstand nothing!' Mike yelled. 'You are on my land in my shack and you owe me three hundred dollars . . .'

'I don't owe you anything,' Victor said, looking coldly at Mike. 'That is what you misunderstand. I have paid you every month, the first day of the month, fifty dollars.'

'Victor!' Mike whispered, his hands dropping to his sides. 'Victor, what are you saying . . .?'

'I have paid the rent. Please do not bother me any more.' Calmly Victor turned his back on Mike and turned two handles on the coffee urn. Steam, in a thin little plume, hissed up for a moment.

Mike looked at Victor's narrow back, with the shoulder blades jutting far out, making limp wings in the white shirt. There was finality in Victor's pose, boredom, easy certainty. Mike shook his head slowly, pulling hard at his mustache. 'My wife,' Mike said to the disdainful back, 'she told me not to trust you. My wife knew what she was talking about, Victor.' Then, with a last flare of hope, 'Victor, do you really mean it when you said you paid me?'

Victor didn't turn around. He flipped another knob on the coffee urn. 'I mean it.'

Mike lifted his arm, as though to say something, pronounce

warning. Then he let it drop and walked out of the shack, leaving the door open. Victor came out from behind the counter, looked at Mike moving off with his little rolling limp down the road and across the cornfield. Victor smiled and closed the door and went back and opened the paper to Walter Winchell.

Mike walked slowly among the cornstalks, his feet crunching unevenly in the October earth. Absently he pulled at his mustache. Dolores, his wife, would have a thing or two to say. 'No,' she had warned him, 'do not build a shack for him. Do not permit him onto your land. He travels with bad men; it will turn out badly. I warn you!' Mike was sure she would not forget this conversation and would repeat it to him word for word when he got home. He limped along unhappily. Farming was better than being a landlord. You put seed into the earth and you knew what was coming out. Corn grew from corn, and the duplicity of Nature was expected and natural. Also no documents were signed in the compact with Nature, no leases and agreements necessary, a man was not at a disadvantage if he couldn't read or write. Mike opened the door to his house and sat down heavily in the parlor, without taking his hat off, Rosa came and jumped on his lap, yelling, 'Poppa, Poppa, tonight I want to go to the movies, Poppa, take me to the movies!'

Mike pushed her off. 'No movies,' he said harshly. Rosa stood in a corner and watched him reproachfully.

The door from the kitchen opened and Mike sighed as he saw his wife coming in, wiping her hands on her apron. She stood in front of Mike, round, short, solid as a plow horse, canny, difficult to deceive.

'Why're you sitting in the parlor?' she asked.

'I feel like sitting in the parlor,' Mike said.

'Every night you sit in the kitchen,' Dolores said. 'Suddenly you change.'

'I've decided,' Mike said loudly, 'that it's about time I made some use of this furniture. After all, I paid for it, I might as well sit in it before I die.'

'I know why you're sitting in the parlor,' Dolores said.

'Good! You know!'

'You didn't get the money from Victor.' Dolores wiped the last bit of batter from her hands. 'It's as plain as the shoes on your feet.'

'I smell something burning,' Mike said.

'Nothing is burning. Am I right or wrong?' Dolores sat in the upright chair opposite Mike. She sat straight, her hands neatly in her lap, her head forward and cocked a little to one side, her eyes staring directly and accusingly into his. 'Yes or no?'

'Please attend to your own department,' Mike said miserably. 'I do the farming and attend to the business details.'

'Huh!' Dolores said disdainfully.

'Are you starving?' Mike shouted. 'Answer me, are you starving?'

Rosa started to cry because her father was shouting.

'Please, for the love of Jesus,' Mike screamed at her, 'don't cry!'

Dolores enfolded Rosa in her arms . . . 'Baby, baby,' she crooned. 'I will not let him harm you.'

'Who offered to harm her?' Mike screamed, banging on a table with his fist like a mallet. 'Don't lie to her!'

Dolores kissed the top of Rosa's head soothingly. 'There, there,' she crooned. 'There.' She looked coldly at Mike. 'Well. So he didn't pay.'

'He . . .' Mike started loudly. Then he stopped, spoke in a low, reasonable voice. 'So. To be frank with you, he didn't pay. That's the truth.'

'What did I tell you?' Dolores said as Mike winced. 'I repeat the words. "Do not permit him onto your land. He travels with bad men; it will turn out badly. I warn you!" Did I tell you?'

'You told me,' Mike said wearily.

'We will never see that money again,' Dolores said, smoothing Rosa's hair. 'I have kissed it good-bye.'

'Please,' said Mike. 'Return to the kitchen. I am hungry for dinner. I have made plans already to recover the money.'

Dolores eyed him suspiciously. 'Be careful, Mike,' she said. 'His friends are gangsters and he plays poker every Saturday night with men who carry guns in their pockets.'

'I am going to the law,' Mike said. 'I'm going to sue Victor for the three hundred dollars.'

Dolores started to laugh. She pushed Rosa away and stood up and laughed.

'What's so funny?' Mike asked angrily. 'I tell you I'm going to sue a man for money he owes me, you find it funny! Tell me the joke.'

Dolores stopped laughing. 'Have you got any papers? No! You trust him, he trusts you, no papers. Without papers you're lost in a court. You'll make a fool of yourself. They'll charge you for the lawyers. Please, Mike, go back to your farming.'

Mike's face set sternly, his wrinkles harsh in his face with the gray stubble he never managed completely to shave. 'I want my dinner, Dolores,' he said coldly, and Dolores discreetly moved into the kitchen, saying, 'It is not my business, my love; truly, I merely offer advice.'

Mike walked back and forth in the parlor, limping, rolling a little from side to side, his eyes on the floor, his hands plunged into the pockets of his denims like holstered weapons, his mouth pursed with thought and determination. After a while he stopped and looked at Rosa, who prepared to weep once more.

'Rosa, baby,' he said, sitting down and taking her gently on his lap. 'Forgive me.'

Rosa snuggled to him. They sat that way in the dimly lit parlor.

'Poppa,' Rosa said finally.

'Yes,' Mike said.

'Will you take me to the movies tonight, Poppa?'

'All right,' Mike said. 'I'll take you to the movies.'

The next day Mike went into town, dressed in his neat black broadcloth suit and his black soft hat and his high brown shoes. He came back to the farm like a businessman in the movies, busily, preoccupied, sober, but satisfied.

'Well?' Dolores asked him, in the kitchen.

He kissed her briskly, kissed Rosa, sat down, took his shoes off, rubbed his feet luxuriously, said paternally to his son who was reading *Esquire* near the window, 'That's right, Anthony, study.'

'Well?' asked Dolores.

'I saw Dominic in town,' Mike said, watching his toes wiggling. 'They're having another baby.'

'Well,' asked Dolores. 'The case? The action?'

'All right,' Mike said. 'What is there for dinner?'

'Veal,' Dolores said. 'What do you mean "all right"?'

'I've spoken to Judge Collins. He is filling out the necessary papers for me and he will write me a letter when I am to appear in court. Rosa, have you been a good girl?'

Dolores threw up her hands. 'Lawyers. We'll throw away a fortune on lawyers. Good money after bad. We could put in an electric pump with the money.'

'Lawyers will cost us nothing.' Mike stuffed his pipe elaborately.

'I have different plans. Myself. I will take care of the case myself.' He lit up, puffed deliberately.

Dolores sat down across the table from him, spoke slowly, carefully. 'Remember, Mike,' she said. 'This is in English. They conduct the court in English.'

'I know,' said Mike. 'I am right. Justice is on my side. Why should I pay a lawyer fifty, seventy-five dollars to collect my own money? There is one time you need lawyers – when you are wrong. I am not wrong. I will be my own lawyer.'

'What do you know about the law?' Dolores challenged him.

'I know Victor owes me three hundred dollars.' Mike puffed three times, quickly, on his pipe. 'That's all I need to know.'

'You can hardly speak English, you can't even read or write, nobody will be able to understand you. They'll all laugh at you, Mike.'

'Nobody will laugh at me. I can speak English fine.'

'When did you learn?' Dolores asked. 'Today?'

'Dolores!' Mike shouted. 'I tell you my English is all right.'

'Say Thursday,' Dolores said.

'I don't want to say it,' Mike said, banging the table. 'I have no interest in saying it.'

'Aha,' Dolores crowed. 'See? He wants to be a lawyer in an American court, he can't even say Thursday.'

'I can,' Mike said. 'Keep quiet, Dolores.'

'Say Thursday.' Dolores put her head to one side, spoke coquettishly, slyly, like a girl asking her lover to say he loved her.

'Stirday,' Mike said, as he always said. 'There!'

Dolores laughed, waving her hand. 'And he wants to conduct a law case! Holy Mother! They will laugh at you!'

'Let them laugh!' Mike shouted. 'I will conduct the case! Now

I want to eat dinner! Anthony!' he yelled. 'Throw away that trash and come to the table.'

On the day of the trial, Mike shaved closely, dressed carefully in his black suit, put his black hat squarely on his head, and with Dolores seated grimly beside him drove early into town in the 1933 family Dodge.

Dolores said nothing all the way into town. Only after the car was parked and they were entering the courthouse, Mike's shoes clattering bravely on the legal marble, did Dolores speak. 'Behave yourself,' she said. Then she pinched his arm. Mike smiled at her, braced his yoke-like shoulders, took off his hat. His rough grey hair sprang up like steel wool when his hat was off, and Mike ran his hand through it as he opened the door to the courtroom. There was a proud, important smile on his face as he sat down next to his wife in the first row and patiently waited for his case to be called.

When Victor came, Mike glared at him, but Victor, after a quick look, riveted his attention on the American flag behind the Judge's head.

'See,' Mike whispered to Dolores. 'I have him frightened. He doesn't dare to look at me. Here he will have to tell the truth.'

'Shhh!' hissed Dolores. 'This is a court of law.'

'Michael Pilato,' the clerk called, 'versus Victor Fraschi.' 'Me! Mike said loudly, standing up.

'Shhh,' said Dolores.

Mike put his hat in Dolores' lap, moved lightly to the little gate that separated the spectators from the principals in the proceedings. Politely, with a deep ironic smile, he held the gate open for Victor and his lawyer. Victor passed through without looking up.

'Who's representing you, Mr Pilato?' the Judge asked when they were all seated. 'Where's your lawyer?'

Mike stood up and spoke in a clear voice. 'I represent myself. I am my lawyer.'

'You ought to have a lawyer,' the Judge said.

'I do not need a lawyer,' Mike said loudly. 'I am not trying to cheat anybody.' There were about forty people in the courtroom and they all laughed. Mike turned and looked at them, puzzled. 'What did I say?'

The Judge rapped with his gavel and the case was opened.

Victor took the stand, while Mike stared, coldly accusing, at him.
Victor's lawyer, a young man in a blue pinstripe suit and a
starched tan shirt, questioned him. Yes, Victor said, he had paid
each month. No, there were no receipts, Mr Pilato could neither
read nor write and they had dispensed with all formalities of that
kind. No, he did not understand on what Mr Pilato based his
claim. Mike looked incredulously at Victor, lying under solemn
oath, risking Hell for three hundred dollars.

Victor's lawyer stepped down and waved to Mike gracefully.
'Your witness.'

Mike walked dazedly past the lawyer and up to the witness
stand and round, neat, his bull neck, deep red-brown and
wrinkled, over his pure white collar, his large scrubbed hands
politely but awkwardly held at his sides. He stood in front of
Victor, leaning over a little toward him, his face close to Victor's.

'Victor,' he said, his voice ringing through the courtroom, 'tell
the truth, did you pay me the money?'

'Yes,' said Victor.

Mike leaned closer to him. 'Look in my eye, Victor,' Mike said,
his voice clear and patient, 'and answer me. Did you pay me the
money?'

Victor lifted his head and looked unflinchingly into Mike's
eyes. 'I paid you the money.'

Mike leaned even closer. His forehead almost touched Victor's
now. 'Look me *straight* in the eye, Victor.'

Victor looked bravely into Mike's eyes, less than a foot away
now.

'Now, Victor,' Mike said, his eyes narrowed, cold, the light in
them small and flashing and gray, 'DID YOU PAY ME THE MONEY?'

Victor breathed deeply. 'Yes,' he said.

Mike took half a step back, almost staggering, as though he
had been hit. He stared incredulously into the perjurer's eyes,
as a man might stare at a son who has just admitted he has
killed his mother, beyond pity, beyond understanding, outside
all the known usage of human life. Mike's face worked harshly
as the tides of anger and despair and vengeance rolled up in
him.

'You're a godam liar, Victor!' Mike shouted terribly. He leapt down from the witness platform, seized a heavy oak armchair, raised it murderously above Victor's head.

'Mike, oh, Mike!' Dolores' wail floated above the noise of the courtroom.

'Tell the truth, Victor!' Mike shouted, his face brick red, his teeth white behind his curled lips, almost senseless with rage, for the first time in his life threatening a fellow-creature with violence. 'Tell it fast!'

He stood, the figure of Justice, armed with the chair, the veins pulsing in his huge wrists, the chair quivering high above Victor's head in his huge gnarled hands, his tremendous arms tight and bulging in their broadcloth sleeves. 'Immediately, Victor!'

'Pilato!' shouted the Judge. 'Put that chair down!'

Victor sat stonily, his eyes lifted in dumb horror to the chair above his head.

'Pilato,' the Judge shouted, 'you can be sent to jail for this!' He banged sternly but helplessly on his desk. 'Remember, this is a court of law!'

'Victor?' Mike asked, unmoved, unmoving. 'Victor? Immediately, please.'

'No,' Victor screamed, cringing in his seat, his hands now held in feeble defense before his eyes. 'I didn't pay! I didn't!'

'Pilato,' screamed the Judge, 'this is not evidence!'

'You were lying?' Mike said inexorably, the chair still held, axlike, above him.

'Mike, oh, Mike,' wailed Dolores.

'It was not my idea,' Victor babbled. 'As God is my judge, I didn't think it up. Alfred Lotti, he suggested it, and Johnny Nolan. I am under the influence of corrupt men. Mike, for the love of God, please don't kill me. Mike, it would never have occurred to me myself, forgive me, forgive me . . .'

'Guiness!' the Judge called to the court policeman. 'Are you going to stand there and let this go on? Why don't you do something?'

'I can shoot him,' Guiness said. 'Do you want me to shoot the plaintiff?'

'Shut up,' the Judge said.

Guiness shrugged and turned his head toward the witness stand, smiling a little.

'You were lying?' Mike asked, his voice low, patient.

'I was lying,' Victor cried.

Slowly, with magnificent calm, Mike put the chair down neatly in its place. With a wide smile he turned to the Judge. 'There,' he said.

'Do you know any good reason,' the Judge shouted, 'why I shouldn't have you locked up?'

Victor was crying with relief on the witness stand, wiping the tears away with his sleeve.

'There is no possible excuse,' the Judge said, 'for me to admit this confession as evidence. We are a court of law in the State of Illinois, in the United States. We are not conducting the Spanish Inquisition, Mr Pilato.'

'Huh?' Mike asked, cocking his head.

'There are certain rules,' the Judge went on, quickly, his voice high, 'which it is customary to observe. It is not the usual thing, Mr Pilato,' he said harshly, 'to arrive at evidence by bodily threatening to brain witnesses with a chair.'

'He wouldn't tell the truth,' Mike said simply.

'At the very least, Mr Pilato,' the Judge said, 'you should get thirty days.'

'Oh, Mike,' wept Dolores.

'Mr Fraschi,' the Judge said, 'I promise you that you will be protected. That nobody will harm you.'

'I did it,' sobbed Victor, his hands shaking uncontrollably in a mixture of fear, repentance, religion, joy at delivery from death. 'I did it. I will not tell a lie. I'm a weak man and influenced by loafers. I owe him three hundred dollars. Forgive me, Mike, forgive me . . .'

'He will not harm you,' the Judge said patiently. 'I guarantee it. You can tell the truth without any danger. Do you owe Mr Pilato three hundred dollars?'

'I owe Mr Pilato three hundred dollars,' Victor said, swallowing four times in a row.

The young lawyer put three sheets of paper into his briefcase and snapped the lock.

The Judge sighed and wiped his brow with a handkerchief as he looked at Mike. 'I don't approve of the way you conducted this trial, Mr Pilato,' he said. 'It is only because you're a working man who has many duties to attend to on his land that I don't take you and put you away for a month to teach you more respect for the processes of law.'

'Yes, sir,' Mike said faintly.

'Hereafter,' the Judge said, 'kindly engage an attorney when you appear before me in this court.'

'Yes, sir,' Mike said.

'Mr Pilato,' the Judge said, 'it is up to you to decide when and how he is to pay you.'

Mike turned and walked back to Victor. Victor shrank into his chair. 'Tomorrow morning, Victor,' Mike said, waving his finger under Victor's nose, 'at eight-thirty o'clock, I am coming into your store. The money will be there.'

'Yes,' said Victor.

'Is that all right?' Mike asked the Judge.

'Yes,' said the Judge.

Mike strode over to the young lawyer. 'And you,' he said, standing with his hands on his hips in front of the young man with the pinstripe suit. 'Mr Lawyer. You knew he didn't pay me. A boy with an education. You should be ashamed of yourself.' He turned to the Judge, smiled broadly, bowed. 'Thank you,' he said. 'Good morning.' Then, triumphantly, smiling broadly, rolling like a sea captain as he walked, he went through the little gate. Dolores was waiting with his hat. He took the hat, put Dolores' arm through his, marched down the aisle, nodding, beaming to the spectators. Someone applauded and by the time he and Dolores got to the door all the spectators were applauding.

He waited until he got outside, in the bright morning sunshine down the steps of the courthouse, before he said anything to Dolores. He put his hat on carefully, turned to her, grinning.

'Well,' he said, 'did you observe what I did?'

'Yes,' she said. 'I was never so ashamed in my whole life!'

'Dolores!' Mike was shocked. 'I got the money. I won the case.'

'Acting like that in a court of law!' Dolores started bitterly toward the car. 'What are you, a red Indian?'

Dolores got into the car and slammed the door and Mike limped slowly around and got into the other side. He started the car without a word and shaking his head from time to time, drove slowly toward home.

DOGS AND FLEAS

John Lutz

'He's out there,' Doris said to Mead Blasingame, 'and he looks ready to talk deal.'

She was referring to high-powered criminal defense attorney Horton Lang, whose present notorious client was the unofficial chieftain of crime in Bayville, Willie Stark.

But if Lang was a successful defense attorney, Mead Blasingame was just as successful – if not as rich – in the role of Bayville's most effective prosecutor. Willie Stark wouldn't be the first upper-echelon criminal to be convicted because of Blasingame's expertise with the law, and with juries. A short but erect and handsome man still in his forties, with black hair and blue, painfully earnest eyes, he might have been cast as Sir Lancelot had he been as actor instead of a lawyer. Sometimes, in fact, Blasingame thought of himself as a knight in the service of justice.

He sat at his wide oak desk and looked at his assistant, Doris Jones. She was more to him than a paralegal; he considered her invaluable in research and jury selection, and from time to time she provided an audience for his dramatic Theatre of the Law.

Mounted on the wall behind Doris was the framed homily that Blasingame's mother had continually quoted to him in his youth: 'Those who lie down with dogs will rise up with fleas.' Blasingame had heard her say it so often that it had stuck. He believed it, and it was the reason he was a prosecutor.

From the beginning of his law career, he'd refused to act as a defense attorney. He knew he couldn't detach himself emotionally from the human scum he might have to defend in court. He feared that if he did mount an effective legal defense and got someone he believed actually guilty acquitted, he'd be responsible for that person. And some of the guilt, some of the evil, would rub off on him like soot. He'd be more like his client than before the acquittal, and he'd be a *de facto* accomplice in future misdeeds. It was a prospect he couldn't think about with dispassion.

'Mr Blasingame? Mead?'

Doris was looking down at him, a pretty blonde woman with a heart-shaped face, creamy complexion, and clear gray eyes; beauty masking such a wicked intelligence.

'Sorry, Doris. Mind wandered. Tell Lang to come in. He can talk deal all he wants, but the cards have already been dealt, and we have the aces.'

She smiled as she went out. A moment later, she ushered Horton Lang into the office, then left the two of them alone.

Blasingame stood up, smiled, and shook hands with Lang, then motioned for him to sit down in the comfortable black leather chair angled to face the desk. After Lang had sat, Blasingame sat back down, made obligatory small talk, then waited patiently for his visitor to get to the point.

Lang was a sixty-eight-year-old man with expensive gray suits, gray hair and eyes, and expressive bushy gray eyebrows that sometimes writhed like caterpillars. The skin stretched tautly over his long, hawkish face which had a gray tint to it. Looking at all that gray, the much younger Blasingame wondered when age would finally begin to slow Lang's clever mind, play tricks with his recall. If it occurred during the Willie Stark case, Blasingame would take full advantage of it.

Stark deserved the death penalty twenty times over. He was the kind of man Blasingame hated, the kind who'd dealt his own warped idea of justice through the barrel of a gun. This time, he hadn't used a gun, though, and someone had seen him.

'Mr Stark has permitted me to begin the process of plea bargaining,' Lang said.

Blasingame raised his eyebrows. "Permitted" 'you?'

'Yes,' Lang said seriously. 'He wants to plead not guilty because he isn't guilty. But he knows the weight of the evidence, misleading as it is, is against him. What would you say to a reduced charge of unintentional manslaughter?'

'I'd say no. We have a witness who saw your client behind the wheel of the car that struck and killed George Blake, then deliberately backed over him to make sure he was dead. Stark had the motive –'

'Which was?' Lang softly interrupted.

'Blake saw him shoot two women to death in cold blood, prostitutes who worked for him indirectly and wanted out of their agreement. He made examples of those women. First with a gun, then he mutilated them with a knife in case any of their co-workers might be mulling over the same liberating ideas.' Blasingame felt himself getting angry. Always a mistake. He lowered his voice. 'Your client, Willie Stark, is an animal.'

'Your witness, Laurie Stone, is herself a prostitute,' Lang pointed out. 'The jury won't believe a woman like that, and you know it.'

Blasingame stood up behind his desk. 'We'll have to find that out in court.'

Lang sighed, smiled, and stood up, buttoning his double-breasted suitcoat across his narrow body. 'You should bend sometimes, Mead. You've lost a few because you refused to bend. You're going to lose this one.'

'We both know better, Horton.'

Lang's smile turned vaguely sad, as if he couldn't understand Blasingame's hopeless position but could easily cope with it. Then he nodded and walked from the office.

A few minutes later, Doris knocked, then stuck her head in. 'Deal?' she asked.

'No deal. Our witness is going to put Lang's client on the road to his execution, and Lang knows it. He has nothing to deal.'

Doris grinned. 'Such a pit bull you are.'

Blasingame knew she was right. Knew *he* was right.

He wished he could concentrate entirely on Willie Stark, but that wasn't the nature of his job. Crime begat crime begat crime. Bayville needed Blasingame.

'Willie Stark isn't our only case,' he said, as if Doris had maintained that it was. 'Bring me the file on Martin Vinton.'

Vinton had been the girls' volleyball coach at the junior high school Blasingame's own twelve-year-old daughter, Judith, attended. He'd been accused of molesting more than a dozen students. Photographs and videotapes of him with some of the girls had been found in a search of his house. The evidence against him was overwhelming.

Blasingame was almost as eager to convict Vinton as he was to nail Stark for murder. The infuriating part was that while Vinton was in jail awaiting trial, Stark was walking around free on bond. Stark had better legal counsel. And he'd drawn the lenient Judge Rudy Moss. Judges these days!

Blasingame sometimes daydreamed about when he'd become a judge.

He was eating lunch in Ollie's Café near the courthouse when a short, heavyset man with close-cropped gray hair and pink-rimmed blue eyes sat down across from him. He had on a wrinkled brown suit, checked shirt, and red tie, and he smelled like cheap deodorant or cologne.

He smiled with yellow teeth that tilted inward at an odd angle, as if long ago he'd been struck hard in the mouth. 'I'm Benny Natch, Mr Blasingame.'

Blasingame was sure they'd never met. He liked to dine alone, and he resented this intrusion. 'We don't know each other, Mr Natch. If you want to make an appointment to see me in my office –'

'That wouldn't work for what I have in mind,' Natch said. He blatantly helped himself to one of Blasingame's French fries. Blasingame sat very still and began to worry.

When Natch had finished chewing and swallowing the French fry, he said, 'I'm here as a sort of emissary from Mr Vinton.'

'The child molester,' Blasingame said.

'Allegedly.' Natch consumed another French fry. 'The point is, Mr Blasingame, that one of the young girls allegedly involved with Natch, and who allegedly posed quite willingly for photographs and videotaping, is your daughter Judith.'

A cold, deep fury took root at Blasingame's core. A vacuum that somehow fed a fire. It was all he could do to restrain himself from reaching across the table and strangling Natch. 'No one is alleging that,' he said in an icy voice that surprised even him with its calmness.

'I am,' Natch said. 'But it doesn't have to go any further, Mr Blasingame.'

'I don't believe you,' Blasingame said.

Natch smiled. It was ugly. 'That's why I brought one of the photographs,' he said. And he laid the photo on the table next to Blasingame's iced tea.

Blasingame stared at it in disbelief, then snatched it up before anyone else might see it.

'Keep that one,' Natch said cheerily. 'It's only one of lots of prints. Then there's the video she stars in.'

Blasingame actually edged close enough to grab Natch, but he didn't. His fingers twitched.

Natch flashed his nasty smile. 'You'd like to kill me, I know.'

'I would,' Blasingame admitted. He lowered his hands beneath the table, out of sight.

'That's understandable; you're blaming the messenger. But we've both got your daughter's interest at heart here. If Mr Vinton is acquitted, all prints and tapes of Judith will be destroyed.'

'I should take your word for that?'

'You've got no choice. But think about it; why would Mr Vinton double-cross you? Even if he did continue to have something on you, if he used it, he'd be risking prison. The child pornography case against him could be reopened. There could be as many counts against Mr Vinton as there are girls he's involved in his . . . er, activities.'

Blasingame had to admit it made sense. 'Blackmail,' he said with distaste.

'More like reasonable accommodation. Is it a deal?'

The two men stared at each other.

'Let's put it this way,' Natch said, 'since I've probably got more experience at this sort of thing than you. You cooperate, and we never have to talk or even see each other again. If Mr Vinton walks away a free man, everything involving your daughter gets destroyed. But if he gets convicted, there'll be more videocassettes and photographs of her floating around, not just Bayville but the whole country, than you can imagine. And don't consider raiding Mr Vinton's premises to confiscate those photos and tapes. They're in the possession of his attorney.'

'You?' Blasingame asked.

'Me. Who, if it comes down to it, will certainly deny this conversation ever took place.'

'Are you working in concert with Vinton's defense attorney?'

'No. Only you, I, and Vinton will know about this agreement and how it relates to whatever develops during the trial.'

He nodded pleasantly to Blasingame, then stood up.

'Those are terrifically good French fries,' he remarked, and walked away.

Blasingame agonized over the conversation with Natch for almost a week. The Vinton case was fast approaching on the docket; he'd have to make up his mind soon.

Judith, his blonde, petite only child, acted as if nothing were wrong, yet Blasingame had seen the photograph. He could sense when people were telling the truth, and he believed Natch. Judith's normal behavior didn't fool Blasingame. He'd seen multiple murderers behave like saints, and he'd sent them to hell.

He said nothing to Judith; he knew he couldn't be positive Vinton and Natch would actually destroy all the tapes and photos of her if Vinton walked away free. Yet, even if they didn't, Judith might still put everything behind her and live an untroubled and fulfilling life despite her youthful mistake. Blasingame also knew that once the pornographic material was spread across the country, she would be marked for life.

At night, he would lie motionless in bed, listening to his sleeping wife, Ann, breathing deeply and evenly beside him. He'd chosen not to burden her with what Natch had told him. What had happened to Judith was something that for all concerned needed to be buried deep and kept secret. So they could pretend it hadn't happened.

On Friday, he visited the motel where the police were guarding Laurie Stone, the eyewitness in the Willie Stark case.

She was an attractive woman with red hair and an edged hardness that was already beginning to penetrate her youth like protruding bones. Blasingame realized with alarm that she was twenty-one, not even ten years older than Judith.

She paced back and forth on the worn blue carpet. Though it was just past noon, the drapes were closed and the lights were on in the tiny room.

'I'm scared, and I feel cooped up, Mr Blasingame,' she said. 'You don't realize what it's like, hiding like this, staying in one spot when you know somebody like Willie Stark is moving around out there, him and his killers, looking for you. I don't know if I can hold out another month till the trial.'

'Stark doesn't know where you are,' Blasingame assured her. 'Or how to find you. And the police are on the alert if he would happen to locate you. You're well protected.'

She shook her head and brushed back a strand of red hair.

'You don't know Willie Stark. Really vicious people like him, they think of ways to get things done. And he's desperate.'

'You're the only one who can convict him, Laurie. We need you so we can arrange his appointment with the executioner and put him away until he keeps it. He won't be able to hurt anyone then. You're not going to let us down, are you?'

'You don't understand. People like you just don't understand people like Willie Stark!' She made a face as if she might begin to cry, and her hands began to tremble. 'I'll try not to let you down, Mr Blasingame, but you gotta protect me!'

'You have my promise,' Blasingame told her. Then he surprised himself by adding, 'For whatever it's worth.'

As he left the motel, he checked and made sure the police guards were still at their posts.

Horton Lang sat again in the black leather chair before Blasingame's desk. This time, Blasingame had sent for him – and asked him to bring his client.

Standing with his back against the wall, Willie Stark looked the part of the regional king of crime. The dark side of royalty. He was forty-five, tall, broad, dark, with a prognathous jaw that would always need a shave. His chalkstripe blue suit looked expensive and fit perfectly. Blasingame had heard somewhere that Stark had his suits tailored so a gun in a shoulder holster wouldn't spoil their lines.

'I want to talk to Mr Stark alone,' Blasingame said.

Lang looked surprised. 'I'm not sure – '

'Why not?' Stark interrupted. 'Leave us alone for a few minutes, Horton, okay?'

Lang didn't say it was okay, but he left the office.

Stark sat down in the black leather chair and stared at Blasingame with eyes that would have made a shark's seem warm. But there was a glint of curiosity in them that wouldn't be seen in a shark's.

'Yours isn't the only case I'm trying,' Blasingame said.

'I'm not surprised,' Stark said. 'You're a busy and ambitious prosecutor, maybe even with a shining political future.'

'And you might have a very limited future.'

'Might,' Stark agreed. He settled back in the chair and waited.

'I'm also prosecuting a man named Vinton,' Blasingame said, 'a child molester.'

'Those guys should be hung by their –'

'We agree on that,' Blasingame said. 'An attorney named Natch talked to me about some photographs and videotapes of my daughter. They're Vinton's, but they're in Natch's possession.'

Stark looked interested. 'Your daughter, huh? Why would you tell me this, counselor?'

Blasingame said nothing.

'They trying to blackmail you?' Stark asked softly.

Blasingame swiveled in his chair and stared out the window. 'I have a dilemma. My daughter would be ruined if Vinton were convicted and that pornographic material was widely circulated. But if he *isn't* convicted, he'll be free to molest more children.'

'He definitely should go to prison,' Stark said. He sounded sincere. 'I've played the game hard, but I never harmed a kid. They should be out of bounds.'

'Including my kid?' Blasingame asked.

Stark shrugged. 'Sure. But you've gotta put Vinton inside the walls. I'm afraid your daughter got the short straw, counselor. Bad luck.'

'I talked to the eyewitness who can send you to the executioner,' Blasingame said. 'She's scared.'

'I'm not surprised, the kind of lies she's been telling.'

'So scared she might not testify if she gets just a little more scared.'

'It's your job to reassure her, isn't it?' Stark said.

Blasingame nodded. 'I wouldn't want her harmed, even if she did get too frightened and refused to testify. Do you understand that?'

Leather creaked as Stark leaned farther back in the chair. He looked at the ceiling, then at Blasingame.

'If she refused to talk once, she'd refuse again,' Blasingame said. 'Especially if no one bothered her.'

Stark continued to stare at him, then nodded. 'True enough.'

'We agree that Martin Vinton should be in prison,' Blasingame said.

He began to straighten papers on his desk. The only sound was the soft, intermittent whirring of Doris's printer in the outer office. Then even that ceased.

The silence began to take on weight.

'That it, counselor?' Stark asked, after almost a minute had passed.

Blasingame didn't look up from the papers.

'That's it,' he said.

Two days later, Blasingame caught it on the ten o'clock TV news. Benjamin Natch, an attorney in Pineburg, a small town fifty miles south of Bayville, had been found stabbed to death in his office. He'd apparently been tortured. His safe and combination-lock fireproof file cabinets had been opened, but authorities couldn't say what, if anything, had been removed.

Blasingame used the remote to turn off the television, then glanced over at his wife, Ann, talking on the phone at the other end of the room. He wondered how Natch had been tortured, and he shivered. Something truly frightening stirred at the core of his mind.

Then Judith walked past in the hallway. She glanced in and smiled and waved to him. Her smile was the warmth and light of his life; he knew she was the only person he loved unconditionally. Maybe he'd done the right thing, the only thing possible, after all.

He told Ann he had some work to do at the office, then went out to his car and drove to the motel to confess to Laurie Stone that he honestly couldn't guarantee her total safety if she testified against Willie Stark. If she chose not to testify and Stark went free, he, Blasingame, would understand and personally see to it that she had money to start a new life in another city.

That was all she needed to hear, something to tilt her one way or the other.

By the next morning, she was gone.

Everything dropped into place like destiny. A furious and incredulous Martin Vinton was convicted of child molestation, contributing to the delinquency of a minor, and trafficking in child pornography. The judge complied with the jury's recommendation and sentenced him to thirty years in the state penitentiary.

And three weeks later, Willie Stark left the courtroom a free man. Blasingame had mounted a competent defense, but without his key witness a conviction was impossible. He was glad to see that Stark avoided his eyes as he left the courtroom to be congratulated by admirers.

So Stark was free, but Vinton was in prison. Win one, lose one. Maybe that was the most you could expect in today's complicated world, even if you were Sir Lancelot jousting with the forces of darkness.

It had worked and continued to work. The next week, Blasingame and Ann pulled Judith out of the junior high school and enrolled her in a private girls' school in the next state. She was resistant at first, but within a month she wrote that she was making good grades and was happy. When six months had passed, she'd become co-captain of the field hockey team and was running for class president.

Also at the end of that six months, Blasingame learned from a police contact that Laurie Stone had been found dead from an overdose of barbiturates in her apartment in Chicago.

Blasingame felt a thrust of pity, and perhaps guilt. But there was no reason to think Laurie Stone hadn't committed suicide. The pressure on her must have been unbearable. The powers she'd ascribed to Willie Stark bordered on the supernatural, and her fear probably never left her. So the woman's short and tragic life had ended in suicide, like so many others who'd chosen the wrong path. She was doomed from the night she'd witnessed the murders. Her death had nothing to do with Blasingame.

The next morning, he read in the *Bayville Register* that Martin Vinton had been strangled to death with a length of electrical cord in prison. An investigation was proceeding, but prison officials had few leads.

Blasingame knew how prison investigations were carried out. Child molesters were at the bottom of the pecking order in prisons. No one mourned Vinton's passing, and no one would talk. The identity of the inmate who'd killed him would never be discovered.

Blasingame felt a weight rise from his chest when he read about Vinton's death. Judith was completely safe now, from Vinton's wicked knowledge of her, from Vinton himself if a lenient parole board had moved to set him free before his full term was served.

So that was the end of the problem. It had played itself out and was finally over.

Blasingame didn't like to admit it, but it was possible that crime paid.

It was early the next spring, and Blasingame was in the middle of prosecuting two men who'd been passing through Bayville and shot to death a family of five, including infant twins, when Doris entered his office wearing an odd expression and told him Willie Stark was in the anteroom and wanted to see him.

Blasingame smiled with a confidence he didn't feel and told her to send Stark in.

Stark had put on about twenty pounds and had a deep, even tan, as if he'd just returned from the tropics. He looked healthy and prosperous in his expensive beige suit and white shirt, yellow silk tie. He wore two diamond rings on each hand, one of them a pinky ring. Gold cufflinks flashed as he sat down and rested his huge hands on the chair arms. Something about his attitude bothered Blasingame. Then he realized what it was. Stark was acting almost as if this were *his* office.

'Counsellor,' Stark said, still smiling, "I've got a favour to ask of you concerning a case you're working on. I know you won't mind.'

Blasingame fought off a wave of nausea. He knew he would mind, and he knew it wouldn't be the last favour he'd do for Stark. A shadowy part of his mind he seldom visited had long feared this day. He was trapped. He had no choice.

'Does the favour have to do with a murdered family?' he asked.

'Bingo!' Stark said.

Looking into the future, Blasingame saw only a darkness that horrified him.

He reached for the gun in the second drawer, then brought it up and rested it in front of him on the desk.

Stark had recognized something in Blasingame's eyes and stopped smiling. 'Don't act in haste and repent at leisure, counselor,' he said in a soft, level voice. His smile returned, but it was forced and cold.

Blasingame raised the gun to eye level and sighted along its barrel. He knew the basic truth of maxims, but Stark's was far too late.

'There's no way you can do this, counselor. It isn't in you. It's not the way you were raised.'

Beyond Stark's tan features and stiff smile, Blasingame could see his mother's framed, wise words mounted on the wall.

He began to itch all over.

SPEEDBALL

Brian Hodge

He had become the same sort of temporal landmark as John Kennedy had once been, but for a generation of cynics. This new breed, disillusioned with politics and nurtured on pop culture. Used to be, everyone could answer the same question: *Where were you when you heard that Kennedy's head came apart?* Which is not such a prevalent character trait any more. *I* certainly can't answer, too young at the time, seven years old and about as cognizant of things presidential as I was of things sexual. Who knew, who cared? Of what possible use are those to a seven-year-old?

But I remember where I was when someone told me that John Belushi was dead. The memory is etched like the inscription on the back of a locket, to be hung about my neck. Like an albatross.

These things I kept to myself, though, while looking at his grave. I was not alone, and while Shelby and I had kept passionate company this whole autumn trip, there were places I would not let her. Things I would not say. Had that problem a lot. I don't think it mattered to her. I seem drawn to the type to whom it never does.

John Belushi had been buried on Martha's Vineyard, March 9th, 1982. Four days after his death; eight and a half years ago. He and his wife had owned a house here, but from what I gather, he spent the bulk of his time elsewhere . . . Los Angeles, New York, movie sets. His loss. A genuine oasis of Atlantean beauty and tranquility, Martha's Vineyard. A mutant triangle of an island, moored south of Massachusetts along with Nantucket and a few other piddly islands. Massachusetts proper hooks back around north into Cape Cod, like a shrimp tail, as if snubbing these lesser pretenders.

Downeast crust and blueblood elitism. I didn't belong here, and in his soul, Belushi never did either. But here he found peace, a commodity all too scarce for the living.

Massachusetts, the state that gave the country the Kennedys: a dynasty founded on a bootlegger's fortune, rising above that with pride and stoic hope, only to sink into borderline disgrace, awash in scandal and alcoholism. What goes around comes around. Funny, with some people, the way it always comes back to substance abuse. I'm certainly not one to point fingers, not with the very special relationship I have with George Dickel sour mash, but then again . . . I'm not the dead one.

Shelby regarded the grave with a cocked head, one hand cupping an elbow, the other hand at her chin. Studied, classic. Behind large-frame glasses, her eyes were serious. She moved with a cautious ease, black hair knotted in a simple twist over one shoulder, standing very straight. Courtroom posture. I suspected a charm school's influence in her early years, suppressed but not entirely overcome.

Back home in south Florida, she was a public defender, champion of the oppressed and the scum of the earth. My existence was far more ignoble, maintaining that grand old tradition of yellow journalism at its most wretched. *The National Vanguard* was the sort of paper generally bought in supermarket checkout lines. I take a bizarre pride in knowing my work is part of the national diet.

No idea what I represented in Shelby's life, not even sure what she represented in mine. Oddly enough, we met while both on the job, at the gonzo bizarro trial of a guy who made videotapes of himself with an Alsatian – porno, of course – then put them in his neighbours' mailboxes at night. The guy showed up in court his first day wearing a Lassie T-shirt. Shelby hadn't had a chance. I always wondered who she'd pissed off to get assigned *that* one.

Maybe I was the sexual court jester she needed to counteract day-in, day-out dealings with those aforementioned oppressed and scum of the earth. No talk of love, of commitment, of anything as far away as next week, even. It was primarily a hormonal thing we had going. Ain't life grand?

So here we were, on vacation from our real lives at the other end of the nation. Mid-October, a leisurely drive through New England to witness its transition into autumn. Last week, Shelby had curled onto her side in bed, turning her back on me forever as she watched heat lightning flicker in a humid Florida sky. Finally said she wanted to see leaves changing colour. I was a native, and never really missed that. She wasn't, and did, and in that moment it was like watching her peel back years and the mileage of the courtrooms and their great cattle call of justice . . . and find there was a poetic little girl inside who could still marvel at the simple brilliance of oaks and sugar maples.

Shelby was more human to me in that moment than she ever had been. And I wished I could return the favour.

The gravesite, Abel's Hill Cemetery. Belushi's grave was not alone in more ways than one. Yes, it had the company of other stones, but it also bore the attention of those who sought it just as I had. A few trinkets and notes had been left behind. Offerings from pilgrims who had come east, or north, or south, out of a melancholy yearning to see all that remained to be touched.

Shelby looked at it, then at me, and I knew what she was thinking. It was like a little shrine.

'I once saw a piece of pop art,' she said. 'Someone had painted the NBC peacock and highlighted an axis of feathers so that it looked like a cross. With Belushi in a loincloth, nailed to it with syringes.'

'Belushi dying for our sins? Now that's a little much.'

'It's easy to deify a dead legend. As long as they die young enough.'

'So when's the cutoff point?'

Shelby shook her head. 'Don't know, I don't know. But we only indulge the *young* and reckless. Old and reckless is just pathetic. Do you think anybody would deify Frank Sinatra if he was found dead of an overdose? It would never happen.'

'Too late, he's working against handicap,' I said, grinning. 'Frank's *already* old and pathetic.'

She shifted, see-sawing her weight back and forth, grinning back, rather lopsided, conceding the point. 'Ah, but there was a time, though . . .'

I thought about it, deification, that whole process by which the prematurely dead are kept forever young in the national consciousness. Like some sort of spiritual archive. Maybe it wasn't so much deification as a romanticism, probably of all the wrong things, but the forbidden allure *did* have its own undeniable appeal. Vaudevillian wisdom, carried to the extreme: Always leave 'em wanting more.

I remember reading about a sign someone had tacked up out here shortly after Belushi's death. Some wiser soul, I think, who saw through more bullshit and misguided romanticism than I'll ever recognize: *He could have given us a lot more laughs, but noooooo.*

I knelt to the grave, reached for the offerings left behind. A Quaalude imbedded in clear Lucite, like a paperweight. A little Samurai sword letter opener. A collection of ticket stubs, their dates, printed in a computerese font, years old; tiny capsulized reviews had been scrawled beside the movie names: *Continental Divide: Not bad. The Blues Brothers: Loved it. Neighbours: Sucked big-time.*

And, of course, the notes. Three, at the moment, sheets of paper folded into tight squares. I wondered: Did someone come out here periodically to gather these sad little efforts at communication with a dead legend? Were they collected and cared for in some sepulcher?

I grabbed one of the notes, looked back at Shelby. 'Do I dare?'

'Legally, you're in the clear. I don't know about morally.'

I unfolded the note. The needle had snapped off my moral compass a long time ago.

And I read. A few lines of lament, sorry you're gone, man, but you're not forgotten, hope you can see the Samurai sword I left behind, see it from somewhere, and that you like it. Signed simply with initials, L.R.

The next one was a poem, definitely penned by a feminine hand, and young, too. Or hopelessly gridlocked into romantic immaturity. Her i's were dotted with little hearts. Crystal Hemmings, of Pittsburgh. Probably got to know Belushi after the fact. *Saturday Night Live* reruns, courtesy of cable TV.

This was just too fucking sad.

I read the third one. Read it again. And again.

John,

I figure I'm due for Heaven, cause I already done my Hell on earth. I thought I could live with this. The only person I could ever lie to was me.

You're dead and I'm sorry. My fault, man. My guilt. My doing. Wherever you are . . . forgive me?

Tim

And didn't these scant few lines read like a confession of sorts? Or was that just wishful thinking, more muck I could rake up and flesh out into a full and sordid tale?

A little of both, probably.

Whoever this Tim was, he wasn't the only one who couldn't lie to himself. And here Shelby and I had said we'd leave our other lives back in south Florida for a while. I tried to pretend I didn't really notice the inevitable disappointment in her eyes as I pocketed the note.

We spent the night on the Vineyard in a hotel that had once been some lofty manor house. We slept with windows open to the night, breathing cool Atlantic air that smelled and tasted and felt far different than it did down home. Like it came from an entirely different ocean. The next morning we took a ferry back to the mainland and set south again. Seeing John Belushi's grave, bunking on an island, these had been spur of the moment ideas the day before. Shelby had seen her New England leaves, hopefully gotten her fill, as far north as Vermont. Real life and careers awaited at the other end of I-95.

These were a lot more certain than what awaited us in the form of one another. But I'm used to that kind of uncertainty. I find it adds a perverse spice to the interpersonal.

We didn't stop for breakfast until Providence, Rhode Island. Shelby indulged me while I set off on foot, and found a shop called The Book Worm. Used stock only; you want new, go someplace else. The door swatted a delicate overhead bell to announce my arrival, and the air within was richly musty with the dry air of old pages. Thousands of them, millions, waiting to be turned.

I pawed through shelves and stacks of nonfiction. In The Book Worm, it appeared that alphabetical order was merely a loose suggestion, nothing to break sweat over. I began in the W's, finally found two copies of what I wanted, one in the T's and the other a few spines away surrounded by U's. I selected the less dog-eared and battered of the pair, filed the other one where it belonged, and paid for my prize.

Carried it outside into crisp October air, just pleasant enough to make me forget that pungent essence of old words. Everything's a tradeoff.

'What did you buy?' Shelby asked when I met her at the car. Nor was she empty-handed herself; she had used the time to browse through an antique store and carried a small brass nautical-looking lamp. Probably half my weekly salary.

So I showed her the paperback. *Wired*, by Bob Woodward. The short life and fast times of John Belushi. I had one at home, read five years before, and a fat lot of good it did me there.

'Research,' I said.

She smiled, and it was one of indulgence. I had four years on her, and sometimes in her presence I still felt like a terminal kid, ready to be sent to the principal's office for spitwad warfare. Only in her case, I was ever more willing to bend over and grab my ankles.

'The sleaze-monger rears his oily head,' she said, and unlocked her car door. I followed, obedient. She drove a Saab. I drove a Plymouth with noisy brakes. Which one would *you* want to take north?

The atlas quoted almost 1500 miles between Providence and home. We'd do it in three days. And Shelby would drive the bulk of it. Which would leave me with a lot of reading time.

I'd already caught the scenery on the way up.

At some point years ago, a stretch of Florida's southeastern Palm Beach county got tagged with the label of 'Tabloid Valley.' Seven main supermarket tabs in the country, and six of them are published within less than twenty miles of each other. Not quite as prestigious as California's Silicon Valley, but you do what you can. The intelligentsia's dissenting opinions to the contrary, it still isn't as bad as toxic waste. Go ask the folks living around Three Mile Island which they would rather have.

The National Vanguard comes out of Delray Beach. A large, stolid building of Spanish architecture, stucco and arched portals and red tile roof. We, the inmates, call it Taco Hell. My first day back at work after our leaf-viewing field trip to New England, I was in the office of my boss. Janice Fletcher, Celebrities Editor. Regarded affectionately around the building as the world's only known case of permanent PMS.

Janice stared through bifocals at the note I had brought back from Martha's Vineyard. Memorizing? Her salt and pepper hair was pulled back into a bun so tight her forehead nearly screamed.

'And for this we should send you to Los Angeles?' She was not amused. 'How do you know this isn't some kid from Boston or wherever, he talks to his TV to old reruns and thinks John Belushi answers him?'

As if I had a persuasive rebuttal to that one? I let it slide and fired off Exhibit B, tossing my speedily-read backup copy of *Wired* onto her desk. Decorated inside with numerous swathes of yellow highlighter.

'Do you remember anything more than the headlines about Belushi's death?'

Janice looked long and hard at the book's cover. And I knew she was focusing on the author's name. Bob Woodward. Looking up at me from below, then, all grim mouth and condescending eyes. As if to say, *Delusions of grandeur, Mike, is that what's going on here?* She didn't need to remind me that he and Carl Bernstein had won a Pulitzer for the *Washington Post* in 1973, for breaking open a little thing called Watergate. *So you think you could find out something* he *couldn't, is that it?*

In a nutshell, yes. We all have to dream, don't we?

I don't know precisely what her problem with it was. Here at Taco Hell, we didn't exactly operate with standard journalism ethics, two sources to back up every allegation. Give us a whiff of anything, real or imagined, and we'd run with it.

Maybe Janice had a denial of just where she was working, and those delusions of grandeur were her own. At least I *knew* I wrote for a scandal rag that few with more brains than an oyster took seriously. But *The Vanguard* could be a weird place, as if some of the power brokers here secretly longed for respectability. And Janice had this irritating sense of righteous duty from time to time.

But maybe that's why my own inertia had done an about-face. Because so did I. That wistful longing to do something that would truly matter. Uncover that dirt, blow the dust off that closeted skeleton, and make a difference for once in my life.

It hadn't been all *that* long ago when I believed this wasn't merely possible, but obligatory. That when the legal system dropped the ball somewhere along the way, in the investigative end or before the judges, we in the information business were the court of last resort. That we were the ones who could still right the wrongs when all the other agents of justice had failed.

'Enlighten me,' Janice finally consented.

'Belushi was in L.A. at the time, ostensibly working on a script he had in development, but mostly finding excuses *not* to work on it. He was staying at a bungalow at the Chateau Marmont, off Sunset. But there's only one person's word in the world that says just how Belushi died: Cathy Smith. Sure, you got a lot of backup support, all these other people that knew what was going on, those last days of his life when Belushi was on a binge. The man was going through thousands of dollars worth of hard drugs. During his last five days or so, he was mixing cocaine and heroin and injecting it. It's called a speedball. Or rather, Cathy Smith was doing it for him. It's mainly her testimony that says how he died. Everything else is just coroner's reports, that sort of thing.'

I took a breath, trawling for facts. I'd tried memorizing all this last night and earlier in the morning. Making a pitch for something like this looks bad enough without crutching yourself with notes. 'The day he died, she shot him his last speedball, say, three-thirty in the morning. He showered and slept off and on after that. She checked him around ten-fifteen and he was okay. Next thing anybody knows, his physical trainer finds him dead around two hours later.'

'Do you think Cathy Smith was lying?'

I shrugged. 'It's possible, but maybe that's all she knew. She took off for Canada, gave this exclusive interview to *The Enquirer* for fifteen grand, saying how she was the one killed John Belushi. Later she denied that. But as far as anyone's telling, that's the way it happened. Maybe she's not so much lying as in the dark about something. Hell, she was a junkie herself, a part-time dealer. An aging groupie who'd pretty much been chewed up by her own life. Her priorities would have been . . . limited.'

I could see wheels turning in Janice's head. Forge on.

'But all through what Woodward was able to piece together of Belushi's last few weeks, months, there was a lot of time unaccounted for. Times he would just take off. Nobody could watch him all the time, nobody could keep up with him. With enough cocaine, the man could keep going strong for nearly two weeks, no sleep. So who's to say that at least one of his lowlife friends didn't slip through the net?'

'Tim,' she said, and snapped a red fingernail against the note. 'Who went all the way to Martha's Vineyard to try clearing his conscience.'

'It's a cry for help,' I deadpanned. 'I think he wants to unload.'

Janice rolled her eyes. Yes, sometimes I tried her patience. 'So are you thinking this Tim was just another player in an accidental overdose? Or is your fertile brain tipping all the way into some full-blown conspiracy theory here?'

I just rocked on my heels and let her have that smile I sometimes unleash. That gosh-I'm-so-charming smirk. All I needed was a hat at a rakish tilt.

I explained to her that, actually, there were two film projects in which Belushi was involved, that certain unknown parties might not have wanted made. The first being *Kingpin*, an idea of Belushi's to base a film on the life of a New York druglord named Mark Hertzan with whom he had gotten friendly. The studios weren't interested, but Belushi was gaining more clout, and enough contacts to go outside the Hollywood mainstream into independent film making. Just a month before Belushi's death, Hertzan was gunned down execution-style in his apartment building. File this one under unsolved; Belushi himself admitted it might have had something to do with the *Kingpin* project.

The other film was far more of a definite go, a script called

Moon Over Miami. Louis Malle was spearheading this one, a story inspired by the Abscam case in which FBI agents posed as Arabs ready and willing to bribe Congressmen for favours. Malle's vision was a black comedy that would demonstrate just to what depths spit-and-polish FBI agents would stoop: hiring criminals to incriminate their Congressional targets, in order to boost the Bureau's public image. Not the most flattering portrayal of the nation's top law enforcement agency.

So I pitched it all, I pitched it hard, and I pitched it from as many directions as I possibly could. It's a numbers game. You batter your head against a wall in enough strategic locations, you're bound to smash through eventually.

'Where would you start, once you got out there?' Janice said.

'Rollie Newkirk.' I braced, waiting for the bomb to drop.

Rollie Newkirk had spent six or seven years affiliated with *The National Vanguard* as a Hollywood contact. Gossip columnist was probably the most apt label to hang on him, but even that didn't seem quite right. Gossip columnist, you think of a certain tacky glamour, Rona Barrett, like that. Rollie didn't come close to even measuring up to her dubious level.

Remember high school? There's usually one kid who saunters into the bathroom and takes a long leisurely piss, then takes forever to wash his hands. Always with a slightly cocked head, tipping that ear for best reception so he doesn't miss any potentially juicy conversations by people who wouldn't ordinarily talk to him on the best day of his life.

Take that kid, add fifty pounds and half as many years, plop him down in Hollywood, and you have Rollie Newkirk.

'I guess he's a start,' Janice said, and sighed.

So I had it, just like that. And hadn't even really had to fight that hard. Nor use my secret weapon, a line penned while driving to work, to shame her into seeing it my way . . .

If *The Enquirer* could pay $15,000 to a junkie, at least *The Vanguard* could allot me that much to go find another one.

A couple days later, I jetted cross-country, out of Miami and into the Burbank Airport. Took a cab down to Hollywood, and my hotel, then stretched out on the bed. Luxury, after spending a full workday's equivalent in a United Airlines coach.

First time I was out here, maybe a dozen years ago, it was a real eye-opener. *Hollywood*, the name alone conjures glamour on an epic scale, but such fancies are an anachronism from a bygone era. The bus station is full of rude awakenings. Runaways and other naive hopefuls, bored by Kansas or wherever, ready to see their names in lights. They're more likely to have police portraits done in chalk on pavement.

At least it ensures the pimps a steady influx of fresh faces.

New numbers had to be invented for the sleaze factor here. South Florida certainly has no shortage of things sleazy, but it seems different there. South Florida seems younger, fresher, its tawdriness taking on more of an adolescent naughtiness. Hollywood has been around longer, lying there between desert and ocean like a whore long past her prime, her cunt dried up like an old gulch. But still tough, make no mistake. Still vicious, still chewing up innocents who come seeking her favours.

Rollie Newkirk was expecting me; I'd called his last known number a few hours after getting the go-ahead from Janice . . . had to give Rollie time to rise and shine. I called him again once I had arrived and we did brunch the next day. Sidewalk cafe on La Brea called Charmaine's. He picked it, and once I saw the prices, I knew why: there was never any doubt but that I was paying.

'Kiss kiss,' he said when I got there, joined him at a little square table. Rollie was all in gray, thinning hair combed back into a short limp ponytail, with plump cheeks crinkling into a dimpled smile. He looked like a Buddha after an image makeover. Rollie had been seated on a far perimeter, next to the hedges. A definite nobody. I checked carefully for hornet nests while sitting, and he clucked at my clothes. 'Oh dear, I see you're *still* dressing like an off-duty lifeguard.'

'Rollie,' I greeted. Tight smile. 'And I see you're still ducking that HIV-positive test.'

'Vicious, vicious,' he said. 'You must pick that up from working too long around Janice Fletcher. How *is* she?'

'Mellowing.'

I'd been there all of fifteen seconds before some stuffy young ramrod of a waiter arrived with a clip-on tie for me. His name was probably Thad. Gazing with vaguely regal distaste at my blue and green shirt; at least it didn't have palm trees on it. Maybe I should have made the effort to tuck it in. He left the clip-on hanging cockeyed, and Rollie eyed all this with bemusement.

'Oh, I didn't *tell* you about dress standards . . .?'

I shook my head no. 'Must have slipped your mind.' Rollie, jeez. He could still be a real bitch.

Menus were a long time in coming. Oh that Thad, being fussy again. When he *did* come back, he wouldn't even tell us his real name, that he would be our waiter this morning. I had no idea we were *that* detestable. I hoped Charmaine's had at least put him on combat pay for dealing with our obviously distasteful ilk.

I saw no point into getting straight down to business right off. Wait until the food came, at least, when most of Rollie's attention would be focused onto our table. For the time being, he had to show off for me, or perhaps himself, discreetly waving to select newcomers. They all carried portable cellular phones. None of them I recognized; shows you how much I know about Hollywood politics. But then, a lot of them seemed to have the same reaction to Rollie. After he waggled his fingers and flashed his pinkie ring at one tanned, gray-haired gent, the fellow turned to his companion – a niece or granddaughter, I'm *sure* – and hunched his shoulders.

I pretended not to notice. Let him salvage one or two shreds of dignity.

I found it easy to laugh inside at him . . . for maybe a minute. Then I just felt depressed, watching him try to maintain this facade of his own creation, perhaps trying to outrun that grossly unpopular kid he must have been a few decades ago. Desperately attempting to achieve whatever immortality or notoriety he could, so that when he died, he might warrant more than a standard single column inch in the *Los Angeles Times* obituaries.

Didn't I want the same thing? And wasn't I scoring about as well?

I hunted for other thoughts to fill the void. Wondering who had worn this tie before me. Maybe some noble eccentric, too talented to consider such trivialities before leaving home. Had I ever seen Spielberg wearing a tie? Maybe Thad would let me keep it as a souvenir.

He brought our food at last, bless him. I let Rollie get a couple bites down before I got to work.

'How good is your memory?' I said.

'Speak in timeframes, love, timeframes.'

'Let's go back eight and a half years. Spring of 1982.'

Rollie sat up straighter, tilted his head back. Three chins waggled at me. 'Oooo, we *are* dipping back into ancient history now, aren't we? I remember there *was* a 1982. What of it?'

'John Belushi's overdose.'

Rollie looked bored, disappointed even. He flipped his chubby hand north. 'I do believe there's a dead horse up on Santa Monica, if you'd like to go flog that one awhile, too.'

'Bear with me, would you? Who's picking up the check, anyway?' Mister diplomacy. 'Belushi's O.D. Surely there was a lot of talk flying around about it at the time.'

'Oh, dearheart, tell me about it.' Rollie leaned across the table, eyes wide. Confidantes, that was us. He even forgot about his food; I must have struck a vital nerve. 'That man was a frightening legend in his own time.'

'You remember hearing anything about anyone he might have been hanging around with at the time, name of Tim?'

Rollie pursed his lips, tapped his fork against the china. Ting ting. 'Tim Matheson? He –'

'Yeah, he played Otter in *Animal House*. No, not that one, a different Tim, I don't have a last name. We're probably talking about a junkie, or close to it.'

Rollie leaned back in his seat, sitting taller all of a sudden. He'd dropped out of gossip mode and gone straight to shrewd. It was going to cost me, this much I knew.

'So we're dealing in information now, are we,' he said, high and delighted. 'Just how much is this worth to you and our dear Janice, so far away?'

I leaned one way, then another, made a show of contemplation. 'I can't say offhand, Rollie, but . . . you point me in the right direction, and I can arrange some sort of consultation fee.'

He leaned back again, looking skyward, lacing plump fingers

and pulling them apart. Repeatedly. 'It's a start. Of course . . .
I'd have to go through my notes. And this *is* eight and a half years
ago we're talking about. This could be a time-consuming process,
why, it could take . . .'

I rolled my eyes. The gossiping Buddha had me by the short
hairs and he knew it. 'And I suppose I could see my way clear to
adding a processing fee to speed things along.'

'Ooooh, we do speak the same language, don't we.' He beamed.
'Now, just what sort of context am I looking for, in regards to this
Tim-no-last-name? What's he supposed to have done?'

I'd thought about this already: should I tell Rollie the angle I
was working? It wasn't the kind of thing you wanted to deposit in
a rumour factory like him. On the other hand, he had already
dealt himself in for substantial self-interest. If he knew the stakes,
he would undoubtedly find them all the more juicy, and work all
the harder.

Sure, why not. What's a little scandal-talk among friends?

So I laid it out for him, bare bones. No need for the persuasive
arguments that had been necessary with Janice. And the further I
went, the more Rollie began to regard me in some new light. I
wasn't sure I liked it. It fell dangerously close to an ogle.

When I wrapped it up, Rollie leaned back with hands folded
over his ample belly. Happy Buddha. 'I always did love the way
your mind works. I never told you that, did I?'

I said nothing. I could always take a compliment.

'I can't promise you anything, Mike,' he then said, and it was
like a completely different Rollie. As if a genuine human being
were in there, peeping out for the moment. 'Only that I'll check
my files and see if I can come up with something for you.'

I could ask for no more. So from my wallet I took a business
card – the *National Vanguard* logo didn't generally impress
people so much as amuse them – and scribbled out my hotel
number, slid it across to him. Rollie pocketed it and I assumed
our business this morning was done.

After brunch was eaten, Rollie left first – busy, busy – and I sat
for a while, smoking two cigarettes and lowering the property
values. Never was Thad more attentive, so close to evicting us,
yet so far, one down and one diehard to go. On his third tight-

jawed trip to ask if there was anything else I required, I finally
tossed three twenties and a five onto his tray to take care of the
bill.

'One thing,' I said. 'Can I keep the tie? I've really come to envy
your sartorial taste.'

'By all means . . . *do.*' His jaw could have cracked walnuts.

'Great,' I said, and rose. I peeled off a hundred dollar bill,
folded it into quarters, and slipped it into the pocket of his
starched white shirt. 'And this is for you, Thad. You've just
been an absolute peach this morning.'

He looked down at his pocket, at me, pocket, then me again.
Blinking. I do believe I'd caught him off-guard. But he quickly
recovered, and that haughty fusspot countenance returned.

'My name's *Tad,*' he said, as if I were cretin of the year.

I just smiled.

Sure, I remember where I was when someone first told me that
John Belushi was dead.

I'd followed him ever since the fall of 1975, when *Saturday
Night Live* debuted. In college at the time, at Gainesville, and the
show quickly became one of those ritualistic totems for myself
and my friends. Gathering in apartments or houses rented en
masse, awash in celebration of the weekend. Or we'd catch it in
bars, places packed and generating enough noise to rival a factory,
but come 11:30, silence would descend so the TV could be heard.
Ill-mannered louts who persisted in noisy distraction were
quickly dealt with by mob mentality.

Chevy Chase went on to be the first star to emerge out of the
repertory company that made up the Not Ready For Prime Time
Players. One season, then the jump to feature films and leading
man status. I knew he'd eventually drift into comfortable ruts and
diminish into mediocrity. He was too smug. And played one basic
character: himself.

No, for me, from the very beginning, Belushi was the one I
tuned in to see the most. *He* was the embodiment of anarchy
incarnate. The bottled outrage, the short fuse, the comedic rhino
with a ferocious edge and no restraint. He was the one that
defined the true excitement of live TV, because he was a gifted

menace to himself and everyone around him, and you never knew what he might do next.

I hated it when he and Dan Aykroyd decided to leave the show after the fourth season. No more weekly fix, but I understood and respected their reasons. Hollywood had opened up to them, and they had outgrown the show. Bigger and better spectacles ahead? I certainly hoped so.

But I noticed something different in those next few years, maybe because I had grown more worldly myself. The nature of the work changed, grew flaccid and safe. And I could watch Belushi giving an interview to some shellacked TV personality profiler, and catch the occasional glimpse of desperation in his eyes – a look wholly removed from any mania of comedic intensity. As if the laughter wasn't enough anymore, or he didn't trust it, or believe it was there at all.

At least, I think now that I did at the time. Maybe I'm just fooling myself with 20/20 hindsight. Wouldn't be the first time.

But I do know this: On Friday, March 5, 1982, I was with friends. Three years out of college and working in Tampa on the staff of an alternative weekly press. No sacred cow was safe from our righteousness, and we fashioned ourselves young journalistic anarchists, devoted to some credo of free expression and principled anger I can't even fully remember anymore. Fridays we generally knocked off early, and that particular one several of us met at one couple's house and devoted several hours to sensimilla via an ornate bong. Friday afternoon became evening, hazy and mellow.

One of my fellow writers went on a pizza and beer run, came back in twenty saying he'd heard on the radio that John Belushi had fatally overdosed in L.A. I refused to believe until I heard it from Dan Rather's lips during a CBS news update after we'd flipped on the TV. Imagine. Dan Rather. I had refused to believe my friend until he had Rather backing him up.

I knew right then I was a sellout.

But it got worse, as this nosedive evening wore on, injury upon insult. I sat on the floor in this dumpy house, realizing that this was the first true loss of applicable culture I had experienced. The first one to really hit home and *hurt*. Yes, I'd loved Boris

Karloff's movies as a kid, and when he died I was sorry, but he could have been my grandfather. Hendrix, Joplin, Morrison . . . they were gone before I was old enough to appreciate their music. And John Lennon didn't count; the Beatles were already history by the time I awakened musically, and by then, newer bands played harder, louder, faster.

And while some would say it was for the best, for the first time I really felt like a full-blown adult.

It's overrated.

Rollie Newkirk called me the day after our brunch, said he had struck out regarding the name Tim. Still, he had a suggestion, gave me the name of a limo driver he had talked to years ago. She had lugged Belushi around on a few occasions, nights of high speed endless thrills, get the limo and go from there. Anything could happen, he could wind up anywhere.

Then Rollie asked if I wanted to join him for an afternoon swim at his apartment's pool. I pictured some crumbling marble depravity with spouting water nymph statues and free-roaming peacocks, and begged off. Sorry Rollie, forgot my special L.A. trunks. The ones with the stainless steel codpiece and butt armour.

It took several phone calls to track down Joyce Fulton, the driver. She was apparently a nomad on the limo circuit. Rollie knew her agency as of 1984, and I took it from there, shifting into legal mode. It's a routine I frequently run, introducing myself as the attorney and executor of the estate of some recently-deceased philanthropist. In this case, said eccentric philanthropist recalled a particularly pleasant chauffeur named Joyce from a few years ago, and he wanted to remember her with a bequest. Could I please be directed to her next employer?

It couldn't fail. Most drivers, from the longest stretch limo to the lowliest taxi, believe that next passenger might turn out to be another Howard Hughes, earmarking them for future gratitude. Never mind that Howie had fourteen-inch toenails by the end, his money spends just the same. As incentive, I said I'd be sure to tell Joyce who had helped direct me to her. Everyone believes in the possibility of finder's fees, too.

They volunteered the information quicker than if I had used thumbscrews.

Joyce Fulton had driven for four firms since 1984, and when I at last reached her present employer, I shifted out of legal mode and into customer. Ordering a limo for that night, and asking if it would be possible to request her. She had come recommended by a former client of a month or so ago, I explained. They were quite accommodating. The customer is always right.

I had her pick me up around nine o'clock. She phoned my room from the cellular to let me know she had arrived, and was standing at reasonably military erect posture beside an open door once I set foot outside the hotel. I smiled, shrugged, and slid in. The door shut after me with such a gentle clunk it was almost a caress. When Joyce returned to the driver's seat, she seemed so far away we might as well have been in different area codes. The partition between us was wide open; at least I wouldn't have to call her back.

'Where are you looking to go?' she asked.

'I don't know. Anyplace is good.'

'Ah, another one of *those*,' she said, though cheerfully enough. 'Okay. Got anybody you want to impress?'

'Sure. How soon can we be in Miami?'

'Uh *huh*,' Joyce said. 'How 'bout *I* pick the circuit?'

I told her lead on, and the limo slid out into traffic like a great maroon yacht. It's quite the decadent sensation. I pilfered the bar right away, clinked bottles around and fixed a margarita just so I could say I'd used a blender in the back of a moving automobile. I turned the TV on, flipped through some channels, found a titty station that must've been relayed in via satellite feed. This limo company thought of everything. I left it there with the sound off. Looked like a Ginger Lynn video. Ah, the classics.

'You don't have to wear the chauffeur's cap if you don't want to,' I said.

'Sorry, company regulations.'

I frowned. 'I'll give you twenty extra dollars to lose the cap.'

'Deal,' she said, and whipped it aside.

So, she could be bought. This I took as a good omen.

And I liked her already. Joyce looked to be in her early forties, give or take. Hair dark and not-quite-shoulder length, with a side part. Her tailored gray uniform fit well; Nautilus workouts, I would have bet. Good tan and just enough faint smile lines for character.

I let her run the tour guide spiel for a while. Here's Mann's Chinese Theatre, here are the La Brea tar pits, there goes Century City. That's where D.W. Griffith built his own vision of Babylon in 1915. She went through it all with easy familiarity, and I'd pop in with questions now and then to let her know I was paying attention.

Babylon? What a portent.

'This bar is understocked,' I told her an hour into this aimless ride. 'There's no George Dickel.'

'Well it's your own fault.' By now we were comfortable enough for mild chastisement. 'You should have asked for it when you made the reservations this afternoon. It would've been waiting for you.'

No problem, I told her, just find a liquor store. Idling in the lot, I tried to talk her into joining me for a drink, but company regs got in the way again. I understood, and needled her long enough into breaking down and letting me buy a couple bottles of mineral water for her. Twist of lemon. Of course.

'Mind if I sit up front?' I asked when I came back out with sack in hand. 'I hate shouting all that distance.'

'It's your ride, Mikey. Do what thou wilt.'

I brought up a glass and a bucket of ice, and the passenger side front was mine. Joyce wheeled us back onto La Cienega, north-bound. Let's go slumming, I suggested, see how Beverly Hills looks these days, so she steered us toward Coldwater Canyon Drive.

'They probably told you I requested you specifically. Didn't they.' Time to cut through one layer of bullshit, at long last. I had plenty more to spread.

'Yep. Happens sometimes.'

I smiled across the front seat at her. Still seemed too far a distance. 'Just so they could meet you?'

That twining road with lots of Southern California's prime real estate lost some of her attention. She looked at me with one wary eyebrow cocked. 'Just what's going on with you, Mike? How about you tell me that right now.'

'I'm doing a book,' I said, 'and I was hoping to interview you. An earlier resource said you might make a good one yourself.'

'Oh yeah?' She brightened considerably. Smiling anew.

I expected as much. Say you're from a newspaper, and I don't care if it's *The New York Times* or *The Washington Post*, and as often than not, warning lights go off in the subject's head. Defenses rise. The *60 Minutes* Syndrome, I call it. All of a sudden you're Mike Wallace, barging in with cameras rolling, ready to wreak havoc on lives and careers. But say you're writing a book, and people want to be included.

That longing for immortality again, I imagine. Books don't line the bottom of a birdcage the next day.

'What's it about?' Joyce asked.

'Loosely, about cultural shifts. The way what used to be more underground culture insinuates itself into the mainstream, becomes gradually more accepted. I'm really fascinated by the punk and post-punk culture out here.'

Joyce sputtered a laugh. 'You don't look like a punker.'

'I don't look like a cultural anthropologist, either.'

'No, you don't. More like –'

'An off-duty lifeguard, right?'

All at once, Joyce looked straight at me with widening eyes. 'Oh lord, Rollie Newkirk sent you!' she wailed. 'Didn't he? That used to be one of his favourite lines.'

Mayday, mayday, I'm dying here. I got her through it, though, talked her down, told her hey, he was just a source, I was no more fond of the man than she apparently was, we'd met once at a party, and in his own unctuous way, he *was* one of the more memorable ones there that night. She bought it, and the more the lies rolled off my tongue, the worse I felt about it. Joyce Fulton was a genuinely fine lady, and my bullshit potential was wholly undeserved.

I really should tip heavily a bit later.

She took the limo around onto Mulholland and back down Beverly Glen, and I went on.

'I'm interested in doing a chapter or two on John Belushi. I know he was wanting to do some punk-influenced work that he never got to film. Rollie said you used to drive him some nights. I was wondering where he used to go, who he used to see from that sort of scene.' I had no idea if this was the milieu where my unknown complicitor lurked or not, but it made sense. Heroin use is a definite counterculture vice. 'And specifically, I'm looking for a guy Belushi would have known, named Tim. I talked to this guy, oh, probably five years ago and made notes – this was even before I ever thought of doing this book – but I lost all the notes in an apartment fire. Psychotic girlfriend, you know how it goes. But that's all I remember: Tim.'

Ah, what a silver-tongued weasel I could be.

Joyce drummed fingers on the wheel, thinking. Then, 'Just Tim, huh? Big city down there, Mike.'

I shrugged. 'That's okay.' I patted the seat. 'Big car.'

She wheeled back down into the sleaze factory and started me on a junket of clubs and nightspots whose patrons probably saw the light of day only rarely. Taking a definite walk on the wild side. Following the footsteps of a dead comic genius.

If I've learned one thing at *The National Vanguard*, it's that if you really want to know someone's life, you root through their garbage like a pig after truffles. It's all in there. But the problem this time was that the trash had been taken out eight and a half years ago. The best I could do was retrace the man's most likely footsteps and see what turned up.

And this much I knew: John Belushi had been heavily into the underground club scene. By now, lo these many years later, a lot of the places Joyce said she had taken him were gone. They live and die according to whim and trend. This week's fashion is next week's anachronism. But the people? Some grow out of it, some die. But some hang with it year after year after year. The hardcores.

And so with Joyce pointing me in the right direction, then waiting with the limo, I did not go gentle into that good night, but I went just the same. It was like a tour of Dante's Inferno, only paved.

They were generally places with all the genteel charm of a broken cinder block. With minimalist decor and music, either live or from a DJ booth, at airport runway sonic levels. I'd generally work my way to the bar and wait for a bartender who appeared to be a veteran, been at this game a few years.

Typical scenario: I'd order a drink and tip well. Sit there with a folded twenty between my fingers like a cigarette and try not to look like a bunboy or a lech readying for a proposition. And when I had their full attention, however long it would take, I'd leap right in: 'How'd you like to get your name in a book?'

Whether or not it worked, I'd at least usually score points for originality. And when it did, we'd talk, I'd hit my litany. Tim, anybody know a Tim, used to be an acquaintance of John Belushi? Sometimes I'd crap out entirely, but sometimes I'd come away with referrals. A tedious business, this. No wonder private detectives charge three hundred per diem for legwork.

I went at it all the rest of that night, until nearly every place was closed, and had Joyce take me right back out the next night so I could do it some more. Following leads, talking to waste cases whose memories ran the foul risk of being as foggy as an English moor. I actually did get steered toward a couple of Tims who claimed they'd known Belushi. One even had the picture to prove it, a worn and faded shot pulled with care from a wallet. The two of them, one younger, the other still alive, standing in some unknown club, faces cranked up with the intensity of celebration either liquid or chemical.

But neither of these Tims was the one I was looking for. *Humour me,* I'd say to them, then ask for a sample of their handwriting. No match either time, but by then I knew already. It was in their eyes that they had no connection with what I had come here for.

By the end of the third night, I was almost willing to give up, pack it in. Worn out, smelling of sweat and stale smoke; sore of feet and numb of ears. But mostly, overwhelmed by that peculiar noxious sense of failure that sets in around three, four in the morning when you can't sleep. When that fathomless sense of the dead of night comes to call, makes you re-evaluate your life. What the hell was I doing out here? It was times like this when I felt like a buzzard, picking the last tattered scraps away from the dead, the dying. Telling myself what the hell, they don't need them anymore, why not take them and put them on display.

The fourth estate. How noble. How constitutionally protected.

Maybe Joyce sensed this in me by the time she got me back to my hotel. Sat there as the engine idled, wearing with a light and easy smile – I still hadn't returned to the back seats – and then she did a rimshot with one hand on the steering wheel. 'So we gonna do this all over again tomorrow night, Mikey?'

'Don't know,' I mumbled.

Her brow creased, all concern. 'Aw come on. You're a fun date. And none of this Dutch treat for *you* no, you're a first class guy all the way.'

I smiled, leaned back in the seat a moment with burning eyes. 'There'll be others, you're young . . .'

She switched off the engine, reached over and smacked me lightly on the shoulder. 'Come on. Get out. Walk a minute.' And then she was out the door. Seconds later, so was I. I'd long relieved her of the obligation to open doors for me.

Joyce got me scooted along and moving, a slow leisurely amble, the speed preferred by those with nowhere to go and all the time in the world to get there. Moving past a sidewalk gauntlet of shrubs and palm trees, fronds stirring overhead. Not much foot traffic in this neighbourhood, this time of night.

'You know,' she said, 'far be it from me to tell a writer how to do his job . . . but it seems to me you're expending a lot of time, energy, and money to find one minor source for a book. Are you sure this guy's that important?'

'You'd be surprised.'

'Or are we,' she said, very even, very knowing, but without judgment, 'even going to be in a book at all?'

I probably knew it was coming, doubts on her part. In two nights, I'd gotten the sense that Joyce Fulton was as sharp as she was discreet. 'Have you been talking to Rollie today?'

'No. And don't worry, I won't ask. I don't even think I want to know. It's easier that way. When you *don't* know. When these lives that cross your own don't leave any traces behind. That way, later, when you hear what's happened to them . . . or what they did to themselves . . . it doesn't hurt.'

I said nothing, just walked at her side, listening to her voice, softer now than in the limo. And I wondered about her, who she really was. She'd told me nothing and I hadn't asked. But I had complied mental stats, just the same. I had her divorced, twice. One kid from the first marriage, a son. Around fifteen, sixteen by now. Splitting time equally between Mom and Dad, and she missed him terribly that other half of the time.

I didn't think I wanted to know how right or wrong I was.

'I genuinely liked him,' she finally said. 'Belushi. He was just too intense for his own good. He ran me hard and ragged sometimes . . . but in the end, he was always a gentleman. There've been quite a few I can't say that about.'

We had turned around by now, heading back toward the limo. I tried reconciling all those varied John Belushis people spoke of into one package. The addict. The gentleman who could be so sweet and disarming. The tyrant who at times bullied and badgered those with whom he worked. The star who had a weekly per diem living rate of $2500 built into his movie contracts, even though his accountants paid all his bills – the studios and everybody else *knew* it was for cocaine. Oh, it's just John, it keeps him going in front of the cameras, he needs it.

I tried to picture him his last weeks. Distraught over a script called *Noble Rot* he had worked on that was reviled by Paramount as unworkable. He had nearly alienated himself from almost everyone concerned in trying to ramrod it through into production by sheer force of his will. And speedballing those last five days of his life . . . getting high with a little help from his friends.

How many friends had it taken?

There were so many unknowns here. Cathy Smith's help with procurement and the needle notwithstanding, Belushi's death still went down as an accidental O.D. Maybe, maybe not, if there was a wild card named Tim in the deck. But Hollywood is a town that hides its secrets well, right from the very beginning. In the early twenties, when William Desmond Taylor was shot in his home, his friends, lovers, and associates swooped down upon the house to rid it of anything scandalous before reporting to the police. When William Randolph Hearst blew out producer Tom

Ince's brains during a yachting excursion, newspapers and even the San Diego District Attorney dismissed the death as due to acute indigestion.

Why should anything change? The two main motives to kill were still love and money. Apply that to Belushi's two back-burner projects. *Kingpin*, the druglord script? Some unknown player had too much cash at stake to allow that kind of possible exposure. *Moon Over Miami*, the Louis Malle film? The FBI or other conservative factions in those new years of the Reagan presidency loved their image too much to see it tarnished any more.

Or maybe it really was accidental, and Tim was just the street hustler who sold the last doses of heroin to Cathy Smith.

Joyce and I had reached the front of my hotel, and it was one of those oddly awkward moments when I felt I wanted to kiss her goodnight, and had no right to even think it. Maybe all this would look clearer after sleep. Deep and dreamless.

'So . . .' she said. Popping her cap on, the first since last night. She grinned wryly. 'See you tomorrow night?'

And I nodded. 'Wouldn't miss it.'

There are probably sadder things in the world – in fact, I know there are – but at the time, nothing seemed sadder than an aging punk rocker. It's a persona best worn by youth; the young come by anger naturally. But let a decade or more go by, and there comes a time when you can't even remember what it was you once were so angry about.

Tim surfaced on the fifth night, late, after I'd spent hours running a slalom that sent us back and forth over twenty mile stretches or more. A bouncer here knew a doorman there who thought he'd met a waitress somewhere else who remembered meeting a punk musician named Tim Frenzy who might have claimed he knew John Belushi. Or something like that. After so long, this food chain of bottom feeders tends to blur.

The end of the road, a Culver City club named Nine-One-One. The emergency phone number, I liked that. I wandered in as I'd done countless other places, these past four nights that seemed a lot longer. Maybe because I'd seen too many desperate people looking for that break they would never get. It nibbles away at you after a time.

The music was loud, barbaric, formless, angry. Didn't *anybody* out here play reggae? I tipped the bartender ten just to point him out, Tim Frenzy, and there he was onstage. Guitar player, all bones and sweat, flailing away at his axe with a glazed intensity that didn't allow much for tracking the rhythm. He had this kind of little boy lost quality that was at definite odds with the lines in his face.

Three thousand miles, several thousand dollars, Rollie Newkirk and Joyce Fulton and a cast of nameless hundreds, and this was the guy? I was seriously underwhelmed. Of course I didn't know at the time, he was just one more contender.

I waited until the band – they called themselves Chili Fart – took a break, then bribed my way to the club's backstage area. An extra beer in hand to break the ice, help Tim replace those precious bodily fluids dripped out front. I flagged him down in a narrow hallway, dim and hot and stale.

'Drink up,' I said in greeting, and handed the bottle to him. His other three mates looked irked, as if I'd breached etiquette. Hard old world, guys, sorry. 'Talk to you a minute?'

Tim glanced me up and down, eyes flat as a lizard's but less alive. 'You from a record company?' Maybe just the tiniest flicker of hope still alive in his voice.

I shook my head. 'Sorry. I represent other interests.'

I caught a bit of deflation in him, one more pinprick in a dream that must have been losing air for years. He waved the others off, and lingered alone with me in that dismal hallway.

'So what, is this, like private shit, or what?'

'Depends,' I said. 'Did you happen to do any travelling back east a couple weeks ago?'

He was silent, but this time I knew I had something. It was probably easier to detect in him than it would have been in most of the others. *Any* sign of life in a dead face and pair of eyes is cause for note. I reached into my pocket for that folded sheet of paper, and he watched my hands with a dull amazement. And a fatalistic dread.

'Yours, right?' I held it before his eyes. This was no time to innocently question. Questions would tip him off as to just how little I actually knew. *'Right?'*

Tim nodded, leaning against the wall in abrupt exhaustion. Shaking his head like he couldn't believe it, yet at the same time could, wasn't this just his luck, his life? And I looked at this miserable failure of a musician, with the bruises and scars of needles old and new along his arms, and I wondered which of us was the more world-weary. I'll see your arms and raise you my liver.

'You don't look like a cop.'

'Doesn't mean I'm still not curious.' And then, just to goose it along, 'You satisfy that curiosity, I can make it worth your while.'

God help us both. He looked more alive in that instant than he had since I'd seen him. The starving dog after the bone.

'There's a room here somewhere,' Tim said, looking down the hall, 'maybe we should . . . you know, privacy?'

He tried doors and I followed, and from out front, music from some bass-heavy club stereo rattled the floor. Tim opened one door and stepped inside. Scarcely a room, more of a walk-in utility closet. We shared it with mops and buckets, cleansers cruel to the nose. And whatever small creatures scuttled unseen behind boxes.

'I tune my guitar in here.' Tim grinned. With his red eyes and soured teeth, he was a walking death's head. 'I like it cause it reminds me of my first apartment. Takes me back, you know. Nothing like those . . . those first days, right?'

I guess anything can be shellacked with nostalgia and called romantic.

'How'd you *find* me, man? I didn't even sign my last name to that thing, did I?'

'Why don't you tell me *your* story first.'

Tim's hands were shaking, with the occasional nervous twitch of his shoulders, and his beer began to foam. I gave him a cigarette to calm him. Smoking in a closet full of solvent fumes, oh we were bright boys.

'I don't even know who the fuck you are.'

I shrugged. 'Does it matter? You went a hell of a long way to make an apology to a grave.'

'Yeah, well, I was in the neighbourhood, okay?' Tim upturned a large metal bucket, sat on its rusty bottom, took a long drink and dragged the cigarette into ash. 'My dad kicked it in Boston, okay? Hadn't seen him in eight years, figured I might as well not fuck up my last chance, right?' He laughed. 'And that asshole, you know he didn't leave me a fucking thing in the will. Just like him, and I could *use* it, too, could use some cash to cut some new demos, we wrote some decent stuff this year, you know? Did you hear it out front?'

I told him yeah, yeah. Gold record debut for sure. But non-commercial. He liked that.

Tim smoking, both of us in clouds. He shut his eyes and I felt the anguish by osmosis. Dead dreams, glimpsed through that cruel magnifying glass of time. All the accumulated regret of one breed and another.

Tim looked up, and he was ancient. 'I killed him and I was glad to do it at the time. Motherfucker, he said . . . one time said he was gonna help the band I was in. Get us on *Saturday Night Live* and maybe a record deal. I mean, why not, I believed him, he was helping those guys in Fear, he got *them* on *SNL* for a fucking Halloween show.' He ground the butt beneath a scabrous boot tip, did a horribly repugnant Belushi parody: 'I trusted him to keep his promise, but noooooo.'

'And so you shot him up that last time, yourself?'

'Cathy Smith, she'd already left. I knew where he was staying at the Marmont, he told me once, said come by, bring my guitar, we'd write some tunes. I found him in bed that morning. Man, I don't even think he knew it when I popped him in the arm.' Again with the death's head grin. 'Junkies give the best shots.' And then, something worse than that grin. The ghost of old premeditation. 'That's what I said to the guy paid me to go in there and do it.'

It was like waking up in a whole new world, hearing that. I leaned in closer. 'Who?'

Tim spewed a bitter little laugh. 'Think I cared back then? I was *pissed!* I had a right to be *heard!* Then some guy hears me talking one night, knows I'm pissed at Belushi for going back on his word on me, he offers me three grand to do a job like that?

Hell yes I'm gonna take it, I'd've done it for nothing if I'd thought it up myself. I didn't ask who he was . . . I just took the money. And I didn't leave nothing behind . . .' His voice was losing that bitterness. His head hung, and I believe if he'd been able, he might have cried. 'I shouldn't have done it, you know. I mean . . . he was just trying to get by, I couldn't see that then, he was just as big a mess as anyone, and *nobody'd* fucking help him . . .'

I stood watching Tim wrestle with his conscience, wondering how I could use this. Wondering how I could ever bring myself to spill this guy's story across a front page. And knowing that somehow I *would* find a way. As always. I'd gone to a lot of trouble to find him, hadn't I?

Remember that tidbit of Chinese wisdom? Be careful what you wish for, for you may get it.

I never learn.

The sound of bootheels thudding steadily down the hall knocked Tim from his bleak reverie. 'I gotta get back onstage, but you pay me, I can tell you what I know, I remember that morning, I remember it real good. You *are* gonna pay me, aren't you, you said you'd make it worth my time, that means money, don't it?'

He sat on that bucket clutching a bottle as empty as his eyes, only the bottle didn't plead. He looked sadder than Judas.

'Yeah,' I finally said. 'I'll pay you.' Some quick calculations in my head, some quick reductions, too. It wouldn't take much to hook this one. 'I'll pay you a thousand dollars cash for exclusive rights. Contract and everything.'

And Tim smiled with the sick hope of a cancer patient, waking up to one more day of life. Tomorrow, his place, and he told me where he lived. But make it afternoon, give him time to sleep, okay?

Sure. I could wait. I'd been hoping for it anyway, a chance to sit him down with a tape recorder, and a list of more incisive questions than I was able to come up with on the spot.

When I rejoined Joyce and the limo, to return at last to my hotel, I rode the rest of the way in the back.

* * *

That afternoon I took a cab to Tim's West Hollywood apartment. Someone other than Joyce doing the driving felt odd. We had dissolved our impromptu partnership for good last night, as I left her sitting behind her wheel in bewilderment over just what I had found inside Nine-One-One. She wanted to know, I honestly believe she did. But I couldn't tell her, and she could never ask.

Tim lived in the dingy squalour of some fifth-floor walkup. In this building's halls it was always dusk. I stood knocking at his door and got no answer. No sound from within, either, at least nothing to carry over the building's ambience. The crying babies and blaring TVs and radios and domestic turmoil leaking from other lives, behind other doors.

His door was unlocked. I needed no more invitation.

It was hot inside, with a subtle stuffy reek of aged laundry and sheets too long without changing. And beneath it, worse, the stink of emptied bowels. I knew Tim was dead even before I saw him stretched diagonal across his iron frame bed. The loose tourniquet still around his bicep and the spike still in that battered vein. On a rickety bedside table sat a spoon with the impromptu cotton filter balled up, and a candle had burned into a stub.

Oddly enough, he didn't look much more dead now than he had when he was still upright at the club.

And in a strange way, I think I actually felt a measure of relief.

The gentle footsteps came from off to my right, and the guy walked evenly out from what I presumed was the bathroom. Startled, you bet I was, but I don't think I was afraid at first because of how utterly benign the man looked. A simple slacks, shirt, and tie combo, of obvious label quality. Neat sandy hair, thinning at the temples, and his face had that taut smoothness of one or two trips under the knife for cosmetic tucks.

He stopped a few feet before me and we stared, and there was no doubt but that he was in charge. And if I tried to run, well, so much for me. His eyes were that cold and hard.

'In some rivers in the Amazon Basin,' he said, 'there lives a tiny little fish called the candiru. And the Indians know better than to piss in the river, because these fish can home in on a stream of urine, and they're so powerful and fast, *they can swim up the stream of urine.*' He looked quite delighted to be sharing this with me. 'The candiru lodges inside the urinary tract, with spiny barbs. It's supposed to be quite excruciating. The fish can only be removed by surgery.'

He looked at me a long time, measuring me up. The longer he stared, the more I felt myself dwindling. At last he nodded sadly.

'*You* have been pissing in the wrong river.' He spread his hands and fingers wide, it's showtime. 'And here I am.'

'How about –' My voice was trembling a bit and I didn't like that at all. 'How about I zip right up and go back where I came from.'

He appeared to consider this at great length. Cracking his knuckles, and I saw just how truly strong his hands looked. With long fingers, all bone and sinew, and I didn't want to see this man with his shirt off.

'Your name is Michael Lancer, you live in Delray Beach, Florida, and you've worked for a supermarket rag called *The National Vanguard* since April of 1983. You have no savings account, no CDs, no money markets or mutual funds, only a checking account with the First National Bank of Miami, and as of ninety minutes ago, it had a balance of four hundred sixteen dollars and eighty-one cents. Have I made my point?'

I nodded. Whoever had sent this guy up five floors to silence my one and only witness had long arms indeed.

He walked closer and lay one firm hand on my shoulder, and while I wouldn't give him the satisfaction of shaking, I still felt about ten years old in his presence. He steered me to a chair and sat me down, facing a window and Hollywood by day. He stood behind me with a hand on either shoulder and I wondered if it would be a bullet in the back of the head, or a quick snapped neck. And why I couldn't muster up enough courage to at least go down fighting.

'This is a huge city, Mr Lancer. But if you ask enough questions to enough people about the wrong subject, you still attract the kind of attention you'd rather not have. But that's all right. That's why troubleshooters are paid so well. Your bank balance? Why, I've made that much standing here talking to you just since you've been in the chair.'

The pressure on my shoulders grew stronger, as he kneaded the bunched muscles for a moment.

'I'm not going to kill you,' he finally said. 'Because I know why you're here, and so do your editors, I'm sure, and if you were to turn up dead, even if it looked like an accident, well, the way you people work and think, it would only validate your reason for being here.

'So what you're going to do is, you're going to fly home and say nothing of me, nothing of Tiny Tim over there, nor will you write a word about us. Because I'll be buying your piece of shit tabloid from now on, every week, and if I see anything I don't like, anything at all that hits too close to home as I judge it . . . then someday, someone's going to walk into your apartment and they'll find that I've been there. And that your heart is just one of several organs missing.'

I think it lost a beat or two hearing that one.

'So you be the judge, Michael Lancer. You decide whether it's worth it or not.'

The grip on my shoulders suddenly eased off, and I heard footsteps pacing away from me, and in no way would I turn around to check on this cultured apparition. I sat facing the window, eyes shut, hearing auto horns drifting up five floors, hands rigid as they clenched the edge of the chair beneath my things. I think he stopped somewhere near the door.

'There are planes leaving for Miami all the time. Find one of them by tonight. And in the meantime . . . if you don't have anything to do . . . go see a movie.'

Gone.

It was a long time before I could move. Some crusader for the sordid truth I made, no? Sitting there on the verge of losing sphincter control, keeping company with a corpse who already had. Top of the world, ma.

And when I finally readied to leave, I thought I could at least call in an anonymous tip. Somebody please run by and clean up this dead junkie. He wasn't much, but he doesn't deserve to lie around in his own filth. I found a scrappy little towel and used it to lift the phone receiver. And put it down.

Disconnected.

Once upon a time, years ago, director John Landis, who was at the helm of *Animal House*, the only profitable, hit movie that John Belushi was in, had an argument with Belushi's manager. Get him off the drugs, Landis argued. 'You can't make money off a corpse.'

I figure that one should be carved on the tombstone.

That's what it's really all about out there: the bottom line. Black ink versus red.

In flight between L.A. and Miami, I had plenty of time to put things together to my own satisfaction. To contemplate those calming drinks on my drop-down tray. No George Dickel on the flight, but I made do just fine.

Kingpin? *Moon Over Miami*? I'd been looking too far afield for motives to kill the man. The best one was right there in his own celluloid world.

John Belushi was the wrong guy in the wrong place at the wrong time, with unlimited access to all the wrong chemicals. But he made us laugh for all the right reasons. He was a man who didn't know how to compromise, and who could absolutely not be controlled. By anyone. The same quality that made him such a brilliant comedian was the same thing that made him such a terror to work with at times.

So what happens, I had to wonder, when you have a guy like that, out of control on a personal level? Whose movies are declining in quality because of poor judgment, whatever, and who can*not* be brought up short on a leash?

How do the power brokers react, the *real* players, the financiers and comptrollers who handle the purse? The ones who pay closest attention to that bottom line. When do they decide that enough is enough, that someone involved in a project insured against loss in case of non-completion is worth more dead than alive?

I think I know, at least in one instance.

Hollywood has never been kind to the renegades in its midst.

Genius requires a singular vision, whereas films are group effort. There's a long, ugly tradition of that Hollywood system breaking the backs of giant renegade talent. Eric Von Stroheim, Orson Welles, Frances Farmer, Dennis Hopper . . . they found out the hard way. Only four of many.

I'm sure the methods employed over the years are as varied as the reasons why. But it all distills down to the same fundamental: Someone doesn't play the game the way they're supposed to.

Enough time has passed since John Belushi's death to notice the difference in his contemporaries. Those with whom he made razored moments of dangerous comedy, with an edge, without rules. Live on a studio stage in New York. But look at them now, those who can still be seen. A few gems scattered here and there in their careers, but it's mostly been downhill in terms of quality. From mediocre to dismally unfunny. But they play the game, take no risks.

It's safe.

Is it any wonder the best work anymore tends to come from unknowns, working in independent corners, or other countries, with budgets the size of a simple Hollywood catering bill?

Maybe it's just as well. In the long run, I don't think anybody really wins the game out there. You either lose money, or your soul. Maybe your life is the cheapest of all, in a town where everything's for sale.

Shit. What was I going to give Janice back at Taco Hell in return for her expectations and cash allocation? Because she would most definitely demand a return on her investment. I felt sure I could whip up a rough outline before touchdown in Miami. It's a long flight, and I tend to work well under pressure.

So. The *Kingpin* angle, or the *Moon Over Miami* angle, which was it going to be? Either one would be just as fictitious.

And, so far as I was concerned, safe.

Once upon a time, I used to think I had ideals. That I would never allow myself to get caught up in playing those games where all I was was a spinning cog in some larger machine. I used to think I knew how to avoid a destiny like that.

But noooooo.

THE PARDON

James Grippando

The vigil had begun at dusk, and it would last all night. Clouds had moved in after midnight and blocked out the full moon. It was as if heaven had closed its omniscient eye in sorrow, shame or just plain indifference. Another six anxious hours of darkness and waiting, and the red morning sun would rise over the pine trees and palms of northeast Florida. Then, at precisely 7 a.m., Raul Fernandez would be put to death.

Crowds gathered along the chain link fence surrounding the state's largest maximum security penitentiary. Silence and a few glowing lights emerged from the boxy three storey building across the compound, a human factory of useless parts and broken spirits. Armed guards paced in their look out towers, silhouettes in the occasional sweep of a searchlight. Not as many onlookers gathered tonight as in the old days, back when Florida's executions had been front page news rather than a blip next to the weather forecast. Even so, the usual shouting had erupted when the black hearse that would carry out the corpse arrived. The loudest onlookers were hooting and hollering from the backs of their pick-up trucks, chugging their long-neck Budweisers and brandishing banners that proclaimed GO SPARKY, the nickname death-penalty supporters had affectionately given the chair.

The victim's parents peered through the chain link fence with quiet determination, searching only for retribution, there being no justice or meaning in the slashing of their daughter's throat. Across the road, candles burned and guitars strummed as the names of John Lennon and Joan Baez were invoked by former flower children of a caring generation, their worried faces wrinkled with age and the weight of the world's problems. Beside a cluster of nuns kneeling in prayer, supporters from Miami's

'Little Havana' neighbourhood shouted in their native Spanish, 'Raul es inocente, inocente!'

Behind the penitentiary's brick walls and barred windows, Raul Fernandez had just finished his last meal – a bucket of honey-glazed chicken wings with extra mashed potatoes – and he was about to pay his last visit to the prison barber. Escorted by armed correction officers in starched beige-and-brown uniforms, he took a seat in a worn leather barber's chair that was nearly as uncomfortable as the boxy wooden throne on which he was scheduled to die. The guards strapped him in and assumed their posts – one by the door, the other at the prisoner's side.

'Barber'll be here in a minute,' said one of the guards. 'Just sit tight.'

Fernandez sat rigidly and waited, as if he expected the electricity to flow at any moment. His bloodshot eyes squinted beneath the harsh glare as the bright white lights overhead reflected off the while walls of painted cinder blocks. He allowed himself a moment of bitter irony as he noticed that even the guards were white.

All was white, in fact, except the man scheduled to die. Fernandez was one of thousands of Cuban refugees who'd landed in Miami during the Mariel boat lift of 1980. Within a year Fernandez was arrested for first degree murder. The jury convicted him in less time than it had taken the young victim to choke to death on her own blood. The judge sentenced him to die in the electric chair, and after a decade of appeals, his time had come.

'Mornin', Bud,' said the big guard who'd posted himself at the door.

The prisoner watched tentatively as a pot-bellied barber with cauliflower ears and a self-inflicted Marine-style haircut finally entered the room. His movements were slow and methodical. He seemed to enjoy the fact that for Fernandez every moment was like an eternity. He stood before his captive customer and smirked, his trusty electric shaver in one hand and, in the other, a big plastic cup of the thickest looking tea Fernandez had ever seen.

'Right on time,' said the barber through his tobacco-stained teeth. He spat his green slime into the cup, placed it on the counter, and took a good look at Fernandez. 'Oh, yeah,' he wheezed, 'you look just like you does on the TV,' he said, pronouncing *TV* as if it rhymed with *Stevie*.

Fernandez sat stone-faced in the chair, ignoring the remark.

'Got a special on the Louis Armstrong look today,' the barber said as he switched on his shaver.

Curly black hair fell to the floor as the whining razor transformed the prisoner's thick mop to a stubble that glistened with nervous beads of sweat. At the proper moment, the guards lifted Fernandez's pant legs, and the barber shaved around the ankles. That done, Fernandez was ready to be plugged in at both ends, his bald head and shaved ankles serving as human sockets for the surge of kilovolts that would sear his skin, boil his blood, empty his bowels, and snuff out his life.

The barber took a step back to admire his handiwork. 'Now, ain't that a sharp lookin' haircut,' he said. 'Comes with a life-time guarantee too.'

The guards snickered as Fernandez clenched his fists.

A quick knock on the door broke the tension. The guard's keys tinkled as he opened the door. Raul strained to hear the mumbling, but he couldn't make out what was being said. Finally, the guard turned to him, looking annoyed.

'Fernandez, you got a phone call. It's your lawyer.'

Fernandez's head snapped up at the news.

'Let's go,' ordered the guard as he took the prisoner by the arm.

Fernandez popped from the chair.

'Slow down!' said the guard.

Fernandez knew the drill. He extended his arms, and the guard cuffed his wrists. Then he fell to his knees so that the other guard could shackle his ankles from behind. He rose slowly but impatiently, and as quickly as his chains and armed escorts would let him travel, he passed through the door and headed down the hallway. In a minute he was in a small recessed booth where prisoners took calls from their lawyers. It had a diamond-shaped window on the door that allowed the guards to watch but not hear the privileged conversation.

'What'd they say, man?'

There was a pause on the other end, which didn't bode well. 'I'm sorry, Raul,' said his attorney.

'No!' He banged his fist on the counter. 'This can't be! I'm innocent. I'm *innocent!*' He took several short, angry breaths as his wild eyes scanned the little booth, searching for a way out.

The lawyer continued in a low, calm voice. 'I promised you I wouldn't sugarcoat it, Raul. The fact is, we've done absolutely everything we can in the courts. It couldn't be worse. Not only did the Supreme Court deny your request for a stay of execution, but they've issued an order that prevents any other court in the country from giving you a stay.'

'Why? I want to know *why*, damn it!'

'The court didn't say why – it doesn't have to,' his lawyer answered.

'Then *you* tell me! *Somebody* tell me why this happening to me!'

The line was silent.

Fernandez brought his hand to his head in disbelief, but the strange feeling of his baldness only reinforced what he'd just heard. 'There has . . . some way . . . look, we've gotta stop this,' he said, his voice quivering. 'We've been here before, you and me. Do like the last time. File another appeal, or a writ or a motion or whatever the hell you lawyers call those things. Just buy me some *time*. And do it like quick, man. They already shaved my fucking hair off!'

His lawyer sighed so loudly that the line crackled.

'Come on,' said Fernandez in desperation. 'There has to be *something* you can do.'

'There may be one thing,' his lawyer said without enthusiasm.

'Yeah, baby!' He came to life, fists clenched for one more round.

'It's a billion to one shot,' the lawyer said, reeling in his client's over-reaction. 'I *may* have found a new angle on this. I'm going to ask the governor to commute your sentence. But I won't mislead you. You need to prepare for the worst. Remember, the governor is the man who signed your death warrant. He's not likely to scale it back to life imprisonment. You understand what I'm saying?'

Fernandez closed his eyes tightly and swallowed his fear, but he didn't give up hope. 'I understand, man, I really do. But go for it. Just go for it. And thank you, man. Thank you and God bless you,' he added as he hung up the phone.

He took a deep breath and checked the clock on the wall. Eight minutes after two. Just five hours left to live.

It was 5.00 a.m. and Governor Harold Swyteck had finally fallen asleep on the daybed. Rest was always elusive on execution nights, which would have been news to anyone who'd heard the governor on numerous occasions emphasizing the need to evict 'those hold over tenants' on Florida's overcrowded death row. A former cop and state legislator, Harry Swyteck had campaigned for governor on a law-and-order platform that prescribed more prisons, longer sentences, and more executions as a swift and certain cure to a runaway crime rate. After sweeping into office by a comfortable margin, he'd delivered immediately on his campaign promise, signing his first death warrant on inauguration day in January 1991. In the ensuing twenty-one months, more death warrants had received the governor's John Hancock than in the previous two administrations combined.

At twenty minutes past five, a shrill ring interrupted the governor's slumber. Instinctively, Harry reached out to swat the alarm clock, but it wasn't there. The ringing continued.

'The phone,' his wife grumbled from across the room, snug in their bed.

The governor shook himself to full consciousness, realized he was in the daybed, and then started at the blinking red on the security phone beside his empty half of the four-poster bed.

He stubbed his toe against the bed as he made his way toward the receiver. 'Dammit! What is it?'

'Governor,' came the reply, 'this is security.'

'I *know* who you are, Mel. What's the emergency?'

The guard shifted uncomfortably at his post, the way anyone would who'd just woken his boss before sunrise. 'Sir, there's someone here who wants to see you. It's about the execution.'

The governor gritted his teeth, trying hard not to misdirect the anger of a stubbed toe and a sleepless night toward the man who guarded his safety. 'Mel – please. You can't be waking me up every time a last minute plea lands on my doorstep. We have channels for these things. That's why I have counsel. Call *them*. Now, good – '

'Sir,' he gently interrupted, 'I – I understand your reaction, sir. But this one, I think, is different. Says he has information that will convince you Fernandez is innocent.'

'Who is it this time?' Harry asked with a roll of his eyes. 'His mother? Some friend of the family?'

'No, sir, he . . . well, he says he's your son.'

The governor was suddenly wide awake. 'Send him in,' he said, then hung up the phone. He checked the clock. Almost five-thirty. Just ninety minutes left. *One hell of a time for your first visit to the mansion, son.*

Jack Swyteck stood stiffly on the covered front porch, not sure how to read the sullen expression on his father's face.

'Well, well,' the governor said, standing in the open doorway in his monogrammed burgundy bathrobe. Jack was the governor's twenty-six year old son, his only offspring. His mother had died a few hours after his birth. Try as he might, Harold had never quite forgiven his son for that.

'I'm here on business,' Jack said quickly. 'All I need is ten minutes.'

The governor stared coolly across the threshold at Jack, who with the same dark, penetrating eyes was plainly his father's son. Tonight he wore faded blue jeans, a brown leather aviator's jacket and matching boots. His rugged, broad-shouldered appearance could have made him an instant heart throb as a country singer, though with his perfect diction and Yale law degree he was anything but country. His father had looked much the same way in his twenties, and he was still lean and barrel-chested. He'd graduated from the University of Florida, class of '65 – a savvy sabre-fencer who'd turned street cop, then politician. The governor was a man who could take your best shot, bounce right back, and hand you your head if you let your guard down. His son was always on guard.

'Come in,' Harry said.

Jack entered the foyer, shut the door behind him and followed the governor down the main hall. The rooms were smaller than Jack had expected, elegant, but simple, with high coffered ceilings and hardwood floors of oak and inlaid mahogany. Period antiques, silk Persian rugs and crystal chandeliers were the principal furnishings. The art was original and reflected Florida's history.

'Sit down,' said the governor as they stepped into the library at the end of the hall.

The dark-panelled library reminded Jack of the home in which he'd grown up. He sat in a leather armchair before the stone fireplace, his crossed-legs fully extended and his boots propped up irreverently on the head of the big Alaskan brown bear that his father had years ago stopped in its tracks and turned into a rug. The governor looked away, containing his impulse to tell his son to sit up straight. He stepped behind the big oak bar and filled his old-fashioned glass with ice cubes.

Jack did a double take. He thought his father had given up hard liquor – then again, this was the first time he'd seen him as *Governor* Swyteck. 'Do you have to drink? Like I said, this is business.'

The governor shot him a glance, then reached for the Chevas and filled his glass to the brim. 'And *this*,' he raised his glass, 'is *none* of your business. Cheers.' He took a long sip.

Jack just watched, telling himself to focus on the reason he was there.

'So,' the governor said, smacking his lips. 'I can't really remember the last time we even spoke, let alone saw each other. How long has it been this time?'

Jack shrugged. 'Two, two and a half years.'

'Since your law school graduation, wasn't it?'

'No,' – Jack's expression betrayed the faintest of smiles – 'since I told you I was taking a job with the Freedom Institute.'

'Ah, yes, the Freedom Institute.' Harry Swyteck rolled his eyes. 'The place where lawyers measure success by turning murderers, rapists and robbers back on the street. The place where commie bleeding heart liberals can defend the guilty and be insufferably sanctimonious about it, because they don't take a fee from the vermin they defend.' His look soured. 'The *one* place you knew it would absolutely kill me to see you work.'

Jack held on tightly to the arm of the chair. 'I didn't come here tonight to re-plow old ground.'

'I'm sure you didn't. It's much the same old story anyway. Granted, this last time the rift grew a little wider between us. But in the final analysis, this one will shake out no differently than the other times you've cut me out of your life. You'll never recognize that all I ever wanted is what's best for you.'

Jack was about to comment on his father's presumed infallibility, but was distracted by something on the bookshelf. It was an old photograph of the two of them together on a deep-sea fishing trip, in one of their too-few happy moments. *Lay into me first chance you get, Father, but you have that picture up there for all to see, don't you?*

'Look,' said Jack. 'I know we have things to talk about. But now's not the time. I didn't come here for that.'

'I know. You came because Raul Fernandez is scheduled to die in the electric chair in' – the governor checked his watch – 'about eighty minutes.'

'I came because he is innocent.'

'Twelve jurors didn't think so, Jack.'

'They didn't hear the whole story.'

'They heard enough to convict him after deliberating for less than twenty minutes. I've known juries to take longer than that to decide who's going to be foreman.'

'Will you just *listen* to me,' Jack snapped. 'Please, Father' – he tried a more civil tone – 'listen to me.'

The governor refilled his glass. 'All right,' he said. 'I'm listening.'

Jack leaned forward. 'About five hours ago, a man called me and said he had to see me – in confidence, as a client. He wouldn't give me his name, but he said it was life and death, so I agreed to meet him. He showed up at my office ten minutes later wearing a ski mask. At first I thought he was going to rob me, but it turned out he just wanted to talk about the Fernandez case. So that's what we did – talked.' He paused, focusing his eyes directly on his father's. 'And in less than five minutes he had me convinced that Raul Fernandez is innocent.'

The governor looked skeptical. 'And just what did this mysterious man of the night tell you?'

'I can't say.'

'Why not?'

'I told you: He agreed to speak to me only in confidence, as a client. I've never seen his face, and I doubt that I'll ever see him again, but technically I'm his lawyer – or at least I was for that conversation. Anyway, everything he told me is protected by the attorney–client privilege. I can't divulge it without his approval. And he won't let me repeat a word.'

'Then what are you doing here?'

Jack gave him a sobering look. 'Because an innocent man is going to die in the electric chair if you don't stop the Fernandez execution right now.'

The governor slowly crossed the room, a glass in one hand and an open bottle of scotch in the other. He sat in the matching arm chair, facing Jack. 'And I'll ask you one more time: how do you *know* Fernandez is innocent?'

'How do I *know*?' Jack's reddening face conveyed total exasperation. 'Why is it that you always want more than I can give? My flying up here in the middle of the night isn't enough for you. My telling you everything I legally and ethically can tell you just isn't enough?'

'All I'm saying is that *proof*. I can't just stay an execution based on . . . *on nothing* really.'

'My word is worth nothing, then,' Jack translated.

'In this setting, yes – that's the way it has to be. In this context, you're a lawyer, and I'm the governor.'

'No – in this context, I'm a witness, and you're a murderer. Because you're going to put Fernandez to death. And I *know* he's innocent.'

'*How* do you know?'

'Because I met the *real* killer tonight! He confessed to me. He did more than confess. He *showed* me something that proves he's the killer.'

'And what was that?' the governor asked, genuinely interested.

'I can't tell you,' Jack said. He felt his frustration rising. 'I've already said more than I can under the attorney–client privilege.'

The governor nestled into his chair, flashing a thin, paternalistic smile. 'You're being a little naive, don't you think? You have to put these last minute pleas in context. Fernandez is a killer. He and everyone who knows him is desperate. You can't take anything they say at face value. This so-called client who showed up at your door is undoubtedly a cousin or brother or street friend of Raul Fernandez's, and he'll do anything to stop the execution.'

'You don't *know* that!'

The governor sighed heavily, his eyes cast downward. 'You're right.' He brought his hands to his temples and began rubbing them. 'We never know for certain. I suppose that's why I've taken to *this*,' he said as he reached over and lifted the bottle of scotch. 'But the cold reality is that I campaigned as the law-and-order governor. I made the death penalty the central issue in the election. I promised to carry it out with vigour, and at the time I meant what I said. Now that I'm here, it's not so easy to sign my name to a death warrant. You've seen them before – ominous looking documents, with their black border and embossed state seal. But have you ever really *read* what they say? Believe me, I have.' His voice trailed off. 'That kind of power can get to a man, if you let it. Hell,' he scoffed and sipped his drink, 'and doctors think *they're* God.'

Jack was silent, surprised by this rare look into his father's conscience and not quite sure what to say. 'That's all the more reason to listen to me,' he said. 'To make sure it's not a mistake.'

'This is no mistake, Jack. Don't you see? What you're *not* saying is as significant as what you're saying. You won't breach the attorney–client privilege, not even to persuade me to change my mind about the execution. I respect that, Jack. But you have to respect me, too. I have rules. I have obligations, just like you do. Mine are to the people who elected me – and who expect me to honour my campaign promises.'

'It's not the same thing.'

'That's true,' he agreed. 'It's not the same. That's why, when you leave here tonight, I don't want you to blame yourself for anything. You did the best you could. Now it's up to me to make a decision. And *I'm* making it. I don't believe Raul Fernandez is innocent. But *if you* believe it, I don't want you feeling responsible for his death.'

Jack looked into his father's eyes. He knew the man was reaching out – that he was looking for some reciprocal acknowledgment that Jack didn't blame *him*, either, for doing *his* job. Harold Swyteck wanted absolution, forgiveness – a pardon.

Jack glanced away. He would not – could not – allow the moment to weaken his resolve. 'Don't worry, Father. I won't blame myself. It's like you always used to tell me: We're all responsible for our own actions. If an innocent man dies in the electric chair, you're the governor. You're responsible. You're the one to blame.'

Jack's words struck a nerve. The governor's face flushed red with fury as every conciliatory sentiment drained away. 'There's *no one* to blame,' he declared. 'No one but Fernandez himself. You're being played for a sucker. Fernandez and his buddy are using you. Why do you think this character didn't tell you his name or even show you his face?'

'Because he doesn't want to get caught,' Jack answered, 'but he doesn't want an innocent man to die.'

'A *killer* – especially one guilty of this sort of savagery – doesn't want an innocent man to die?' Harry Swyteck shook his head condescendingly. 'It's ironic, Jack – but sometimes you almost make me glad your mother never lived to see what a thick-headed son she brought into this world.'

Jack quickly rose from his chair. 'I don't have to take this crap from you.'

'I'm your father,' Harry blustered. 'You'll take whatever I –.'

'No! I'll take *nothing* from you. I've never asked for anything. And I don't want anything. *Ever*.' He stormed toward the door.

'Wait!' the governor shouted, freezing him in his tracks. Jack turned around slowly and glared at his father. 'Listen to me, young man. Fernandez is going to be executed this morning, because I don't believe any of this nonsense about his being innocent. No more than I believed the eleventh-hour story from the last "innocent man" we executed – the one who claimed it was only an accident that he stabbed his girlfriend' – he paused, so furious he was out of breath – 'twenty-one times.'

'You've become an incredibly narrow-minded old man,' Jack
said.

The governor stood stoically at the bar. 'Get out, Jack. Get out
of my house.'

Jack turned and marched down the hall, his boots punishing
the mansion's hard wooden floor. He threw the front door open,
then stopped at the tinkling sound of his father filling his empty
scotch glass with ice cubes. 'Drink up, governor,' his voice
echoed in the hallway. 'Do us all a favour, and drink up. Drink
yourself to *death*.'

He slammed the door and left.

Death was just minutes away for Raul Fernandez. He sat on the
edge of the bunk in his cell, shoulders slumped, bald head bowed,
and hands folded between his knees. Father José Ramirez, a
Roman Catholic priest, was at the prisoner's side, all in black,
save for his white hair and Roman collar. Rosary beads were
draped over one knee, an open Bible rested on the other. He was
looking at Fernandez with concern, almost desperation, as he
tried once more to cleanse the man's soul.

'Murder is a mortal sin, Raul,' he said. 'Heaven holds no place
for those who die without confessing their mortal sins. In John,
chapter twenty, Jesus tells his disciples: "Whose sins you forgive
are forgiven them, and whose sins you hold bound are held
bound." Let me hear your sins, Raul. So that you may be
forgiven them.'

Fernandez looked him directly in the eye. 'Father,' he said with
all the sincerity he could muster, 'right now, I have nothing to
lose by telling you the truth. And I'm telling you this: I have
nothing to confess.'

Father Ramirez showed no expression, though a chill went
down his spine. He flinched only at the sound of the key jiggling
in the iron door.

'It's time,' announced the guard. A team of two stepped inside
the cell to escort Fernandez. Father Ramirez rose from his chair,
blessed Fernandez with the sign of the cross and then stepped
aside. Fernandez did not budge from his bunk.

'Let's go,' ordered the guard.

'Give him a minute,' pleaded the priest.

The guard stepped briskly toward the prisoner. 'We don't have a minute.'

Fernandez suddenly sprung from his chair, burrowing his shoulder into the guard's belly. They tumbled to the floor. 'I'm innocent!' he cried, his arms flailing.

A barrage of blows from the other guard's black jack battered his back and shoulders, stunning the prisoner into near paralysis.

'You crazy son of a bitch!' cried the fallen guard, forcing Fernandez onto his belly. 'Cuff him!' he shouted to his partner. Together they pinned his arms behind his back, then cuffed his wrists, then his ankles.

'I'm innocent,' Fernandez whimpered, his face pressing on the cement floor. 'I'm *innocent!*'

'The hell with this,' said the guard who'd just wrestled with the condemned man. He snatched a leather strap from his pocket and gagged the prisoner, fastening it tightly around the back of his head.

Father Ramirez looked on in horror as the guards lifted Fernandez to his feet. He was still groggy from the blows, so they shook him to revive him. The law required that a condemned man be fully conscious and alert to his impending death. Each guard grabbed an arm, and together they led him out of the cell.

The priest was pensive and disturbed as he followed the procession down the brightly lit hallway. He'd seen many death row inmates, but none was the fighter this one was. Certainly, none had so strongly proclaimed his innocence.

They stopped at the end of the hall and waited as the execution chamber's iron door slid open automatically. The guards then handed the prisoner over to two attendants inside who specialized in executions. They moved quickly and efficiently as precious seconds ticked away on the wall clock. Fernandez was strapped into the heavy oak chair. Electrodes were fastened to his shaved head and ankles. The gag was removed from his mouth and replaced with a steel bit.

All was quiet, save for the hum of bright florescent lights overhead. Fernandez sat stiffly in his chair. The guards brought the black hood down over his face, then took their places along the gray-green walls. The venetian blinds opened, exposing the prisoner to three dozen witnesses on the dark side of the glass wall. A few reporters stirred. An assistant state attorney looked on impassively, smirking. The victim's uncle – the only relative of the young girl in attendance – took a deep breath. All eyes except the prisoner's turned toward the clock. His were hidden behind the hood and a tight leather band that would keep his eye balls from bursting when the current flowed.

Father Ramirez stepped into the dark seating area and joined the audience. The guard at the door raised his eyebrows with surprise. 'You really gonna watch this one, Padre?' he asked quietly.

'You know I never watch,' said Father Ramirez.

'There's a first time for everything,' the guard quipped.

'Yes,' said Ramirez. 'There is, indeed. And if my instincts are correct, let's hope this is the *last* time you kill an innocent man,' Then he closed his eyes and retreated into prayer.

The guard looked away. The priest's words had been pointed, but the guard shook them off, taking the proverbial common man's comfort in the fact that *he* wasn't killing anyone. It was Governor Harold Swyteck who'd signed the man's death warrant. It was someone else who would flip the switch.

At that moment, the second hand swept by its highest point, the warden gave the signal, and lights dimmed throughout the prison as twenty-five hundred volts surged into the prisoner's body. Fernandez lunged forward with the force of a head-on collision, his back arching and his skin smoking and sizzling. His jaws clenched the steel bit so tightly his teeth shattered. His fingers pried into the oak armrests with so much effort that his bones snapped.

A second quick jolt went right to his heart.

A third made sure the job was done.

It had taken a little more than a minute – the last and longest sixty-seven seconds of this thirty-five-year-old's life. An exhaust fan came on, sucking out the stench. A physician stepped forward, placed a stethoscope on the prisoner's chest, and listened.

'He's dead,' pronounced the doctor.

Father Ramirez sighed with sorrow as he opened his eyes, then lowered his head and blessed himself with the sign of the cross. 'May God forgive us,' he said under his breath, 'as He receives the innocent.'

BEST IN THE BUSINESS

Tom Sweeney

Today of all days, Bill Morrell didn't want to be late for work. He was running early this morning, but still swung his Lincoln Navigator to the left and zipped past the semi-trailer that filled the centre lane. Old Man Denslow had scheduled a special meeting of all partners and associates today, and office rumour had it that he intended to announce a new partner in his law firm. That plum would probably go to the lead associate, whose position would then be up for grabs. Bill Morrell planned on being chosen the next lead associate, accelerating his career here in Springfield directly into the fast lane. It would also help take his mind off that media-circus trial going on in the capital.

Once past the truck, Morrell had a clear view of the road ahead, just as he liked. What was the point of having an SUV if you couldn't sit above traffic? The first glimpse of Springfield each morning still inspired him: a dozen or so tall buildings outlined against the sky, as if sprouting from the ubiquitous soyabean fields, looking like the Magical City of Oz. To Bill, when he first saw it three years ago, it was Oz. And Mecca and Camelot, all rolled into one. Nothing at all like LA, this was the place his wife had declared would help them to escape the past and find a better future.

'We'll start new,' Elly had said. You'll be back on top in no time. You always could do anything you put your mind to. Even Sheila noticed that.'

Just inside the Beltway underpass, a car behind him flashed its high beams. He glanced back incuriously, noticing a woman driving a small red car, but the moment's inattention caused him to miss seeing the blue Buick entering the freeway until almost too late. Screaming in on the left on-ramp with no visible intent to slow down or merge, the Buick had forced him to move over to the middle lane. In the midst of this manoeuvre, the red sports car pulled up on his left, tight on the Buick's bumper.

Morrell flashed a look of annoyance at the red car, but the annoyance turned to surprise when he saw his daughter behind the wheel. Light, fly-away blonde hair, slightly hooked nose and strong chin. That profile he could never forget.

Sheila? Alive? He knew it. He'd always known it!

Before Morrell could honk or catch her attention, she blew by, squeezing through the tiny gap between Morrell's Navigator and the Buick. A sudden flash of brake lights, a zig in front of the Buick, a zag back in front of the truck, and the red car was out of sight as suddenly as it had appeared.

Sheila! So he'd been right all these years. It had to be her. One quick glimpse of her profile was all he had gotten, but it was enough. The woman in the car was his daughter.

But then, where had she been all this time? Why would she have left home without saying anything? Why hadn't she been in touch even once?

No, he must have been mistaken. His wife was right. Sheila was dead, and he needed to get on with his life. Still . . .

Oh, what the hell! Morrell pushed on the accelerator and aggressively wove his way through traffic, blowing by his intended exit. A twisting pain lanced his gut at the thought he'd never make it to work on time, but he didn't take his foot from the gas pedal.

He had almost caught up to her when an old Ford pickup moved left into the passing lane for no reason that Morrell could see. It left him effectively pinned in – a concrete barrier loomed on the left, a solid row of cars stretched out on the right, and an old geezer doing fifty-five in front of him. Morrell slowed to a crawl. Seething, he poked along for almost two miles before a slight gap opened to his right.

Screeching across two lanes of traffic, Morrell took up the chase again. The red car was nowhere in sight, and he could only hope that it was still on the freeway. He briefly considered giving up the chase and going to work, but he tightened his grip on the steering wheel and doggedly drove on. He was beyond downtown now and traffic thinned dramatically. Free of the pack, he increased speed. Ninety. Ninety-five. Cars on the other side of the freeway passed by in a multi-coloured blur, but he remained focused on the cars ahead, searching for the red sports car.

Ha! There she was, in the right lane. He almost overshot her. She eased onto the exit ramp, and Morrell slowed in time to make the exit. Getting the cumbersome SUV under control, he slipped in behind her, tailgating her as she turned right onto Lincoln Avenue. They went through one, two, three green lights. The fourth was red. As she braked, Morrell jammed over to her right and jacked to a stop beside her at the light.

Slowly, deliberately, he turned toward her and stared. The profile was a perfect match. Yes. All this time she'd been alive! Then, the girl in the car glanced his way. Viewed from the front, she bore no resemblance to Sheila.

Morrell slumped at the wheel. A horn honked behind him and he realized that the light had turned green. The red car was nowhere in sight, but so what? It wasn't Sheila.

Of course not. Sheila was dead, her body identified by X-rays of her legs. The X-ray prints of the unique double-compound fracture she had suffered in first grade matched the X-rays taken of the legs of the headless and armless corpse that was found two weeks after Sheila had disappeared.

At the next light, Morrell made a U-turn and headed back toward the freeway. To downtown and work. He looked at his watch. He should be in the office now. Today was the wrong day to show up late. He could kiss the lead associate position good-bye now. So much for getting on with his life.

Traffic heading back into the city wasn't heavy this far out, allowing him to do exactly what he told everyone he never did – think about Sheila.

The body had been hers. Had to have been. The Grand Canyon T-shirt, the only piece of clothing that remained on the dismembered body, he had bought for her the year before. She'd been wearing it that Saturday morning when she'd left for the library. Because of the amputations, there obviously weren't fingerprints or dental work available, but the leg X-rays were conclusive.

Traffic started to back up, and since everyone seemed to want to be in the passing lane, Morrell moved to the extreme right of the freeway. Gotta keep moving, adjusting to the new situation. Just as Elly had said: 'You can't hang on to her forever, Bill. Life goes on, and sometimes you just have to move on with it.'

Tears welled in Morrell's eyes as he acknowledged his daughter's death for the first time. His rationalizations now seemed absurd, his clinging to the fact that the doctors wouldn't swear that the X-rays absolutely and irrefutably identified his little girl. The medical report was laced with words to indicate their belief that the body examined was Sheila Morrell. Words like, *The slight differences observed are easily within parameters of normal healing and growth.* And, *Odds of a similar injury occurring to someone else are so remote as to be non-existent.*

The doctors wouldn't swear that such an injury could never happen to anyone else. It wasn't impossible, just so unlikely as to defy the laws of probability. The medical report wasn't ironclad, but the language was plain enough to Morrell and anyone else with any sense. Besides, the insurance company paid off on her policy, and that ought to be proof enough. Especially to a lawyer like himself.

Morrell straightened in his seat. And a good lawyer he was, too. A damned good lawyer. One of the best in the business. He'd blown today's promotion, but there'd be others. And he'd get the next one. That was a promise. He'd do it for Sheila.

For her memory.

He sighed heavily and slumped momentarily, but quickly squared his shoulders. I'll do it for you, Sheila. I'll be the best lawyer in the business and I'll do it for your memory.

Traffic became sluggish and slowed until it came to a dead stop, but Morrell had a purpose in life for the first time in years. Driving the last half-mile in the breakdown lane, Morrell took his exit and wound through the downtown maze. One block from his office, he was almost broad-sided by someone speeding through the intersection at least five seconds after the light had turned. Jeez, why don't they arrest these guys? Someone's going to be killed.

Morrell filed the data away in his mind. It would be good background in case he ever had to sue someone who ran a red light and rammed his client. Then he could expound from first-hand experience on the dangers of being hit broadside. He also filed away the fact that drivers ran lights with impunity, in case he ever had to defend someone who ran a red light and rammed someone else's client.

He was still thinking about these possibilities as he walked into his office. He hoped to slip in unnoticed, but his secretary immediately flagged him down. 'Thank goodness you're here. Mr Denslow has been in twice looking for you.'

Damn. But then, it needn't be bad news. Old Man Denslow wouldn't come down twice unless he wanted – needed – Bill to be at that meeting. Lead associate?

At the end of the hallway, he was ushered immediately and smoothly into Denslow's office by a male executive secretary, who then stood by the door. A half dozen associates were seated along the wall behind the table. No one looked directly at anyone else, and no one spoke.

The four senior partners trooped in, followed by Denslow himself. When all were settled, Denslow spread a folder open in front of him and said, 'Congratulations, Bill, on the Branstad case. It was a fine piece of work.'

'Thank you, Mr Denslow, but it wasn't that difficult. Any one of the junior associates could have done as well.' He knew he was stepping out on a limb, questioning the senior partner's judgment in assigning a case, but Morrell didn't want any more of those traffic cases. He was taking charge of his life again, and it felt good.

Denslow didn't take offense, however. 'Not so, son, not so. Any one of them could have won the case, perhaps, but not with your flair.' He held up a well-manicured hand. 'Don't tell me it's just a W in the Win/Loss column. It was more. Her driving skills not withstanding, our Mrs Branstad is the great-aunt of our esteemed Lieutenant Governor. People in high places were quietly watching the courtroom, and our firm shone.

'It was a case we had to win, and we had to win it with panache. And you did both.' Denslow beamed. The partners beamed. The associates beamed on the outside, but their eyes showed their fear that the lead associate position was going to Morrell.

Morrell did a slow burn. *They could have told me about the Lieutenant Governor*, he thought. *I would have performed my heart out*. Then the light came on. He *had* performed his heart out. Now, belatedly, he recognized the case for what it was – a test. Probably he had been tested with other cases before, but this was the final exam, manoeuvres with live ammunition.

Denslow continued, 'We all appreciate the remarkable job you've done in the last three years, and we all wanted to thank you. But we have an even bigger issue. A new case has been offered to us which could catapult the firm to national recognition.'

He paused, then spoke for effect, enunciating each word clearly. 'We have the opportunity to defend The Butcher, as the media calls him. I guess the first thing we need is a new appellation for the reporters to use.'

Morrell frowned at this and had trouble breathing, but the partners all chuckled in unison. The associates laughed politely.

'At any rate, though he was supposed to go to trial upstate in the capital, the wild media coverage caused the State to order a change of venue. The public defender succeeded in getting it transferred here after I offered the firm's pro-bono services in the public interest.

'It'll be a long, though job, but not hopeless.' He looked around the room, and his paternal gaze settled on Morrell. 'And we've selected you to be lead attorney.' Ignoring the disappointed faces of the associates, he added, 'The man who could pull this one off could be our next partner.'

Morrell expelled the air from his lungs with a soft whoosh. Partner. Talk about putting your life and career on the fast track. But the Butcher? He shook his head once and looked to the head of the table. 'I'm afraid that won't be possible.'

Morrell paused for a long heartbeat, perversely enjoying the frowns from around the table. 'The Butcher, does he not rape and mutilate his victims, cutting off heads and hands and sometimes entire arms? Yes?'

Without waiting for an answer, Morrell continued, 'Gentle-

men, you have no reason to know this, but three years ago in
California my daughter was murdered. She had been raped, and
her head and arms cut off.'

There were gasps and scuffling of chairs from around the table.
Morrell slightly raised his voice and continued, 'She was identified by X-rays of unique breaks in both her legs. A young punk
from out East was arrested, but the police were unable to break
his alibi and the jury acquitted him. For what it's worth, I don't
think he was guilty, anyway.'

Denslow broke in, 'My God, Bill. We're sorry. We had no idea.
Of course you won't represent The Butcher. In fact, you should
take a sabbatical. Or a change in venue yourself. I could place you
temporarily with my brother's firm in Atlanta, and you could
return here and resume your position when the trial ends.'

Every fibre in him demanded that he take Denslow up on the
offer to go away, to isolate himself from the pain sure to be
dredged up in the trial of the man who most likely murdered
Sheila.

But no. Was he going to get on with his life, or be forever stuck
in the past? He *had* to stay here in Springfield. He had to face
down his demons now, here. Forget the past and look to the
future. Focus on being the best lawyer he could possibly be.

That thought stopped him cold. Be the best lawyer he could be.
Wouldn't that be accepting a case that could make him a partner?
Just what made a good lawyer, anyway? Figure that one out and
do what had to be done to be the best lawyer anyone could be.
Only then would he be free of the past.

Once again, Elly had the key. 'I've never understood how you
could detach yourself from your clients,' she used to tell him.
'How you could defend those horrible people you knew were
guilty.' He explained to her that detachment from one's client
was not a shortcoming, but a gift. It was what made him the
effective lawyer he was. And the better lawyer he was about to
become.

'Mr Denslow,' he said slowly, 'The past is past. I can't change
that. I can only move forward to do the job for which I was placed
here on Earth: to be a lawyer. The best lawyer I can be.'

Denslow sat back, face unreadable, giving Morrell nothing.

The partners sat as statues. The associates squirmed, watching Denslow and the partners for some clue on how to react.

Morrell continued, 'And what makes a good lawyer? To be a good lawyer requires one to have a certain detachment about guilt and innocence, crime and retribution. To be a great lawyer naturally requires more detachment. What then, must it take to be a top lawyer?'

Morrell paused for effect and to group his thoughts. He knew that he was fighting for more than this assignment. He was fighting to free himself of his past. All that had gone before had led to this moment. Denslow, who had become his life's judge, maintained impassive silence.

As though giving a summation to a jury, he said, 'To be one of the best lawyers in the world requires the most detachment, the ultimate in applying the law in defense. Look to history: John Adams defended the British soldiers who perpetrated the Boston Massacre, soldiers who had shot his countrymen and neighbours. Why? Not because they were innocent, but because everyone in this country deserves legal counsel in their defense. John Adams had the necessary detachment. So, gentlemen, do I. I will defend The Butcher.'

Denslow's mouth quirked in sour puzzlement at Morrell's words. 'I'm not sure the country is quite ready to see you defend your daughter's murderer,' he said.

'I'm not defending my daughter's murderer any more than John Adams defended his neighbour's killers. I'm defending a man accused of a crime, who is still innocent until proven guilty.'

Denslow shook his head. 'If you take this case, the story of your daughter is sure to surface. And then what happens? We lose the case and we'll be accused of railroading the man for personal interests. We win the case, and the PR might be even worse. No, I can't have you on this case. I can't even have you in this city. You can go to Atlanta or I'll accept your resignation. Sorry, Bill.'

I'm not down yet, thought Morrell. This is the trial of my life and I'm not going to lose it.

'I agree,' he said, to put himself apparently in Denslow's corner. 'If I'm in Atlanta, there'll be no reason for the media to tie me to the trial. But once there, I can follow the trial closely.'

Denslow frowned and looked at his watch. Morrell hurried on, 'There are all kinds of downside issues to a trial like this that you couldn't possibly know about. I went through one of these trials three years ago, watching from the prosecution's side. I can help with those issues, give you the inside track.' He noted with relief that Denslow's eyes jumped at the mention of an inside track.

Morrell had more to say, but sometimes a lawyer can say too much. A time always came to conclude, and this was the time. He leaned back, his lawyer instincts telling him that he'd won.

Denslow looked around the table, his face giving away none of his thoughts. Morrell waited, but he wasn't worried. He'd presented his case perfectly. Finally Denslow smiled and smacked a palm on the conference table. 'You're better than a great attorney, Bill. You're one of the best in the business.' He looked around at the partners and opened his briefing papers. 'All right, then, Bill will advise us and pull the strings from Atlanta. Here's how we'll handle it on this end.'

Morrell listened to Denslow outline the strategy for the trial, but his thoughts were on a sixteen-year old girl wearing a Grand Canyon T-shirt.

I'll win this one for you, Sheila, he thought.

BAIL HEARING

Morris Hershman

The judge took off his court robe and sat down back of the desk. 'I'll decide whether or not to allow bail,' he said. 'I want to hear your side of it in private, young man.'

'Yes, Judge.' Tony Greer's dark, troubled eyes were narrowed. 'As long as I don't have to double-cross nobody, whatever you say goes.'

'You pulled a hold-up, Tony. Tell me about that.'

'Well, I was told to do it.' Tony gave an expressive little shrug. 'I never expected I'd get reamed.'

'That's pretty surprising. I've sat in Juvenile Court for five years now, and I've seldom had to pass sentence on a juvenile offender who took it for granted he'd never get caught.'

'I'll tell you why, in my case.' Pride inflated Tony's body, making him look older than his sixteen years. 'Nobody in my gang ever did a day's term in prison.'

'Gang.' The judge nodded and glanced down at the papers on his desk. 'The Imperial Kings.'

'I've wanted to join up for as long as I could remember.' Tony smiled. 'In my neighbourhood, you can't run alone, so you might as well run with the gang that makes you feel safest, and that's the Imperial Kings.'

The judge felt a little guilty himself, as he generally did when he saw some of the underprivileged coming before him in court. Probably he was too sensitive. He forced himself to look stern.

'And I suppose you didn't like any of it.'

'I liked everything I did with the Imperial Kings,' Tony Greer said. 'The girls were great, and the joy-popping was fun, and any guy who followed orders was supposed to be safe from jail.'

'You haven't become a narcotics addict, I hope.'

'On my word I haven't, Judge.'

More reliable than the boy's word was his neatness, his self-control. The judge pursed his lips.

'About the robbery,' he began.

'Well, in order to get initiated I was told I'd have to do two things. The first one was to walk up to a policeman and steal a bullet from out of his belt.' Tony Greer winced at the memory. 'I was scared, but there wasn't no trouble.'

'Was it sensible?' the judge felt he had to ask.

'For a guy who wants to be on the safe side and join the Imperial Kings, Judge, it was sensible.'

The judge could have made a couple of clever remarks, but he didn't. 'What was the second thing you had to do in order to become a member of the gang?'

'*That* was it, Judge – robbing Mr Brodsky's fish store without wearing a mask. Well, I walked right in and did it. That's about all, Judge, except that I was identified and I'm here. But not for long. Any guy with the Imperial Kings, let alone a prospective member, don't serve a jail term.'

'And you won't name one member of this gang, even if it means reducing the inevitable sentence,' the judge said, recalling what was on the probation officer's report. 'As you haven't been initiated into this gang, you wouldn't be betraying an oath.'

Tony Greer shook his head firmly.

The judge said, 'Co-operate with the Youth Squad and name the boys who belong to this gang, and you might even be freed on probation. Otherwise, you'll be put into a reformatory until you reach the age of twenty-one.'

'Nobody who works with the Imperial Kings ever serves a sentence. I won't do a day's stretch in any reformatory.'

'Not even if it means your getting a small bail, so that you can spend a few days in freedom before your trial comes up?' The judge waited for a reply. When it wasn't forthcoming he sighed resignedly and said: 'Tony, your parents have been very straightforward and convincing in their talks with me. As a result I've decided, against my better judgment and entirely for their sakes, to set the bail at a low figure.'

'I haven't been under arrest for a day, even,' Tony said, grinning. 'See what I mean, Judge? I won't do no stretch.'

'I'm sure I'll hate myself for it as soon as I've signed the papers,' the judge said, making his voice stern to show that he wanted to be thought of as a harsh arbiter of justice, after all. 'Wait outside with the bailiff.'

When the court clerk arrived a few minutes later, the judge said, 'I'm sending Greer back to spend a few more days with his young hoodlum friends, but you can't set an unreasonably high bail in a first-offense juvenile case. It would be harsh – unjust.' He added with a profanity that was rare for him when he was away from the golf course, 'What in hell else could I have done?'

'I managed to get away for an hour,' Tony Greer said eagerly to Peter Santos, gang leader of the Imperial Kings. 'Can't we make the intiation fast? You guys'll never know how much I want it.'

'Sure, Tony, sure,' Santos said. 'We'll make a circle right now and get it over with . . . Get in a circle, you guys.'

Fourteen boys hurriedly formed a circle, with Tony and Santos in its centre.

'We all know that Tony has been loyal, and that he might have to do a reformatory stretch on account of it.'

Tony put in, 'I know you guys will keep me from taking a fall.'

'We've never had anybody connected with us put in a day at any reformatory,' Pete Santos said. 'That's because we know that the cops would have years to work on any guy, and they might get names out of him sooner or later and then put heat on the rest of us. The reason we've all been around so long is that the cops don't have any opportunity to find out who we are.'

'I'd never give a single name,' Tony started.

'The Imperial Kings can't afford to take chances, even on our newest member,' Santos said, then added, 'Sorry, kid.'

Tony Greer's chest had automatically begun swelling with pride, but that was before the knife found his heart.

THICKER THAN WATER

Henry Slesar

Vernon Wedge didn't want to see the old man. Olga, his secretary, gave Blesker a sub-zero reception, but he sat on in the attorney's waiting room. His shoulders were rigid, his crooked fingers interlaced, his chalky face a portrait of stubbornness and determination. Finally, Vernon had to yield.

'Sit down, Mr Blesker,' he said wearily, pointing to the leather chair in his office. 'I know why you're here; my phone's been ringing all morning. Four newspapers, a youth worker, even a settlement house. What have you got, anyway, an organization?'

The old man looked befuddled. 'Please,' he said. 'I just come about my boy . . .'

'Yes, I read the newspapers. And I suppose you think your kid's innocent?'

'He is!'

'Naturally. You're his father. Have you talked to him since it happened?'

'I came from the prison this morning. They're not treating him good. He looks skinny.'

'He's only been in custody a few days, Mr Blesker, I doubt if they're starving him. Look,' Vernon said testily, 'your boy is accused of knifing another kid in the street. That's what happened. You know how many witnesses there are? You know what kind of evidence the district attorney has?'

'I know he's innocent,' the old man said. 'That's what I know. Benjy's a good, serious boy.'

'Sure,' Vernon frowned. 'They are all good boys, Mr Blesker, until they start running with a street pack. Then they're something else.' He was almost shouting now. 'Mr Blesker, the State will pick an attorney for your son. You don't need me.'

'I have money,' Blesker whispered. 'The family, we all got together. I run a fuel oil business; I'm selling the big truck. I can pay what you ask, Mr Wedge.'

'It's not a question of money –'

'Then, it's a question of what?' The old man was suddenly truculent. 'Whether he's guilty or not? You decided that already, Mr Wedge? From reading the newspapers?'

Vernon couldn't meet the challenge, it was too close to the truth. He *had* prejudged the case from the newspaper stories, and knew from the accounts that this was one client he could live without. His record was too good. What was worse, he had lost his last client to Ossining. Every criminal lawyer is allowed a few adverse verdicts; but two in a row?

'Mr Blesker,' he said miserably, 'will you tell me why you came here? Why did you pick me?'

'Because I heard you were good.'

'Do you know what happened in my last case?'

Obstinate: 'I heard you were good, Mr Wedge.'

'You told every reporter in town that you intended to hire me. That puts me in a very compromising position, you know that? And you, too. Know how it'll look if I turn you down? Like I think your boy is guilty, that the case is hopeless.

'I didn't mean any harm,' the old man said fumblingly. 'I just wanted to get the best for Benjy.' He was getting teary. 'Don't turn me down, please, Mr Wedge.'

Vernon knew a lost cause when he saw one; perhaps he had known from the start how this interview would end. His voice softened.

'I didn't say your boy is guilty, Mr Blesker. All I say is that he's got a bad case. A very bad case.'

Motionless, the old man waited.

'All right,' Vernon sighed. 'I'll think it over.'

The police blotter had Benjy Blesker's age down as seventeen. He looked younger. The frightened eyes gave him a look of youthful bewilderment. Vernon wasn't taken in by it; he had seen too many innocent, baby-faced, icy-hearted killers.

The boy's cell was clean, and Benjy himself bore no marks of ill-treatment. He sat on the edge of the bunk and kneaded his hands. When Vernon walked in, he asked him for a cigarette.

Vernon hesitated, then shrugged and offered the pack. 'Why not?' he said. 'If you're old enough to be here . . .'

Benjy lit up and dropped a tough mask over his boyish features. 'You the lawyer my old man hired?'

'That's right. My name is Vernon Wedge.'

'When do I get out of here?'

'You don't, not until the trial. They've refused bail.'

'When's the trial?'

'Don't rush it,' Vernon growled. 'We need every minute of delay we can get. Don't think this is going to be easy.'

Benjy leaned back, casual. 'I didn't cut that guy,' he said evenly. 'I didn't have anything to do with it.'

Vernon grunted, and pulled a sheet of handwritten notes out of his pocket.

'You admitted that you knew Kenny Tarcher?'

'Sure I knew him. We went to Manual Trades together.'

'They tell me Kenny was a member of a gang called The Aces. You ever run with them?'

'With that bunch?' Benjy sneered, and blew a column of smoke. 'I was a Baron. The Barons don't mix with those bums. You know who they take into that gang? A whole lot of –'

'Never mind,' Vernon snapped. 'We can talk about your social life later. You were a Baron and Kenny was an Ace, so that made you natural enemies. You had a rumble last month, and this Kenny Tarcher beat up on you pretty good. Don't give me any arguments about this, it's ancient history.'

Benjy's mouth was quivering. 'Look, Mr Wedge, we don't have that kind of gang. You know Mr Knapp –'

'The youth worker? I just came from him.'

'He'll tell you about the Barons, Mr Wedge, we're not a bunch of hoods. We got a basketball team and everything.'

Vernon smothered a smile. 'Why do you carry a knife, Benjy?'

'It's no switchblade, Mr Wedge. It's more like a boy scout knife; I mean, they sell 'em all over. I use it for whittlin' and stuff like that.'

'Whittling?' It was hard to hide the sneer. The end of Benjy's cigarette flared, as did his temper.

'Look, whose side are you on? I didn't stick Kenny, somebody else did! I swear I didn't kill him!'

'Take it easy. I'm not making accusations, kid, that's the court's job. Now sit back and relax. I'm going over the story, from the police side, and then you can tell me where they're wrong. Every little thing, understand?'

Benjy swallowed hard. Then he nodded.

'It was ten minutes to midnight on June 21,' Vernon said, watching him. 'You and two other guys were walking down Thurmond Street; you came out of a movie house. Kenny Tarcher came out of the corner apartment building on Thurmond and Avenue C. You bumped into each other, and there was some horseplay. The next thing that happens, you and your pals start running down the street. Kenny falls down and tries to crawl to the stoop of his house. There were two people on the steps. They saw you running. They saw Kenny die, right in front of them. He had an eight-inch gash in his stomach . . .'

Benjy looked sick.

'Ten minutes later, the cops caught up with you in your old man's fuel supply store on Chester Street. The knife was still in your pocket.' He paused.

'I didn't cut him,' the boy said grimly. 'All the rest of that stuff, that's true. But I don't know who cut Kenny.'

'Who were the other two guys with you?'

'I never saw 'em before. I met 'em in the movies.'

'Don't give me that!'

'What the hell do you want from me?' Benjy bellowed. 'I tell you I don't know those guys! One of them must have done it, I didn't! When I saw he was hurt, I ran. That's all it was!'

'You had the knife –'.

'I didn't use it!'

'That knife is Exhibit A,' the lawyer said. 'You know that, don't you? The witnesses saw you holding it –'.

'Leave me alone! You ain't here to help me!'

Vernon got up.

'I am, Benjy. The only way you can be helped, kid. I want you to cop a plea.'

'What?'

'I want you to plead guilty. Believe me, it's the only sensible thing to do. You put this case to a jury, I swear you'll be spending the rest of your life in a cage. Plead guilty, and the worst you'll get is twenty years. That's not as bad as it sounds; you'll be eligible for parole in five.'

'I won't do it!' Benjy screamed. 'I'm innocent! I'm not goin' to jail for something I didn't do!'

'I'm talking sense, kid, why won't you listen?'

'I didn't do it! I didn't!'

Vernon sighed. The corners of his mouth softened, and he dropped a hand on the boy's shoulder.

'Listen,' he said gently. 'I really want to help you, son.'

For a moment, Benjy was still. Then he threw off the arm of sympathy, and snarled at the attorney.

'I'm not your son! I got a father!'

Like father, like son, Vernon thought wryly, looking at the mulish mouth and marble eyes of the old man. He was sure Blesker had a softer side. Under other circumstances, he would smile and tell jokes and hum old-country tunes. Now, faced with the lawyer's blunt advice, he was hard as a rock.

'You've got to talk some sense into him,' Vernon said. 'He doesn't know what's good for him. If he pleads guilty to murder in the second degree, the judge will be lenient.'

'But he goes to prison? For something he didn't do?'

'You're his father, Mr Blesker. You're ignoring facts.'

'The facts are wrong!' Blesker put his fists on his knees and pounded them once. When he looked up again, there was a new mood in his eyes. 'You tell me something, Mr Wedge –'

'Yes?'

'You don't like to lose cases, am I right? That's what they say about you.'

'Is that bad?'

'If my boy pleads guilty, you don't lose nothing. You still got your good record, right?'

'Do you think that's my only reason?'

Blesker shrugged. 'I'm only asking, Mr Wedge. I don't know nothing about the law.'

Unable to refute this accurate estimate of his inner thoughts, Vernon tried to summon up an angry denial and failed. He shrugged his shoulders.

'All right,' he said grudgingly. 'So we plead Not Guilty. I'll do everything I can to make it stick.'

Blesker examined his face for signs of sincerity. He seemed satisfied.

Vernon came to the courtroom on opening day with a heart as heavy as his brief case. Surprisingly, the first day didn't go badly. Judge Angus Dwight had been assigned to the bench. In spite of his dour look, Vernon knew him to be scrupulously fair and sneakily sentimental. Wickers, the prosecuting attorney, was a golden-haired Adonis with a theatrical delivery, a keen mind, and an appeal for the ladies. Fortunately, the impanelled jurors were men with only two exceptions, and they were women far past the age of coquetry. During the first hour, Wickers' facetiousness in his opening remarks drew a rebuke from the judge concerning the seriousness of the affair; Vernon's hopes lifted a notch.

But it was his only good day. On the second afternoon, Wickers called a man named Sol Dankers to the witness chair.

'Mr Dankers,' he said smoothly, 'you were present at the time of Kenneth Tarcher's slaying, isn't that so?'

'That's right,' Dankers said heavily. He was a hard-breathing, bespectacled man with a red-veined nose. 'I was sittin' on the stoop, when these kids start foolin' around. Next thing I know, one of 'em's stumbling to the stoop, bleedin' like a pig. He drops dead right at the feet of me and my Mrs. I was an hour gettin' the bloodstains off my shoes.'

'Is that all you saw?'

'No, sir. I seen that boy, the one over there, runnin' away with a knife in his hand.'

Then it was Vernon's turn.

'Mr Dankers, is it true your eyesight is impaired?'

'True enough. I'm sixty-two, son, wait 'til you're my age.'

He drew a laugh and a rap of the gavel.

'It was almost midnight on a street not particularly well lit. Yet

you saw a knife –' he pointed to the table where Exhibit A rested –
'that knife, in Benjamin Blesker's hand?'

'It was sort of flashin' in the light, if you know what I mean.
But to tell you the truth, I wouldn't have noticed if Mrs Danker
hadn't said, "look at that boy, he's got a knife!" '

The crowd buzzed, and Vernon frowned at the inadvertent
hearsay testimony. The damage was done; he didn't even bother
to voice a complaint.

Mrs Danker testified next; there was nothing wrong with
her eyes, she said stoutly, and she knew a knife when she saw
one. It was the third witness who did the most harm. He was
Marty Knapp, a dedicated youth worker serving the neighbourhood.

'No, Benjy isn't a bad kid,' he said thoughtfully. 'But he had a
temper. And he never forgave Kenny Tarcher for the beating he
gave him.'

'Then in your opinion,' Wickers said triumphantly, 'this *might*
have been a grudge killing? Not just a sudden scuffle or un-
planned assault, but a deliberate, cold-blooded –'

Vernon was on his feet, shouting objections. Judge Dwight
took his side at once, but the impression was indelible in the
collective mind of the jury. When Vernon sat down again, he felt
as forlorn as Benjy Blesker looked.

On the eve of the fourth day, he went to see him.

'What do you say, Benjy?' he said quietly. 'You see the way
things are going? I'm pulling out the whole bag of tricks, and I'm
not fooling anybody.'

'Try harder!' Benjy snapped.

'If I knew how to work miracles, I'd work one. Look, this state
doesn't like to hang kids, but it's happened before –'

'Hang?' the boy said incredulously. 'You're crazy!'

'Even if you got life, know what that means? Even if you got
paroled in twenty years, you'll be thirty-seven years old, almost
middle-aged, with a record.'

There were tears flooding Benjy's eyes. It was the first sign of a
crumpling defense, and the lawyer moved in swiftly.

'Plead guilty,' he said earnestly. 'Plead guilty, Benjy. It's not
too late.'

The boy's head snapped up.

'No!' he screamed. 'I didn't do it!'

The fourth day was the worst of all. Vernon railed mercilessly at the prosecution witnesses. He called Dankers a weak-eyed, boozing liar. He forced Mrs Dankers to admit that she hated the neighbourhood kids, and the Barons especially. He got Knapp, the youth worker, to recite every detail of Benjy's good record. But through it all, the jury shifted restlessly, bored, irritated, obviously unimpressed by the 'character' testimony, eager only for facts, the bloodier the better.

Wickers gave them what they wanted. Wickers treated them to a blow-by-blow reenactment of the stabbing. He bled for them. He clutched his stomach. He put the victim's mother on the stand. He let her cry through ten minutes of pointless testimony, until even Judge Dwight got sick of the spectacle. But it was working. Vernon, jury-smart, knew it was working.

The trial was almost over. Wickers, waving the knife under Benjy Blesker's nose, got him to admit that it was his, admit that he was never without it, admit that he had it in his pocket – maybe even in his hand – the night of the slaying. It was his curtain-closer. Wickers sat down, the prosecution's case stated.

One more day, and it would be finished.

There was a weekend hiatus before the trial resumed. Vernon Wedge spent the time thinking.

It was the old man's fault, he thought bitterly. It was old man Blesker who was behind all the trouble. His faith in Benjy was the indomitable, obstinate faith of the fanatic. Even if the boy was guilty, concern for his father would prevent him from admitting the truth.

'The funny thing is,' he told Olga, his secretary, 'if I was on that jury, I wouldn't know how to vote.'

Olga clucked.

'You don't look well,' she said. 'You look anaemic. When this is over, you ought to see a doctor.'

'A headshrinker, that's what I ought to see.'

'I mean a doctor,' Olga said firmly.

It was then that the idea was born. Vernon looked at his secretary queerly, and stood up behind the desk.

'You know, it's a thought. Maybe I ought to see one. You remember Doc Hagerty?'

'No.'

'Sure you remember! On the Hofstraw case, 1958 –'

'But *he's* not the kind of doctor I mean. I mean a good all-around G.P.'

'I'm going out,' Vernon said suddenly. 'I'll be at the Dugan Hospital if you need me. But don't bother me unless it's urgent.'

He found Hagerty in the basement laboratory of the Dugan Hospital. Olga was right: Hagerty was no chest-thumping, tongue-depressing practitioner; he was more biochemist than physician. But he was what Vernon needed.

Hagerty was a white-haired man with shoulders rounded from years of bending over microscopes, and he smelt vaguely of sulphur. He turned out to be ignorant of the trial. Vernon summarized the facts briefly, and then talked about blood.

'You mean there were no benzidine tests made?' Hagerty said quickly. 'Of the murder weapon?'

'Yes,' Vernon admitted, 'and the test proved negative. There weren't any bloodstains on the knife, you understand, it was clean. The prosecution claims that all traces were wiped or washed off. It's never been much of an issue up till now. But I once heard you talk about a more sensitive test than benzidine –'

'There is,' Hagerty grunted. 'Benzidine is the standard blood test in this city, but there's another one. It's a lot more delicate, in my opinion, and it's not always employed. It's called the reduced phenolphtalein test, and depending on a couple of factors, it might be just what you're looking for.'

'The quality of the blade metal, for one thing. And even if the metal is porous enough to retain microscopic particles of blood, it may be impossible to determine *whose*. If your boy ever cut his finger, or somebody else –'

'What do we have to do? Vernon said excitedly.

'Get me the knife.'

'That's impossible. It's court property at the moment.'

'Then get me half a dozen like it.'

The lawyer spent all of Saturday morning searching for the weapon's counterpart. His mental picture of it was sharp; he recalled every curlicue on its handle; he even remembered the letters at the base of the blade: B.L. CO. USA.

He finally found one in a dingy variety store four blocks from the scene of the stabbing. The proprietor had exactly five left in stock; he took them all.

There was a two-hour wait that afternoon before he could see Hagerty again; when the white-haired doctor joined him in the laboratory, he didn't apologize.

'I have the solution all ready,' he said crisply. 'You sure this is the same make of knife?'

'Positive.'

Hagerty sprung the large blade. Then he removed a bottle of whole blood from a cabinet, and dipped it inside. Vernon swallowed in revulsion as Hagerty wiped the blade clean with a soft cloth, and marked the knife with a pencil.

'Any trace?' he said, offering it for examination.

'Clean as a whistle.'

Hagerty brought all five blades to a beaker filled with a murky liquid. Vernon helped him open all the knives, and they were ready for the demonstration.

'Mix 'em up good,' Hagerty said. 'It's like a magic trick; you shuffle 'em up, I'll find the one.'

Vernon scrambled the knives. Then, one by one, Hagerty dipped them into the solution.

The third one turned the liquid pink. It was the knife that had been marked.

'It works,' Vernon breathed. 'It really works.'

'The metal is porous. If there were bloodstains on it from years ago, this test would show it up.'

'Thank you,' Vernon said humbly. 'You've saved my life, Doc.'

'*Your* life?' Hagerty said dryly.

When Vernon entered Benjy's cell, the boy was reading a pulp magazine with intense concentration. He seemed detached, disinterested. Vernon understood it; he had seen this before in the condemned.

'Listen to me,' he said harshly. 'Listen good. I have an idea that might save you but I have to know the truth.'

'I told you everything –'

'There's a test,' the lawyer said. 'A test that can determine whether or not there was ever blood on that knife of yours.'

'So?'

'I propose to make that test in court on Monday. If it's negative, the jury will know you didn't kill Kenny Tarcher.'

'I don't understand that kind of stuff –'

'I'm not asking you to understand,' Vernon said tautly. 'If you stabbed that boy, a solution is going to turn pink and you can kiss your freedom goodbye. What's more, if you ever cut *anybody* with that knife, even yourself, it'll turn pink.   So
I want you to tell me now. *Was there ever blood on that knife?*'

'I told you I didn't cut him!'

'You moron!' Vernon shouted. 'Do you understand my question? Was there ever blood of *any* kind on that knife?'

'No! It was brand-new. I never cut anybody with it.'

'You're sure? Absolutely sure?'

'I told you, didn't I?'

'This is scientific stuff, boy, don't think you can fool a test tube!'

'I said it's clean!'

Vernon Wedge sighed, and stood up.

'Okay, Benjy. We'll see how clean it is. We'll give it a bath. And God help you if you lied to me.'

On Monday, Wickers rose to make his final peroration. He was bland-faced, a picture of confidence. Vernon looked at the vacant faces of the jurors, waiting for their emotional rubdown. But he wasn't going to allow it.

He stood up, and addressed Judge Dwight.

'Your Honour, something occurred over the weekend which I consider of paramount importance to this case. I ask the court's permission to introduce new evidence.'

'Objection,' Wickers said calmly. 'The defense has had sufficient time for the introduction of evidence. I suggest this is a delaying tactic.'

Vernon looked defeated, but he was only playing possum. Judge Dwight prompted him.

'What sort of evidence, Mr Wedge?'

'It's a demonstration, Your Honour,' he said weakly. 'In my opinion, it will clearly establish my client's guilt or innocence. But if the court rules –'

'Very well, Mr Wedge, you may proceed.'

Quickly, Vernon undid the clasps of the black box in front of him. He removed the wide-mouthed beaker, and then the foil lid that covered it. He brought the murky solution to the bench that held the trial exhibits.

'And what is this?' Judge Dwight said.

'This, Your Honour, is a chemical solution specifically formulated for the detection of blood.'

The courtroom buzzed; on the prosecution's side of the room, there was a hurried consultation.

Vernon faced the jurors.

'Ladies and gentlemen, Exhibit A in this case is the knife which presumably killed Kenneth Tarcher. This is the knife which was in the possession of Benjamin Blesker the night of the slaying. Yet not one shred of testimony has been heard during this trial concerning the vital factor of blood.'

He picked up the knife, and sprung the long, shining blade.

'This knife!' he said, waving it in the air. 'Look at it carefully. It has never left the court's possession since my client's arrest. Yet this clean, shiny blade can still tell a story of guilt or innocence. For as every biochemist knows, there is an infallible test which can determine whether an object of such porous metal has *ever* been stained with even one drop of blood!'

He poised the knife over the mouth of the beaker.

'Ladies and gentlemen, I intend to prove once and for all whether I have been defending a boy falsely accused, or a lying murderer. I intend to dip this blade in the solution. If it turns pink – you must punish him for his guilt. If it remains clear – you must do what is just, and set him free.'

Slowly, he brought the knife down.

'Your Honour!'

Wickers was on his feet, and Vernon halted.

'Your Honour, objection! Objection!'

'Yes, Mr Wickers?'

Wickers' eyes flashed angrily. 'Defense counsel is acting improperly. The police laboratory has already made the standard benzidine test of the weapon and found no bloodstains on the blade. We admit that the knife has been cleansed –'

'Your Honour,' Vernon said loudly, 'the sensitivity of this test far exceeds the benzidine – '

'This performance is irrelevant, immaterial, and completely improper!' Wickers whirled to the jury. 'At no time during this trial has the prosecution denied the absence of blood on Benjamin Blesker's knife. Any so-called "test" that corroborates this is completely gratuitous, and is intended as pure theatrics to mislead and befuddle the jury! I demand this farcial demonstration be stopped!'

There was a moment's silence. Vernon looked up at the judge hopefully, waiting.

Dwight folded his hands.

'Mr Wedge, I'm afraid you're not in a position to qualify as an expert in forensic chemistry. And, as Mr Wickers says, mere corroboration of the police laboratory report is gratuitous evidence that cannot be properly admitted. Therefore, the objection is sustained.'

'But Your Honour – '

'Sustained,' Judge Dwight said gravely. 'You cannot make the test, Mr Wedge.'

His summation was the briefest of his career.

'I believe Benjamin Blesker is innocent,' he said wearily. 'I believe this because of a test I was not permitted to make. This boy knew that the results of this test might have condemned him, yet he told me to proceed. No guilty man would have allowed it; no innocent man would have had it any other way.'

The jury was out less than an hour. When they returned, they declared that Benjamin Blesker was innocent.

Vernon was permitted the use of an adjoining chamber for a meeting with his client. It wasn't a victory celebration. The boy seemed stunned, and the happiness in old man Blesker's face looked more like sorrow. When the lawyer entered the room, he stood up shakily and held out his hand.

'God bless you,' he whispered. 'Bless you for what you did.'

'I didn't come to be congratulated,' Vernon said coldly. 'I wanted to see you both for another reason.'

The bailiff entered, and placed the beaker on the desk. When he left, Vernon took the knife out of his pocket, and put it down beside the beaker. The old man picked it up and looked at the weapon as if he had never seen it before.

'Wickers was right,' Vernon said flatly. 'What I did out there was theatrics. I didn't want to make the demonstration; I was counting on the prosecution halting it.'

'You didn't want to?' Blesker said blankly. 'You didn't want to make the test?'

'I could have gotten an expert, a real one, like Doc Hagerty. But I didn't want to take the chance; if this stuff had turned red . . .' He looked at the beaker and frowned. 'No,' he said. 'The risk was too great. If Wickers had played along, I would have been forced to do it. But I figured they would object, and the jury would be impressed the right way. They were, thank God.'

Blesker let out a long sigh.

'But now there's something we have to do,' Vernon said. 'Something to satisfy us all.'

'What do you mean?'

Vernon looked at the boy. Benjy wouldn't meet his eyes.

'I still don't know the truth,' the lawyer said. 'I don't know it, and neither do you. Only Benjy here knows it.'

'You can't mean that! You said yourself – '

'Never mind what I said out there. There's only one way we can really know, Mr Blesker.'

He held out his hand.

'Give me the knife, Mr Blesker. We're going to make the test the judge wouldn't allow. For our own sakes.'

'But why?' the old man cried. 'What difference does it make?'

'*Because I want to know*! Even if you don't, Mr Blesker, I want to know!

'Give me the knife,' Vernon said.

Blesker picked up the knife. He touched its cool blade thoughtfully.

'Of course,' he said.

Then, slowly, he drew the blade deliberately across the back of his hand. The sharp edge bit deep. Blood welled like a crimson river in the cut and stained his hand, his cuff, his sleeve, the surface of the desk. He looked at the wound sadly, indifferently, and then handed the dripping weapon to the attorney.

'Make your test,' he said dreamily. 'Make your test now, Mr Wedge.'

And as Vernon stared at him, he removed a crumpled handkerchief from his pocket and wound it about his injured hand. Then he took his son's arm, and they left the room together.

WHEN RANDOLPH WOKE UP

Kevin L. Donihe

(Prologue)
Mom served cookies on the living-room floor.

Perry Mason flickered in the background.

And Randolph Jacobs sat on a mat in front of the TV, drinking chocolate milk and staring up at Raymond Burr.

The black and white images enraptured Randolph Jacobs. He closed his eyes and watched himself slide into Mr Mason's shoes. The world melted and Randolph smelled the courtroom and inhaled Mr Mason's cologne.

His cologne.

Mom didn't mind. At least Randolph was a quiet boy.

(Forty-Five Years Later)
Randolph surveyed himself in the mirror and found his tie straight and his jacket neatly pressed. He brushed the dandruff from his shoulder, grabbed his car-keys from a rack, and began the day.

On route to the Washington County courthouse, Randolph fell behind a line of vintage cars. In the mix, Packards jostled with classic Mustangs for prominence. A few older models – some of which seemed to date from the twenties – sputtered alongside.

Such nice cars, Randolph marveled and redirected his attention to the radio. He soon found himself singing along to *Raindrops*.

Five minutes later – with old melody still on his lips – Randolph pulled into the parking lot of the country courthouse. He parked his car in the assigned space and stretched before climbing the marble steps. At the flight's summit, Randolph opened the door and immediately noticed someone had remodeled the courthouse's main-hall. Drastically so. Modernism had given way to a more utilitarian layout – the carpet ripped up in favour of black and white tile.

Randolph was perplexed, but he assumed stranger things had happened. He found himself preferring the new arrangement. It was stark and simple – the way he felt a courthouse should look. He still felt sorry for the labourers and wondered how hard they must have worked to alter the layout is so little time.

He pressed on before pausing by a water-fountain. Randolph leaned over for a drink and looked up at a posted lithograph. It was a collage of Norman Rockwell reproductions. He wasn't surprised.

Randolph wiped his lips. He turned to walk away but almost ran headlong into the young woman standing behind him in line.

He looked up at her face. Her hair. Her slinky black dress. Her long cigarette holder.

'Hi, big handsome. You got a light for me?'

'I'm sorry,' Randolph replied. 'We don't smoke in the courthouse.'

'Since when?'

'I'm not sure. Sometime in the 80s?'

'Details, details, details,' the vamp moaned. 'What's a girl to do? My brother's on trial for murder and you won't even let her have one teensy-weensy cigarette.'

'I'm sorry. But those aren't my orders.'

'You're not going to let my brother swing, are you?'

'Who's your brother?'

'Your client.'

'Which one?'

The vamp laughed. 'I understand, Mr Mason. You play your games and I'll play mine.'

'I'm sorry. You must have me mistaken for someone else. My name is Randolph Jacobs.'

'I see. You just go on and do your job. I'll be waiting out here when you're all done.'

Randolph turned away.

The girl was overwrought. Frighteningly so. Randolph tried to think nothing more of it even as he heard the other people in the hall call out Mr Mason's name.

'Hello, Mr Mason.'

'Fine morning, Mr Mason.'

'Glad to see you, Mr Mason.'

Randolph wondered who around him could be the popular Mr Mason and why he seemed to be the only one there with no prior knowledge of the man. Assuming Mr Mason must be walking close behind, Randolph spun around.

And saw nobody.

'Good morning, Mr Mason!'

'Nice day, Mr Mason!'

'Great tie, Mr Mason!'

He continued down the hall. Randolph attempted to ignore the others, but they refused to stop addressing his unseen colleague.

'Nice hat, Mr Mason.'

Randolph couldn't help but realize the last comment had been addressed directly to him.

'Did you just call me, Mr Mason,' he turned to the lady and stammered.

'Of course I did, silly.'

Randolph quickly spun away and let his fingers play over his face. The rugged and noble contours were unfamiliar.

And – at the moment of realization – Randolph ran screaming to the bathroom.

Randolph Jacobs leaned over the basin. He turned on the spigot but the cold water merely stung his cheeks.

His legs collapsed. His face fell into the sink and Randolph tasted the grit and soap-scum. There he remained until he heard the bathroom door swing open.

Randolph lifted his head. He had no idea how long he had spent with his face in the sink but was certain only a few minutes had elapsed. He forced his lips into a smile as the man paused to wash his hands in the adjoining basin.

'Would you happen to know the time?' Randolph asked and cringed, his voice as unfamiliar as his face.

'11:17, sir.'

'Thank you,' Randolph offered.

'You're welcome, Mr Mason.'

Randolph groaned and the bathroom door swung on its hinges. The man's footsteps melded with other hallway sounds and faded from ear-shot.

He considered slamming his head against the sink, but drew in a deep breath instead.

If this is hell maybe it would best to play the game. Conformity offers the least resistance. Better than suicide.

Randolph instinctively agreed and, at that second, everything went black.

An instant later, Randolph found himself in his customary seat in a non-customary court. All the women around him wore bee-hive hairdos. The men sported glasses with rims that matched their well-shorn hair. Each smoked unfiltered cigarettes.

He couldn't quite recall how he had gotten from the basin to the courtroom. He knew he was somehow *there*. But that was good. Randolph didn't know how he would respond if the judge chastised him for lateness. He couldn't remember Mr Mason ever having that problem.

Randolph reached up and touched his cheek. It felt damp. He wondered if anyone would be able to see the water.

If only he had a few more minutes to compose himself.

Somewhere in the distance, Randolph heard the bailiff announce the judge's entry. He felt himself rise. When the judge banged his gavel, Randolph wondered if the hammer had crashed against his skull.

'You may cross-examine the witness.'

Randolph cleared his throat and vacated the seat. His feet felt heavy. He wondered how strange it all must look to an outside observer. Randolph quickly swivelled his head to the left and to the right.

Everyone else seemed to be following the script perfectly – and that only complicated matters.

To his left, he noticed a camera. This was no dress rehearsal. The lens followed him to the witness stand and Randolph knew this take was going to print.

Cool it down, he thought to himself. *Just follow the script. Do what Mr Mason would do.*

'So,' Randolph began, pulling words out of thin air. 'Do you recall what you were doing when the crime in question was committed?'

'You asked that question yesterday,' smirked the witness.

Randolph felt the sweat as it formed. He spun around and saw a group of primly attired men nod disapprovingly. He assumed they were continuity experts.

Damn, I've already been spotted. Keep paranoia down. Keep paranoia down. Go on, Randolph, ask a question!

'So', Randolph stammered without realizing what he was saying, 'would you say that a murderer is a bad person?'

The witness glared. 'What kind of question is that?'

'Just answer the question.'

Good save. Just try to stay authoritative.

'Yeah. I would say a murderer is a bad person.'

'And would you also say that . . .'

Randolph's neck bristled. He stopped, turned around, and immediately realized why he felt so ill at ease. Everyone sat, looking cross, as he struggled by the witness stand. He felt the collective weight of the stare and it proved too much.

'Damn you all! I can't do this if everyone's judging me!' he shouted, pumping his fists at the extras.

'You're not supposed to say that,' the witness said, breaking character. 'The Director will not be pleased.'

To his left, the gavel banged so furiously it sounded tribal.

Over and above the judge, Randolph heard the silence give way to screams and commotion. He heard the script-writers ruffle their pages as the studio chiefs made threatening calls. He saw the vamp storm in and complain how she never had the opportunity to finish her lines.

'Cut! Cut! Cut! This will never do!' Boomed a voice over the intercom. 'Bring the actor to my office. Immediately!'

Before Randolph could protest, the best boy pulled him away from the set and pushed him through various corridors until they stopped by an office.

Alan Smurtz, Director

The plaque above the door read.

The best boy opened the door and Randolph saw a suited man standing by a desk. Randolph couldn't help but notice the dueling scar running down his right cheek.

'Come in, Randolph,' the Director said, motioning with his hands.

Randolph decided to do as he was told.

'I'm sorry you forced me to bring you here. When you were a kid you didn't know Perry Mason was just an actor. But you've broken with the script.'

Randolph shook his head. 'I don't care what you have to say. I *demand* to be taken back!'

'You're the only one who can fill that order, I'm afraid. I just coordinate things here and make sure everything's going according to plan.'

'My being here isn't *according to plan*!'

'Oh, you think you can be Perry Mason and grandstand like *this?* We have rules here, you know.'

'Your rules are absurd!'

'And why's that – if I may ask?'

'Because this isn't supposed to happen!'

'In your world, perhaps that's the case.'

'*Your* world?'

The Director laughed. 'We are not aliens, if that's what you're thinking. I was only being metaphorical when I said we were from different worlds.'

'I don't want metaphors! I just want you to tell me where I am!'

The Director tapped his knuckles against his desk and knocked down a shot of whisky.

'You know, sometimes it's good to have a little alcohol buzz. You can really let loose and tell an actor just what you think.'

'You dragged me here!' Randolph shouted.

'That's because you were too *stupid* to ask! We had to *come and get you*.'

'That's criminal abduction!'

The Director moaned and tossed down another shot. 'Don't you see? There's no crime here. We're all just kids playing. And you just so happened to ruin it all by throwing rocks.'

'I didn't throw anything!'

'I was being metaphorical again,' the Director sneered.

'Can't you say anything without confusing me? I'm supposed to be in court now! That's all that matters! I don't have to play make-believe anymore. I'm a lawyer. I *realized* my goal.'

'Oh really? When you were a kid did you fantasize about Perry's enormous wealth? Did you relish the thought of his three car-garage? No, you loved him because he was a true defender-of-justice. Are you, sir, a true defender-of-justice in your present capacity as attorney?'

'As far as the law allows.'

'As far as the law allows!' The Director scoffed. 'And what's that supposed to mean? I think I know. It means you *compromised*.'

'What are you trying to say?'

'Simply that you're not Perry Mason. Far from it. You fell short of your childhood innocence so I don't understand why you would pass up this opportunity. All you got to do is follow the script. It's so simple even a three year-old could do it. Consider this your last chance.'

'Damn you,' Randolph spat. 'Haven't you been listening! I don't want this dream! I've changed. Everybody changes!'

'I haven't,' the Director replied.

'But I have! Take me back!'

'Is that what you really want?' The Director sighed.

'Yes.'

'Then so be it.'

Before Randolph could react, the best boy slipped a blindfold around his eyes. The script-writers hoisted him onto their shoulders and carried Randolph from the office before tossing him into the rear of a limousine. In the front seat, the director smiled.

'We're be bringing you back home, now. And don't worry about missing your case. We'll take you back to last night.'

It seemed as though they drove for hours before the Director threw open the door and tossed Randolph to the street just outside his suburban home.

(*Back in the Real World*)
Randolph dusted off his clothes and panned his gaze across all that had been restored.

He saw his kids throwing rocks at each other by the swing-set.

He saw his mailbox overflowing with bills and responsibility.

Through the kitchen window, he saw his wife cooking another tasteless meal and realized that she would later request another round of equally tasteless sex.

Randolph turned away from the house to call out to the Director, but the limo had already turned a curve and driven out of sight.

THE CASE OF THE CRYING SWALLOW

Erle Stanley Gardner

I

Perry Mason, tilted back in his walnut desk chair, was studying a recent decision of the state supreme court when Della Street, his secretary, opened the door from the outer office, advanced to the desk and quietly laid ten crisp one-hundred-dollar bills on the blotter.

Mason, too engrossed to notice what she was doing, continued his reading.

Della Street said, 'A client sends his card.'

Mason straightened in the swivel chair and for the first time caught sight of the money which Della Street had so neatly spread out.

'He said his name was Mr Cash,' Della Street explained. 'Then he handed me ten one-hundred-dollar bills and said these were his cards.'

Mason grinned. 'So the black market begins to turn yellow. What does Mr Cash look like?'

'He's a floor walker.'

Mason raised his eyebrows, glanced at the cash. 'A *floorwalker?*'

'No, no, not a department store floorwalker! I mean that he's a floor *walker*, the same as you are. He paces the floor when he's worried. He's doing a carpet marathon out there right now.'

Mason said, 'I don't know whether civilization is breaking down the character of our criminals or whether the black market operators haven't been in business long enough to develop intestinal stamina. The bootleggers were a tougher breed. My own opinion is that these black market operators simply haven't had time to become accustomed to the fact that they're on the other side of society's legal fence. Give them another eighteen months and they'll be as tough as the old gangsters.'

'He definitely *isn't* a black market operator,' Della Street said positively. 'He's distinguished-looking, has a slight limp, is deeply tanned and . . . and I've seen him somewhere before. Oh, now I have it. I've seen his picture!'

'Give.'

'Major Claude L. Winnett, polo player, yachtsman, millionaire playboy. When the war came, he quit being a playboy and became an aviator, bagged a whole flock of German planes and then was captured, liberated last fall, discharged because of his wound, returned to his doting mother and . . .'

Mason nodded. 'I remember reading about the chap. He got a citation or something. Didn't he get married?'

'About four or five weeks ago,' Della Street said. 'That was where I first saw his picture – in the paper. Then again last week a reporter for the society supplement paid a visit to the Winnett home – one of the old-time country estates with stables of polo ponies, riding trails, hedges, private golf courses . . .'

'Show him in,' Mason said. 'But let him know first that you've placed him. It may save time.'

Major Winnett, lean, fit, bronzed, and nervous, followed Della Street into the office. The excitement and anxiety of his manner were more noticeable than his slight limp. A well-modulated voice and patrician bearing made his surrender to emotion all the more impressive.

'Mr Mason,' he said as soon as he was in the room. 'I had intended to keep my identity a secret and ask you to represent another person. Now that your secretary has recognized me, I'll put my cards on the table. My wife has disappeared. She needs your help. She's in trouble of some sort.'

'Tell me about it,' Mason said.

Major Winnett reached into his inside pocket, took out a folded piece of letter paper and handed it to Mason.

The lawyer opened the letter and read:

Claude, my darling, there are some things that I can't drag *you* into. I thought I had a way out, but I guess I didn't. Our happiness was such a beautiful thing. But beautiful things are always fragile. Don't worry about anything. I am responsible, and I am not going to let you suffer because of what you have done for me. Good-by, my darling –
MARCIA

'What does she mean by saying she's responsible and not letting you suffer because of what you have done for her?' Mason asked.

Major Winnett's manner was uneasy. 'My marriage was not exactly in accordance with the wishes of my mother. I went ahead with it despite her objections.'

'Spoken objections?'

'Certainly not.'

'Yet your wife knew of them?'

'Women feel many things without the necessity of words, Mr Mason. I want you to find her and straighten things out for her.'

'And then report to you?'

'Certainly.'

Mason shook his head.

For a moment there was silence, broken only by the faint rumble of traffic and the breathing of Mason's client. Then Major Winnett said, 'Very well. Do it your way.'

'When did your wife leave?'

'Last night. I found this note on the dresser about midnight. I thought she had previously retired.'

'Is there any reason why your wife would have been vulnerable to what we might call an outside influence?'

'Absolutely not – if you mean blackmail.'

'Then tell me why your wife wasn't free to come to you with her troubles.'

'I don't know, unless it's on account of my mother.'

'What about her?'

'My mother is a very unusual person. When my father died, a dozen years ago, Mother stepped in and took charge. She is living in a bygone era. She has old-fashioned ideas.'

'The proprieties?' Mason asked.

'Not so much the proprieties as . . . well, class distinctions, the aristocracy of wealth and that sort of thing. I think she would have been happier if I had married someone more in our own set.'

'Who, for instance?'

'Oh, I didn't say any particular person,' Major Winnett said hastily.

'I know you didn't. That's why I'm asking you.'

'Well, perhaps Daphne Rexford.'

'You think this caused your wife to leave?'

'No, no. Not directly. My mother has accepted Marcia into the family. Whatever may have been Mother's ideas about the marriage, Marcia is now one of us – a Winnett.'

'Then suppose you tell me what you mean when you say "not directly." '

'Marcia would have done anything rather than subject me to any notoriety because she knew how my mother felt about that. You see, Mr Mason, we live in a large, rather old-fashioned estate surrounded by hedges, with our private bridle paths, high wire fences, locked gates, no-trespassing signs and all the rest. The more the world moves in a way that meets with the disapproval of my mother, the more she tries to shut that part of the world out from her life.'

'Anything unusual happen within the last few days?' the lawyer asked, probing his client's mind.

'A burglar entered our house Tuesday night.'

'Take anything?' Mason asked.

'My wife's jewelry, valued at perhaps twenty-five or thirty thousand dollars, although I don't suppose a person could get that for it. It had been insured at fifteen thousand dollars.'

'Had been?' Mason asked.

'Yes, my wife cancelled the insurance. As it happened, only the day before the burglary.'

Major Winnett glanced almost appealingly at the lawyer.

'Cancelled her insurance,' Mason said, 'and then twenty-four hours later the burglary took place?'

'Yes.'

'And you fail to see any connection between those two facts?'

'I am certain there is none,' Major Winnett said hastily. 'My wife's reasoning was absolutely sound. She had carried this insurance policy and paid high premiums on it while she was living in apartments and hotels because she wanted to keep her jewelry with her and wanted to wear it. But when she married me and came to live in Vista del Mar, it seemed hardly necessary to continue paying high premiums.'

'Tell me more about that burglary and why you didn't report it to the police.'

'How did you know we didn't report it to the police?'

'Your facial expression,' Mason said dryly.

'That was purely on account of the fact that my mother . . . well, you know, the newspaper notoriety and . . .'

'Tell me about the burglary,' Mason said.

Major Winnett spoke with the rhythm of a man who is carefully choosing his words. 'I am a sound sleeper, Mr Mason. My wife is not. On Tuesday night I was awakened by the sound of my wife's scream.'

'What time?'

'I didn't look at my watch at the time but I did look at it a few minutes later, and as nearly as I can place the time, it was around quarter to one.'

'How long had you been in bed?'

'We retired about eleven.'

'And you slept until your wife screamed?'

'Well, I have, in the back of my consciousness, a vague recollection of a swallow crying.'

Mason raised his eyebrows.

'You are, of course, familiar,' Major Winnett went on hastily, 'with the famed swallows of the Mission of San Juan Capistrano?'

Mason nodded.

'The nesting place of those swallows is not confined to the Mission. They get more publicity at the Mission because they leave on a certain day and return on a certain day. I believe that the time of their return can be predicted almost to the hour. A very unusual sense of keeping a calendar. How they are able to return year after year . . .'

'And you have some of those swallows at your house?' Mason interrupted.

'Yes. They are a nuisance. Their nests are built out of mud and are fastened to the eaves. Our gardener knocks them down as soon as he detects the birds building, but in case one of them eludes his vigilance and the nest is built, then we don't disturb it, because the birds lay eggs very soon after the nests are built.'

'Go on,' Mason said.

'Well, this particular swallow's nest was located in a very unfortunate place. The main residence at Vista del Mar is a large Spanish-type house with the tile roofs and a white exterior. Our bedroom is on the second floor with a projecting balcony. The tile projects out over that balcony, and the birds had made their nest in such a place that if a man climbed over the balcony rail, he'd be within a few feet of the nest.'

'And a man did climb over that rail?'

'Evidently that is what happened. We found a ladder that had been placed against the side of the house. The intruder had climbed up the ladder. In doing so, he disturbed the swallows. When they're disturbed, they have a peculiar throaty chirp.'

'And you heard that?'

'I either heard it or dreamed that I did. My wife doesn't remember it, and she is a much lighter sleeper than I am, but I don't think I was mistaken.'

'Then you went back to sleep?'

'Apparently I did. I remember hearing the protestations of the swallows but, although I was aroused from a sound slumber, I didn't thoroughly waken. I dozed off again and was soon in a deep sleep from which I was awakened by my wife's scream.'

'She saw the burglar?'

'She was aroused by some noise in the room. She saw this man standing at her dresser. At first she thought I had gone to the dresser for some purpose and she started to speak to me. Then she looked over and saw that I was in my bed . . .'

'There was enough light for that?'

'Yes. A late moon was giving some light.'

'What happened?'

'The man heard the motion – some sound of the bedsprings, I guess. He darted out to the balcony. My wife screamed and that wakened me, but it took me a few seconds to get oriented, to realize where I was and what was happening. By that time the man had made his escape.'

'And you think the swallows were crying because the man disturbed them?'

'That's right. When he entered the building, he must have climbed over the balcony rail and touched the nest.'

'When did your wife cancel the insurance?'

'Monday afternoon.'

Mason toyed with his lead pencil, then asked abruptly, 'What happened Monday morning?'

'We all four breakfasted together.'

'Who's the fourth?'

'Helen Custer, my mother's nurse.'

'Your mother isn't well?'

'She has a bad heart. Her physician feels it's advisable to have a nurse in the house.'

'She's been with you long?'

'For three years. We consider her very much one of the family.'

'You breakfasted and then what?'

'I wrote letters. My mother . . . I don't know exactly where she *did* go. Marcia went riding.'

'Where?'

'Heavens, I don't know. One of our bridle paths.'

Mason said, 'I believe it rained Sunday night, didn't it?'

Major Winnett looked at him curiously. 'What,' he asked, 'does that have to do with it? . . . I mean, what is the significance?'

'Skip it.' Mason interrupted. 'What happened next?'

'Nothing. My wife returned about eleven.'

'When did she tell you she was going to cancel the insurance?'

'That was just before lunch. She telephoned to the insurance company, and then she wrote them a letter confirming her action.'

'Did you notice anything unusual in your wife's manner?'

'Nothing.' Major Winnett said so swiftly that it seemed the answer had been poised on his tongue, waiting merely for Mason's question.

Mason said, 'Well, it's ten-thirty. I want to get Paul Drake of the Drake Detective Agency. We'll make a start out at your place and go on from there. I'll leave here about eleven. Does your mother know your wife has left?'

Major Winnett cleared his throat. 'I told her my wife was visiting friends.'

'How will you account for us?' Mason asked.

'How many will there be?'

'My secretary, Miss Street, Paul Drake, the detective, myself, and perhaps one of Mr Drake's assistants.'

Major Winnett said, 'I'm working on a mining deal. I can explain to my mother that you're giving me some advice in connection with that. Your detective wouldn't mind posing as a mining expert?'

'Not at all.'

'You'll come to the house and . . . will you want to stay there?'

Mason nodded. 'I think we'd better. And I'll want photographs and a description of your wife.'

Major Winnett took an envelope from his inside pocket and extracted nearly a dozen photographs. 'I brought these along. They're snapshots. She's twenty-five, redheaded, bluish-gray eyes, five feet two, a hundred and fifteen, and as nearly as I can tell from checking the clothes that are left in the closet, she's wearing a checkered suit, sort of a gray plaid. It's the one that she's wearing in this picture.'

Mason studied the photographs, then reached for the envelope. 'All right,' he said, 'we'll be out. You can go on ahead and see that all necessary arrangements are made.'

II

The city of Silver Strand Beach lay in a sheltered cove on the lee side of a peninsula. The Winnett estate dominated this peninsula, its wire fences with forbidding no-trespassing signs stretching for some two and a half miles. The Spanish-type house, perched on the summit some five hundred feet above the ocean, commanded a view in all directions.

Mason's car swept around the last curve in the gravelled

driveway and came to a stop in front of the imposing house as he said to Paul Drake, 'I think the cancellation of that insurance policy is, perhaps, the first indication of what she had in mind, Paul. And I think that may have some connection with the horseback ride she took Monday morning.'

Paul Drake's professionally lugubrious face didn't change expression in the least. 'Anything to go on, Perry?'

'It rained Sunday night,' Mason said. 'It hasn't rained since. If you could find the path she took, it's quite possible you might be able to track her horse.'

'For the love of Pete, do I have to ride a horse?'

'Sure. Tell the groom you'd like to ride. Ask him about some of the bridle paths.'

'I can't see anything from a horse,' Drake complained. 'When a horse trots, I bounce. When I bounce, I see double.'

'After you get out of sight of the house, you can lead the horse,' Mason suggested.

'How about me?' Della Street asked.

'Try to get acquainted with the nurse,' Mason suggested, 'and take a look around.'

Major Winnett himself answered Mason's ring; and the swift efficiency with which he installed them in rooms, then introduced them to his mother and Helen Custer, the nurse, showed that he had already made his preliminary explanations.

When Drake departed for the stables, after having expressed his spurious enthusiasm for horseflesh, Major Winnett took Mason on a tour of inspection.

Once they were alone in the upper corridors, Major Winnett asked quickly and in a low voice, 'Is there anything in particular you want to see?'

'I'd like to get familiar with the entire house,' Mason said guardedly. 'But you might begin by showing me *your* room.'

Major Winnett's room was on the south side. Glass doors opened on the balcony, from which the ocean could be seen shimmering in the sunlight.

'That's the swallow's nest?' Mason asked, indicating a gourd-like projection of mud which extended from the tiles just above the balcony.

'That's the swallow's nest. You can see that a person climbing a ladder . . .'

'Was the ladder already there?' Mason asked.

'Yes. The handyman had been doing some work on a pane of glass on the side of the bedroom. He had left the ladder in position that night, because he intended to finish it the next morning. Damn careless of him.'

'In that case,' Mason said, 'your thief was an opportunist, since he didn't bring his own ladder.'

'Yes, I suppose so.'

'One who was, moreover, apparently familiar with the house. How about your servants?'

'You can't ever tell,' Major Winnett said. 'Particularly these days. But I *think* they're all right. Mother pays good wages and most of the help have been with her for some time. However, she *is* rather strict at times and there is a certain turnover.'

'You own virtually all of the land on this peninsula?'

'Quite a bit of it, but not all of it. In a moment we'll go up to the observation tower and I can show you around from there. Generally, we take in about three-fourths of the peninsula. There is a strip out on the end where the county maintains a public campground.'

'The public can reach that camp without crossing your estate?'

'Yes. Our line runs along by the grove of trees – beautiful oaks that offer a place for picnics. Picnickers are always scattering papers and plates around. We try to persuade them to go on down to the public campgrounds on the end of the peninsula.'

'So anyone who came out here at night would have been definitely a trespasser?'

'Quite definitely.'

'And having taken that risk, must have had some specific objective in mind, and would, therefore, if he were at all prudent, have arranged some manner of reaching his objective?'

'Yes, I suppose so.'

'Therefore,' Mason went on, 'either your burglar must have been someone who knew that the ladder was here, or else it was an inside job.'

'But how could anyone have known the ladder was here?'

Mason said, 'If you can see the camp and the picnic grounds from here, it is quite possible that someone in the camp or picnic grounds could see the house.'

'Yes, the house is quite a landmark. You can see it for miles.'

'And perhaps a man, looking up here about dusk and noticing that a ladder had been left in place, would have decided it might be worthwhile to climb that ladder.'

'Yes, I suppose so. However, Mr Mason, I can't see that there is the slightest connection between the theft of my wife's jewelry and her disappearance.'

'Probably not,' Mason said.

They finished their tour with a trip up a flight of stairs to the place which Major Winnett described as 'the tower.'

Here was a belfry-like room, fifteen feet square, with plate-glass windows on all sides. In the centre, a pair of eighteen-power binoculars attached to a swivel on a tripod could be turned and locked in any position.

'In times past,' Major Winnett explained, 'when there was more merchant shipping up and down the coast, we used to enjoy looking the boats over. You see, these binoculars can be swung in any direction. Now I'll point them toward town and –'

'Just a minute,' Mason warned sharply, as Major Winnett reached for the binoculars. 'They seem to be pointed toward that grove of trees. If you don't mind, I'd like to look through them.'

'Why, certainly. Help yourself.'

Mason looked through the powerful prismatic binoculars. The right eye showed only a blur, but the left showed a shaded spot under the clump of big live oaks where the road crossed a mesa before dipping down through a little canyon to again come into view as it swung out toward the picnic and camping grounds on the extreme tip of the promontory.

'There's no central focusing screw,' Major Winnett explained. 'You have to adjust each eyepiece individually. Perhaps . . .

'Yes, so I see,' Mason said, removing his eyes from the binoculars.

'Here is what I mean,' Major Winnett went on. 'You simply screw this eyepiece . . .'

Mason courteously but firmly arrested the major's hand. 'Just a moment, Major,' he said. 'I want to look at that right eyepiece.'

'Someone must have been tampering with it. It's way out of proper adjustment,' the major said.

'The left eyepiece is at zero adjustment. I take it that means a perfectly normal eye,' Mason said, 'whereas, on this right eyepiece, there is an adjustment of negative five. I take it those graduations are made so that a person can remember his own individual adjustment for infinity and adjust the binoculars readily.'

'I suppose so. The figures represent diopters.'

'And an adjustment of negative five certainly blurs the entire –'

'That can't be an adjustment,' the major interposed. 'Someone has idly turned that eyepiece.'

'I see your point,' Mason said and promptly turned the eyepiece back to zero. 'There,' he announced, 'that's better.'

It was now possible to make out details in what had before been merely a patch of shadow.

Mason swung the binoculars to the picnic ground and could see quite plainly the masonry barbecue pits, the tables and chairs. Beyond them, through the trees he caught a glimpse of the ocean.

'A beach down there?' he asked.

'Not a beach, but a very fine place for surf fishing.'

Mason swung the binoculars once more toward the clump of trees and the wide place in the road. 'And you say people picnic there?'

'Occasionally, yes.'

'From that point,' Mason said, 'one could see the house quite plainly with binoculars.'

'But the binoculars are up here.'

'Not the only pair in the world surely.'

The major frowned. Mason turned the glasses on a moving object and saw a magnified image of Paul Drake walking slowly along a bridle path. The short, somewhat cramped steps indicated that his brief experience in the English riding saddle had been more than ample. The detective was leading the horse, his head bowed as he plodded along the bridle path.

III

Mason waited until he saw Major Winnett leave the house, walking toward the stables. Then the lawyer quietly opened the door of his room, walked down the corridor to Winnett's bedroom, crossed the balcony and climbed to the rail.

The entrance to the swallow's nest was too small to accommodate the lawyer's hand, but he enlarged it by clipping away bits of the dried mud with his thumb and forefinger.

From inside the nest came faint rustlings of motion. An immature beak pushed against Mason's finger.

The parent swallows cried protests as they swooped in swift, stabbing circles around the lawyer's head, but Mason, working rapidly, enlarged the opening so he could insert his hand into the nest. He felt soft down-covered bodies. Down below them, his groping fingers encountered only the concave surface of the nest.

A frown of annoyance crossed the lawyer's face. He continued groping, however, gently moving the young birds to one side. Then the frown faded as the tips of his fingers struck a hard metallic object.

As the lawyer managed to remove this object, sunlight scintillated an emerald and diamond brooch into brilliance.

Mason swiftly pocketed the bit of jewelry and drew back from the fierce rushes of the swallows. He dropped to the floor of the balcony and returned to the bedroom.

Back in the bedroom, he made a swift, thorough search of the various places where small objects might be concealed. A sole leather gun case in the back of a closet contained an expensive shotgun. Mason looked through the barrels. Both were plugged with oiled rags at breech and muzzle.

Mason's knife extracted one of the rags. He tilted up the barrels, and jewelry cascaded out into his palm, rings, earrings, brooches, a diamond and emerald necklace.

Mason replaced the jewelry, inserted the rag once more and put the gun back in the leather case, then returned the case to the closet.

Preparing to leave the room, he listened for a few moments at the bedroom door, then boldly opened it and stepped out, retracing his steps toward his own room.

He was halfway down the corridor when Mrs Victoria Winnett appeared at an intersecting corridor and moved toward Mason with stately dignity and a calm purpose.

'Were you looking for something, Mr Mason?' she asked.

The lawyer's smile was disarming. 'Just getting acquainted with the house.'

Victoria Winnett was the conventional composite of a bygone era. There were pouches beneath her eyes, sagging lines to her face, but the painstakingly careful manner in which every strand of hair had been careful coiffed, her face massaged, powdered, and rouged, indicated the emphasis she placed on appearance, and there was a stately dignity about her manner which, as Della Street subsequently remarked, reminded one of an ocean liner moving sedately up to its pier.

Had she carefully rehearsed her entrance and been grooming herself for hours to convey just the right impression of dignified rebuke, Mrs Victoria Winnett would not have needed to change so much as a line of her appearance. 'I think my *son* wanted to show you around,' she said as she fell into step at Mason's side.

'Oh, he's done that already,' Mason said with breezy informality. 'I was just looking the place over.'

'You're Mr *Perry* Mason, the lawyer, aren't you?'

'That's right.'

'I had gathered from what I read about your cases that you specialize mostly in trial work.'

'I do.'

'*Murder* trials, do you not?'

'Oh, I handle lots of other cases. The murder cases get the most publicity.'

'I see,' she said in the tone of one who doesn't see at all.

'Nice place you have here,' the lawyer went on. 'I am very much interested in that observation cubicle on top of the house.'

'It was my husband's idea. He liked to sit up there. Didn't I hear the swallows crying out there?'

'I thought *I* heard them too,' Mason said.

She looked at him sharply. 'We try to keep them from nesting here, but occasionally the gardener fails to see a nest until it is completed. Then we don't disturb the nest until after the young birds have hatched. They're noisy and talkative. You can hear them quite early in the mornings. I trust they won't disturb you. Are you a sound sleeper, Mr Mason?'

They had paused at the head of the stairs. Mrs Winnett apparently did not intend to go down, so Mason, standing poised on the upper stair tread, used strategy to terminate the interview.

'My friend, Drake, is looking over the horses, and if you'll pardon me I'll run down and join him.'

He flashed her a smile and ran swiftly down the stairs, leaving her standing there, for the moment nonplussed at the manner in which the lawyer had so abruptly forestalled further questions.

IV

In the patio, Della Street caught Perry Mason's eye, gave him a significant signal and moved casually over to the driveway where she climbed into the car and sat down.

Mason walked over. 'I think Paul Drake has something,' he said. 'I'm going down and look him up. He's just coming in on the bridle path. What have you got?'

'I can tell you something about the nurse, chief.'

'What?'

'In the first place, if a woman's intuition counts for anything, she's in love with the major – one of those hopeless affairs where she worships him from a distance. In the second place, I think she has a gambling habit of some sort.'

'Races?'

'I don't know. I was up in the cupola just after you were. There was a pad of paper in the drawer of the little table up there. At first it looked completely blank. Then I tilted it so the light struck it at an angle and I could see that someone had written on the top sheet with a fairly hard pencil so it had made an imprint on the sheet under it. Then the top sheet had been torn off.'

'Good girl! What was on the sheet of paper? I take it something significant.'

'Evidently some gambling figures. I won't bother to show you the original at this time, but here's a copy that I worked out. It reads like this: *These numbers* on the first line, then down below that, *led*; then down below that a space and 5"5936; down below that 6"8102; down below that 7"9835; down below that 8"5280; down below that 9"2640; down below that 10"1320.'

'Anything else?' Mason asked.

'Then a line and below the line, the figure 49"37817. That looks like some sort of a lottery to me. I learned Mrs Winnett has been up in the cupola lately, and since *she'd* hardly be a gambler, I assume the nurse must have written down the figures.'

Mason said thoughtfully, 'Notice the last three numbers, Della, 5280, 2640, 1320. Does that sequence mean something to you?'

'No, why?'

Mason said, '5280 feet in a mile.'

'Oh, yes, I get that.'

'The next number, 2640 feet is a half mile, and the last number, 1320 feet, is a quarter mile.'

'Oh, yes, I see now. Then that double mark means inches, doesn't it?'

'It's an abbreviation of inches, yes. What does this nurse seem like, Della? Remember I only barely met her.'

'Despite her muddy complexion, straight hair and glasses, her eyes are really beautiful. You should see them light up when the major's name comes up. My own opinion is this nurse could be good-looking. Then Mrs Winnett would fire her. So she keeps herself looking plain and unattractive so she can be near the major, whom she loves with a hopeless, helpless, unrequited passion.'

'Look here,' Mason said, 'if you've noticed that within an hour and a half, how about Mrs Victoria Winnett? Doesn't she know?'

'I think she does.'

'And hasn't fired the nurse?'

'No. I think she doesn't mind if the nurse worships the ground the major walks on but doesn't presume to raise her eyes to look at him, if you get what I mean.'

'I get it,' Mason said thoughtfully, 'and I don't like it. Wait, here comes Paul now.'

Drake, walking stiffly, joined them.

'Find anything, Paul?' Mason asked.

'I found something,' Drake conceded, 'and I don't know what it is.'

'What does it look like, Paul?'

'In the first place,' Drake said, 'you can easily follow her tracks. She took the lower bridle path. After the first quarter mile, there's only one set of tracks going and coming. They were made when the ground was soft and they go down to a road and a gate that's locked. I didn't have a key, but I could see where the horse tracks went through the gate and down onto the road, so I tied up my horse and managed to squeeze through the fence.'

'Any tracks around those trees, Paul?'

'An automobile had been parked there,' Drake said. 'There must have been two automobiles. That's the only way I can figure it out, but I still can't figure the tracks right.'

'How come?'

Drake took a small thin book from his pocket. 'This is a little pocket book which gives the tread designs of all makes of tyres. Now an automobile that had some fairly new tyres was in there. One of the wheels was worn too much to identify, but I identified the track of a right front wheel. Then the track of the other front wheel and the other hind wheel and . . . well, there I bogged down, Perry.'

'What do you mean?'

'Of course, you have to understand it's a little difficult trying to get those tracks all fitted into the proper sequence. They . . .'

'What are you getting at?' Mason said.

'Hang it, Perry, I got *three* wheels.'

'And the fourth was worn smooth?'

'Not that – what I mean is, Perry, that I got three wheels *on a single side*.'

Mason frowned at the detective. '*Three* wheels on a side?'

'Three wheels on a side,' Paul Drake insisted doggedly.

Mason said rather excitedly, 'Paul, did you notice a circular spot in the ground, perhaps eight or ten inches in diameter?'

'How the deuce did you know that spot was there?' Drake demanded, his face showing bewilderment.

Mason said, 'It was made by the bottom part of a bucket, Paul. And the three tracks on each side were all right. That's the way it should be.'

'I don't get it.'

'A house trailer,' Mason explained. 'An automobile and a house trailer were parked under the trees. The waste water from a trailer sink is carried out through a drain to the outside. A bucket is placed there to catch the water as it runs off.'

'That's it, all right,' Drake admitted, then added morosely, 'I'm kicking myself for not thinking of it, Perry.'

Mason said, 'It now begins to look as though Marcia Winnett had kept an appointment on Monday with someone in a house trailer. And that seems to have been very much a turning point in her life.'

Drake nodded. 'On Monday – that's a cold trail, Perry.'

'It's the only one we have,' Mason pointed out.

V

Mason, studying the tyre tracks, said, 'It was an automobile and a house trailer, Paul. The round place which marks the location of the spout bucket can be taken as being approximately in the middle of the trailer. You can see over here the mark of an auxiliary wheel attached to the front of the trailer to carry part of the weight while the trailer was parked. That enables us to estimate the length of the trailer.'

Drake said, 'The trailer must have been backed in between these trees, Perry.'

Mason started prowling along the edge of the fence. 'Took some clever handling to get it in there. Let's look around for garbage. If the trailer remained here overnight, there are probably some tin cans . . . potato peelings, stuff of that sort.'

Mason, Della Street and Drake separated, covering the ground carefully.

Abruptly Della said, 'Chief, don't look too suddenly, but casually take a look up there at the big house on the hill. I think I saw someone moving in the glassed-in observation tower.'

'I rather expected as much,' Mason said, without even looking up. 'However, it's something we can't help.'

Drake exclaimed, 'Here it is, Perry, a collection of tin cans and garbage.'

Mason moved over to where Drake was standing. Here the water from the winter rains, rushing down the ditch at the side of the road, had eddied around one of the roots of the big live oak and formed a cave which extended some three feet back under the roots of the tree.

Mason, squatting on his heels, used two dry sticks to rake out the articles.

There were three cans which had been flattened under pressure, some peelings from onions and potatoes, waxed paper which had been wrapped around a loaf of bread, an empty glass container bearing a syrup label, and a crumpled paper bag.

Mason carefully segregated the items with his sticks. As he did so he kept up a running fire of conversation.

'That flattening of the cans is the trick of an old outdoorsman,' he said.

'Why flatten them?' Della inquired.

'Animals get their heads stuck in cans sometimes,' Mason said. 'Moreover, cans take up less room when they're flattened and require a smaller hole when they're buried. This little garbage pit tells quite a story. The occupant of the trailer must have been a man. Notice the canned beans, a can of chili con carne, potatoes, bread, onions – no tomato peelings, no lettuce leaves, no carrots, in fact, no fresh vegetables at all. A woman would have had a more balanced diet. These are the smallest cans obtainable and . . . hello, what's this?'

Mason had pulled apart the paper bag as he talked. Now he brought out a small oblong slip of paper on which figures had been stamped in purple ink.

Della Street said, 'That's a cash register receipt from one of the cash-and-carry grocery stores.'

Mason picked up the receipt. 'And a very interesting one,' he said. 'The man bought fifteen dollars and ninety-four cents' worth of merchandise. There's a date on the back of the slip and this other figure refers to the time. The groceries were bought at five minutes past eight on Saturday morning. It begins to look, Paul, as though this is where you take over.'

'What do you want me to do?' Drake asked.

Mason said, 'Get a room in the hotel at Silver Strand beach. Open up something of an office there. Get men on the job. Get lots of men. Have your men buy groceries. See if the printing on the slip from any cash register matches this. If it does, try to find out something about the single, sun-bronzed man who purchased fifteen dollars and ninety-four cents' worth of groceries at five minutes past eight on Saturday morning. A sale of that size to a man just a few minutes after the store opened might possibly have attracted attention.'

'Okay,' Drake said. 'Anything else?'

'Lots else,' Mason said. 'Della, where's that slip of paper, the copy you made of what you found in the observation tower?'

Della ran to the glove compartment and brought back the square of paper on which she'd made the copy.

Drake looked at it, then said, 'What is it, Perry?'

'Stuff Della found in the observation tower. What do you make of it?'

'Some sort of dimensions,' Drake said. 'Here's this number 8 inches and 5280 feet, 9 inches and half a mile, 10 inches and quarter of a mile. What's the idea, Perry? Why should the inches run 5, 6, 7, 8, 9, 10, and . . .?'

'Suppose they aren't inches?' Mason said. 'Suppose they're ditto marks.'

'Well, it could be.'

'Then what?' Mason asked.

Drake said, 'Then the numbers could have something to do with a lottery of some sort.'

'Add them up,' Mason said dryly.

'The total is already here,' Drake said. '49"37817.'

Mason handed him a pencil.

Della Street, leaning over Drake's shoulder, was the first to get it. 'Chief,' she exclaimed, 'the total isn't correct.'

'I knew it wasn't,' Mason said. 'I didn't know just how much it was off, however. Let's find out.'

Della Street said, 'The total is . . . Wait a minute, Paul, I'll get it . . . 45"33113, but the total that's *marked* there is 49"37817.'

'Subtract them,' Mason said. 'What do you get?'

Della Street's skillful fingers guided the pencil as she hastily wrote down numbers and performed the subtraction. '4"4704,' she said.

Mason nodded. 'I think,' he said, 'when we get this case solved, we'll find the important figure is the one that *isn't* there. Bear that figure in mind, Paul. It may turn up later.'

VI

Perry Mason took the steep stairs to the observation tower two at a time.

There was no one in the cupola. The binoculars, however, had once more been swung so that they were pointing to the grove of trees where the trailer had been parked. Mason placed his eyes to the binoculars. The left eye showed a clear vision, the right was blurred.

Mason bent over to study the adjustment on the right lens, saw it was set once more at negative five, then he changed the focus on the binoculars.

As he did so, he heard motion behind him and straightened abruptly.

Mrs Victoria Winnett was standing in the doorway. At her side was a slender brunette in riding clothes whose face showed startled surprise. Mrs Winnett's face showed no expression whatever.

'I hardly expected to find *you* here,' Mrs Winnett said to Mason and then, turning to the young woman at her side, said, 'Miss Rexford, permit me to present Mr Perry Mason, the lawyer.'

Daphne Rexford favoured Mason with a smile which went only as far as her lips. Her eyes showed an emotion which might have been merely nervousness, might have been panic.

Mason acknowledged the introduction, then said, 'I'm fascinated with the view you get from here, Mrs Winnett.'

'My late husband spent much of his time here. The place does hold something of a fascination. Daphne loves it.'

'You're here frequently?' Mason asked Daphne Rexford.

'Yes, I study birds.'

'I see.'

'But,' she went on hastily, 'since you're here, I'll postpone my bird study until some other time.'

'On the contrary,' Mason said, 'I was just leaving. I wanted to get the lay of the land.'

'He's working with Claude on a mining deal,' Mrs Winnett hastened to explain to Daphne Rexford. 'There's a mining engineer with him. And Mr Mason has his secretary. You'll meet them if you're over for dinner tonight.'

'Oh, thank you, but I . . . I don't think I can make it for dinner tonight. If Claude's going to be busy . . . Where's Marcia?'

'Visiting friends,' Mrs Winnett said dryly. '*Please* come.'

'Well, I . . . I should . . .'

Mason said as she hesitated, 'Well, I must get down and hunt up my client. After all, I must earn my fee, you know.'

'I feel quite sure you will,' Mrs Winnett said with a certain subtle significance. 'Come, Daphne, dear. Draw up a chair. What was it you were saying about swallows?'

Daphne said hurriedly, 'Oh, there's a meadowlark! I think there must be a nest down by that bush. I've seen that same lark so many times in that exact position . . .'

Mason quietly closed the door and walked down the stairs.

Major Winnett was in the drawing room. He looked up as Mason crossed toward the patio. 'What luck?' he asked.

'Progress,' Mason said.

Major Winnett's lips tightened. 'Can't you do better than that? Can't you give me something definite? Or are you just running around in circles?'

'A good hound always runs around in circles to pick up a scent.'

'Then you haven't anything definite yet?'

'I didn't say that.'

'You intimated it.'

Mason slid his right hand down into his trousers pocket and abruptly withdrew the diamond and emerald brooch he had taken from the swallow's nest.

'Seen this before?' he asked, extending his hand.

Major Winnett stiffened for a moment to rigid immobility. 'It looks . . . Mr Mason, that certainly is similar to a brooch my wife had.'

'One that was stolen?'

'I believe so, yes.'

'Thank you.' Mason said and slipped the brooch back into his pocket.

'May I ask where you got that?' Claude Winnett asked excitedly.

'Not yet,' Mason told him.

The telephone rang sharply. Major Winnett moved over to the library extension, picked up the receiver, said 'Hello,' then turned to Mason. 'It's for you.'

Mason took the telephone. Drake's voice said, 'We've got something, Perry.'

'What?'

'That oblong slip of paper from the cash register. We've located the store. The girl that was on duty remembers our party. We've got a good description now. With that to go on, we had no trouble picking up his trail in a trailer camp. He registered under the name of Harry Drummond.'

'There now?' Mason asked.

'Not now. He pulled out early yesterday morning. I've got men covering every trailer camp anywhere near here. We should pick him up soon. We have the license number and everything. And here's a funny one, Perry. There's a jane looking for him.'

'You mean . . .?'

'No, not the one we're interested in, another one. She's brunette, snaky, young and tall, and she was asking the cashier about him earlier in the day. Had a good description. Wanted to know if such a man had been in.'

'Are you located there in the hotel?'

'Yes. I've fixed up an office here and have half a dozen men out on the job, with more coming in all the time.'

Mason said, 'I'll be right up.'

'Okay, be looking for you. Goodbye.'

Mason heard the click at the other end of the line but did not immediately hang up. He stood holding the receiver, frowning at the carpet.

Abruptly he heard another sharp click and the telephone bell in the library extension gave a little tinkle.

Mason dropped the receiver into place and turned to Major Winnett. 'I take it,' he said, 'you have several extensions on the phone?'

'Four,' Major Winnett said. 'No, there's five. There's one up in the observation tower. I almost forgot about that.'

'Thank you,' Mason said, and then added after a moment, 'so did I.'

VII

Paul Drake was talking on the phone as Mason entered the suite of rooms Drake was using for headquarters. In an adjoining room Della Street, a list of numbers at her elbow, was putting through a steady succession of calls.

'Come in, Perry,' Drake said, hanging up the receiver. 'I was trying to get you. We're getting results fast.'

'Shoot.'

'Our party is a man thirty-eight years old, bronzed, wears cowboy boots, a five-gallon hat, leather jacket, Pendleton trousers, rather chunky and has a wide, firm mouth. The license number of his automobile is 4E4705. He's driving a Buick and has quite an elaborate house trailer painted green on the outside with aluminium paint on the roof. Up until Saturday morning he was in the Silver Strand Trailer Camp. He left Saturday, showed up again late Monday night, pulled out again Wednesday morning and hasn't been seen since.'

'How did you get it?' Mason asked.

'Just a lot of legwork.'

'Give me the highlights.'

'We located the store that has that cash register – the only one in town. Cash register gives the time and date of sale, the amount of the items and the total. This sale was made shortly after the store opened Saturday morning, and the cashier remembers the man's general appearance. She particularly remembered the cowboy boots. We started covering trailer camps and almost immediately picked up our trail.'

'What are you doing now?'

'I've got operatives scattered around with automobiles covering every trailer camp, every possible parking place for a house trailer anywhere in this part of the country. We're working in a constantly widening circle and should turn up something soon.'

Mason took out his notebook. 'The number is 4E4705?'

'That's right.'

'Then our mysterious observer in the observation tower made a mistake in addition. Remember, we were looking for a number 4"4704. The first number must have been 4E4705 and ditto marks were beneath the E. The real total then should have been . . .'

He was interrupted by a knock on the door, a quick staccato knock which somehow contained a hint of hysteria.

Mason exchanged glances with Drake. The detective left the desk, crossed over and opened the door.

The woman who stood on the threshold was twenty-seven or twenty-eight, a tall brunette with flashing black eyes, high cheekbones and an active, slender figure. A red brimless hat perched well back on her head emphasized the glossy darkness of her hair and harmonized with the red of her carefully made-up lips.

She smiled at Paul Drake, a stage smile which showed even, white teeth. 'Are *you* Mr Drake?' she asked, glancing from him to Mason.

Drake nodded.

'May I come in?'

Drake wordlessly stood to one side.

His visitor entered the room, nodded to Perry Mason and said, 'I'm *Mrs* Drummond.'

Drake started to glance at Mason, then caught himself in time and managed to put only casual interest in his voice. 'I'm Mr Drake,' he said, 'and this is Mr Mason. Is there something in particular, Mrs Drummond?'

She said, 'You're looking for my husband.'

Drake merely raised his eyebrows.

'At the Silver Strand Trailer Camp,' she went on nervously. 'And *I'm* looking for him *too*. I wonder if we can't sort of pool information?'

Mason interposed suavely. '*Your* husband, and you're looking for him, Mrs Drummond?'

'Yes,' she said, her large dark eyes appraising the lawyer.

'How long since you've seen him?' Mason asked.

'Two months.'

'Perhaps if you want us to *pool* information, you'd better tell us a little more about the circumstances and how you happened to know we were looking for him.'

She said, 'I'd been at the Silver Strand Trailer Camp earlier in the day. The man promised me that he'd let me know if my husband returned. When your detectives appeared and started asking questions, he took the license number of their car, found out it belonged to the Drake Detective Agency and . . .' She laughed nervously and said, 'And that is where I started to do a little detective work on my own. Are you looking for him for the same reason I am?'

Mason smiled gravely. 'That brings up the question of why you're looking for him.'

She gave an indignant toss of her head. 'After all, I have nothing to conceal. We were married a little over a year ago. It didn't click. Harry is an outdoors man. He's always chasing around on the trail of some mining deal or some cattle ranch. I don't like that sort of life and . . . well, about two months ago we separated. I sued for divorce.'

'Have you got it yet?'

'Not yet. We had an understanding about a property settlement. When my lawyer sent my husband the papers, he sent them back with an insulting note and said he wouldn't pay me a red cent and that if I tried to get tough about it, he'd show that I didn't have any rights whatever.'

'Why?'

'I don't know.'

'And you want to find out just what he means by that?' Mason asked.

'That's right. And now suppose you tell me what *you* want him for. Has he done something?'

'Is he the type who would?' Mason asked.

'He's been in trouble before.'

'What sort of trouble?'

'A mining swindle.'

Drake glanced inquiringly at Mason.

'Where are you located?' Mason asked Mrs Drummond.

'I'm right here at the hotel. And don't think they're the ones who told me about Mr Drake's being here,' she added hastily. 'I found that out by . . . in another way.'

'You spoke of *pooling* information,' Mason said suggestively.

She laughed and said, 'Well, what I meant was if you find him, will you let me know? And if I find him, I could let you know. After all, he shouldn't be difficult to locate with that trailer, but I want to catch him before he can get out of the state. If I can find out where he is, I have – some papers to serve.'

'You have a car?' Mason asked.

She nodded, then added by way of explanation. 'That is one thing I salvaged out of our marriage. I made him buy me a car, and that's one of the reasons I want to see him. The car's still in his name. He agreed to let me have it as part of the property settlement, but in his letter to my lawyer he said he could even take the car away from me if I tried to make trouble. Does either of you gentlemen have any idea what he meant by that?'

Mason shook his head and Drake joined in the gesture of negation.

'Perhaps,' Mason suggested, 'we might work out something. You see, even if your assumption is correct that we are looking for your husband, we would be representing some client in the matter and would naturally have to discuss things with that client.'

'Is it because of something he's done?' she asked apprehensively. 'Is he in more trouble? Will it mean all his money will go for lawyers again, just like it did before?'

'I'm sure I couldn't tell you,' Mason said.

'That means you won't. Look, I'm in room six-thirteen. Why don't you ask your *client* to come and see me?'

'Will you be there all during the evening?' Drake asked.

'Well . . .' She hesitated. 'I'll be in and out. I'll . . . I'll tell you what I'll do. I'll keep in touch with the hotel and if there are any messages, I'll be where I can come and get them.'

She flashed them a smile, moved toward the door with quick, lithe grace, then almost as an afterthought turned and gave them her hand, glancing curiously through the open door of the adjoining room to where Della Street was seated at the telephone. Then she gave Mason another smile as the lawyer held the door open for her, and left the room, walking with quick nervous steps.

Mason closed the door and cocked a quizzical eyebrow at Paul Drake.

'The guy's wise,' Drake said. 'That means we haven't much time, Perry.'

'You think he was watching his back trail?'

Drake nodded. 'She's an alert little moll who knows her way around. This man Drummond has done something that he's trying to cover up. He left her to watch his back trail. She hypnotized the man who runs the trailer camp and then when my man showed up in an agency car —'

'But how about her asking questions at the cash-and-carry, Paul?'

Drake snapped his fingers. 'Shucks, there's nothing to *that*. That's the way she builds up a background for herself. After all, she —'

The telephone interrupted. Drake picked up the receiver, said, 'Drake talking . . . Okay, let's have it . . . When? . . . Where? . . . Okay, stay on the job . . . We'll be right down.'

Drake hung up the receiver, saying. 'Well, that's it. We've got him located.'

'Where?'

'Little down-at-the-heel trailer camp in a eucalyptus grove about three miles from here. Not much of a place, autocourt cabins in front and, as an afterthought because there was lots of room, the owner strung up some wires and advertised trailer space in the rear. The conveniences aren't too good and it's patronized mostly by people who want to save two bits a day on the regular parking rate. The chief advantage is lots of elbow-room. The grove consists of several acres, and if a man wants to walk far enough to the bath and shower, he can pick his own parking place for the trailer.'

'Any details?' Mason asked.

'One of my men just located it. The trailer came in yesterday night. The man who runs the place was busy selling gasoline at the time, and the driver of the car called out that he'd come back and register later. He tossed the man a silver dollar and the man told him to park any place he wanted to where he could find a plug for his electric connection.'

Mason said, 'Let's go. Della, you stay here and run the place. We'll telephone you in half an hour or so.'

They drove down to the trailer camp in Mason's car. Drake's operative, lounging casually in the door of one of the auto cabins, gave the detective a surreptitious signal and pointed toward the adjoining cabin.

Registering simply as 'P. Drake,' the detective rented the vacant cabin, then settled down with Perry Mason. A few moments later Drake's operative came across to join them.

'Ever met Pete Brady?' Drake asked Mason.

Mason shook hands, saying, 'I've seen him once or twice before around your office.'

'Glad to know you,' Brady said to Mason, and then to Drake, 'I'm not certain but what the guy who runs the place is getting a little suspicious. I asked too many questions.'

'What's the dope?'

'The trailer's out there attached to the car. So far, I haven't had a glimpse of the man who is in it, but it's the license number of the car we want okay – 4E4705.'

'Let's take a look around,' Mason said.

'You'll have to take it easy.' Brady warned. 'Just sort of saunter around.'

'How about the gag of buying a trailer?' Drake asked. 'Have you used that?'

Brady shook his head.

'We'll try that,' Drake said. 'You can wait here for a while. What's the guy's name who runs the place?'

'Elmo, Sidney Elmo.'

'Did he see you come over here?'

'No. I waited until he was selling gas.'

'Okay. Stick around. I'll go tell the bird that we heard one of the trailers here was for sale. He won't know anything about it. That gives us an opportunity to go sauntering around looking them over.'

Five minutes later when Drake returned, Mason joined him and they walked slowly out past the line of somewhat dilapidated cabins into the eucalyptus grove. Late afternoon shadows made the place seem cold and gloomy. The ground was still moist from the rain and the drippings of the trees when ocean fog enveloped that portion of the country.

'There's the outfit,' Drake said. 'What do we do? Go right up and knock and ask him if it's for sale?'

Mason said. 'Let's try one of the other trailers first. We can talk loud enough so our voices will carry over here.'

'Good idea,' Drake said.

'Take this one,' Mason suggested.

The two walked over to the small homemade trailer Mason had indicated. It was parked about a hundred feet from the green trailer. Electric lights showed a well-fleshed woman in her late forties cooking over the stove. On the outside, a man was taking advantage of the failing light to tinker with the bumper on the trailer. There was an Oklahoma license plate on the car.

'This the outfit that's for sale?' Mason asked.

The man looked up, a long, thin mouth twisted into a smile. He said with a drawl, 'I ain't saying yes, and I ain't saying no. You want to buy?'

'We're looking for a trailer that we heard was for sale here.'

'What sort of a trailer?'

'We just heard it was a good one.'

'That's the description of this job all right.'

Drake interposed, 'You're not the man who spoke to the manager of the Silver Strand Trailer Camp and said he wanted to sell, are you?'

'Nope. Fact is, I'm not particularly anxious to sell. But if you wanted to buy it, I'd be willing to listen.'

'We're looking for a particular trailer that's for sale,' Mason explained. 'How about that green one over there? Know anything about it?'

'No. It just came in last night.'

'Don't suppose you've talked with the people who own it?'

'I ain't seen 'em. They haven't been around all day.'

Mason said, 'That looks like it. Let's go over there, Paul.'

'Take it easy,' Mason said as they approached. 'Ever use a house trailer. Paul?'

'No. Why?'

'The steady weight of the trailer has a tendency to wear out springs. So most trailers are equipped with an auxiliary wheel which can be screwed into position when the trailer is parked.'

'There isn't any here,' Drake said.

'That's just the point. Furthermore, no spout bucket has been put out under the spout. And to cap the climax, the cord hasn't been connected with the electric outlet.'

'What are you getting at, Perry?'

By way of reply, Mason knocked loudly on the trailer door. When there was no response, the lawyer tentatively tried the knob.

The door swung open.

There was still enough afternoon light to show the sprawled figure lying on the floor. The dark pool eddying out from under the body showed little jagged streaks of irregularity, but its ominous significance could not be misjudged.

'Oh-oh!' Drake exclaimed.

Mason stepped up and entered the trailer. Carefully avoiding the red pool, he looked down at the body. Then he bent over, touched the high-heeled cowboy boot, moved it gently back and forth.

'Been dead for some time, Paul. Rigor mortis has set in.'

'Come on out,' Drake begged. 'Let's play this one on the up-and-up and notify the police.'

'Just a minute,' Mason said. 'I . . .' He bent over, and as he did so a shaft of light struck his face.

'What's that?' Drake asked.

Mason moved slightly so that the beam of light struck his eyes.

'That,' he announced, 'is a hole in this trailer, directly in line with the window of that Oklahoma trailer. Light from the window over there where the woman is cooking comes through the hole in this trailer. The hole could have been made by a bullet.'

'Okay, Perry. Let's notify the police.'

Mason said, 'First I want to find out a little more about that Oklahoma trailer.'

'For the luvva Mike, Perry, have a heart! You're in the clear on this one – so far.'

Mason, moving cautiously, left the trailer. He hesitated a moment when he stepped to the ground. Then he carefully polished the doorknob with his handkerchief.

'That's removing evidence,' Drake said. 'There are other prints there besides yours.'

'How do you know?'

'It stands to reason.'

'You can't prove it,' Mason said. 'The murderer probably wiped his fingerprints off the door just as I did.'

Mason walked back to the trailer with the Oklahoma license. The man, still bent over the bumper at the rear of the trailer, seemed to be working aimlessly, stalling for time. The position of his head indicated an interest in what had been going on over at the other trailer.

'That the one?' he asked as Mason approached.

'I don't know. No one seems to be home.'

'I ain't seen 'em leave. They couldn't go very far without their car.'

'Seen any visitors over there?' Mason asked casually.

'Not today. There was a young woman called last night.'

'What time?'

'I don't know. We'd gone to bed. Her headlights shone in the window and woke me up when she came. I sat up in bed and looked out the window.'

'See her plain?'

'Yeah – a redhead. Checkered suit – trim-looking package.'

'She go in?'

'I guess so. She switched off her lights and I went back to sleep.

Woke me up again when she left. Her car backfired a couple of times.'

Mason glanced at Drake. 'I'd like to find these people.'

'I think there's only one – a man. He drove in last night and had quite a bit of trouble backing the trailer around. You take one of these big trailers and it's quite a job to park it. You try to back up and everything's just reversed from what it is when you're backing just a car. We went to bed pretty early and sometime after I'd got to sleep this other car came up. What really woke me up was head-lights shining in my window. I looked out and seen this woman.'

'Remember what sort of car she was driving?'

'It was a rented car.'

'How do you know?'

'From the gasoline rationing stamp on the windshield.'

'Your wife didn't wake up?'

'No.'

'How long have *you* been here?' Mason asked.

'What's it to you?'

'Nothing.'

'I thought not,' the man said, suddenly suspicious, and then after a moment added, 'You're asking a lot of questions.'

'Sorry,' Mason said.

The man hesitated a moment, then, by way of dismissal, turned back to the bumper.

Mason glanced significantly at Paul Drake. Silently the two walked away.

'Okay, Paul,' Mason said in a low voice. 'Get Della on the phone. Tell her to put operatives on every drive-yourself car agency within a radius of fifty miles and see if we can find where the woman rented the car. When we spot the place. I'll handle the rest of it.'

'I don't like it,' Drake said.

'I don't like it myself,' Mason told him. 'But the young woman who called there last night was Marcia Winnett.'

'And her car backfired,' Drake said dryly.

Mason met his eyes. 'Her car backfired, Paul. And in case it ever becomes necessary, remember that the only person who heard it said it was a backfire.'

Drake nodded gloomily. 'Not that *that* will do any good, Perry.'

'It keeps us in the clear, Paul. You don't rush to the police to report that someone's car backfired.'

'When you've discovered a body, you do.'

'Who knows we've discovered any body?'

'I do.'

Mason laughed. 'Back to the hotel, Paul. Try to trace that car. And just to be on the safe side, find out where Mrs Drummond was last night.'

VIII

The last task Mason had given Paul Drake turned out to be simple. Mrs Drummond had been trying to locate her husband in the nearby trailer camps all the evening before, and she had arranged with a police officer who was off duty to accompany her.

Locating the rented car in which the girl in the checkered suit went to the trailer camp was another matter.

Despite all of Drake's efficiency, it was nearing eight o'clock when his detectives uncovered the lead Mason wanted. A man who operated a car rental agency in one of the coast cities, some twenty-five miles from Silver Strand Beach, had rented a car to a young woman who wore a checkered suit and who answered the description of Marcia Winnett.

Drake looked up from the telephone. 'Want my man to try to pick up the trail from there or do you want to do it, Perry?'

Mason said, 'I'll do it, Paul. And it might be best to let your man think that that isn't the trail we want.'

'Okay,' Drake said, and then into the telephone, 'Describe her, Sam. Uh-huh . . . uh-huh, well, that's not the one. Keep working. Cover those other agencies and then report.'

Drake hung up the phone. 'Want me to come along, Perry?'

'Della and I'll handle it.' Mason said. 'Start calling your men in. Let them feel it turned out to be a false lead. And you'd better start checking on Mrs Drummond, Paul. I wouldn't like to have her show up right now.'

Drake nodded and said solicitously, 'Watch your step, Perry.'

'I'm watching it. Come on, Della.'

The man who operated the car rental agency which had furnished a car to Marcia Winnett was not particularly communicative. It took diplomacy to get him in the mood to talk. Even then he confined his information to bare essentials.

He had never seen his customer before. She gave her name as Edith Bascom. She said her mother had died and it was necessary for her to use a car in connection with handling the estate. She was registered at the local hotel.

'Do you check on these stories?' Mason asked. 'Or do you just rent cars?'

'Sometimes we just rent cars. Sometimes we check.'

'What did you do in this case?'

'Cars are scarce now,' the man said. 'We checked.'

'How?'

The man picked up a daily paper dated the day before and indicated the obituary column. Mason followed the man's finger to the stereotyped announcement of the death of Mrs Shirley Bascom and the statement that funeral arrangements would be private.

Mason said, 'I guess that covers it all right.'

'What's your interest in it?'

'I'm a lawyer.'

'I see. Well, she's okay. Rather upset on account of her mother's death, but a nice girl. You'll find her in the Palace Hotel, two blocks down the street.'

'You checked on that?'

'I told you cars are scarce,' the man said. 'I checked on it.'

It was but a matter of routine for Mason and his secretary to get the number of the room which had been assigned to Edith Bascom. Two minutes later Mason was knocking on the door.

There was no answer. Mason tried the knob. The door was locked.

Mason made a swift survey of the hall, stooped and held out his hands. 'Step on my hands, Della. Take a quick look through the transom.'

She braced herself with a hand on his shoulder, caught the lower ledge of the transom and peered through.

Mason, with his right hand on her hip, steadying her, felt her body stiffen. Then she was scrambling to get down.

'Chief,' she said in an ominous whisper, 'she's stretched out on the bed. She's . . . terribly still.'

'Lights on?'

'No, but the shade is up and there's enough light coming in from the electric sign in front to make out the form on the bed.'

Mason said, 'There's a spring lock on the door . . . Better take another look, Della. See if she's breathing and . . . hold it. Here comes a chambermaid.'

The chambermaid who wearily approached was aroused only momentarily from the lethargy of overwork by the bill Mason pushed into her palm.

'My wife and I seem to have left our key downstairs. If you could let us in, it would save us a trip down . . .'

'It's against the rules,' she said, then added tonelessly, 'but I guess it's okay.' Producing her passkey, she clicked back the latch on the door.

Mason boldly pushed open the door, stood aside for Della to enter, then followed her into the dimly lighted room and closed the door behind him.

Della Street crossed over to the woman lying on the bed, as Mason groped for her pulse.

'She's alive!' Della Street said.

'The light,' Mason said crisply. 'Pull the curtains first.'

Della Street jerked down the shades, ran over and switched on the light.

Mason glanced at the bottle of sleeping tablets by the side of the bed, picked up the newspaper on the floor and glanced at it.

'She must have taken them yesterday,' Della said. 'We'll need a doctor and –'

'This afternoon,' Mason interrupted curtly. 'This is a late edition of the afternoon paper.'

He dropped the paper, shook the sleeper and said, 'Towels, Della. Cold water.'

Della Street grabbed towels and turned on the cold water in the bathroom. Mason slapped Marcia Winnett with cold towels until the eyelids flickered open.

'What is it?' She asked thickly.

Mason said to Della Street, 'Run down to the drugstore, Della. Get an emetic. Have room service send up some black coffee.'

'How about a doctor?'

'Not if we can avoid it. Let's hope she hasn't had the tablets down long enough to get the full effects. Get an emetic.'

Marcia Winnett tried to say something, but the words were unintelligible. She dropped back against Mason's shoulder.

Mason calmly started removing her blouse. Della Street dashed from the room, headed for the drugstore.

Thirty minutes later Mason and Della Street assisted Marcia Winnett from the bathroom. There was a dead, lacklustre look about her eyes, but she could talk now, and the coffee was beginning to take effect.

Mason said, 'Concentrate on what I'm telling you. I'm a lawyer. I'm retained to represent you.'

'By whom?'

'Your husband.'

'No, no, he mustn't . . . he can't . . .'

Mason said, 'I'm *your* lawyer. Your husband retained me to help you. I don't have to tell him anything.'

She sighed wearily and said, 'Let me go. It's better this way.'

Mason shook her once more into wakefulness. 'You went riding Monday morning. You talked with a man in a trailer. He made demands on you. You had to have money and have it at once. You didn't dare to ask your husband for it.'

Mason waited for an answer. She made none. Her eyelids drooped and raised as if by a conscious effort.

Mason said, 'You went back to the house. You cancelled the insurance on your jewelry because you were too conscientious to stick the insurance company. You arranged to have some repairs made to a window on the side of your bedroom so a ladder would be handy. You got up in the night, went out to the balcony, and dumped your jewelry into the swallow's nest. Then you started screaming.'

Her face might have been a wooden mask.

Mason went on, 'You had waited until Tuesday to stage the burglary. You knew that it would be too obvious if it happened Monday night, the day you had cancelled the insurance. Wednesday morning you found an opportunity to get most of the jewelry out of the swallow's nest. There was one piece you overlooked. Now then, suppose you tell me what happened after that.'

She said, with the drowsy calm of one who discusses a distant event which can have no personal bearing, 'I wanted to kill him. I can't remember whether I did or not.'

'Did you shoot him?'

'I can't remember a thing that happened after . . . after I left the house.'

Mason glanced at Della Street, said, 'If I'm going to help you, I have to know what hold that man had on you.'

'His name is Harry Drummond. He was my first husband.'

'You were divorced?'

'I *thought* I was divorced. There were reasons why I couldn't go to Nevada. I gave him the money. He went to live in Nevada.

'From time to time he sent me reports of how things were coming. Twice he asked for more money. Then he wrote me the divorce had been granted. He was lying. He'd gambled the money away. There never had been a divorce.'

'When did you find this out?' Mason asked.

'Monday morning,' she said. 'He was clever. He'd kept in touch with me. He knew I rode down along that bridle path. He parked his trailer there. Mrs Victoria Winnett doesn't like to have people camp there, so I rode down to ask whoever was in the trailer to please move on down to the public campgrounds.'

'You had no idea who was in the trailer?'

'Not until Harry opened the door and said, "Hello, Marcia. I thought it was about time you were showing up".'

'What did he want?'

'Money.'

'And he threatened you with – what?'

'The one weapon Claude couldn't stand, notoriety.'

'So you promised to get him money?'

'I promised to get him my jewelry. He had to have money at once. He said someone was putting screws on him for cash.'

'You were to meet him there when?'

'Wednesday morning.'

'So you manipulated this fake burglary on Tuesday night after cancelling your insurance on Monday. Then you took him the jewelry. Did he ask you how you had managed to secure the jewelry?'

'Yes. I told him the whole story. I told him it was all right to pawn it because the Winnetts wouldn't report the burglary to the police.'

'And then what happened?'

'I can't remember.'

'What can't you remember?'

'I can't remember a thing from the time . . . from the time Harry took the jewelry. He made some sneering remark, and I remember becoming very angry and then . . . then my mind went entirely blank.'

'Did you have a revolver with you when you went down to the trailer Wednesday morning?' Mason asked.

'Yes.'

'Where did you get it?'

'From a bureau drawer.'

'Whose gun was it?'

'I don't know. I think it was . . . Mrs Winnett's gun – pearl-handled. I thought I might need some protection. It was a crazy idea. I took it along.'

'Where is that gun now?'

'I don't know. I tell you I can't remember a thing that happened after I gave him the jewelry and he made that sneering remark.'

'Did he make some further demands on you? Did he tell you you had to meet him at an isolated trailer park last night?'

'I don't know. I can't remember.'

'*Did* you meet him there?'

'I can't remember.'

'Did you,' Mason asked, "rent an automobile from a drive-yourself agency about two blocks down the street?'

Her forehead puckered into a frown. 'I seem to have some faint recollection of doing something like that, but I . . .' She shook her head. 'No, it eludes me. I can't remember.'

Mason said impatiently, 'Why don't you come clean? You were clever enough to read the obituary notices and pretend to be the daughter of a woman who had just died. I'm trying to help you. At least tell me what I'm up against.'

'I don't know. I can't remember.'

Mason motioned toward the bottle of sleeping tablets. 'And you thought you could take this way out and it would help?'

'I don't know. I guess I must have been . . . perhaps I was nervous. Perhaps I hadn't been sleeping at all and I just took too large a dose. I can't remember.'

Mason turned to Della Street. 'Willing to take a chance, Della?'

She nodded. 'Anything you say, chief.'

Mason said. 'Put her in a car. Take her into Los Angeles. See that there's plenty of money in her purse. Take her to a *private* hospital. Under no circumstances give *your* name or address. Put on the rush act. Tell the first nurse you meet that this woman accosted you on the street and asked you to help her find out who she was. That you think it's a racket of some sort, but that she seems to have money, and if she needs any assistance, the hospital is the place where she should be able to get it. Then turn and get out of the door fast.'

Della nodded.

Mason turned to Marcia Winnett. 'You heard what I said?'

'Yes . . . I . . . you mustn't take chances for me. I know that I must have killed him. I can't remember the details, Mr Mason, but I killed him. I *think* it was in self-defense. I can't remember.'

'I know,' Mason said gently. 'Don't worry about it. Remember you're a widow now. Don't get your memory back, and the next time you see me remember I'm a stranger. I'm going to try to help you. Get started, Della. Drive with the window open. Let her get lots of cold air. Get her to a hospital.'

'How'll *you* get back?' Della asked.

'I'll have one of Drake's men pick me up.'

Della looked at Marcia with cold contempt. 'If you ask me,' she blurted indignantly, 'this act of hers . . .'

Mason gently closed one eye in an owlish wink. 'Take her to the hospital, Della . . . and be sure you get out from under.'

IX

The gravel on the driveway caused the wheels to slide as Mason slammed on the brakes. The car skidded at a sharp angle and Mason didn't even bother to straighten it out. He snapped off the lights and the ignition, leaped out and headed up the steps of the Winnett mansion, pushed open the door, and strode into the drawing room unannounced.

Mrs Victoria Winnett and Daphne Rexford were lingering over liqueurs, talking in low voices.

Mrs Winnett's smile was distantly friendly. '*Really*, Mr Mason,' she said, 'you're rather late – for dinner.'

The lawyer merely nodded, glancing at Daphne Rexford.

Mrs Winnett's reached for the bell. 'I presume I can get you something,' she said. 'But after this, if you don't mind –'

'Let the food go,' Mason said. 'I want to talk with you.'

The finger which had been touching the bell remained motionless. She said, '*Really*, Mr Mason,' in a voice that indicated a polite rebuke.

Daphne Rexford hurriedly arose. 'If you'll excuse me, I have a telephone call I want to make . . .'

'Sit down, my dear. After all, I can't permit this human tornado to come bursting in on our tête-à-tête with . . .'

Mason caught Daphne Rexford's eye and jerked his head. She made a feeble attempt at a smile and left the room.

'Really, Mr Mason,' Mrs Winnett said, her voice now quite cold. 'My attachment to my son is such that I am willing to make all the allowances for his friends. Even so . . .'

She let her unfinished sentence carry its own meaning.

Mason drew up a chair and sat down. 'Where's the major?'

'He was called out about twenty minutes ago.'

'You're fond of Daphne Rexford, aren't you?'

'Of course.'

'Was she in the observation tower Monday?'

'Really, Mr Mason. I'm not on the witness stand.'

'You're going to be.' Mason said.

'I'm afraid you've been drinking.'

'If you think this is a joke,' Mason said, 'just keep on stalling. Time is precious. The officers may be out here any minute.'

'Officers?'

'Officers. Cops. Bulls. Detectives. Plain-clothes men. Newspaper photographers. Walking around here with their hats on, throwing cigarettes on the rugs, taking flashlight pictures with captions – "Society Leader Insists on Innocence".'

That last did it. Mason saw her wince.

'You're a good poker player, but you can't bluff now. This is a showdown, Mrs Winnett.'

'Just what do you want?'

'To know all that you know.'

She took a quick breath. 'I know some trouble has developed between Marcia and Claude. I think that Marcia has left him. I hope she has.'

'Why?'

'Because I don't feel that they are destined to be happy together . . .'

'No, I mean why has she left him?'

'I don't know.'

'Make a guess.'

'I can't.'

'You know something about what happened on Monday?'

'On *Monday?* No.'

'Was Daphne in the cupola on Monday?'

'I think she was.'

'Did she come to you and tell you anything about what she saw either Monday or Wednesday?'

'Mr Mason, you're being impertinent!'

Mason said, 'You've found out something about Marcia. You thought she had involved the family good name, and took it on yourself to try to avoid notoriety. Your attempt backfired. I'm trying to find out just how badly it backfired.'

'You can't prove any of these things you're saying, Mr Mason.'

'That,' Mason said, 'is only because I haven't the facilities at my command that the police have. The police may prove it.'

'They won't,' she said coldly. 'I have told you absolutely everything I know.'

Mason pushed back his chair, started for the door which led to the patio, then abruptly whirled, tiptoed swiftly back to the drawing room door, and jerked it open.

Daphne Rexford, plainly embarrassed, tried to pretend she had just been approaching the door. 'Heavens,' she said, laughing, 'I thought we were going to have a collision, Mr Mason. You seem in a hurry.' She tried to push easily on past him.

Mason barred her way. 'You were listening.'

'Mr Mason, how *dare* you say anything like that?'

'Come in,' Mason said. 'Let's have it out. Let's . . . no, on second thought, I think I'll talk with you alone. Come on.'

Mason took her arm. She drew back.

Mrs Winnett said, 'Mr Mason is completely overstepping the prerogatives of a guest. I dislike to ask him to leave in my son's absence, but . . .'

Mason said to Daphne Rexford, 'Police are going to be swarming over the place before midnight. Do you want to talk to me or do you want to talk to them?'

Daphne Rexford said over her shoulder to Mrs Winnett, 'Good heavens, Victoria, let's humour the man! I'll be back within a few minutes.'

Without waiting for an answer from Victoria Winnett, she smiled disarmingly at Mason and moved away from the drawing room. 'Come on, where do you want to talk?'

'Over here's good enough,' Mason said, stopping in a corner of the library.

Daphne Rexford stood facing him. 'What,' she asked in a low voice, 'are the police going to be investigating?'

Mason met her eyes. 'Murder.'

'Who . . . who was killed?'

'Let's talk first about what *you* know,' Mason said. 'You're the one who has the trick right eye. Mrs Winnett has been covering up for you.'

'I'm afraid I don't know what you mean.'

'Whenever you look through the binoculars,' Mason explained, 'you have to move the right eyepiece quite a distance in order to see clearly, don't you?'

'What if I do?'

Mason said, '*You* were the one who was watching Marcia on Monday. What did you see?'

'Nothing. I –'

'Were you here Monday? Were you in the observation cupola?'

'I believe I was.'

'You're over here quite a bit?'

'Yes. Victoria and I are great friends. She's an older woman, of course, but I like her. I like what she stands for and –'

'And like to be near Major Winnett and see as much of him as you can?'

'Certainly not,' she said indignantly.

'We'll let it go at that for the time being,' Mason said. 'Now, about Monday, what did you see?'

'Nothing. I –'

'You were up in the tower?'

'Yes. I go there quite frequently. I study birds, and I write poetry. I can get inspiration up there, and –'

'And keep an eye on Major Winnett's wife when she's around the grounds, I suppose?'

'Mr Mason, that's unfair and untrue.'

'All right. You saw her Monday. What did you see?'

'I . . . nothing.'

Mason said, 'You saw her go into that orange trailer that was parked down in the trees. You watched her –'

'It wasn't orange. It was green.'

Mason grinned at her.

'All right,' she said. 'Don't think you're trapping me. I just happened to notice Marcia riding, and then I saw a house trailer parked in the trees.'

'Did you see her go in?'

'I saw her tie up her horse and walk over toward the trailer. I wasn't interested. I returned to the poetry I was writing.'

'How long was she in there?'

'I don't know.'

'Why did you watch her?'

'I didn't watch her. I was looking at birds.'

'You had a pencil and a pad of paper up there with you?'

'Yes, of course. I told you I write poetry. One doesn't write on the walls, Mr Mason. I keep pencil and paper in the drawer of the table up there.'

'You used the binocular to get the license number of the automobile. You marked it down, didn't you?'

'No.'

'When were you up there last writing poetry?'

'Why . . . why, today.'

'Do you go up there every day?'

'Not every day, but quite frequently.'

'Have you been up every day this week?'

'I . . . I guess I have. Yes.'

The telephone rang, a sharp, strident, shrill summons.

Mason waited, listening, heard the butler answer it. Then the butler walked with unhurried dignity across the library to the drawing room and said something to Mrs Winnett. She arose and went to the telephone. Mason heard her say, 'Hello, Claude darling . . . Yes, dear . . . he's here . . ., I'm afraid, Claude, that there has been some misunderstanding. Mr Mason's activities are hardly such as one would connect with a mining matter. He has shown quite an interest in what Marcia –'

Mason walked over, gently pushed her aside, took the receiver from her hand and said into the telephone, 'Okay, Major, I've got it now. Get out here at once.'

Major Winnett's voice was harsh with anger. 'Just what do you mean, Mr Mason? I'm afraid that you and I –'

Mason interrupted. 'Your mother is trying to protect somebody. Daphne Rexford is trying to protect somebody. There's only one person I can think of whom they'd both go to such lengths to protect. That's you. If you get out here fast, we *may* be able to beat the police to it.'

'What do you mean?'

'You know damn well what I mean,' Mason said and hung up.

X

Major Winnett's limp was more noticeable as he moved across the drawing room to confront Perry Mason. 'I don't know exactly what's been going on here,' he said angrily. 'I don't know what prerogatives you have assumed, Mr Mason. But as far as I'm concerned, our relationship is ended.'

Mason said, 'Sit down.'

'I'm waiting to drive you to town, Mason, in case you don't have a car. If you do, I'll go with you to your room and you can pack up.'

Mason said, 'As nearly as I can put things together, you had previously discovered the trailer parked down in the trees. You were suspicious. You went up to the observation tower and saw Marcia go to the trailer and then later on saw the car and trailer go away. You took down the license number of the car. You looked up the man who owned that car. After that you kept a pretty close watch on what was going on.

'You didn't say anything when Marcia canceled the insurance on her jewelry and then had such an opportune burglary. You were very careful not to call the police because you knew the police would tab it as an inside job. You let your wife think it was because your mother didn't want any notoriety, but you got the jewelry and hid it in that twelve-gauge shotgun. After that you kept a pretty good watch on your wife. Where did you get the jewelry?'

'Mason,' Winnett said coldly, 'in case you don't leave this house at once, I'm going to call the servants and have you put out.'

Mason brushed aside Major Winnett's angry statement with a gesture. 'You'll have to hire more servants, then,' he said, and went on. 'When the trailer came back on Wednesday and Marcia went down there the second time, you decided to investigate. When you got down there, you found you had a fight on your hands. You killed Harry Drummond. Then you locked up the trailer, came back to the house and waited until dark. Then you took the trailer with its gruesome evidence of murder, drove to a trailer camp –'

'Mason, watch what you're saying. By heaven, I'll throw you out myself!'

'– parked the trailer,' Mason went on, as smoothly as though Major Winnett had said nothing, 'but only after some difficulty, then got out and went home. Then you felt it would add an artistic touch to have two shots fired so the *time* of the killing could be definitely fixed. So you went back, sneaked into the trailer park, stood in the dark *outside* the trailer and fired two shots in the air.

'You didn't realize that Marcia had been following you, and when she heard those shots she naturally thought you had killed Drummond out of jealousy, decided that she loved you too much to let you take the rap, and so skipped out. That's the reason you didn't go to a detective agency to get someone to try to find your wife. You wanted a lawyer who specialized in murder cases, *because you knew there was going to be a murder case.*'

Major Winnett snapped his fingers. 'A lot of half-baked theories!'

'You see,' Mason went on, 'you made a couple of fatal mistakes. One of them was that the first shot you fired missed Drummond and went clean through the trailer, leaving a hole in the double walls that clearly shows the direction taken by the bullet. When you parked that trailer in the automobile camp under the eucalyptus trees, it was dark and you didn't take the precaution of noticing where a bullet fired under such circumstances would have hit. That was a mistake, Major. As it happened, the hole in the trailer was lined up absolutely with the window of an adjoining trailer.

'At first the police will think the shot might have been fired from the other trailer. Then they'll make a more careful investigation and find that the direction of the bullet was the other way. Then they'll know that the murder wasn't committed there at the trailer park. There's another little thing you hadn't thought of. At the time you moved the trailer, the body had been dead for sometime but the pool of blood hadn't entirely coagulated. Near the centre of the pool there was blood that was still liquid. It spread around when the trailer swayed from side to side in going over irregularities in the road. That is what gives the pool of clotted blood the peculiar appearance of having little jagged streamers flowing from it.'

Major Winnett was silent and motionless. His eyes were fixed on Mason with cold concentration. The anger had left his face, and it was quite plain the man's mind was desperately turning over Mason's words.

'So,' Mason went on, 'you knew that when the police started to investigate, they would find the dead man had been Marcia's first husband. You knew they would then start looking for her. When they found that she had skipped out, you knew what would happen. And so, you came to me.'

Major Winnett cleared his throat. 'You made a statement that Marcia had followed me. Do you have any evidence to back that up?'

Mason said, 'It's a logical deduction from –'

'That's where you're wrong. Come to my room. I want to talk with you.'

Mason said, 'You haven't much time. The police have found the body. They're going to be out here looking for Marcia as soon as they have completed an identification and checked up on the man's history.'

'All right,' Winnett said, 'come with me. Mother, you and Daphne pretend you haven't heard any of this. I'll talk with you later.'

Major Winnett led the way to his room, opened a portable bar and took out a bottle of Scotch.

Mason refused with a gesture, then when Winnett had poured out a drink, the lawyer reached over and poured half of that drink back into the bottle. 'Just enough to give yourself a bracer,' he warned, 'not enough to give you a letdown afterward. You're going to be talking with the police pretty soon. Start talking with me now.'

Winnett said, 'I didn't know Marcia went to visit the man in the trailer on Monday. I did know that Marcia went to the trailer on Wednesday.'

'*How* did you know?'

'I was watching her.'

'Why were you watching her?'

'Someone told me she had been to the trailer on Monday.'

'Who?'

'My mother.'

'What did you do?'

'After she left the trailer on Wednesday, I went down there to see who was in the trailer and see why my wife was having a rendezvous.'

'What did you find?'

'I found the man dead. I found Marcia's jewelry spread out on a table in front of him. I realized what must have happened. I saw that one shot had gone into the man's heart. One had apparently gone past his head and into the wall of the trailer.'

'All right,' Mason said sarcastically, 'it's your story. Go ahead with it. What did you do then?'

'I took Marcia's jewelry and locked up the trailer. I came home. I waited until after dark, then I moved the trailer to a trailer camp I knew of, where I parked it. I got out and left the trailer and walked to where I had parked my own car earlier in the day. I had driven home before I realized that I could completely throw the police off the scent by letting it appear the murder had been committed late that night in the trailer camp. So I returned, stood near the trailer, fired two shots into the air, then ran to my car and came back home. I thought Marcia was in bed. But when, after a couple of hours, I went up, I found she wasn't there, that she had left that note. That's why I came to you. I wanted your help. That's the truth, so help me.'

Mason said, 'You wrote down the license number of that automobile. Later on you tried to cover it up by adding some words and some figures. Then you added the total –'

'Mr Mason, I swear I did not.'

'Who did then?'

'I don't know.'

'Someone wrote down the license number of the car,' Mason said, '4E4705, then tried to camouflage it by working in a number of other figures and writing at the top *These numbers called* – but a mistake was made in the addition. I . . . wait a minute . . .'

Mason stood motionless, his eyes level-lidded with concentration.

'Perhaps,' Major Winnett suggested, 'it was . . .'

Mason motioned him to silence, then, after a moment, picked up the telephone, dialed the hotel where Drake had established an office, and when he had Drake on the line, said, 'Hello, Paul.

Perry talking. I think I've got it. There wasn't any mistake in the addition.'

'I don't get it,' Drake said. 'The total should be 49"37818. Actually it's 49"37817.'

'And that figure is right,' Mason said. "The number we want is 4E4704.'

'But the license number was 4E4705.'

Mason said, 'What happens when you have two cars? You are given license numbers in chronological order. Look up license number 4E4704. You can start your search in room six-thirteen there at the hotel. Make it snappy.'

Mason slammed up the telephone receiver and nodded to Major Winnett. 'We've got one more chance. It's slim. The next time you go to a lawyer, don't be so damn smart. Tell him the truth. Where's your mother's room?'

'In the other wing at the far end of the corridor.'

'And the nurse's room?' Mason asked. 'That must be a communicating room?'

'It is.'

Mason said, 'Let's go.'

Helen Custer, answering their knock, seemed somewhat flustered. 'Why, good evening. I, ah . . . is there something . . .'

Mason pushed his way into the room. Major Winnett hesitated a moment, then followed. Mason kicked the door shut.

'Police are on their way out here,' Mason said to the nurse.

'The police? What for?'

'To arrest you.'

'For what?'

Mason said, 'That's up to you.'

'What do you mean?'

Mason said, 'Playing it one way, it's blackmail. Playing it the other way, it's being an accessory after the fact on a murder charge. You'd better take the rap for blackmail.'

'I . . . I . . . why, *what* are you talking about?'

Mason said, 'I've practiced law long enough to know that a man should never torture clues to make them point in the direction he thinks they should go. When that column of figures added up to 49E37817 and I thought it should have been

49E37818, I assumed a mistake had been made in the addition. It wasn't a mistake. You marked down the number *Cal* 4E4704. You wanted to preserve that number but you didn't want anyone to think that it had any significance, so you added the words at the top, *These numbers,* and then inserted *led* after the *Cal,* so that made it read. These numbers called. Then you added other numbers after that number and then totaled the sum. Now then, you probably have less than five minutes to tell us why you wrote down 4E4704.'

She glanced from Mason to Major Winnett. There was dismay in her eyes. 'What makes you think I –'

Mason took out his watch, said, 'If the police get here first, you'll be an accessory after the fact. If you use your head, you *may* be able to get by with a rap for attempted blackmail.'

'I . . . I . . . oh, Mr Mason. I can't . . .'

Mason watched the hand ticking off the seconds.

'All right,' she blurted. 'It was yesterday morning. I was looking for Mrs Victoria Winnett. I thought she was up in the observation tower. I went up there. She wasn't there. The binoculars were adjusted so they pointed down to that grove of trees. I just happened to look through them and saw the trailer. A light coupé was parked beside the big Buick that was attached to the trailer. A man and a woman were having a struggle of some sort. The man tried to strike her and the woman reached into her blouse. I saw the flash of a gun, then another flash. The man staggered back and the woman calmly closed the door of the trailer, got in her car and drove away.

'Through the binoculars I got a look at the number of her automobile. It was Cal 4E4704. I wrote it down on a piece of paper, intending to tell the police. Then . . . well, then I . . . thought . . . I . . .'

'What did you do with the pieces of paper?' Mason asked.

'After a moment I realized that perhaps I could . . . well, you know. So I changed the focus on the binoculars back to –'

'So what did you do?' Mason asked.

'I didn't want that number to seem too conspicuous. I had written Cal 4E4704, so I wrote down other things, just as you said.'

'The first number you wrote on a single sheet of paper that was on the table and not on the pad. When you wrote the rest of it, you had placed the paper on the pad.'

'I . . . I guess I did.'

Mason pointed to the telephone. 'Ring up police head-quarters,' he said. 'Tell them what you saw. Tell them that it's been bothering you, that you thought you should have reported it to the police, but that Mrs Winnett is so opposed to any form of publicity that you didn't know just what to do; that tonight you asked Mrs Winnett about it and she told you to telephone the police at once; that the reason you didn't do so before was because the trailer was gone when you looked again and you supposed that the man hadn't been hurt and had driven the trailer away.'

'If I do that,'' she said, "then I . . .'

'Then you stand about one chance in ten of beating the rap all around,' Mason said grimly. 'Don't do it, and you're stuck. What did you do – actually, I mean?'

'I looked up the license number. I found that the car was registered in the name of a Mrs Harry Drummond. I located her, and while I wasn't crude or anything . . . I wanted to open up a beauty shop and . . . well, she agreed to finance me.'

Once more Mason pointed to the telephone. 'Get police headquarters. Come on, Major. Let's go.'

Out in the corridor Major Winnett said, 'But how about my wife, Mason? How about my wife? That's the thing that bothers me. That –'

'And it damned well should bother you,' Mason said. 'She must have seen you driving the trailer Wednesday night and followed you to the place where you parked it. She went in, found Drummond dead and thought you had been trying to avenge the family's good name. You can see now what happened. She gave Drummond money to get a divorce. He told her he'd secured one. She married again. Drummond made the mistake of also marrying again. When the blowoff came, his second wife threatened to prosecute him for bigamy unless he gave her money. The only way he had to get money was to put the heat on Marcia. She was too conscientious to ask you for money or to try to stick the insurance company for money, so she staged a fake burglary, cached her jewelry in the swallow's nest, then turned over the jewelry to him. When the second Mrs Drummond came for her money, all her husband had to offer her was jewelry. She thought it was hot. That started a fight and she shot him. And probably shot him in self-defense at that.'

'But how am I going to explain – about moving the body?' Major Winnett asked.

Mason looked at him pityingly. 'You're not going to explain one damn thing,' he said. 'What do you think you have a lawyer for? Get in my car. Leave the nurse to put the police on a hot trail.'

XI

It was nearing midnight when Perry Mason and Paul Drake walked into metropolitan police headquarters with a description of Marcia Winnett and a series of photographs.

'Of course,' Mason explained to Sergeant Dorset, 'the major doesn't want any publicity. She had a spell of amnesia several years ago. He's afraid it *may* have returned.'

Sergeant Dorset frowned down at a memo on his desk. 'We've picked up a woman who answers that description – amnesia – a hospital telephoned in the report. How does it happen *you're* mixed in the case, Mason?'

'I handle the Winnetts' business.'

'The deuce you do!'

'That's right.'

Dorset regarded the memo on his desk. 'The county teletype says a man named Drummond was murdered. Mrs Winnett's nurse saw it all, phoned in a report. She had the license number of the murder car, Drummond's wife's.'

'Indeed,' Mason said, his voice showing courteous interest, but nothing else. 'May we take a look at this amnesia case now? The major is very anxious.'

'And,' Dorset went on, 'when the county officers picked up Drummond's wife, she swore that not only was the killing in self-defense, but that the nurse had been blackmailing her. The nurse called her a liar Mrs Drummond's confession puts her in a poor position to claim blackmail. I understand the county is so pleased with having cracked the murder case they're washing their hands of all the rest of it.'

Mason glared at Sergeant Dorset. 'Will you kindly tell me what all this has to do with Major Winnett's wife?'

Dorset sighed. 'I wish to hell I knew,' he said, and then added significantly, 'but I'll bet a hundred to one we never find out now.'

Mason said, 'Come down to earth. That murder case is county. The sheriff's office wouldn't like a city dick sticking his nose in.'

Dorset nodded. 'And by the same sign the way you've arranged it, the amnesia case is city and the county men won't mess around with *that*.'

He regarded the lawyer with a certain scowling respect.

Mason said very positively. 'I don't see what the murder has to do with all this if the sheriff's office has a solution and a confession, but one thing I do know is that if you have Major Winnett's wife here she's suffering from a nervous ailment and if you make it worse with a lot of fool notions, you'll wish you hadn't. Do I get her now, or do I get a *habeas corpus?*'

'Hell, you get her now,' Dorset said disgustedly. 'I can't help feeling that if I knew everything you'd been doing in the last twelve hours I'd get a promotion, and if I try to find out, I'll be back pounding pavements. Damn it!'

He picked up the telephone and said into the transmitter, 'Send that amnesia case number eighty-four on the night bulletin up to my office.'

WAITING FOR ALAINA

O'Neil De Noux

LaStanza stopped beneath one of the black wrought iron street lights common to the lower French Quarter and rechecked the address written inside the high heel shoe he carried in his left hand. Printed on the inner cushion in blue ball-point pen ink was the address 1212 Dauphine. He tucked the red high heel under his left arm, loosened his dark blue tie and pulled his portable police radio from the rear pocket of his dress black pants.

He called his sergeant. '*3124 to 3122.*'

'*Go ahead.*'

'*I'm at the house.*'

'*10-4.*'

LaStanza turned off the radio and slipped it back into his rear pocket. He wiped his brow with the sleeve of his gray sport coat. Even with the sun down, it was still steamy in New Orleans. The humidity hovered near a hundred percent. He crossed Dauphine and stood in front of a prim yellow, two-story wooden house with a large brass '1212' plaque next to its shuttered front door. He eased through the wrought iron gate, took the four steps up to the front gallery and rang the bell. Hiding the high heel behind his back, he withdrew his credentials and waited.

The door opened. LaStanza recognized the tall, blond haired man in the smoking jacket and cravat, a brandy snifter in his left hand.

'Police,' LaStanza said, opening his credentials for the man. 'I'm Detective LaStanza. Homicide.'

The man's green eyes opened slightly. His eyes were more aqua than LaStanza's light green eyes. His faint moustache looked as finely tended as his house. LaStanza's thick Sicilian moustache was longish, like his dark hair, and in need of a trim. Smiling the man said, 'It's about time we met.'

LaStanza nodded, slipping his ID folder back into his inside coat pocket.

The man moved aside and said, 'Come on in.'

LaStanza noticed the bandage on the man's right hand. He kept the shoe hidden as he stepped into a pristine hardwood foyer with beige walls decorated with mini-Audubon prints. The place smelled faintly of lemon cleaner. The brisk air-conditioned air felt great.

The man closed the door and led LaStanza into a living room to the right.

'You look like you could use a drink?'

'No, thanks,' LaStanza said. 'I'm working.'

The living room had a comfortable feel, wall-to-wall carpet, two thick sofas, a roll top desk, cut glass lamps and huge Audubon prints on each wall. Typically, its ceiling was fourteen feet high. The man sat on one sofa and waved LaStanza to the other.

The man was Boyd Perez, from an old Castilian family. Boyd was related to a gangster who used to rule Plaquemines Parish, that old segregationist political boss, Leander himself. Boyd was the citified version, slick, rich, powerful, a successful real estate attorney and leading realtor with a background in loan sharking, gambling and prostitution. Now, middle aged, Boyd was 're-spectable money.'

'I thought you were Alaina,' Perez said, slipping LaStanza that same oh-so-friendly smile.

'Oh, my cousin's coming over?'

'She should be here at eight.' Perez glanced at the thin gold watch on his left wrist.

LaStanza pulled his radio out and put it on the dark wood coffee table between the sofas. Then he sat on the sofa facing Perez and placed the red high heel on the coffee table between them. He watched the aqua eyes and caught a slight glitch when he man looked at the high heel.

Smiling now, Perez rose and said, 'You sure I can't get you something?' On his way to the wet bar at the far end of the room, Perez added over his shoulder, 'I'm going to freshen my drink.'

'Go ahead.' LaStanza watched him, wondering – *if a policeman came into my living room and placed a woman's high heel on my coffee table. I'd have to ask.* LaStanza felt the leopard inside now, prowling back and forth, back and forth in anticipation.

'You know Alaina's told me so much about you,' Perez said, pouring himself a double brandy. 'I feel I know you.'

'She's told me a lot about you too.'

Perez moved back smoothly, his eyes shifting to the high heel. He smiled again, his little moustache curling up above his thin lips.

'I suppose I should ask what that shoe is doing on my table.'

LaStanza picked up the shoe and leaned forward as Perez sat, handing it to the man.

'Take a look at what's inside. Don't worry about the finger-print powder. It rubs off.'

Perez craned his neck forward, but did not touch the high heel. Studying what was inside for a moment, he looked up at La-Stanza and the glitch was back, but only for a second. It was a small glitch, like facial tick.

LaStanza returned the shoe to the table and sat back. Perez took a sip of his freshened brandy. LaStanza waited. It was an old homicide trick. Wait long enough and people will restart the conversation, automatically. It was the polite thing to do.

'I suppose I'm supposed to ask why my address is written in that shoe?'

'That's what we'd like to know.' LaStanza crossed his legs, letting his coat fall open. He adjusted the holster of his two-and-a-half inch barrel, stainless steel Smith and Wesson .357 magnum on his right hip.

'Whose shoe is it?'

'We don't have her name yet,' LaStanza said, his eyes fixed on the aqua eyes. 'We found her body next to the Governor Nicholls Street Wharf a short while ago.'

'Body?'

'Yes, she was murdered. That's my specialty, you know. Homicide.'

Perez took another sip. His eyes narrowed. Placing the snifter on the table, he shook his head and said, 'Strange.'

'She was about five-three, about a hundred pounds, a real looker. Except she's sort of blue now.' LaStanza watched him.

Perez stared at the shoe, his hands at his sides, palms down on the sofa.

'She was wearing a tight red dress.' LaStanza waited again.

Perez looked up at him and said, 'I have no idea who she could be. Uh, could have been.' He picked up the snifter but didn't take a drink. He rolled the brown liquid around in the glass, crossed his legs and leaned back on the sofa. Looking at his watch, he said, 'Alaina's going to be here soon.'

He looked back at LaStanza and said in a deep, controlled voice, 'Would you like to see the place?'

'Sure.'

The old house had been restored beyond its original beauty. It reeked of new money. LaStanza followed Perez through the living room to a study that also smelled of lemon cleaner, through a narrow hall into a spacious rear kitchen with a picture window that revealed a serene patio out back. Beyond the patio were the slave quarters which were completely dark, illuminated only by the lights of the tree-lined patio.

'It's too hot to sit outside,' Perez said, waving his bandaged hand.

There were black wrought iron benches out on the patio, among the banana trees and two large magnolias. Perez explained about the original Spanish architecture of the place, as they stepped back around to the stairs that led upstairs.

'There are three bedrooms upstairs,' Perez said on their way back to the living room. 'You sure I can't get you a drink?'

LaStanza shook his head, moving past Perez to sit again on the sofa facing the man.

'Alaina tells me you live on Exposition Boulevard. In a mansion.'

LaStanza took out his pen and note book from his coat pocket. He wrote down a quick description of Perez and the house.

'Alaina tells me your wife is one of the wealthiest women in Louisiana.' Perez sat and crossed his legs again. 'I met her father once. Bankers, aren't they? Her family?'

LaStanza looked up and said, 'So you have no idea why your

address would be written in the shoe of a murder victim.'

Perez picked up the snifter, took a sip and said coolly, 'No. But excuse me for asking. If you're so rich now, why do you still work?'

'I like it. And I'm good at it.'

'Ah, a natural talent.'

He's being cute now.

'I was well taught. My partners are very, *very* good.'

Perez took another sip. 'Was there anything written in her other shoe?'

'We haven't found it. Yet.'

Perez's eyes didn't even flinch this time. Looking LaStanza in the eye he wouldn't even blink. The leopard liked that, a staring contest.

He didn't know her other shoe was missing. So where is it? His mind's clicking right now. Wondering where it is.

LaStanza waited.

'So let me get this straight,' Perez said, returning the snifter to the coffee table. 'You find my address in a dead woman's shoe and deduce that I am somehow involved in her . . . demise.'

'Real policemen don't deduce. We use inductive reasoning.'

'What's that?' Perez brushed a piece of lint from his dark slacks.

'Arriving at a solution that fits all the evidence. We have your address in her shoe. That's part of the evidence we need answered.'

Perez shrugged and looked away, a slight smile on his face again.

'So that's how you solve murders. Indusive reasoning.'

'Inductive. That, and the fact that criminals usually make mistakes. Most are pretty dumb.'

'No plastic bags over the head?' Perez put his arms up on the back of his sofa. 'No beating witnesses with telephone books? Rubber hoses?'

'You watch too much TV, counsellor.'

LaStanza ran his hand over his moustache and said. 'You hear about it all the time, in the News. Like the man who killed a cab driver last week.'

Perez squinted his eyes and shrugged.

'Along the lakefront. He forgot he gave the cabby his address when he got in. It was the last entry in the cabby's log book.'

Perez nodded and said, 'Stupid.'

And you couldn't do anything stupid, right?

'Just yesterday a man over in Treme shot his ex-girlfriend's new boyfriend with the same revolver he used to kill a burglar two years ago. As if we don't keep bullets to compare against bullets from unsolved murders. Same gun. Same shooter.'

Perez looked at his watch. 'It's not like Alaina to be late.'

'What happened to your hand?'

'Scratched it on a thorn,' Perez said quickly, a little too quickly. He reached for the snifter and added, 'Out in the patio.'

'Thorn? On a magnolia tree?'

'One of those banana leaves.'

'Oh.'

Perez straightened out his dinner jacket and uncrossing his legs. 'When I went to law school, they told us most murders are committed by people who know each other well.'

'Murder among friends and associates,' LaStanza said. 'Eighty percent of murders are like that.'

'What about the other twenty percent?' Perez's voice dripped with concern.

'Stranger murders. Son-of-Sam. Ted Bundy. The Boston Strangler.'

'Yeah.' There was more concern in the voice.

'Son-of-Sam's in jail for life. Bundy was fried in Florida. The Boston Strangler died in prison. They were all caught.'

'Not Jack The Ripper?'

He's being cute again.

'We've learned a lot since then.'

'Ah,' Perez stood up and said, 'Well I'd like to help you, but I don't know anything about this.' He waved at the shoe.

'Mind if I wait for my cousin?' LaStanza said, slipping his note pad back into his coat pocket. 'I haven't seen her in a while.'

'Sure.' Perez let out a sigh and sat back down.

'Where's your car?' LaStanza asked.

The glitch was back. This one was not as subtle as the others.

'Uh, in the garage.'

'You still drive a black Jaguar?'

Perez nodded and reached for the snifter.

'So, what happened to the other shoe?' LaStanza asked.

Perez said nothing.

'Did you keep it as a souvenir?' And there it was, heavy in the air. The leopard had said it. LaStanza watched.

Perez narrowed his eyes again, lifted the snifter and then smiled. 'Alaina never told me you were so funny.'

'Remember the Slasher?'

Perez nodded as he drank.

'That was my first case in Homicide. He kept the brassieres of his victims. When we caught him, I found the bras in his apartment.'

'I suppose you're going to ask to search next.'

'Actually no.' LaStanza shot him a cold smile. 'You must think I work alone. While we've been talking, my partners have been canvassing the neighbourhood. They're outside right now. You'd think that *someone* would have seen a woman in a red dress come in here.'

LaStanza took the note pad from his pocket, opened it and put it on the table next to the high heel. He noticed how Perez stared at it.

'I'm not going to ask you to search. My sergeant should be here in a minute with search warrants for your house, your car, your garage, your slave quarters and you.'

Perez looked at his watch once again and said, 'She's late!' Looking back at LaStanza he dropped his voice an octave and said, 'What do you mean a *search warrant* for me?'

LaStanza let the question linger a moment, like a breath of hot air before answering. 'Hair. We're going to need some of your hair and blood and skin.'

It wasn't a glitch this time. It was a full second pause. Perez crossed his legs and said, 'Run that by me again.'

LaStanza waited. He could see the tumblers rolling behind Perez's eyes.

'It doesn't figure. A search warrant for me.'

'You know what I mean, Counsellor. Our victim scratched her

killer. She had skin and blood beneath her fingernails.' LaStanza moved his gaze from the aqua eyes to the bandage on Perez's right hand. 'You know about DNA fingerprinting, counsellor?'

Perez cleared his throat and nodded slightly.

'If you had sex with her or if you left skin or blood under her fingernail, it's as conclusive as a fingerprint.'

'I know about DNA!'

'Pubic hairs getting mixed together. Seminal fluid. You know, the typical debris of sexual intercourse.'

'The only *debris* you'll find here came from your cousin!'

If he thought that would rile LaStanza, he was sorely mistaken. Alaina was a big girl, had been for a while. Miss Louisiana at eighteen, she had so many boyfriends LaStanza could never keep up. If she didn't sleep around, he'd be shocked.

But, since Perez thought he was cute, LaStanza brought out he leopard again. 'Where do you think we'll find the other shoe?'

'What makes you think you will?'

'You were surprised when I told you it was missing. You're wondering right now if it's in your bedroom, or slave quarters, or the patio where it fell off when you carried her out to your garage or if it's in the trunk of your Jag.'

Perez rose and straightened his jacket.

'Can you feel it?' LaStanza asked.

'Feel what?'

'Feel us closing in on you.'

'You are not funny any more! I let you come in here because you're Alaina's cousin and you accuse me of all this. Without one shred of evidence. Furthermore . . .'

'It was such a small mistake,' LaStanza interrupted. 'Who would have thought to look in her shoe?'

Perez went back to his watch once again. 'Now what's Alaina going to think when she gets here, with policemen all over my house.'

LaStanza picked up the note pad and went back to writing a summary of their conversation.

'What are you writing?'

'I'm getting your quotes straight.'

'OK. Write this down. I don't know why *any* woman, particularly your redhead in a tight red dress, would have my address in her shoe.'

LaStanza stopped writing and looked up. He shot Perez the eye of the leopard, the dagger-in-the eye Sicilian stare. He felt the leopard pacing again.

'Suppose,' he said, 'she didn't like to carry her purse. She didn't want to forget your address.' He watched Perez's eyes. They looked like gazelle eyes, blinking as they stared back at him. 'And I never told you she was a redhead.'

'You did too!'

The leopard answered in a deep guttural voice. 'No. I didn't.' Perez tried squinting, tried looking tough.

'I said she had a red dress. I never told you she was a redhead.'

'Yes, you did. You came in here and said you found a redhead in a tight red dress strangled next to the Governor Nicholls Wharf.'

LaStanza leaned his hands along the back of the sofa and grinned. 'I never said she was strangled. I just said she was blue.'

He reached forward, picked up his radio, flipped it on and called his sergeant. '*3124 to 3122.*'

'*Go ahead.*'

'*You with the judge?*'

'*10-4.*'

'*Well,*' LaStanza knew he had to talk fast. '*He hasn't copped out yet. He told me he never saw her. But then he told me she had red hair and was strangled when I didn't tell him she had red hair or how she died.*'

'*Stand by.*'

Perez looked as pale as the Audubon heron on the wall behind him. LaStanza watched him. He didn't move. LaStanza felt his own heart racing, picturing old Judge LeBeau sitting in his robe reading over the warrants, like a character from one of those Dickens books. Probably had a nightcap on his bald head.

If he was a betting man, he'd bet LeBeau would okay the warrants. On the corner of Judge LeBeau's desk in the old jurist's chambers was a miniature electric chair.

'*3122 to 3124.*'

'*Go ahead, sarge.*'

'*It's enough for the warrants. We're 10-8.*'

There was an immediate knock on the door.

'That'll be the cavalry,' LaStanza said. 'You want me to let them in?'

Perez let them in. LaStanza watched from the doorway of the living room as his two plainclothes partners moved in, followed by two crime lab technicians carrying portable, red vacuum cleaners and large black cameras.

Perez stood stiffly in his foyer, ten feet from his open front door. LaStanza wished the man would rabbit. Please, he thought, please run. LaStanza, an all-state miler in high school would love to run down the smoking jacket gangster.

After what must have been the longest ten minutes of Perez's life, LaStanza's supervisor arrived. Sergeant Mark Land, rumpled and sweaty in a close-out-sale brown suit, handed Perez the legal sized papers. Land was an oversized version of LaStanza with the same dark hair and full moustache, except the large Napolitano Italian looked more like a grizzly, especially when angry.

'We have a search warrant for this residence,' Mark said, 'and for your garage, your vehicle, patio and slave quarters.' Mark looked up at Perez and added, 'We also have a warrant for blood and hair and skin. We'll have a medical technician meet us at the Detective Bureau. You understand?'

Perez examined the papers in his hands. He cleared his throat and said, 'I want to call my lawyer.'

'You can do that from our office. Right now you are instructed to sit on your sofa and wait.' Mark tapped the papers. 'It's standard procedure during search warrants. We have the right to detain all occupants of the house. Is anyone else here?'

Perez shook his head and said, 'No.' He moved back to the sofa and sat heavily on it. He reached for his drink, hesitated, then grabbed it and took a stiff belt. LaStanza sat back across from him and waited. He watched two drops of perspiration work their way down the sides of Perez's face.

He heard the men moving around the house, drawers opening and closing, doors opening and closing. Perez stared into his drink for the longest time, then looked around his room. He finally looked at LaStanza and said, 'Alaina isn't coming is she?'

LaStanza shook his head no. 'I called her before I came.'

Perez let out a long sigh.

Mark stepped into the doorway. He grinned at LaStanza and immediately the phrase, 'like a shit-eating bear came to mind.' Mark held up a plastic bag with a red high heel in it. LaStanza looked back at Perez who had closed his eyes.

'Where'd you find it?'

'Garage.'

'Anything written inside?'

'Just a name. Body. Same blue ink. Wanna see?'

LaStanza rose and looked at the show, then withdrew his handcuffs from his belt at the small of his back. 'All right,' he told Perez. 'Stand up.'

Perez shot a quick look at Mark. The burly sergeant spoke to Perez as if he was talking to a four-year-old. 'Now counsellor, you're going to have to go with Detective LaStanza like a good little boy, while we process the crime scene.'

Mark stepped over to LaStanza, put a friendly arm on his junior partner's shoulder, leaned over and whispered in LaStanza's ear, 'Boy, did we get lucky on this one, or what?'

'You can say that again.'

Mark did, whispering the same phrase in LaStanza's ear, the silly bastard.

Perez stood slowly. LaStanza quickly cuffed the man's hands behind his back and then searched him. He wanted to grab the smug son-of-a-bitch by the throat and strangle him and leave him on a rat infested wharf. He never told Perez about the rat bites on the victim's feet.

'You know,' he told Perez as he patted him down. 'The mistake you made wasn't the shoe at all. It was denying you knew her.'

Perez blinked at him and then tried smiling. 'You can't use anything I said against me. You didn't advise me of my rights.'

LaStanza laughed and let the leopard answer. 'Counsellor, you know your rights better than I do. I wanna see you convince a judge you didn't know you had the right to remain silent. Anyway, my report's gonna say I read them to you at the beginning.'

He could see the muscles working behind Perez's clenched jaw.

LaStanza leaned close, an inch away from Perez's ear and whispered. 'You know your biggest mistake? Your biggest mistake was letting me in.'

HARD GETAWAY

Robert J. Hoyden

Serving a summons in Seattle is definitely not a job for just anybody. After having been a process server in this town for about twenty years I considered myself somewhat of an expert. I figured I pretty much had seen everything that this tough, gritty business can toss at you. That was until I was once again called upon to serve papers on Fat Mike, a notorious and evasive deadbeat. I had tracked down and unloaded legal papers on Fat Mike at least three or four other occasions, each time being tougher than the previous service. Needless to say whenever I caught up to him he was less than thrilled. In fact he took it quite personal. I imagined that Fat Mike was involved in more litigation than most major law firms in Seattle. He was repeatedly getting sued for bad debt, breach of contract or a host of other treacherous acts that landed him in judicial hot water. He was a nasty fellow and he made it a point to stay out of sight of process servers. In fact, he had a reputation that made most process servers cringe when called upon to chase after him.

So after one of my clients, a Seattle attorney, asked me to serve a summons on Fat Mike still again I decided to take along an associate process server. I called upon my friend Billy Middleton, who was also a long-time veteran in the business. Though most process servers are lone wolves by nature occasionally a back-up server was warranted; as a bodyguard, if nothing else.

I dialed up his cell phone and we agreed to meet at the Merchant's Café. The Merchant's billed itself as Seattle's oldest saloon and eatery, built shortly after the Great Fire of 1889. It was situated smack in the middle of Seattle's historic Pioneer Square. We agreed on a drink and a meal – hopefully not our last.

Billy and I sauntered into the rustic cafe. I dropped my body onto a creaking stool at the bar near the front entrance and Billy sat down next to me. I watched as a pretty woman passed by outside the entrance.

'Well, Billy,' I said, turning my attention back to him, 'how have you been?' Middleton and I had been friends for better than ten years. He had a handsome, chiselled face, brown, shaggy hair and broad shoulders. And like me he preferred wearing old vests and khakis.

At that moment a gum-chewing, comely-looking, dark-haired bartender approached us. 'What'll it be, boys?' she said in a sharp and sexy New York accent.

'I'll do a Ballard Bitter,' I said, referring to a micro beer brewed in Ballard, a sleepy bedroom community Northwest of downtown Seattle.

'And you, smiley boy,' she said to Middleton, who nearly always wore an infectious smile.

'Ditto,' he said to her. As she started to walk away he looked back at me. 'Not too shabby, Cooper. I still wouldn't mind finding an occupation where I didn't have to put my life on the line every day.'

'I hear that.'

'But, as you know, the money is pretty good in this racket, I love being my own boss and setting my own schedule. Not to mention a little adventure from time to time,' he said with a smile.

The two beers arrived in thick, sturdy mugs, foam slowly trickling down the sides.

'Speaking of adventure one of my clients wants me to serve Fat Mike again,' I said.

'The house mover?'

'That's him.'

'And, I suspect you want me to assist you in this endeavour?' he said with raised eyebrows.

'What are friends for?'

He laughed. 'Yeah, I'll help you, Coop. But it'll cost you a beer when we are done – assuming we don't get killed.'

'It's a deal.'

I took a hearty slug of my brew and said, 'Speaking of this business, Billy, wasn't Ted Bundy a process server at one time?'

Middleton was quiet for a moment as he thought about the question. 'As I recall the story, Coop, he was a messenger and not a process server. But, he did operate here in Seattle. Christ, I wonder if Bundy killed any of those women while he was out delivering papers. Man, that's a freaking thought if I ever had one.'

'Process servers already get a bad rap for doing this nasty work. Then along comes a Bundy or some other loser. We're going to need to hire a public relations firm, Billy.'

My friend laughed. 'So, Cooper, if I recall Fat Mike is hard to pin down. You sure he is going to be around?'

'Reasonably. I called his office, spoke to some woman and using the ruse of wanting to talk to him about a job I managed to glean from her that he was due in this afternoon about 4:00 p.m.'

'You're in charge of this one, Coop. I'm along for the ride.'

'As my bodyguard,' I added.

'Now you're talking two beers.'

'No problem. Let's chow down and then check it out.'

We enjoyed a much spirited conversation, a nice leisurely dinner and each downed another Ballard Bitter. We squared up the tab and after leaving a healthy tip headed off on our dangerous adventure.

It was around 3:45 p.m. as Billy and I, speeding southbound down Interstate 5 in my Ford Ranger truck, exited onto Highway 518, a major arterial heading West into Burien, another Seattle bedroom community. After passing a giant flatbed truck with the surly-looking driver eyeballing us we took the first exit, which delivered us into an area known as Riverton Heights. At the exit's stop sign we turned left onto South 154th Street, past the Riverton Heights post office, motored another half-mile or so and took a hard right onto 24th Avenue South. As I turned onto 24th I glanced in my rearview mirror to see the flatbed lumbering slowly along about three hundred yards behind us. At that point we cruised down 24th, closing in on our next stop, an area known as Tur Lake. As we turned left onto South 142nd Street a monstrous Boeing 777 roared overhead and made its descent toward the runway at Seattle-Tacoma International Airport, less than one mile away. The airport was locally referred to as 'Sea-Tac.'

'Cooper, I recall that after you caught up with Fat Mike the problem sometimes was not him so much as his . . .

'Employees,' I said.

'Yeah, his employees. I think their average IQ is about 13, roughly the intelligence of zucchini but, man, are they a rowdy lot.'

After about seventy yards along South 142nd I whipped a hard left and bounded onto a dusty, pothole-riddled road. Bouncing forward we finally skidded to a halt in an enormous cloud of dust. The haze poured into the open windows causing us to cough and spit out dirt particles. I swept a hand in front of my face in an attempt to clear the air.

'Christ, Cooper, we should have driven up in a Sherman tank,' Middleton said, also sweeping away the floating debris.

After cranking on the emergency brake we escaped the truck, leaving the keys in the ignition and the engine running for a possible quick getaway.

With summons in hand I met Billy in front of the truck. The dust cloud had dissipated and we stood looking at a large, double-wide mobile home about thirty yards away, tucked under some lifeless parched trees. Off to the right of the mobile home was a large knoll of loose dirt and behind that a sprawling pasture and Tur Lake. There were several battered and useless vehicles and dismembered automobile parts strewn about. There were at least two operating vehicles and a motorcycle in front of the mobile home.

'You know what Fat Mike looks like, right, Cooper?'

'Oh, yeah. I nailed him a few times myself,' I said, folding the papers, tucking them into my vest's inner pocket and starting toward the mobile home. Middleton was close on my heels.

At the base of the steps and porch, which was encircled by a wooden trellis, I stopped and peered at the door. It was slightly ajar and I could hear talking and laughing inside. The voices were deep and ominous – like a room full of drunken lumberjacks. I looked at Middleton. 'Ready?'

After getting his nod I started up the stairs. I pulled the creaking screen door, pushed open the front door and in we boldly tramped. The screen door slapped shut as we started through the kitchen. Dirt, soiled newspapers, spare parts, tires and other garbage were scattered around. Greasy tools and small machinery lay on the floor. The wallpaper was shredded and smeared with grime. The place reeked of cigar smoke, beer and rotting garbage. Clearly a charming place, I mused.

Then we came into a large, open room. The talking and laughing immediately ceased as Middleton and I stepped into view. Six very brawny, dirty, scruffy and annoyed-looking men sat around a huge circular wooden table. Each had a beer can in front of him. There were three or four empty cans lying crushed into little aluminum balls in the middle of the table. One guy took a long swig from his beer and another guy heartily scratched his crotch.

'What the hell do you want?' one of the oafs belted out as he eyed us.

'Lighten up, buddy,' I said, stepping closer. The pack of them scanned the two of us up and down. They gaped at us as if we were cops.

'I betcha you're fucking pigs, ain't ya,' the rude one said.

I stepped a bit closer to him and looked him in the eyeballs. It was important not to be intimidated by their actions. Though admittedly it is hard to act tough when you are in a room full of cutthroats; of whom any two could probably mop us with our asses. 'No, man, we are not cops,' I said.

'So what do you want,' he asked with a hint of civility. He appeared to be calming down.

'Is Fat Mike around?'

'He's in the other room. He'll be out in a moment. Sit down over there,' the rude dude said, pointing to a smelly, ripped up couch.

Middleton and I chose to stand, towards the exit and across from the curious crew. Billy, trying to break the malevolent atmosphere, said, 'So, boys, what does it cost to move a house?'

Two of the goons laughed at Billy's obvious ignorance. 'It all depends on how big the place is and how far we need to move it,' one of them chortled through crooked and stained teeth.

'Oh, of course,' Middleton said, placating them.

The first oaf was still unhappy with our presence. 'What do you want Fat Mike for?' he asked.

'I'll just talk to him,' I said. 'Do you mind?'

Springing out of his seat, the rude guy who was bigger and uglier than the others, came over to me, pointed a finger near my face and said, 'Yeah I friggin' mind, asshole. Mike is my brother and I mind his business.'

I stood my perilous ground and looked into his eyes. 'No problem.'

He backed up a few steps, then said, 'I don't think I like you. You look familiar and I don't connect your face to a good time, either.'

The door Middleton and I entered swung open and another filthy joker came in. 'The flatbed is here,' he announced. He looked at Middleton and me and stepped directly to Fat Mike's brother, who was still scowling. The joker whispered to the brother and then put a handful of something into his hand.

Middleton leaned into my ear and whispered, 'That's the flatbed driver we saw minutes ago out on South 154th, Cooper.'

I didn't respond. I was looking at the ugly brother who was glowering at me and dangling my truck keys over his head. 'Expecting a fast getaway, boys?'

'Ah, no, actually, my . . . uh . . . my . . . ignition wires are faulty,' I bullshitted.

The ugly brother called my bluff. 'You liar. You dickheads are up to something.' He tossed my keys into the middle of the table where they clinked into a roundly crushed beer can.

A few of the sitting house movers bristled, chuckled and rustled in their chairs. They were hoping for some action. I looked at Billy who was rolling his eyes.

Then from the back room Fat Mike emerged. He was as fat and foul-looking as his thugs. Double rolls of fat drooped under his chin; he must have weighed four hundred pounds or more. Fat Mike saw me and his face immediately lit up.

'COOPER!'

I seized the opportunity. Out of my vest came the legal papers. I flipped them in the air and tossed them over the middle of the table. They spread open, scattered and drifted onto the table. 'You been served, Mike!'

Those words detonated the room. Amidst flying paper I heard many unpleasant variations of 'asshole' and 'motherfucker'. Chairs screeched against the floor and then slammed against the walls. Full cans tumbled to the floor and beer gushed all over. I started to push Middleton to get the hell going.

'Cooper! The keys! The keys!' Billy uttered as he stumbled toward the exit in the kitchen.

'Damn!' I had already forgotten about the stupid keys. In the jumble of mass confusion I took at least three steps towards the table. I felt a solid hand clamp onto the scruff of my neck. I spun around, breaking the grip, and placed a row of knuckles in the ugly brother's rude mouth. He took the blast, his knees buckled and he flung back and crashed into a wall. I reached the table, swatted a crushed beer can out of the way and snatched the keys. I pushed away from the table and turned to bolt into the kitchen. The flatbed driver was in my path.

'You ain't going no place, chump,' he said.

'Oh, yes he is,' said Middleton as he whipped the driver around by the shoulder and walloped him in the gut and followed with a jarring left hook to the jaw. The blast sent the driver sprawling across the table amidst flying cans and spilled beer.

Billy was about three steps in front and there were at least four hoodlums three steps behind me as we all rumbled through the kitchen. As I dashed by the sink I swept my arm across the cluttered counter top and brought a wave of cans, glasses, paper and cartons cascading into their paths. One guy jumped over the stuff and the others were slightly delayed in their pursuit.

Middleton was outside and running towards my truck when I blasted out the screen door. I tried to step outward and possibly leap, but two heavy hands latched onto my shoulders, dragged me back and turned me around. All I saw was a blurring fist and all I felt was a rock hard jolt to my jaw. My entire body lifted into the air and my arms flung back as I plunged with a violent smashing of wood through the trellis which enveloped the porch. It felt like thirty minutes as my body sailed through the air. I came down with a savage collision into the hard, dusty ground.

Though the shit was totally knocked out of me I could see that Middleton was back to help. He jumped and brought a heel crushing into the face of one of the pursuers who was nearest me. As he came down on his toes he tossed a fake left and followed with a jabbing right fist into the nose of another guy who was quite close. He turned, grabbed me near an armpit and hustled me along.

I was in pain, half-running and half-stumbling, as I used his support to get to the truck. Amazingly, I still held the keys tight in my palm and I dropped them into Middleton's open hand. He ushered me to the passenger side of my truck and instead of running around the vehicle he dived over the hood and fell into the dirt. As he came up, the ugly brother, with a trickle of blood on his chin from my previous punch, was standing there. A clenched fist came up to his face, there was a click and a stiletto blade snapped up. Middleton took a step back and slightly knelt into a defensive posture. Quickly he reached down, grabbed a handful of dirt and powdered the brother's face and eyes. The brother coughed, sputtered, spit out dirt and groaned. Middleton's driving right fist laid the man out cold. Instantly Billy was in the truck, key in the ignition and it jumped to life.

One of the goons approached my side. His hand was starting to come in my window. I snapped open the door, swung it wide open and caught the joker in the windpipe. He grabbed his throat, gurgled and fell back.

Middleton had the truck in reverse and it spewed dirt, dust and pebbles in all directions. He jammed the stick into first gear and lunged forward. Suddenly the truck stopped dead. 'Damn! Look!' Middleton pointed.

The recently arrived flatbed truck was blocking the entire access road onto the poperty! Middleton quickly looked around and seeing three people clambering after us, punched the shifter in reverse and backed up. He stopped, cranked it back into first gear and with a startling rebel yell he surged forward and right at the thugs. His scream and the charging truck forced them to dive and leap for their lives. I held onto the dashboard and my door. We bounced wildly toward the knoll of dirt. Middleton had a crazed, damn-the-torpedoes look on his face.

'Watch the dirt, Billy!' I screeched. 'I don't think it will give way.'

'It fucking better!'

With a mighty blast we exploded into the dirt knoll. The front of the truck dipped, burrowed into the top of the pile of dirt and came back up like the bow of a ship taking on a great wave. My head snapped back and a colossal mushroom of dust swirled about us. We went up and over the knoll and came hurtling down onto the other side. Middleton blazed a new path into the pasture. A couple of cows, about fifteen yards away, protested our sudden appearance but wisely moved out of the way.

Middleton abandoned all caution as we banged, rattled and bounded across the pasture. A few ducks and other birds lifted off Tur Lake in fright as we created a loud commotion. Middleton looked in the rearview mirror and I turned around. About fifty yards away four or five very upset people were running and shouting and waving their arms. Fat Mike stood on the porch, legal papers in hand, looking through the shattered trellis. They quickly vanished in the cloudy distance.

THE NEW LAWYER

Mike Wiecek

Tom Baker wasn't exactly working late when the phone rang, but everyone else had already left. He'd passed the bar and hung out his shingle only three months back. A dingy cubicle between a bondsman and a penny-stock huckster, with one receptionist for the floor and rent due weekly, was the best he could afford.

'Baker Law Offices,' he said, trying to sound stentorian and professional.

The man on the other end was whispering and panicky.

'I think I need a lawyer,' he said. 'I had a little car accident . . . I might have killed someone.'

Tom's heart leaped. A criminal case at last!

'Ok, go slow,' he said. 'What happened?'

'I was driving along and this guy ran out and it was dark, and I didn't see him, and there was this awful crunching thwacking sound and when I looked back he was just lying there –'

'Take it easy,' said Tom. 'Let's think about this. He ran in front of you, no warning, on a dark street – hard to say it was your fault.'

'Well . . . I might have been going a little fast.'

'Speeding?'

'Maybe. Like maybe, I don't know, 50 or 60 miles an hour.'

'On a residential street?' This didn't sound so good.

'There was no traffic!'

Tom considered. 'OK, you were speeding. Still, it's probably no more than manslaughter, since there was no intent.'

The man hesitated. 'Does it matter, you know, *why* I was speeding? Like if my wife was in labour in the back seat, that would be, like, a good reason, right?'

'A great reason!' Suddenly Tom could see headlines – the trial would probably get out-of-state coverage on a story like that. He'd make his reputation on this case! 'Did she deliver before you got to the hospital?'

'No, no,' said the man. 'That was just, like, an example. Actually, well, this is kind of hard to say . . . listen, you're my lawyer, you don't tell anyone my secrets, right? I don't want to get into more trouble over this explanation.'

'Absolutely. Confidentiality is fully protected by attorney-client privilege.'

'Good. Well, what I did, I was off to see this guy, my former business partner.' The man paused. 'Thing is, I had just found out he'd stolen $150,000 from our deal! And I was so angry, I guess I was rushing over to his house, and I was probably going to, well, shoot him.'

'What?' As fast as he assimilated that, Tom started thinking, talk shows! TV interviews! A book deal! 'Did you tell anyone that?'

'Just a couple guys at the bar . . . I might have had a few beers beforehand.'

Tom winced. 'So they'll probably testify. But I have to say, in point of law, it really doesn't matter – this dope runs out in front of you, it's not your fault, no matter what you were thinking about.'

'Well, there's one more thing . . .' The man's voice trailed off.

'Yes?' Tom could barely restrain his excitement.

'This is so screwed up . . . thing is, the guy I ran over, he's the one I was going to murder anyway.'

'Huh? What?' Tom couldn't say anything else.

'But I didn't mean to do it that way! Like, I was going to his house to *shoot* him, I didn't expect him to run in front of my car five miles from there. See what I mean?'

Tom thought, I can win this case! Not only is the publicity going to make me famous, but I know exactly how the law works – there was a question like this on Morrison's Criminal Law final. The DA doesn't have a chance!

'Immaterial,' he said. Movie rights! 'The relevant fact is that you didn't want to kill him when it happened. *Wilcox vs. Indiana*, 1973. Also *Malverna vs. Adams*, and of course *Gluckheimer*. Your state of mind is what matters, and I think we can prove absence of intent. For that matter, we might even be able to beat the manslaughter. Even if there were witnesses, it was dark, we can undermine their credibility.' He was scribbling rapidly on a legal pad. 'Let's see, we have to get started immediately, so you can turn yourself in before they arrest you. Where are you now?' He paused. 'Hello? Are you there?'

There was no answer – the man had hung up. He frantically dialled callback, but the call had come from a blocked line. In dismay, Tom watched his dreams of fame implode.

Martin slipped back into the classroom apologetically, trying not to disturb the hush of students hunched over their bluebooks.

'Long time in the bathroom, weren't you?' Professor Morrison glared at him. 'You only have twenty minutes left to finish the exam.'

'Sorry,' said Martin as he sat down, the cellphone pressing his hip pocket. 'I think I can finish right up.'

FROM "WHITE RUSSIAN"

Michael Hemmingson

I

That morning, before we pulled the bank job, I had a bad feeling. Something in my gut told me it was all going to go wrong.

I wasn't listening, of course. No one ever does.

I should've never gone over to Paul's. Paul was married and had kids. He had two daughters, eight and nine. His wife, Winona, greeted me at the door in a tank-top and khaki capri pants. She had a plan – Winona *always* had a plan. She'd play coy and aloof when it suited her, but there was always some deal cooking in her brain.

'He's in the shower,' she told me, closing the door. She was all smiles. 'He *just* got in.'

I nodded.

'Think: by this afternoon, we're going to be rich.'

'Yeah,' I said.

'Or . . .'

'Or?'

'Or maybe we'll be free.' She moved my way, and wanted a kiss. I hated it when she took these chances.

I was really nervous about the job.

Paul came out of the shower half an hour later, drying his hair with a pink towel. 'Ready to go get rich?'

'Yeah,' I probably said.

'Go do it,' Winona giggled. 'I wish I could be there.'

'Patience, patience.' Paul went to the fridge and got out a beer. 'Helps the nerves. Hey,' he said to me, 'wanna drink? Your favourite? We have Kahula and vodka.'

'And milk,' Winona said.

I shook my head. I never pass on a White Russian, but today was an exception.

Winona stayed home, watching TV, while her husband and I went to rob a bank.

There was a third man in our crew. Hank. He was waiting at a bus stop when we picked him up. I was driving. I was to be the getaway driver. The car was an old Ford Cutlass we'd picked up for a few hundred bucks, barely holding together and wearing stolen license plates. Hank was pumped up, and he had a pistol tucked in his pants. I didn't have a gun. I didn't see any reason why I needed one.

'Rock'n'roll,' Hank said, rubbing his goatee.

'This is going to be *so* easy,' Paul said.

I'd known Paul since we were kids. We'd gone to school together in Sacramento.

Paul had gotten into some trouble with the law before, had done some time; nothing serious, a few months (I'd done eleven months for possession of and conspiracy to sell crystal meth). But there were things he got away with, mostly embezzling money or stealing merchandise from various employers over the years. We'd get drunk and he'd tell me how he fucked over his bosses and got away with it. I think Paul was more seduced by the idea of committing a crime without paying the toll, rather than the actual financial benefits *of* the crime.

He was working in a pawn shop. He knew that every Thursday his boss took that week's proceeds to the bank himself. 'It's always at least twenty, thirty grand,' Paul said. 'That, and whatever else is in the bank, which should be plenty, we'll walk away with a good chunk of change.'

But there was something else. His boss had a mistress, and one afternoon rushed out to meet her. He left his keys behind. One was a key to a safe deposit box. Paul ran across the street to the hardware store and made a copy of it.

Paul told Hank and myself that his boss had often bragged about the diamonds he had in that box.

'It's all just waiting there for us to grab,' he'd said.

Yes, the idea of it was seductive. I was unemployed. I'd been having a hard time keeping down jobs since my eleven month stretch. It's not easy for former drug dealers to become regular working-class citizens.

'After the bank job,' Winona said the last time we had sex, 'I'll ditch Paul and we'll go somewhere and start fresh.'

'What about the girls?' I asked.

'Paul can take care of them. I love my girls, I do, but this life isn't for me, Cork. I'm twenty-six-years-old! I'm not suppose to be so – *domestic*.'

She wanted to do something daring like move down to Los Angeles and try her hand at an acting career.

Later, she had a different idea. She was worried about the bank job. She didn't think it'd go down right.

This was her plan, in her own words: 'When those two yahoos go in, take off. *Don't* think, just *drive*. Come back here and get me. I'll be packed. I'll clean out the bank account and we'll split. They won't have a get-away car, they'll get caught and do time. We'll be on our way to freedom.'

I parked a half a block down from the bank. Paul got a gym bag from the trunk, which had a short-barrelled pump-action shotgun, and a .357 Smith and Wesson. Hank was bouncing up and down. 'Fucken relax,' Paul said. Then they walked to the bank.

They *strolled*.

Sitting there, I began to panic. I almost said the hell with it, and drove away. I guess I should have. I should have done what Winona wanted. She was waiting for me and our new life, packed and ready. But that was my best friend in there. I didn't give fuck-all about Hank, but Paul and I grew up together.

I couldn't do it.

I couldn't leave him in there.

I could screw his wife, yeah; I could plan on splitting with her, yeah. But I couldn't abandon him in the middle of a job.

Fuck me.

I don't know what went on in the bank. They were in there for exactly nine minutes. They both came rushing out like Tasmanian devils and jumped into the car. There weren't alarms going off like I thought there'd be. Not audible ones, anyway.

'GO GO GO!' Paul was yelling.

I floored it.

Then there was the sound of police sirens . . .

'You get the money?' I asked.

'Ohhhhhh, do we got *money*!' Hank said.

'You get the diamonds?' I asked.

'Yeah, I got them,' Paul said. He grinned.

'*Let's get the fuck out of here*!' Hank screamed.

'We're cool, we're cool,' Paul said. 'Corky, we cool?'

'We're cool,' I said, and turned a corner real fast, almost losing control, where I crashed right into a Volkswagen bug that was also speeding and running a red light. I saw the woman in the bug, she was young and blonde and had small dark eyes. I saw her fly out her windowshield and land on the pavement. There was a lot of blood in my eyes because my forehead met my windshield.

There was steam and smoke from the engine.

Police sirens.

Paul and Hank getting out of the car and running.

Black.

Voices.

Uniforms.

Black.

I woke up in the back of a paramedics van. Tubes in my arm, my nose. Voices. Black.

My last thought: *This is all fucked-up –*

I woke up in a hospital room. My chest was bandaged. There were two uniformed police officers there, and another one in a suit and tie.

'You awake now, Mr Byrd?' the suit and tie asked me, sitting down by the bed with a smile. The metal chair was much too small for his bulky frame. I knew the guy worked out a lot, like cops are known to do. He had a very nice suit, and I wanted to tell him this.

It was hard to speak, and I was in pain. 'Yeah, sure.'

His smile went away. 'I'm going to read you your rights.'
It was fucked-up, all right.

II

I was still in the hospital bed when the public defender came by to visit me. He must've been in his mid-twenties, already balding, with bad patchy skin. He was carrying a lot of files with him.

'Mr Byrd?'

'Corky,' I said.

'My name is Darrell Even. I'm your lawyer. I mean, if you want me to be.'

'You're a public defender?'

'Yes. Do you have access to an attorney?'

'No,' I said.

'How you doing?'

'All right, I guess.'

'I hear you broke three ribs.'

'That's what they tell me.'

He grinned. 'I guess it could've been worse.'

'So tell me what I'm facing.' I wasn't in the mood for chitchat, and I'd dealt with free lawyers before.

His grin went away. 'Nancy Davenport is dead.'

'Who?'

'The woman whose car you crashed into.'

The blonde girl. 'She's dead?'

'I'm afraid so. And the D.A. wants to charge you for it.'

'I didn't mean to kill her.'

'But you did, in the act of a crime. There's the bank robbery, and the assault on the bank security guard.'

'I had nothing to do with that.'

'You were a part of it,' Darrell Even said. 'Look, here's the deal: give them the names of your two accomplices, they'll go easy on you.'

'What's easy?'

'They'll drop the armed robbery charges, and the assault. You'll have to do some time for vehicular manslaughter.'

'No,' I said.

He nodded. 'Very well. I'll let them know.' He got up and left.

The next morning, I was transported to jail and booked. I was moving slow. My body hurt. My jailers didn't care. I was given the standard dark blue coveralls to wear, and a plastic package with toothpaste, a brush, and a black comb. I was assigned a cell with two other fellows. I had the bottom bunk. I laid down and closed my eyes.

It wasn't easy to relax in jail, it never is. One of my cellmates was eighteen, Asian, he'd been picked up for joyriding. He'd never done time before. He was nervous. He started crying. He was lucky he was with two fellows who didn't mind his crying. I understood how he felt – I felt the same way the first time I went in.

The other guy, a little older than me, was pacing back and forth. He said he was coming down off heroin, which wasn't a good thing. He was in for stealing a radio at a store he'd just had a job interview at. He didn't know why he stole the radio. He was arrested because he had a lot of priors. 'I'm going to get a felony mark for that fucking radio,' he kept saying, walking back and forth, sweating out the drugs.

One smelly and sweating, one whining and crying. I closed my eyes and tried to imagine myself somewhere else.

A few hours later, my name was called on the intercom. I was told I had a 'pro visit.' I was expecting the public defender in the visiting room. Sitting at the grey metal table was a slender, dark-haired woman in a suit. She held out her hand.

'Mr Byrd,' she said, 'I'm Linda Henry, your lawyer.'

'What happened to Darrell Even?'

'I'm not a PD,' she said. 'I've been retained.'

'By who?' I asked, but knew I didn't have to.

She smiled. 'Let's just say by someone who has a vested interest in what happens to you.'

I nodded. 'So how is Paul?'

She just smiled.

'You can tell him I'm not a rat,' I said. 'They offered me a deal for names, but I didn't take it.'

'The DA wants to charge you with armed robbery, but that's a bunch of horse puckey. That crap won't fly.' She crossed her legs. Nice legs, but sex was the furthest thing on this jailbird's mind. 'You weren't in the bank. You weren't armed. You were driving the getaway car, and that makes you an accessory. They can charge you with that, and they could get it. You'd do a year. Six months, maybe. You didn't rough up the security guard, that they can't charge you with. It's the vehicular manslaughter that you need to worry about.'

'How much time would I get?'

'Well, this is the thing. I just talked to the DA. He's thinking of going for murder.'

I could feel the blood leaving my head. 'Murder?'

'More bullshit, but it could be a problem. He wants to argue that your intentional reckless driving, which was premeditated, put the general public at risk, resulting in the death of a citizen.'

'Oh shit.'

'We can beat that. But manslaughter . . .' She shook her head.

'So what's the story?' I asked.

'Arraignment is tomorrow morning. We could make a deal, get it over with, no trial.'

Yeah, I figured Paul wouldn't want me to go to trial; I might chicken out at the eleventh hour, name names.

'What kind of deal and how much time?' I asked. My mouth felt very dry.

'Vehicular manslaughter alone. Drop the reckless and assault. Seven years, you'll do three to five, get out on parole. If we do this deal tomorrow, it can work. Go to trial, guilty on the same, you could get twenty-five to fifty.'

This wasn't quite sinking in. Prison time. But I knew there was no avoiding it. They had me in here, and I was going to be in here for a good time.

Linda Henry added, 'One month from now, I will send you a copy of your bank account statement. Currently, you have a balance of $12.46. Next month, it'll be a considerable amount more.'

'How much?'

'More than $12.46.'

At nine-thirty the next morning, in arraignment court, I

pleaded as told, according to the deal. The process was very quick, as quick as the death of the blonde in the bug.

A month later, Linda Henry mailed me a copy of my bank statement. The balance read $5,012.46. I felt cold and sick.

I called the lawyer from the prison phone.

'How can I help you, Mr Byrd?'

'Five grand for seven years?' I said. 'That's *all*?'

'I don't understand.'

'I don't know how much money they got, but I know he grabbed the diamonds. I *know*, Ms Henry, that my third of the heist is worth damn more than *five thousand dollars*.'

'I still don't understand,' she said distantly.

'How do you do it? You're an attractive woman, you seem to have it together. But you have no problem representing crooks. You know your client is a bank robber –'

'I think we should terminate this conversation, Mr Byrd.'

'Just one more thing,' I said. 'Relay a message to your client. I still won't rat him out. I don't operate that way. But when I *get* out, he and I are going to sit down and talk about the money. And so are you and I.'

I slammed the phone down. I'd just been screwed, by both my best friend and a lawyer.

I wasn't in the least surprised.

THE FORMULA

Marc Lodge

Ann Whalington Britain, senior partner in the law firm of Haverly & Carwick, frowned at the tall young associate sitting on the other side of her desk. 'An unfavourable result in this case, Jem, could cost the firm its largest client.' She carefully laid a manila file folder on the opposite side of the wood surface and leaned back.

Jeremy Thomas Anderson returned a nervous smile and fingered a suspender as he looked at the file label: BI ENTERPRISES V. NEWSOME. He glanced out the window of Britain's fortieth floor corner office. Ten blocks away across the Queenston skyline, the famous triangular logo of BI Enterprises on the company's world headquarters building was at his eye level. BI was a billion dollar conglomerate, one of the largest companies in the South. Haverly & Carwick, H&C to the cognoscenti, was a four hundred lawyer firm, with billings in the millions, but BI still accounted for some fifteen or twenty percent of the firm's total revenue.

She couldn't be serious. 'I've never worked on one of their matters,' Jem said. He was only three years out of Duke law school, long enough to value experience over academic achievement but not long enough to have gathered that experience.

Britain toyed with her gold fountain pen. 'We have one of these every five years or so. Just a nuisance, I'm afraid, but it has to be handled. BI worries about it because it involves Buffo.' She sniffed with a disapproving air. 'BI began this case in-house. As usual, they need us to bail them out.'

Jem took notes on his legal pad as she talked. He himself used a disposable pen from the firm's supply room.

'You know about Buffo, I assume.'

'The car wax.'

'To BI, it's more than just a car wax. They consider it the
foundation of their empire. Silly, really, with the airline and the
chain of auto supply stores and the railroad involvement and all
the other transportation tie-ins, but for historical reasons, I
suppose, they consider Buffo sacrosanct. When a claim like this
one comes along, alleging ownership of the formula to Buffo,
everyone over there quakes in their boots.'

'Isn't the formula a big secret? They keep it locked up somewhere?'

Britain rolled her eyes. 'At the world headquarters on Benson
Street. In a concrete vault, fifty feet below the surface of the
earth, with a twenty-four hour armed guard. The Constitution
should have such protection.'

Jem waited. She looked out at the BI Tower. 'It's a strange
client in some ways,' Britain said. 'The founder still goes to the
office several times a week. If he whispers, they jump. He's like a
god over there.' She smiled. 'A little like Mr Carwick here. They
were very close.'

Eldridge Kingston Carwick, the Carwick of Haverly & Carwick, was another part of the mingled BI/H&C legend. Mr
Carwick had been the lawyer for the founder, Randall Jessup,
a soap salesman who had invented Buffo in his garage, then
displayed a marketing genius and sense for synergistic acquisitions that became the object of worship in the nation's leading
business schools. At ninety, Jessup ranked among the twenty
wealthiest Americans on lists that, according to rumour, failed to
take into account the bulk of his fortune, which was buried in
densely layered trusts and holding companies.

Mr Carwick had created that structure and, allegedly, had
amassed his own substantial fortune from an early investment in
BI. He was past ninety himself but came to the firm offices almost
daily. Ann Britain currently was BI Enterprises' chief outside
lawyer, but Eldridge Carwick remained the founder's closest
personal adviser.

Britain's phone buzzed. She listened for a moment, said, 'Give
me five minutes,' and hung up. She frowned at Jem. 'The damn
Louisville takeover again.' Jem smiled sympathetically.

Britain spoke briskly. 'Look at the file. This fellow Newsome began to sell a car wax and called it Buffum. BI's trademark people filed for an injunction. Newsome's lawyer, some clown named Tolbert, has filed a bogus counterclaim. The gist is that Newsome has ownership rights to Buffo, that this is the same formula as Buffo, and that BI has infringed his property. Obviously a desperation ploy, clearly barred by the statute of limitations.'

She shrugged. 'He'll follow it with a request that we produce the Buffo formula. They always do.' She shook her head at the foolishness of it all. 'Check with the file room; by now, we have an automatic pattern in these cases. You'll need to depose Newsome, investigate his claims, then prepare a motion for summary judgment. You can find some briefs in the files; just update them. If Newsome has any money, ask for attorneys' fees to discourage this sort of thing.' She picked up the phone, dismissing Jem. 'Give me a memo on your plans, then we'll talk, then we'll squash him like a bug.'

Tim Newsome toyed with the collar of his green knit golf shirt and stared at Jem with a wrinkled brow. 'I don't understand the question.'

His lawyer, Bertrand Tolbert, grunted; his fleshy jowls hung nearly to the open dirt-stained collar of his white shirt. 'Whaddya say?' he growled.

Jem sighed. Newsome was a young man with an open face that invited instant trust. Jem believed his story so far, but as the firm taught, he tried to maintain a skeptical tone in his questions, that would, of course, not appear in the written transcript. He rephrased the questions. 'You claim this is your grandfather's formula, correct?'

Newsome nodded.

'You have to answer out loud so she can take it down.' Jem pointed to the court reporter.

'It is my grandfather's formula,' Newsome said.

'How did it come into your possession?'

'My mother died last year. We found it in the attic, in a box of things that came from her father.'

'Who is we?'

'My sister and I.'

Tolbert groaned. His waist shifted from one side to the other as he pushed himself up in his chair, then settled back down. 'You already asked that, kid. Several times. Let's get on with it.'

'I can conduct my own deposition, thank you.' Jem flipped through his legal pad, then looked at Newsome. 'How did you know what it was?'

'It said "Formula for Buffo" across the top. And I am a chemical engineer. I recognized the ingredients.'

'Do you have it here?'

'No.'

Jem turned to Tolbert. 'For the record, we would like that paper produced.'

'You really want it attached to this transcript?'

'No. Keep it separate.'

'Fine. We will produce it at the same time as you produce the formula for the version of Buffo that your client manufactures.'

'Don't be ridiculous.' Jem glared at Tolbert. 'Your client is the one who claims to have obtained the formula. We are entitled to the basis for that claim.'

'Your client started this litigation, counsellor. Put up or shut up.'

Jem's patience began to wear thin. This had been three hours crammed into Tolbert's office – Tolbert had no conference room – and Jem was attempting to juggle his files and legal pad on his lap and the floor while asking questions. Only the court reporter appeared comfortable. The fat lawyer had refused to come to the adequate surroundings at H&C. Typical plaintiff lawyer crap.

Jem glanced at the court reporter. She sat blank-faced at her steno machine. He wondered if she realized when he made a mistake.

'Let me go at this a different way,' he said, ignoring the 'Awww, jeez,' from Tolbert. 'You have never seen the formula for Buffo, have you, Mr Newsome?'

Newsome phrased his answer carefully. 'I have never seen the formula that BI uses.'

'Then on what basis do you contend it is the same as the one in your mother's attic?'

Newsome began to tick points off on his fingers. 'One, the end products look and perform identically, except for colour. BI added colouring. Two, I have a friend at a gas chromatography lab. He tested both; they are identical except for insignificant trace elements. The colouring again. Three, everyone in my family knows that my grandfather invented Buffo.'

'How do you know that?'

'My grandmother told us. She said my grandfather and Jessup were friends and partners. Grandfather made the first batches of Buffo in his garage. Then Jessup stole the formula'

Jem looked at Tolbert. 'For the record, that is of course hearsay.'

Tolbert waved his hand. 'This is a deposition, counsellor. Come on, get on with it.'

Back to Newsome. 'How exactly did this alleged theft happen?'

'I don't know.'

'If it happened, it was more than fifty years ago, wasn't it?'

'It was whenever Buffo was invented.'

'Did your grandfather pursue this in court?'

'He died.'

'What about your grandmother?'

'She was afraid.'

'Is she alive?'

'No.'

In another hour, Jem ran out of questions. Tolbert followed him to the door. 'Kid, tell your bosses they better settle this one. Fast. 'Cause your client ain't gonna like it when word gets out. Or when we get mad and release our formula to the press.'

'Is this blackmail, Bertrand?'

'Gimme a break, kid. Run on home to mommy and tell them to settle.'

'Assuming hypothetically that I knew the formula, I would have to say that it cannot be confirmed by gas chromatography'. Dr Carrington Timmons leaned back in his office chair with a smug expression and looked at where the office window would have been on any other floor of the BI World Headquarters building. For security purposes, this floor, the lab floor, had no windows.

'Why not?'

'Because that process reveals only certain compounds and elements *after* combination. It does not show what went into the stew, as it were.'

'But if they are identical except for traces . . .'

'It could be the traces, my boy. That could be the distingushing feature. Soap is soap, wax is wax, except for traces. The traces are what make Buffo special.'

Jem searched the man's face for signs of deception or doubt; he found none. The chief chemist looked back at him with a bland expression. 'Could you test this other stuff for me?' Jem asked finally.

Timmons displayed his first moment of hesitation. 'We need special authorization to put Buffo through a gas chromatograph.'

'Why, if you can't recreate it from the results?'

'Company policy, my boy. But I will look into it. Leave me a sample.'

'The grandfather's name was Will Brunstone.' Jem handed the BI archivist a paper with the man's name and possible date of death.

She looked at it dubiously. 'I'll see what I can find. Unfortunately, some of our earlier holdings are not well indexed. I've asked for more staff, but the priorities are in the airline, they say.'

'Would it help if we went through the files? I have people who can do that. Our paralegals, you know.'

She hesitated. 'I'm afraid not. Not without authorization. Company policy, you know.'

The firm's chief files administrator, Eloise Smoot, laid a four inch printout on Jem's desk. 'These are the files on the computer. They go back to World War II.' She opened a box of three by five index cards. 'These are the pre-war files. We haven't bothered to put them on the computer.'

Jem leafed through some of the index cards. They were

yellowing, written in a flowing old-style script. Some corners crumbled in his hand. He looked at Eloise.

She shrugged. 'I'm afraid the rats got to some of them over the years. In the old building. We asked the firm to give us the people to put these on the computer, too, but priorities, you know. We can barely keep up with the new matters.'

'They're not in alphabetical order?'

'No. By lawyer, chronologically. Most of the BI files are under Mr Carwick – he was the chief BI lawyer back then. The company was called Buffo International then, you know. Until they bought the race track and the tire company.'

He looked at the Carwick cards, about two inches of them, and picked one at random. Eloise pointed to some numbers written in the corner. 'This is the box number for the archives. Then we have another list that correlates box numbers with warehouse shelf. They're usually right; sometimes we find a mistake.'

'What happens then?'

She shrugged. 'Then it's lost.'

He spent an hour sorting through the cards. Most of them said 'Buffo.' He asked for all the files.

'Give us a week,' Eloise said when he gave her the list.

The files arrived from the warehouse, and Jem deposited them and Miranda Beliz into a small conference room. 'Sort them out,' he said. 'Sorry. We're looking for any references to Brunstone or the formula for Buffo.'

Miranda was a very imaginative paralegal who had wanted to be a lawyer until she began to work in a law firm and discovered what lawyers do all day. Now she wanted to be a librarian. She rolled her eyes and surveyed the mountain of corrugated boxes that were stacked against the wall.

'If anything squeals at me when I open the box,' she said, 'I quit.'

Jem grinned. 'All for the firm.'

In his office, he had a message to call May Curtin. He could not recall who she was until he recognized the phone number: the BI archivist.

'We have located some very early correspondence files for the years you requested. I went through them and saw only one reference to a William Brunstone: a letter to a Mrs Brunstone offering sympathy for her husband's death.'

'Can you send it over?'

She hesitated. 'This is from the founder's personal file; I need authorization for that.'

'I'll have legal call you.'

Legal was a classmate of Jem's from law school. Legal also was dubious. 'I don't know about the founder's files. Let me check with the general counsel.'

Britain studied Jem's memo as he sat staring at the BI logo. She muttered to herself and made notes in the margin. When she finished, she looked up at him. 'Have they answered our interrogatories yet?'

'I gave him a few more days. They're due next week.'

'See what they say, then we'll decide.' She flipped through the memo. 'Forget the chromatograph; BI will never allow it. They're too nervous about the formula.'

'I asked for Newsome's test results.'

She nodded. 'That might do it, if we can believe him. Now, the founder's files, that's the big problem?'

'Yeah. Apparently there's some reference to Brunstone, but the archivist is afraid to produce it. I need you to talk to someone over there.'

Britain shook her head in amusement. 'I told you – a strange client.' She sighed and looked at her watch. 'I have a meeting with them this afternoon on the merger; I'll talk to the man then.' She looked at the memo again. 'How long until you have the motion ready?'

'I need the interrogatory answers, and the response to the requests for admission. Probably a couple of weeks after that.'

'Keep it moving. They'll start to show some interest if I ask for the founder's files. We don't have any reason to doubt the result yet, do we?'

'Can't guarantee a summary judgment. There may be issues of fact. But we do have the statute of limitations argument.'

'Don't tell them there may be factual issues. We'll deal with that after we see your motion.' She rose. 'Have you talked to Mr Carwick yet?'

'No.'

'See him. If this Brunstone really did exist, he might know something about him.'

Jem could not tell if Mr Carwick's head shook from palsy or as a negative gesture. Then he worried that the old man might not have understood him. He was about to ask again when Mr Carwick said, 'Brunstone. What was that first name?'

'William. William D.'

'Billy Brunstone.' He tapped his fingers lightly on the desk. 'It sounds familiar, but . . .'

Jem began to speak, but Mr Carwick raised a single finger. 'A chemist, I believe. Or a baker. Some sort of fellow who fooled around with chemicals. Died in a fire. Sad, very sad. I might have gone to his funeral. What about him?'

Mr Carwick apparently had forgotten Jem's explanation. He was ninety-three, after all. 'His grandson claims that this Brunstone knew the formula for Buffo.'

The old man chuckled. 'Nonsense. He was a baker or a cook or something. Buffo is car wax. Randall would never tell him the formula.' He cocked his head as if a memory came to him. 'That's right. Randall lived next door to Billy Brunstone. It was a very close call, I tell you. A very close call.' He rose and stood precariously, peering at Jem. 'Thank you for coming in . . .'

'Jem.'

'Yes, of course. James. Thank you for coming in, James. I have enjoyed talking with you.'

As he listened to Tolbert over the phone, Jem pictured the fat lawyer's sweat-soaked collar. 'Kid, where's your settlement offer?'

'There won't be one.'

'Come on. Timmy isn't greedy here. Just give him enough to let him think he got justice, and we'll be on our way. You can't take the chance, kid.'

Jem decided to try to talk some sense into him, although it probably would be futile. 'BI's policy is not to settle cases like this. They can't afford to open the floodgates. Even if you had a claim, it's barred by the statute of limitations. You're talking, fifty, sixty years here.'

'Which statute of limitations?'

'Take your choice. Contacts. Conversion or misappropriation of trade secrets. Whatever your claim is. Nothing survives that long.'

Tolbert snorted in his ear. 'Kid, lift your head out of the law books and look around. Your client can't afford this.'

'Where are my interrogatory answers?'

'Screw those. You know how much work it is to answer those things? Oppressive. Burdensome.'

'Tell it to the judge.'

'No. I'll tell it to you. I'm sending you some stuff, kid. Look at it and call me. With your offer.'

Miranda wrinkled her nose as she held the paper between her thumb and forefinger.

'Watch your desk,' she said. 'It has some sort of grime on it.'

Jem turned it delicately to read it. It was a brownish carbon, shiny and brittle from 1937. He read aloud. ' "Memo to File. From E.K. Carwick. Certain documents formerly herein have this date been transferred to File 'Brunstone. W. D.'" '

He looked at Miranda. 'What file did this come from?'

'It was labeled "Jessup, Randall, Miscellaneous." One of Mr Carwick's files.'

'Okay. Where's the Brunstone file?'

'There isn't one that I see. Either in the boxes or in the card index.' She waved at a spot on her dress. 'Look at that. I searched through every box. There's some sort of dust that just sticks to you.'

'Did you ask Eloise?'

'She has no record of it. She said maybe Mr Carwick would know.'

'What else was in the Jessup file?'

She shook her head. 'Miscellaneous, Like it said. A few letters about buying some property, some dispute with the phone company about a bill, a few memos about meetings.'

Miranda rummaged through her briefcase. 'I found some other references to William D. Brunstone.' She pulled more papers out and piled them on Jem's desk. 'Here is his death certificate. A fire at his house. Here's a copy of a newspaper article about it. The cause was unknown, but they said he had a laboratory in his garage, and they speculate it started there. It was in the middle of the night.'

Jem glanced at the article while she rummaged through her papers. The fire was in 1937. The firm had been founded only a year before.

Miranda produced another photocopy. 'Here, this is interesting. The alarm was called in by his next door neighbour, Randall Jessup. I guess it's *the* Randall Jessup. This was before Buffo, wasn't it?'

The earliest Buffo files were from 1938; from Jem's readings, the product had taken off during World War II. 'I wonder if there's some way to check.'

She produced more papers. 'Here's the chain of title to both properties; I ran the owners through letter purchases. Here are birth certificates for Newsome's mother. She is in fact Brunstone's daughter, so that part is true, at least. And she did die last year.'

'A file? Brunstone?' Mr Carwick wrinkled his brow. The shaking grew more pronounced. He gazed at a picture on his office wall; a landscape of the early BI headquarters now preserved as a museum on the company's headquarters campus. After a moment, the gaze became a stare, and Jem worried that he had drifted off.

Suddenly Mr Carwick snapped his head straight up. 'Yes,' he said as if Jem had just entered the room. Then he turned, pulled a key from his vest pocket, and opened a locked file drawer in the credenza behind him. He bent over, his nose no more than an inch from the file labels, and pawed through them, muttering the entire time. From the other side of the desk, Jem could not make out the mutters or see the files.

Mr Carwick grunted and shut the file drawer, carefully locking it. 'No, James,' he said. 'No Brunstone. I seem to recall that name, but it's been a very long time, you know. Was the file memo dated?'

'Yes, sir. Nineteen thirty-seven. It was in the old style files, the ones by lawyer.'

'Yes, that was very long ago then. We changed filing systems in 1958, as I recall. June. When Mrs Halstead came to the file room. I remember her saying to me. "Mr Carwick," she said, "we have to modernize this system." Now, of course, we have the computers. They began in 1974. One of the earliest systems in a firm this size, I believe . . .'

Jem left twenty minutes later, educated in the history of the firm's filing techniques but unenlightened as to the location of the files.

The delivery from Tolbert sat on his desk. It was copies of three single-page documents and several handwritten pages held together by a binder clip.

The first page had been copied with a blank paper over most of it. The only legible portion was the top: 'FORMULA FOR BUFFO' was written in block printing across the page. Under it, in new ink, was 'Kid, your client won't like it if I produce the real formula, so I have redacted the rest of this to save your butt. Thank me later. Tolbert.'

Another single page document was a letter:

COPY
April 12.
Dear Jessup,
Re our discussion. I propose a fifty-fifty split of both profits and costs of operation; my capital contribution to be the formula and initial supplies, yours the advertising matter, postage, etc. We both contribute the 'elbow grease' until revenues support salaries. For the nonce, we can work out of my garage. Your idea about promoting this product as a 'secret' formula is nonsense. I plan to take immediate steps to apply for a patent, which will provide

ample protection to us for an adequate period of time.
Keep the lawyers out of it. Perhaps you can afford to pay
them, but I certainly cannot. This will serve as our
agreement. Sign below to confirm.

It was unsigned.
The last page was another letter:

April 20.
My dear Mrs Brunstone.
Please accept my deepest sympathy over the untimely death
of your husband in the tragic fire that so shocked us all.
Billy was a dear friend, and we shall all miss him.
    My best to you and the children. Please do not hesitate to
call on me if I can provide you with any assistance whatsoever.

Sincerely,
Randall Jessup.

Jem leafed through the clipped pages. The cover sheet was a piece
of Tolbert's letterhead with the handwritten words 'From Brunstone Lab Notes.' The remaining dozen sheets were photocopies
of a different handwriting – he thought it was the same as the first
letter – and appeared to deal with tests of various mixtures of car
wax. Each entry contained a time and date statement, from the
spring of 1937. On the last page, the entry read: 'Monday, April
15, 1937, 10 A.M. Final Formula – Mix 132 – Clear and hard
drying. Prepared production samples, per RJ instructions sent to
EC in advance of meeting tomorrow.'
    There also was a report from a gas chromatography laboratory
company. The two samples submitted were identical in all significant respects, it said.

Miranda had left for the night; the conference room smelled of
the musty file folders and the dusty boxes from the warehouse.
He rummaged through the file cabinet and found her copies of
the newspaper clippings. The fire was described in one dated
Wednesday, April 16, 1937.

A local baker perished last night in a conflagration that destroyed his house and outbuildings and threatened those of neighbours.

William D. Brunstone, 25, of 144 Jellicoe Street was found in the ashes of his garage, following a blaze that required four companies of local fire fighters to bring under control. The garage was destroyed completely in the fire, which apparently was fed by chemicals stored by the deceased, an amateur chemist. The main house also suffered significant damage, according to fire officials, and will require demolition for safety purposes.

Two firefighters suffered minor injuries, and several others were treated and released for smoke inhalation. Brunstone's wife and children were away visiting relatives at the time.

The fire apparently started in the garage, according to neighbours who alerted the fire department at 11:55 p.m. It spread rapidly and threatened houses next door. 'I was at a church social with a group of several hundred individuals,' said next door neighbour Randall Jessup, 'and arrived home to find the firemen hosing down my roof. They would not let me in.'

Jessup, a friend of the deceased, speculated that the fire began with a laboratory experiment gone awry. 'He was constantly mixing things up in there,' Jessup stated.

Brunstone was a baker and entrepreneur, according to his friend and lawyer Eldridge Carwick, who expressed shock and dismay at the death. 'He was an outstanding member of the community and will be sorely missed.'

Other friends and associates echoed Mr Carwick's sentiments . . .

Jem had lifted his hand to knock on Britain's closed door when the senior lawyer's secretary saw him and shook her head in alarm. She bustled up to him and spoke in a whisper. 'She is in conference and can't be disturbed.'

Jem looked at her cubicle. A husky man in a black suit leaned against her desk. Another man, in the same outfit, lounged against the file cabinet wall, staring at the closed office door. Both men appeared bored but alert. Jem bent closer to the secretary and whispered back, 'This is important.'

'Mr Carwick is in there.' She looked over her shoulder at the men and lowered her voice even more. 'With Mr Jessup.'

'Jessup?'

She nodded in awe. 'He came in about ten minutes ago. Mr Jessup almost never goes anywhere, you know. So it's a real feather in Ms Britain's cap.'

Jem had started away when Britain's office door opened. She glanced at him in surprise, then nodded to the men in the secretarial cubicle. They pushed past Jem into the office and emerged, one holding the door, the other pushing a wheelchair containing a desiccated figure with an old fashioned car blanket across its knees. They left without a word.

'James.' Mr Carwick nodded to Jem as he passed. He had an old file folder tucked under his arm. Jem could make out 'B-R-U-N . . .' on it. Britain tapped him on the shoulder and gestured toward her office.

'The client has decided to settle this Newsome case.'

'Why?'

She shrugged. 'It's the client's call. Apparently Mr Carwick happened to mention it to Mr Jessup, and he decided that's what he wants to do. I don't know why exactly, but I speculate that he is nervous about this formula disclosure nonsense. Did you talk with Mr Carwick about that?'

'Not about the formula.'

'Then maybe he looked in the file himself. Mr Carwick takes quite an interest in the BI matters. Anyway, I told you they were sensitive about it. I am ordered to negotiate with Tolbert myself. So send up the file, and I'll take care of it. Thank you for your help.'

He turned to leave.

'Jem,' she stopped him. 'You did a fine job, and they should have let you finish. But sometimes clients get a weird notion. Mr Carwick was impressed with your work. He made me promise to use you on other BI cases.'

Mr Carwick was in his office in the dim light of dusk. The folder labeled BRUNSTONE was on his desk. He looked at Jem with a squint. 'What is it, James?'

'What happened to Billy Brunstone, Mr Carwick?'

Carwick emitted a dry chuckle. 'He died. Playing with fire.
You should never play with fire.'

'Was it his formula?'

The old man ignored him. His voice grew distant, his eyes less
focused. 'Greedy, too. Sometimes when you want too much, you
end up with none. He should have taken the twenty-five percent
that Randall offered. Half, that was too much. Randall could get
the money somewhere else. And he did, after Billy died.'

'Was it his formula?

'The product doesn't matter, James, it's what you do with it.
Marketing, that's the key. This secret formula nonsense, that's
just marketing. Randall had everything lined up – customers,
endorsements. Then Billy got greedy. He thought the formula
was worth half. Hell, Randall's a genius. We could have put lard
in that jar and Randall would have sold it. Anyone with any sense
could see that.'

'Did Randall Jessup start the fire?'

'The way to grow a law firm, James, remember this when
you're older, the way to grow a law firm is to grow the client. Get
a client with vision, one who will grow, and nurture that client.
That's what we did here, Barton Haverly and I. Gave Randy
some seed money, took some stock, and kept his business by
giving him good service.'

The old man leaned back in his chair now, staring at the ceiling.
'Time to time, Randy would make noises about hiring some other
law firms. It's like a marriage. You have good days and bad days.
But then I'd have a little chat with him and remind him of our
history together and certain of our services in the past and then
we'd kiss and make up. But he's an old man now, in that wheelchair, and I'm an old man and before long, neither one of us will
be around to keep the marriage together.'

He looked at Jem with a sharp, appraising glare. 'Britain can't
do it. She cares too much about mergers and airlines, and not
enough about the core business. Never forget the core business.'
He sighed and shook his head. 'And you're too young. Hell,
you're not even a partner. But I suppose you can keep your
mouth shut, can't you?'

'Yes, sir.'

'I searched your desk. You've kept your mouth shut so far, haven't you?'

'Yes, sir.'

The old man stood. 'Give me some legal advice, boy. Tell me about the attorney–client privilege. If a client confesses a crime to me, can I tell anyone?'

'No, sir.'

'That's good legal advice, James. I came to you for advice. and you rendered it. That makes me your client, so to speak, for purposes of the privilege, doesn't it?'

'I suppose so.'

'Then here.' Mr Carwick slid the folder across the table to Jem. 'This will help you make partner, boy. Keep it locked up. Read it-once, and never use it unless you need to keep BI in line.'

Jem looked him in the eye. 'Did Mr. Jessup start that fire?'

Mr Carwick laughed soundlessly. 'Hell, no. He was at a church social with hundreds of witnesses. We made sure of that. Just one of the services that bound the marriage.' He worked. 'You take the ingredients for Buffo and put a couple of them together then put a match to the mix – you have a regular bomb, James. It's very simple. Anyone could do it. Even you or I could, if we had enough at stake.'

'Where were you that night, Mr Carwick?'

'As always, James, I was acting in the best interests of the client.' He turned and stared at the BI logo across the skyline. Jem rose, began to speak, then walked from the office.

Mr Carwick called to him: 'Read the file, Jem.'

That night, Jem read the file.

UNREASONABLE DOUBT

K.L. Jones

Cindy Adams had never sat on a jury before. She wanted to do a good job, so she paid very close attention. The judge was a grumpy old man who reminded Cindy of her boss. She had the feeling he wasn't really as mean as he seemed to be. On the other hand, she was sure she wouldn't want to be a defendant before him.

'Ladies and gentlemen of the jury,' the judge said. 'Now that you have been sworn to hear the evidence in this case, it is time for the lawyers to present opening statements. The one thing you must remember at all times during this trial is that the State must prove the defendant's guilt beyond a reasonable doubt. That standard is the foundation on which our system of justice is based. Now with that in mind, I call upon Ms Daniels, the assistant state's attorney to present her opening statement.'

'Thank you, Your Honour,' Daniels said.

As she spoke, the prosecutor moved across the courtroom until she stood just a foot or so from the jury box. To Cindy the young woman on the other side of the rail seemed cold and professional.

'Members of the jury,' the prosecutor said. 'My job is to make you believe that the defendant, Kelvin Stouter, is a murderer; that he in fact killed his wife, Diane. This is not a typical murder case because we cannot tell you where the body is. Our case is built on what we call circumstantial evidence. But once you have heard all the evidence I am sure that you will be convinced beyond a reasonable doubt of Kelvin Stouter's guilt. Just listen to the witnesses, and judge what they say. Use your common sense and I am certain you will arrive at the right verdict. Thank you.'

Abruptly the woman turned her back on the jury and stalked back to the table across from the jury. As she did so, one of the two men who sat at another table next to it rose and advanced toward the jury.

'Your turn, Mr Olson,' the judge said.

Robert Olson introduced himself to the jury as the attorney for the defense. Cindy was a little surprised that he seemed so young. He, too, stood close to the jury and Cindy had the feeling he was looking right at her. He projected a certain warmth as he too urged the jurors to pay close attention to what they would hear.

'And if you do,' he said in conclusion, 'you will not only have a doubt as to my client's guilt, you will have serious doubts as to whether or not Diane Stouter is dead.'

'Now that you've heard from the lawyers,' the judge said, 'It is time for the state to present its case. Are you ready, Ms Daniels?'

'Yes, your honour. Our first witness will be Arlene Cates, the deceased's sister.'

'Objection,' Olson said raising angrily from his chair. 'We don't know if Mrs Stouter is dead. That's something the state still has to prove.'

'Your point is very well taken, Mr Olson,' the judge said.

'I'll withdraw the remark,' the prosecutor said, smiling. To Cindy it was obvious that the woman was playing some kind of game, that she knew exactly what she was doing.

Mrs Cates was a well-tailored woman in her early thirties. She began her testimony by stating that she was the sister of Diane Stouter and that she had last seen her sister on September 12th when they had eaten lunch together at the Rockway Inn.

'We had lunch together every Thursday,' Mrs Cates said.

'When was the next time you spoke with your sister?'

'She called me late the next Tuesday night. She'd had an argument with Kelvin, and was very upset. She said she was afraid.'

'Afraid of whom?' Ms Daniels asked.

'Her husband, Kelvin Stouter.'

'Did you have lunch with your sister the following Thursday?'

'No,' Mrs Cates said. She spoke deliberately and to Cindy it seemed the witness were struggling to maintain herself. 'I never saw or heard from my sister again.'

Mrs Cates went on to relate that she had gone to Rockway Inn and waited until 12:30. She then called the Stouter home but there was no answer. She waited for another half hour and then called Kelvin Stouter at work.

'He seemed unconcerned. All he told me was that he didn't know where Diane was.' Again Mrs Cates seemed on the verge of tears.

'That night,' she went on, 'I went over to their house.'

'What happened there?'

'At first Kelvin didn't want to let me in. He said the place was a mess. He said he still didn't know where Diane was. We were standing at the front door. After a few minutes he let me into the hall.'

'Could you see into the kitchen from that hallway?' Ms Daniels asked.

'No,' Mrs Cates said. 'I couldn't. The kitchen door was closed. I'd never seen that door closed before.'

The rest of Mrs Cates' testimony concerned her calls to the police about her sister. Then it was Mr Olson's turn to question the witness. Cindy was surprised at how few questions he asked. Only one seemed really important.

'Now, Mrs Cates, your sister told you that she and Kelvin had an argument. Isn't it true that she told you the argument was caused by the fact that she was having an affair, and Kelvin had just found out about it?'

'No,' Mrs Cates had said. 'That is not true.'

Cindy thought the answer came too fast.

The rest of the witnesses called by the prosecution were police officers. To Cindy their testimony seemed precise and professional. They told about a series of calls from Mrs Cates and several calls they made to Kelvin Stouter who simply told them he did not know where his wife was. The last witness was Detective Levinson, a homicide investigator.

'I didn't get involved in the case,' Levinson said, 'until a car registered to Mrs Stouter was found. The car was in the airport parking lot and had been there for three days. The keys were in the ignition.'

'Was there anything else unusual about the car?'

'There were blood stains on the driver's door. There was also quite a lot of dried blood found in the trunk. The blood was found to be type O-positive. That's the same type as Mrs Stouter.'

Levinson testified that after examining the car, he went to the Stouter home. Kelvin Stouter told him that he didn't know where Diane was, but suggested she might have run off with a man she was having an affair with. Stouter didn't know the man's name and wasn't able to give any details about the affair or the man.

With Stouter's approval, the police searched the home.

'Did you find anything unusual?'

'First of we found a closet full of woman's clothes. No empty hangers. If Mrs Stouter ran off, it looked as if she didn't take anything.'

'What else?'

'Well, the kitchen seemed to have been cleaned pretty thoroughly, but our lab people found a stain in one of the corners. They said it was blood. Type O-positive.'

The courtroom was exceptionally silent after Levinson's statement. Cindy waited, anticipating something but she didn't know what.

Ms Daniels stood and faced the jury.

'The State rests,' she said.

The first two witnesses for the defense were simply character witnesses. They had known Kelvin Stouter for years, and simply could not believe him capable of any act of violence, especially not against his wife.

After this testimony Olson spoke briefly with his client, then stood up to face the jury.

'Our last witness,' he announced, 'will be my client, Kelvin Stouter.'

Cindy watched as Stouter moved across the courtroom.

He did not look at the jury until he was sitting in the witness chair. Stouter's testimony was brief. He made no attempt to explain the blood stains in the car or in the kitchen. He admitted having a fight with Diane before she disappeared. It was over the fact that she was seeing another man.

'Kelvin,' Olson asked, 'did you kill your wife?'

'No,' the defendant said. 'I don't believe she is dead.'

His voice broke.

'I love her. And I wish she'd come home.'

'With that,' Olson said, 'the defense rests.'

'Very good,' the judge said. 'It is now time for the lawyers to present closing arguments. After that it will be up to the jury to decide the case. Ms Daniels, whenever you are ready.'

The prosecutor moved across the courtroom and placed her notepad on the rail that separated her from the jurors. She summed up the testimony that the prosecution had presented, and concluded by saying: 'If Diane Stouter isn't dead, why hasn't she been in touch with her sister? Why did she leave her clothes at home? If Kelvin Stouter didn't kill his wife, where is she?'

The prosecutor was replaced by Robert Olson, counsel for the defense. He spoke without notes, pacing back and forth before the jury as he argued his client's case.

'The prosecution asks where is Mrs Stouter,' he said, pausing directly in front of Cindy. Dramatically he looked at his watch. 'Soon we'll have an answer to that question.'

As she looked at Olson, Cindy could also see Stouter sitting at the defense table, nervously toying with a pencil. His eyes were down and Cindy was unable to read the expression on his face.

'That door,' he said gesturing toward the courtroom door, 'will open in the next ten seconds, and Mrs Stouter will walk into this room . . .'

A buzz started among the spectators.

'What is this nonsense,' Ms Daniels said rising from her chair. Almost involuntarily, she looked over her shoulder to the door.

'Ten seconds, your honour,' Olson said as the judge looked rather startled.

Cindy's eyes moved almost involuntarily from Olson to the courtroom door. Out of the corner of her eye she was aware of Stouter still playing with the pencil, his eyes down.

Cindy waited for something to happen. Nothing did.

Following a moment of silence, Olson began to speak again.

'I have to apologize,' Olson said. 'I've mislead you. Mrs Stouter, so far as I know, will not be in court. But I did notice that all of you on the jury looked to that door. I believe everyone in the courtroom looked toward the door. You wouldn't have done that if you were convinced beyond a reasonable doubt that Diane Stouter was dead.'

'Mr Olson, a courtroom is no the place for playing games,' the judge said.

'With all due respect, your honour,' Olson said. 'I was just trying to make a point. And I think I did. Thank you, ladies and gentlemen of the jury. I am sure that you will do your duty when you retire to the jury room.'

After the arguments the judge read instructions to the jury telling that they could only consider the evidence they heard testified about and reminding them that if they had a reasonable doubt of the defendant's guilt, they should acquit him. The jury was then led into a small room just off the courtroom.

The first vote in the jury room was eleven to one. Cindy was the only holdout. The foreman asked her to explain her reasoning. She did and the next vote was unanimous.

After being thanked for their service, and discharged by the judge Cindy retrieved her coat and purse from the jury room. She was one of the last jurors to come back into the court room and when she did so, she was surprised to see a group of jurors talking with the defense attorney.

'She's the one turned us around,' one of them said pointing to Cindy.

Olson came toward her. Cindy froze, tense until Olson smiled. She sensed that he, too, was nervous. 'You don't have to talk to me,' he said, 'but I am curious. I know you looked at the door, just like everybody else.'

'Yes,' Cindy admitted. 'Even the judge and prosecutor looked at the door. You really were quite persuasive. I really expected to see Diane Stouter come into court.'

'So how could you vote guilty?'

'Well, you weren't quite right when you said everybody looked toward the door. One person didn't.'

Olson waited.

'Kelvin Stouter.' Cindy said. 'He never looked toward the door. He was the one person in the courtroom who was certain his wife would not be coming through those doors.'

A MURDER COMING

James Powell

Fog is always there and never here. When the man in the fur-collared overcoat and homburg reached the CNR tracks the fog had moved to the edge of the lake. When he reached the lake and the sagging wharf the fog stood a bit off from shore.

For a moment the man stared out fretfully across the water. Then he noticed someone on the edge of the fog at the end of the wharf and quickly picked his way out to him. 'Did Alcott send you for me?' he asked. 'My name is Watford.'

The other man was staring down into a rowboat. He looked up slowly. His face was broad and stubbled with white. 'No,' he said. His breath smelled of alcohol.

'Damn!' muttered Watford and hurled a ball of paper off into the fog. ('Would you mind delivering this, Judge?' the station-master had asked, handing Watford his own telegram in which he had answered Alcott's curious wire and announced his arrival time.) The fine, drifting rain had started up again. 'Five dollars to row me out there,' said Watford. The man looked at him with soft unblinking eyes. Watford drew a banknote from his wallet and held it under the man's nose. 'If you don't know where Alcott's place is, I can show you,' he said.

'Not many people on the islands this time of year,' said the man.

'Five dollars,' said Watford, who didn't care to discuss the comings and goings of a future provincial minister of justice with a local inhabitant.

The man shrugged and tucked the money in a pocket of his mackinaw. He stepped down into the boat and drew it up tight against the pilings. With a strong hand under Watford's elbow, he helped – almost lifted – him down. Then, as his passenger arranged himself in the bow, the man untied the boat and pushed off. Before the oars were in their locks the fog had closed in and the wharf had disappeared.

Now nothing was visible beyond the boat except a dark rim of water tufted with mist. At intervals shapes emerged from the fog and then slipped back into it. Watford, who felt the cold off the water almost at once, hunched inside his coat and thought of crocodiles and Loch Ness. 'Your boat's taking water,' he said suddenly, noticing the water lapping around his dapper little feet.

The man at the oars had been watching him with an expression as placid as a cow's. Now he shook his head.

'Don't tell me all this is from the rain,' insisted Watford.

The man shook his head. 'The boat's taking water.'

'That's what I said,' snapped Watford.

The man shook his head again. 'It's not my boat.'

Watford frowned. 'Well, we could still use a can or something to bail with,' he said uneasily.

'Try your hat,' the man suggested.

As he groped for a cutting reply, it occurred to Watford that the man wasn't staring as much as offering his face to be recognized. 'Have you and I met before?' he asked.

'You once sentenced me to be hanged, Judge,' said the man. 'If you call that a meeting.'

Watford leaned forward curiously, searching the slack cheeks, the pitted skin, the water-blue eyes. The man grinned shyly. Then holding the oars in his armpits, he took a drink from a bottle in a brown paper bag. Watford refused the offered bottle with a disdainful shake of the head. Then he shook his head again, perplexed.

The man started to row again. 'Edward McSorley,' he said.

'Ah, yes,' said Watford, brightening. In the late forties McSorley, a small-town hardware store owner, had been convicted of the murder of his wife. In the course of the trial it was also revealed that the McSorleys were The Shouting Bandits, bank robbers whose brief career had made them the darlings of the southern Ontario press. In fact, McSorley claimed his wife wasn't dead but had run off with their accumulated loot.

Watford gave an abrupt laugh. 'McSorley, remember the

witness, your peeping tom neighbour who saw you came up behind your wife that night and choke her with your arm? Remember how you answered that when you took the stand? You said . . .'

' "My wife is a judo expert," ' repeated McSorley gravely. ' "I often let her practise on me after dinner." '

Watford forced a frown. 'Not that I approve the commuting of your sentence, McSorley,' he said. 'The death penalty is a last bastion of the grand style in this all too colourless world. In his heart even the simplest of murderers sees the justice of an eye for an eye. Isn't that so?'

'Don't look at me. I didn't kill my wife,' said McSorley.

'I had hoped we could speak frankly,' said Watford. 'After all, you've served your time.' He paused. 'You have, haven't you?'

'Twenty-five years,' said McSorley, peering over his shoulder into the fog.

'Good for you,' said Watford. 'But now that the time has come to rehabilitate yourself, here's a tip: talk about the bloody deed at the drop of a hat. I mean it. If you ask me, our prisons should emphasize the teaching of communications skills – public speaking, first-person narrative, dramatic reading with gestures, and all. You see, so few of us actually get to kill in white heat. The man on the street thirsts to know what it's like. I confess to a certain curiosity myself.'

McSorley rested on his oars. 'Maudie's still alive,' he said. 'And the only thing I learned in prison was this.' He lunged forward, a hunting knife in his upraised hand. Wide-eyed with fear, Watford fell backward across the bow. The knife arced down and stopped just short of his throat. 'I learned you don't do it like that,' said McSorley. With one hand he pulled Watford back into his seat. 'You come up like this.' He arced the knife up from the bottom of the boat and pressed it against Watford's stomach. 'Want me to go through that one more time?' he asked earnestly. 'Are you sure you got it?'

'I got it,' whispered Watford hoarsely.

After a doubtful moment McSorley said, 'I guess you'd better do some bailing.' Watford crushed his Homburg into a scoop and started throwing water over the side. McSorley watched, mildly interested, lounging back on his seat, legs crossed and an elbow on the gunwale. He took a drink, then another.

Watford bailed. 'You have to admit you had a fair trial,' he said hurriedly, regretting the squeak in his voice. 'Eminently fair, as I recall. The evidence was all there. Oh, perhaps Brownish could have made more of prosecution's failure to positively identify those bone fragments in the incinerator as your wife's.'

'He giggled a lot,' observed McSorley.

'Yes,' panted Watford as he bailed, 'Brownish was famous for his little giggling fits in the courtroom. But he came from a fine family. We all forgave him a lot for that. Poor Brownish. He died several years ago, or perhaps you hadn't heard. Walked into an open manhole in broad daylight.'

The boat was now bailed out. Watford's fingers were like sticks from the cold. The icy water had set his wrists aching. He started to throw the sodden wreckage of his hat over the side.

But McSorley wagged the knife. 'Why don't you put it on?' he said.

Watford put on the hat. The leather sweatband made him shiver. Water trickled down his face and the back of his neck. He had the sudden urge to cry.

'Here's to Brownish,' toasted McSorley, raising the bottle to his lips. 'We're having a wonderful time and wish he was here.' Then he handed the bottle to the unhappy Watford.

Watford braced himself, tilted the bottle, and choked in surprise. 'Cognac?' He pulled down the bag to read the label.

'Special occasion,' said McSorley.

As he handed the bottle back Watford remembered with a start that it was Alcott who had prosecuted McSorley's case. He cleared his throat nervously and said, 'Say, this isn't the old routine where the released murderer hunts down the person he's supposed to have killed and then murders him before the very eyes of the judge and prosecutor who convicted him? The ironic part, you see, is that he can't be tried twice for the same crime.' He added almost hopefully, 'Is that what all this is about?'

'I couldn't kill anybody,' said McSorley. 'I'm just not a violent person. Now, Maudie is a violent person. Once I saw her break a man's nose with her forearm,' McSorley looked at the knife as though seeing it for the first time. He offered it to Watford. 'Here,' he said sheepishly, handing the judge the knife.

Watford's heart pounded. Was it a trick? He had to force himself to take the knife. Had McSorley just wanted to humiliate him? Clenching the knife, Watford looked the man in the eye defiantly and swept the wet Homburg off his head and over the side. McSorley grinned meekly.

Breathing easier now, Watford said, 'All right, let's get going. We can't sit here all afternoon.' Watford had never had the exhilaration of ordering anyone to do something at knife point before. Frightened, he pushed the knife deep in his pocket and folded his arms. 'What is it you want, McSorley?' he demanded.

McSorley rowed in silence. Finally he said, 'At the trial nobody asked why we were called The Shouting Bandits.'

'It was hardly relevant,' said Watford. A small island with a single pine tree slid by in the fog. Alcott's island wasn't far now. 'Proceed,' said Watford. 'Consider yourself asked.'

'I guess the first time I met my wife is the best place to begin,' said McSorley. 'She was the new bank teller just arrived in town, a big-boned, broad-shouldered woman with this hard-of-hearing problem and a voice like a bugle. But too vain to wear a hearing aid. Funny, because she was plain as a post. Kicked out of the School of Library Science at the University of Western Ontario because of it – her hearing, not her looks.' He faltered. 'I'm not telling it right,' he said helplessly. 'I guess maybe prisons should teach those communications skills you talked about.'

McSorley pulled on the oars thoughtfully, as though ordering things in his mind. 'Hardware stores smell of things with weight to them,' he began again. 'But banks smell like courtrooms, all paper and dried-up ink.'

'More matter and less art, McSorley,' said Watford.

'When my turn came at the teller's window that first day, Maudie blared right out, "Speak up there, Mr Man. You're not in church," ' said McSorley in a rush. 'Everybody turned. The bank manager stuck his head out of his cubbyhole. But what really hit me like a load of bricks was that she was right. I mean I'd been whispering in the bank all my life and so'd my father before me.

'The next day, Sunday, I spent walking the few streets of the town trying to figure out what to do. After two generations of whispering how could I put things right and become my own man again? All of a sudden there was Maudie coming out of Fallows Tourist Rooms with a fibre suitcase, fired from the bank and heading home to Sarnia.

'Well, there weren't any buses on Sundays, so I offered to drive her. It was in the car that I laughed and shouted and guessed the only way for me to get my own back was to rob the bank. Maudie punched my arm and shouted that was the best damn idea she'd ever heard and to count her in. She felt banks had given her a raw deal. And libraries, too. But we both agreed there was more money in robbing banks.

'The next thing I knew I was visiting Maudie regularly in Sarnia where we'd sit around and shout about robbing banks. You wouldn't really think that could lead to wedding bells, but it did. On our honeymoon we sneaked back to town in masks and robbed the bank. That's when she broke the bank manager's nose. He didn't jump when she shouted "Jump!" A violent person, Maudie. 'For the next few months, Mondays meant close up the hardware store and rob a bank. By God, nothing makes you speak right up in a bank like knowing you've robbed it! But I'd had my fill. Besides, they elected one captain of the River Street Merchants (Northside) hockey team with Monday practices and a good chance that year of beating our Southside rivals. So I said, "Hold the phone, Maudie."

'She didn't like that a bit. I could hear it in her voice after dinner when she'd get me in a full Nelson, snap my neck, and say, "Tomorrow we're going to rob a bank. One and done." "No, now Maudie," I'd say, "enough's enough." But love curdles fast when you've built a marriage on robbing banks.'

Watford said, 'So according to you she took the money and ran. But why make it look like you'd killed her?'

'I'm somebody to be reckoned with,' insisted McSorley. 'I rob banks just because I'd whispered in them. She had to be afraid of what a guy like that would do if she stole his share. So you were supposed to kill me. But you didn't.'

'God knows I tried,' said Watford. 'I wasn't the one who commuted your sentence.'

'Anyway, the big question now in her mind is what a guy like me is going to do to make up for those twenty-five years I spent in jail,' said McSorley.

'So you've really found her then,' said Watford.

'I put a private detective on that,' said McSorley. 'She owns a place called Echo Lake Lodge about forty miles from here – just a couple of ratty cabins for fishermen and a three-stool lunch counter.' He smiled. 'Tell you what I did: when I got out I bought an old car and paid her a visit, just a wave and a smile and hanging around outside, just giving her the jumps.'

A dark shelf loomed ahead of them in the fog. Alcott's landing. 'If that's what this is all about, I wouldn't advise you trying to harass Mr Alcott and myself,' warned Watford. 'We have friends with the police who'd be happy to extend themselves on our behalf.'

'I'm not going to bother you any more, Judge. Honest,' promised McSorley. 'Just let me finish what I was telling you. You see, I knew she couldn't take much of the waiting, and wondering what I was going to do. She'd have to come after me. And so there she was, padlocking the lunch-counter door behind her and there I was driving off in a cloud of dust. I let her chase me until I caught her, Judge. Now I've got her where she can't get away.'

'Why tell me all this?' demanded Watford.

McSorley edged the boat up against the landing. 'Because you're a judge,' he said. 'Because you say when people have the right to kill and when they don't.'

'I've already told you you've got a murder coming, so to speak,' said Watford, standing up.

McSorley helped him out of the boat and onto the landing. 'The trouble is I'm just not a violent person,' he said. 'So I let her chase me until she could taste my blood and then I put her where she couldn't get away. When the police come looking they'll find her. Or her body.'

Watford looked down at him. 'Her body?' he asked.

McSorley grinned. 'Well, you see, Judge, I told her a lie. I told her I'd hired a couple of guys to kill her.'

'Figuring on scaring her to death?' asked Watford contemptuously. He stuffed his hands in his pockets and started to walk away. Then he stopped and pulled out the knife. 'Here. This is yours,' he said.

But McSorley had already pushed off. 'That's all right,' McSorley said gravely. 'You just remember what I told you.' He arced his fist down. 'Not like that. Like this.' He arced his first up. 'Mr Alcott never did get that straight.'

Watford gave a puzzled frown. Then something moved in the fog. Someone was coming down the landing toward him. 'Alcott?' he called doubtfully, for Alcott was a small man with a quick step.

'Alcott?' he called again.

McSorley rested his oars and sat there on the edge of the fog. He held up the bottle in a little salute and before putting it to his lips said, 'You'll have to shout louder than that, Judge. A lot louder than that.'

THE ADVENTURE OF THE NEFARIOUS NEPHEW

Michael Mallory

Although he was quite slender, Sir Peter Swindon managed to puff out his chest like a pigeon while strutting like a popinjay, his white periwig standing in for a bird's natural crest. I have no doubt that this posturing was impressing some within the courtroom, though I felt it bordered on the comical.

'Now then, Dr Watson,' he said, absently brushing his moustache with the edge of his monocle, 'you were engaged by Scotland Yard to examine the body of Humphrey Jafford, were you not?'

'I was,' my husband answered from the witness stand.

'And what did your examination reveal?'

From one coat pocket John withdrew a small notebook, and from the other, a pair of spectacles that he had only recently been required to obtain. Using the detailed terminology of the medical profession, he went on to describe the gruesome fact that Mr Jafford had died as the result of a severe blow to the head from a heavy object. 'Judging from the position of the body and the direction of the blood flow from the wound,' he added, 'it seems clear that Mr Jafford was facing his attacker, and fell backwards upon receiving the blow.'

'Facing his attacker,' Sir Peter mused. 'And why should he not face his attacker, since he knew him so well.' This statement was pointedly directed towards the defendant, Owen Jafford, the victim's nephew. Strikingly handsome, if somewhat dandified, Owen Jafford was marked by one curious fluke of nature: despite his youth, his hair, which was worn on the longish side, was almost totally white.

But if the prosecutor's objective was to rattle the defendant with his accusation he failed, as young Jafford merely looked away in bored fashion.

'Is it possible, Dr Watson,' Sir Peter went on, 'that a heavy, silver-headed walking stick, much like the one the defendant carries, could have been the object that was used to kill Humphrey Jafford?'

'It is possible, yes.'

'I see. Was there anything else that you observed while examining the deceased?'

'Yes. The placement of the wound, on the right side of the head, indicated that his assailant was a left-handed man.' I looked back at the now-frowning defendant and noticed that he was indeed holding his walking stick with his left hand. 'And then there was the matter of his closed fist,' John offered.

'Pray, explain yourself, doctor,' Sir Peter said.

'The late Mr Jafford's left hand was tightly clenched, a muscle contraction that does not occur naturally in death. It occurred to me that he might have been grasping something in his hand at the time of his death, so I asked Inspector Laurie to pry the man's hand open.'

'And what did the inspector find?'

'Hairs,' John said. 'White hairs.'

Sir Peter turned to glare once more at Owen Jafford. 'White hairs found in the hand of a man who had been killed by a left-handed assailant; the evidence speaks clearly for itself, m'lud,' he announced. 'I put it to the court that, having been informed of his dying uncle's intentions to disinherit him, Owen Jafford took it upon himself to speed along his uncle's appointment with the angels before any new will could be drawn up. The two argued, may even have struggled, ergo the hairs in Humphrey Jafford's clenched hand. The encounter rushed to a deadly conclusion when Owen Jafford raised his stick' – and here the prosecutor thrust his hand dramatically in the air – 'and struck!'

The spectators in the court chamber collectively gasped at the theatrics.

'Thank you, Dr Watson,' Sir Peter concluded and returned to his table.

It was now time for Mr Strang, the counsel for the defence, to strike back at John's damaging testimony, which, I feared, was in for a severe raking. I was therefore quite surprised when the opposing barrister calmly announced: 'May it please the court, m'lud, I have no questions for Dr Watson.'

'Indeed, Mr Strang?' remarked the grim-faced Judge Wilkins, who seemed quite surprised himself. 'Very well, Dr Watson, you may step down.'

John did so, striding to the back of the courtroom to take a seat beside me. I squeezed his hand in support of a job well done. While I knew John had offered expert testimony in many cases in the past, I had never before seen him in this environment. In fact, this was my first experience with the criminal court system of Great Britain. I would not have been here at all were it not for my desire to be near John at all times during this break in his successful lecture tour.

Mr Strang then announced: 'I would like to summon to the stand Lady Emmaline Belgrave,' and the confused reaction of Sir Peter indicated that he knew nothing of this surprise witness.

A small, elegant woman of middle years, clad in a fine crushed velvet dress the colour of berries, made her way to the stand. Mr Strang bumbled along behind her, revealing a natural Pickwickian sort of dignity that stood in contrast to the affected theatrical pomposity of his opponent.

'Now then, Lady Emmaline,' he began, 'you have heard it stated that Humphrey Jafford met his untimely death on the evening of January the twelfth, 1904, sometime between eight o'clock, when his servant delivered a brandy to him in his library, and half-past eleven, when the same servant checked upon him.'

'Oh, yes, indeed,' she chirped.

'And at that time, Lady Emmaline, where were you?'

'I was at the Royal Opera House in Covent Garden.'

'Were you alone?'

'Quite.'

'While you were there, did you see anyone who is perhaps in this courtroom?'

'Oh, yes,' she said, smiling, 'I saw that young gentleman over there, Mr Jafford.'

A loud rumble of murmurs now broke out within the court-room, prompting the judge to call for order. When it had been restored, Mr Strang continued.

'How long were you at the opera, Lady Emmaline?' he asked.

'Curtain rings up exactly at eight, so I must have been there from about half-past seven,' she replied. 'I like to sit in my box and watch the comings and goings of the other patrons. Since it was Wagner night, the curtain did not ring down until nearly midnight.'

'And Owen Jafford was there the entire time?'

'Oh, yes, the entire time.'

'So there is no way he could have been in Earl's Court on that evening, murdering his uncle.'

The witness shuddered. 'How dreadful, even to contemplate.'

'Thank you, Lady Emmaline,' the portly barrister said, returning to his seat. John, meanwhile, leaned over to me and whispered into my ear: 'There's a development for you!'

It was abundantly clear, however, that Sir Peter was not about to take this development peacefully. He virtually leapt to his feet and approached the stand. 'Lady Emmaline, prior to the evening when you say you saw the defendant at the opera, had you ever met him before?'

'Oh, no,' she replied.

'Indeed? How was it, then, that you came to notice, and keep under surveillance for nearly four hours, a man of whom you had no prior knowledge?'

'As I said, I like to watch people from my box. It so happens that I have been looking for a walking stick to get as a gift for my husband, Lord Belgrave. When I noticed Mr Jafford take his seat, I said to myself: "That young man is carrying the exact walking stick I have been seeking.' I made it a point to seek him out after the opera to ask him from whence he had obtained it. I fear the other patrons must have thought me the victim of a robbery, for I ran after him calling, "Young man, please stop!" '

A titter of gentle laughter ruffled the crowd at this. Sir Peter, however, seemed not amused. 'M'lud,' he said, 'in light of this unexpected testimony, I beg the court time to reevaluate our case.' I noticed a smugly satisfied smile on the face of Mr Strang.

'Very well,' Judge Wilkins ruled, 'we shall reconvene at ten o'clock tomorrow.' As Sir Peter walked back to his chair, I noticed that he faltered slightly, and for a moment I thought it might be more theatrics, but the concerned expression on John's face convinced me otherwise. Within seconds we were at his side.

'Has the pain returned?' John asked.

'Only slightly,' Sir Peter responded, though his ashen face told a more serious tale.

'I insist on giving you a thorough examination,' my husband said. 'Chest pains are not to be ignored.'

'Accompany me to my office, then, for I have no time to follow you to yours.'

Even though the walk from the Old Bailey to the Inner Temple was an easy one, John decided that a coach ride would be best for the ailing barrister. Once within the Temple, I waited in a clerk-filled antechamber while John conducted his examination in Sir Peter's private office, after which I was allowed inside.

'I have warned you, Sir Peter, against the continued strain of too many cases in succession,' my husband was saying. 'After this one it is imperative that you rest.'

'After I forfeit this one, you mean,' he said gloomily, all traces of the former popinjay having disappeared.

'The defendant does appear to have a strong alibi,' I stated.

'That woman was lying, Mrs Watson,' he replied, 'The evidence against Jafford is simply too strong, as Strang must have realized, which is why he has miraculously produced an eye-witness at the eleventh hour to put him in a different place altogether.'

'Please, Sir Peter, you must not excite yourself,' John cautioned.

'But can't you see that the young scoundrel is going to get away with it?' the barrister cried. 'I have until tomorrow morning to try and break this alibi, or the case is lost.'

'Perhaps you could beat Lady Emmaline's statements down on the stand,' John suggested.

'No, no, no, you saw how she charmed everyone in the courtroom. I would come off as a reprehensible bully. The question we should be asking is, why would a woman of her station be lying for a young rotter? She must know him, somehow. If only I could prove that, it would destroy her story. But how could I be expected to do it by ten o'clock tomorrow?'

'Well, it will do absolutely no good to work yourself into a froth,' John said. 'I am going to prescribe a sedative for you so that you will at least get a decent night's rest.'

'Dr Watson, if you could guarantee that you would have the solution to my problem by the time I awaken tomorrow morning, I would gladly ingest anything,' Sir Peter said. 'If not, I must continue to work, through the night if necessary.'

'I accept the challenge,' I blurted out, prompting John to turn and stare at me, open-mouthed. 'Before the clock strikes ten tomorrow, you shall have an answer.'

'But how could you . . . ah, I see,' the barrister said, his eyes darting back and forth between John and me. 'You shall get Sherlock Holmes to work on the problem, eh?'

'If he is available. Right, darling?' I said, watching John's face begin to redden.

'Fair enough,' Sir Peter said, suddenly relaxing. 'Go ahead, Dr Watson, do your worst.'

John stepped out to talk to one of the law clerks, sending him to the nearest chemist for a powder. After instructing Sir Peter as to its administration, he escorted him to the street and hailed a coach to carry him to his home. Then, and only then, did John speak to me.

'What in heaven's name did you mean by promising to solve his case for him?' he demanded. 'And what is this business of getting Holmes involved! You know perfectly well he is off somewhere on this American crusade of his and cannot even be contacted!'

'John, I did not promise that Mr Holmes would be involved,' I said. 'I suggested that he may help if he were available, which, as we know, he is not. Nor did I say that we would solve Sir Peter's case. What I said was that we would have an answer for him. The answer might well be, "Sorry, we cannot help you." '

John was glaring at me now, and doing a rather good. impersonation of a smoldering log in a fireplace. 'Oh, don't look at me that way, dear,' I protested. 'You saw the state the poor man was in. This was the only way he would have agreed to your prescription.'

John sighed. 'Yes, you may be right. Still, I don't like to see him get his hopes up only to be dashed.'

'Then we must do whatever we can to see that his hopes are not dashed,' I replied.

Since John had to return to his surgery that afternoon (rather than atrophy as a result of his recent absence, his practice had seemed to grow), he headed off in one direction and I another. I arrived home, chilled from the brisk January weather, to find Missy, our maid, dusting the bookshelf. 'Thank you, dear, for cleaning this off for me,' I said, pulling down the Debrett's that we had somehow acquired, yet rarely used.

I quickly found the entry for Lord Hugh Belgrave, but discovered it to be less than revealing, being largely concerned with his lineage. It did, however, confirm that his lordship had taken a wife named Emmaline, a union which produced a son named Richard. I read the entry over and over, looking for some kind of clue, which, of course, was not there. Then, as Missy continued her chores, I sat back and tried to imagine what Sherlock Holmes would do in this situation, given the scanty facts. The answer came quickly.

I snatched up yesterday's edition of *The Times* and turned to the theatre listings. A cry of delight escaped my lips (which rather startled poor Missy) as I read the schedule for the Royal Opera House.

When John arrived home several hours later, he was surprised to find me in evening wear. 'Where are we going?' he asked.

'To the opera, John,' I replied. 'It's Wagner night.'

A light, but not altogether unpleasant, snow salted our clothing us as we stood in a queue at the box office of the opera house. Our seats were not particularly good, though to be honest, I have never been much of an enthusiast for Wagner, favouring less portentous music. But witnessing the performance was only a secondary reason for my presence. After searching the entire house bottom-to-top, I finally spotted Lady Emmaline, in an upper lodge box, seated next to a young man. I kept my attention focused on her throughout most of the first act, and at the first interval, watched as she and her companion exited through the back. Quickly rising from my seat, I started to slide past John.

'Where are you going in such a hurry?' he asked.

'I must not lose Lady Emmaline,' I responded.

'I am coming with you,' he said, rising himself.

'No, she might recognize you from the trial. I must do this alone.' Leaving him, I made my way up the aisle and entered the crowded foyer, where the chances of finding one person in particular seemed impossible. Being rather tall, however, I was able to peer over the heads of most of the multitude. Before long I spotted Lady Emmaline Belgrave standing at the bar next to her young companion, who was sipping a brandy. As I fought my way through the throng to get to them, I realized I had but one quick chance to try and obtain the information I was seeking. I also realized that now was not the time for subtleties. 'Lady Emmaline, isn't it?' I called, as soon as I was within earshot, and the woman turned to me.

'Yes?'

'I thought so,' I said, wedging myself next to her. 'Perhaps you don't remember me, but we met through a mutual friend, Owen Jafford.'

But before she could reply, her young companion spun around and faced me. 'Do we know you, madam?' he demanded.

'Dickie,' she scolded, 'don't be so dreadfully rude.'

'I am sorry,' I went on. 'I was just telling Lady Emmaline that we have a mutual friend, Owen Jafford – '

Dickie Belgrave's darkly handsome face melted into a black scowl. 'Never heard of the blighter,' he said sharply, 'and I will thank you, madam, to mind your own business. Come along mother, let's go back.' She was still protesting as the young brute pulled her through the crowd towards the stairs.

It was obvious to me that the name Owen Jafford meant something to Dickie Belgrave, something he chose not to acknowledge.

I quickly returned to John, who was chatting amiably with another patron. 'Darling, let's go,' I said, excitedly.

'But we have only seen one act,' he replied.

'Please, John,' I entereated.

'Oh, very well.' Excusing himself from his previous conversation, he accompanied me to the coat room.

In the freezing cab on the way home, I told him of my encounter with Lady Emmaline though, to my surprise, he failed to share my excitement. 'That was a rather foolhardy thing to do, Amelia,' he uttered. 'You tipped them off to your game.'

'There was no time to do anything else,' I protested. 'But if Sir Peter put Dickie Belgrave on the stand – '

'Belgrave would deny knowing Jafford, just like he denied it to you,' John said. 'And being the son of a peer, he would be believed.' Then taking my icicle hand in his, he added gently: 'I am sorry, Amelia, but the law requires proof, not merely intuition. It may be true that Lady Emmaline and her son are both lying, but how can you prove it? Ah, here we are.' The cab pulled to a stop in front of our home.

Spending the time required to prepare for bed in silent rumination, I had to accept the fact that he was right. We had failed. More precisely, *I* had failed, and Owen Jafford was soon to be a free man.

'Aren't you coming to bed?' John asked.

'I think I will stay up for a bit and read,' I said. 'Maybe it will drive away this horrid sense of frustration.' From the shelf I selected Mr Dickens' *Christmas Books*, which I had been meaning to reread since the yuletide, and turned to my favourite among these tales, *A Christmas Carol*. I savoured the familiar prose until my eyes began to tire and droop, and with growing effort I read the description of the second midnight spirit:

> *Its hair, which hung about its neck and down its back, was white as if with age; and yet the face had not a wrinkle on it, and the tenderest bloom was on the skin.*

Whether I had actually dropped off into sleep or not, I do not know. All I can recall is suddenly sitting up, vividly awake, a light beam having been switched on in my mind. I had found the flaw in Lady Emmaline Belgrave's testimony!

Being of generous nature, I let John sleep rather than rushing into the bedroom and waking him up with the news, though I myself tossed and turned excitedly throughout the night. Early the next morning, however, we were en route to the home of Sir Peter Swindon to tell him of my realization. His initial reaction was all that I had hoped for.

'That is brilliant, Mrs Watson!' he cried, but then ruined it by adding: 'If only you were a man, you would make a splendid lawyer.' Why, oh why is it that so many men would just as soon accept the existence of Mr Wells' Martian invaders than believe that a woman is born with a brain? I opened my mouth to respond to him, but before I could, he let out a gasp and clutched his chest, then slowly sank down to one knee.

'Sir Peter!' John cried, rushing to him and helping him off the floor to a nearby couch.

'This is the worst one yet,' gasped the lawyer.

'We must get you to the hospital immediately,' John declared.

'But the case . . . ' Sir Peter croaked.

'The case is not worth risking your life over,' John replied, sternly. 'The judge will simply have to delay the proceedings until you are well.'

A sardonic smile rose through the fear and pain on the lawyer's face. 'Strange would not let that go unchallenged,' he uttered. 'He is holding all the cards at present, and would protest that this was nothing more than a confusion tactic. He would badger Wilkins for a dismissal, and likely get it.'

As I watched and listened helplessly, an idea began to form in my mind, one that was so audacious, so riotous, that I tried to push it out, but it would not go. 'Perhaps I can help,' I offered. 'What if I were to question Lady Emmaline in court?'

'You?'

'Yes, along with a few visual aids such as . . . well, might I borrow a suit of yours, Sir Peter?'

'A suit?' he queried. 'You mean you wish to appear before the Bench posing as me?'

I wanted to tell him that I was simply attempting to meet his own criteria for legal acceptability – namely, being of the male sex – but I fought the urge down. Instead I said: 'I know it probably sounds insane – '

'Because it is insane,' John interjected. 'You must forgive my wife, Sir Peter. She was an actress in her youth and sometimes forgets that all the world is not a stage.'

I was about to rebuff John's comment when I noticed that Sir Peter was regarding me with renewed interest. Through the pain, I thought I detected a shining curiosity in his eyes. Playing up to this interest, I said: 'This may be the only chance to bring Mr Jafford to justice.'

'Do you think you could do it?' he asked.

'No,' John returned, 'I positively forbid –'

'Yes,' I answered firmly, ignoring my husband. 'I watched you yesterday in court, observed your manner and stance. As we are roughly the same height, it would be a matter of removing my cosmetics, fixing my hair, fashioning a moustache and lowering my voice. And I have experience, of course – I once understudied the role of Portia.'

'I know why you are doing this, Amelia,' John said conspiratorially, 'and I assure you, you do not have to prove anything to either of us.'

'Whatever do you mean, darling?' I asked, innocently.

'Amelia, we are talking about the King's Bench!' John suddenly cried. 'The Old Bailey is not a theatre!'

'Don't be too sure, old fellow,' Sir Peter said, ending the argument.

I quickly dressed in an old tweed suit of Sir Peter's and set about duplicating his visage over my own. Letting down my hair, I flattened it as much as possible and hid the excess under the shirt collar. Soot from the fireplace turned my auburn tresses black like Sir Peter's, and I carefully trimmed some ends, which I attached under my nose with paste to create a moustache. In his closet I found an old, rather dusty, periwig and an unused monocle. Strutting like a popinjay, I made my entrance into the living room.

'God help us,' John muttered. 'The resemblance is better than I would have predicted, but still, you will never get away with it.'

'People tend to see what they expect to see,' Sir Peter said, adding: 'It just might work.'

It was that quietly-spoken encouragement that carried me all the way to the Old Bailey where, less than an hour later, properly robed and bewigged, I faced an audience consisting of judge, jury and on-lookers (including, I noticed, Dickie Belgrave). I silently prayed, then called Lady Emmaline Belgrave to the stand. Immediately, Judge Wilkins interrupted.

'Counsel for the prosecution does not sound like himself today,' he said, frowning, and for a moment I fought down panic. I recovered well enough to say: 'I fear I am catching cold, m'lud.'

'I see,' he acknowledged, albeit skeptically.

'Lady Emmaline,' I began, 'yesterday you testified that you had never before met, or even seen Owen Jafford prior to the opera.'

'That is true,' she confirmed.

'Where were you when you first noticed him?'

'In my regular box in the loge.'

'And where was he?'

'Down below, on the orchestra level.'

'Quite a distance,' I noted, strutting and fiddling with the monocle, while trying to keep my face down. 'And tell me again what you thought upon seeing Mr Jafford?'

'I said to myself: "That young man is carrying the exact walking stick I have been looking for." '

'Ah, yes, and then you told us that you ran after him shouting, "Young man, please stop." '

'That is true.'

I took a deep breath. 'I confess, Lady Emmaline, that I do not understand that. Anyone truly seeing Owen Jafford for the first time, especially from the distance of a loge box or from behind, would be excused for assuming that he was an elderly man, since his hair is white. Yet, by your own testimony, you knew him to be a young man, and even used that term to call after him – or so you claim. There is only one way, Lady Emmaline, that you could have assumed that Mr Jafford was a youth of less than thirty, and that is if you had already been acquainted with him.'

A murmur went through the courtroom.

'Well, I . . . I . . .' she stammered.

'What is the truth, Lady Emmaline?' I demanded. 'How long have you known Owen Jafford? Long enough to lie on his behalf?'

What followed was chaos. Mr Strang jumped up and began shouting objections, while at the same time, Lady Emmaline turned to her son and called out, 'What should I say, Dickie?'

Leaping to his feet, Owen Jafford shouted back: 'Say nothing, you senile old cat!'

'How dare you speak that way to mother, Jaffie!' Dickie shouted back, and within seconds, the august proceeding had been reduced to a shambles. Through all the shouting, however, I was able to hear Lady Emmaline's excited testimony, which was directed towards the judge. 'They told me it would cause no harm to pretend I saw Jaffie at the opera,' she was saying. 'They said it was the only way Jaffie would be able to get the money he owes my Dickie.'

Judge Wilkins, meanwhile, was pounding his gavel to the breaking point in the attempt to bring about order. Once it had finally been restored, he announced: 'The prisoner at the bar will be remanded into custody until such time as I have had the opportunity to confer with counsel for both sides. I wish to see the prosecutor immediately.' With that he stepped down from the bench and motioned for me to follow.

With considerable trepidation, I followed him to a surprisingly austere chamber located behind the courtroom, which was furnished only with a desk, two chairs, an odd framed painting or two, and an array of filled bookcases. He began to remove his robes and wig, and bid me do the same. The game was over. Slowly, and trembling with fear, I removed the garments and pulled the pasty moustache from my lip.

The judge's gaze turned into a stare, then a gape. 'Good God!' he said, 'I knew you weren't Swindon, but I had no idea you were a woman! Who in blazes are you, and where the devil is the real Swindon?'

Hesitantly, I introduced myself and explained that Sir Peter had suddenly taken ill and was under the care of my husband, emphasizing that John was vehemently opposed to my impersonation. There was no sense in ruining my husband's reputation as well.

'The doctor is a sensible man,' he said.

'I know that, my lord,' I said, softly.

'On the other hand, without this decidedly brazen act of yours, we would never have got the goods on Jafford, would we?'

'You, too, believed him to be guilty?'

'As sin. And quite honestly, were I prosecuting this case, faced with these peculiar circumstances, I might have condoned such extreme measures myself in order to convict the blackguard.'

'Is that why you did not expose me at once?'

He shook his head. 'I did not expose you because I did not want to turn my courtroom to a circus until I figured out what your game was. But then I became rather interested in your line of questioning.' Having said that, his face became quite stern. 'But I must caution you in strongest terms not to attempt this again. Given the circumstances, the high regard in which I hold your husband and, frankly, the results, I am willing to overlook this absurd charade. But I will not be so forgiving in the face of any future assaults on the integrity of the Bench. And one more thing: you are not to tell another living soul what you have done here today. Is that clear?'

'Perfectly, my lord, and thank you,' I said, sighing with relief.

The reaction from the excitement in the courtroom was still at such a pitch in the hallways of the Old Bailey that I was able to wedge past an army of reporters and slip out of the building unnoticed. Equally anonymously, I boarded the omnibus that carried me home.

John would demand a complete explanation of course, as would Sir Peter, though aside from them, I anticipated no difficulty in complying with Judge Wilkins' command for silence. For even if I were to tell anyone of my escapade in court, who would believe it?

PRAYER DENIED

Jeremy Russell

I pulled up to the Sternwood mansion in my cream-coloured Mercedes 360 at 10:54 Wednesday morning. I wasn't supposed to arrive until 11:00, but I despise being late. I also hate being early. More than anything I hate it when I am not noted for my punctuality.

The L.A. sunlight was nearly white with an innocent early fall grace. I used my extra few minutes to check myself in the mirror. My slate gray suit was immaculate, except for one wrinkle near my right armpit which I quashed immediately. I leaned down and pulled my black silk socks up tight against the hair on my calves, then sat up again and adjusted my red and blue abstract tie, wondering if it weren't maybe too loud after all. I scratched myself behind the ear and decided I was everything the well-dressed attorney should be when calling on thirty billion plus dollars.

Vivian Sternwood's man let me in and led me down an enormous featureless hallway to an antechamber of sorts with deep green furniture on a dark hardwood floor. Mumbling something, he left me staring at a painting of what could only have been a young Mrs Sternwood in a gilt frame surrounded by Civil War sabres and crossed rifles.

In her picture she was a beautiful woman, the kind that you expect to meet at a Beverly Hills cocktail party or see wrapped in a towel in an ad for shampoo – pale skin and freckles, dark blonde hair and altogether as wholesome as a loaf of whole-wheat bread. There was a look in her eyes, however, that made you wonder what she thought of the painter. Maybe she just didn't like sitting still for that long. Funny that he'd captured that, they usually paint that kind of thing out, don't they? I was just stepping closer to read the signature when a voice said, 'Mrs Sternwood will see you now, Mr Zweben.' It was the man who'd met me at the front.

We went through a few doors into a heated room. Although it was in the high 70s that day, somebody had a fire going. A bundle of twigs wrapped in blankets had been propped up in a chair beside the fire. It took me a second to realize that Mrs Sternwood was the bundle. The man left us as soon as I was in the centre of the room and as soon as he was gone a frail hand emerged from the blankets and curled its fingers in beckoning. It was like a greeting from the boatman at the River Styx. Once I was around to the side of the chair, I could see a face protruding from a hole in the blankets. One thing I can say for Mrs Vivian Sternwood, she had all her teeth. You could see them right through her cheek.

'Well,' she said rather bitterly after I had watched her without sound for about thirty seconds, 'have you gotten a good look?' Mumbling some small apology, I turned and looked into the fireplace at the two burning logs. 'Oh, don't be sorry, Mr Zweben, there is little as fascinating to the young as the old, and I am exquisitely old. Please, tell me about yourself.'

I put my hand behind my head and tugged at the short hairs beneath my skull a moment before answering. 'I'm thirty years old and unmarried. I am an associate at Gutman & Royce.'

'But in line to make partner, I assume.'

I shrugged. 'Perhaps.'

She grinned. 'They don't send just any associate to Mrs Vivian Sternwood upon her personal request.'

'What *is* the nature of your request, Mrs Sternwood?'

She motioned for me to sit. 'Let me ask you a series of questions to see where you stand. That's what they teach you in law school isn't it?'

'What's that?'

'The Socratic method.'

'With a twist.' The wood in the fire crackled. I was starting to sweat from the heat and I adjusted my collar.

'If you're hot, feel free to remove your jacket. You needn't worry about offending me.' I did so instantly, loosening my tie as well, an unprecedented manoeuvre on my part, but it was hellishly hot in that room.

When I'd loosened my tie, Mrs Sternwood asked me: 'Have you ever thought about the nature of supernatural evil?'

I failed to keep my eyebrow from riding up. 'I don't think about things that . . . I don't think about. I mean, that I don't believe in.'

'I see, a practical man. Good. I wouldn't want to engage some new age spiritualist twit.' She waited a moment and when I didn't say anything, she said, 'Well, I hope at least that you are a pragmatic skeptic and not one of those denial junkies who has to screen everything that doesn't agree with his preconceived, usually provincial, philosophy.'

'You'll find me open-minded.'

'Not too open-minded to be pragmatic?'

'Why don't you tell me what it is you want to tell me and see how I react?' I suggested as gently as I could.

'Very well,' she said. 'Go over to the table, you'll find a parchment there.'

'A parchment?' I put my hands on my knees and stood up with a little huff. On the table across the room, a small three-legged obsidian-topped antique table barely higher than my thigh that looked lonely without a couch nearby, there was a ragged slip of torn brown paper in a plastic slipcase. I picked it up and examined the yellow veins of decay that wrapped the edges like worms. There was something scrawled in a cracked and dried brown ink, but it was so messy as to be totally illegible. I turned back to the woman in the cocoon. 'So?'

'It's a contract,' she said looking into the fire, her face sideways to me. 'A contract I wish to break.'

I took the paper back over to my chair near her, loosening my collar still more and fanning it in the heat. 'What's this all about, Mrs Sternwood?'

'How old would you guess I am?'

Scratching the side of my face, I sighed. 'Eighty-five? I don't know. Maybe ninety.'

'Not even close.'

I shrugged. 'So, are you going to tell me or should I guess again?'

Her smiled dimmed. 'I'm beginning to dislike your tone.'

'I'm sorry about that Mrs Sternwood, but nothing about this interview has been straightforward and everything about it has been abstruse and frustrating. You ask me three different ways my opinion of the supernatural, then tell me you want me to help you break a contract I can't read, and then you start in on the guessing games. How would you respond in my position?'

'Keep in mind, Mr Zweben, I am paying for the privilege of this interview.'

'Yes you are, but I'm not getting much more out of it than that,' I said bluntly. Immediately I hedged, as it's good to do with a client, 'I'm just telling you this to help you. Because, well, I'm only here to help you.'

After I'd spoken, she closed her eyes and didn't move for some time. I wasn't sure if I had offended her or if she were merely thinking about what to say next. Perhaps both. I wasn't used to potentially offending my clients, but nothing about this interview was normal. Maybe it was the loose collar that was throwing me off. 'Excuse me,' she said. 'I'll start again. I was born in 1842.'

'That would make you one hundred and fifty-eight years old, Mrs Sternwood.'

'That's exactly how old I am.' I opened my mouth to interject that it wasn't possible, but she held up a cool hand and said, 'Please. I have a story to tell. I was born in Atlanta, Georgia and my parents were not rich. My father moved there to work for the Fulton Company when they opened a branch there in 1837. There was a lot of money in railroads then, something like being involved in the Internet now I suppose, but he was just a clerk. My mother was a housewife. All women were housewives. I lived a dull life, slaveless in contrast to the rich around me, until the Civil War started when I was twenty-two. Then everything was very exciting for about two years and very scary for about two more. The fear culminated when Sherman brought his army to burn Atlanta to the ground. Both my parents were killed that night and I awoke alone in the scarred wilderness somewhere behind the Union Army. Bodies were all around me, not exactly piled up, but laying here and there like discarded clothing. Worse, the countenance of Satan was on the land. You may not know what I mean, pray you never do.'

'You'd had a terrifying experience,' I rationalized.

'No,' she said, 'the devil had come to collect the souls of the dead. We were not a good people, and he was harvesting us. You understand? This was not my imagination.' She paused with her eyes shut again, then reached up into her mouth with a bony hand draped in gnarled skin. The hand seemed to disappear into her mouth just as if she were trying to swallow it and I sat up involuntarily. But as quickly as she made it disappear, she twisted fast to the left and jerked it free again. It returned with a bloody molar between forefinger and thumb. Demure as an aristocratic vampire, a trickle of blood slathering down her chin, she examined the tooth – red roots, white enamel and what was either a cavity or an old mercury filling – then she threw it into the fire. 'I'm one hundred and fifty-eight years old and I'm falling apart.' She sighed. 'After wandering hungry for several days, drinking from streams, I came across a patch of ground that might once have been the garden in someone's plantation and I dug the earth for anything. I bloodied my fingers on rocks I thought were tubers. There was nothing the Union hadn't dug up and destroyed. That's when it came to me, the knowledge that I had another option. That we all have another option, one we rarely recognize, one that Religion has trained us to ignore, but that I had been reminded of by the vision and presence of Satan.

'And a man came walking out from some shrubs. Quite an ordinary looking man. He handed me a pen and that parchment. But there was no ink for the pen. I had to use my own blood to sign the contract. "Write what you want," he said once I had pierced my inner elbow with the sharp tip of the pen. I wrote that document that you hold in your hand and I gave it to him. He nodded, signed it himself and gave it back to me. Without speaking further, he left me there with my contract. Within an hour I was found by some people heading North and I went with them to Chicago, where one thing led to another and gradually what I had requested came true.'

She stopped and waited for my reaction. I decided that since she was insane, I would have to humour her. 'Well that explains a lot,' I said, trying not to sound strained. 'About your wealth and age and everything.'

She looked at me like I had only just crawled up from the muck of evolution and was destined for a quick extinction. 'Does it? Well, I want rid of it. I don't care for any of it anymore. As you probably already know, you should never make a false move when making wishes and I made a bad mistake.'

'Why would I know anything about that?'

'Everybody knows. It's in all the fairy tales. I wished for immortality, but I forget about eternal youth. Stupid wasn't I? Now I want out of it,' she went on. 'I'm tired out. I guess the devil knew all along. He's very patient. Evil can wait. But if he's going to win after all, at the very least, I want my soul back. No reason that he should get everything, is there? I want out of the contract.'

'As your attorney,' I said, loving the sound of it, 'I have to advise you not to pursue this lawsuit. It will get thrown out of court and at the possible cost of considerable embarrassment to you and to Gutman & Royce.'

'We'll take it before Judge Maxine Cross, she won't throw it out,' Mrs Sternwood said with the kind of conviction that can only come of having a Judge in one's pocket.

I stood up. 'Can you provide me with the text of this, uh, parchment?'

'Yes, I remember perfectly.' Funny how those schizophrenic realizations will stick with you, I thought. 'But I'm tired now. I'll fax it to you tomorrow.'

'Here's my card.' She took the card in a hand so dry it could have belonged to Tutankhamen. I was afraid it was going to break off.

Catherine Gutman is all flabby fat, soft fat, and at times bulbous bits of it ooze out of her clothing. Her neck is a collapsed pink curtain of flesh, layered heavily upon itself, and she has a great soft egg of a belly above which she pulls the waistband of her skirts. She has tiny feet which she wedges into tiny shoes that end in even tinier heels, making her legs look like upside down traffic cones, somewhat melty. Furthermore, she has the stink and menace of the mid-West about her. You can see it in her coifed mane and endless painted nails. She looks like nothing so much as an evil cowgirl, especially with the damp end of half an unlit cigar clenched between her teeth, which is exactly how I found her when she called me into her office after I'd been back from the Sternwood mansion for about an hour.

She says she quit smoking years ago, but will never give up the bliss of masticulating expensive tobacco. 'I'd like to know how it went today.'

'I guess you know all about her sold soul and all of that,' I said. 'Well she means to get it back.'

'She wants you to file against Satan?'

'That's right. She wants to file for injunctive relief for the removal of immortality.'

'I was afraid of that. This could be . . . this is a sticky. It could be very embarrassing for her and more importantly for the firm. I don't want it in the papers. Doesn't she understand that it'll just get thrown out of court?'

'I explained that to her. Her idea was to make sure it gets before Maxine Cross.'

'Pulling favours?' Ms Gutman put a hand into the fat under her chin. 'You've got to make sure that this case looks good.'

'Ms Gutman, excuse me, but . . . I understand why you might feel it's in the best interests of the firm to play along, but do you really expect me to file a complaint – a complaint with *my* signature on it – against Satan?'

'I want you because you're the only one around here who could pull it off. You'll be nice to Mrs Sternwood, even if she is a bit crazy. You'll be young and handsome and that will help. You won't laugh at her, because you understand power and you're not yet as arrogant as the rest of us. And more importantly, you'll find a plausible defendant.'

'She needs a psychiatrist not an attorney.' Ms Gutman squinted so that the fat puffs crowded around her eyes until they were nothing more than a dark gleam. I cleared out some phlegm from the back of my throat. 'Well, I do enjoy a challenge. As it turns out, there was precedent for Mrs Sternwood's case. In 1971 a man named Gerald Mayo filed a lawsuit, a desperate *in forma pauperis* civil rights action, against "Satan and his staff" who allegedly placed deliberate obstacles in plaintiff's path and caused his downfall. Obviously, Gerald Mayo was a lunatic, but his case against Satan placed several interesting legal precedents in the path of Mrs Sternwood's lawsuit, since, ultimately, it was "Prayer Denied" for Mr Mayo.'

She took her cigar out of her mouth and pointed it at me violently, holding it in her left hand between her first and second fingers. 'Just make sure that the case is settled out of court.'

As soon as she was gone, I called Denny from the Research Department. If it was worth doing, it was worth doing right, I thought. He said he'd be up in fifteen minutes.

He came in my office with his tie loose and one of the buttons in the middle of his shirt undone. I didn't ask why, I figured he probably didn't know himself. At least he came in on the dot of fifteen minutes. He sat opposite me, looking concerned, serious, attentive, while I explained the Sternwood case to him. I concluded, 'which is why I need you to look up everything on the devil for me. I want a comprehensive history and get me any rare books, you know, the kind that they always talk about in stories, the one's with lots of disturbing imagery and pentagrams and arcane languages. I don't care if you have to order them all the way from Oxford. I don't care if you have to hire some archeologist to dig them up à la Indiana Jones. The more skullduggery the better. Also, get anything you can on modern cults. I mean names, addresses, phone numbers, websites, recent crimes. I want to be able to pull these people into court. Bikers, cultists, pagans, rock stars, California bird worshippers, I don't care. Make sure you put Charles Manson on that list. He's still alive isn't he? I want you to get me something by Friday, Saturday at the latest. Can you do that?'

He said: 'You're taking it seriously then?'

'Well, we've made a decision to treat it seriously, that's different than taking it seriously.' I switched from watching his eyes to looking at the unbuttoned button to looking at his eyes again. 'Hell, take it any way you want. The point is we need to put on a good show for the richest woman in the world. She must have a hand in the pies of half of our clients. If she gets seriously displeased with us . . .'

I gave him a pointed look.

Abruptly he noticed the button and buttoned it in one swift movement. His tie however remained loose.

That night I dreamed of Vivian Sternwood. Younger even than she looked in the portrait in the hall, she wandered aimlessly in what had very recently been a battlefield. Although the bodies around her, and the broken wagons and abandoned cannons, appeared real enough, the soot smudging her face was a trifle too particularly applied, like stage make-up. Her dress was torn in all the most demure places. She picked among corpses, kneeling here and there in appropriate panic, evidently searching for something.

I watched her tour the sour field in her cinematically burnt and torn cloth, turning the dead with her toe and digging through satchels. As she became increasingly agitated, she would push at a pile of bodies and root through their clothing like a ghoul, then run to the next pile. Sometimes she wouldn't even bother to stand again, but merely crawl on hands and knees to the next corpse.

It took her a long time, but eventually she pulled open a knapsack and found what must have been some bit of bread, although it looked like a twisted tuber in her grubby hand.

She lifted the bun or root and began a pledge, the pledge of her soul for survival, while behind her a long snake crawled out of the knapsack. 'I don't care what I have to do,' she told the wind and the sky. 'I only care what I get.'

The next morning at 10:00 Mrs Sternwood's fax came sliding out of the machine. She had hand written her transcription of the contract, but at least it was in ink and not blood.

> With this writ I do deed my soul to Satan upon my death in exchange for wealth and immortality.
>
> V. Sternwood

When I finished, I scanned the fax into the computer and tossed it in a file on the desk. Although arguing souls is tricky, there was no doubt that 'immortality' and 'upon my death' together formed a clear contradiction, which resulted in no exchange of goods. If

Satan gave her immortality, then she kept her soul, which meant
Satan got nothing. It would be easy enough to dissolve in court if
it ever came to that, because there had not been an exchange. But
it took me less than a second to decide I wasn't going to bring that
up with Mrs Sternwood. She was crazy and rich and what she
needed was to be humoured. That meant entertained. Massaged.
I had done it for clients before, lead them on, told them what they
wanted to hear while racking up the billable hours.

I picked the phone off the stand near my desk, held the handset
to my face and dialed the Sternwood number rapidly from
memory. The man who had led me through the house took
my information and got Mrs Sternwood for me.

'Yes?' she asked with a voice like stale bread crust.

'I got your fax just now. I think we've got him on Fraud in
which case we can get around the Parol Evidence Rule.' There
was a silence. At last she ordered me to explain myself. 'Well, I
considered the thought that it would be either impractical or
impossible for him to, ah, possess your soul, but my figuring was
that that would mean you would have to repent. And I'm not at
all sure how the law views repentance. What I'm saying is that if
your soul were pure, you might be able to wiggle out without the
law getting involved at all. Get it? But, I'm assuming that since
you brought the case to us, you aren't interested in a religious
conversion.'

'Quite right,' she snipped.

I listened to her breath for a little while, it was like listening to a
rat chew saltines. Then I started again slowly: '. . . okay, that
leaves a couple of things. Why don't we discuss this in person?'

'Come on Sunday.' Having said this, she hung up immediately.

Denny came in my office like he'd been waiting for me to get
off the phone. He had a concise history of the devil with him, said
he'd stayed up all night on it and sat down to tell me about
demonic roots in Mazdaism, where the devil was known as
Ahriman, and Mithraism, as well as early Judaism. He seemed
excited. 'I learned that he was only gradually phased into early
Christianity,' he began eagerly, 'you know, as they sought a
binding element in the face of persecution and finally, in a
reversal, Satan became the excuse for the persecution when

Christianity became the dominant socio-political model. They used him as an excuse for everything from the Crusades to the Inquisition.'

A little of Denny's enthusiasm bled into me and I found myself poring through the history papers after he left. The more I read, the more I saw parallels to the law and the more I saw those parallels, the weirder I felt. I started to ask myself questions beginning with 'what if?' Like, what if Vivian Sternwood really did make a deal with the devil? On the one hand, I had to ask these questions, but the more I considered them the crazier it made me. Each question opened up new questions. I'd never known much about religion, never cared for it much, and having it thrust so abruptly on my undefended mind was startling, to say the least. Suddenly I started to think about supernatural evil. Mrs Sternwood's question still lingered in my mind like the bad after taste of something spoiled.

What made the biggest impact on me was the fact that the concept of a fallen angel was only really formalized in about 200 B.C., long after the concept of an evil deity was more or less theorized. So, then I wondered, what really is the devil's relation to God. It seemed to make a big difference to how the contract was to be enforced. From my reading I was able to determine that there are three ways to understand Satan. Either he's doing God's work or work that God has approved, as in the Book of Job, or he is a fallen angel rebelling against God, as in *Paradise Lost*, or he is God's enemy and an entirely separate entity from God, which would be the Manichean viewpoint. Each of these would mean something different for Mrs Sternwood's lawsuit. For example, if Satan is subservient to God then his contracts are presumably enforced by God; if on the other hand Satan is rebelling against God then we would think that Satan's contracts are not enforceable except through the trickery and deceit of the devil himself. If Satan, however, is a deity himself, separate but equal or slightly less than equal to God, then his contracts might or might not be enforced depending on the state of the conflict between the two. They might, for instance, have treaties which allow satanic contracts to be enforced in God's dominion under certain circumstances. I should think that those circumstances would include the general malevolence of the soul being bartered and so on.

Denny had also provided me with a list of promising devil worshippers and cultists that he'd obtained from a source in the Police Station, but I wasn't sure that they believed in the sanctity of demonic contracts or whether the Judge was going to allow them to defend their deity in absentia. If only Anton Le Vay hadn't died. If anyone could have made it work it was the high priest of the Church of Satan. He might even have given me a run for my money.

That night I dreamed that Scarlet O'Hara was trapped in the wilderness and forced to eat the dead body of Rhett Butler and their daughter. Among mouthfuls she said: 'I don't care *(gulp, chew)* what I have to *(munch)* do, I will never be hungry *(chew, swallow)* again.'

On Sunday I arrived at Mrs Sternwood's house at 2:24 p.m. and was led right into her sweltering living room with its roaring fireplace. She swivelled her head at me sharply with fierce eyes and jabbed a finger at the chair across from her. I took it.

'I don't want to waste any time being pleasant. Just give me the document to review and tell me what I'll need to know to understand the legalities.'

'All right then.' I reached into my briefcase. 'I've thought through and rejected several Causes of Action. For instance, Duress. You could argue that you made the decision under the threat of, well, starvation. But throw that out, because there was no threat from the devil toward you. No food was exchanged. You had a root already if I recall.' That was from my dream, but she didn't deny it. 'So Duress is, if not out, at least difficult to argue. Undue Influence, but that's not neat enough. If we're going to take the devil to court, let's make it as neat as possible, I say. It would be infinitely better if he just settled.'

At this point she interrupted me. 'Never mind what we can't do, Mr Zweben, what is it we can do?'

'Our Causes of Action are a Breach of Contract and a Breach of the Covenant of Good Faith and Fair Dealing. But first I have to tell you, you're not the first person to try suing Satan. In the only other case in the legal record involving the devil, Gerald Mayo versus Satan and His Staff, it was alleged that Satan had "on numerous occasions," I'm quoting now,' I said, looking down at the papers, '"Caused plaintiff misery and unwarranted threats, against the will of plaintiff, that Satan has placed deliberate obstacles in his path and has caused plaintiff's downfall." Which, interestingly enough, may be semantically correct. The term "Satan" means "obstacle" in early Hebrew. God would put a Satan in someone's path. Later, Satan was a type of angel that God would send to impede the path of the unrighteous. More importantly, the Court agreed that the complaint revealed "a prima facie recital of the infringement of the civil rights of a citizen of the United States," I'm quoting again, "the Court has serious doubts that the complaint reveals a cause of action upon which relief can be granted by the court." In other words, they doubt their power to affect him. Mayo Prayed to proceed *in forma pauperis* –'

'He prayed?'

'Yes. When you ask the court for anything, you Pray. It's a technical term you understand, nothing Religious. You Pray for monetary damages; you Pray for injunctive relief. Whatever you want, you Pray for it. In this case, Mayo was Praying for the court to pay his fees and provide him assistance.'

'What does this have to do with my case?'

'Well, we have to argue around these precedents to get your case accepted. Luckily the case is only persuasive authority and not binding. And the devil's existence is irrelevant to the case as is Ronald McDonald's when we sue him as a corporate entity. Many entities of dubious existence are sued, even dead people are sued. However, there are three things we need to argue or prove to the court. First, that Satan or agents acting on his behalf live in the United States, at least part time, or have some minimum of contact with it, which I plan to show by bringing various, uh, expert witnesses. I haven't met with them yet, but a few in my files look promising. It would, of course, be easiest if I could just bring Satan into court, but I doubt he'll show. Which is the source of the second problem. How do you serve Satan with a subpoena? Any thoughts?'

She closed her eyes, contemplating my question. 'I'm . . . not . . . sure . . .'

'Let me read some more. ". . . official reports disclose no case where this defendant," *id est* Satan, "has appeared as defendant. There is an unofficial account of a trial in New Hampshire where this defendant filed an action of mortgage foreclosure as plaintiff. The defendant in that action was represented by the preeminent advocate of that day" . . . I'm not sure exactly who that was, but in any case . . . "and raised the defense," ' at this point I recall waving my hand about meaningfully, "that the plaintiff was a foreign prince," *id est* The Prince of Darkness, I assume, "with no standing to sue in an American Court. This defense was overcome by overwhelming evidence to the contrary." I repeat overwhelming evidence to the contrary. I do not know what this evidence was that proved Satan to be a resident of the United States and more particularly New Hampshire, but I think we can be pretty confident that we can nail down the first point. The second point, as you admit, is much trickier. How do you serve Satan with process? There is some possibility that we might be able to get authorization to serve by publication, it's done at times, but that leaves us with the question as to which publications are we sure that Satan will see. But let's come back to that puzzle.

'There was a third reason that that case was thrown out. Gerald Mayo wanted to his suit to be a class action. To sue on behalf of all who suffer at the hands of Satan. We don't have to worry about that.' I waited, but she didn't open her eyes, so I went on again. 'I have a plan for serving process. Well, not a plan, just a thought. You see, we can use the techniques that the cultists, I mean expert witnesses, recommend. If their testimony is convincing than it might be said that the subpoena had appeared in Hell, in the hands of the devil himself, even if we didn't actually see it happen. This would probably require some cheap theatrics, but it can be done. The other means is to utilize more orthodox religious methods. I mean an exorcism or something involving priests and chanting. Again theatrical, but those witnesses will be more credible.'

'Are you making fun of me?' she asked softly, opening her left eye. In it the fire bucked like an epileptic firefly.

The question stopped me short. I suppose I had been making fun of her a little, but not consciously. It was just that the whole thing was so absurd and I couldn't help but sound somewhat sarcastic.

I coughed. 'You're right, perhaps we should just publish our summons in the *Wall Street Journal.*' She didn't say anything, so I assumed it was all right. 'If we get our complaint to the court accepted, then we have to convince them that the contract is invalid and fraudulent, which would get us around the Parol Evidence Rule.'

'And what, pray tell, is that?'

'It has to do with what is admissible. You see, usually only the final form of a contract is admissible. In other words, the written form. In this case, your bloody parchment. That is what the Parol Evidence Rule states, it says nothing that alters the terms of the contract may be brought into evidence. However, if the oral agreements do not modify or alter the terms of the contract, but only define them, well then not only are they admissible, but important to a full understanding. So, what I'd like to do is allow the oral contract, the oral agreement, what was said between you and Satan, to be brought to bear. He said, "write what you want," did he not?'

'Yes,' she sounded confused.

'Well, did you get what you wanted?'

'No.' I could hear the confusion starting to lift.

'You wrote immortality and wealth with the assumption, based on the verbal agreement that you would get what you wanted out of these simple words. Write what you want. What you thought you wrote was not what he thought you wanted. There was a miscommunication. I mean, what are immortality and wealth if not a means by which never to go to Hell? Never to experience any deprivation. Never to –'

'I get the point.'

'So you see, the contract is voided. You only ever wrote it under the assumption that you would never go to Hell. And yet you are living in Hell now. So it was all wrong. And on the other hand, if Satan claims that he did not intentionally doom you to life, as it were, then we've got to argue Ambiguity surrounding

the term immortality. Does it include eternal youth or not?
However, there is one thing that you should know, because,
well . . .' I cleared my throat. 'The standard that we will be held
to is that of an omniscient third party. It's the standard for
determining Ambiguity in contract law. And when I started to
imagine an omniscient third party in relation to Satan, I couldn't
help but think of God, he being omniscient and a third party to
this particular dispute; more particularly, he being the only third
party that can legitimately be considered omniscient. And I
thought, well why does God allow Satan to make these kinds
of contracts anyway? So, I got to reading the Bible.'

She interrupted: 'You're kidding?'

'No, no, I did. I read the part where Satan appears to tempt
Jesus in the Desert, because it's Satan's big moment. I read it a
couple of times, four or five. It starts by saying that Jesus was led
by the Spirit into the wilderness to be tempted by the devil. Not
unlike what happened to you, in a sense, or what happened to
Scarlet O'Hara in *Gone with the Wind* right before intermission.
Assuming that we have an omniscient and omnipotent God and
all that, then Jesus was put in the way of temptation, not just that
but he was *tempted*. Granted he resisted the temptation, but it was
not simply an act of temptation by the devil, not according to the
Bible, it was actually the feeling of temptation in Jesus.'

Mrs Sternwood sighed a sudden, moist sigh. 'So what?'

'Well, it shows that God, *id est* an omniscient third party, has
given special powers to Satan. The power to tempt Jesus Christ
himself! Which doesn't give the rest of us much of a chance at all,
does it? I mean, we may try to live like Jesus – as the saying goes,
"What would Jesus do?" – but we aren't really expected to be him.
I mean, he died for our sins. He forgives us. I think that fact speaks
to the unconscionability of the contract. It's one thing to be
tempted by the Tempter and even to succumb to the temptation,
but it's another thing for him to be able to hold us to a contract
based on his temptation. Even an omniscient third party like God
can see that, don't you think? Which is why we have redemption,
absolution and forgiveness, I mean as church doctrine.'

'But God does give Satan the power to enforce a contract.'

'Yes, but he shouldn't. And that's what I will tell the court.

Unless,' I laughed, 'we find out more about why he's got that power during Discovery. But even if we win I'm not sure how the court can enforce any of this on Satan.' I hadn't planned to say that, it just came out. And once I had started I couldn't stop. 'You have considered the fact that most sane people accept that Hell is metaphorical?' I had come across this argument several times in my reading. 'They say it exists in our minds.' I pointed at my head. 'The devil is a personification of Evil. Our, uh, shadow. Our dark side.' Now I was talking to myself more than her, still trying to answer that question that she had posed to me in the beginning. What is the nature of supernatural evil? 'By obeying our negative desires we make a Hell for ourselves, which, I think, is really true, I mean . . .' Although it felt like I had a lot more to say, I looked up at that moment and saw she was gazing at me strangely, insanely.

'You don't believe me?' Before I could respond, she climbed to her feet, dropped her blanket and raised her arms to reveal her withered, naked body. It was like something left out to mummify in the desert or decaying in an airless tank, a corn husk curling with age and moss. Bits of her were peeling like paint on an old house. Her public hair was missing a patchwork of tufts. Shocked, I stood out of my chair fast enough to knock it over with the backs of my legs. 'Do you think this is metaphorical?' she said. 'Is this a Hell I created for myself in my mind, Mr Zweben, or is this a curse?'

I was about to answer, although I couldn't tell you what I planned to say, when suddenly my cell phone erupted in bleats. I held up the pointer finger of my left hand. 'I'd better take this,' I said, putting the phone against my face with my right hand. 'Hello?'

'Osmond. I've got something. You have to come get it right now, though.'

'Denny? Is that you? What are you talking about?'

'I need you to meet me right now.' His voice had as much anxiety as a cat locked in a travel crate.

'I don't know,' I said, looking up at my client. She had lowered her arms to her sides, but was still horrifyingly naked. 'Uh, yeah, okay, where?'

'The Starbuck's on the corner near the office. You know the one? Not the one down the street, but the one right on the corner?'

'Yes, yes, I'll be right there.' I hung up. 'That was my research assistant. Something big. Immediate. Gotta go.' I started off towards the door with stiff, long-legged strides. She didn't try to stop me.

Denny was at the coffee shop ahead of me looking worse than usual. He was sitting by the window in a rumpled shirt and no tie, and his hair didn't look like it had been washed or combed since the last time he'd slept in it, which could have been a few days ago judging by the circles under his eyes. He motioned his hand at me once as I came in the door, then put a to-go cup in front of his mouth. I nodded and ordered a cup of coffee. They gave it to me in a glass.

'Take it,' said Denny before I'd even had a chance to sit down. He was pushing a parcel across the table at me. 'Take it, I don't want it.' He put the cup in front of his mouth again. The package was wrapped in brown paper stamped 'airmail.'

'What is it?' I asked, setting aside my glass and starting to pick at the tape.

'Don't open it here!' he said, shocked, throwing aside his coffee so that it sloshed all over the window beside us.

'Watch it.' I knocked a droplet off the space above my suit pocket with my pinky nail.

'Take it home and open it,' he said, standing up. I saw that he'd managed to cover most of his right thigh with coffee and immediately felt sorry for him. I opened my mouth sure that the word 'Denny' would spring out of it in a concerned if slightly petulant tone, but before it could, he interrupted. 'Just – I don't ever want to see it again. Okay?'

I got home at six minutes to five. I wandered into the office and set the parcel on the desk. I had to slide my mouse pad and keyboard out of the way to set it down. Inside it was a big leather-bound dictionary of a book. It was in Latin, naturally. I didn't know Latin. Well some Latin, but not enough to read it. I wondered if Denny could read Latin. But that was stupid, because he hadn't even opened it.

I continued to look at the book while I mused. There was a lot to look at in it other than Latin. There were pictures from old Germanic woodcuts of serpents, witches with black cats, and diagrams of such exquisite detail that they would have made Aleister Crowley proud. The whole book looked to have been made by hand, probably by monks somewhere in the Black Forest in the twelfth Century. But that's just a guess. The calligraphy was beautifully done, all in red and black.

Then I found a page with a picture of a devil in a pentagram. He was an ugly bastard with hooves and goat's legs and a goat's head, horns, forked tail, sinister grin and fingernails like ice picks. A grin started to spread on my face as I looked at it. This case was a sure loser, a career stopping atrocity, and the woman was just mad enough to force me to go through with it. So I thought, what the hell? – maybe I could just have a little fun on my way out, get myself remembered. Fancy devil summoning might impress the courtroom quite a bit. Or it could get me laughed right the hell out of court, no pun intended. But part of me was starting to enjoy the idea of making a fool of myself very much.

The problem was what part of me?

I've never been that kind. I don't tell jokes, because I'm afraid people might laugh at me. I was tired, I told myself. Under a great deal of stress. I would be thinking rationally in the morning. But after a few hours wandering the house, drinking chamomile tea and watching late-night television, even masturbating, I couldn't get to sleep.

After awhile I was back in front of that book looking at those witches summoning up that ugly demon and suddenly I just started reading the Latin, butchering the pronunciation, but letting it spill out as fast as I could. It rolled off the tongue fairly well, although not a word made sense me. Don't ask me why I did it, I was out of my mind, that's all.

When I finally stopped, the door behind me – the closet door – opened with a slow extended creak that sent a shiver of pure adrenal fear arching up my spine. I spun the chair and sat facing the dark mouth of my closet. There was nothing to see, it had just swung open . . . but the timing of it. I rubbed my eyes. Maybe I could sleep now I'd got that off my chest. I started to stand when it suddenly occurred to me that someone was standing in the darkness of the open closet doorway.

My heart rushed up my throat at a thousand throbs a second and I stiffened straight, my hands lifting off the arm rests. A cold sweat broke out on the back of my neck just as sudden as if I'd been sprayed with an aerosol canister. 'Who the fuck?' I managed.

'No,' said a keen voice, soft and high, 'don't get up.' A man in a very nice suit of some cut I've never seen before stepped out of my closet. 'I don't mean to be rude.'

'How long have you been in there?' I demanded, standing up. He was a full five inches shorter than I am and had a small moustache like that Agatha Christie character, the one from Belgium, you know, a moustache that curls at the end. But his skin was yellow; he looked Lebanese or something. He held out a card. 'I don't care who you are, get the hell out,' I said, reaching out to grab his shoulder. The look in his eyes made me stop.

He said: 'Now then, Mr Zweben. I am here on a matter of great concern to my – would you take the card please.' I took the card. On it, it said 'Bud Azazel, attorney at law.'

'You-you're kidding?'

'No joke.'

'Azazel? They considered making that the prime signifier.' I was quoting the history that Denny had put together for me. 'It was in the running right up there with Beliar. Satan only won out because the word appears more often and at more critical points in canonical texts.'

'That's my name,' he said with a slight grin. 'But I can assure you that I am not Satan. As I started to say, I am here on a matter of great concern to my employer. Satan.'

'You're Satan's attorney?' I tried to think of something sarcastic to say, but couldn't.

He chuckled under his breath.

I picked the cordless off its cradle. 'I'm calling the police.'

'I'll be gone before they get here and besides, I'm not going to hurt you. I only want to speak with you.'

I held the phone at ready, my finger on the blue PHONE button. 'It's four-forty two in the morning.'

'You set up the appointment.' He motioned at the book on the table. 'Now then, since you're in such a hurry to have me go back where I came from, I'll be brief and blunt. It's in your best interests, by which I mean the best interests of your client, if you drop the case now.'

'And why is that?'

'Because, she can't win it. Her soul is as black as night, if you'll pardon an old man a cliché.' He took a pair of spectacles and a piece of paper out of his pocket. 'Just look at this analysis,' he said, putting the wire-rimmed glasses on his nose. 'Her total quotient of evil actions is far and away enough to send her to Hell anyway. And she may think that her sorry immortality is worse than Hell but, speaking as one who knows, she is far from suffering real damnation.' He held the paper close to his nose and looked at it through his spectacles. 'She's got to have total repentance before she can get anywhere near the pearly gates and that's assuming you can even win in court, which I seriously doubt. Why just look at these numbers.' He showed me a yellowing paper covered in charts and graphs and oiled with the sweat of his palm as if he had spent a lot of time poring over it in disbelief. 'She's had more than enough time to accrue sins, Mr Zweben. And the rules of the contract, the, uh, fine print, state quite clearly that no repentance counts while under terms. So, really, there's just no way for her to get out of going to Hell if she breaks the contract, not when you consider the fact that she'll die as soon as it has truly been severed.'

'So, she breaks the contract, she goes to Hell and it's as simple as that?'

'Yes, and what's more she is well aware of that fact. She knows what an evil woman she is. You can see that if you look right here in the "Denial" column, the only low numbers on this page.'

Ignoring the paper, I went on, 'But why does Satan want contracts like these? If she would just be going to Hell anyway and the contract keeps her from dying?'

'Well; Mr Zweben, Satan's motivations are beyond me, really, but I can say this. He is always trying to stand in the way of God and these contracts help him to do that. They're enforceable, just as God's word is enforceable – in the beginning there was the word, you know. He's using the covenant structure against God, which is nice for him, really. But that's neither here nor there, because the real point is, this lawsuit will only hurt your client. I wanted to make sure that you were aware of that.'

I sat back against the desk and put the phone beside me. 'Well, she may want to prove a point anyway. One lawyer to another. But I have a question, about the fine print, would you be able to supply me a copy of that?'

He turned away evasively, giving me a profile of his short, upturned nose. 'You'll have to request that in Discovery. It's not exactly in document form, but I assure you the rules are quite firm and eternal. They have to be to please a certain omniscient third party.'

'Okay, well, at least tell me how they were delivered so that I can help my client make the right choice.'

'Well,' he said somewhat abruptly, 'it's all doled out to her unconsciously before she signs, Satan enjoys being fair for some reason, and she gets reminders when she sleeps. The devil deals in dreams. Fantasies and the nightmares both. I can assure you she knows the fine print, really.'

'Maybe she does – although I doubt dreams will stand up in court – but, even if they did, she may not know what's best for herself. What I want to know is if there's any way she can get out from under the contract without us having to go to court. Yes, it seems it would be better for everybody if it didn't go to court.' Of course a moment before I had been madly thinking just the opposite, but Bud's appearance had sobered me up a bit.

'I'll tell you, Mr Zweben, there is one way. She can transfer the contract to someone else. I mean, if she performs the right rituals. And if that's all, I'll go now, I've had my say.'

'Yes, you'd better go,' I said, feeling suddenly sleepy. He went into the closet then and closed the door behind himself. When I went and opened it a moment later, it was empty.

Two weeks later we were sitting in Judge Maxine Cross's chambers; it was 12:06 in the afternoon when she walked in

the door, her face a Greek mask representing 'this is not funny at
all.' She sat down opposite an enormous desk and fixed her cool
green eyes on me first as if to say she hated me most of all, then
looked over at Mrs Sternwood. 'Hello Vivian,' she said. Ms
Gutman, in all her glorious mid-western Jell-O, was with us,
but the judge never looked at her and I imagined that they had
some old enmity. 'What's going on?'

'I'm doing something I should have done a long time ago,'
Vivian said proudly. She was dressed impeccably in a pinstriped
pants suit, but looked as if she might melt out of it at any moment.

'You'll make a fool of yourself.'

'I am a fool.'

'Yes, I could agree with that.' Then she looked at me again. 'I
have you to thank for this?' she said, holding up the complaint
that I had filed. 'I especially like the part about a generalized
sense of evil. How did you put it? The desire to spend two dollars,
just to make sure someone else doesn't get one? I'm paraphrasing,
but that's the gist anyway.' She paused to flip through my
complaint. 'Very clever,' she said, although it sounded like she
meant the opposite. 'I'm not sure I understand this parallel
you've drawn between Eve and Scarlet O' Hara, but I did enjoy
what you said about her digging up the "root" of all evil at the
end of the first part.' Suddenly she began to quote me: ' "And so
we call the personification of this American evil, and indeed of
evil itself, Satan by name, to task for the lie that he has pervaded,
id est the Fraud that you can live and not grow old." I enjoy your
flourish here with the i.e., how *appropriate* to leave the Latin
intact.' She threw the complaint on the table with a loud slap.
'The court will hear opening arguments, dates will be set immediately, talk to my clerk,' she said before marching out.

And so began another round of waiting and writing, filling and
waiting. Until at last our day in court arrived. Gutman and Royce
would rather have settled, but the cults refused. The Dark Lord
wouldn't have it, I suppose.

On my way out the door to go to the courthouse I suddenly
remembered the book that Denny had been so anxious to be rid
of. It was sitting open on my desk where I had left it a month
before. Odd to think that I hadn't touched it, or used my

computer, or sat in my desk chair since that night. I'd been thinking of the incident with Azazel as a dream and, as for the book, I hadn't forgotten about it, in fact it was often in my thoughts, but it was like it hadn't really existed and I was suddenly remembering that it did. On a whim I picked it off the table and as I did something small and white fluttered to the floor.

It was a card that said 'Bud Azazel, attorney at law,' but I was late for court.

The courtroom was called to order. The Defense, a shaggy lawyer named Simon Simonson from a dingy little law firm that the cultists had chosen to represent them, rested early. And even as they rested, I found myself reading that passage from the book. I still didn't understand the Latin, but when it was done I felt filled with a strange energy, as if I were listening to foot-tapping music and wanted suddenly to dance. I went to the front of the room and said the things that I had planned to say, but said them hurriedly. Then all at once, not knowing quite what I was saying, I blurted, 'Your honour, I call Satan to the stand.'

A non-descript but finely dressed man in the back of the room stood up and came forward down the centre aisle. No sooner had he materialized than the court was in an uproar, everyone stood up to see who this crazy fool was. Maxine Cross pounded her gavel and screamed for order. This did nothing to quiet the din, through which the devil strolled with stiff military gait towards the front of the room. Not until she called for the marshals to clear the courtroom did the shouts and ejaculations, loud prayers, singing of hymns (much of which was later noted in the paper as coming from people who previously considered themselves atheists or agnostics) finally taper off to harsh whispers of "be gone" and eventually silence. I suppose for this audience the thought of missing a showdown between a lawyer and Beelzebub was more horrible than the actual presence of the demonic in their midst.

And so my interrogation of Satan began.

The Plaintiff calls Satan.
(Witness Sworn)

By Mr Zweben:

Q. State your name for the record.

A. John Semyaza

Q. But you are Satan?

A. Yes, such is my title.

Q. What do you mean by title?

A. Satan is like 'king' and Hell mine as a king his king-dom, although I know mine own is but a heap of ruins. 'Twas a studied punishment, a death beyond imagination that banished me there.

Q. You don't deny that you are Satan then?

A. No.

Q. And you're suggesting in your convoluted archaic speech that you were made Satan of Hell as punishment for crimes against God. Do mean to suggest that you repent of the evil that you have done?

A. That I had not done a thousand more. Even now I curse the day – and yet I think few come within the compass of my curse – wherein I did not some notorious ill as kill a man, or else devise his death, ravish a maid, or plot the way to do it, accuse some innocent, and forswear myself, set deadly enmity between two friends, make poor men's cars break their axles, set fire on apartment buildings in the night, and bid the owners quench them with their tears. Oft have I digged up dead men from their graves, and set them upright at their dear friends' door, even when their sorrow almost was forgot, and on their skins, as on the bark of trees, have with my claws carved in Roman letters, 'Let not sorrow die, though I am damned.' I have done a thousand dreadful things, as willingly as one would kill a fly, and nothing grieves me more than I did not do more.

Q. So you would consider yourself a villain then? A villain who not only perpetrated great crimes, but continues to perpetrate them.

Mr Simonson: Objection your honour, he's leading the witness.

Court: Sustained. One question at a time, please.

Q. Okay. Do you consider yourself a villain?

A. Ay, like a black dog, as the saying is.

Q. Do you continue to commit heinous acts?

A. I don't expect to answer that, although I am not ashamed. I do take the fifth, as is said.

Q. And where were you on the evening of September 2, 1864?

A. Damned.

Court: The witness will kindly keep a civil tongue.

A. I meant no disrespect, your honour. I *was* damned.

Q. You were in Hell?

A. Ay, I was where all the infections that the sun picks up from bogs, fens and flats are made by inch-meal a disease.

Q. Do you deny having any relations with Vivian Sternwood on that evening?

A. I do. But I do not deny sending an associate to her side. Fetch me that flower, said I, fetch me this herd, and be thou here again ere the leviathan can swim a league.

Q. And to whom did you say this?

A. Some subsidiary demon, I do not recall exactly.

Q. Why did you send this demon to her?

A. Because her bright eyes did break each morning against my window and she led her life toward me, but would not yet let me feed upon the sweetness of her noble beauty, which was ever meant for Him who resides above.

Q. Must you speak so convolutedly?

A. Ay, I must. And besides, methinks it matches the logic of your questions.

Q. Did you indicate just now that her soul, that is the soul of Vivian Sternwood, was destined for God?

A. All souls are destined for God, lest some evil intervene. For He is forgiving. More forgiving than we are to ourselves.

Q. I take your meaning to be that God is forgiving. Let the record state the witness indicated that God is forgiving just now. What is your relationship with God?

A. There is none but Him whose being I do fear. He hath wisdom that doth guide His valour to act in safety. My genius is rebuked, as it is said Mark Antony's was by

Caesar. Upon my head He placed a fruitless crown and put a barren sceptre in my grip, thence to be wrenched eventually no doubt, depending on His will alone.

Q. The Lord giveth and the Lord taketh away?

A. So some say. But from me, I think, he only taketh.

Q. Do you resent God, then?

A. He has hurt me more than he had voided me. For now I stand as one upon a rock, environed with a wilderness of sea, who marks the waxing tide grow wave by wave expecting ever when some envious surge will in his brinish bowels swallow him.

Q. Explain more precisely what you hoped to gain from Mrs Sternwood on that evening?

A. Her soul.

Q. And did you?

A. Ay, a contract for it.

Q. Why would you want such a contract? Why not just corrupt and kill her?

A. Where be the sport in that?

Q. If you are sporting, why send a 'subsidiary demon' to obtain her signature?

A. Her soul may have been bound for Him, but her eyes, as I said, did on me oft alight. Desires burned in her hotter than my fires. Yet there is that which makes a man a coward. A man cannot steal, but it accuseth him. A man cannot lie with his neighbour's wife (or husband), but it detects him. 'Tis a blushing, shame-faced spirit that mutinies in a man's bosom. It fills a man with obstacles to my kingdom. Although it is turned out of towns and cities, and this country's especially, for a dangerous thing and every man that means to live well endeavours to trust to himself and live without it, I feared that it might interrupt her course to me. And so set I to have my guarantees.

Q. Okay, I'm sorry, I'm trying to follow you. I really am. I'm sure we're all trying hard to follow you. But you're talking in riddles. Do I have to guess? If I have to guess, I guess conscience. You feared her conscience. Is that correct?

A. Oh, those pangs have dragged many from my drain.

Q. I'll take that as a yes. So, you wanted a contract that would keep her from Heaven and bind her to Hell despite her own desires?

A. Ay.

Q. And what did you think of the contract with which your 'subsidiary demon' returned?

A. I shall answer thusly, the raging rocks and shivering shocks shall break the locks of prison gates and Phibbus car shall shine from far and make and mar the foolish Fates.

Q. Okay now, that's Shakespeare. You're quoting Shakespeare. I recognized that one, it's from the funny one. With the fairies. *Midsummer Night's Dream*. You haven't been quoting Shakespeare this whole time have you? I'm going to ask the question again and this time a simple No or Ay will suffice, okay? Were you satisfied with the contract?

A. No.

Q. Why not?

A. I enjoyed and hoped at lust's majesty. But I was cheated by her dissembling nature. I gave this one too much leeway with the text of it.

Q. So you think that there was something wrong with the contract that you arranged?

A. Ay, but I am subtle, false and treacherous. I laid inductions dangerous and by drunken prophecies, libels and dreams wrought I a new arrangement for a fairer maid.

Q. Who was this person?

Mr. Simonson: Objection your honour, the question is irrelevant.

Court: Sustained.

Q. Well, let me ask this then. There was something in the contract that made you want to break it and write a new contract?

A. Ay.

Q. What was that?

A. She is now old and altogether joyless. She was crushed before I knew the nectar of her sweet deceit. It was time that wrought this ruin.

Q. Are you immortal?

A. Ay.

Q. Do you age?

A. No.

Q. And how is it that you are immortal, but do not age when despite the immortality that you granted Vivian Sternwood she continues to age?

A. The evil that men do lives after them, the good is oft interred with their bones.

After Satan's appearance in court the papers were sure to get a hold of the whole thing and the Judge, knowing what was coming, called Ms Gutman and me into her office. She had us sit and stood over us with her arms crossed. We waited under her hateful gaze for several minutes.

'I put up with the cults and their "expert witnesses," ' she said at last. 'It was a mockery, but I stood for it for Vivian's sake. But after today. I don't know where you got him, whether he's an actor or merely insane, but – Catherine, did you know that was going to happen?'

Ms Gutman shook her jowls seriously, all of her bulbs quivering. 'Honestly, Maxine, I had no idea.'

'So it was just you then?'

I sighed. 'It really was the devil, though.'

'You expect me to believe – '

'Couldn't you feel it? The countenance of evil in the courtroom? Semyaza is a name for Satan from the first Book of Enoch in which God's original batch of angels lust after the daughters of men – which answers at least one question, Satan was a fallen angel after all. Mrs Sternwood asked me what I thought the nature of supernatural evil was and I didn't know.' I stood up and turned to look at Ms Gutman. She showed her disapproval by moving her cigar butt around in her face with her hand as though she were using it to stir putty. 'But now I do. Evil is dormant in each of us, that's the first thing that Mrs Sternwood taught me, it's in there waiting for the proper temptation to prompt us to act against others' and our own best interests, but that is only evil. Supernatural evil comes from outside of us, radiates from somewhere, Hell I suppose, perhaps from the lap of Satan himself and motivates that dormant evil. It is all around us, the hidden stuff of the universe, but you won't find it in a rock, you won't find it in a cloud, only in *living things*. Why does everything that lives have to take to live, to steal, stalk and kill? Even plants strangle one another in their vain struggle for the sun. Because the call to life is really the greed of life, supernatural evil, that which drives the locusts to breed, feed and starve in waves.' I was getting really excited now, waving my arms around. I don't know what came over me; everybody knows it's a bad idea to harangue a judge. 'It is the beast that eats its own young; the snake eating its tail. The foundation of life is the simultaneous impulse to immortality and self-destruction. Immortality being the temptation and self-destruction being the result.'

'I'm sanctioning you,' said the Judge. 'Rule 11. A frivolous lawsuit. And since you believe in Satan, Mr Zweben, or pretend to, I've decided to transfer the contract to you. That's your sanction for turning my courtroom into a circus.' She turned away from me and towards the exit, flipping closed her glasses as she went. 'That should please your client, Catherine.'

She left us.

Ms Gutman regarded me coolly, wiping her upper lip with the pad of her thumb. 'You know what, Osmond, I hope you do believe in Satan. I really do. I hope you believe in him the way the victim believes in his voodoo curse. And I hope he gets you.' She started to go, then stopped and, finally, waving at me as dismissively as a queen waving off a peasant, she said, 'And, of course, you're fired, too.'

The next day, I called Mrs Sternwood. I had to find out more about what I could expect from my newly acquired contract. Whatever was going to happen, I hadn't felt any difference yet. I listened to the phone ring and I imagined the man walking down that long hall from the overheated room where he'd probably just been serving the mistress some chilled celebratory champagne. When he finally answered and I asked him to put me through to her, he said, 'Mrs Sternwood died last night, sir, but I am glad that you called. It seems she mentioned you in her will.'

MY BONNIE LIES . . .

Ted Hertel, Jr

Shortly before I graduated from law school, my great-aunt Anna took my arm and pulled me aside at a cousin's wedding. 'Why do you want to be a lawyer, Bonnie? All lawyers are liars.'

I reminded her of the honoured tradition of such great attorneys as Lincoln. I told her of the proud profession of well-respected men and women who held to the truth and sought justice in all they did.

'Bah! Remember Nixon. Get out while you still can.'

From that moment on I vowed to be honest and straightforward with my clients, my fellow attorneys, the judges I would appear before, and the public at large.

That, of course, was my first lie.

When I graduated, I became an associate with a large, prestigious, law firm. I was paid more money in a year than my father had earned in the seven years it took for him to put me through college and law school. In return the firm expected me to live there twenty-four hours a day in order to bill the absurd number of hours I had to meet to remain on the partnership track. Billing fifty hours a week does not mean working fifty hours a week. More like a hundred, actually. Something always interrupted the day: a cold call from a securities broker; the two-hour, three martini lunch, so fashionable in those days; the continuing legal education classes; or the pro bono work the firm also expected of associates.

So I learned creative billing. Our minimum billable unit was a quarter hour. It took only a minute to read a letter? Bill it at '0.25'. A three-minute phone call? Another quarter-hour on the time-sheet. Thirty to forty-five minutes on a brief? An hour. The little lies became the necessities of staying sane.

There were no fax machines when I first entered the practice. It was easy to tell the complaining client that her work was actually done and would go out in the mail that night. Of course, I would then do it and get it to the post office for last pickup. Even backdating the bill became standard operating procedure. The advent of the fax gave birth to a new lie: 'Oh, my secretary is out sick today. We'll fax it to you first thing in the morning.'

Next, I found myself encouraging frail, elderly clients to appoint me as the personal representative of their estates. Funny how soon afterwards they died – and how quickly their probate assets were eaten up. Those legal fees will kill a person . . .

Did I have any regrets? Only that I didn't have more frail, elderly clients.

Eventually I left the firm and set up my own, Cunningham Law Offices. I shifted my focus from a civil practice to helping people I believed were wrongly accused of a crime, assuming, of course, they had enough money to convince me of their innocence. Over the fifteen years of my criminal defense work, I had rarely lost a case. Further, I had developed quite a reputation for getting the job done right the first time. There aren't a lot of second chances in criminal law. So I worked – and I worked hard. After all, it's the duty of the lawyer to use every means to keep wealthy clients out of prison.

When they weren't jetting around the world, Paula and Gene Fischer appeared nearly every week on the local society pages. Gene owned a computer consulting company. Paula, according to the papers, did nothing besides serve on the boards of several charitable organizations. The Fischers lived on a sprawling, secluded estate on Shore Drive. They had everything money could buy.

So it was with some degree of surprise that I saw a panic-stricken Gene Fischer barge into my office without an appointment that Monday morning. A recent newspaper article covering the exclusive Carillon Ball had described him as 'fashionable and strikingly handsome,' which upon meeting him turned out to be an understatement. Tall, broad-shouldered, and very tan, he was dressed to kill, which turned out to be the perfect attire for what he had to tell me. I stood to greet him and directed him to one of the leather chairs facing my desk. He started right in, just as if we were old friends.

'I killed Paula. Late last night. She was –'

'Whoa! Stop right there. Just so you understand, I only represent people who are innocent.'

'Well, then you obviously can't help me.'

'That's not what I said at all. I merely want you to know that if I take your case, it'll be because I believe you aren't guilty. You obviously haven't been arrested or you wouldn't be sitting here.'

'Let's just say that so far I haven't been caught. When the police find me, they'll arrest me.'

'And why will they do that?'

'I told you: because I killed my wife.'

'Yes, I understand that you believe, wrongly of course, that you killed your wife, but why will the police believe that?'

'Well, for one thing, somebody saw me do it.'

'That's the sort of mistake an amateur makes –'

'I'm hardly a professional.'

'Of course you're not. What I'm saying is an amateur believes an eyewitness to a crime is infallible. Quite the contrary, actually. Witnesses are generally unreliable – and the police can easily be convinced of their mistakes once a professional, like me, presents the true facts to them. Now, tell me what you think happened.'

Fischer related that over the last ten years of their marriage he had become more obsessed with his business and less absorbed with his wife. Between their frequent trips Paula filled her life with committee work, he had assumed. However, within the last year or so she had become careless, raising Gene's suspicions. Phone calls were abruptly terminated when he entered a room. Several times in the past few months he had tried to reach her at this or that committee meeting, only to be told she had called with some excuse for not attending. Yet when they talked later, Paula would tell him all about how much had been accomplished at the meeting.

Although Fischer suspected his wife's affair, he wasn't in a position to make an accusation since he himself had begun an affair some months earlier with a young woman named Karen Goodrich. She was 'beautiful and about as smart as a couch cushion.' A mutual friend had introduced Paula and him to Karen at a party. Gene and Karen found they had a lot in common, not the least of which was an interest in his money. They met secretively several times a week for an expensive meal and sex.

Last night Fischer had come home with a migraine from a business meeting. He heard some noise out in the back yard and, upon investigating, saw Paula and Karen, both very naked, caressing each other in the hot tub. They did not see Gene, however, until he walked out of the patio doors with the gun from the study in his hand.

'Betrayed, not only by my wife, but also by my mistress.' I didn't point out the obvious irony in that statement.

'My only mistake was not making sure the gun was fully loaded. I shot Paula twice and then the damn thing just "clicked". I wish there'd have been at least one left for the other slut.'

'So, let me get this straight. You were at a business meeting last night and left because you weren't feeling well. You stopped at Del Mondo's for dinner, had a few too many drinks – not a good thing with a migraine, I'm sure you know – saw a couple of people you know, and finally went home. Because you'd been drinking, you took a cab home. When you got there, the driver helped you to the house. You heard some noise around back, so you both went to the rear yard. You and the cabbie found your wife dead in the hot tub, with her girl friend standing over her holding the still smoking gun. She saw you and, thinking you were next, you took off until you could come here this morning. Right?'

'What the hell are you talking about? That's not what I said!'

'No, but I'm convinced that's what happened. I told you I don't represent the guilty. Bad for the reputation to lose all those cases, you know. Since I am in fact representing you, it follows that you are innocent. All those drinks at Del Mondo's apparently left you very confused. I have a rather straightforward defense litany for my clients: "You don't have a wife. If you have a wife, she's not dead. If she is dead, she wasn't murdered. If she was murdered, you didn't kill her. If you did kill her, you were crazy." We know the first three aren't true in your case, so we'll approach it from the fourth line of defense, namely, you didn't kill her. It's never necessary to get to that "crazy" one, by the way.'

'Maybe you're the one who's crazy . . .'

'I assure you that I'm not, as you'll see when we discuss my fee: $100,000, whether we go through trial and appeal or I pick up that phone right now and get any potential charges dropped.'

'A hundred grand for a phone call . . .'

'Better that than spending it and the next two years fighting these ridiculous charges. In fact the sooner you're out from under suspicion, the happier you'll be and the more you'll believe I earned my fee. Which I need in full up front. And yes, I will take your cheque.'

As he handed it to me, I told him I hoped to call him in a few days with good news. In the meantime he should do his best to stay out of sight of the police and in touch with me.

Actually, it didn't even take that long. Two days later Gene Fischer reappeared in my office, looking slightly less fashionable and handsome than he had on his first visit. He sat in the same leather chair in front of my desk, rubbing his face as he waited for me to start talking.

'The cops have the real killer. They picked her up last night.'

'That can't be. That just can't be.'

'But it is. The police arrested Karen Goodrich at her home.'

'She – she saw me kill Paula.'

'That's what her story is, but we know that's just not possible, is it? The cops have proof that she did it.'

'I don't understand.'

'It's all very simple. She killed her. She got caught. That's it.'

'There has to be more.'

'You're a detail person, I see. Okay, it seems that this woman and your wife were seen in Del Mondo's several hours before you arrived. The same maitre d' who seated you –'

'I didn't go to Del Mondo's!'

'I'm sorry, but I really have to believe the witnesses who saw you and her and Paula.'

'You said eyewitnesses were unreliable.'

'True, one or two could be wrong, but they can't all be mistaken.'

'But I didn't . . . did I?'

'I'm sure all that alcohol must have affected you. That's why the cabbie drove you home – and a good thing he did, too. So don't worry about it. Now, let's see, where . . . oh, yes, the maitre d', the staff, and most of the customers heard the two of them fighting during dinner. She was screaming and crying because Paula had told her that it was over between them. Seems Paula didn't want to risk losing all that money you were constantly lavishing on her. Goodrich said something trite like if she couldn't have Paula, no one could. Then she stormed out of the place. They tell me Paula was rather calm, even finished her dinner.

'Apparently, your wife went to your house and eventually got into the hot tub. That's when Karen showed up with the gun. She must have gotten it from the study. I understand that's where you kept it. Just two bullets, but they did the trick. That must have been about the time you showed up with the cab driver. Did you hear the shots?'

'Of course I did. I was there when I shot her!'

'You mean, when you heard Karen Goodrich shoot her.'

'I don't know what I mean anymore.'

'Turns out you rushed out of there with the cabbie and he took you back to Del Mondo's where you'd left your car. You'd sobered up pretty well by then – a shock like that can do it. He said he'd call the police and you took off. By the time he called the cops, Goodrich had already gotten to them with a story about your having shot Paula. But it turns out that her prints were all over the gun. Yours weren't. Curiously, the gun had been missing from the police lab for a couple of hours, but they found it after a little looking around. And of course, I informed the police that you and the driver had arrived in time to see Goodrich standing over Paula with the gun in her hand. Naturally, you were too distraught to call the police yourself. I told them I'd bring you in for a statement in a day or two. I'll help you get your thoughts in order before we go see them.

'So, you see, it's really all over.'

Gene stood to go and I rose along with him, accompanying him to the door. I thought about mentioning that the maitre d', his staff, the customers, and the cab driver were all former clients of mine, that they all owed me an occasional favour for my having gotten them out of a tight situation of one kind or another over the years. But all I said was 'By the way, Gene, one day, I may need a favour from you, maybe something as simple as saying you ate at a particular restaurant at a certain time. I'm sure you'd have no problem with that . . .'

Ashen-faced, he nodded, then left the office without saying a word.

The day after I stood by Gene Fischer's side as he gave the police his statement, my phone rang again.

'I need your help. I've been arrested.'

'Tell me about it.'

'I've been framed for murder. My name is Karen Goodrich.'

Naturally, I took her case – and her hundred grand.

As I've said, I only represent the innocent.

TOMORROW'S VILLAIN

Mat Coward

For a short while, following the death of my daughter, I became something of a national hero.

It helped that I was an ordinary bloke – a self-employed electrician – and not what the papers call a 'toff.' The papers hate toffs, which is odd, given that the papers are staffed almost exclusively by toffs.

It helped even more that I was a lone father. Lone mothers are, even these days, still subject to a certain moral ambiguity: is she in that position deliberately? Or did she at least bring it on herself? But a father, struggling bravely against both nature and society to raise a child all on his lonesome – why, he's halfway to being a saint already.

So when Nadine (named for the Chuck Berry song) died in a back street in the West End of London, all I had to do was fight back the tears on live TV and I was instantly canonized.

I made the usual press conference appeal for witnesses, remembering with some guilt as I did so that whenever I'd watched such performances on TV in the past, I'd always assumed that the person making the appeal was the guilty party.

Nadine died one week after her eighteenth birthday, of a rare allergic reaction to the chemicals contained in an anti-rape spray. Normally, so the coroner later declared, this would not have led to a fatality; however, there was evidence at the death scene of a scuffle, during which, it was surmised, her assailant had held the canister close to her face and emptied its entire contents directly into her mouth and nose. Her death, essentially from respiratory failure, had followed rapidly. I was astonished to learn that Nadine carried such a spray – she loathed all weapons – but I supposed that no parent ever knows their children as well as they think they do.

Within seventy-two hours of my daughter's death, the police made an arrest: a twenty-one-year-old, black, male shop assistant, Horace Jones. The next day's papers described him variously as Nadine's 'live-in lover' and 'steady boyfriend'. I'd never heard of him.

A black, male killer, a white, female victim; a brave but grief-stricken dad. We were news, the three of us.

These events happened in November, so they were still fresh in the public's mind when a national radio station ran its annual 'Man Of The Year' phone-in poll. I won. That made me laugh. I mean, *really* laugh – laugh with real amusement. I was the Man of the Year for having lost my daughter. If I'd had two daughters, and they'd both been killed, would I have been elected Pope?

Horace Jones denied all charges, both at the time of his arrest, and a few months later, during his trial. His denials were not believed, and he was duly sentenced to life imprisonment.

His trial put me back in the headlines, and my heroic status was confirmed and even enlarged. I really believe that, at that moment, I could have stood for Parliament with some hope of success. Nadine was a victim, Horace Jones was emblematic of all that was wrong with modern Britain, and I was . . . well, I seemed to be, for no reason that was ever clear to me, the symbol of all that was *right* with modern Britain.

Jones' lawyer lodged an appeal against the conviction. As it happened, I knew the lawyer, Teddy Edwards; had known him, at least, some years earlier, when we'd served together on a local anti-apartheid committee here in Maidstone. About a week after Jones began his sentence, Teddy phoned and asked to see me. I agreed; I was still in that stage of grief where I wanted more details, more information, more understanding of what had happened.

'He's not guilty, Jack,' Teddy said as we sat drinking tea in my empty kitchen. 'I'm sorry, I know that probably isn't what you want to hear, but I have to tell you: I have no doubt in my mind at all that Horace Jones did not kill Nadine.'

It wasn't what I wanted to hear, of course, and it wasn't what I'd expected to hear. 'You have to say that, don't you, Teddy?' I replied. 'A lawyer – you've got to believe your clients are innocent. That's how it works, surely?'

He shook his head. 'Not at all, Jack. Not like that at all. Ninety-nine per cent of my clients are thieves and liars and worse. I have to *accept* that they're innocent if that's what they choose to tell me, but I'm not required to *believe* it. I represent them to the best of my ability, because that's my job – and because,' and here he paused for a self-deprecating chuckle, 'and because, now that I'm a middle-aged, middle-class solicitor, I actually do believe in the system. I'm not the radical I once was, Jack. Well, which of us is? I think our system of law is, over all, a good system. And it can only work as long as even the most heinously guilty arsehole gets the best defence the system can provide him with. But no, I don't usually believe their pathetic fairy stories.'

'So what's different this time?' I asked.

He sat forward in his seat, and started ticking off items on his fingers. 'OK. Right. Basically, I think Horace has been lynched. He's black, Nadine was white. She was a lovely girl training to be a nurse, he's just some inner city nobody with a petty criminal record; possession of drugs, some minor thieving. It's a match made in Hell.'

'Just because ignorant people wanted him to be guilty doesn't mean he *wasn't* guilty,' I said.

'No, sure, good point.' Teddy looked tired and sweaty. He'd aged a lot in the few years since I'd last seen him. Much of his hair had gone, and his suit was irreversibly rumpled. It was a reasonably expensive suit, so I assumed the rumpling came from within. He took a packet of cigarettes out of his pocket and waved it at me. 'Do you mind if I smoke?'

'No, of course not.'

'Really,' said Teddy, 'say if you do.'

I shook my head, and stood up to find him an ashtray. 'Nadine smoked.'

'They all do, don't they?' he said, lighting up gratefully. 'Teenage girls. My wife says the ones you want to worry about are the ones who don't smoke. You can guarantee they're doing something much worse.'

Teddy went back to talking about the case, putting forward his arguments concerning Horace Jones's innocence, but after a while he noticed that I wasn't hearing him.

'Christ, Jack, are you all right?'

It was the smell of the cigarette. Before Teddy, the last person who'd smoked in that house had been Nadine. For some reason, when everyone came back here for the funeral meats, all the smokers were careful to take their cigarettes out into the garden, even though there were ashtrays on every surface in the kitchen and living-room. A kind of bizarre, turn-of-the-century mark of respect for the dead: don't let them see you smoking.

When the snake of aromatic grey and white smoke from Teddy's cigarette coiled across the table between us and up into my brain, I instantly and absolutely broke down. From a man of flesh, holding things together, I turned into a bowl of dry cornflakes: shattered, jagged, formless. And then soggy, as the tears flowed. I wasn't sobbing: I was just sitting there, staring straight ahead, while the tear-water poured out of my eyes like beer from a tap.

Teddy helped me through to the living-room. He drew the curtains, put the lights on, poured us both a scotch from an almost full bottle on the sideboard. I'd hardly been in the living-room since Nadine died. I felt out of place, almost a visitor in my own home, and I think that helped me regain control of my tear ducts.

After a while, I was ready to resume the conversation. Teddy wasn't smoking any more.

'I don't know how much of the trial you took in, Jack. I don't imagine legal niceties were uppermost in your mind, but let me tell you – and you don't have to take my word for it, I'll get you a transcript of the trial – there was basically no evidence against Horace. No serious evidence.'

'Then how did he get convicted?' I asked. 'You said just now you believed in our system of law.'

'Yeah, sure, but compared to *what* – that's the question.' Teddy rubbed his hands over his scalp, making the little hair he had left stand up in tufts. He looked like a baby that's just woken up grumpy from an afternoon nap. 'To an idealist, a thing is either perfect or terrible. But a realist sees things in context. All

I'm saying is, if you were an innocent man, with no money, charged with a terrible crime, where would you rather be tried: Britain or America? Britain or China? Britain or Spain?'

'But this time the system got it wrong. That's what you're telling me?'

'I'm sure of it.'

'OK,' I said, the details of the evidence given in court coming back to me. Teddy's assumption was understandable, but wrong: in fact, I had taken in, and retained, every word of that trial. As long as the trial went on, Nadine still existed. People still spoke of her, and what does being alive mean other than being talked about? 'As I recall, there were two main pieces of physical evidence. First of all, the wounds to your client's face . . .'

'Right,' said Teddy. 'The nail scratches. The wounds were the right age, and they came from a woman's hand, or to be precise from false nails – fun nails, they're called these days – we didn't contest that, but remember that the prosecution was unable to say that they came from *Nadine's* nails. And that's not just a technicality, Jack.'

'The wounds were said to be made by a woman of Nadine's height.'

He shrugged. 'She was of average female height. Means nothing.'

'All right. What about the fingerprints?'

'The clincher, as far as the jury was concerned,' Teddy admitted. 'Horace's prints were on the canister of anti-rape spray. Nobody else's, not even Nadine's. He says, as you'll remember, that he and Nadine had met in a pub in Covent Garden a month before her death, right?'

'And that they'd seen each other "as friends only" several times during that month. Yes, I remember.' So much for the press reports that she'd been killed by her 'Black Live-In Lover'. 'But when your barrister asked him in court if, during that time, he had handled the spray can, he couldn't say, could he?'

'Not *couldn't* say,' said Teddy. 'Wouldn't say. And that's crucial, Jack. You know that barristers never ask questions they don't already know the answer to?'

'I've heard it said.'

'Well, we thought we knew the answer to that one. We thought Horace was going to reply that Nadine had spilt her handbag once when they were out together, and that he had helped her re-pack it. Hence the single set of his prints on the spray.'

'So why didn't he?'

Teddy shook his head. 'Don't know. Actually, yes, I think I do – because it was a lie. I don't think that is how his prints got on there, and he is the kind of bloke – something of an innocent, religious upbringing – that he's just not willing to tell a lie. Even to save his neck.'

Now I shook my head – the scotch was clouding my mind a little. I hadn't had a drink since the day of the funeral. 'But if even you think he's lying about the anti-rape spray . . .'

'My guess is that he knows something about what happened, but he's not willing to say it. So, to avoid lying, he just says nothing. Or else, *I don't know, Sir,* which amounts to the same thing.' Teddy stood up. 'Look, Jack, I'm sorry. I've given you a bad evening. I'll let you get some kip, now. But can I talk to you again? I really think it's important.'

'Of course you can,' I said. 'I'm always happy to talk.' *About Nadine,* I didn't need to add.

Teddy sent me the trial transcript, and I read it, feeling a jet of life squirt up through my body every time I saw the word *Nadine* in print.

The prosecution's case was straightforward. Horace and Nadine first met in a pub in Covent Garden. They went out together several times over the next few weeks, to pubs, ethnic restaurants. They did not sleep together. They chatted about the things they had in common: football (she was a West Ham fanatic, my daughter), exotic food and 1960s rhythm and blues music.

On the night of her death, they had been drinking in a pub off the Charing Cross Road. At closing time, they walked towards Leicester Square Tube staion, taking a short cut through an unlit alley. There, Horace demanded sex. Nadine refused. Horace persisted, to the point of attempted rape (her clothes were in disarray when she was found). She tried to use the anti-rape spray on him, but he took it from her and turned it on her, forcing it into her mouth and nose. When he saw the effect this had on her, he panicked and ran. She was found dead by an off-duty ambulance driver about forty minutes later. At around that time, a blood-splashed black youth was seen running in a nearby street.

Horace Jones was a suspect from the start of the investigation, according to the prosecution's version of events. Detectives learned of his existence from some girls at Nadine's college, and heard from the same source that he and Nadine had been seen 'arguing violently' in a Covent Garden wine bar the night before her death. He was described as 'a big, strong man' which caught the detectives' attention, since it had already been noted that the method of death probably ruled out a female killer, a short man, or a weakling.

When taken in for questioning, Horace denied killing Nadine, or fighting with her, or attempting to rape her, but he declined to give an account of his movements during the crucial hours. He also refused to explain the scratches on his face, and when, on the second day of questioning, he was confronted with the finger-print evidence, he offered no comment. At the end of the second day, he was charged with murder.

The police did everything by the book: no doubt about that. It's clear from the interview transcripts that they went to great lengths to persuade Horace that he ought to be represented by a lawyer – 'Don't need a lawyer, man. I got no lies to tell' – and the interviews were interrupted repeatedly for tea breaks, and on three further occasions so that Horace could be seen by the duty surgeon, 'as the prisoner appeared to be in a state of considerable emotional shock.'

They'd got their man, and they weren't going to lose him through a procedural error. Or else maybe they were just good cops, trying to do the job properly. I suppose that's not impossible, after all.

'Have you read it?' said Teddy on the phone.

'I have.'

'Great. Thanks. Listen, sorry to have to, you know, put you through –'

'That's OK. Don't worry.'

'OK, great.' A pause, during which I wondered whether there were any cigarettes in Nadine's room. I'd never smoked, not even as a kid, but it would be nice to smell that scent again. 'Listen, Jack – I'd like you to meet him. Horace: I'd like you to talk to him.'

I almost dropped the phone, as my heart stopped pumping and my limbs froze. *Meet him?* 'Is that . . . would that be allowed?'

'Oh yeah, yeah, listen – yeah.' Teddy was gabbling. In gratitude, I suppose, that I wasn't screaming at him. 'I mean, you know, a prisoner's allowed visitors. Up to him who they are.'

'And he's willing?'

Teddy laughed. 'About as willing as you are, Jack! But, yes, he'll see us. If you think you're up to it.'

How much easier it must have been in the days of capital punishment, I thought. At least back then the ghosts were all dead.

'So you've read the evidence, what do you think?' We were in Teddy's car, driving to the prison. 'There's not much to it, is there?'

'I agree it's a bit thin,' I said. 'But if Horace didn't do it, and he wasn't there, then why wasn't he able to offer a more convincing defence? Some sort of alibi, or something.'

'I'm hoping,' said Teddy, who seemed a lot more nervous than I was, 'that we'll find that out today.' I, by contrast, was not hoping for anything in particular. Why was I there? The ususal reason: to prolong the existence of Nadine.

'You won't get a word out of our Horace,' said the prison officer who checked our papers. 'He's the tall, dark, silent type.' When the guard clocked my name, he gave me a look that only just fell short of naked contempt. That was an omen, if I'd been in a state to notice it. But all such thoughts fled my head the moment I sat down opposite Horace and looked into his eyes for the first time.

I knew straight away that he hadn't killed my daughter.

It wasn't anything to do with him. It wasn't that I looked upon Horace and knew him incapable of murder. It was rather that I looked at Horace and knew *Nadine* to have been incapable of being murdered by him.

Nonsense, of course. Irrational, meaningless. I understood that then no less than I understand it now, but that understanding didn't change what I knew. One thing that having your daughter murdered does for you – did for me, at any rate – is it liberates you from the rules of rationality. If you know something, you just know it, and you don't ask how or why. I had already accepted the utterly impossible fact that my only child had predeceased me; after that, accepting any lesser impossibility was child's play.

Teddy introduced us – as if we needed it! – and then sat with his chair slightly behind mine, leaving the two of us alone in a room full of chattering, grieving men and women.

'All right, Horace,' I said, without preamble. 'You didn't kill Nadine. So who did?'

Horace said nothing, just stared at me with the eyes of a disinterred corpse. He didn't blink, and he didn't look away.

'Do you think your need not to tell is greater than my need to be told? Is that it, Horace? Because if so, then there's nothing I can –'

He blinked. Once. It was one of the most effective interruptions I have ever been subjected to. I stopped talking, and waited.

At last, he said: 'I don't want to tell you. Being in here is better than telling it. It's terrible in here, but it's better than telling it.' But he did tell us his story, even so. Not all of it – not even then – but enough.

A week later, Teddy and I held a press conference. Teddy gave a broad outline of the case for an appeal hearing, while I answered follow-up questions from the reporters – all of which were of the idiotic 'How do you feel?' variety. My well-rehearsed answer was simple: I felt it was wrong that a man should be in prison for a crime he hadn't committed. I felt that those actually responsible for my daughter's death should be brought to justice. Beyond that, I had no comment to make.

The Campaign For Justice For Horace Jones was formally launched, with Teddy as its Treasurer and me as its Secretary – and thus, within the space of a day, I passed from being yesterday's hero to being tomorrow's villain.

To the news papers, I was no longer an ordinary working

bloke; I was a 'self-employed businessman'. I was no longer a
brave lone father, struggling to raise his beautiful daughter; I was
now a 'divorcee loner,' who had raised a 'wild child'. (The fact
that my ex-wife had died in a motor accident shortly before our
divorce had been finalized, and that I was therefore technically a
widower, went unmentioned).

I was, above all, no longer that quiet, unassuming dad who
bore his bereavement with solemn dignity. Now, I was that crazy
do-gooder who wanted to let a murdering monster out of jail to
kill again. (A *black* monster. The word was always there, even
though it rarely appeared in print.)

One journalist – who I later discovered was all of twenty-two
years old, fresh down from Oxford, and a niece by marriage of the
proprietor – wrote an op-ed piece in the *Daily Telegraph*, telling
the world (and, incidentally, me) precisely what it was that I was
doing, and why. The *what* was putting my 'white liberal conscience' and 'knee-jerk pro-ethnic bias' before the 'natural love a
proper father feels for his child'. And the reason I was doing this
was, as far as I could make out, because that was what white
liberals did.

It was all a case of 'political correctness gone mad,' the writer
concluded (demonstrating that what she lacked in empathy she
made up for in cliché-mongering), and furthermore it was this
'false prioritization, born of middle-class guilt and enforced by
the liberal theocracy,' that had led to the breakdown of family-
based, Christian society. And so on: I'm sure you're familiar with
the script.

Daft, I know, but it was that word 'liberal' that annoyed me
most. I have never been *remotely* liberal; I am a socialist son of
socialist parents. My daughter was a socialist. My great-grand-
father was arrested seven times during the General Strike. If
Lucinda Buckteeth-Jodphurs, or whatever the silly little bitch's
name was, wanted to get into a liberal-despising contest with me,
she'd better be prepared for a heavy defeat. My wife, now, she
was a liberal. Probably one of the reasons we split up – I don't
mean because we argued about politics, but because, being a
liberal, she had no moral impediment to abandoning her husband
and child to pursue self-fulfilment.

Smart comedians, bored with their usual diet of bent politicians and ugly TV celebrities, made neat little gags at my expense. They couldn't be accused of racism, of course, because they were being *ironic*.

It wasn't only the mass media that took an interest in me. Someone painted 'Wog Lover' in large, ironically black letters on my garage door. Of the two attackers, I found I had more respect for the spray-painter than for the *Telegraph* girl. They were both saying the same thing, after all – *exactly* the same thing, make no mistake about that – but at least the painter didn't try to disguise himself with the false-beard-and-moustache of education, privilege and logorrhoea.

I left the legend on the garage door, didn't try to clean it off. I decided instead to treat it as a compliment. 'Wog Lover'? Sure, why not? I *do* try to love my neighbour: that's how I was brought up. It's how my daughter was brought up.

Besides, if I'd cleaned it off, someone would only have put it back, wouldn't they? I could have been out there with a bucket and scrubbing brush every day for the rest of my life.

There was much more in a similar vein, but it's not worth listing. No-one actually hit me or put a bomb through my window. As for the rest – well, if you want the truth, being a national villain was considerably less irritating than being a national hero had been. At least I could get my car out of my garage without first clearing several dozen bouquets of damn lilies away from the door.

'I'm really sorry,' Teddy said one night over a beer, in my living-room. The campaign to secure an appeal hearing went on for two years – a much quicker process than it had been in the recent past, Teddy was always at pains to point out. In America they bury their mistakes, he'd say. At least Horace is still alive.

'You're sorry for what?' I asked, though I knew what he meant.

'All this. If I'd known it was going to be so hard on you –'

'You'd have done it anyway,' I said, putting an end to the discussion. Because he *would* have done it anyway, and he'd have been right to do it, so what was the point of pretending otherwise?

The appeal hearing revealed the usual tragic, tawdry story of errors and evasions. It wasn't so much a case of evidence being deliberately hidden in order to frame the innocent – more a case of facts which didn't fit being ignored, so as not to ruin a good theory. Evidence, for instance, suggesting that there had been more than two people involved in the scuffle which led to Nadine's death. Evidence which showed that Nadine's death might have been caused by one strong man, or by a number of smaller, weaker people acting together.

Everyone does that, don't they? Leaves out the bits that don't fit. Cops do it, politicians do it, school teachers, scientists, sports commentators.

In the dock, this time, Horace told the story that he had told me when I visited him in prison.

'Nadine and me, we were friends, OK? Nothing more. I don't care if you all believe that or not, that's the truth. That is the *truth*. I'm not gay or nothing, but she already had a boyfriend. She was seeing a married man.'

That was the bit he hadn't wanted me to hear, because of what had happened between me and Nadine's mother. He was right: I didn't want to hear it. I didn't want to hear evidence, in a court of law, that I had raised a daughter who was merely human, not perfect.

'The night she died, the night they killed her, she and I had a drink, and then she went to meet this fellow, John.'

Don't call her *She*, I wanted to say. If you call her Nadine she still exists.

'He was supposed to be a meeting in Birmingham, but he wasn't, he was meeting her at a hotel in Hampstead. But when we split up after our drink, and she was going to one Tube and I was going to another, I followed her. I decided to follow her, because . . .'

During a long pause, no-one in the court tried to prompt him.

'. . . I wasn't her boyfriend, OK? Whatever everybody thinks. I just followed her because I was – because I decided to follow her to see if, you know. Just to *see*. When she turned into that alley, near the Tube, I saw that I wasn't the only one following her. There was four girls, four young women, and they were following her too. I saw them. They had this can of spray, I didn't know what it was then, just a can of something. The main girl, the leader, she was wearing gloves. I saw what they did, and I ran up to them and I was shouting at them to stop and I tried to grab the can, but one of the girls, she raked my face with those long nails. I couldn't see too good, there was blood all in my eyes, and I . . . I ran off to get help. To get some help, you see? For Nadine.'

That was the bit he hadn't wanted *anyone* to hear. That was why he had gone to prison for a crime he hadn't committed: to avoid telling the world that he had run from four girls.

'I don't think they meant to kill her. I think they just meant to beat her up. But she . . . Nadine collapsed when they sprayed that stuff in her face.' Another long, uninterrupted pause. 'I ran off to get help.'

A young black man – a young black *male,* as the newspapers always say – running through the streets of the West End, blood running down his face, shouting about murder. He couldn't find a policeman, and no citizen was brave enough to help him. Are you surprised?

By the time he got back to the scene, Nadine was dead.

'I went home,' Horace concluded. He was asked by the Crown's barrister and by his own why he had simply gone home, why he hadn't stayed with the body, called the police called an ambulance? I don't know why they asked: surely the answer was obvious. The poor kid was ashamed.

Horace Jones did not receive a proper pardon, but he was released on a technicality. He went to live, Teddy told me, with a distant relative somewhere in the Midlands. He changed his name. He refused to sell his story to the newspapers, which means that if the reporters ever do catch up with him they'll consider it their solemn duty to rip his life to shreds. I only hope that by then he's got a life worth ripping.

I never saw him again, except for briefly in Teddy's office, immediately after his release, when I just had time to ask him one question.

'People saw you and Nadine arguing the evening before she died. What were you arguing about?'

He gave me that dead stare. I didn't know if he was going to answer, until he spoke. 'Football,' he said.

'Football?'

'I don't like football. I like cricket. In cricket you get fair play.'

I've no idea if that was the truth. Could have been, I suppose. Funny thing is, Nadine and I used to have that same argument. I'm a cricket man, myself.

On the steps of the appeal court, a police spokesman announced that 'as far as we are concerned the case remains closed' – police code for, 'Of course the bastard was guilty – we wouldn't have arrested him otherwise, would we?' But they were humiliatingly forced to abandon this position only a few days later, when one of the girls involved in the attack on Nadine broke ranks, and turned herself in at her local police station, accompanied by her family lawyer.

She hadn't been directly involved in the violence, she said. Leading the attack had been her best friend, the wife of the man Nadine was seeing, along with the wife's two sisters. They'd set out to teach Nadine to 'keep her filthy hands off other women's blokes' but 'it had all gone horribly wrong' and she could 'no longer live with the guilt.'

She was charged with a lesser offence; the other three were charged with murder. Their case is due to be heard early next year. And I, naturally, am a public hero once again. I am the courageous, loving father who fought for an innocent boy's freedom against the forces of bigotry and ignorance. My drive is full of bouquets again. I hate it. I'm thinking of moving, changing my name, going abroad. But I'm afraid that to do so would be to surrender to cynicism, and I am determined not to do that. Cynicism is the triumph of death and futility, and I won't willingly become its ally.

Of course, to some I am still a 'Wog Lover,' and poor Horace is still a murdering savage who got away with it. A Conservative MP, hiding behind the parliamentary privilege of immunity to the laws of slander, told the House of Commons that in his opinion the police had acted correctly throughout, only to have their actions 'second-guessed by subversives,' and that Horace Jones was 'a guilty, guilty man with a soul as black as tar.'

To my astonished delight, the MP's party leadership disowned him, his local activists turned against him, and his career fell into a terminal decline. So, then: there *are* still good people in the world. Perhaps I'm even one of them, since the campaign to free Horace began, for me, as a means of keeping Nadine's name alive – but somewhere along the way it became something else: a desire to prove that in a world full of shrugged shoulders, it is still possible to give witness to the simple, concrete difference between right and wrong.

I try to remember that, I mine that thought for whatever comfort it contains, now that the whole business is over and done with, now that my daughter Nadine finally does not exist, and can never exist again.

CRUEL AND UNUSUAL

Carolyn Wheat

New York City, November 1994

It was a typical Ambrose, Jeffers file: thick as the Manhattan telephone directory, every page neatly aligned, colour tabs for the sixteen exhibits at the end. Avery Nyquist had thumbed through hundreds of case files in her seven years as an associate with the prestigious firm, read thousands upon thousands of legal documents, digested millions of words designed to throw a cloak of legalistic obfuscation over the simplest fact.

Never had she read, or even imagined reading, the words of Petitioner's Exhibit 'A'. They lay before her, their coal-hard reality sending a chill through her. It was as though a black widow spider had walked across the pristine surface of Avery's designer desk.

'. . . there to be taken to a place determined by law, to be subject to execution by means of the electric chair, until he shall be pronounced dead by a duly authorized coroner of the state of Wyoming.'

A death warrant. She was looking at a death warrant. A piece of paper, duly signed, stamped, and filed with the county clerk, a piece of legal paper just like all the thousands of papers she'd read in her legal lifetime. Only because of this paper, a boy would die.

She had been asked to do many things since her first day at the most prestigious law firm on Wall Street. Work from eight in the morning until midnight, then show up bright and eager for more at seven the next morning; argue a major securities fraud appeal before the Court of Appeals in Albany, then dash to a top-secret merger negotiation on Maiden Lane that evening – and be fully prepared for both, facts, figures, and legal precedents at her polished fingertips; visit a hapless junior arbitrageur at the Metropolitan Correctional Centre, then go to an elaborate sushi lunch with Japanese bankers and know just the right things to say to both.

But this was too much.

Avery stared at the file for a few more minutes, considering her options with the same cool detachment she brought to her client's affairs. Could she afford to say no? And if she could, how should she do it?

At last, sighing, she ran a hand through her shoulder-length blonde hair, pushing it back from her forehead in a gesture her colleagues would have identified at once as signifying Decision Mode. She pushed herself back from the polished desk and hefted the file. Heavy. Too heavy.

She marshalled her arguments as she strode down the hall toward her mentor's office. Harrison Jeffers III had always supported her at the firm, had always recommended her for the tough assignments other partners doubted she was ready for; he had run interference for her on those few occasions where her suggestions fell on deaf ears. Surely he would see how absurd it was to waste her valuable time and talent on a case more suited to a Chambers Street criminal lawyer.

It took all of thirty seconds for Avery to see that her optimism was unfounded. The deep wrinkle between Hal's eyebrows became a canyon as he listened to her carefully worded reluctance to handle the case.

'Avery,' he began, in the near-condescending tone he'd used when she first arrived at the firm, a bright-eyed, eager law graduate. 'I wouldn't have assigned you the case without good reason.'

His ice-blue eyes looked into hers. She was supposed to lower her lashes, defer to his masculine authority, agree that of course he was right and she'd been a fool to question his wisdom.

But that was not how she'd earned the respect of one of the sharpest minds on Wall Street.

She kept her eyes locked with his. 'I am probably the best securities fraud litigator in this country,' she said. 'I know more about the Securities and Exchange Commission's rules than people who've spent twenty years at the SEC. I know Blue Sky Law better than the people who deal in speculative stocks. I have the complexities of civil RICO at my fingertips.' She paused to let her words and her air of confidence sink in. Then she went for the jugular of her argument.

'So what am I doing representing a berserk teenager who killed his family with a shotgun? In Wyoming, no less?' She softened the challenge with a smile and a shake of her head. She could afford a touch of femininity so long as she didn't let it detract from her edge.

'You're fulfilling this firm's commitment to *pro bono* litigation.' Hal leaned back in his custom leather swivel chair, puffed on his pipe, and waited for her comeback. He was, as usual, enjoying the verbal tennis match.

So was she. Leaning back in the client chair, which was three inches closer to the ground than Hal's, she copied his pose of leisured ease. They had all the time in the world, and she was his equal. Those were the messages her body language sent across his uncluttered ebony desk.

She crossed expensively stocking legs. 'I know what *pro bono* means. It's the legal equivalent of Mobil Oil sponsoring a public television program on the environment. It's the WASP version of Yom Kippur: one day's atonement for a year of sins. I understand all that. What I don't understand is why this case isn't being handled by a two-year associate hungry for litigation instead of one with a desk already piled with matters that should have been conferenced yesterday.'

'For one thing, you've already been to the Supreme Court,' Hal said. He took the predictable three puffs on his pipe before continuing. 'I want someone who can go before the Court and *argue*, not sweat bullets because he's finally made the big time. Someone who won't be awed by just being there. Someone who –'

Avery raised a weary hand. 'All right,' she conceded. 'Understood. You want experience. So why not let me supervise one of the younger associates from here, then fly down to D.C. on the day of argument? That way, you'll get the benefit of my experience and I'll still have time for my important cases.'

Hal raised an eloquent eyebrow. 'A young man is about to be electrocuted by the state of Wyoming, and that's not an "important" case?'

'You know what I mean,' she retorted. 'Important to the firm.'

'Important to your career,' he countered, but his tolerant smile took the sting out of the words.

'That's always been the same thing,' Avery argued. She abandoned her pose of leisured ease and leaned forward in her chair. 'What's good for the firm is good for my career, and vice versa. That's the way it should be. And that's why this is different: it doesn't matter to the firm, and it could even damage my career by taking me away from cases I should be prioritizing.'

She didn't bother to add what they both knew, that it could damage her career if she didn't win in court. And the odds of winning a death penalty case in the present political climate were very low indeed.

Hal sighed. He laid his now-cold pipe on the marble ashtray that flanked his left arm. 'I had hoped never to hear you use language like that, Avery,' he said, more in sorrow than anger. 'There is no such word as "prioritize".'

Avery grinned. This was the Hal she'd always loved to do battle with – the nitpicker, the elitist, the world-weary cynic. Surely descending into a discussion of syntax meant she'd won her point. Her shoulder muscles relaxed in anticipation of victory; she considered asking her mentor if he wanted to share a late lunch at Fraunces Tavern.

'The thing is, my dear,' Hal said, his tone one of patient finality, 'I made a promise to a friend. A very old friend. I said I would send my best lawyer on this case. And that, I'm afraid – or rather, I am not afraid, I am in fact pardonably proud to say – is you.'

Cody, Wyoming, June 1987

Mr Farkas was a practical man. He kept saying so, over and over, in a louder and louder voice, as if no one else in the jury room could come close to him in the matter of practicality.

Mr Dundee didn't care how practical Mr Farkas was. He was tired of being bullied, and his weariness showed in the droop of his eyelids and the cutting edge of his tongue. 'Give it a rest, Farkas. We all know where you stand. Give someone else a chance to talk, will you?'

Farkas grunted. 'If they say something worth listening to,' he grumbled.

' "Something worth listening to," ' the little teacher with the pageboy hairdo echoed, 'I suppose that means something you agree with.'

'I'm tired of hearing a bunch of crap about how that kid isn't responsible for what he did,' Farkas retorted.

The teacher's favourite technique was to repeat what others said and put little quotation marks around it, give it an ironic twist that mocked and speaker. ' "A bunch of crap," ' she repeated, her tone speculative, 'I don't think I've ever heard that particular phrase before. I'm not at all certain you can actually have a bunch of –'

'I wouldn't mind going home sometime in the next decade,' the tall thin man with the goatee interjected.

Mrs Barstow couldn't remember all their names. Twelve jurors meant eleven names she had to hold in her mind all at once. Mr Farkas she had no trouble remembering; he was a florid man with a big mouth who reminded her of that actor who always seemed to play generals in 1950s' movies. She couldn't remember the actor's name anymore, but Mr Farkas looked and sounded just like him, all bluster and noise.

Mr Dundee was black. Well, not black exactly, more like coffee with cream. He worked for the post office and Mrs Barstow could just see him doing it, could picture him standing behind the counter making little jokes while he waited on people. He was the kind who'd show up during the Christmas rush with a fuzzy Santa Claus hat. The kind who when you asked for a special stamp, he'd open the drawer and look for it, not just snap that they were out of those and couldn't she see there were people waiting behind her.

No wonder Mr Dundee thought Tyler Baines was innocent. He was the kind of man who thought the best of people.

The others she tended to think of by looks or occupation. There was the schoolteacher and the man with the goatee and the pregnant girl and the two young men with Mexican names; she could never remember which was Hernandez and which was Lopez. One worked in a garage, but she couldn't remember for the life of her what the other one did. There was the bottle blonde – although Mrs Barstow had to admit they made hair dye a lot more natural now than they had in her day; you couldn't really tell except that this girl didn't have the complexion that went with real blonde hair.

The last three jurors were closer to her own age. One was a widow; the other two, in that strange coincidence that happened on juries, had both worked for Montgomery Ward. They lunched together everyday, exchanging stories about people they had known in common. Mrs Barstow thought one looked familiar from her own shopping days, but she hadn't said anything. The other one looked like somebody she wouldn't have wanted to return something to.

The widow was speaking her mind. '. . . have to remember what that doctor said about Tyler's ability to control his impulses. The boy is just not like other people. We can't forget that.'

Farkas snorted and was about to put his two cents in when one of the Mexicans jumped in. 'Man, I don't know about them doctors,' he said with a shake of his head. 'I don't want to sound like I'm ignorant or nothing, but I can't accept that some kid blows his father and sisters away with a shotgun and we gotta let him go on account of what some doctor says.'

'But if he didn't know what he was doing,' the nice Montgomery Ward lady said, 'Then he shouldn't be found guilty.'

There were too many people talking. Too many egos vying for attention. Mrs Barstow leaned back on the hard chair and closed her eyes, trying to recapture her sense of herself. She tended to lose herself when there were too many voices in the room.

The sour-faced Montgomery Ward's clerk nudged her. 'You have to try to stay awake, dear,' she said in a tone that put Mrs Barstow's teeth on edge. 'I know it isn't easy at your age, but you owe it to the rest of us to make an effort.'

Mrs Barstow, at seventy-five, was the oldest member of the

jury. She sensed the defense attorney hadn't wanted her, but she was the second alternate and he was probably out of preemptory challenges. She remembered preemptory challenges from Court TV; she was proud of all the things she'd learned from that program. She'd always thought she'd like to be a court buff when she got old, and now she could do it without leaving her couch. She liked watching trials, liked hearing from the lawyers about why they were doing what they were doing. Some lawyers were slick and smart and she felt they weren't to be trusted, although she would certainly want them in her corner if she were ever in trouble. Others were just like regular people, only they talked faster. They were never at a loss for words, lawyers; that was what she admired most about them. They never stood in front of store clerks, groping for the name of the thing they wanted, the thing they knew perfectly well what it was, could draw a picture of, except that they couldn't remember what you called it.

She opened her eyes. She would have liked to tell Miss Monkey Ward to keep her comments to herself, that she hadn't been asleep and wasn't going to fall asleep and didn't need any officious reminders from prune-faced old bats like her. But although she remembered the word 'officious' when she was thinking to herself, there was always the danger that what she wanted to say wouldn't be what she actually said when the time came.

Washington, D.C., December 1994

'If you can give me one good reason – one, count them, *one* – why we need some Wall Street yuppette on this case, I'll –' Max Jarvis sawed the air like an old-time actor as he paced the tiny office on Wisconsin Avenue. The walls were lined with towers of cartons whose weight lay heavy on the bottom box, which bent under its load. The desks were littered with legal papers, cardboard coffee cups with logos of Greek diners on the side, computer printouts listing cases spewed out by the legal research program in the corner. On the wall behind Max's desk a hand-lettered sign read 'Cruel and Unusual, Attorneys at Law.'

' – cool down, Maxwell,' the lazy Southern voice drawled. 'I got a favour comin' from a friend up North, and this is what he's givin' me for Christmas. A nice shiny WASP who can argue our case without the old farts on the bench goin' "Here come those crazy death penalty fanatics" the minute she opens her mouth. Someone who can help us lift Tyler Baines from the mire of all the other boys scheduled to die this year. Someone who can get us a little ink and won't look half bad on Court TV. A new face, Max, that's what she is. And a new face is what we need on this one.'

Max Jarvis fixed his partner and friend with the look that had earned respect on the streets of Bensonhurst and said, 'And what's wrong with our faces? You make a good appearance on the tube, Ren. Those wide blue eyes, that John-Boy Walton accent. The six o'clock news bunnies eat it up like shoo-fly pie.'

Renshaw Craley leaned forward, his large bony hands clasped in an attitude of prayer. 'We agreed once upon a time, old buddy, that we would do whatever it took to save our clients from the chair. *Whatever* it took. And if it takes us using a Wall Street designer suit with real pearls and a head of hair that cost more than our monthly salaries combined, then so be it. So be it, for Tyler's sake.' Ren's horsey face was dead serious, his blue eyes bored into Max's as he repeated, 'for Tyler's sake, Max.'

Max took in a lungful of dusty air and whooshed it out. 'Okay, I get the point, Ren. Tyler Baines is gonna fry if we don't pull a rabbit out of our hats. And you think our hats are empty and we need a new face. Well, I think we've won our share of cases – big cases, newspaper cases, not just penny-ante shit – and I know we've got more knowledge and experience with the death penalty than anyone else in this country, so –'

'A slight exaggeration, Maximilian,' Ren interrupted. 'The ACLU has a few good lawyers working on Death Row, the NAACP Inc. Fund are no slouches, and even Amnesty International –'

'All right.' Max lifted an exasperated hand. 'Jeez. Let me finish my point, okay? Which is that no Wall Street hotshot, male or female, white, black or green, can come in here and do anything like the job on this case that we can do. So what the fuck do we need her for? And don't give me that we suddenly need a pretty face instead of good lawyering.'

Ren Craley spun around in his swivel chair, pointed to a picture on the wall. It was an ordinary family picnic – at first glance. When you looked closer you saw that two of the boys were Asian, one girl had tiny crutches under her arms, and the beaming blond parents couldn't possibly have given birth to all the children of various colours and ages that surrounded them at the picnic table.

'The Baineses were mighty special people,' he said, his Southern accent deepening as he spoke. 'Folks thought highly of them, even the ones who didn't think it was right for them to adopt outside their own kind. Face it, partner, Lonnie and Dora Baines were nigh unto saints in West Hamburg, Wyoming. And Tyler blew them away. Just picked up his foster daddy's shotgun and sprayed shot all over that little house with the picket fence. Got two of his sisters as well, one nine and one twelve. And the mother maimed for life. Add to that the fact that people out West don't hold much with the insanity defense, and you've got Tyler practically sitting in the electric chair even as we speak. He's dead, Maxeleh, dead meat. Unless we can pull that rabbit from our hats. And yes, I'm counting on a fresh face, a female face. To get people thinking that a nice-looking young woman wouldn't take a case like Tyler's if she didn't think the boy was seriously screwed up.'

'Like using a woman on a rape case,' Max said. He'd slowed his pacing and said the words as though thinking out loud. 'Yeah, it could work. It's sexist bullshit of the worst kind, but it could work.'

'So you're with me, finally? You'll help show our new associate the ropes?' When Max didn't answer at once, Ren repeated his earlier plea. 'For Tyler.'

Max nodded. 'For Tyler.'

Cody, Wyoming, June 1987

The man with the goatee was the foreman. Mrs Barstow knew Mr Farkas thought he should be the foreman, and was bitterly disappointed when the others chose the bearded man instead. She herself had voted for Mr Dundee, who after all was trusted to run an entire post office.

'Perhaps we should take another vote,' the goateed man said, trying vainly to infuse a little enthusiasm into his voice.

'What for?' Farkas demanded. 'It will just come out the same way it did last time and the time before that and the time before that. Six for conviction, six for acquittal.'

'They were such a wonderful family,' the pregnant girl whispered. 'I saw them on television once. A real inspiration, that's what they were.'

This was true, but it didn't stop Mr Farkas from giving the girl a hard glare. 'That kind of talk isn't helping one bit,' he blustered. 'Who cares what kind of family they were? Lonnie Baines and those two little girls are dead and that no-account Indian kid of his did it, and that's all she wrote.'

Both Mexicans and Mr Dundee opened their mouths to protest and Mrs Barstow couldn't blame them one bit. Whatever Tyler Baines had or hadn't done, it had nothing to do with his being an Indian.

Or did it? The schoolteacher began to talk about Foetal Alcohol Syndrome and how it was more prevalent among children of Native American ancestry. Mr Farkas's red face wasn't the only one to scowl at her terminology; here in Wyoming, most people still said Indian, even if they said it with a hint of defiance, as if daring those Eastern liberals to make something out of it.

'I don't give a good goddamn how much rotgut whiskey that little brat's momma drank when he was in the womb,' Mr Farkas exploded at last. 'He killed Lonnie Baines and those children in cold blood, for God's sake.'

'I don't see how this discussion is furthered,' the widow said in a shaking voice, 'by taking the name of the Lord in vain.'

'Oh, Christ,' Mr Farkas muttered, wiping his brow with a limp handkerchief. 'Haven't we got more important things to talk about?'

Mrs Barstow could see that the widow had every intention of telling Mr Farkas that in her view there was precious little that was more important than respecting the Lord.

Mommy was afraid Tyler would get the gun, like he did before.
That was what Melissa, the ten-year-old, had said. Melissa was
born without a foot, but you'd never know it to watch her walk.
They could do such wonderful things these days, Mrs Barstow
thought, but then she thought about Tyler and how nobody
could do any thing for him, and she decided maybe things hadn't
changed all that much.

What could it have been like, Mrs Barstow wondered, to be a
little ten-year-old with only one foot and a brother who might
find the shotgun and blow the whole family to bits?

Why did a family with a son that hard to handle keep a gun
anyway?

The answer to that one was easy; it came to Mrs Barstow
unbidden. *This is Wyoming; we need our guns.* That was what her
late husband had said every time she begged him to get rid of the
gun that stood for thirty years behind the kitchen door, in the
little hallway they called the mudroom. He needed a gun, he said,
in case a coyote came prowling around the garden, or in case a
cougar attacked their dog, or in case – well, just in case.

In case mad killers came out of the mountains and tied them
both up and slit their throats with her carving knife. Like that
farm family in Indiana that funny little writer wrote the book
about.

Thinking about the funny little writer brought back images of
Junior: blond and elfin, not at all like her or her husband. Some
people joked that Junior had been left by elves, with his wispy
golden hair and pointed ears and heart-shaped face.

Tyler found my money and stole it, the Vietnamese boy named
Peter had said. *I hid it, but he always found it.*

Mrs Barstow could sympathize with that. Hadn't her big
cousin Annie always found things she hid? Annie came to the
ranch in summer; she was two years older and shared Mrs
Barstow's room. She seemed to think that gave her the right
to take anything she fancied, so Mrs Barstow took her most
precious things and hid them in places she didn't think Annie
would look, but Annie always did. She always did, and she always
found them, and she always broke or ruined them.

Ma said it was okay because Annie was their guest and you had to be nice to guests, but Mrs Barstow never thought it was right, and when she became a mother she knew she would never let anyone steal from Junior no matter what. Guest or no guest, her child would come first.

Did Dora Baines feel the same way? She and Lonnie had two children of their own, two blood-children in addition to the adopted family. Did they make a distinction between their own children and the little guests?

She couldn't blame them if they had, especially when it came to Tyler. It was one thing if your own blood-child turned out bad, but when you had a bad one and he wasn't really yours, you couldn't be blamed for wishing he'd never come into your life.

A fragment of testimony came back to her. Just a little wisp of a phrase; for a moment, she couldn't even remember who'd said it. '. . . considering bringing a suit to compel the agency to resume custody due to a failure to disclose a material fact.'

Long words. Legal words. Thank goodness for Court TV; Mrs Barstow knew that *compel* meant to make somebody do something, and that *failure to disclose* meant that someone had kept something a secret. *A material fact* meant that it was a big secret, an important omission – like the agency not telling the Baineses their adopted boy might have been born with Foetal Alcohol Syndrome.

Had the Baineses been trying to send Tyler back to the orphanage?

It didn't sound as if the orphanage wanted him back.

Washington, D.C., February 1995

'The first trial ended in a hung jury in 1987, Your Honour,' Avery explained. 'One of the jurors was taken ill during deliberations and the alternates had already been discharged. On retrial in 1988, the State of Wyoming managed to convince twelve jurors that Tyler Baines was legally sane within the meaning of Wyoming law despite a documented history of Foetal Alcohol Syndrome.'

Ren Craley leaned over the makeshift judge's bench and

stepped out of character. 'I'd watch that hint of sarcasm if I were you, Avery,' he said. 'You know, that part about the state "managing to convince twelve jurors." That kind of stuff's been known to piss off the Supremes.'

Max Jarvis nodded; he looked about to add something, but Avery glared at him and he shut up. It was bad enough to be lectured by a backwoods lawyer who'd probably read cases by kerosene lamp, but she didn't have to take back-seat lawyering by two guys instead of one.

Still, it made a lot of sense to moot-court the argument as often as possible before the big day. Ren and Max sat at a long table, shooting questions at her while she tried to stick to the argument she'd prepared while at the same time answering their concerns. It was the only way to prepare for appellate argument; pretend you were before the court and field as many questions as your colleagues could come up with.

'Here's a Sandra Day O'Connor question,' Max said with a wicked grin. 'Counsellor, how do you respond to the State's argument that your client received all the due process of law he's entitled to because the jury was permitted to consider the Foetal Alcohol Syndrome in the second trial?'

'Your Honour is correct that the jurors were told they could take into account the medical history of Tyler Baines,' Avery replied, trying for the same deferential tone she intended to use on the real Supreme Court, 'but the defense contends that the judge's charge effectively undermined the impact of the medical testimony by not directing the jurors to consider Foetal Alcohol Syndrome a form of insanity under Wyoming law.'

'Oh, so this case isn't about the Foetal Alcohol Syndrome as such,' Ren Craley drawled. 'Instead it's about the precise wording of the judge's charge. Is that your contention, Counsellor?'

Avery shot the tall Southerner a sour glance. 'Is that supposed to be Rehnquist or Scalia?' she asked.

'Take your pick,' Ren replied. 'They're both going to stick it to you.'

Cody, Wyoming, June 1987

We couldn't have a normal life, Dora Baines had sobbed. She wiped away her tears with a hand that had only three fingers; her adopted boy had blown the others away with the shotgun. *Tyler was getting too big for me to discipline. He got mad at Sarah and broke her arm; she's only five years old.*

Five years old and blind, Mrs Barstow recalled. A Romanian orphan who'd been left to die in a miserable institution.

'They wanted him dead,' Mrs Barstow said softly to herself. 'They needed him dead. It was the only hope they had for a normal life.'

Her eyes filled with tears. *A normal life*; that was what she and her husband had had after Junior died. A normal life, a life that wasn't spent caring for a child who demanded every minute of your time and gave nothing in return because he had nothing to give. A child they labelled autistic, a child who would never hold a job or get married or even laugh at a joke.

The gun was hidden where Tyler wouldn't find it.

But Tyler found everything; there was no hiding place he couldn't ferret out.

The gun wasn't loaded. At least Peter, the Vietnamese boy, had sworn it wasn't supposed to be loaded.

What good an unloaded shotgun would be against marauders from the mountains Mrs Barstow couldn't say, but Peter had insisted the shells were kept in another, quite separate, hiding place.

A hiding place little Melissa had testified Tyler knew about, because he'd found the money she'd been saving for a new Barbie. He'd stolen it only a week before the night of the gun.

The gun was supposed to be unloaded; the shells were supposed to be hidden.

But when Tyler Baines ran for the gun, grabbed it and pointed it at his adoptive family, it had been loaded and deadly.

Why? Mrs Barstow let the question nag at her while the others argued diminished capacity. Why had the gun been left where the family must have known Tyler could find it? Why had the shells been hidden in a place he'd only recently raided?

Why had a jar of sparkling water been left on the picnic table where Junior could pick it up and drink from it?

She thrust her fist into her mouth to stop the involuntary cry. The sour-faced Montgomery Ward's clerk gave her a suspicious look.

Mrs Barstow leaned back against the hard chair and murmured something about feeling faint. Mr Dundee stood up and walked over to the water cooler, where he filled a little paper cup and brought it back to her. She took it gratefully and sipped; the water felt good going down even if it did have a hard time getting past the lump in her throat.

They had set him up. The family had set Tyler Baines up.

That was not a phrase she'd learned on Court TV, but it was a good one anyway.

Mr and Mrs Baines had wanted Tyler to go for the gun. They had come to the end of their rope. Everyone knew Tyler's temper; everyone had said it was only a matter of time before he killed someone out there on the ranch.

No one would have blamed Mr Baines if he'd been forced to kill his son, if he'd defended himself and his family from the boy he couldn't control.

Tyler's gun wasn't supposed to be loaded. He would brandish a weapon and scream at his parents; his father would shoot him in self-defense, then sob as the gun in the boy's hand proved to be empty. It would all be a horrible mistake.

Washington, D.C., April 1995

'She did a good job, Max,' Ren Craley said. 'You can't blame her for what the Supremes did.'

'Yeah, I suppose,' Max agreed. At least, his words agreed. His face said something else. 'She didn't have her heart in it, though. If one of us had argued Tyler's case, we'd have shown some passion, for God's sake.'

'Do you really think that would have impressed anybody, Maxie?' Ren countered. His blue eyes were sad. 'Hell, boy, we feel passion for all the poor fuckers about to die in the chair or the chamber or whatever, and what the hell good does our passion do any of them?'

'Nine-zip,' Max said, tossing the *Washington Post* onto the battered desktop. 'Not one dissent. Not even Ginsburg, and you know she hates the death penalty. Nine-fucking-zero and our little yuppette is back on Wall Street making the world safe for hostile takeovers and it doesn't matter to her one bit that an Indian kid with the I.Q. of a turnip is about to –'

Ren held up a large, bony hand. 'Peace, Maxeleh. What's done is done. I have here in my hand a case about a girl in Tennessee who met up with the wrong guy and the two of them knocked off a Seven-Eleven. Boyfriend held the gun, but she drove the gateway car and now she's looking at the chair. He's already been fried; you think we got a chance of getting her life without parole instead?'

Max Jarvis' answer held a world of cynicism. 'We might if you don't get any of your fancy Wall Street friends to help us out.'

Cody, Wyoming, June 1987

It was a terrible mistake, Mrs Barstow had told the deputy when he came to the house the day Junior died. She'd told nothing more nor less than the truth, but he'd misunderstood her and kept on misunderstanding her no matter how hard she tried to tell them: it was a terrible mistake.

Of course it was, dear; now don't you worry about a thing. Junior's in a better place now, dear; it was all for the best.

She had grown to hate being called 'dear' – it was what people called you when what they really meant was *shut up*.

They thought she meant it was a terrible mistake that Junior drank the Drano thinking it was soda water. This was before they made it blue so children could see it wasn't water; the liquid in the jar had been clear and bubbly and it ate Junior's entire gullet right out and he died a horrible writhing death.

But that wasn't the mistake she was talking about. She meant it was a mistake for her late husband to think that getting rid of Junior would return their lives to normal.

The Baineses had made the same mistake. Life without Tyler was supposed to be normal, but here they were coming into court at Tyler's trial, every one of them lying about the truth, every one of them mourning a husband and father and two little girls who wouldn't have died if they hadn't been so set on becoming normal again.

You couldn't go back to normal once your life was changed by someone like Junior or Tyler; she knew that now.

New York City, April 1995

Avery Nyquist folded her expensively manicured hands on the cool surface of the ebony desk. She gazed with expectant calm into Harrison Jeffers III's appraising eyes. She pretended indifference to what her mentor at Ambrose, Jeffers was about to say, but inwardly she swelled with pardonable pride.

'I'm pleased to be able to offer you a partnership in this firm,' Hal said in his rich voice. 'The partners met last night and I want you to know the vote in your favour was unanimous. No dissenting votes. Everyone here knows what you've accomplished here in the last seven years, and we're eager to welcome you to partnership rank.'

Partnership. The Holy Grail of Ivy League law graduates turned Wall Street associates. Seven years of working one-hundred-hour weeks, of playing tennis at one a.m. with someone who worked the same gruesome hours at Simpson, Thatcher, of dashing to JFK to meet a client between flights from London to Hong Kong, of choosing clothes, jewelry, hairstyle with one end in view: does it look like it belongs on an Ambrose, Jeffers partner? And now the Holy Grail was hers.

She smiled at the man across the desk from her, the man who had helped make it possible. Helped, not waved a magic wand for her. She'd earned it, but earning wasn't everything in the cutthroat world she worked in. There were, she knew, equally hardworking lawyers at the firm who were in the offices of other partners being told they weren't quite partner material.

As she opened her mouth to thank Hal, her eye caught the

headline in the morning's *Law Journal:* HIGH COURT RE-
FUSES TO OVERTURN DEATH PENALTY IN CASE OF
WYOMING YOUTH, it read. The subhead went on: Unanimous Court Leaves Issue of Foetal Alcohol Syndrome Defense
to Lower Courts; Baines to Die Tomorrow.

Tomorrow? Wasn't there one more stay, one more appeal?
She'd have to call Ren, find out what he and Max intended to do
now. The Supreme Court had affirmed, but surely another
habeas to the District Court, or perhaps a motion for rehearsing
before the Wyoming Supreme Court . . .

'Avery, are you listening to me?' Hal's tone held an edge
underneath its bantering surface; he wasn't used to being tuned
out by those lower in the pecking order.

'Sorry,' she murmured. 'I just didn't know I'd lost that case.'
She gestured at the neatly folded *Law Journal* on his desk.

'Which case?' Hal asked, then followed her eyes to the newspaper. 'Oh, that,' he said, shaking his head. 'I should have
mentioned it. You can go ahead and say "I told you so," ' he
invited. 'You said it was a dead loser. Maybe I should have
listened to you and sent somebody else to Washington.'

When she got home, Avery promised herself, she'd call Ren
Craley to commiserate with him about the decision, to bitch
about the fact that is wasn't even a real opinion, just a quickie
affirmation which would give the State of Wyoming a green light
to go ahead and snuff out Tyler Baines' young, meaningless life.

She had a sudden, vivid recollection of the gleam in Ren's deep
blue eyes as he talked law, force-feeding her with every nuance of
the Supreme Court's vagaries on the subject of the death penalty.

He cared.

That was the difference between Ren Craley and the man
across the ebony desk, the man who'd taught her everything she
knew about surviving on Wall Street. That was the difference
between Ren Craley and all the men she'd ever dated, ever done
business with.

Ren cared.

That was the difference between Ren and her, she realized with
a suddenness that wiped away the triumph of making partner. He
cared.

She didn't. Not really. Not about this man who'd treated her like a precocious child whose achievements reflected well on him, not about the SEC hearing she'd attended earlier that afternoon or about the IRS consultation she was going to have in the morning. She didn't give a good goddamn about any of them.

She didn't even care about making partner. Once upon a time, it had meant everything to her, but now that it was here, all she could think about was that big, stupid boy being strapped into the electric chair. Could he understand what was happening to him and why? He had picked up a gun in rage; could he know that stone-sober people doing their jobs were going to take his life because there was a piece of paper that said they should?

'Avery?' Hal's voice came to her from far away, sounding concerned. 'Are you feeling all right?'

She shook her head. No, she wasn't all right. She didn't know why, exactly, but she was far from all right. She got up from the deep leather chair and made her way, with increasingly swift steps, to the ladies' room. She headed into the nearest cubicle, sat down on the commode, and burst into noisy tears.

Cody, Wyoming, June 1987

Mrs Barstow tuned in to the heated argument still going on in the smoke-filled room. Only two jurors smoked, and they'd voted to separate for smoke breaks, but this was Wyoming, and you didn't tell men they couldn't light up when and where they wanted to out here in the West. Oh, maybe in California, but that wasn't the real West.

Mrs Barstow didn't mind the smoke; her late husband had puffed himself to death and the smell was a familiar reminder of the days when she'd shared a life with another person. Funny how the smell of something that caused death made her feel alive.

She had to tell them. She had to make them see.

'It all went so wrong,' she said, shaking her head. 'So terribly wrong.'

'It went wrong from the day those do-gooders took that kid into their house,' Mr Farkas said.

'No,' Mrs Barstow replied. 'That's not what I mean. The gun was in the wrong place.'

'Yes, dear,' the nice Montgomery Ward clerk said in her saccharine tone. 'If they'd hidden the gun better, Lonnie Baines and the two little girls would be alive today. But that doesn't help us decide about the insanity plea, now, does it, dear?'

Why couldn't they understand, she wondered, as she stared at first one face and then another. They all looked at her with varying degrees of concern on their faces, concern that said they had no comprehension of her words. They knew she was upset about something, and that upset them, but they had no clue what she was talking about.

'It was just like Junior,' she said, certain that would explain everything. As the words left, she reached a trembling hand to her mouth as if to recall them; she had never before spoken of Junior to strangers.

She wasn't sure she could do it now. But then she thought about that boy, that hulking dark-eyed boy with his straight Indian hair and expressionless face and dim brain, the boy who was going to be sent back if anyone would take him, only nobody would. The boy who had reached for a gun his parents had made certain would be where he could find it. She had to go on, for his sake.

She tried. She said the words over several times, in several different ways, trying to make the others understand about the gun and about the Baines' terrible need to rid themselves of the boy they'd tried unsuccessfully to tame.

The words wouldn't come the way she'd planned. She got mixed up, too, calling Tyler Baines 'Junior' and trying to explain about the bubbling water that had eaten him up from the inside and how wrong her late husband had been – as wrong as Lonnie Baines.

She began to cry. It had been so long since she'd even thought about Junior, so much longer since she'd said his name, the name that brought back the reality of him.

'This is too much,' the little schoolteacher had said. 'This is really too much for the poor old thing.'

'Yes,' Mr Dundee agreed. '"We've got to tell the judge we're deadlocked. It's cruel and unusual punishment to keep us here when we're never going to come to a verdict.'

'No,' Mrs Barstow wailed, 'let me finish. You have to let me explain.' Her breath was coming in little pants; she felt weak and strange. Why couldn't they shut up and listen? Why wasn't there enough air in this little room? Why did juries need twelve people, twelve months, twenty-four eyes, too many voices and legs and arms?

Too many.

Dizziness swept over her; the words she needed to say about Tyler Baines crawled into a corner of her brain and fell asleep. She let her head fall to one side and was horrified to realize that spittle dripped down her cheek.

What was happening to her?

'My God, she's having a stroke,' the little school teacher cried. 'Somebody call the guard. We have to get her to a doctor.'

Mr Farkas ran from the room. The others bustled and exclaimed and reached for her as though their touch could restore her. The nice Montgomery Ward's clerk took out a handkerchief and wiped her chin as gently as you would a baby's.

She opened her mouth to tell them, to make them see what she'd seen, but all that came out were gabbled sounds that reminded her, horribly, of Junior.

'Don't worry, dear,' the nice Montgomery Ward's clerk said, patting her hand. 'It's almost over. We'll get you out of here, dear, don't you worry.'

'Cruel and unusual punishment,' Mr Dundee repeated. Shaking his head.

Washington, D.C., June 1995

'If it please the Court,' counsel for the petitioner began, 'the execution of Rosalee Jenkins Pruitt is contrary to the Sixth Amendment to the Constitution of the United States of America because –'

'Too wordy,' Max Jarvis cut in, stabbing the air with a stubby finger. 'We need to stay polite but cut that down to the bare minimum.'

Avery Nyquist ran her fingers through her hair and turned exasperated eyes on her new partners. 'Is he always this nitpicky?' she asked Ren Craley.

The tall, bony lawyer smiled, showing huge horse teeth. 'Yeah, he's a real pain in the behind, but you'll get used to him, Ave.'

I'll get used to him, Avery thought. And I'll get used to working twenty hours a day trying to keep people alive, and I'll get used to shopping at Penney's instead of Sak's, and using a drugstore rinse on my hair instead of consulting a master colourist, and I'll get used to working in an office the size of a telephone booth instead of one with a view of New York Harbour. And I'll get used to a steady diet of Supreme Court arguments and last-minute stays and visits to Death Rows all across the country.

I'll get used to caring.

But will I ever get used to the idea that a piece of paper, stamped in triplicate, can take a man's life as surely as a loaded shotgun?

No, she wouldn't.

She hoped she never would.

ABUSE OF PROCESS

Howard T. Rose

It looked like such a nice day out. The evidence was the view from my office window. I thought I should be at the beach, or maybe on a boat, rather than work. But it was Wednesday, one-thirty, just after lunch, I'd had a corn beef sandwich and a pint of beer. The woman sitting in my office, a prospective client, didn't look like she was having a good day. She was in her late twenties, dirty blonde hair pulled back, dark circles under her eyes. She was wearing white slacks and a black blouse. Her perfume was nice. I know I'd smelled the brand before, I just couldn't remember where and when.

'My ex-boyfriend is suing me,' she said, 'and I don't know what to do.'

Her name was Tara Flowers. She'd called the firm I worked for, was transferred to me. I told her I'd give her a free half-hour consultation.

'When were you served with the summons and complaint?' I asked.

'Two weeks ago. I have thirty days, right? That's what the piece of paper said. If I don't answer in thirty days, it says: "You could lose the case, and your property and wages may be taken from you without further notice from the court." ' She was reading the printed matter on a summons she held in her hands.

I said, 'Don't worry about that. Let me see the paperwork.'

She handed over the legal documents. Everything seemed to be in order, plus there was a Notice of Case Assignment. Judge Holloway. I shook my head. He'd been on the bench before I was born.

The cause of action was abuse of process. The litigant was one Ethan Porter, represented by August Yannick, Attorney at Law.

'Ethan Porter is your ex-boyfriend?'

'Yes,' Tara Flowers said.

'How long were you together?'

'Three years.'

'Live together?'

'Two years.'

I read through the three-page complaint, alleging that Tara Flowers had abused the process of the legal system by filing for and receiving a restraining order. Porter claimed that he was never properly served with the temporary order and the Order to Show Cause, that he didn't know about the hearing, and that Tara Flowers erroneously received injunctive relief against him. He also claimed she lied about everything in her application for a restraining order, which alleged physical abuse and threats of more abuse on his part.

'Did you lie?'

'How can you ask that?' she said.

'Because I need to know.'

'*No*,' she said.

'What about serving him with the papers?'

'I don't know what that's all about. I paid this process server thirty bucks to serve him.'

'Did he?'

'I suppose so. He sent me a proof of service in the mail.'

'Which you gave to the court at the hearing, and the judge, or commissoner, accepted it?'

'Yes,' she said.

I nodded. Lawsuits of abuse of process are generally brought against attorneys or administrative agencies, but they can be filed, in legal theory, on citizens. A case for abuse of process needs to meet three criteria: clear facts that a legal process was misused, that it was done willfully, and that there was an ulterior motive (such as malice). Porter's complaint was alleging all three.

I explained this to Tara Flowers.

'I did what I thought was right,' she said. 'He was harassing me, calling me, sending me letters. I called the police, they said he hadn't outright made any threats and there was no evidence of any threats, and they couldn't do anything, but if I got a restraining order they could. I debated a long time, but I couldn't take it anymore, so I finally went and got it. I paid a man to serve Ethan, a process server. Ethan didn't show up to court. The next thing I know, I get this lawsuit.'

'Who served you?'

'The Marshal.'

'Porter is alleging that your motives for getting a restraining order were malicious and done to hurt him.'

'That's outrageous,' she said.

'What were your motives?'

'To protect myself. For my peace of mind. He knows how . . . I am. He knows that what he was doing was driving me crazy. *This* is even driving me more crazy. He's not going to take my car and garnish my wages, is he?'

'No,' I said softly. Clients always ask that. I think the media distorts the nature of the growing litigation problem, and people become far too terrified of what they don't know.

'I also got this the other day.' She pulled an envelope from her purse. 'This is why I started looking for a lawyer.'

She handed me the envelope. The return address, and the address on the enclosed stationary, was from August Yannick, Attorney at Law. It was typed on an electric typewriter, same as the complaint. An attorney who uses a typewriter and not a computer immediately tells me what kind of attorney they are.

The letter was a settlement proposal, for $10,000.

'Ten grand,' I said, folding the letter up.

'Ethan knows I have twelve in the bank,' she said. 'My life's savings.'

'So what do you want to do?'

'What can I do?'

'There are several options,' I told her. 'First, you can settle.'

'Give that asshole ten thousand?'

'No. We could make a counter-offer.'

'Why? Why should I give him *any*thing?'

'You shouldn't. I'm outlining your options. We can try to settle this and get it over with now, or we can fight it, which will drag on over the course of this year, maybe next year as well. Either way, I'm sorry to tell you this, it's going to cost you money.'

'What if I just ignored it all? Moved out of town?'

'You don't want to do that. If the case goes into default, he'd get a judgement against you. Then he could screw up your credit rating, garnish your wages, maybe seize your bank account.'

'That jerk,' she said. 'This isn't fair.'

'No,' I said. 'It usually isn't.'

'What will it cost me to fight this? How much do you charge?'

'My retainer is eight hundred dollars. I charge one hundred seventy-five an hour, plus filing fees.'

'What will it cost in the long run to fight this?'

'Depends.'

'On what?'

'On how far it goes. He's paying a lawyer too. He could give up a few months down the road.'

'A rough guess, please.'

'Anywhere from three to seven thousand.'

'And if I offered him one thousand now, to go away, it would cost me less?'

'Sometimes that's how it works.'

'If I win, doesn't he have to pay me back?'

'The court would order him to, but it may not be easy to collect. But you'd then have a judgement on him.'

'And I could ruin *his* credit and garnish *his* wages?'

'You could try and collect on the judgment, yes.'

'The hell with him,' she said. 'I won't pay him *one dime*. I won't give him the satisfaction. I'd like to hire you to fight this.'

'You don't need to answer the complaint. We can delay this a bit – file a motion for demurrer.'

'What's that?'

'Basically, attack the legal validity of the complaint. If the motion is sustained, the suit will be null and void. But he could re-word it, or re-file, but that'll cost him money as well.'

'Let's do that,' she said, and got out her checkbook.

I had a date that night with a woman who was a police officer. We'd been on several dates so far and I was thinking there was a possibility of a relationship here. On this date, that idea died as quickly as a motion for a summary judgement. It just wasn't there. She knew, I knew it, and we parted ways with a friendly kiss and, 'Well, see you around.' I wasn't thinking too much about Tara Flowers and her case, other than a fleeting thought that her boyfriend was a fool for having let her go, she was quite attractive; also, her boyfriend was a fool for suing her. Lawsuits over relationship matters never get anyone anywhere, other than continuing the pain.

I went home, watched TV, drank some vodka (to numb my own pain and loneliness) and fell asleep while a re-run of *Matlock* was on.

I found a note to myself on a yellow stick-it on my desk: *Call August Yannick*. I called him later that afternoon. He didn't have a secretary. I wondered if he worked out of one of those little offices downtown, or maybe his home.

'He sounded like he was eating lunch, a sandwich perhaps. 'Who you say you are?'

'Lawrence Jacobs,' I said. 'I'm representing Tara Flowers.'

'Who?'

'Your client, Ethan Porter, is suing her. I'm representing her in this case.'

'Oh yeah. She screwed-up the proof of service. Clear matter of abuse of process. Does she want to settle?'

'No.'

'Then why you calling me?'

I said. 'To see if you can talk some sense into your client. This case will go nowhere. He's just prolonging the –'

'This is a strong and solid case of a vexatious woman misusing the legal process,' he said. 'And I'll get a judgment if we go to trial.'

'If,' I said. 'I plan to demur.'

He laughed. 'On what grounds?'

'Insufficient facts stated for a cause of action.'

'There are no defects on the complaint's face, Jacobs. A demurrer is just a delay tactic that I'll make clear to Judge Holloway, and get you sanctioned. Go ahead and file your motion. I'll see you in court.'

He hung up.

It was worth a try.

Five weeks later, the hearing for the demurrer commenced. I told Tara Flowers she didn't need to go, these were short hearings, but she wanted to be there. Her ex-boyfriend wasn't at the hearing, however; August Yannick sat alone. He was five foot seven and about three hundred pounds. He wore an old, cheap pale blue suit with several stains. He had a five o'clock shadow at ten-thirty a.m.

I leaned over and said to Tara, 'At least your ex isn't here.'

'I knew he wouldn't,' she said. 'He has a criminal record. He hates courts and judges, makes him nervous.'

'Funny for a guy who files a lawsuit.'

Judge Holloway came out, we stood, he sat, and we sat.

He was an old judge, like I said, with striking blue eyes and neat silver hair. 'Gentleman,' he said, looking at both of us. 'I'm overruling the motion for demurrer.'

'Your honour!' I said, standing.

'An objection, Mr Jacobs?'

'This is a nuisance suit,' I said. 'A man harassing his ex-girlfriend and –'

Yannick didn't stand when he cut me off: 'Such an allegation by opposing counsel isn't appropriate for this kind of hearing. This hearing is about the fact of the complaint and whether the facts in the complaint constitute a cause of action, and not a forum to argue any indifference or inferences as to the mind set of either parties.'

I look at him and wanted to say, 'What?'

The judge said, 'The fact that there is question of improper proof of service, and that the Defendant, Flowers, obtained legal relief that could be questionable, and couched in ulterior motive, is grounds for a cause of action for abuse of process. The demurrer is overruled.' Before I could say anything, he added, 'I won't entertain any further oral argument, counsellor.'

At least he didn't sanction me.

As the next moving parties took their places before the judge, Tara said, 'What does this mean?'

'The complaint stands,' I said.

'I don't understand.'

'At this point, we can do three things: make another motion to strike the complaint, but that may prove to be futile; appeal the judge's decision, because it was a rather hasty one; or answer the complaint and make the slow crawl toward trial.'

'All of which will cost me money,' she said.

'I'm afraid so.'

'The hell with it. I'll pay him off.'

'Tara,' I said.

'Offer him a thousand dollars.'

'Are you sure you want to do this?'

'I *don't* want to do it,' she said, 'but I don't want to be bothered by this anymore and I don't want it costing me *thousands* instead of one.'

'Very well. Wait here.' Yannick was leaving the court room. Actually, he was waddling. In the corridor, I called out to him. He stopped. He was sweating. As I got near him, I could smell him. 'My client wishes to make a settlement offer.'

'Shoot,' he said. His breath was bad, too.

'Five hundred.'

'Five hundred grand?' He whistled. 'I didn't think she was loaded.'

'Five hundred dollars.'

'You're insulting me,' he laughed. 'That won't even cover my client's expenses.'

'Yes it will,' I said. 'You probably charged him all of three hundred dollars. He gets away with two hundred profit. And he's not in this for money. I know that, you know that. He only wants to hurt her. He can rest assured with the satisfaction that he has.'

Yannick made a face, waving a hand, like I was crazy. 'A grand. Make it a grand, and maybe we can talk business.'

I kept my poker face. 'I think my client may go that high.'

'Well, I need to talk to my client first. He may not accept it.'

'He'll have to.'

'If he does, we'll transact the whole matter tomorrow, what do you say?'

'Just let me know.'

I started to turn and Yannick said. 'Hey, Jake, your client, that Tara Flowers, she's some fine looker.'

I didn't say anything to that.

'Really fine, like something out of one of my fantasies,' he said. 'You plugging her?'

'Your conduct is a bit untoward,' I said.

'Hey, I like women,' he said.

I gave him a look, and hoped he could see in my eyes what I really wanted to say.

'I'd be giving her the ol' salami if I were you,' he said, turning and waddling off. 'Mr Porter said she was a tiger in bed. Boy oh boy,' and he whistled.

Later that day, Yannick called my office and said his client accepted the settlement offer and wanted it in a cashier's check. I called Tara at home, she said she'd bring the cashier's check by on her lunch break tomorrow. I told her by five o'clock the lawsuit would end and she could go on with her life.

'Yeah, right,' she said, and hung up.

Tara Flowers never showed up with the cashier's check. I tried calling her at work, she wasn't there. Hadn't come in today, I was told. I tried calling her at home. I got her voice mail.

'Tara,' I said, 'I was just wondering where you were so we can get this taken care of.'

Yannick kept calling on the hour. I had the firm's receptionist tell him I was in an emergency meeting. He kept calling, and I couldn't put him off any longer.

'Are we going to do this or what?' he said.

'There's a problem.'

'A problem?'

'My client didn't show up with the money.'

'She change her mind?'

'I don't know. I haven't spoken to her.'

'It's four-fifteen, Jacobs.'

'I know.' It was four-twenty by my watch.

'Seems like we won't get this done today,' he said. 'Tell your client that tomorrow the settlement price is fifteen hundred.'

He hung up. People were hanging up on me a lot these days.

I tried calling Tara again. Voice mail.

On my way home, I dropped by her apartment. She didn't live that far from me, up on a hill, an area where a lot of university students called home. I went to her door. When I knocked, it creaked open. 'Tara?' I called. 'Tara Flowers?' Nothing. I went inside. A spare apartment. 'Tara?' I could smell it before I got to the bedroom: she was lying face down on the bed, wearing only her bra and part of a ripped skirt. A torn blouse was on the floor. Her eyes were still open, looking at the wall in dead terror.

The universe operates in mysterious ways – evidence of this was the officers that responded to my 911 call (in less than three minutes); they were the policewoman I'd been casually dating a few weeks back, and her partner, a beefy Hispanic guy donning a crew cut. They took one look at Tara, concluded she was dead, and called for the ME and homicide detectives.

'Did you kill her?' the beefy Hispanic cop asked me. He looked ready to throw me to the floor and do a hog-tie.

'Shut up, George,' my policewoman friend said, 'he didn't kill anyone.'

She took me outside, shaking her head. Her name was Nancy. Officer Nancy Prescott. 'Larry,' she said, 'what have you gotten yourself into?'

'She was my client,' I said, and explained to her the situation.

'You think her boyfriend did it?' Nancy said.

'Ex-boyfriend,' I said. 'She had a restraining order on him, he was suing her, I'd say he's a likely suspect.'

'Wasn't she going to pay him money?'

'Maybe he didn't like the amount. Maybe he didn't want to settle. Because that would be the end. He didn't want it to end.'

'So he comes over here and kills her.'

'Yes.'

She nodded. When the MEs and homicide dicks arrived to seal off the apartment and start collecting evidence, she told one of the plainclothes cops the story she'd gotten from me. Then the cop got the story from me again, which was the same that I told Nancy. Tara had apparently been strangled to death, that's all I was told.

'They'll pick the ex-boyfriend up tonight,' Nancy said to me, 'if he's home.'

'He'd be a fool if he was,' I said.

'*If* he did it,' she said. 'Listen, I know this has to be rough.'

'Not at all,' I said, 'happens all the time. A client of mine gets murdered once a month.'

'After you give all your statement fifty times, let's get out of here. My shift is just about up. We can get a drink.'

'That'd be nice.'

We had quite a few drinks later on, starting at a bar, then we picked up some beer and tequila at the liquor store and went to my place. I lived in a condo, on the sixteenth floor. I liked the view from my window, looking over the city. So did Nancy. We were standing on the terrace, and we were both quite drunk.

'If we're not careful,' Nancy said, 'we'll fall off.'

'Can you fly?'

'I'm not SuperCop. We'll go splat.'

I looked down and had vertigo, more from the booze than the height. 'It's a long way down.'

She was smiling, leaning against the metal guardrail, wearing tight jeans and a t-shirt, gun and badge on her hip. 'You have such a great home here.'

'It's okay.'

'*Okay*. How much did this put you back? Three hundred grand? More?'

'I don't remember.'

'You're lying. You forget that I'm a cop and I can tell when someone's lying.'

'You forget that I'm a lawyer and I can deceive people, make them think I'm telling the truth when I'm lying and vice-versa.'

'You make good bucks being a shyster,' she said.

'I do all right.'

'Better than me.'

Then we were kissing. We were kissing a lot.

'Listen, Larry,' she said, touching my chest. 'I know we haven't exactly hit it off, but I do like you.'

'That's nice,' I said. 'I like you too.'

She giggled. 'We're both pretty wasted.'

'Yeah.'

'I have tomorrow off, I can get hung over.'

'I don't.'

'Take tomorrow off,' she said. 'Or do you mean you don't get hung over?'

'I think I will,' I said. 'Take tomorrow off, and take the hangover.'

'Let's go to the bedroom,' she said.

'Okay,' I said.

She took my hand.

I was feeling pretty bad later the next morning. On the other hand, I was feeling pretty good, waking up next to Nancy and remembering last night. As I took a shower, she made some phone calls. I was drying my hair while she explained that Ethan Porter had been released several hours after he was detained and questioned.

'Seems he has a solid alibi,' she said. 'He was doing day labour at a construction site. There were two dozen men there who saw him all day, from six in the morning until five that afternoon. ME places Tara Flowers' death between eight a.m. to noon.'

'So he may not have done it.'

'No.'

'What if he rushed over to her place during his lunch break? Knowing she'd be there, quickly killing her, then zipping back to work. I did construction one summer when I was in law school. We took early lunches. Let's see, you start at six a.m., say lunch is around ten . . . that'd put him in the right time-frame.'

She shook her head. 'Uh-uh. Someone in homicide already thought of that. Lunch was at ten-forty-five, when the roach coach showed up at the construction site. Porter had to borrow five bucks from a guy to get something to eat. Porter stayed around the site to eat.'

'So we don't know who the killer is,' I said.

'You and I don't. I don't know what homicide has come up with yet. Do you have any ideas who else hated her?'

'No, I . . . wait.' I said.

'What?'

'I didn't even think of this.'

'What, Larry?'

'You're off-duty, but you're still on duty, right?'

'A police officer is always on duty.'

'Good. You get to be a cop today.'

'This is my day off.'

'Take a shower, get dressed, we have somewhere to go.'

'Tell me what this is about.'

'I will on the way.'

In my car, I told her.

Porter's complaint alleged that he had not been properly served with the Order to Show Cause and Temporary Restraining Order, that the papers were not served on him personally, and placed under his door on a day when he was out of town. He included, as an exhibit, an airline ticket to San Francisco, placing him on the flight at the time the process server said he served Porter. This was a possible problem, so I had called the process server at his office. He worked alone, his name was Joey O'Rourke, his business was Rocket Fast Attorney Support Service. His Yellow Pages ad claimed: *We always serve, quickly and on time*. I had called him. I had told him who I was, told him about the lawsuit and what Porter claimed, and the evidence he had.

O'Rourke had breathed heavily into the phone. 'Look, I don't want to talk about this.'

'What do you mean?' I'd said. 'Tell me, did you or did you not place the papers under Porter's door, and did you or did you not personally serve him like you're supposed to?'

'You know, that guy's lawyer called and tried to squeeze money out of me. Said I was in trouble for perjury. I told him to shove it. And I'm telling you to shove it. If Flowers wants to squeeze me for money, she can try. They can all go to hell.'

He'd screwed-up, and he wasn't going to admit it. 'I can subpoena you into court,' I'd said.

'Do it,' and he hung up.

I'd decided to check at the City Recorder's Office on Joey O'Rourke's registration as a process server, and to operate a business. I was told that while Rocket Speed Attorney Support Service's business license was up to date, Joey O'Rourke had not renewed his process server's registration number nor his required $2,000 bond, both of which expired three months ago.

This wasn't good. Nine times out of ten, a process server can get away with slipping documents under the door when no one is home, because most people don't know the intricacies of legal procedure when it comes to service, and in cases like restraining orders, nine times out of ten, the other person isn't going to show up for court, just as Ethan Porter had not. Seldom are these little inaccuracies in legal process challenged, unlike this case at hand. It was, therefore, conceivable that Ethan Porter didn't, in fact, know about the hearing, and that's why he hadn't gone. I doubted this, but in court, it would look plausible. That and the fact O'Rourke was not legally supposed to be serving court papers would hinder Tara Flowers' defense quite a bit. I could've argued that the fault lay with the process server, since he didn't perform his job, opening a good negligence suit for Tara, but Porter was also alleging that *she* knew he hadn't been properly served, and *she* conspired with O'Rourke in issuing a false and perjurous proof of service. Such an accusation was a long shot, but it still put my client in an unfavourable light.

I had decided not to bring the matter up with her. I had decided to keep quiet about it and wait and see what August Yannick had up his sleeve. It was his trump card, his best evidence, and I didn't want to give him any more ammunition.

Rocket Speed Attorney Support Service had a small office in a building that had over a hundred small offices, two blocks from the courthouse. Tara Flowers must've looked in the Yellow Pages and saw that Rocket was the closest process serving business in the area. The door was locked, and no one answered.

'We'll wait,' I told Nancy.

'Yeah. How long? I'm starving. Can't you hear my stomach growling?'

We didn't have to wait long. Fifteen minutes later, a man in shorts and a t-shirt arrived and opened the door. He was stocky and had blonde hair. I'd say he was thirty.

'Mr O'Rourke?' I said. Nancy and I followed him inside. A very tiny office, with a computer, typewriter, and a fax machine.

'Yes?' he said. 'Can I help you both?' He smiled, all business.

I pointed to the stack of legal papers on his desk, waiting to go out and be served. 'I hope you renewed your registration and re-posted bond to be farming those out,' I said.

His smile went away. 'Excuse me?' He was nervous now. I could've been an investigator for the county, or the D.A.'s office.

I said, 'Why did you do it, O'Rourke?'

'Who the hell are you?'

'Why did you murder Tara Flowers?'

Nancy gave me an incredulous look. So did Joey O'Rourke.

'Get out of my office,' he said.

'You killed her, didn't you?' I said. 'She was a threat to your livelihood, so you killed her, leaving Ethan Porter with nobody to sue.'

He moved toward me. 'If you don't leave, I'll knock some teeth out of that stupid mouth of yours.'

'That would be assault and battery,' Nancy said, 'and you don't want to do that, guy.' She flashed her badge.

'This is Officer Prescott, Joey,' I said.

He sat down, dazed. 'Oh God.'

'You killed her,' I said.

'I didn't kill anyone.'

'Sure you did.'

'You're her lawyer, aren't you? We talked on the phone last month.'

'You were testy with me, you hung up.'

'This has been a nightmare,' he said. 'I wish that woman never stepped into my door. Thirty bucks for a lousy TRO and it's been nothing but a pain in the ass.'

'So you killed her.'

'Why do you keep saying that?!'

'I know you hadn't renewed your registration number and bond,' I told him. 'What would happen if a judge found that out? That's several violations of the Business and Professions Code, Joey. You would've been fined, you may have been banned from working as a process server in the state, and the matter could've been referred to the district attorney's office for criminal charges. And Tara Flowers could've had a good case for professional negligence. You knew that a lawsuit was pending, filed by her ex-boyfriend. You knew that if it went to trial, you would've been called to the witness stand and everything would've come to light. This was something you couldn't let happen. You were following the progress of the case. You discovered that, two days ago, my motion for demurrer was denied. You got scared. You decided to murder Tara Flowers. Kill her, the case doesn't proceed, she doesn't sue you, and your mistakes aren't aired in open court.'

'That's insane,' he said.

'But true.'

'Nancy's hand was hovering near her gun.

'I didn't kill the woman!' he yelled, and slammed his fist on the desk. 'I heard about it on the news and I said: "Jesus, it's her." '

'Officer Prescott here can bring you in, and you can confess,' I said. 'Nice and clean. What do you say, Joey?'

'I was out in the field all day, serving papers,' he said. 'I can account for every minute of my time. I didn't go near that woman, I had no intention of going near her, I wish I'd never taken her job, and *I didn't* kill her and I wish you'd leave me alone.'

He was telling the truth.

'A nightmare,' he said. 'And the other lawyer, this Yannick guy, he keeps trying to extort money out of me. Says he'll tell the judge and D.A. that I wasn't operating a legal business. Look, okay, so I lapsed, but after you called me last month, I went down and renewed my registration and posted a new bond. It hurt my pocket, business has been slow, I just got divorced, my mortgage is in default, this is why I lapsed, but I'm up to date, I'm legal and current, and I just wish everyone would leave me alone.'

'I tell you what,' I said. 'Think about it, and if you feel like confessing, you know where the police station is.'

'I didn't do anything to anyone,' he said softly.

Nancy followed me out.

'Larry,' she said, 'what was that all about?'

'Just a poor schmuck trying to make a living,' I said, feeling bad, remembering my days as a starving student . . . hell, even a

starving lawyer, when I'd take any case, some of them I'm
ashamed of today.

'You think he was telling the truth?' she asked.

'Yeah.'

'You had a pretty good line of reasoning for a motive.'

'Hey, I went to school with some tough professors.'

'He seemed like he was telling the truth.'

'He was. He didn't kill her.'

'That leads us back to square one.'

'Sorry for dragging you to this.'

'You were hoping he'd break down and confess, I'd make the
arrest and get a promotion.'

'Something like that.'

'Tough break, kid.' She took my arm.

'Let me buy you lunch,' I said.

'It's a deal.'

The next day I was sitting in my office, looking over some
interrogatories for another case, trying to put Tara Flowers
out of my mind. My phone rang.

'Hey, counsellor,' Nancy's voice said, 'give me some legal
advice.'

'Shoot.'

'Never say that to a woman with a gun.'

'What are you doing? Where are you?'

'I'm drinking coffee and eating donuts,' she said. 'What else
does a cop do on her break?'

'Now this legal advice . . .'

'I'm feeling randy –'

'How lucky for Randy.'

'Would you shut up. I'm feeling frisky – yeah, lucky Frisky. I
go both ways. I don't want to go home after work. I don't want to
go to a bar where a bunch of cops hang out.'

'What do you want to do?'

'I want to play,' she said. 'But who wants to play, too? Can you
give me advice?'

'I have a bottle of great white wine at home, unopened,' I said.

'Yeah?'

'So why don't you, after your shift, come on by, we'll open the bottle, we'll consume it, and we'll see if maybe I'm feeling both randy and frisky, or we can role-play that I'm Randy and you're Frisky, and . . .'

'And?'

And I didn't say anything more.

'I'll be there at six-ish,' and she hung up.

At least my love-life was looking better.

I was having lunch with one of the partners of my firm and she had to talk about the murder of my client, and how we could use this to our advantage for publicity. 'Even weird publicity is better than none,' she laughed. I mentioned that I hated the fact that a sleazy lawyer like August Yannick had gained the upper hand on me.

'Yannick?' she said. 'August Yannick?'

'The one and only. You know him?'

'Of him. I thought he'd been disbarred.'

'He seems to be in practice.'

'I heard he had been, or was up on some charges. He's slime.'

I wondered if it was possible that Yannick, like O'Rourke, was in business when he wasn't supposed to be. It wasn't as if judges and law clerks checked on the status of every attorney's bar number.

I called the State Bar when I got back to the office and inquired of August Yannick's standing. I was informed that five investigations for misconduct and unethical practices were under way, but he was still a member of the Bar. I knew he wasn't going to be for long, if he was found to be at fault in the investigations. I also knew he was probably having a hard time getting clients with that kind of smear. Yannick didn't advertise, and none of the referral services recommended attorneys who were under investigation.

'Oh boy,' I said.

I called August Yannick. I got his answering machine.

'We need to talk, you and I,' I said.

I parked my car in the garage at my condo building. I was thinking of that bottle of wine, and felt someone come up behind me, and felt something cold and blunt jab into my side.

'Yes, we need to talk.' I could smell his breath before he spoke. 'I have a gun on you,' Yannick said. 'Let's go up to your pad, and let's be smooth about it.'

I was smooth. We took the elevator. Yannick hummed along with the elevator music: 'You and Me Against the World.' We stopped on my floor, got out, went to my door, and walked in.

'Hey, nice pad,' he said. 'Real nice. Better than my one-bedroom hole in the wall.'

'Can I turn around?'

He stepped back. 'Sure.'

I looked at him. He was holding a silver-plated snub-nose.38.

'You killed Tara Flowers,' I said.

'I didn't mean to.'

'What happened?'

'It doesn't matter. I needed that grand. I know it's not much, but these days, to me, it is. I needed to get the hell out of Dodge, and a grand would do it. Now that she's dead, no grand. But it looks like you can afford that, maybe more. So I guess this is a stick-up, Mr Jacobs. I know you probably don't have a grand here, but let's say you give me your bank card and pin number, and your credit cards as well. Maybe anything valuable you have here.'

'And you'll just leave? No. You'll kill me. You came here to kill me. I know too much.'

'You went and talked to O'Rourke yesterday. He told me when I called him again –'

'To get money from him.'

'I knew you were on to something, if you didn't already know.'

'You can't run forever, Yannick,' I said. 'Turn yourself in. Hell, I'll even be your lawyer.' A moment of insanity here . . .

'You're not good enough, I already proved that I can beat you.' He turned his head. 'Nice terrace. Why don't we step out and get some fresh air?'

We went out and onto the terrace. The sun was starting to set. I squinted my eyes. He was too close for ease, gun and bad breath.

'Nice view,' he said. 'Long way down.'

I was feeling that vertigo again.

'I could push you off,' Yannick said. 'Horrible way to die. Shoot you, the impact will cause you to fall back, and fall over the rail.'

'Are you trying to scare me?' I said.

'Yes. Is it working?'

I didn't say.

He smiled. 'It is.'

'Did you scare Tara Flowers?'

'I wanted the grand. I wasn't going to split it with Porter. I never was. It's funny how this came about. I met Porter in a bar. I was drinking my way into a sorry state, and Porter was all riled up. We got to talking. Told me about this ex-girlfriend and how she'd put a restraining order on him. I asked details, and found out the service was illegal. I told him I was a lawyer and that he had grounds to sue. I told him I'd take his case on contingency. He liked the idea. 'I'll teach her to mess with me," he said. "Yes, mess with her back", I said. I asked if she had money. He said she had over ten grand in the bank.'

'So you figured this was easy money.'

'Now you get it.'

'I know about the misconduct investigations,' I told him. 'I know you'll probably be disbarred.'

'And that I'm hurting for business and cash and I need to start anew.'

'But why kill her?'

'When you said she wanted to settle, I called her. She was home. I went over there. I told her I'd take the cheque now and leave and it'd be over with. But she got suspicious and wanted to call you. I had to yank the phone out. I told her I'd take the cheque and some nookie. I mean, she's a looker all right. I was getting excited, let me tell you. But she had to put up a fight. I didn't mean to strangle her. I just wanted her to stop screaming.'

The vertigo was getting worse and my adrenaline was pumping. The sun glared off his gun.

'So what will it be?' he said. 'The money, the credit cards, or do you go squish on the pavement?'

'I'll give you the money,' I said, knowing I was going to die regardless.

The front door burst in. Nancy was there, in a firing stance, her gun drawn, her badge out, wearing jeans and a wind beaker.

'FREEZE!'

Yannick yelped, turned, and fired. A bullet lodged into the wall, over Nancy's head. She fired three times, all three bullets entering Yannick's huge chest and stomach, inches away from me. I was glad Nancy was a good shot. The impact of bullets to flesh pushed Yannick back. The metal guardrail unhinged and he went down. I heard his descending yell, like when Wylie E. Coyote always plummets into a steep canyon.

Nancy pulled me inside. 'Are you okay?'

'Yeah. Nice shooting.'

'Who was that?'

'A fellow lawyer. Tara's killer.' I looked at my watch. Seven minutes after six.

'I knew something was wrong,' Nancy said. 'I parked my car and just happened to look up and see two men on a terrace. I thought one looked like you. It was you. Then I saw light flash off a metal object in the other man's hand. I knew what that object was so I rushed up here.'

'My hero,' I said. 'You saved me.'

'He killed Flowers?'

'It's a long story,' I said.

'You'll be telling it fifty times tonight,' she said.

'Don't remind me.'

'What a mess, Larry.'

'We better call the police,' I said.

'I'll call it in. Would it be uncouth to open that bottle of wine before they get here?' She smiled.

'Probably bad protocol, and downright rude, but who cares?' I opened the bottle while Nancy made the call.

DELISA

K. Anderson Yancy

Softly caressing Lynn's back, I sat on the bed watching her; feeling the warmth radiating from her brown skin penetrating my suit and caressing me with her love. As I leaned over and kissed the nape of her neck, half-asleep she stirred, placing her left hand in my lap, the engagement ring sparkling in the light. 'You're leaving already?'

'We takeoff in a moment.'

'It's so early.'

'*Good Morning America* wants me in their L.A. affiliate by 3:30. The Supreme Court's announcing its decision at 8 a.m. D.C. time.'

With a universe of hope and optimism she whirled to face me. 'Do you think they're going to say we're human?'

Smiling I took her in my arms. In their comfort she was unable to see the profound sadness cross my face when I told her. 'I think it'll go well.' And for a little longer, her hope was preserved.

Sitting in the dark, I watched the lights of the L.A. skyline skimming below us. The view along with the sounds of the craft were hypnotic and calming, a temporary oasis from the madness of my life. I tried to force myself to focus and rehearse for the interview, but, unable to concentrate, my mind strayed wildly.

I glanced across our craft to see Shawn sitting catty-cornered from me, reading with a frightening intensity as he raced through the output of the monitor in his left hand. Nearly continuously, his thumb depressed a button on the side of the machine and responsively, soft variations in its light pattern reflecting off his face changed, evidencing the maddening rapidity with which the pages scrolled.

I remembered Shawn removing the text, *Moshe Dyan and The Formation of The Nation of Israel,* from a section in his valise containing works on the French Resistance, Abolitionism and biographies on Martin Luther King, Gandhi, Malcolm X, John Brown, Ho Chi Minh, Charles DeGaulle, Erwin Rommel, Napoleon Bonaparte and a legion of others.

I'd always been intrigued by Shawn's duality. He was reading a book on a warrior who ruthlessly fought for his people's independence. I understood why Shawn would be drawn to the acts of freedom fighters. But it was interesting that Shawn, a devout pacifist, had held an interest in warfare for as long as I'd known him. Maybe it was related to that morbid fascination some people have about looking at accidents? Or maybe it was Shawn's attempt to come to an understanding of humanity?

Knowing his great, life-long love for history, it surprised me when we graduated from high school and he went on to earn his Phd. in genetic engineering, continuing on to become one of the leaders in the field and author of the definitive works on the science. We never spoke about it, but I wondered if for him this was an attempt to understand himself.

On that day there was something different about him and for the first time I wondered if the study of these warriors was also a way for Shawn to come to terms with himself.

Reflecting on this and everything else I turned to look out the window and I could feel that Shawn took a break from his text to study me, seeking to unravel the complex strands of my existence.

After a while he smiled warmly. 'Alpha Cetus Three to Richard.'

From the distance I responded. 'I read you five by five.'

'Congratulations again!'

'Thanks.'

Still out there somewhere I returned to the window and we sat in silence.

'So, when do I become an uncle?'

Unable to breach the distance I answered, 'We still need to set a date for the wedding,' then returned to the beyond.

'You look worried? Whatever the decision is, it's been made all you can do –'

'No, it's just pre-game jitters. I'm trying to play out as much of
it as I can before I get there. Mentally interviewing myself. Going
over what I'll say for a favourable court decision or an unfavourable one. And wondering if this interview is really going to be
non-hostile.'

'They promised.'

'They always do. I've been lied to too many times to believe
them. This show's in the business of selling news. The Delisa are
the hot product.'

'Don't worry. How they intend to use us and the Supreme
Court's decision will ultimately become clear. You can only
prepare so much, but you have to act once you know.' He grinned
broadly and winked. 'That's one of life's secrets.'

'You've just heard the U.S. Supreme Court's ruling on Daniels v.
CalGenTek. We're pleased to have Richard Harrison here today.
Counsellor Harrison represented Daniels before the High Court.'
Smiling, Katie turned from the camera to face me. 'We're glad
you could join us.'

'Thanks for inviting me.'

'I'm certain you're disappointed the court ruled the Delisa
were not human?'

Detached and dispassionately I replied, 'No.'

She looked perplexed. 'No?'

Calmly and with a hint of indifference I answered. 'No. . . . I
was disappointed when Chicago lost the Super Bowl.' With each
word my calm slowly faded and my passion rose. 'I was angered
when my best friend slept with my wife. I was outraged when the
Hadistas waged a campaign of genocide against the Salmays . . .
There's no word for what I feel now. I'm certainly *not* disappointed the court didn't *legally* acknowledge the Delisas' humanity.'

Enamoured with my passion, Katie tossed aside her interviewer's impartiality. 'I certainly agree with you. The court said the
trade in Delisa is a logical extension of the Doctrine of Commercial Adaptability. What does that mean?'

'When a business manipulates the DNA of a species so that the
altered life form serves a new commercial purpose, they're

granted a patent – an exclusivity – and the right to place it on the market.

'The Delisa are a genetically engineered species, derived primarily from human DNA that's been combined with the genes of a number of plants and animals. From their inception, they've been considered domestic animals. Not because they're predisposed to be more barbaric or untamed than we are . . .'

She smiled. 'I've found them to be innately peaceful.'

'They are. No Delisa has ever harmed a human or another Delisa. They're considered animals simply because the 14th Amendment to the U.S. Constitution prohibits enslavement of humans.'

Katie crossed her legs. 'So by augmenting human DNA and selling those beings, people can engage in a morally and constitutionally forbidden practice?'

Full of fervour I uncrossed mine and leaned into her. 'Precisely. Slavery is outlawed. Animal ownership is not. The only physical difference between the Delisa and us are the composition of our eyes. *They're* stronger, smarter. When I was eight, I didn't know what calculus was, let alone multi-integral calculus.'

'Apparently, the court, in part, based its decision on CalGenTek's documents, which demonstrated their intent to develop the Delisa as an inferior life form.'

'The name Delisa comes from the first two letters of the words *DE*rivative *LI*fe *SA*pien. Undisputedly, they are a derivative life form. That's not the same as an inferior one. CalGenTek's documents also indicated they were attempting to create a genetically superior species, but the court ignored those when it rationalized its decision.'

'Interesting.'

'The average employer is always looking for the cheapest source of qualified labour. The rolling depression during the beginning of this century, as our trade barriers decreased and industries fled to lower wage third worlds was proof of that.'

'So when CalGenTek was creating the Delisa, they had a ready market for cheap, intelligent labour.'

'A labourer that cheap is called a slave. Sadly, another part of this nation's scarlet past has been repeated. These . . .' I searched for the correct term and as it flowed from my mouth another of our words took on a permanently profane meaning. '. . . Jurists have again blemished the social accomplishments we've made this decade, carrying us into as dark a period as that which followed the Dred Scott decision, when the enslavement of Africans and their descendants was legitimized.'

Katie reflected on my comments. 'I hope not.'

'So do I.'

'It led us into a war that nearly destroyed our nation. With our current technology we could destroy our civilization.'

'And our species.'

Katie shivered involuntarily. 'Not a pleasant thought.'

Returning to her interviewer persona, she glanced into a camera. 'Earlier we agreed to allow CalGenTek to comment on the decision. Joining us from their headquarters in Los Angeles, we have Wendy Muse. Good Morning, Wendy.'

'Good morning, Katie.'

'What's your reaction to the High Court's decision?'

'We're pleased. It validates what we've said all along. The Delisa are animals.'

'With this out of the way, do you plan on increasing your marketing efforts?'

'To a degree. A few weeks ago Borat Industries announced a breakthrough in robotics that makes it uneconomical for us to continue to raise Delisa as labour.'

I grinned. *There's more than one way to win a war!* I'd invested a lot of resources in that company.

'So it looks like Mr Harrison has won after all?'

'Not exactly. In Asian countries they're a recently discovered delicacy, with a popularity that's spreading rapidly. Though, to most westerners, the idea of eating Delisa will no doubt remain repugnant.'

Unbelieving, Katie asked. 'You eat Delisa?'

Smoothly she answered. 'No. I've never tried it, but I've been told they taste like veal.'

Katie and I made no attempt to hide our disgust.

Oblivious to our emotions or just ignoring them Wendy continued. 'We can obtain a high enough price to continue to raise them *ex vitro* and then after their gestation period is complete ship them off to market.'

Whistling a happy tune, a blood splattered CalGenTek worker came through a door behind Wendy. Seeing the camera, he fell silent and hurriedly left. The videographer followed a hunch and sprinted through the doors, deftly avoiding Wendy and the worker as they attempted to intercept him, his camera continuing to transmit what he saw while he struggled to evade them and other approaching workers. It was a slaughterhouse filled with Delisa in various stages of butchering and packaging.

Katie stared at the monitor in wide-eyed horror, while I closed mine and softly said, 'My God.'

Livid, and without hesitation Shawn stormed out the studio and irrevocably initiated the actions foretold in a prophecy made long, long ago by Mary Shelley in her warning, *The Frankenstein Monster*.

Not long after Shawn had told me, 'You can only prepare so much, but you have to act once you know.' He did.

Still in the suit and sunglasses he'd worn to *Good Morning America*, Shawn calmly walked into CalGenTek's lobby. His mind riveted on his mission, he remained unaffected by the sense of wonderment and awe most visitors felt.

The anteroom was impressive resembling the waiting room of royalty. The carpet plush and hand woven. Fine art hung from the walls and sat on exquisite furniture. Given the company's eminence as a leader among the giants of the economic monarchy, all was fitting.

Even the flora displayed in the atrium was emblematic of its stature. Undulating, genetically engineered plants, creatures that also possessed the physical characteristics of animals.

Some were truly beautiful.

The *Parrot Bushes* were monuments to the artistry of genetic engineering.

The *Jenkins' Trees*, a mixture of human, squid and pine traits were clearly a garish abomination, a mockery of nature, a testament that the field of genetic engineering ran unchecked and things were designed merely because they could be.

The Atrium teemed with these and a multitude of lives indicative of the vast array of entities CalGenTek had created and implanted into all aspects of our existence.

Unimpressed, Shawn shifted his gaze from the creatures and paused on the security officer absorbed with the urgency of his tasks as he sat behind a marble desk in a large oversized chair vaguely resembling a throne.

The man noted Shawn. 'Sir, I'll be with you in a moment.'

Shawn coughed and with great warmth responded with a soft raspy voice. 'Please take your time.'

The man returned the smile and swiftly shifted his concern to the immediacy of his duties, while Shawn casually walked to the building directory and floor plans to study them.

Finished the officer looked toward him. 'My friend, thank you for waiting. May I help you?'

With an even softer, coarser voice, Shawn mumbled. 'Yes, can you –' He quickly turned, broke out in a violent coughing attack and for a moment was unable to speak.

The guard bent closer. 'Pardon?'

The tint of Shawn's glasses and the officer's reflection in them masked the malevolent, discordant bursts exploding in Shawn's eyes as he bent closer to speak.

Covering his mouth, Shawn turned away, coughed, shook his head to say I'm sorry and touched his neck.

The guard smiled. 'That's okay. I have a touch of the flu myself.'

Again, the two bent closer together. Like a viper Shawn struck out with both hands, grabbed the man's head and slammed it into the marble security counter. Blood ran from the deep fracture in the guard's forehead forming tiny rivulets as the fluid flowed around lacerations and shattered skull fragments.

Shawn removed the man's pistol and ammunition clips, then hid them under his suit. Passing on the purple visitor's badges lying on the counter, he took the guard's neon orange employee ID and attached it to his jacket's breast pocket.

Quickly, Shawn removed the guard's sports coat as he stuffed him under the desk. Using it, he wiped the counter clean of blood, tossed it underneath the station and returned the chair to its normal position, blocking a clear view of the corpse entombed there.

Genuinely remorseful for killing the guard, Shawn stared at the man's crypt, bowed and made the sign of the cross. Sensing someone was watching him, Shawn swiftly shot up and quickly scanned the room, while reaching for his weapon.

There was no . . . one.

He saw them – the *Jenkins' Trees*.

Standing in the simulated sunlight of the arboretum, they'd witnessed his deeds and now deliberated his judgment.

Shawn was shocked. He figured as distant cousins, they were self-aware. But, he'd never realized their true extent.

Analysis complete, closing their eyes they bowed to him in what Shawn knew was an acknowledgement of solidarity with his manifesto. When they returned upright and opened their eyes, Shawn closed his and returned the salute to his kindred.

Done, Shawn composed himself as if nothing had happened, walked through the lobby to a tastefully ornate wooden-leather door and held the guard's ID to a recognition plate adjacent to it.

Hearing a light musical tone and a soft click signaling the unlocking of the security door, he turned the handle and entered.

Shawn strode through the entrance and immediately entered a corridor made of two huge bay windows. Floored by the realization of what they contained, he faltered and stopped. Awed, he spoke to himself in a low whisper. 'My God.'

On both sides technicians, humans and Delisa, worked on the 'Mamas' – artificial wombs from which generations of Delisa were born. The birthing units stood in perfect lines, a transparent battalion of soldiers, faithfully executing their orders – 'be fruitful and multiply.' To Shawn it looked as if this army continued around the world to the other side and if not for him, they'd form an unbroken ring.

His eyes fell upon the unborn children. Saddened and repulsed, he dwelled on them as a cascade of thoughts and emotions covering the hideous indignities his people had suffered and the horrendous future of further dehumanization awaiting them.

Their debasement had started here at CalGenTek and these young Delisa evidenced this company and humanity's desire to strip away even their most basic right.

Not even a mother?

Like a crop, they were arranged in sections of varying maturity, ranging from embryo to adult. Shawn had heard the Delisa growth cycle could be expedited in these wombs. But as he watched a section of embryos explode into foetuses, he came to a new understanding of the meaning of the term expedite.

The embryos' older siblings watched the outside world with angelic innocence.

Sorrow snared Shawn, as he thought of their future.

Deliberately he reached for his weapon, as their fate flashed before him. After a fierce internal struggle, he released it and forced himself to wait.

Masking his true feelings, nonchalantly Shawn continued toward his destination.

Arriving, he was surprised and pleased to see the *Good Morning America* news crew still there, involved in a heated argument with human security and other CalGenTek personnel.

Shawn removed his glasses, revealing a malevolent, discordant micro-universe in which all its stars were going nova. Drawing his automatic pistol, he selectively fired on the crowd.

Screams enveloped the weapon's bursts as bullets pierced neon orange CalGenTek employee ID's, dropping the guards as they reached for their pistols, while others ran or dived to the floor for sanctuary.

For a moment Shawn grinned to himself, as he surveyed the carnage thinking the employee badges made great targets.

With the CalGenTek staff down, he ceased firing, and in the silence of the sobs, studied the bloody floor littered with dead and dying CalGenTek workers while the *Good Morning America* staff cowered.

He'd spared the news crew; his message needed a conduit. Training his weapon on them, he spoke.

'Come.'

In shock the crew continued to cringe on the floor.

'Come or die!!!!'

He aimed and they hurriedly complied. 'Good choice. Turn your camera on me. We've got history to make.'

Shawn then took his weapon off them and burst through the door where he'd witnessed the butchering of his kindred and fired on new targets.

Fuming, I sat at a table in the jail's interview room, waiting.

The door creaked open and I looked up to see Shawn manacled and shuffling in under the cautious observations of his armed escorts.

'Please unchain him.'

The senior officer answered for the group. 'God no! He butchered 19 people –'

'Butchering baby Delisa!'

'I don't care what he was doing! It was illegal and it took nine people to –'

'As you are well aware, I'm his attorney and fully within my rights to make this request. And if you'd like to continue in this line of employment, I'd suggest you reach into your pocket or wherever you keep the key, remove it and release him.'

For a long while we glared at one another. Finally, the officer gave in. 'I'll release *it*.'

I glanced at the officer's badge. 'Thank you, Sergeant Johnson, 59836. I'll insure your . . . cooperation is noted by the appropriate supervisors.'

The jailer unchained Shawn and rebuked my comment by slamming the door after he and his staff exited.

Finally alone, I snapped at Shawn. 'Jesus Christ! Do you know what you've done?'

'Killed nineteen murderers!'

'And badly damaged the movement! You know, people have been after me for years and you, you've handed me to them!'

'I'm sorry.'

'Sorry? I'm going to lose everything. I've been slapped with a civil law suit for each of your victims – living and dead. Because, I'm technically your owner.'

Shawn's face filled with remorse. He started to speak but stopped.

In that instant my rage was replaced with profound sorrow. 'I'm sorry. You know I don't care about those things.'

'I know.'

'It's just what I – we've been able to accomplish with them. The colonies . . .'

The room grew silent for a moment, as the magnitude of our losses sunk in.

I looked at my brother. 'I've never really thanked you for all the help you've given me with the Delisa.'

'Why? You did it for me.'

'I did it for us. I couldn't stand by and let you be treated like property. I hate to admit this, but to my parents your mother was just a servant. Not even that. Just something else they owned . . .'

'I know.'

'Hell, they only showed *me* slightly more affection than the staff.' I felt my eyes begin to tear and fought desperately to stop it, but unable to hold them back I let them flow. 'I miss your mom. The times with you and her are my best memories . . . As far as I'm concerned she was my real mother.'

Tears rolled down Shawn's face as he listened and reflected. He walked to me. 'I love you.'

'I love you too.'

We embraced. 'I'm scared.'

'Me too.'

'They've got us. I don't know what I can do.'

'I know whatever you do will be your best.'

The filled court sat in silence, rapt with deep anticipation as the prosecutor approached the jury.

Seated next to Shawn at the defense table, I glanced discreetly at my watch, then looked at the opposing counsel and thought, *There's not much I can do. This'll be a mercifully quick trial, done before the day is.*

I sat intense and focused studying him, while Shawn shifted nervously in his seat complicating the tasks of the press artist rapidly sketching us.

'Ladies and gentleman of the jury. On August 8 of this year,

Shawn Harrison walked into a CalGenTek laboratory here in Los Angeles and with forethought and malice bludgeoned one guard before proceeding through the facility slaughtering human after human until he was finally subdued.

'On that day Shawn Harrison committed 19 counts of murder in the first degree.

'Let me review the law for you.

'Section 189 of the California Penal code states "All murder which is perpetrated by means of a destructive device or explosive, knowing use of ammunition designed primarily to penetrate metal or armour, poison, lying in wait, torture, or by any other kind of *willful*, *deliberate* and *premeditated* killing, or which is committed in the perpetration of, or attempt to perpetrate, arson, rape, robbery, burglary, *mayhem* or any act punishable under section 288 is murder of the first degree.'

'Section 187 defines murder as "the unlawful killing of a human being with malice aforethought . . ." '

Shawn bent into me and whispered. 'Twelve humans. So much for a jury of my peers. Thanks Richard. But, there's not much you can do. At least it'll be mercifully quick. Over before the day is.'

'Shawn, I'll think of something.'

The judge dismissed the witness as I made notes on my legal pad.

Shawn reached over and tapped me on the shoulder. 'I'm sorry. The prosecutor dragged this out for five weeks, to make himself famous at your expense. If anyone else had represented me, they'd have finished in five hours.'

The Judge glanced at us, wondering. No doubt trying to determine what my defense might be. Without a doubt she would make that discovery at the same time I did. She shifted her attention to the prosecutor.

'Does the prosecution intend to call additional witnesses?'

'No, your honour. The prosecution rests.'

He grinned smugly, glaring at me as he took his seat. Locking eyes, we silently duelled as I watched the man's orbs radiate intense arrogance and cruelty. I dismissed him and as I looked away I saw Shawn's eyes playing a hopeless melody and I saw my answer, just as the Judge moved us to the defense phase of the trial.

'Counsel for the defense, are you ready to present your case?'

I stood. 'No Your Honour.'

'Counsellor, you've had ample time to prepare.'

'If I may Your Honour. Defense motions for judgment of acquittal.'

'On what basis.'

'My client is charged with murder. This charge is historic for two reasons. First, no Delisa has ever been charged with murder.'

'Objection Your Honour! Lack of relevance! This is a court-room, not a history class.'

'And, I am the judge, not an attorney before her. Overruled. Will the prosecution please be seated? Counsellor Harrison, please get to the point.'

'Yes Your honour. Secondly, this court follows the common law definition of murder, which is the killing of a *human* being by another *human* with malice. And I'm certain you're aware of the recent U.S. Supreme Court's ruling that the Delisa are not *human*. Accordingly, this . . .' I made a dismissive motion to-wards Shawn. '*Animal* cannot be charged with murder.'

I could see the judge silently weighing my argument. There in the silence whispers erupted throughout the courtroom. When I resumed they terminated abruptly.

'If I may Your Honour?'

'Continue.'

'This court has only held the owners of domestic animals responsible for the injuries they caused, if their masters were *aware* of the animals' dangerous propensities. Until now, no Delisa had ever harmed a human. Additionally, masters have absolutely no responsibility to trespassers for the injuries their domestic animals inflict.'

'I'm not certain I follow you.'

'Now, if the Delisa were reclassified as wild animals, their owners would be entirely responsible for the damage they do. But only if the injuries are the result of their creatures' abnormally dangerous characteristics. However, under this scenario, the ownership of wild animals is normally limited to rural areas. Delisa ownership would be forbidden in cities –'

'Objection, Your honour! Relevance! This information has no bearing on the case.'

I grinned at her. 'Your honour, I was only providing additional information on animal-owner liability to aid you in making a decision –'

She fixed me with a stern gaze and I prepared for the reprimand. 'I know what you were doing, Counsellor Harrison. This is a criminal court. Defense of the Delisa's claim to freedom and your civil law suits are *not* to take place in this court. Do I make myself clear?'

'Yes, Your honour.'

Caught, I offered no further argument and thought, a partial victory is better than a complete defeat. She realized I was using her court and the press coverage as my own forum. My brief speech had allowed me to use the First Estate as I began defending the law suits I'd been served with because of Shawn. But more importantly, it launched the next stage of the Delisas' try at humanity. Reclassifying them as wild animals would severely limit the places they could be enslaved.

'The prosecution's objection is sustained . . . Mr Harrison.'

'Yes, Your honour.'

'I want to review your argument. You're requesting that your client be acquitted for murder and related charges because murder is the killing of a human being by another human being and that your client is not human and accordingly can not be charged with murder and the other crimes.'

'Yes, Your honour. That's correct.'

'You're right. Motion granted. Case dismissed.'

She pounded her gavel and with that freed Shawn.

Pandemonium exploded throughout the court. Some cheered the decision. Others decried it. Shawn was invigorated and his tone took on a sense of finality and malevolence.

'We will be free. And, our humanity will be recognized.'

Deeply saddened by what I knew was coming, I repacked my things as I spoke. 'For a while, a legal loophole will allow you to openly conduct war against the Sapiens and it will lead to your freedom and your humanity . . . But, maybe some wishes are better left unanswered. Unfortunately for you and the rest of the Delisa, humanity's not a lofty goal to aspire to, it's a depth to sink to.'

Light from candle flames danced upon the walls to the rhythm of soft romantic music as Lynn and I sat around the dining room table. A partially carved, roasted chicken lan in the centre surrounded by an array of side dishes.

Despite the mood and the company, I just couldn't eat my dinner. It wasn't that my mind was elsewhere. The problem was that it *wasn't*.

Like a child trying to avoid eating something he disliked, I used my fork to move the food around on my plate.

It was the chicken.

It was hideous.

And just having it on my plate contaminated everything else. God, what I would have given for a mountain of mashed potatoes to hide it all under.

Lynn held her wine glass, watching, appraising my actions.

'You don't like it, do you?'

'No, it's good.'

'You haven't tasted anything.'

'It is good.'

'How do you know?'

'Lynn, you know I love your cooking. But I can't eat this. That chicken looks so gross.'

Her eyes flashed to anger though the rest of her remained calm and I knew I'd chosen the wrong words, but still I continued.

'It only has two legs and two wings and no tails.'

'That's because it's all natural. You've been eating that genetically engineered food all your life. Who knows what that stuff does to your body?'

'Geneng food is all natural, to me. Not this.'

'Try it. You might like it.'

I looked at my plate. No doubt my expression said exactly what I was thinking. *NO WAY!!!!*

'Please.'

I glanced at Lynn and she returned such a sweet, inviting look I had no choice and I acquiesced. Taking my fork I lifted a piece of white meat towards my mouth, just as a chime played a haunting melody. Overly enthusiastic, I downed my fork and the chicken on the plate and jumped from the table. 'THE DOOR!'

I could tell Lynn was peeved, so I swiftly darted back to the table, took her face in my hands, and kissed her on the lips.

'I love you. Even though you tried to poison me.'

She smiled and I walked to the door. Opening it, I saw Shawn and Melissa, his Delisa lover.

For a moment we all stood in apprehension and silence.

Not knowing what else to do, I invited them in. Nervously, they entered. Very worried, Lynn came to us.

Shawn glanced at our table and made small talk. 'I see you had one of those all natural chickens too. Yeah, Melissa tried to kill me with one of those today.'

'Kill you? You had three servings.'

'I didn't want to hurt your feelings and I didn't want the chicken to have died for nothing.'

We laughed. Melissa playfully punched him in the arm and the silence returned.

I broke it. 'Shawn, are you –'

'Yeah.'

'Don't do th –'

'I can't wait around like some caged, rabid dog, until they figure out some reason to come pick me up and put me to sleep.'

'You're protected here.'

'I am. But what about the rest of my people. I've had a good life. Thanks to you. I've lived better than most humans. But, slavery is wrong and I must do, what I must do.'

'We can attack it on other legal grounds. Justice –'

'Justice! Where do you find justice? We don't have a justice system. We have a legal system and they're two separate things. This legal system only gives you what you can afford to buy. And, it will never produce justice.'

Lynn glanced from Shawn to Melissa. 'You don't agree with his plans?'

'I don't know. We haven't accomplished much at all playing by the rules. Something else has to be done.'

'Not this.'

'Then what?'

Lynn had no answer. Tears slowly formed in her eyes. Responsively, we all joined her. Melissa and Lynn hugged, as Shawn extended his hand to shake, goodbye. I grabbed it and we embraced.

'Shawn . . . take care my brother.'

'Take care, my brother . . . You know you have to distance yourself from me. Forever.'

I shook my head no, but my tone and words spoke the truth. 'I know . . . Forever.'

DRAWING THE LINE

Ian Creasey

During the twenty one minutes it takes to name all the alleged murder victims, no network dares to enrage the bereaved by cutting to commercials. It makes for surprisingly gripping television. The camera pans round the court and picks out all the actors in the drama, subtitles providing background so that no voice-over drowns out the roll-call of the dead. Here's the judge, famously relaxed: he's known for his twin habits of occasionally closing his eyes to aid concentration, and suing for libel anyone who suggests that he has fallen asleep. Here's the prosecutor, a rising star: this is his first high-profile case. Has he applied a touch of make-up in fear of TV's unforgiving glare? You can't decide. Opposite him sits the defence, nicknamed St Jude after the patron saint of lost causes: this may be the toughest case yet in her long career. Then there are the minor players, functionaries and security guards each granted a brief moment of celebrity by TV's roving eye.

Wherever the camera goes, the accused cannot escape scrutiny. He is constantly on-screen in an inset box bordered by prison bars. He is calm inside his virtual cell, but his appearance does him no favours. Tall, muscled, short-haired – if you saw him on the street you might instinctively touch your wallet. Even before the evidence, it doesn't look good for him: the TV graphic shows that the prosecutor has won convictions in 73% of his cases to date, but the defence has only won acquittals in 14% of hers.

With the confidence born of an excellent record and a cast-iron case, the prosecutor swaggers about the court like a pirate captain about to hang a mutineer from the yard-arm. 'It began with a simple break-in,' he says, displaying slides of a fingerprint found on the window, and a fingerprint from the defendant. After a stretch, a rotate and a tweak for 'pressure compensation', he superimposes them to show that they're identical. But you're not convinced by this special effects trickery, and there hasn't been much action yet, so you flick through the channels to see if anything else is on.

There isn't, and you switch back to see a black and white video, instantly recognizable as security camera footage. A tall figure walks down a corridor, carrying a hold-all. He doesn't seem completely confident of the way, for he stops to consult a sign on the wall. As he looks around, and listens for any approaching footsteps, the camera gets a clear view of his face. The prosecutor stops the tape for a moment, and juxtaposes the freeze-frame with a photograph of the accused, to demonstrate that the right man is on trial. Then the tape continues, with occasional jumps where footage from different cameras has been spliced together.

The intruder reaches his destination. The sign on the door is barely legible due to the slight fuzziness of the picture; the prosecutor informs the court that it reads, 'Emergency generator. No admittance to unauthorized personnel.' The door is evidently locked, but the intruder has come prepared. His body blocks the view, so the camera doesn't show exactly how he does it, but he swiftly has the door open. He steps through and pulls the door closed behind him. For some reason there is no security camera in the emergency generator room, but the prosecutor fills in with photos taken afterwards, which show an impressive amount of damage.

'At this point,' he says, 'members of the jury may be wondering why the defendant wasn't apprehended before he could commit the murders. After all, he's been clearly visible on security cameras for some time, and the damage to the emergency generator could not have been done quietly. Let's have that answer from the security guard on duty that evening.'

The witness is well into middle age and looks stout rather than beefy. You think he's in no shape to apprehend anyone, let alone someone as young and fit as the accused. He has to be told to speak up, and after the introductory formalities the nub of the matter is reached.

'We were playing cards – me, Father Francis, Doctor Lindsey, and Ernie.' He spills out the names as if eager to spread the blame.

'Where were you playing cards?'

'In the day-room.'

'Could you monitor the cameras from there?'

'No, you have to be in the control-room for that. But it's cold down there, so we always used to sit in the lounge.'

'So you didn't see the intruder, because you weren't watching the video monitors. Did you hear any unusual noises?'

'I did hear something, but I thought it was coming from outside. It's a rough area, you know. I didn't want to go out and confront a gang if they were just trashing someone's car. I use the bus myself.'

The prosecutor sighs. 'No further questions.'

The videotape continues. The intruder emerges, having wrecked the emergency generator, and makes his way to the main power room, which isn't even locked up. Here there is a camera, and although the angle isn't ideal, the figure can be seen taking two devices out of his hold-all and carefully placing them underneath the huge black transformers. After kneeling down to make final preparations, he stands up, gives a satisfied nod to the empty room, and walks out rather more quickly than he came in.

The prosecutor doesn't bother to show the intruder retracing all his steps back to the break-in point, and instead the footage from the power room keeps rolling, the clock ticking over at the top. Nothing happens for ninety seconds, but during this period tension in the court accumulates like a static charge. Even the judge sits up. The prosecutor takes his glasses off and puts them back on again. Only the defendant appears relaxed. He has been impassive throughout the previous evidence, but now he permits himself a faint smile. You reflexively brace yourself.

The phone rings, and you leap up as if it's given you an electric shock. As you explain that no, you don't have time to answer a few questions – not even if there is a prize draw – you look back at the TV, but when it finally comes the explosion is a disappointment. There's a brief impression of movement at the bottom of the picture, then the image collapses into static.

'The tape ends there,' says the prosecutor, 'because the security system, like everything else, went down when the power room was blown up, and as the stand-by generator had already been sabotaged, it took several hours to restore the electricity. By then, of course, all the damage had been done. This act was murder, plain and simple. Maybe it wasn't as personal as killing someone with a knife or a bullet, but the effects were just as lethal. Here are some pictures taken by the police when they arrived.'

These photographs are also in black and white, illuminated by flashlights, and the first ones simply show row upon row of beds, occupied by recumbent figures wired up to shadowy, mysterious apparatus. No lights glow on these dead machines, and the meters all rest at zero. Then a few close-ups show the occupants more clearly. They're almost all extremely old, and undignified in death, with glassy eyes, lolling tongues, and miniature rivulets of drool soaking their identical pyjamas and night-dresses. The flashlit monochrome photography, the zombie-like appearance of the ancient corpses, the sinister aspect of the defunct life-support machines – all these factors make the macabre images linger in your mind like half-remembered scenes from an old horror film.

Next morning all the papers have the same photo on the front page, the defendant's faint grin during the replay of the deadly explosion. Only the headlines differ: 'Smile of A Monster', 'No Remorse', 'The Face Of Evil'. Intrigued by 'You Be The Judge', you find it refers to photo-montages of the accused hanging on the gallows, sitting in the electric chair and awaiting a lethal injection. It's a poll on how he should be executed, without even the caveat 'if he's found guilty'.

On breakfast TV's *Rewind*, the experts are convinced that the case is already lost.

'When he smiled, he signed his own death warrant,' says a man in a beige suit. His tie is beige too, with a pattern of black microphones. 'The jury will remember that smile of smug self-satisfaction, and it'll convince them that he's guilty.'

'But what has the defence been doing to prevent that? Nothing! She should have been challenging the evidence.' You vaguely remember this guy as the chief defence lawyer in a couple of big trials a few years ago.

'How could she? It seems pretty clear-cut,' says the anchor-man.

'That's precisely my point. It seems clear-cut because it hasn't been challenged. She should have questioned it – then even if her points were largely bogus, it would still have created what I call the "aura of doubt".

'She must have a strategy in mind, surely.'

'I presume she'll argue for not guilty by reason of insanity. It looks like the only option, if she's not going to dispute the facts.'

The beige suit exclaims, 'Hah!'

'Trevor?'

'That's a complete cop-out. I don't care whether he's of sound mind or not, he's still done it, and should face the full punishment of the law.'

The star lawyer tries to interject, but the anchorman cuts him off.

'Let's go to the phones on that point. Is insanity an excuse? Is it justice to punish someone who doesn't know what they're doing? The lines –'

You have no desire to hear dozens of cabbies ringing in to demand the execution of the feeble-minded, so you switch channels to the trial. The court is filling up and everyone is frisked with meticulous thoroughness, as today the defendant takes the stand. He's obviously been told not to smile again, as he now maintains an impassive mask.

The prosecutor waits for silence. He clearly intends to build anticipation as the shuffling and whispers slowly die down, but the judge spoils the effect by telling him to get on with it. He flushes and says tartly, 'I *intend* to get on with it, and I'll come straight to the point.' He turns to the defendant. 'Did you pull the plug?'

'Yes.'

The prosecutor lets this hang for a long moment then, just as the judge leans forward, says, 'No further questions.' He sits down and although he doesn't look at the defence team, he's palpably thinking, *Get out of that!*

The cameras zoom in on St Jude, who's almost the only person in the courtroom not wearing black; instead she's opted for a dark blue power-suit, which complements her steel-gray hair. She clearly has another unenviable task, and can only ask the question in everyone's mind.

'You've just admitted cutting off the electricity. How do you justify pleading not guilty to the charges of murder?'

'Murder requires the victim to be alive. These alleged victims were not alive at the time.'

There is a disbelieving intake of breath all around the court, and you laugh scornfully. Is this the best she can come up with? No wonder she doesn't win many cases!

'Not alive in what sense?'

'Not alive as in *dead*. The earliest experiments with electricity showed that it could make a severed frog's leg kick. More advanced technology can apply the same principle to people, but that doesn't mean they're any more alive than those dead, dissected frogs.'

The defendant's calm voice and blank, expressionless face are far more shocking than a madman's grin or a video bad guy's sneer. There are gasps and cries of 'Shame!' from the public gallery, and a scuffle breaks out as the stewards try to stifle the outraged relatives. When they restore order, the defence begins presenting her evidence, professionally enough but with an air of going through the motions.

'Ladies and gentlemen of the jury, you have seen pictures taken after the explosion, but not the scene beforehand. Several months earlier, however, a TV documentary crew visited the nursing home. That footage was never aired – until now.'

The contrast with the earlier pictures is striking. This video has colour and sound, and after all the previous grainy, badly lit, black and white shots, the film's professional polish makes it look hyper-real, like God's own view.

The tape begins with an establishing shot of the locale: discount warehouses, obsolescent factories converted into student flats, and half-empty office developments boasting luxurious interiors at low low rents. The camera zooms in to the nursing home's exterior, lingering for a few seconds on the sign,

'Applecroft Retreat', cheerily illustrated with the shrubs and flowers conspicuously absent in the landscape outside. Then it cuts to several dull interviews guaranteed to cause an itchy flipping finger in homes the world over. Only Father Francis has any presence, his eyes radiating sincerity as he denounces the evil of euthanasia.

'Life is sacred,' he says. 'It is a gift from God, and should not be callously thrown away to suit the whim of the moment or the pockets of the greedy. Our residents receive loving care, and every treatment that medicine can provide, including the latest generation of Total Life-Support Machines.' He expands on this theme, continuing although he must have known that anything past the first ten seconds would never reach the screen. But he's a natural, and you think that he could do very well as a tub-thumping TV evangelist.

Finally, the film shows the residents themselves, row upon row of them, sleeping peacefully in metal-framed beds (the white paint just beginning to peel), wired up to machines emitting soothing hums in vast polyphonic harmony. Or are they sleeping? It's a shock when the camera begins to move down the hall, and you see that many of the apparent sleepers have open eyes, focused far above the ceiling as if looking for heaven.

The cameraman knows his trade. The viewpoint is just low enough to make the life-support machines tower imposingly, and the beds blur into the distance like an exercise in perspective. As the slow tracking shot reaches the end of an interminable hall, a muffled noise hints at life and passion somewhere: a pan leftward reveals the day-room, but there's only odd job man Ernie watching the races on TV. The camera enters an elevator, emerging at another floor full of more dormitories. The upper levels contain residents older and more frail than those below, their reclining forms almost obscured by the enfolding Total Life-Support Machines of which Father Francis boasted. These appear more lively than the patients, their flickering lifesign displays and flashing green lights making them look like fruit machines awaiting a final jackpot. Perhaps it's an illusion, but the twitching meters appear to show a curious synchronisation of heartbeats. The voiceover discusses the recent advances in medicine leading to the TLMs, but on the third floor the narrator runs out of prepared text and begins to improvise, talking about the ancient legend of the Sleepers under the Hill, and anything else that enters his head. And then he simply shuts up, and the film is now silent except for the throbbing drone of the machines, becoming even more eerie thereby.

There's a large amount of raw footage. The scenes are lengthy because unedited, but the lack of action makes them seem even longer. The cumulative effect is of a slow-motion, frozen world, reminding you of nightmares in which you can't move no matter how you try. And with a shudder you're suddenly convinced that the residents are all silently screaming, struggling to escape but being held down by the machines, which are, after all, state of the art.

By now you're so used to the motionless, echoing halls that the sight of a visiting family is a surprise. The camera keeps its distance from the encounter, but it's obvious that the adults in the party are well used to the state of their relative and make only a token attempt at communication before settling down to have a good gossip across the bed. The child, perhaps, has not been here before. She keeps tugging at the hand of the unresponsive old man, until finally she gets a resounding slap and is told not to touch. But when her wails have died down, she begins to call out as if she can wake him up, although his eyes are already open. 'Grandpa . . . Grandpa . . . *Grandpa!*'

Fade to black.

The producer is called to testify that the footage is genuine and a fair representation of conditions inside the home. He says that the film was never transmitted because it was 'too depressing'. It's certainly depressed you. You switch the TV off and walk to the shop, lingering to feel the sun on your skin. On the way you decide to ring the relatives you only ever see at Christmas, as if you can reach out to stop them declining into senility. But when you get back you put the kettle on first, and then you don't quite get round to it.

The next few days address the central point of the defence's case. Could the nursing home residents have been murdered if they were effectively dead already? Life and death are apparently simple concepts, easily expressed in one chunky syllable, but the boundary between them is anything but simple. Technology constantly pushes it back and forth, blurs it, and defies anyone to label the results. When exactly does life start? When does it end? Call a philosopher! One has been found to act as an expert witness, but despite having to discuss these ideas with generations of students, he isn't very good at explaining them to you. And his dress sense –! You're not surprised when *The Makeover Show* devotes an entire edition to fusty academics.

So far you've been horrified, then puzzled, but when the medical evidence starts you're just plain bored. The defence and prosecution each bring on their experts, in an arms race of ever-increasing seniority and prestige. Brain death, PVS, coma recovery . . . arcane terminology pours out devoid of context or meaning.

On *Rewind* the anchorman says, 'Trevor, it sounds like the victims died of KBJ: Killed By Jargon.'

'That's right, Richie. The courtroom tape already has a caption showing how long the trial has lasted, but it needs another caption telling us how many acronyms have been used – if only for the spread-betting people.'

'The defence is doing her job of raising doubt, as I advocated all along: she's just doing it a bit late.' The lawyer was faintly patronising, as if pleased at the progress of a slow pupil.

Trevor shook his head. 'There's no doubt in my mind – he murdered them.'

'The only people who died were those connected to the TLMs. Do you want to prosecute doctors every time they switch off someone's life support machine?'

Trevor repeats an already notorious quote from the trial's testimony: ' "It isn't murder if it's committed by licensed professional after proper consultation," ' but he can't quite keep a straight face.

'Surely an act is right or wrong in itself, not áccording to who does it?' says the anchorman. 'Let's –'

– *go to the phones*, you silently complete. You already know what callers will say: you've seen the T-shirts overprinted with simplifying slogans.

During final esoteric legal wrangles, coverage switches to the lively demonstrations outside the court, where the accused is either a hero of the Right to Death cause, or a terrorist who if freed will come round to your house and shoot your granny. Although both factions claim to respect life, they look like they'd quite like to kill each other given the chance. At least abortion clinics are enjoying a rare respite, as the local pro-lifers are all besieging the court for the duration.

'What's happening here?' says the reporter doing vox pops.

'We're lighting two hundred and seventy three candles in memory of the victims brutally murdered by that bastard in there.'

'Will you protest against the death penalty, if that's the outcome of the case?'

'Of course not!' says the pro-life spokeswoman. 'An eye for an eye –'

But she's interrupted by a splashing sound, as the opposition hose down the candles. She smiles radiantly at this propaganda gift, and holds up one of the few candles to survive the wetting. 'That's what will happen to vulnerable people everywhere, if given the official sanction of a not guilty verdict. You stop being productive –' She blows out the candle.

The hose operator is disowned by the pressure group to which he belongs, but appears on a daytime chat show to argue the case for the defence, heckled by bereaved relatives who couldn't get seats in court.

'Those candles were in pain, man. They needed sheets of glass just to protect them from the wind. It was a merciful release.'

An egg arcs down from the stalls and impacts on his jeans. Without missing a beat he says, 'And battery farming as well, that's just another symptom of a sick society. It's all connected. Your values are warped if –'

You switch over from this knockabout debate just in time to hear the judge ask the jury to reach a verdict. Your finger hovers over the remote as he speaks. 'Please press one for not guilty, two for guilty, three to hear evidence again . . .'

THE DETECTIVE AND THE BLUNT INSTRUMENT

Lyn McConchie

Luisa surveyed her paperwork and moaned softly. Being a detective in the Los Angeles Homicide and Burglary Squad was an interesting job – at the time when her paperwork wasn't climbing towards the ceiling. What she needed right now was a crime. That way she could get out of the office and turn some of her reports over to Andi to be typed. She glanced up as the phone rang. Her hand shot out to seize it in hope. Yes! A murder. She sighed, grabbed up half a dozen of the reports and dumped them on Andi's desk as she passed.

'These have to be typed up by tomorrow night. I can't stay. Call me if there's anything you need clarified in any of them.'

Andi grinned. 'That's what I'm here for.'

'I know.' Luisa gave her a nod as she hurried for the door. She did know but Andi was always busy too and Luisa hated to add to it. If she was going to be in the office she felt she should do some of her own paperwork. Packett had his car waiting by the door since it had started to rain heavily.

'Where to?'

'Out Canyon Road, turn left and it's that unsealed road that goes right on over past Washout. The woman there said her husband had been murdered by an intruder. She said she's in a wheelchair, she has no car, she's terrified and could we come as fast as possible.'

'She rang us direct?' Packett said with interest. 'Most people either ring the emergency number or their local station.'

Luisa nodded, that had struck her too. Once they arrived and could ask, the explanation was simple. Mrs Alston had originally been Patrolwoman Mary McCarthy. Luisa vaguely remembered the case. Mary had been on the beat almost six years and was an up and coming officer. She'd only been married a year when in attempting to stop a getaway car she'd been run down and dragged half a block. She'd chosen to retire on a part-pension. Not that the set-up here looked like someone on very little money.

'So, you heard your husband yelling, then he went quiet and you saw someone running away. You followed them a short distance trying to see who it was. Then you returned to find your husband battered to death. You called us at once. Is that all correct?'

'Yes. I might as well tell you up front. Mike got into arguments with people. He liked to control things and he got furious if he couldn't.' She spun her small electric scooter. 'He wrote to complain about a lot of things. He had files you might like to look over.'

Packett was checking the scene, making notes, and keeping an eye out for the team's arrival. Luisa studied the sprawled body. The man had been good-looking. About thirty, black hair, blue eyes, wiry body. He'd been well-dressed in casual clothes. It looked as if two blows had been struck but they'd know more about that once the pathologist had done his job. Rain drummed on the roof. This far into the hills it had started raining here a hour earlier. Two magnificent dogs in large wired-in runs were barking angrily at Packett. Luisa followed Mary to the next room where the woman opened a large cabinet. Inside neat ranks of files were colour-coded.

'Here. That will give you a few suspects.'

Luisa picked out several letters at random and read them. It certainly would. She dug a little deeper. Each file contained a last sheet headed 'Resolution'. Some were filled out. In most cases it looked as if the 'Resolution' would provide some wonderful motives. She made a rough estimate of the files and groaned. At a guess there must be several hundred people with cause to dislike Michael Alston.

She remembered something she'd wanted to ask. 'Isn't it very isolated up here not to have a car?'

'We both have cars. I had an accident with mine and Mike's is in for servicing.'

'Oh, thank you.' Luisa studied another letter and became engrossed. Mary had left Luisa to get on with the job. She'd take the opportunity to check up on the woman herself. She rang a source who always knew things.

'Mary McCarthy? Oh, yes. That's the one who was run down by bank-robbers. She was left in a wheelchair, right?'

'Right. I need to know what else you can tell me. For instance there seems to be a fair amount of money around. Whose is that?'

The source chuckled. 'It's Mary's and I bet her husband doesn't like that a lot. I met him a few times. He's the sort of man who just has to control whatever's happening. Mary won the money in a lottery before she met him. She was smart. It was a lot, a real big strike. She put it all into a trust. She gets the interest but once she dies the capital gets spread around. Some to family, some to charities she was interested in and some to our Police fund. She made him sign a pre-nuptial agreement. If he leaves her he gets nothing. If he stays he gets to live very well.'

'What if she throws him out?'

'Same thing. He gets nothing.'

'What if she dies?'

'As I understand it, he gets what she's left him in the will. About a million plus the property they live in. That's worth a fair amount.'

Luisa looked around her. 'Another million, I'd say. Maybe more depending on how far these grounds stretch.'

'Fifty acres I'm told.'

Luisa bit back a gasp. Fifty acres! Okay, so right now the city hadn't reached here although the land was within county boundaries. But there was a road, and in another ten years the land would be worth tens of millions. But then, in ten years a will could be changed. After learning this she wouldn't be surprised if Alston had murdered his wife. But he hadn't.

'When did you see Mary last?'

There was a long pause. Then, 'You know, it must be several months. She used to drop in every few weeks. She's been ill a lot of course. She seems to catch everything going and her husband liked her to himself. But I know Jack was saying he hadn't been out there for a while either. He's her old partner.'

Something clicked in the back of Luisa's mind. 'Check around. See who has seen her lately or who saw her last and when.'

She hung up slowly then went to work her way through Michael Alston's files. Almost every one yielded names which would have to be checked out. But Luisa was waiting to talk to the pathologist and read all the crime scene reports. Once they'd arrived she sat down to read quietly. The pathology report was simple. Two blows. The first one would have stunned the man although he appeared to have stayed on his feet. The next one had smashed his skull. The instrument had been something like a flat-sided baseball bat. Long and heavy. Neither blow had broken the skin so there'd be no blood to be found as evidence. The perp was probably around five eleven and quite strong from the angle and power of the blows. He'd struck the first from behind, the second from the front.

Luisa turned to the scene reports and Mary's statement. Mary had no idea where the man had come from. Possibly he'd left a car down lower and hiked up on foot. From the very brief glimpse she'd had he was around six foot, white male, with dark shaggy hair. She hadn't been able to see if he was carrying anything as he plunged into the surrounding brush. The reports from the people living down around the start of the road were odd. Several of the women had been home all day. None had seen or heard a car around the relevant times.

They'd had the dogs in. None had appeared able to find a trail. If the man had walked all the way in he should have left some-thing, but then, it had been raining hard. She turned back to Mary's statement. Why hadn't the woman let her own dogs chase the man? Here it was. Mary had stated that she'd gone after the intruder a short distance, then gone to her husband, seen he was dead and rung the Police. The rain had started a good half an hour before the killing. She'd felt it better not to let the dogs out in case they damaged any trail and also there was a high fence around the inner property. To have the dogs chase the man she'd have to go down and open the gate. Yes, there was an electric eye which usually did that. It had stopped working days earlier and her husband hadn't got in someone to fix it as yet.

Amongst the papers there was one from Packett who'd talked to a woman responsible for the Alston medical records. She hadn't been specific, just mentioned that Mary did seem to have had a number of minor accidents lately. Luisa plowed through other reports starting to develop unpleasant suspicions. No one who knew Mike Alston had liked him. A good many people had very good reason to actively dislike him. And perhaps a woman who had to live with a man like that, even be partly dependent on him, might come to like him still less. Which brought up a point about their financial set-up she wanted to check.

Her source was talkative. 'I told you. If she tosses him out he gets nothing.'

'What if he sues on the grounds he'd done nothing?'

'Well, that could get a little more complicated. If he convinced a Judge he'd been dumped maliciously and without cause, he could be entitled to half.'

'What? Half of everything?'

'Ah huh. Even the trust if he got the right judge. It isn't as if it's family money.'

Luisa hung up thinking about that. A smart man. A man who liked to live well and to control everything around him. He couldn't leave or he'd lose out. He couldn't do anything to get himself thrown out. But if he could make it look as if he'd been badly treated or if his wife died – or if he combined those ideas. What if he'd started isolating Mary, keeping her friends out, keeping her in. Causing apparent accidents. If she did realize what was going on and forced him to leave he'd have a good claim so long as she couldn't prove anything. And if she didn't realize in time – he'd inherit.

That would mean Mary had killed him and that was impossible. They'd checked. The electric scooter she used could travel well over smooth ground and inside the house. But Mary could never have used it to dispose of the weapon. Still. Just in case, she'd eliminate Mary from her inquiries. Elwood reported back on that a couple of days later. Packett was off chasing up some of those Mike Alston had injured.

'I can't find anything except more evidence this Alston was a bastard. It looks as if either he was trying to set someone up for a big lawsuit or he was trying to kill his wife. The woman's been electrocuted once, had two car accidents and several falls. Nothing provable but if it was me it was happening to I'd have got suspicious a long time back. The seat on that scooter of hers can be cranked up so that she's the right height to have hit him. That's so she can reach things on high shelves more easily. The batteries provide the power for that as well as movement.

'But there's no weapon, Lieutenant. I had the team in and we scoured the place. If it was there we'd have found it. The pathologist said that even with the skin unbroken if it had been wood there'd have been traces of some sort. Nothing's been burned. I checked that scooter and the wheels were just normally dirty. Nothing like what they'd have been if she'd gone down to the gate. They hadn't been cleaned in the last couple of days either.'

Lusia nodded. She thought of that herself. Mary could have let the dogs out with orders to carry a weapon well away before dropping it.

'I checked out the electric eye too. It was out when you arrived and according to the servicemen it seemed to go out a lot. He wondered if kids were coming up and vandalizing it. He repaired it the day after Alston was killed and he's confirmed it wasn't working when he saw it.'

'Okay, thanks. Looks as if Packett may be the one with leads.'

The trouble was that there were too many of them. At times it looked to Luisa as if half of L.A. had cause to dislike the late Mr Alston. Mary's sister had moved in with two small children. They'd added a maid whose husband lived with her and would do minor repairs for cash. Luisa called, admired the dogs, chatted casually to the sister, and considered possibilities. They'd eliminated most of the suspects. Those still around had motive and no alibi but there was no proof either. It was Luisa's belief that Mike Alston had been trying to kill his wife – or collect big on a lawsuit. Either way he'd have come out with a lot of cash as opposed to the nothing he'd get if he just left.

Mary wasn't a fool. She'd been a good cop, street-smart and

intelligent. She must have known what was going on even if it had taken a while. How would she react? If she tried to divorce Mike without proof of any wrong-doing he'd have taken her to the cleaners. Mary had grown up with a father who loved cars, and taught her all he knew. The garage which had checked her car after the accident said they could prove nothing but in their opinion it could have been tampered with. Mary could have guessed that too. She'd have seen all the options Luisa saw.

If Mary wanted to keep the money and her life they only came down to one. Michael Alston had to die. But where was the weapon? Without that they had no case and no hope of the CPS ever considering one. Luisa shuffled the papers thoughtfully. Even if they found a weapon they were unlikely to convict Mary unless the weapon was something peculiarly hers. There were too many other red herrings a good lawyer could drag in. She'd leave things alone. If they found a weapon she could act. Until then she'd only make a fool of herself and alienate a lot of good cops trying to prove Mary had anything to do with it.

Over the next few weeks the case petered out. No new leads, no new suspects. It ended up in pending a month later. Luisa had sent Elwood back one last time. They'd searched the brush with dogs and found nothing. They'd waited until everyone but Mary was out and gone through the house, out-buildings and grounds again with a fine-tooth-comb. Mary had sat, bland-faced on her scooter and said nothing. Luisa had even checked with doctors. They'd been positive. Mary had considerable upper-body strength and could have struck the blows. But there was no way she could walk.

If she ever had used a weapon she could not have disposed of it. Three meticulous searches had found nothing that could be proved to have been it. How could a crippled woman who couldn't walk, couldn't leave the immediate grounds, have disposed of a weapon? The simple answer was, she couldn't. No matter what Luisa suspected, she had to be wrong. Up in the hills the Alston property was for sale. Mary was taking her mother and sister on a cruise, then returning to buy elsewhere. The dogs would go to kennels.

Luisa called one last time. Mary was polite, but casual. Yes, she understood the police had been able to arrest no one. That was how it happened sometimes, wasn't it. She shrugged and for a fraction of a second something showed in her eyes. Mike had probably brought it on himself. He didn't treat people very well. A lot of them hadn't liked him much. She showed her visitor out. Luisa went quietly. But unable to leave it alone she continued to think about the case sometimes when she was home.

The solution came to her finally when she was around enjoying a barbecue with friends. They had dogs, big ones like Mary's beasts. Jerri was in the kitchen as Luisa watched.

'I'll just feed the dogs. That way they won't be begging while we eat.' She opened the refrigerator. 'Darn, I forgot to thaw any meat. Oh, well. They can have some of the old stand-by. They don't mind that being warm.' She turned to remove an item from the freezer. Luisa's eyes opened wider.

'What's that?'

Jerri looked down at the length of something which looked like plastic-wrapped wood. 'This? It's dog food. Because it's flatter than most types it thaws in the microwave quickly.' She grinned as she tucked it into the machine. 'There's another advantage to this type. The latest kind has edible wrapping as well.'

Luisa stared at the dog food. The flattened roll was over two foot long. At one end there was a long strong-looking loop of pale dirty-brown string to carry it. The wrapper said it weighed three kilos. Frozen solid, held by the string loop and swung, it would make a killing weapon. Somehow Luisa thought it had.

'How long does it take to thaw a whole length?'

Jerri looked slightly puzzled. 'About half an hour, why?'

'I just wondered.' Not that she was wondering any longer. Mary had waited for both cars to be away and the gate inoperable. Had her husband had another accident in mind? Or had it been Mary who'd damaged the gate a few days earlier that time? It could even have been Mary every time for that. It didn't matter. She'd waited for it to rain. Then she'd cranked the scooter seat up high, taken the length of frozen dog food from the freezer and nailed her husband. She'd claimed she'd started after the killer for a short distance before returning. To have had to traverse half the house to reach her husband after that.

Instead she must have put the dog food into the microwave at once and waited as long as she dared. Then she'd rung Homicide. Of course she'd rung them. Her own police station was closer. She'd want as much time as possible. It had taken them more than the half hour to reach her on top of any time she'd already gained. Luisa grinned unwillingly. They had no hope of proving any of it. She was sure Mary would have herself covered as to where and how she'd got the dog food. Even if they showed that she'd had some once it proved nothing.

However Luisa knew. The other proof too would be long gone but she remembered now. Mary had met them at the door with her hands empty. Later as she talked alone with Luisa in her husband's study she'd been fiddling with something. Nothing noticeable at the time. Nothing memorable. Just a length of brownish rather grubby-looking string.

WHEN I'M DEAD AND GONE

Martin Edwards

'I hate to think that he might die on such a beautiful day,' said Sylvia Reid.

Sun was streaming through the office window, but dismay clouded her pleasant features. She had been qualified as a solicitor for exactly one month, not long enough to learn to take each client's misfortunes in her stride before moving on to the next buff folder and the next troubling tale.

Death, Harry Devlin wanted to tell her, hurt as much in the depth of the darkest night as at the height of an Indian summer. Too often in the past he had come face-to-face with death – the death of those he had loved as well as of those he had good cause to loathe – and he knew that whether sudden or slow, its constant companions were anger, pain, and despair.

But there was work to be done and all he said was: 'I hate to think that he might die before we've managed to write out his will.'

She frowned. 'No need to worry. Lucy has already typed up the engrossment. Would you like to look it over?'

Harry loosened his tie while he thought about it. Making the most of the good weather, his partner Jim Crusoe had taken his wife and children off to Blackpool, leaving Sylvia in charge of the firm's non-contentious department for the first time since her admission. In truth, she had understood more about the law of property, wills, and probate three months into her traineeship than Harry ever would, but he could not escape the uncomfortable feeling that she still expected him to offer words of wisdom about the legal small print, as well as about how to cope with clients who were despondent, defeated, or about to die.

'If you don't mind,' he said awkwardly.

Sylvia handed him the crisp foolscap sheets and studied his face for a reaction. She was a serious girl and so anxious to do well in her career that Harry marvelled at her decision to stay on with them rather than moving to a rival firm which could offer more training, prestige, and money than Crusoe and Devlin ever could.

He scanned the will paragraph by paragraph. Leonard Justinian (for Heaven's sake!) Routley had not indulged in complex testamentary dispositions, but Harry did not want her to think he was simply going through the motions of glancing at her work. And in any event, since Routley was apparently a solicitor, he would expect the will to be word perfect.

'Pass me *Ibbotson*, please.'

She slid the massive bulk of *Ibbotson on Inheritance* in front of him. It was the nineteenth edition of a monograph which had first appeared when Victoria was in nappies; within the profession, it was better known as *Everything Your Clients Always Wanted to Know About Wills, But Couldn't Afford to Ask.*

Words of warning were uttered on every page. *The draftsman of a will is enjoined to manifest the highest standards of professional care . . . he must regard the desires of the testator as paramount . . . although before death a misapprehension will be susceptible to correction, thereafter, even where all the beneficiaries are sui juris, ambiguous provisions may need to be the subject of a ruling from the court.* The orotund phrasing did not conceal the menace of the message. Harry knew that to err might be human, but it would also expose the firm to a negligence writ. In Jim's absence, they couldn't run the slightest risk of making a mistake.

'I was surprised that Mr Routley hadn't already made a will,' Sylvia said as he leafed through the precedents with what he hoped was a knowledgeable air. 'After all, solicitors know better than anyone else about the problems that can arise on an intestacy. It seems slapdash.'

Harry couldn't help blushing. 'Tell you the truth, I haven't made one myself.'

She goggled at him. 'Why ever not? Superstition?'

'Simply never got round to it.'

He might have added, but didn't, that he had no one close enough to leave all his things to. Besides, who would thank him for a roomful of dog-eared murder mystery paperbacks and scratched sixties LPs which had never been translated to compact disc? And who exactly would mourn him, a man without a wife or family, when he was dead and gone?

Wanting to change the subject, he reached back in his memory for a scrap of legal trivia. 'Anyway, lawyers writing their own wills are notoriously inept. Wasn't it Sergeant Maynard who decided to benefit the profession with a will that raised most of the problems of inheritance law that had perplexed him during his lifetime?'

Sylvia laughed. 'At least Mr Routley's instructions were easy to follow. He wrote them out for the matron at the old people's home to read to me over the phone.'

'Why the urgency? What's the matter with him?'

'Heart trouble, the matron said, complicated by diabetes. Apparently he had a bad do last night. The doctor examined him this morning and says he could go at any time. With the late summer holiday coming up, it's a long weekend, and the poor old man started to get worried that he might not have a chance to put his affairs in order by the time Tuesday came around.'

Harry glanced at a passage in the textbook cautioning of the dangers associated with intellectual incapacity. He had a nightmarish vision of sitting for hour after hour at Routley's bedside, trying to take advantage of a fleeting lucid interval. 'You're sure he's still compos mentis?'

'I did press her about that, especially as we have never acted for him in the past. But she said the doctor was quite definite. And when I go over there later this afternoon to have Mr Routley sign the will, I'll talk it through with him, to make sure I'm happy that he knows what he's doing. In the meantime, his wishes seem clear enough.'

'I see this man he refers to as his good friend, Parbold, pretty well scoops the pool. You know what they say: where there's a will, there's a relative. Has Routley no family at all?'

'The matron says not. He's a bachelor, and when I asked if, nevertheless, he might have any children, she sounded shocked and said that with a gentleman of that calibre, it was absolutely out of the question.'

'Stranger things have happened, but never mind. So there's no one else who might have a possible claim on the estate?'

'She's positive from what he has said to her that there are no brothers or sisters, and she isn't aware of any cousins, however many times removed, let alone nephews or nieces. So that leaves the way clear for Walter Parbold.'

'A bachelor's old boyfriend, perhaps?'

'Maybe, though the matron was so brisk and businesslike, I didn't dare to ask.'

'How much is the estate worth?'

'Too little to attract inheritance tax. There are bank and building society accounts, National Savings, and a few privatisation shares. But not more than sixty thousand in total. A tidy sum, but hardly a fortune.'

'The prices some of these homes charge,' said Harry, 'he probably went in there a millionaire. So – at least there's no problem about covering the specific bequests?'

'None at all. You can see there are several small pecuniary legacies to other residents at the home. He intends to leave his gold watch to his doctor, a local G.P. whose name is Berkeley. All rather trivial in money terms, but I suppose the little things matter a great deal when you come towards the end.'

'Parbold's the sole executor, I notice.'

'Yes, no scope for appointing Jim and yourself, I'm afraid.'

Unspoken was the acknowledgement that a solicitor did not make money out of drawing a will. Profit came with the work on the probate. Routley had no doubt decided that his affairs were easy enough to administer. If Parbold was intelligent and capable, there might be little need to involve a solicitor. And as a lawyer himself, Routley would know better than most what a hole legal fees could make in any estate. On the other hand, if Parbold turned out to be elderly or inefficient, the odds were that he would soon find the burden of executorship too much to cope with alone. The price of professional help was often worth paying. Harry sensed there might still be an opportunity for further business.

'Did you find out whether Parbold is willing to act?'

'Yes, the matron was sure about that. Parbold often pops in to see his pal and he was happy to help.'

'What if Parbold dies before Routley?'

Sylvia flushed. 'I – I didn't ask. I assumed that, since Mr
Routley is in such a poor state, the question simply wouldn't
arise. Do you disagree?'

'Even a sick man may linger on for much longer than anyone
would expect,' Harry pointed out, 'while a perfectly healthy
person can be run over by a bus at any time – especially in view
of the way they are driven round the streets of Liverpool.'

'Shall I give the matron a ring?'

'Not a bad idea.'

She checked the number in the book, but a couple of minutes
spent listening to the answering tone convinced them both that
the Mersey Haven Rest Home was woefully understaffed.
Perhaps all the caregivers were sitting outside, soaking up
the sun.

'What shall we do?' Sylvia could not conceal her anxiety. In
Jim's absence, Routley's will had offered a chance for her to
shine, and now she was afraid that if the unexpected happened
and the residuary gift to Parbold lapsed, it would be her fault.

Harry closed *Ibbotson* with a decisive smack. 'It's too lovely to
stay inside any longer. I don't have any more appointments this
afternoon, and I wouldn't mind making an early start to the
weekend by running over to Otterspool.'

Crestfallen, Sylvia said, 'So you're taking over the file?'

'Not at all. I can scarcely tell a codicil from a cold supper. But if
you're dealing with a retired solicitor, you may find it useful to
have me come along. If any last-minute redrafting is necessary,
we can retype the will at the home. I presume they must have a
typewriter, if not a word processor.'

'And when the poor old man's ready to sign,' she said, brightening, 'we can act as witnesses, if need be. As a matter of fact, the
matron did enquire about that.'

Harry got to his feet. He had become interested in this new
client, even experienced a certain fellow feeling for him. Maybe
when they met, Harry would see in Routley his own reflection in
forty years' time, a retired solicitor with no wife or kids, just a bit
of money in the bank, a few momentoes to leave to acquaintances,
and a host of memories that would die as soon as he did. But none

of this could he explain to the earnest young woman who saw the forthcoming meeting as so much valuable experience.

'Let's move, then,' he said. 'I wouldn't like the old bugger to breathe his last while we're queuing at the traffic lights by Jericho Lane.'

In the years when Gladstone reckoned that peace in Eastern Europe and an answer to the Irish Question were just around the corner, the yellow brick villa which now housed the Mersey Haven Rest Home must have belonged to one of his wealthiest fellow Liverpudlians. At that time, the owner could scarcely have imagined the day would dawn when a development of poky semis would encroach upon the wooded grounds of his home and when on the river which it overlooked not a single oceangoing ship could be seen. Now the building seemed an anachronism. So long had passed since a single family lived here in splendour. Its gentility had faded, and it had become simply somewhere people came to live in peace and quiet before they finally died.

As Harry swung his MG into the drive, he slowed to read the Gothic lettering on a garish yellow signboard.

'High-class accommodation for senior citizens,' recited Sylvia, 'with nursing care provided by qualified staff, supervised by the resident proprietress and matron in charge, Mrs A. Katsikas.' She paused and added, 'I suppose Mr Routley's lucky he can afford it.'

'Not so lucky at the moment,' said Harry, and they both fell silent, contemplating the prospect of advanced years, infirmity, and the black abyss beyond.

He parked on hardstanding at the side of the home, and they headed on foot for the main entrance, past a sun lounge tacked onto the east wing by the kind of builder who would happily have stuck a sauna on the side of the Anglican cathedral. As he walked by the windows, Harry was conscious that he was being scrutinised by an old woman with watery eyes; he saw another half-dozen ancients baking under the glass, fast asleep with their heads lolling on shrunken chests.

At close quarters the building, like its residents, was showing its age. The brickwork needed repointing, and paint was peeling from the woodwork. The front door yielded to Harry's touch and he led the way inside. A small desk in the hall bearing a notice marked ENQUIRIES was untenanted; Harry rang the bell.

At once a wizened face belonging to the owner of the watery eyes poked around the side of the door from the hall to the conservatory. 'Have you any idea who I am?' she demanded.

Harry gave a helpless smile and was forced to admit that he did not.

'I can tell you – in the strictest confidence, mind – that I am Princess Coralie of Monte Carlo,' the old lady said. 'Am I right in thinking I have the pleasure of addressing none other than His Royal Highness, Crown Prince Rupert of Eastern Bohemia?'

Harry had been called many things in his life, but he'd never before had the misfortune to be mistaken for royalty. Aware that Sylvia was controlling her mirth with the utmost difficulty, he was saved from the need to reply by the approach of a plump, comfortable-looking woman in a blue uniform. At the sight of her, an expression of truculent dignity crossed the wrinkled face.

'Hush! Not a word!' the old lady hissed. 'No one must know our secret.'

Harry winked at her and she vanished as swiftly as she had appeared.

'I see you've met our princess,' said the plump woman with a smile. 'You're not a relative, are you, love?'

Harry shook his head. 'I don't like to admit it, but no blue blood flows through my veins. My name's Harry Devlin and I'm a solicitor.' He paused, trying to reconcile the woman's broad Lancashire vowels with the exotic name on the signboard outside. 'You're not Mrs Katsikas, by any chance?'

'Guilty,' she said, nothing his puzzled look with amusement. 'They call me Ada, a good Red Rose name, but my ex-husband was Greek. I met him on a package tour of Corfu. Should have realised that holiday romances don't last much longer than the average sun tan.'

She gave a laugh and shook him by the hand, her ringless fingers pressing into his flesh. 'You're younger than most solicitors I ever came across. To say nothing of your lady friend. Are lawyers like policemen, getting younger all the time?'

Daunted by her roguish manner, Harry said hastily, 'This is my colleague Sylvia Reid. You spoke to her earlier today on behalf of Mr Routley. I thought it would be helpful if we both came. Firstly, in case there's a need to make any last-minute changes to the will. Secondly, to provide a couple of independent witnesses. I gather you thought that might be necessary.'

The matron became more serious. 'Yes, given that we are very short-staffed this afternoon. The holiday weekend, you know. People like to make it into a decent break. But our guests still need to be looked after, of course, and there is some urgency in this case, in view of poor Mr Routley's condition.'

'I understand he may not survive the weekend?'

'That's right. Dr Berkeley was pessimistic this morning. Frankly, something could happen at any moment. I think Mr Routley senses that himself, which is why I needed to call on your services without delay. I hope the instructions were clear?'

'Fine, fine. Is it possible for me to see my client now?'

'Yes, I was with him in his room when your car pulled up outside. He had a sleep after lunch, but he woke up half an hour ago.'

'His mind is still in good shape, I understand?' said Harry.

'Oh yes, there's no trace of dementia, and the drugs he has been taking make him drowsy at times, but don't have any damaging effect on the brain. I know he has been thinking for a while about making his will. It preyed on his mind that he hadn't done so before. But at least it's not a hasty decision. He's very much at peace with himself.'

Harry had never been able to grasp the idea of coming to terms with death. His own end would, he felt sure, fill him with terror as it approached. For him, life was something to cling to and fight for, whatever the cost. He and Sylvia followed Ada Katsikas upstairs in silence.

The matron directed them to a room above the front door. Knocking softly, she said, 'Leonard, it's Ada. The solicitor is here at last.' Turning back to them, she whispered. 'I'll just make sure he's presentable, then I'll call you in.'

A couple of minutes later she reappeared and gave an encouraging nod. 'Yes, I've just made him comfy. He's frail, of course, but able to talk quite clearly. I don't suppose you want me to sit in, but if you do need me for any reason, please don't hesitate to press the button by the side of his bed.'

Leonard Routley lay propped up in his bed. He was solidly built with a good head of grey hair; but for the chalky whiteness of his cheeks, Harry would not have guessed he was close to death.

'Mr Routley, I'm Harry Devlin and this is Sylvia Reid, who works with me. Thanks for instructing us. I'm sorry to hear you're not so grand.'

The old man waved away the words of sympathy with a flap of his hand. In a wheezing but audible voice, he said, 'I know the state I'm in, Mr Devlin. I'm not long for this world, and all I want is to get things settled.'

'You're a fellow solicitor, I gather?'

'For my sins,' he grunted. 'Have you got the will?'

'Here it is. Do you need me to take you through it?'

'I don't think there's any need. If you'll pass my reading glasses, please.'

He indicated a pair of spectacles lying on his bedside chest along-side a faded black and white photographs. Harry glanced at the blurred image: dark-haired young fellow, tall and erect in mortar-board and gown. The passage of perhaps fifty years had made it hard to recognize the breathless old man from the record of his younger days.

'Your degree ceremony?' Harry asked as he passed the spectacles.

'A long time ago,' mumbled Routley as he began to study the will, tracing his finger along each line as he sought to absorb its sense.

'Leonard *Justinian* Routley,' said Harry. 'Is that right?'

'Afraid so. Damn fool name, never come across it anywhere else. Never understood why my parents ever landed me with it.'

'A family connection with the law, perhaps?'

'God knows. Justin would have been bad enough. What else do we have? Ah yes, small gifts to three of the nicest old crocks here, Raymond, Lavinia, and Charlotte, that's right. And to the good doctor, as well. He's done his best for me. With the rest to Parbold, excellent.'

Harry was troubled by something. Absently, he asked, 'He's an old friend of yours?'

'Feel as if I've known him all my life,' said Routley. 'Though truth to tell, we only met after I moved into this place. First-rate chap, never let you down. Deserves it, I can assure you.'

'I'm sure.'

'Well, everything seems all right. Thank Heaven that's done at last. I know I shouldn't have left it so long.'

'We never take the advice we love to give our clients, do we?' said Harry. 'There's just one thing I'd like to ask.'

'Go on.'

'Don't you think we ought to cover the eventuality that Mr Parbold might predecease you?'

The old man stared at him. 'There's no question of that. Walter's as fit as a fiddle. I'm a sick man. Berkeley hasn't beaten about the bush. He gives me a few days at best. Maybe only a few hours, for all he and I know.'

'I appreciate that, Mr Routley, but accidents can happen when we least expect them. If by some stroke of fact, Mr Parbold were the first to die, you'll know as well as anyone the problems that can arise. No executor, no residuary legatee. Messy. I gather you don't have any family.'

'None whatsoever.'

'So applying the intestacy rules to your residue wouldn't achieve anything. The Crown would take the bulk of your estate.'

For a moment Routley bowed his head. He seemed to be dismayed that the point had not occurred to him. 'Perhaps you're right. I suppose I'm not thinking straight. What do you suggest?'

'Is there anyone else you would like to benefit if the worst came to worst and Mr Parbold did not survive you?'

'I suppose . . .' said Routley slowly, 'the doctor would be as good a man as any.'

'You have his full name?'

'Giles Alexander Berkeley,' said Sylvia unexpectedly. 'He happens to be my and my mother's G.P. I've always been rather in awe of him, but there's no doubt he has an excellent reputation. You couldn't be in better hands, Mr Routley.'

'I realise that. All the same, I don't want any delay.'

'No need for any,' she said. 'We can make the necessary alternations in a matter of a few minutes if Mrs Katsikas will let us use her typewriter.'

Harry pressed the bedside bell and the matron came running in. 'No problems, I hope?'

'A minor alteration, that's all.'

The plump woman gave her patient a startled look. 'I hope I didn't make a mistake in writing down your instructions, Leonard. We went through them so painstakingly. I can't believe it's a good idea to chop and change at the last minute.'

'It's nothing, Ada. A technicality, that's all.'

Harry explained the point and asked if Sylvia could type the amendments on the spot.

'Of course, of course. I'm only relieved it's something minor that can easily be attended to. And Dr Berkeley's a good man, even if the point is – shall we say, academic? I know how much Leonard has set his heart on finalising the will this afternoon. Would you like to come this way, Miss Reid?'

'Where did you practise?' Harry asked Routley when they were alone.

'Oh, I was with a small outfit in Greater London,' said Routley. 'You wouldn't have heard of them. And besides, it all seems a long time ago.'

'So you're not a local man?'

'I was raised in Wigan, but we moved down South when I was in my teens. My widowed sister stayed up here and when I retired I decided to move in with her. She died eighteen months ago and it was then that I decided to come to the Mersey Haven.'

'Have you been happy here?'

'First-class place. The matron talks a lot, but she's marvellous. And this is where I met Walter Parbold. Listen, would you mind drawing the curtains? The sun is so strong, it's making me feel faint.'

'Was he in residence when you first arrived?' asked Harry as he moved to the window, but when he turned again, Routley's eyes had closed. He leaned over the bed and was glad to hear steady breathing from its sleepy occupant.

A couple of minutes later, the matron ushered Sylvia back in. 'All done and dusted, Mr Devlin.'

Harry glanced at the retyped will before passing it to Routley, whose eyes had just begun to open.

'Please make sure you're happy with it before I ask you to sign.'

The old man read through his final dispositions before giving a satisfied nod.

'It reflects my wishes. You've done a good job.'

'Sylvia here did all the work.'

The young woman coloured. 'It was very straightforward.'

'At least there were no family complications,' said Harry, 'no hotchpot.'

Routley shook his head. 'A will's an important document. I wouldn't want mine to be a hotchpotch.'

Harry took a fountain pen out of his pocket and watched carefully as his client scratched out his signature with a shaky hand. Then he and Sylvia signed their names underneath and added their descriptions and addresses.

'Do you wish me to keep the original in our archives?'

'Thank you, but no. It will be safe enough here.'

'In that case, if there is a photocopier downstairs, perhaps I could take a copy for my office records?'

'With pleasure,' said Ada Katsikas, beaming. 'Now, I rather fancy you're tired after all this excitement, Leonard. Not used to visitors, are you? I'll show Mr Devlin and Miss Reid out, and I'll bring the will back to you in a few minutes.'

'Goodbye,' said Harry. 'I'm always glad to meet a professional colleague. Perhaps I'll see you again sometime.'

The old man gave a weak smile. 'I'm afraid I don't think I'll manage that, Mr Devlin. But thank you both for your prompt help in my hour of need.'

When they were back in the car, Sylvia said, 'Are you all right?'

'Any reason why I shouldn't be?'

'It's just that you went rather quiet while we were in the rest home and something still seems to be gnawing at you.'

He thought for a moment. 'Let's say I always feel uneasy in the presence of the dying.'

After dropping her off at the station, he did not drive away at once. Rather, he sat in the car park for twenty minutes, letting his thoughts roam. He hadn't told Sylvia the whole truth, but the things that tantalised him were trivial, and he knew it might be unwise to make too much of them. The sensible course was simply to go home and forget about Leonard Routley's will until the time came to send in the bill. But he had never been good about taking the sensible courses in life.

Doubts were lurking in his mind; he could not rid himself of them. Past experience had taught him that he would have no peace until he found answers to the questions he found puzzling. Although, if he were mistaken, he faced at best embarrassment, at worst a charge of professional misconduct, he knew that he had to act – and without delay. He could not live with any other choice.

This time he parked half a mile away from the Mersey Haven Rest Home and made his way there on foot. On the earlier visit he had noticed that a footpath and cycle track had been carved between the housing development and the grounds of the home, and he followed its curving course for a couple of hundred yards until he reached a stretch out of sight of both the houses and pedestrians on the main road.

Conveniently, the new featheredge fence which separated the rest home from the path had already been broken down and there were signs that someone had trampled under the horse chestnut trees which fringed the grounds. For once Harry found himself sending up a silent prayer of thanks for juvenile delinquency. He slid through the gap and, with head bowed to avoid the low looping branches, hurried around the perimeter. Soon he realized he had arrived at a point directly behind the central part of the building and perhaps fifty yards distant from it. On this occasion he had no intention of going in by the front entrance; he must check covertly to find out whether his guess was wide of the mark. He could see dustbins and a gleaming Range Rover, which belonged, he guessed, to Mrs Katsikas. But what caught his eye was a window on the ground floor which someone had left invitingly open.

There was nothing for it but to hope that no one would see him as he broke cover. He dashed to the window, stopping up short of the brick beside it. Panting, he thought ruefully back to his footballing days, when he'd always had the ability to race up from midfield and lose his marker before meeting a cross pulled back from the wing. Nowadays, he would struggle to keep up with the average referee.

No matter. He had reached his destination, and when he stole a quick glance through the window, his luck held. The room was deserted. A moment later he was inside.

Fussy ornaments and knickknacks covered every inch of shelf space and there was a faint whiff of perfume in the air. Even before he heard a light approaching tread in the corridor outside, he realized he'd entered a woman's bedroom.

He could see nowhere to hide. No convenient cupboard or empty wardrobe. He wasn't even able to squeeze under the bed: it was a drawer divan. Holding his breath, he hoped the footsteps would pass by the door and disappear into the distance.

Instead, they paused for a second and then the door swung open.

'Crown Prince Rupert! This is a surprise!'

Harry's heart sank. He would almost rather have been confronted by Ada Katsikas wielding a rolling pin than Princess Coralie of Monte Carlo in coquettish mood.

'Your Royal Highness,' he said, edging round the bed as he tried desperately to remember a chunk of Anthony Hope dialogue. 'I must apologise most humbly for this unwarranted intrusion.'

'Rupert, my dear, you don't have to say sorry to little *me!*'

'You see, I had hoped to leave my card, suggesting that perhaps we could have a longer conversation later this evening.'

The watery eyes were bright with excitement as he moved closer to the door. 'What a marvellous idea!'

He had almost made it. 'Shall we say nine tonight – in the sun lounge?'

'Splendid!'

'Until then, let us say nothing!' He placed his finger to his lips and felt like crying with relief when she nodded and waved a delicate farewell as he peered outside and, seeing the coast was clear, made good his escape.

The corridor led him straight back to the main hall. No one was about. He took the stairs two at a time and within seconds he was standing outside Leonard Routley's door. He listened for a moment, then put his head round and looked inside.

The room was deserted.

He saw that the bed had been remade. There were now half a dozen photographs crammed on top of the bedside table, including the degree picture that Harry had seen on his previous visit. The rest showed a man at different points in his life. There were two studio portraits, one that seemed to have been taken at Ascot, and another where he was shaking hands with a youthful-looking Duke of Edinburgh. The rest were less blurred than the degree photo.

He heard movement and voices outside. No question, they were coming closer. For the second time in five minutes he found himself looking round desperately for a hiding place. Once again he was out of luck.

You would never have made it as an Anthony Hope hero, after all, he muttered to himself.

He had no choice but to brazen it out. Standing by the bed, his arms folded, he watched and waited as the door swung slowly open.

Ada Katsikas was wheeling a frail old man in a chair. For all his pallor, Harry recognised him at once as the man in the photographs. Quite different from the tall chap who had his hand on the matron's shoulder and who, when his now florid cheeks had been coated in white makeup an hour earlier, had been introduced as Leonard Routley.

The matron and her companion came to a sudden halt, their faces drenched in horror at the sight of Harry. Only the old man in the chair, his head lolling to one side, was unmoved.

'Next time you impersonate a lawyer,' said Harry to the man who was not Leonard Routley, 'you ought to mug up more on the jargon we use. As we say in our profession, *res ipsa loquitur*, Mr Walter Parbold.'

'Do you think they actually had murder in mind?' asked Sylvia the following Tuesday. They were sitting in Jim Crusoe's office, with the rain drumming against the windowpanes. The weather had broken in the early hours of Saturday morning and storms had raged the whole weekend long in the best traditions of the British bank holiday.

'Not at all. Both father and daughter were thieves, not killers. Parbold has seen the inside of Walton Jail and Strangeways over the years. Dud cheques, selling dodgy cars, that sort of thing. His daughter doesn't have a record, but the police found she left one or two of the homes where she'd worked as a nurse with scant ceremony after patients' money and belongings started to go missing. Presumably Ada's purchase of the Mersey Haven was funded by their ill-gotten gains.'

'But they couldn't afford the upkeep?' asked Jim.

'Which was why they had to keep their eyes out for a likely mark. Leonard Routley fitted the bill perfectly, because he had plenty of cash, but no relatives who might turn up and start asking awkward questions once he left his estate to a chap he hardly knew.'

'What made you suspect?' asked Sylvia.

'I imagine that his father was a lawyer, too, as his middle name was that of a great Roman jurist.'

'Justinian? I've never heard of him.'

'A sign of the educational times. But I would have expected old Routley to know something about the author of *The Institutes*. And then he seemed to confuse hotchpot with a hotchpotch.'

'I wouldn't even have thought you knew anything about hotchpot,' Jim grunted.

'I'm fine on footnote knowledge, but don't press me for a definition.'

His partner reached for *Ibbotson* and turned to the glossary. '*Hotchpot; a throwing-in to a common lot of property for strict equality of division which requires that advancements to a child be made up to the estate by way of contribution or accounting.*'

'Ah yes,' said Harry, 'it was on the tip of my tongue.'

'I see that once you realised you were dealing with a fake, you could guess the rest,' said Sylvia. 'Ada had cleared out her staff for the afternoon, having arranged for a respectable doctor to confirm that the real Routley was of sound mind . . .'

'He died yesterday, poor old chap. In Ada's room, the police found the will he actually made twenty-five years ago. He had no one he cared much about, so he left everything to a worthy charity. The Distressed Solicitors Association.'

'I keep thinking they ought to make me a grant,' said Jim.

'. . . but why,' Sylvia continued firmly, 'were you so sure that illness hadn't simply caused Routley to forget things that he should have known?'

Harry rubbed his chin. 'I've had more than my share of dealing with death. It has an awful atmosphere all of its own. Horrible, yet unmistakable. But when we walked into that bedroom, my guts didn't churn. I felt fine.'

Outside they heard another rumble of thunder and Harry couldn't help thinking again about the real Leonard Routley and wondering, now that the sad old man was dead, where his soul had gone.

THE SNAKE CHARMER

Janice Law

Almost as soon as he saw the terrible thing that had happened to him, Wilson thought of Bent, Benton Worthy, friend, companion, gambler, lawyer extraordinare. If anyone could help him, Wilson decided, it was Bent, who knew about this sort of thing, and who wouldn't be shocked, not even by the way Dot's head lolled to one side or by the blood or even by the attempt, which, Wilson saw now, should never have been made to rewrite the course of events.

Events had just taken an inexplicable wrong turn. It would be important to convey that to Bent, and old Bent would understand, of course he would, with his roster of clients. The lawyer joked that he was 'Eliot Ness', because he ran the Untouchables – a crack good for a laugh in any suburban living room. If his listeners were in the mood to be serious, Bent could switch gears and talk about Our Legal System and the Right to Counsel in his round, mellow orator's voice. That resonant instrument had a rasp underneath from the vast quantities of good cigars and old bourbon Bent needed to keep in fighting trim, and the distinctive, seductive sound it produced was worth a million dollars to a man with a jury to convince.

Bent would not be put off by the details of the matter, which looked bad, Wilson admitted. The blood, the matted hair, the mashed in front of a Mercedes sedan resting against a phone pole suggested panic and incompetence. But really, looked at another way, those details were in his favour. They showed a certain unfamiliarity, didn't they? They showed that he was not the sort of man to be involved with blood or with the concavity in Dot's skull or with the sound, somehow worse than all the rest, of legs and heels thump, thumping down the front stair.

Had he managed everything perfectly, had there been no mess, no errors, he, Wilson Hargus, would have stood revealed as a cold blooded killer, instead of a victim of circumstances, the only real victim, as he saw it. He'd have to explain that he'd been truly unfortunate.

And he had. Hadn't he warned Dot many times? Hadn't he been patient? He'd explained his position, made everything clear. A man who could make complicated fiscal transactions clear should have been able to get through to Dot. But every time he thought she understood him, every time things were clear and going fine, she would slip away to defy him. In little things, of course, in little things. The first signs, the first hints, are always little things, little things that you have to act on if you want to stay in control and remain on top.

So that was another reason for involving Bent – although, strictly speaking, the lawyer wasn't needed. A Mercedes smashed against a light pole is an accident, a real accident, no matter what happened before. Still, Benton Worthy would be good to have around. Wilson had felt that right away, because Bent understood staying in control. Even when he seemed to be flying, with too many bourbons and too much money riding and a haze of adrenaline in the air, you just had to look at his eyes, and you knew Bent was in there watching all the time. That was the sort of man Wilson would like to be, aimed to be, aimed, really, to exceed, because Bent only knew some things at second hand, while he, Wilson, now had other experiences.

Bent was impressive, nonetheless. Wilson had always enjoyed late nights with Bent, searching out serious action where the bets were big, the girls beautiful, the liquor on the house. Those were the places where Bent knew people, former clients mostly, men with scarred, dangerous faces, casino pallor, runny noses, half contained anger.

Wilson remembered one man – small, thin, pale skinned with paler eyes and large, white hands, *Fleur*, that was his name. *Fleur*, a French name, 'a flower'. Wilson felt sweat on his hands and a queer feeling, a combination of nausea and detachment. He knew that he should be thinking of other things: of what the police had just told him, of how he, the bereaved husband should act, of further explanations, of making clear – why should that be so difficult? – the fact that it was Dot who'd been in the wrong, Dot who'd made his life insupportable, Dot who'd driven him to these unimaginable events.

Instead, he sat in the living room on the burgundy and silver striped couch with his head in his hands and thought about Fleur, standing in the smoke washed glitter and darkness of the casino. Bent had greeted his old client expansively, called for more drinks, and exchanged the usual pleasantries, while Fleur stood impassive, looking as if he was several pints short of blood and several inches too small for his large white hands.

When they finally got away to the craps pit, Wilson asked, 'Who the hell is that?'

Bent gave one of his repertory of odd smiles. With cars driving in and out and sirens in the distance, Wilson thought of the vast variety of Bent's smiles, jolly, conspiratorial, sardonic, warning, sinister. Fleur elicited one of the sinister variety. 'That's a Magician,' Bent said. 'Cross him and he'll make you disappear.'

'He doesn't look . . .' Wilson suggested.

'Appearances are deceiving.' Bent tidied up his piles of chips. 'That guy's one of the best Magicians in the trade.'

Magician, one of Bent's words, like 'wise guys' and 'reptile life' that opened up another world. Bent had a way with words; he possessed a language capable of turning the usual facts of life to theatre and myth. All his pleasures were gaudy; all his friends, colourful, dangerous, larger than life guys.

'So what are you?' Wilson asked him one night.

Bent smiled. 'I'm the Snake Charmer,' he said.

The Snake Charmer had now materialized in the living room, summoned, Wilson recalled after some effort, by a frantic early morning phone call. He remembered the sound of his own voice in the empty living room, as he cried, 'Jesus, Bent! Get over here! Something terrible's happened!'

Now Bent was sitting across from him with all the appurtenances of the successful lawyer, his leather encased yellow legal pad, Mont Blanc pen, Rolex watch, and subtly striped silk suit, Wilson considered the cool alert eyes, the red face, the fleshy folds around the jowls which flared and subsided like the hood of a cobra and thought not of snake charmers but of snakes.

I've hired the very best, thought Wilson, I've hired the real magician who can make all this disappear, *this* being the situation of the moment, where he, Wilson Hargus, was sitting in his own living room with anger and grief and folly, while the local police extracted Dot's body from her smashed up Mercedes and tried to puzzle out certain little anomalies in the position of the corpse and the nature of her injuries.

Soon the investigating team would go upstairs. Wilson saw that as inevitable, where they would poke around, perhaps, until they found the trophy, ugly, bronze, heavy, inscribed *Wesleyan Wrestling 1978*. Though he'd washed and scoured the trophy, it would be bad, just the same, if they found it. Very bad. They had these new tests, chemicals and special lights able to detect the faintest traces of blood.

Wilson knew about them; he watched tv, read the Science *Times;* he just hadn't thought of tests and lights at the crucial moment. Hell, if he'd taken time to think of tests and lights and investigative teams and feeling like hell, Dot would be in the kitchen making breakfast and he'd be getting ready to play eighteen at the country club. But he hadn't thought, so he'd scrubbed the floor, and bundled up the sheets, and thrown them into the wash with all his clothes, which were now dry and back in his bureau and in his closet.

Maybe that was another mistake. Wilson always sent his shirts to the cleaners, and someone might notice that. But if he'd put the shirt back on, the wrinkles would have given him away. That was the hell of the situation: the many unthought of, potentially lethal, details, way too many to keep in mind at a moment of violent horror. It – Wilson thought of the incident as 'it' – should have taken planning. Lots of planning.

And really, nothing had been intended. Wilson could almost, but not quite, convince himself that nothing had been intended. That in the middle of a violent shouting match with Dot, his hand had, of its own accord, escaped his control, lifted the trophy and slammed it into the side of her head. Repeatedly. Which proved, didn't it, that he was innocent, fundamentally innocent? That he was a victim of circumstances, whom Bent could and must help?

'You called me,' said Bent, 'very wise.'

Wilson realized that Bent had many different voices as well as laughs. The one Wilson liked was the invitation voice, the voice Bent used when he called up at eleven p.m., maybe later, breaking into sleep with the sound of excitement and pleasure. 'Hey, Will, wake you? Let's get some action. Hit the casino.'

Or the call might come earlier, say three or so on a Friday afternoon. 'Ya ready?' No introduction, no preamble. 'I got the plane warmed up and I'm thinking Vegas or the islands.' *I'm thinking another life,* was what Wilson heard, an exit from Dot and everything she put him through, a portal to the world of action and magicians and excitement. That was the voice Wilson liked.

'I've got to understand the situation here,' said Bent. This was Bent's business voice, completely different, flat, calm, hiding all its interest. This was the voice Bent used to take apart a prosecution case and to lay out the logic of the defense, holding his fireworks for the summation, when he would suddenly loose his astonishing oratorical powers.

'It was Dot's fault,' Wilson began. He put his face in his hands and did not see Bent's subtly raised eyebrow. 'I thought we had an understanding. But she drove me crazy. Always worrying about bills and never letting up. And she had a boy friend. I think she had a boy friend. Why else would she be so difficult? It stands to reason, doesn't it?'

'Maybe,' said Bent. 'Boyfriends sometimes make women difficult. Or mellow them out. It all depends.'

'It's not like I didn't warn her,' Wilson said.

'Let me understand the situation. Dot was found in her car, right?'

'It was an accident, of course, a terrible, terrible accident,' Wilson said.

'That's the working hypothesis. But there are problems, right?'

'Some,' admitted Wilson. 'There are some problems.'

'Maybe you'll be lucky,' Bent said philosophically. 'Or maybe not. We've got to be prepared.'

That sounded good to Wilson.

'Including my fee.'

Wilson raised his hands. 'There's money.'

'I usually work on a retainer,' Bent said. He mentioned a staggering sum and Wilson swallowed.

'Best to be prepared,' said Bent. 'For every eventuality.'

Their next conversation was in the local jail, a nice modern building suitable for an upscale suburb with a steadily rising crime rate. Wilson wore an orange jumpsuit; Bent was smart in a pale gray summer suit with a pink shirt and an Italian tie. His brief case was a fine oxblood leather, its smooth covering so succulent as to appear edible. Bent set it on the table, sat down in one of the straight chairs, and handed across a pack of cigarettes.

'I've got to get out of here,' Wilson said. 'You've got to get me out of here. I didn't expect I'd be in jail this long. I can't stand the lights, Bent. Lights on all the time.' His hands shook as he lit the cigarette with Bent's lighter. 'And some of the guys in here, Bent, you wouldn't believe.'

'Reptile life,' Bent agreed.

'So you got to get me out. What's the hang up?'

Bent gave a little sigh. It always amazed him how thin a grasp of reality his clients possessed. Mob capos, drug runners, captains of industry, princes of the street – or Wall Street – they were all the same. It made Benton Worthy wonder how the world ran, sometimes. 'We're discussing bail now. But it's going to be high, Wilson. Very high.'

'None of this was my fault,' Wilson said. 'None of this. It was Dot's – Listen, you know what she was like.'

Bent nodded noncommittally. He had recently extracted himself from a twenty-five year marriage. The divorce had cost him a lot of money and considerable effort, but he could afford to be generous. Especially with present opportunities and prospects, Bent knew he could recoup his losses.

'And you know there was a boyfriend.' It made Wilson a little nervous that Bent did not agree more enthusiastically.

'As you have said.'

'There was,' Wilson insisted.

'We'll do our best to ruin her reputation. Juries sometimes

understand crimes of passion. But the victim can only be blamed for so much. There is a delicate line.'

'She drove me crazy,' Wilson said.

'You'd better tell me what happened,' Bent uncapped his pen and got ready to write.

'It was entirely an accident.'

Bent fixed him with a cold stare. 'I am not the police, the prison psychiatrist, or a reporter. I am your legal counsel. You've got to give me the facts. Even the inconvenient ones.'

'I meant,' said Wilson, 'that I did not intend to kill Dot.' He saw their bedroom again, with the rose beige carpeting, the white metal bedstead, the armoire insisted on by the decorator. Wilson disliked both decorator and the armoire and kept his trophies on top of it. The wrestling trophy was the ugliest, and he kept that on the bureau, where it had been handy.

What else? Raised voices, tired arguments, the nauseating sense that while he, Wilson, was struggling, struggling to make a different life, a life of pleasure and control, a life like Bent's, Dot had somehow escaped. That she had succeeded in some subtle way without him and where he had failed.

They argued as a result: about money, sex, the decor of their house; over who to invite and who to ignore. Nothing was too small for them; argument was like oxygen; they needed it to breathe. Then came the night when the mixture was too rich, and hatred flared up like an acetylene torch.

He remembered Dot lying in bed. The lights were already off but the room was lit by the street lamps that kept their neigh-bourhood safe. Wilson remarked on the irony, but Bent just kept writing with his fat, beautiful pen.

'She was wearing her sleep mask,' Wilson said reluctantly; this was a detail that bothered him in a couple ways. 'She's yakking on and on about – I forget what the hell it was about.'

'You better remember,' said Bent.

'Money. You know I've been dropping a bit at craps.'

Bent shrugged. He was in the same boat, but he never dis-cussed his losses with anyone.

'I come out of the bathroom – you know the way the master suite's arranged?'

Bent nodded. Lavish master bedroom with oversized his and her closets flanking a spa sized bathroom ensuite. His customers liked space, they liked size. They liked new. Bent, himself, preferred old, though he sensed his tastes evolving. He'd had a passion for early American antiques, and until the divorce, he'd owned a nice eighteenth century farm house well out in the country. But he'd gotten sick of snow and winter, and lately Bent found himself looking at Caribbean colonial furniture.

Some of the stuff out of the islands was first rate, mostly made by slave craftsmen, which was disagreeable, but the pieces were high quality and came with lots of history. Bent was fond of history, because it gave perspective. Perspective, he thought now, was what Wilson lacked most.

'So I'm talking to her, standing in the doorway where the closets are, and she's lying there with her sleep mask on not even looking at me, for Christ's sake!' Wilson's voice rose as he thought about the dark room, the windows washed with the sour orange of the street light, the pervasive odour of Dot's perfume, and her not listening to him. Not even when he shouted that he'd had enough. No.

It was only when he moved, he must have moved, but he did not remember moving. As in a dream, he was just suddenly somewhere else, standing in front of the bureau, his eyes only half adjusted, the streetlight gleaming down the side of the trophy in his hand.

Dot sat up then and raised her sleep mask. How had she known? It gave Wilson a creepy feeling that he had not known and she had. That he had been so close to disaster and had not realized it, until she said. 'What are you doing?' Sharp, accusatory, as if she'd been in the right all along. As if he was going to have to confess some fault, when she was wrong. when there had to be reasons.

Wilson stopped. 'And then?' Bent prompted.

Wilson drew on the cigarette as if it was the breath of life. 'I don't know. The light by the bed fell over. When I set the lamp back on the night table and pushed the switch, it had already happened.'

He had a very clear impression of the sleep mask lying on the pillow. 'The sleep mask,' he said and Bent said nothing. They both knew that was what had caught him out. A sleep mask with a little drop of blood – that and certain problems with the pattern of injuries – had led to the conclusion that the 'accident' had been staged and the crime scene, the master bedroom of the Hargus residence.

'Then you took your wife downstairs?' Bent asked.

'Down into the Mercedes, yes. I drove out of our cul-de-sac and onto Mountain Avenue. It was still early – two-thirty or three in the morning. Dead quiet.' Wilson started to tremble, as if the morning chill had left a physical memory.

'Foggy. It was foggy.' The big lawns were pale in the mist, the tops of the old trees lost, the 'executive' homes, scarcely visible except for their white-eyed security lights, mindlessly alert. He hadn't had a clear idea of where he was going. Perhaps the woods around the reservoirs, something like that. And then the tree just grew in his mind, shot up and got bigger and bigger until there it was: the half dead elm the neighbourhood had bitched and griped about for years and the damn councilmen had refused to take down. Wilson pushed down the gas pedal. jerked the wheel and, at the last minute, hit the brakes.

The impact shot up his arms like an electric current. The air bag opened, and he panicked for a minute, shouting and flailing around. Then he was back and in control. He mentioned that to Bent, how control returned and he knew what he had to do. He moved Dot over into the driver's seat and repositioned her with her hands on the wheel and left the motor running. He stood for a moment by the side of the road, expecting discovery; then he walked home, cutting through the park and the dark yards.

'You wanted to kill yourself,' Bent said. It was not a question. Wilson shrugged.

'You were in a state of complete shock and horror – post traumatic stress – ' Here Bent paused and made a note to have Elizabeth research everything known about post traumatic stress syndrome. 'You wanted to kill yourself, but you survived. Your head hurt; naturally you were stunned, and you only came to yourself back home. Amazing what the body will do unaided by

the mind. Yes,' Bent added with satisfied note in his voice. 'Yes,
that might do.'

'I need to get out of here,' said Wilson.

Bent ignored him. 'I'll need your medical history. I need
evidence of instability. Alcoholism – you are a bit fond of the
bottle, Wilson. Addictive behaviour? Gambling will take care of
that. Good thing for you, Wilson, that I've led you astray. I think
we can work up a good profile. If we can find Dot a boyfriend,
that's good, too, but you're our main hope.'

'I don't see,' Wilson began.

'Temporary insanity. It's the only way to go. Manslaughter –
manslaughter we might have managed if you hadn't tried to set
up that phony accident. You call the cops, you're all in pieces, you
hit her in an argument – maybe manslaughter. The "accident",
Wilson, the "accident" is the costly thing here. We need you to be
crazy.'

'I'd have to get treatment. I'd still be locked up.'

Bent shrugged. 'Consider the reptile life,' he said.

When Wilson continued to protest, Bent brought up the
clincher. 'Look, the state could bring in murder one and you'd
be looking at death row. I tell you, if I pull this off, if we get
innocent by reason of insanity, it will be the height of my career.
The absolute pinnacle.' He smiled the old Bent smile, full of
enthusiasm, eagerness, and pleasure.

And he was as good as his word. When Benton Worthy
engaged himself, he gave everything he had. His performance
in the State of Connecticut v. Wilson Hargus was a masterpiece.
Even the prosecutor, angry that the jury had returned an incon-
ceivable verdict, had to admit that Benton Worthy was one of the
best. As for Wilson, packed off for what he was sure would be a
short course of psychiatric treatment, he understood that the
Snake Charmer was a miracle worker.

Even after he was off the hook, Wilson relied a good deal on
Bent. His finances would have been a mess if Bent hadn't agreed
to manage everything for him for the duration. Bent even took
care of the sale of the house – overly big, Wilson felt and full of
bad memories.

Bent kept him from making mistakes, too. Natural mistakes,

not the mistakes of a guy out of control, but of a normal person trying to be insane. 'Don't ask about your stock portfolio,' Bent had to tell him. 'For a while you're on another planet. I'll see to everything. Wait until, we're walking the grounds before you ask me anything about the market. Anything!'

For the same reason, Bent never produced any paperwork, not even when they were walking the grounds. 'You can't be obviously rational,' Bent said. Wilson was restricted to scraps of financial news on the day room television. The rest of the inmates preferred the soaps, sports, interminable talk shows. With the bull market roaring along, heading for 9000, with stocks volatile, with opportunities and pitfalls everywhere, there were days that Wilson thought he could, indeed, go mad without a complete market report and access to his computer files.

Whenever Bent visited, Wilson quizzed him about various stock issues, made suggestions, gave advice. Bent always listened attentively, holding his head a little to one side, his cool eyes alert. Every now and then he complimented Wilson on some tip about the market. 'You really are a genius,' he'd say.

Four years after the incident, Wilson Hargus got the good news that he was cured. He hadn't had a drink since the night Dot died; of necessity he'd stayed away from the craps tables. The medical staff complimented him on his 'anger control', on his 'realistic awareness of the issues', on his earnest pursuit of 'his therapeutic goals'. He phoned Bent to let him know. He wanted Bent to rent him a condo, but Bent said, 'Go with a hotel first. Get your feet on the ground. Why tie up money in a place you might not like?' Which made perfect sense.

Wilson was scheduled for release on a Tuesday. He rather expected Bent to pick him up, but the lawyer called the day before and explained that he had to be in court for a big case, not as challenging a case as Wilson's, of course, but interesting. Bent had gone ahead and booked Wilson into a hotel, the Clariton, downtown. Near his office.

Tuesday morning, Wilson shook hands with the orderly, the doctor, a couple of the more tolerable inmates, and walked to freedom. A cab took him downtown, and an hour after leaving therapy sessions and the mind numbing monotony of the day room, Wilson Hargus was standing in a hotel room overlooking the river and the interstate.

After the spartan hospital decor, the room seemed full of pattern – the floral bedspread a jungle laced with greens and purples, the drapes the same wild design. Wilson took off the unfamiliar jacket and tie and threw them on the bed. He switched on the tv and found the financial news.

The room had a mini-bar. Wilson poured himself a beer which was cold and bitter, as curiously unfamiliar as his jacket and tie. He was free. 'I've gotten out', Wilson told himself. 'I'm out and I never have to go back. Dot is gone, and I'm a rich man and I can live as I please.' He liked the sound of that. Not that he'd had doubts. He'd always felt innocent and he'd never expected anything really bad to happen. Not once he put Bent in control.

He called the attorney's office and asked about his belongings, which were all in storage. He told the secretary he'd need his laptop computer and she said she'd have someone drop it off. 'No, it's no trouble,' she assured him. 'Attorney Worthy knew you'd want a computer first thing.'

'And Bent? When will Attorney Worthy be in?'

A pause, the slightest hesitation. 'I think he's to be back by the end of the week.'

'I see. I thought he was in court.'

'End of the week,' she said.

'Listen, I'll need cash. Bent has been handling my affairs.'

'Your hotel has been prepaid for two weeks,' the secretary said. 'Including meals,' and she hung up, leaving Wilson standing, annoyed, with the phone in his hand. But then, he saw the wisdom of the thing. He had just gotten out. He needed to get his legs again, to adjust. The staff at the hospital were very big on adjustment. They would approve, for sure.

Friday morning, Wilson called again. He was tried of watching tv and of room service meals and tired, too, trying to contact his broker. His new broker, that is, for Bent was apparently working through another house now. The office did not know which firm, either. 'Attorney Worthy keeps all that material at home' the secretary told him.

'I expected him back today.' Wilson was exasperated, because the market was in overdrive and there was money to be made. 'I need to get a handle on my financial situation. We're not talking a nickel and dime operation here.'

The secretary murmured soothingly, then put him on hold for another call. When she came back on the line, she said her best advice was to call back later. Attorney Worthy was often late coming in. He said he did his best thinking late in the day.

Wilson knew this was so, but he hung up with a sense of uneasiness, almost of dread. He thought of all the nonsense they'd talked at the hospital, about 'reentry into ordinary life' about the strains of 'leaving the therapeutic community'. The strain wasn't leaving the goddamned 'therapeutic community', it was trying to find where his money had gone. And Bent, too, but Wilson immediately put that idea aside.

He'd trusted Bent with his life and Bent had done the magic act and charmed the jury and saved his life. Without Bent Worthy, he, Wilson Hargus, dissatisfied ex-financial consultant, might be sitting on death row with only delays and appeals between him and a precipitous introduction to the afterlife. No point in over-reacting, but, still, Wilson knew he'd feel a lot better if he could talk to Bent in person.

At six p.m., Wilson stood in his hotel room listening to the phone ring unanswered in Bent Worthy's law office. He called Bent's home, but Bent had moved out ages ago, his wife, his ex-wife, said. He had a condo now, down on the park. In spite of himself, Wilson began to tremble. Bent was just across the park. All the time, he'd been just across the park in the arrogant glassy condo visible behind the trees. Wilson thanked the ex-Mrs Worthy and hurried out into a breezy, early spring night that could pass for November.

Wilson wore his raincoat which was too thin for the chill and walked fast. He cut straight across the damp grass of the park without giving a thought to possible reptile life in the shaded darkness. He passed the fountain with the iron deer and the fleshy indian maidens, avoided the derelicts drinking on the benches and, in fifteen minutes, reached the brightly lit plaza of the condo only slightly out of breath.

The lobby was warm and bright. Nicely veined brown marble

covered the floor and the walls. The large desk at the door had a built in bank of monitors. No escape for Bent here, Wilson thought.

'Benton Worthy's apartment,' Wilson said.

'Your name, Sir?'

When he gave his name, the man asked for some identification. Wilson was irritated and said so.

'There's a package for a Mr Hargus,' the doorman said. 'But I was told I.D. was essential. Mr Worthy was very specific about getting I.D.'

Wilson took out his driver's license. The doorman looked, nodded, and handed over a large manilla folder.

'I still want to see Bent,' he said.

'I'm afraid Mr Worthy has been away for several weeks,' the doorman said. 'But he was very particular you should have that package.'

Wilson turned away with a strong sense of impending disaster. He sat down on one of the caramel coloured banquettes that furnished the lobby and opened the envelope. Inside, he found a cheque book with exactly $10,000 dollars in it and a letter, dated several days earlier, from Bent.

Dear Wilson,

You provided me with two inestimable opportunities. I hope that my success with the first will excuse me for having availed myself of the second. The chance to save you was irresistible. So was the opportunity to enrich myself and escape a situation where my habits and my associates had combined to put me in jeopardy.

As you see, I have not left you destitute, and I am sure that, in a market such as we enjoy at present, a man of your talent will make a swift recovery.

Do not look for me; I will not be back. I've charmed my last snake.

Benton Worthy

FRUIT OF THE POISONOUS TREE

John F. Dobbyn

Trevor Townsend, Judge of the Superior Court in and for the County of Suffolk, Commonwealth of Massachusetts, is, by any measure, a piece of work. We were no more than twenty minutes into the argument on my motion for an injunction against Boston Bank & Trust, one of His Honour's favourite charities, when I could actually count six male gophers tunnelling through the walls of my stomach. Understandable, since the judge had that finely honed bent of the incurably self-satisfied for meeting every legal argument with a barb dipped in the vitriolic oil of sarcasm.

The afternoon break came mercifully at three o'clock. I rose to the bailiff's cry of 'All rise' with the thought of purging my mind with a chocolate blitz at the Bailey's downstairs. The whim died aborning, however, with a crook of Judge Townsend's finger as he departed the bench for chambers. I looked at counsel for the defense for any light she could shed on the summons. She shrugged, smiled, and passed quickly to the free world outside.

Reluctance doesn't begin to characterize my entrance into the judge's chambers. He had shed the robe and sat like Torquemada, ready to welcome the next guest of the Inquisition.

I took his nod as a gracious invitation to make myself comfortable. Tea and macaroons would be served momentarily. Perhaps not.

'Mr Knight, I assume I have your confidentiality. I wish to retain your services to represent my son in a criminal matter.'

There are jump-shifts in conversation that affect the hinge of your jaw, such that you wonder if you will ever get your mouth fully closed again. This qualified. I think it was seeing the unexpectedly human motion of concern on the judge's Mount Rushmore features that brought me back.

'On what charge, Judge?'

'The allegation is murder in the first degree. My son is a junior at Harvard. He attended a party of college students – not Harvard – at an apartment on Beacon Street last evening. The incident occurred there.'

'Where is he now?'

'He is being detained at the Charles Street prison. They're reluctant to depart from the usual bail disallowance in a capital case because of the delicate position of his relationship to a judge. I'm loath to ask special favours for the same reason.'

'Certainly not, Judge. Can't soil the old robes just for the sake of getting the kid out of the reach of every rapist at Charles Street that wants to get back at the old man.'

Actually, I didn't say that. I just nodded.

'May I assume that you will take the case, Mr Knight?'

There are two things you don't do as an attorney. One is appear at a medical convention unarmed. The other is turn down a sitting judge.

As long as I was at the Suffolk Courthouse anyway, my first stop was the District Attorney's office. No need sparring with the assistant D.A.s. The top lady herself, Ms Lamb by name, if not by temperament, would sooner surrender her flesh to the torturers than give up one juicy headline from this case to an assistant.

She was surprised to see me, since nearly all of the criminal practice I took on was in federal court. I had clerked for a federal judge after law school, and a steady stream of indigent appointments came from that source. During my seven years with the firm of Bilson & Dawes (the last two as junior partner), my seniors had harrumphed and scowled over my accepting even federal criminal appointments. It tarnished the pristine image of the three-piece suits who practiced not trial work but civil li-ti-ga-tion. The bearded, whiskey-breathing slouches who frequently populated the firm's waiting room when I took a criminal appointment did nothing to loosen firm policy.

'You've got to be joking. You represent young Townsend?'

I smiled pleasantly in spite of the inference. 'Strange bedfellows, what? Shall we talk business?'

'There's no business to discuss, unless you're offering the full plea of guilty. Have you talked to your client?'

'My next stop. Why are we being inflexible here?'

'Because I'm going to personally walk your boy to the electric chair.'

'Might we go through the inconvenience of a trial first?'

She grinned that half grin that they get when they're holding the real cards.

'I'll give him the formality, if he insists, but when the jury reads his confession . . .' Her hands and eyebrows went up in unison. I hate that gesture.

'He confessed?'

'To every detail. He dictated a statement, read it, signed it, and then went through the whole thing again for the video camera. I'll send copies of both to your office.'

She leaned in for the killer. 'Count on it. He'll burn, at least for this one.'

Youth led me to take the bait. 'You imply there's more?'

'Four unsolved strangulation-rapes in the last two years. I don't suppose you get beyond the financial pages up at Bilson.'

If there was anything soft and cuddly about Ms Lamb as an infant, she had managed to ossify it in her eighteen years at the bar. At five foot eight, one hundred and twenty-five pounds, dark hair in a bun so tight her nostrils flared, she was one lean, mean, prosecuting machine. Not uncharacteristically in the trade, word had it that she was waiting for the case that could transport her to the state house. This one sent up flares.

'I assume the Miranda warnings reared their ugly heads in the process.'

'Right up there at the front.'

'I'd have bet on it. And the autopsy report, you'll be pleased to share it?'

'You'll be the second one to see it.'

Ms Lamb's grinding arrogance made me long for the warmth of Judge Townsend's courtroom.

Charles Street prison affords a cluster of intimate dwellings measuring six by eight, where the accent is less on privacy than on togetherness. It seemed to have been constructed around the era of the Tower of London, and probably shared the architect.

I sat waiting in the attorney's room until I found myself looking up a six foot four inch frame to the palest features I have ever seen on an eighteen-year-old. I've seen feeder goldfish thrown into a tank of piranhas looking more in their element than young master Townsend.

I had been fully prepared to resent him, with his Brooks Brothers tweed over chinos over oxblood loafers (no socks) – the uniform of those who were born to attend Harvard. Oddly, there was a humility in his eyes that did not seem born of his present circumstances. I found, out of reflex, that I liked the boy. I fought against it.

'I'm Michael Knight: Your father asked me to come around.'

I would have said 'represent you,' but I still hadn't gotten used to the idea. He held out a well-muscled hand that clamped mine with authority. I raised an eyebrow. He caught my meaning and forced a shy smile.

'Crew.'

'And pretty good too.' I caught part of the inscription on his T-shirt where the top shirt folded open. Filling in the rest of the letters, my guess was that he had won a regatta singles championship. 'I bet a ring went with that.'

He flushed a little and then seemed to go into himself when he said, 'They took it when I came in. I think they said I could have it when I go to court.'

From his expression, my guess was that remembering past victories made the embarrassment more painful.

I nodded him into the wooden straight-back across the table. He hung over the table like a puppy about to be scolded.

'You want to tell me about it, Trevor?'

'Chip.'

His eyes came up from the table. I didn't blame him for going for a nickname. I only hoped it was not 'off the old block.'

'What happened, Chip?'

He was leaning on elbows wide enough apart to accommodate a Mazda. I noticed that his eyes did not retreat to the table. Good sign.

'I got an invitation from a girl I knew to a party at an apartment on Beacon Street around Berkeley. I guess four or five girls live there. It was mostly a group from different colleges around town. I got there about seven-thirty. Had a couple of drinks. I started to feel dizzy, sick. Someone brought me up to one of the bedrooms. I fell on the bed and went out cold.'

He took a breath before the tough part.

'I woke up about nine . . .'

'How did you know it was nine?'

'There was a clock beside the bed.'

I nodded.

'There was a girl in the room. In the bed. I think we'd been arguing.'

'After you woke up?'

His eyes drifted. He stood up and walked over to the window that was an eighth-inch glass and a quarter-inch grime that had been collecting since John Adams last washed it. His voice was calm and deliberate.

'I took the belt from a terrycloth robe that was lying on the bed. I put it around her neck and tied a slipknot. I pulled it taut until the breathing stopped. I could see her eyes close. She fell backwards on the bed.'

I waited, but there was no more. The wet beads on his forehead belied the quiet tone of voice.

'Why?'

He turned back, almost surprised to see me.

I said, 'Why?'

He thought about it. 'I think we'd been arguing.'

'About what?'

'I can't remember.'

'Was she the one who invited you?'

'No. I didn't know her before last night.'

'What happened then?'

'I must have passed out. I don't remember anything until somebody dropped me onto the bed in my apartment in Cambridge.'

'Any idea of the time?'

'Yes. Ten o'clock. I heard someone say it. It seemed so early, I checked the clock. That was all I remember until the police woke me up. They came sometime early in the morning.'

I jotted down some notes and let it sink in.

'What were you drinking?'

He came back to the chair. 'Some kind of punch. I don't know. I think it was gin.'

'Did you take it, or did someone bring it to you?'

He thought. 'One of the fellas there brought the first one. I took the second.'

'Any drugs?'

He shook his head.

'What was the girl's name, the one that invited you?'

'Sue . . . ah, Sue Banner . . . Bannister. I just met her the week before at a football game. I didn't know her well. She called me the night before to tell me there was going to be a party.'

'Did you know anyone else there?'

'Couple of the fellas went with me.'

He caught me with his eyes before I got the next questions out.

'I appreciate what you're trying to do, Mr Knight, but I did it. There's no point in trying to make a defense. Can we just get it over with?'

What had so far been a perfect loser of a day headed downhill when I got back to the firm. I could read the vicarious pain in my secretary's eyes when she handed me the message slip.

'SEE ME NOW! A.D.'

Ask any associate and most of the junior partners what 'A.D.' stands for, and they'll whisper, 'Angel of Death.' Alex Devlin – 'Lex' to those who are permitted the liberty, which included the Dalai Lama and a few others – is one who suffers not the foibles of juniors gladly. He has a body like Spencer Tracy, a jaw that could plow snow, and a nose that was designed by the man who laid out the Boston streets.

Word had it that he had been the best of the best in the criminal bar. Ten years ago he hung up his spurs and pulled out of criminal defense work entirely. Nobody at my level knows why, and nobody at his level is talking. They say he had a taste for the grape, but then so does half the trial bar.

Actually he didn't hang up his spurs. He traded them for polo boots. After a year in never-never land, the firm recruited him for the courtroom magic that he still performs in the clean arena of civil litigation.

Word of my summons had apparently circulated, because every associate I passed on my way to the gates of hell took one last look at me in life. I smiled the smile of the brave as I entered the inner sanctum.

He was standing at the window, back to me, and even from that angle the aura was formidable. When he turned around, I was moved by the power of the man's presence. It wasn't fear as much as awe.

'You've taken the Townsend defense. Why?'

'I didn't have much choice, Mr Devlin. It was put to me as a command performance. I still have no idea why he wanted me.'

I could feel the heat of his eyes and pitied any witness on cross-examination.

'He didn't want you. He wanted me. Now he's got me.'

The blank look on my face asked the question. He answered it.

'You carry the firm's name. This case will fill the first three pages of the *Record-American* every night. He knew I couldn't afford to stay out of it.'

'If he wanted you, which I don't doubt, why didn't he ask you?'

'He knows I'm out of criminal work.' His shoulders sloped a bit, and I couldn't read the look in his eyes as he sat down at the desk.

'Apparently I'm back in it. What have you got?'

I sat opposite him and took out my notebook. I told him everything I knew about the case. My secretary had handed me a manilla envelope from the D.A.'s office when she gave me the note from Mr Devlin. I opened it and found the signed confession of Chip Townsend and a videotape. I handed over the confession. Mr Devlin read it and threw it back.

'Read it. Tell me if it squares with what he said.'

I ran through it '. . . belt from a terrycloth robe . . . lying on the bed . . . around her neck . . . slipknot . . . pulled it taut . . . breathing stopped . . . see her eyes close . . . fell backwards on the bed.

'That's it. They also got it on videotape.'

I held it up. He gestured to the VCR and television in the corner of the office – standard equipment for trial counsel. I slipped in the tape and turned on the TV. It was a full-body shot of Chip in the D.A.'s interrogation room. After the Miranda warnings, he said his piece.

'I took the belt from a robe that was lying on the bed. I put it around her neck and tied a slipknot. I pulled it taut until the breathing stopped. I could see her eyes close. She fell backwards on the bed.'

The lines over Mr Devlin's eyes told me he caught the same thing I did, but I thought I'd let him say it.

'Let me see that confession again.'

I took it over. He reread it and looked up at me. Something came alive in his eyes. I nodded.

'Check your notes.'

'I just did. Verbatim. He told the story in exactly the same words three times. What are the chances of that?'

He leaned back. His eyes focused vaguely on a framed picture of two teenage girls, but the action was clearly going on inside. I jumped in before the spark of optimism ignited prematurely.

'That's the good news. The bad news is that the D.A. thinks Townsend is the one who committed that string of rape-strangulations. She can only get an indictment on this one, but she'll do everything but show slides to suggest to the jury that he's the serial killer.'

'She does and she'll have a mistrial. What about the autopsy?'

'I spoke to the D.A. We can have it as soon as she gets it.'

He came straight forward with one elbow on the desk and the other hand snatching the phone out of its state of rest.

'She's playing games with you, sonny.'

'Michael, Mr Devlin. I prefer to be called Michael.'

Or maybe I just thought it, while I watched him strangle the phone and punch numbers.

'This is Lex Devlin. Let me speak to Mrs Lamb.'

A pause, but a short one. She was not about to leave the king on hold, even if he did ignore the 'Ms' protocol.

'Angela, Lex Devlin. I'm representing Judge Townsend's son.'

I could hear her heart drop across half a mile of Bell Tel cable.

'Be good enough to fax me the autopsy report. I'll need a full set of pictures too. You have my fax number.'

Another pause for a tactical decision. Again, the king was not to be denied. Whatever she said amounted to 'Yes.'

Mr Devlin wrapped it up with minimum pleasantries and shot me a look. 'Don't let 'em stall you, sonny. The M.E. had *that* report finished before the sun came up. Probably delivered it in his pajamas. Bring it in as soon as it gets here.'

I was back in five minutes with the report and a stack of photos of a young girl, undressed and beaten unmercifully from the waist up.

He scanned the pictures and winced at each new shot. He picked up the medical examiner's report and walked to the window, mumbling what he was reading. I picked the lowlights out of the copy I had made for myself.

Cause of death: strangulation.

. . . Contusions, the result of severe blows, as by a human fist, covering the abdomen, chest, and face, inflicted prior to death, . . . two ribs fractured . . . had been sexually assaulted . . . contusion and depression circling the throat . . . wool fibres found in depression as if garroted by loosely spun cord . . . fifteen centimetre circular contusion at back of neck with pressure fracture of first cervical vertebra . . .

Time of death: eleven p.m.

He was still grumbling when he caught up the phone and punched in more numbers. I thought I had become invisible until he glanced over and said, 'Listen and learn, sonny.'

There were the pat sounds of an official answering voice over the phone.

'Let me speak to the medical examiner.'

More bureaucratic sounds. I wasn't surprised, since the Suffolk County M.E., Dr Max Reinert, was known for the kind of arrogance only an entrenched institution can afford.

'Listen, dear. You walk through the swinging door and whisper two words into his pink little ears – "Lex Devlin." '

My eyebrows must have been somewhere around my hairline, because he shrugged. 'Sometimes you've got to call in old debts, sonny. Remember that when a public official needs a favour.'

He was back to the phone. 'Max. Thanks. One question. How accurate is the time of death on the girl in the Townsend case?'

The baritone voice boomed through the phone like a speaker. 'Right on the money, Lex. Ten minutes either side.'

'How?'

'Three good indicators. Body temperature. She was indoors at room temperature all evening till we got there. The state of rigor confirmed it. Contents of the stomach locked it in. I'd bet my next paycheck on it. More than that, your paycheck.'

I saw the closest thing to a smile I could visualize on Devlin's features. 'Good job, Max.'

Mr Devlin held the phone with his chin while he pressed the hang-up button with one hand and flipped the Rolodex with the other. He punched in enough numbers to get out of state.

'Dr Mayhew, please. Lex Devlin in Boston.'

Mr Devlin hit the speaker-phone button and leaned back. A professional but softly feminine voice came over the speaker.

'Lex, how's my favourite crusader?'

'Damn few holy wars lately, Jean. I need you. Can you give me some time?'

If the pause was for indecision, there was none in the answer. 'When do I book the flight?'

That brought a real grin. 'Soon. First a question. I've got a boy, eighteen years old, charged with the sadistic sex-murder of a young college girl. He confessed.'

'So?'

'Three times in identical words. Says he was at a party, had a couple of drinks, and passed out. He woke up in his apartment much later. The only thing he recalls about the interim is this mesmerized, almost memorized confession. I saw it on videotape. He seems to believe it. A number of things don't square with the confession. He claims to have strangled the girl with a terrycloth belt. Says he did it from the front, since he could see her eyes and she fell backwards. He's firm on that. The M.E. says she was garroted with a cord that left *wool* fibers, probably from the back since there was a major contusion on the back of the neck and a broken cervical vertebra. The time's wrong too. He remembers being home by ten p.m. The M.E. is certain the time of death was ten minutes either side of eleven o'clock. What do you think?'

'I better come and see him. Was he on drugs that night?'

'He says no.'

'Could a drug have been slipped to him?'

Lex looked at me. I nodded and whispered. 'The first drink was brought to him by one of the kids at the party.'

'Yes it could, Jean.'

'There's a possibility the confession could have been suggested to him under a drug like Haldol, the so-called zombie drug. Your boy could have been set up to confess to someone else's doings. Has he been medically tested for drugs, especially the class that induce suggestibility?'

Mr Devlin pointed a finger at me that got my feet in gear double-time.

'Even as we speak, Jean. Thanks. When can you get here?'

The trial was standing room only. I've always thought that the state misses a bet by not charging admission. This one could have sold out Fenway Park.

Ms Lamb bestrode the courtroom like a behemoth, to borrow a phrase. She played society's avenging angel as she led the medical examiner through his paces. She breezed over the facts that didn't square with the confession, and belaboured the details of brutality. The clear and present hope was that the jurors would connect those details with the newspaper accounts of the other four murders without her risking a mistrial.

She put on the boy from the party who found the girl's body around midnight. He did not recall seeing Chip leave the party.

Next in the witness box was a boy by the name of Tom Keating who said that Chip came downstairs in a stupour and asked him for a ride home. He could not pinpoint the time.

Then the *pièce de résistance,* her one-way ticket to the governor's office – Chip's confession. First she played it in living colour in video. Then she introduced it in permanent written form to accompany the jurors during their deliberations.

I was with Mr Devlin at counsel table. When the prosecution rested, he stepped up to the plate, so to speak. He put Chip on the stand first, and actually asked him to repeat his confession, to the surprise and, I must say, delight of Ms Lamb. She couldn't hear it too often. Chip went through it again – verbatim – in that same detached monotone.

Mr Devlin next called Dr Jean Mayhew. She was outstanding. He led her gently, but she knew where to go. She gave the jury a class on the suggestibility of confessions, especially when the subject is under the influence of a particular class of drugs.

'Dr Mayhew, would you tell the jury why such a suggested confession would be convincing?'

She was the voice of scientific reason. 'Because under the right conditions of suggestibility, the person is totally convinced of the truthfulness of the false confession. This is particularly true if a drug like Haldol is used. The subject can't be reasoned with or dissuaded.'

'Thank you, Dr Mayhew.' *From the bottom of our hearts.*

Mr Devlin's summation to the jury was a *tour de force*. He cut a mighty swath through Chip's confession with a recap of Dr Mayhew's testimony, the finding of Dr Burke of Mass General who tested Chip, at my request, and found traces of Haldol in his blood, and finally, a recitation of the inconsistencies between the medical examiner's findings and the confession – the timing of the death, the material used in the strangulation, and the position of the girl as facing away from the murderer during the strangulation. The evidence was circumstantial, but it seemed convincing to me.

Apart from the evidence itself, Mr Devlin was Daniel Webster standing toe-to-toe with the Devil. He could have read from a box of Cheerios, and if I had been on the jury, I would have acquitted

Adolf Eichmann. On the other hand, the members of the jury looked noncommittal.

By the time Ms Lamb finished her strident closing harangue, imploring the jury to ignore apparent circumstantial inconsistencies and believe the defendant's voluntary and repeated confession, it was late in the day. The judge adjourned until the next morning for the charge to the jury and the retiring of the jurors to deliberate.

I started loading the briefcases to take them back to the office. Mr Devlin was sitting beside me in a kind of funk. I chalked it up to the drain of his closing argument, until I heard him mumble through his hands, 'Damn. It's not enough. It's not complete.'

I reached for our set of the medical examiner's blown-up photos, when he took them out of my hand. He sat poring over them while I finished up.

Chip held his gangly cuffed hands out to Mr Devlin before being led back to the Sheriff's van for Charles Street.

'Whatever happens, Mr Devlin, you gave me the best possible defense. You're beginning to convince me, even though I can still hear those words inside of me . . . I'm really grateful.'

He was no youngster, Mr Devlin. The old war-horse used to be able to go all night after a performance like that. So went the stories. But now he was played out. I watched him sink back in the chair at counsel's table with his eyes closed.

He was still there when Ms Lamb ran up to the court clerk and asked to see the judge in chambers. The clerk got permission and summoned Mr Devlin and me to follow Ms Lamb into chambers.

Judge Jeffreys had taken off the robe and was down to the suspenders. He waved us to seats from behind his desk.

'This couldn't wait till tomorrow, Angela?'

'Your Honour, I want to reopen for new evidence. This is critical. I just received it two minutes ago.'

She laid a photograph on the desk and stood back like Prometheus placing fire at the feet of man. The judge cocked his glasses for a closer look. He handed it over to Mr Devlin. I got third look. It was a candid shot of a smiling Chip Townsend roughhousing with a boy in a fraternity T-shirt who had his left arm locked around Chip's neck. The surroundings could be identified as the apartment where the party took place. It didn't take Columbo to spot the old school clock on the wall. In its unsubtle way, it was screaming eleven-thirty. No wonder Ms Lamb had reached seventh heaven. The photo placed Chip at the party after the time of the girl's death. One of the pillars of our defense was his testimony that he was home by ten.

'I take it you can authenticate this photo, Angela.'

'I can, Your Honour. One of the boys at the party was taking candid shots that night. He just realized the importance of this one and rushed it in.'

The judge looked over his glasses at Mr Devlin. He was unruffled, almost nonchalant, but looking into his eyes was like looking through the face of a fine watch at the meshing of intricate gears.

'Could I ask the worthy District Attorney if she spoke to this photographer before today? What's his name?'

'Charles Bingham. Yes, we've spoken before.'

'About the case?'

'Of course. I'd asked him if he could remember Townsend leaving the party. He couldn't. But this photo settles it.'

'Perhaps. When you first spoke to young Bingham, did you ask him to bring to your attention anything he later remembered about the case?'

'Certainly.'

'And therefore he brought in this picture. How did you hear about young Bingham in the first place?'

'The defendant gave his name as one of the people he knew at the party.'

'When?'

'When what?'

'When did the defendant give you his name?'

'He gave it to the police officer when he was arrested.'

His eyes were glowing like coals.

'That's interesting. What occasioned the arrest?'

'We got an anonymous tip that there had been a murder.'

'And that Townsend had committed it?'

'No. Just that he had been one of the male guests.'

Mr Devlin settled back and looked at the judge. I may be

wrong in thinking that a look that signified a single thought passed between them.

'Your Honour, I move to suppress the photo as evidence.'

A steel spring could have come through Ms Lamb's chair without catapulting her to her feet in better time.

'That's absurd, Your Honour. On what grounds?'

The judge nodded to Mr Devlin. 'Would you care to illuminate, Lex?'

'As Your Honour knows, an anonymous tip that doesn't charge a crime is not sufficient to justify an arrest. The arrest was a violation of Mr Townsend's constitutional rights. That arrest led to the defendant's telling the police about young Bingham, which in turn led to his bringing in the photograph. It is, in the poetic phrase of Mr Justice Brennan, ' "the fruit of the poisonous tree." I move to exclude it.'

The granting of Mr Devlin's motion by the judge was the exit cue for Ms Lamb, which she executed in what could best be described as a high dudgeon. She had gone from a lock on a guilty verdict back to a crap shoot. It was anybody's guess which way the jury would go on the evidence.

The photo sat on the desk. Since no one else seemed interested, I picked it up. This case had more whys and hows than a three-year-old.

That night, sometime after midnight, I was in the company of a row of empty martini glasses at the upstairs bar of the Marliave. I was taking my two-thousandth look at the photo, when it grabbed me. The cold air on the dead run to the *Boston Globe* building chilled out the cobwebs. I was cold sober when I reached the photo lab.

The technician of technicians on the night staff was a former client with enough residual gratitude to do a drop-everything favour.

Judge Jeffreys opened the next morning's session with the charge to the jury – an explanation of the law that applied to the case. I slid in beside Mr Devlin partway through it. I had a bombshell, and I had to risk the sting of the court to whisper my discovery.

The judge shot me a look that could have silenced Howard Cosell. Even Mr Devlin gave me a silencing whack on the knee.

I sat there like a monkey on a barrel of rattlesnakes. But if I was edgy, I noticed that Chip Townsend was twice as agitated. Mr Devlin was the calm between two storms.

When the charge ended and the jury left the room, Mr Devlin shushed the both of us and led us to a vacant corner of the courtroom. He gave Chip the nod first. The boyish shyness had hardened, and his voice was an explosive hiss.

'There's supposed to be more evidence. Where's the picture?'

Mr Devlin nodded. 'I figured that was what was eating you.' He looked at me. 'And what have you got for us?'

I leaned in for secrecy. 'I had a friend at the *Globe* do a blowup of this section of the picture. Since Chip was home at ten, the big clock on the wall showing eleven-thirty must have been a setup. They forgot one detail. Look at the watch on the wrist of the kid with his arm around Chip's neck. You can see in the blow-up. It says eight o'clock. That's probably the real time. This was rigged evidence. It proves that someone was trying to frame Chip.'

I had an immediate seconder. Chip was leaning into both of our faces. 'You've got to get the case reopened to get that in. I was framed.'

Mr Devlin looked Chip right in the eyes, but I could feel the fire two feet away.

'Listen to me, you little cockroach, you've played your last game with me. For starters, let's admit among us boys, you raped and killed that girl.'

I looked to Chip for a denial. He was stone silent.

'I think you're a psychotic killer, kid. I think you killed four other girls and got away with it. I know you killed this one. I think you went upstairs with that girl and whatever it is that snaps in your mind went off. Only this time you got carried away in the wrong circumstances. You couldn't just walk away. Too many people knew you had gone upstairs with the girl. When they found the body, you knew they'd come looking for you. That's when you came up with that glassy-eyed confession that didn't quite tally with the facts. You fed it to the D.A., and she was so tickled to get it, she dropped the ball on the rest of the investigation. You even took a dose of Haldol, because you knew sooner or later I'd check you for it.'

Personally, I was blown away, but young Townsend didn't give an inch.

'That photo's got to get into evidence, Devlin.'

Mr Devlin leaned closer, and the heat rose.

'That photo is as phony as you. You had your buddy deliver it so it'd be the last thing the jury'd see. Soon as I saw you and that clock and your pal's arm with the watch up there like a beacon in one cute package, I knew what you had in mind. You figured the D.A.'d bite like a trout, and she did. Since you had us primed to look for a frame-up, you knew we'd catch on to the difference in times. I'd expose the frame-up, and the jury'd acquit. Don't play boys' games with men, kid. I had it suppressed. The jury'll never see it.'

Chip was sputtering. 'You can't keep out defense evidence!'

Mr Devlin walked away. 'I can when it amounts to perjury.'

I caught Mr Devlin in the corridor. 'You've got to tell me. How did you know he was guilty?'

His voice was back to normal. 'That picture the M.E. took of the circular contusion on the back of the dead girl's neck. Two straight lines leading toward each other in the middle of the circle. That bothered me until yesterday afternoon when our grateful client shook hands with me. It perfectly matched the oars on the crest of his championship crew ring.'

Before he walked away, he actually smiled at me. 'That was good work on the photo, sonny. You might be worth something yet.'

I recovered from the glow enough to yell after him, 'What do you think the jury'll do?'

I saw the shoulders go up in a shrug. 'Frankly, I think they'll nail him. We raised some smoke, but don't ever underestimate those twelve sweethearts in the jury box. God bless them, they pay more attention to their instincts than to the lawyers.'

I turned to carry the bags back to the office and get on to other things, when his voice caught me.

'Hey, sonny.'

He turned around on his way out the door.

'As soon as they come in with the guilty verdict, we file a motion for a new trial. This time we defend on insanity. At least he'll avoid the chair. Get on the research now. By the way, what's your first name?'

I've got to admit, it was a great day – despite the guilty verdict.

THE FIRST THING WE DO . . .

C.J. Henderson

'Okay – I got one. How do you get a lawyer out of a tree?'

'Easy,' Hubert told Carmine. 'Just c-cut the rope.'

Everyone laughed. It'd been the same way for the past two days. Actually, as far as New York City was concerned, it'd been that way for the past three months because we had a serial killer running around doing, in the words of the late night talk hosts, 'a valuable public service' by killing lawyers.

It had taken the law a while to notice a pattern because there was a great deal of randomness connected with the killer. He had no recognizable M.O., no signature ear markings. Each time he struck, he varied his technique enough so little pointed to him – except, of course, all the dead lawyers – entertainment attorneys, labour arbitrators, family practice, personal injury, criminal defense or corporate attorneys, it didn't matter – as long as they were a law school graduate, our boy wanted them.

'I'll g-give you one,' answered Hubert. 'A nervous woman goes to her doctor and asks, "doc, can I get pregnant from anal intercourse?" and the doctor says . . .'

'Sure you can, lady,' interrupted Peter Wei. 'Where'd you think lawyers come from?'

As everyone laughed, Carmine pulled his VW bus to the curb several blocks up from the Jacob Javitz convention centre so another of our men could take his position. As Popeye slid out the slide door, I looked at my watch to see if we were still on schedule. I had to. A job as easy as the one we were on, I didn't want to blow.

Once word got out the news had a field day turning the city

upside down. Serial killers have that effect. When our then latest
media curiosity committed a dismemberment, the press dubbed
him, 'The Bar,' in the headline, ANOTHER LAWYER DIS-
MEMBERED BY THE BAR. As always, it stuck. Despite the
fact he killed in cold blood with axes and clubs, with icepicks,
knives or by any other means he could think of – the joke stuck.
One man was thrown off the roof. One woman was made to drink
liquefied lye. Anther woman was battered to death, one hundred
and fifteen bones in her body broken – one at a time – with a block
of marble, another choked to death with a length of barbed wire.
Still, the cute comedy name stuck – and for only one reason. I
think you can guess what it was.

'Come on,' complained Hu. 'Somebody must have a new one.
Give.'

'What do you have if you've got a lawyer buried up to his neck
in the sand?' tried Peter.

'Not enough sand,' answered Hu. 'Try again.'

'How do you know when a lawyer's lying to you?'

'When you can see his lips moving. Try again.'

'How do you save a drowning law . . .'

'Take your fuckin' foot off his head.' Hubert sat forward, then
threw himself back, bouncing off the seat. Slapping his knees
with frustration, he growled, 'Shit. We can't have t-told every
goddamned lawyer joke in the world already. Can we?'

I was happy to let Hu fume in despair while I got the rest of our
people in place. My name is Jack Hagee. I run a small investigations agency. Normally I'm not one to make light of tragedy to
alleviate despair. But this time I'd gotten my share of laughs out
of the legal profession's latest woe – just like everyone else. After
all, nobody likes lawyers – not those they attack nor those they
represent, not the people who trained them, not the people who
sleep with them – nobody. Once upon a time they were a useful
profession, each member judged as an individual. But that was a
long once-upon-a-time ago. Now, thanks to the easy cash to be
made by the simple trick of turning neighbour against neighbour,
they've multiplied like any other dangerous carnivore introduced
into a virgin killing field.

Bred to feed on suspicion and create paranoia they are a useless type of thing – callous and indifferent, monstrous in their appetites and devoid of honour. Because of their ceaseless efforts on behalf of the public, we now live in a country where doctors deny their title rather than risk treating someone dying in the street . . . where city governments give away millions in blackmail payments to hobos . . . where insurance rates are so out of control most towns can't risk taking the chance of having a fireworks show on the Fourth of July.

And, what most people don't understand is how truly different lawyers are from everyone else. The first year of law school consists of nothing but studying case after case in which the person in the right – aka: the one deserving justice – loses in court. Law students are force fed these cases as a way to break down any resolve they might have about doing the right thing. For, in the eyes of those who dispense the law, there is no right and wrong. There is no such thing as justice. There is only the law, and how one can use one's own personal, ever-shifting interpretation of it to free car thieves, muggers and pimps, drug dealers and rapists, murderers, torturers, cannibals and every other breed of vicious, lowlife scum who prey on the masses . . . as long as it increases one's bank balance or prestige.

Not that I should complain, considering it was the Bar that had gotten my agency its current sweet contract. Ten months earlier, the American Bar Association had rented the massive Javitz Centre – a solid acre of ill-conceived glass walls and roofs once called by a former city mayor, 'that glass heap on the Hudson' – for their 'Conference on Proposed Federal Court Fee Shifts.' Aside from not wanting to look like cowards, they'd paid too much for the conference centre to back out once news of the Bar hit the stands. So, to assure its membership they were doing everything possible to protect them, the big boys decided to go for a ton of extra security. Meaning us.

The Javitz has its own security, but for Ernest Malloy, national chair of the ABA subcommittee on civil procedure in the federal courts, that was certainly not good enough. In fact, it didn't take much time in Malloy's presence to realize that, in his opinion, not much of anything good enough for normal mortals was good enough for the lowliest attorney. Armed guards at every entrance,

metal detectors, the finest electronic surveillance money could
buy – not enough. Malloy wanted security on the streets watching
for anyone who might look in some way like a serial killer. It made
little practical sense but, it was what the client wanted so, the
Javitz Centre got it for him. Oliver Costigan, their head of
security, called me, asking me to put together a 7P, 4C, double
ring that would cost no more than $2,500 a day. I told him 'no
problem.'

7P stands for 'seven person.' 4C means one person stationed at
each of an area's 'four corners.' 'Double ring' – floaters making
continual loops. Boring work, but great pay. Ready to earn my
lion's share of it, I got out and headed for my car. Carmine would
circle the centre several times an hour. I would try to stay a half-
block to a block behind him. If anyone called in over their pin
mikes, the van would move in instantly, to either take pictures of
a suspect or offer assistance if things had gotten that far out of
hand.

After we'd been in place for almost three hours one of the
Javitz's security people brought me an announcement.

'Ollie said to come out and get ya, Jack. We may have our boy.'

I gave him a look which told him I didn't appreciate practical
jokes. He gave me one back that said he didn't, either. So far over
thirty 'confessors' had shown up at the Javitz, all claiming to be
the Bar. They were those same sad, misguided fools who appear
at every police station in sight during high-profile cases, trying to
relieve the pressure of some guilt they can't bear by taking on one
they can – like confessing to an axe murder because they can't face
the memory of having screamed at their mother the day she died.
Of course, what'd surprised me was that they were coming to the
convention centre to confess instead of going straight to the cops.
Ollie had explained that one for me.

'Jack,' he'd said with no hint of humour in his voice, 'cops
don't scare anybody anymore because they don't punish anybody
anymore. These guys are looking to make confession, to be
punished. Lawyers, now they hurt people – *they* punish people.
Judges, politicians, they're all lawyers. They've got the power
these days. That's why the loonies are coming to them.'

Curious to see what made this particular loonie so special, I decided to just sit back and see what happened next. It only took us a matter of seconds to reach the room where security was holding the thirtieth Bar to show up since the conference had begun. We entered the room to find Ollie Costigan, an older, even-tempered man with a slightly stooped posture and rock-hard arms and shoulders, both the results of too many years of hard work in hard weather. Ollie was an old time cop, one who'd come up the long way, meaning he'd come up clean. After retirement, Ollie had cast around for a walking-around-money job and had luckily come upon his current post just as it's last owner was leaving it. I'd figured it was all for the best. Ollie Costigan was the type of guy who'd have died without some type of work. Watching him stand over the man in the chair in the centre of the room, the look in his eye told me he was a long way from dying.

'What've you got now, Oll?'

'Somebody's weak sister. She wants a date for the prom but nobody wants to take her.' Ollie motioned two of his men to move in around the suspect. Then he walked me off to one side, saying in a low voice, 'Straight line, Jack, you may be out of a job here.'

'I get to stop working for Malloy? You're breaking my heart. You think this guy's the goods?'

'I don't know. My instincts tell me he's just another Mother Theresa out to do his good deed. But there's a couple of things. First, he knows a lot of crap he shouldn't.'

I almost asked why he didn't just turn the guy in and let New York's finest take care of it when the answer became obvious. Ollie didn't think this guy was actually the Bar but, he couldn't risk releasing the real killer. Then again, he didn't want to put up with the flack he'd catch from the cops if he turned in some crazy. *Poor old Costigan*, he could hear them clearly, *can't tell a loonie from a murderer anymore. Guess he's just a crank, now.*

'And, second,' added Ollie, opening a suitcase on a far table, 'he brought this with him.' Ollie flipped the lid up to reveal a component bomb – a three piece shrapnel affair, one that, in a packed room like the ones upstairs, would have sent broken bits of wire and shredded metal through the fifty or sixty people closest to it.

'Nassssty bit of work,' I said, admiring the hand-wrapping job the wire man had done. Ollie shut the case once more.

'Yeah,' he said, 'well put together. But Bozo here,' Ollie's eyes flashed toward the man in the chair, 'isn't the artist that did it. We called the bomb squad and, yeah, I'll kick his ass into the wagon in a New York minute as soon as they get here but, as to whether or not he's the Bar, well, come on, see what you think.'

Malloy had gotten Ollie access to the police files on the Bar. He'd wanted his security people to have all the information available on the killer stalking him and his flock and he'd damn well made sure he got it. Picking up two thick folders from the table next to the bomb, Ollie preceded me, walking back to the man in the center of the room, asking, 'Now, tell us again, Mr, Mr, ah . . .'

'Cowan. Gregory Cowan.'

'Mr Cowan, why did you come here today with that case over there? You did bring that case on the table with you today, correct?'

'Oh, yes. That was me. I came to kill all the lawyers.'

'Why would you want to do that?'

'For the same reason everyone would do it,' answered the little man, smiling up at us. 'Because I hate lawyers.'

Ollie handed me one of the files as he kept Cowan talking. Knowing what he wanted I started skimming, getting a feel for those parts of the case that hadn't been revealed to the public. Interrupting Ollie's good cop bit, I asked in my best 'tired-but-curious' voice,

'Mr Cowan, did you kill Ms Judith Lerner?'

'I don't . . . was that the one . . . ah, in Scarsdale? Yes, it was. The one with the horrible country club dress, huge white seams running here, and here, with those big puffed-wing sleeves. Buttons at the tips – horrible tacky woman. Yes, I garroted her. With a piece of spiky wire from her own garage. Yes, I enjoyed killing her.'

I looked over the top of the file at Ollie, at Cowan, then back at Ollie. No crime scene photos of Lerner had been released. Cause of death had been given as strangulation but, no mention had been made of the wire, or that it'd come from her husband's barbed wire collection. Those were 'held' facts, points not released in the hope they could be used to prove what they seemed to be proving now. There was no way he could have known about her clothes. Or the wire.

Looking to see exactly what it is we had found, I picked another name. Again, Cowan's memory matched our facts.

'Michel Steffens. The fat one in the red suit – that atrocious red suit. Oh God, yes. You want to know if I think he was killed with a kitchen knife – because that's what it said in the papers. Phooey – I jammed a pair of scissors through his eye. That's how I killed him. Steffens, I mean. Mr Red Suit.' Cowan looked at me strangely, like a teenager going for the bonus point on a quiz rather than a psychotic confessing to a string of murders. He pursed his lips for several seconds, then told us, 'I'm just so bad with names, you see. I'm very good with clothes but, I'm just not that good with names.'

That might have been the case but, something didn't feel right to me. Wanting to test his memory for clothes a little further, I tried another name in the files, asking him about Sandy Connell. Then I asked about Frank Belinito, and then Roger Seran. In all three cases the quiet, unassuming Mr Cowan had either the right answers or very, very close ones – close enough that the missed degrees could be forgiven. After all, who can remember the exact details of every move they make – even their murders.

By the time I'd asked about Belinito, Ollie had settled into the chair next to mine, listening to Cowan's answers, rolling them over in his head. Leaning over toward me, he asked, 'So, what do you think, Jack?'

I searched my head for my best answer. The man had come into the midst of hundreds of lawyers with intimate knowledge that only the killer everyone was looking for should've had. But, despite all of that, I told Ollie, 'I don't think this is the guy.'

'Which,' came a voice from behind us, 'just goes to show what a great horse's ass you are, Mr Hagee.' Without turning – without ever having met the man – I knew that Ernest Malloy had entered the room.

I stood and extended my right hand, greeting our visitor, 'Mr. Malloy, I presume.'

Ignoring me as he would anything not conducive to lining his pockets, Malloy turned to Ollie, demanding, 'Why isn't that man in custody? Why are you wasting time here with this gutter worker?'

'The police bomb squad *has* been alerted, Mr Malloy,' snapped Ollie, in less of a mood for nonsense than I was. 'When they get here there's no doubt Mr Cowan will be taken into very firm custody. As for Jack, I asked him in to help me give our detainee the once over.'

'I hardly see where that's pertinent,' countered Malloy. 'I've been told – the whole centre's heard the news – that this Cowan is the person people have been referring to as the Bar. Is he or isn't he?'

'If you want my opinion, Mr Malloy, and that seems to be what you're asking for – the answer is "no." I don't think so.'

'And why not?'

'Something about him doesn't feel right. I know that's not much to go on . . .'

'Yes,' snapped Malloy, grinning as if he were performing in court. 'I agree. It isn't. I'm told this man knows the intimate details of any Bar murder on record. Is that true?'

'Yes, sir,' admitted Ollie. 'It is.'

'And that he came here with a lethal device he claims freely he intended to set off upstairs during the next general floor meeting?'

'That's right, your honour,' called out Cowan. 'I did.'

'You admit you are the man the media calls "the Bar?" '

'Yes, sir,' answered Cowan, respectfully. 'That would be me.'

'Malloy,' I said, causing the lawyer to jerk around abruptly. 'Almost three dozen guys have shown up here claiming the same thing. I'm sure it's a phenomenon you're used to.'

'Indeed, Mr Hagee. But I'm sure you'll agree that in the case of the typical disturbed individual making false confession, that they can't usually plead their case as convincingly as Mr Cowan.'

'There's a first time for everything, Malloy. Ollie's right about this – something doesn't feel right about this guy. I don't care how much he knows about the Bar's methods.'

'No, you wouldn't, would you?' sneered the lawyer, turning

away from both Ollie and Cowan to face me fully. 'You're one of those "gut-feeling" people, who in the face of all evidence and logic proceeds off on their own track because deep down inside, you just *allllways* know what the right answers are. Don't you?'

'Sometimes it works that way, sometimes it doesn't. That's not the point. Who knows what the answer is here – maybe the real Bar found Cowan and coached him, set this all up just to throw everyone off guard. Who knows? He certainly has planned all his moves carefully enough so far. All I'm telling you is that this is our work, Malloy. This is what we do for a living and as the expert you insisted be hired I'm telling you that I'm sure that guy over there is not your man. He might be working with him but, *he's* not the Bar.'

'You don't fool me,' answered Malloy. Pulling at his jacket sleeve absently, evening out the amount of cuff showing at each wrist, the lawyer said, 'you're protecting your job. Like any greedy teamster you want to keep yourself and your men on the job as long as possible. Well, we'll have no more of that.'

Malloy took one last look at Cowan and then instructed Ollie, 'You'll contact both the police and the press right now and inform them that you have the Bar in custody. And as for you, Mr Hagee . . .' the lawyer grinned just enough to make a straight line of his pencil moustache, 'You and your team are no longer needed. You will cease operations at once and vacate the area. You and yours will not cost those assembled above another cent.'

I stood back, stunned for a moment, then said, 'You're crazy, Malloy. I'm telling you you're making a mistake.'

'And I'm telling you that you may be able to cheat your other clients with vague references to the condition of your intestines and romantic notions about the superiority of instinct over facts, but not me.' Turning back to Ollie, Malloy demanded, 'Mr Costigan, I don't intend to be in this basement when my award is presented. I intend to be upstairs, on stage, receiving it from the head of the New York Bar as it says in the program. There-fore, allow me to be brief. You are an old man who needs this job so let me tell you what you're going to do. You will escort Mr Hagee from the premises – you will see to it that all his people know they are unemployed by,' the lawyer glanced at his watch, 'two o'clock at the latest.'

'Hey,' I yelled, suddenly at my limit, 'Fuck you, Malloy. This kind of nickel-and-dime thinking is what gets people like you killed. Try and remember, it was your fear of the Bar that made you call me and mine in the first place.'

'Yes,' sneered the lawyer, 'and now it's my lack of fear that allows me to dismiss you.' Turning back to Ollie, he snapped, 'Two o'clock and Mr Hagee is barred from the area. If I see him or any of his ilk inside the convention centre I'll see to it you never work again. Do I make myself clear?'

Ollie didn't answer. I could see the steam building within him, pushing him toward making himself clear to Malloy. Not seeing any point in that, I said, 'He understood. Go get your award . . . *lawyer.*'

'Save your epithets, Mr Hagee,' he said back at me over his shoulder, already walking off toward the exit. 'And your false nobility. You'll need the breath to get yourself off Javitz property before Mr Costigan's men are forced to detain you for trespassing.'

And then he was through the doors and gone. Ollie apologized – I told him not to bother. He sent some of his people to find my guys and get them the message to meet me at the front entrance. Then, we both agreed that Malloy was a sack of shit, traded a few lawyer jokes, and I went out to find the boys.

After I told them everything that happened, Hubert said, 'You m-mean we've been screwed by a lawyer?' Slapping his face for comic effect, he finished, 'I'm shocked. By gosh, that's what it is – I'm shocked.'

'Yeah, you and me both,' I agreed. While the others bitched about losing two and a half days' pay so Malloy could grandstand for his budget committee, I thought about what'd happened. On the surface, Malloy appeared to be right – the facts did point directly at Cowan. How, I asked myself, could he not be the Bar?

'Hell with them,' said Hu. 'I got a new joke. One scientist says to another, "we should start usin' lawyers instead of white mice in our experiments." When the other scientist asks "why?" the first one says, "I got three reasons . . ." '

Sure, I thought, the real Bar could've coached Cowan and sent him in as a distraction but, it was such a comic book scenario – risking leaving a man behind who knew who he was, just to gain a distraction? It didn't make any sense. What could he gain? And what was it about Cowan, I asked myself again, that made me want to grasp at such straws rather than just believe he was guilty?

'First, there's a lot more lawyers than white mice. Second, the lab assistants won't get so attached to them. And third, let's face it, there's some things even rats won't do. Of course, sir, it might be very hard to extrapolate our test results to human beings.'

Sir. I heard the word again – heard Hu saying it, heard the others laughing and then heard it again – Cowan's voice talking to Malloy . . . *sir* . . . he'd called him. It clicked in my head . . . whoever the Bar was, he wasn't a man who called lawyers *sir*, especially shitheels like Ernest Malloy.

'Yes, sir, hard t-to extrapolate those test results from lawyers t-to human beings.'

I started running toward the Javitz centre. *Respect*. Cowan had shown Malloy *respect* – something no one would do who really hated lawyers. The little geek had said he hated lawyers and everyone present had believed him because it was such an easy thing to believe. As I closed the gap between myself and the front door, I *knew* that the real Bar was somewhere inside, getting ready to kill Malloy and everyone else around him – not saying *sir* to anyone. I made it as far as the front door when the first of the bombs went off.

How? I wondered as hundreds of the Javitz's intricate glass walls blew out above me. With a noise as loud as God, the roof was flung into the air, tons of transparent plate lifting into the sky for a horrible moment, then racing back to Earth. The slam of it was a terrible sound followed by a moment of silence. Then the sharding crashes began as bloody crystal rained in the streets.

I pressed up against the wall, trying to avoid the deadly torrent, wondering again, *How? When? Where?*

I didn't bother to wonder *Why?* That one I knew.

That one was easy.

WITNESS

Madison Smartt Bell

The day he heard that Paxton Morgan was released, Wilson had
been planning to revise a will. It was a slack period for him and he
didn't expect to be in court until late in the following week, but
he'd come in early just the same. The door to his inner office was
open on the lateral hallway, and he could hear the whisk of a letter
opener as Mrs Veech, behind the front desk, sliced into the
morning mail. Mostly bills or offers of subscriptions, he'd
glanced through it quickly on his way in.

There was a jingle as the front door opened and Wilson raised
his head to listen, but it was a man he didn't want to see, and Mrs
Veech denied his presence. A grumble, sound of pacing, scrape of
a match and a faint distant odour of tobacco. Mrs Veech coughed.
The voice grudgingly inquired if the smoke bothered her. Mrs
Veech said nothing but coughed again, more significantly. Her
allergy to cigarettes was highly selective – Wilson, for instance,
smoked himself. When the front door released a jangle of departure, he picked up his pencil and went back to the will. Mrs
Veech, he could hear, was dealing with the remains of the mail.

'Mr Wilson, did you know they were letting Pax Morgan go?'

He heard her voice without immediately understanding it,
registering only the anxiously rising note at the end. The task
in his hand was complicated, though almost entirely frivolous:
the testament of a woman some forty years old who would
probably live at least forty more, revising her bequests more
or less semi-annually. Still, it was an amusement she could afford
if it pleased her, harmless enough, and he had use for the fee.

He drafted another line or two on the long yellow pad and
broke the point of his pencil. Then the sense of Mrs Veech's
question reached him and he stood up, taking a cigarette from his

shirt pocket as he stepped into the hall. Mrs Veech sat bolt upright in her desk chair, clamping some sort of form in both her hands. Wilson took it from her and walked to the front window, setting the unlit cigarette in the corner of his mouth as he moved. It was a slick gray photocopy of a release form from Central State, with the name of Paxton Morgan typed along with other information and the illegibly scrawled signature of some doctor or official in the lower right-hand corner. He noted that the box for the date was not filled in.

'They might have already turned him out,' Mrs Veech said.

'Or they might just still be thinking about it.' Wilson turned to face her. Round, plain and comfortable, she was a clean fifteen years older than he and normally unfazeable, though now she seemed perceptibly disturbed.

'I wonder who sent us this,' he said.

'There wasn't any cover letter.' Mrs Veech frowned.

Wilson stepped across and picked up the slit envelope from the stack of circulars on the desk and paced back to the window, turning it over in his hands. It was letterhead stationery from the hospital, with his own address unremarkably typed and a postmark from two days before. Absently he folded it in three and peered out the window, around the hanging vines of the plants Mrs Veech had insisted on stringing up there. The office was on the ground floor at the corner of the square, and sighting through the letter *O* of his own reversed name on the glass, Wilson could see a couple of cars and one mud-splattered pickup truck revolving lazily around the concrete Confederate soldier on his high pedestal at the centre. Opposite, the usual complement of idlers lounged around the courthouse steps. The office had a southern exposure, and he could feel a slight sunny warmth on the side of his face through the pane.

'Well, damn their eyes,' he said, and then, as he noticed Mrs Veech again, 'Excuse me.'

Back in his inner office, Wilson lit the cigarette and set it in an ashtray to burn itself out, then began dialing the phone with the butt end of his pencil. In some fifteen minutes he had variously heard that Pax Morgan had already been released, was not going to be released at all, or had never been admitted. He hadn't expected to discover who had sent the anonymous notification, and so was not surprised when he didn't. Although he did learn that a Dr Meagrum was supposed to be presiding over the case, he could not get through to him. He left a message asking that his call be returned. The central spring of his revolving chair squealed slightly as he leaned back, away from the phone. On the rear wall of the room, behind the triangle of clients' chairs, bookshelves rose all the way to the high ceiling, bearing about half of Wilson's law library. Hands laced behind his head, he scanned the top row of heavy books as though looking for something, though he was not. After a moment he tightened his lips and leaned forward again and made the call he had been postponing.

He had the number by heart already because it had once been his own, the Nashville law firm where he'd formerly worked. In those days Sharon Morgan would likely have answered the phone herself, but they used her more as a researcher now, and had hired a different receptionist. She was good at the work, and with the two children there was no doubt the better pay made a difference. Still studying for her own law degree, part time; Pax had never liked that much. Wilson asked for her and waited till she came on the line, her voice brisk, as he remembered it. It had been some months since they had spoken and the first few exchanges passed in pleasantries, inquiries about each other's children and the like. Then, a pause.

'Well, you never called just to pass the time,' Sharon said. 'Not if I know you.'

Wilson hesitated, thinking, What would she look like now? The same. Phone pinched between her chin and shoulder, a tail of her longish dark hair involved with the cord some way. Chances were she'd be doing something on her desk while she waited for him to continue, brown eyes sharp on some document, wasting no time.

'Right,' he said. 'Have you heard anything of Pax lately?'

'And don't care to,' she said, her tone still easy. 'Why would you ask?'

The chair spring squeaked as Wilson shifted position. The distant sound of a typewriter came to him over the line. He flicked his pencil with a fingernail and watched its bevels turning over the lines of the yellow pad. 'And not the hospital either, I don't suppose.'

'Oh-*ho*,' Sharon said. He could hear her voice tightening down, homing in. She took the same grim satisfaction in any discovery, no matter its purport, which was part of what made her good at her job. 'Is that what it is?'

'I'm afraid,' Wilson said, 'they're letting him out, if they haven't already.'

'And never even let me know. There ought to be a law . . .'

'. . . but there doesn't appear to be one,' Wilson said. He picked up the hospital form and read off to her its most salient details. A stall, he thought, even before he was through with it. 'The morning mail,' he said. 'No date, and I don't even know who sent it.'

'Then what are you thinking to do?' she said.

'I've been calling the hospital,' Wilson said. 'If I ever get through to the right doctor, maybe I can convince them to hold him, if he's not already gone.'

'*If*,' Sharon said sharply. 'All up to them, is it?'

'I would call it a case for persuasion,' Wilson said. 'So, did you have any plans for the weekend? I should be able to get in touch . . .'

'I'm taking the children out to the lake.'

Wilson plucked another cigarette from his breast pocket and began to tamp it rhythmically on the old green desktop blotter. 'I don't know,' he said. 'Why not go to your brother's, say? Instead.'

'What would we want to do that for?'

'Look, Sharon,' he said. 'You know, it's to hell and gone from anywhere, that house on the lake. And nobody even out there this time of year.'

'I will *not* run from that –' She interrupted herself, but he thought the calm of her voice was artificial when she went on. 'The kids are packed for it. They're counting on it. I don't see any reason to change our plans.'

'You don't, do you?' Wilson said without sarcasm, and put a match to his cigarette. He supposed he'd been expecting this, or something a whole lot like it.

'Why don't you get a peace bond on him?' Sharon said. 'If he really is out, I mean. Something. Because it ought to be *his* problem. Not mine.'

'I could do that,' Wilson said. 'Try to, anyway. You know what good it'll do, too. You know it better than I do.'

There was silence in the receiver; the phantom typewriter had stopped. Pax Morgan had been under a restraining order that night back before the divorce decree when he'd appeared at the house in Nashville he and Sharon had shared and smashed out all the ground-floor windows with the but end of his deer rifle; he'd made it all the way around the house before the police arrived.

'Well, devil take the hindmost,' Wilson said. 'I'll let you know what I can find out. And you take care.'

'Thanks for letting me know.'

'Take care, Sharon,' Wilson said, but she had already hung up, so he did too.

Shifting the cigarette to his left hand, he picked up the pencil and began jotting a list at the foot of the pad with the blunted tip. Often he did his thinking with the pencil point; he'd discovered that sometimes a solution would appear in the interstices of what he wrote. There were only two items on the list.

-Judge Oldfield   injunction P.M.
-Dr Meagrum   Central State

He added a third.

-call back S.M.

The pencil doodled away from the last initial. The list was obvious and complete, and after he acted on it nothing would be solved. A long ash was sprouting from his cigarette, but he didn't notice until the spark crawled far enough to burn his knuckle.

For the rest of the morning, he worked abstractedly on the will with imperfect concentration. Every twenty minutes or so he interrupted himself to make some fruitless call. Dr Meagrum was perpetually 'on rounds' or 'in consultation.' Judge Oldfield was spending his morning on the bench. Wilson's own phone rang occasionally, but always over something trivial. When he called Oldfield's chambers again around noon, he found that the judge was gone to lunch. He tightened his tie, got his seersucker suit coat down from the hat rack and, with a word or two to Mrs Veech, went out himself.

Circling the square counterclockwise, he passed the Standard Farm Store, the bank and the counterhouse steps, where one man or another raised a broad flat palm to greet him. It was warm out, an Indian summer heat wave, though it was late October and the leaves had already turned. A new asphalt path on the southbound street felt tacky on his shoes as he crossed. A couple of blocks west of the square he was already verging on the edge of time; beyond the long low roof of Dotson's Restaurant there were woods, turned fired-clay red patched with sere yellow, with a few deep green cedars standing anomalously among the other trees.

The fans were on inside the restaurant, revolving on tall poles, fluttering the corners of the checked oilcloths on the small square tables. Judge Oldfield sat toward the rear – alone, for a wonder – behind a plate of fried catfish, hush-puppies and boiled greens. As Wilson approached he put down his newspaper and smiled. 'What wind blows you here, young fellow my lad?'

'An ill one, I'd say.' Wilson sat down on a ladder-back chair. 'Do you remember Sharon Morgan? A Lawrence, she was, before she married.'

'Married that crazy fellow, didn't she?'

'That's the one.' Wilson ordered an iced tea from the waitress who'd appeared at his elbow, and turned back to the judge. 'They're letting him out of Central State, at least that's what it looks like.' He ran down the brief of the morning's activity while Oldfield grazed on his catfish and nodded.

'It worrying you personally?' the judge said when he was done. 'For yourself, I mean?'

'Oh, no,' Wilson said. 'Not hardly. It wasn't me he said he'd kill, was it? I doubt he'd remember much about me. I never knew him any too well. Even while the divorce was going on it was just her he was mad at.'

'So it's the wife – ex-wife, I mean. She's the one with the worry.'

'She's the one.' Wilson frowned down at his hands. There was a small watery blister where the cigarette had burned him, surprisingly painful for its size. He turned the cold curve of the iced tea glass against it. 'She asked me to get an injunction on him. That's why I came hunting you.'

Oldfield took off his fragile rimless glasses, rubbed them with a handkerchief and put them back on. 'That's tricky, old son,' he said, 'when you don't know for sure if he's loose or not.'

'Hard to get good information out of that place, don't you know?' Wilson said. 'Seems like a lot of them are crazy, doctors and patients alike.'

'Must be that's why they call it a madhouse,' Oldfield said with a faint smile. 'Well. She does live in the county now? Full time?'

'She moved here right after the divorce,' Wilson said.

'Just to oblige you, now,' Oldfield said. 'I could sign you a paper. You draw it up. It happens he *is* out, you let me know and we'll sign it and serve it right away. It won't be much of a help to her, though.'

'Don't I know it,' Wilson said. 'But what else do you do?'

'Not a whole lot that you *can*,' said Oldfield. 'You really think she's got call to worry? Not just fretful, is she?'

'Not her,' Wilson said. 'I'm the one fretting. I'm wondering, how can I get a deputy to watch over them for a couple of days?'

'You know you can't set them on her,' Oldfield said. 'Not without she asks for it herself.'

'She won't.'

'She was a pretty thing, as I recall,' Oldfield said irrelevantly. He took off his glasses and rubbed at the bridge of his nose. 'And knew her own mind, or seemed to.'

'You mean she's stubborn.'

'Yes, that's right.'

Wilson stood up. 'I thank you,' he said.

Oldfield smiled myopically up at him, his eyes a light watery blue. 'You ought to stay and try the catfish.'

'Well, I believe not,' Wilson said. 'Not much of an appetite today.'

'A young man like you?' The judge shook his head. 'Must be this heat.'

'Your wife called,' Mrs Veech reported. 'She'll call you back. And that man from Central State, he called. Dr Meagrum.'

'He would have, wouldn't he?' Wilson said, shrugging out of his jacket. 'Wait till I was gone, I mean.'

Mrs Veech sniffed. 'In a tearing-down hurry, too,' she said. 'He was right cross to find you not here.'

'He'll get over it,' Wilson said. 'All right, then, would you make sure for me that Pax Morgan still has his house in Brentwood? We might want to serve a paper on him a little later in the day.'

In the inner office it was a little too warm, though not quite oppressive. He put his coat on the hat rack, cracked the single window and paced for a moment at the far side of his desk. It was a shallow room and the high wall of dark bookbindings seemed uncomfortably close. With a sigh he went back to his seat, lit a cigarette, picked up the will, put it down, lifted a list of the other items on his immediate agenda and then let that drop too.

The urge to pick at the blister seemed irresistible. He tore loose an edge of it, reviewing, in spite of himself, what little he really knew about Pax Morgan. They'd gone to the same high school, but two years apart; Wilson was the younger. Pax had played football – he remembered that – indifferently, in the line. Later on he had inherited money and started dabbling in real estate, or insurance, neither making nor losing much at whatever it might have been. Grown, he was a loud bluff fellow with a ruddy face and crinkly, almost yellow hair. At the large parties where Wilson would occasionally run into him, he was known for drinking too much and becoming not just mush-mouthed but crazily incoherent. The drinking was said to be a factor in his later, more serious breakdowns.

Wilson had gone to Sharon's wedding but he couldn't think if it was before or after it that he'd had the one brush with Pax he remembered with real clarity. Another party, undoubtedly some Christmas gathering, for Pax was wearing an incongruous Santa Claus tie and had managed to get quite drunk on eggnog.

Shuffled together by the crowd, they somehow became embroiled in an argument over deer hunting. Wilson shot duck and dove, rabbit and squirrel, and on his father's farm he might shoot what he had to, to protect the livestock, but he had no taste for shooting deer, which now appeared to be Pax's ruling passion. Wilson was trying to get off the subject, but Pax wouldn't let it drop.

'You've never been blooded,' he said thickly. 'That's your trouble, you've never been *blooded*.' He grasped Wilson's lapel and twisted it, drawing himself unpleasantly near, and Wilson was a little startled by what he himself did next, a trick someone had showed him in the Army. He took hold of Pax's thumb and squeezed the joints of it together, so that the sudden sharp pain made Pax flinch and let go. Reflexively, Wilson took a step backward, jostling someone behind him in the crowded room, but Pax's face went from surprise to a total blank, like a television switched to an empty channel, and so the whole episode was amputated.

Real craziness there, or an early sign of it. Wilson pulled the dead skin back from the blister, creating a small red-rimmed sore. By the time of the divorce, there were many worse examples, enough to fill a dossier. Wilson had never cared for divorce work much, but Sharon was both a colleague and a sort of distant friend, and also it was in the first thin stage of his independent practice. But once it was over he swore off friends' divorces altogether, no matter how bad he might need the work. It had been an easy case in the sense that the outcome was not in real doubt, but it was angry and ugly on Pax's side, and there'd been some bitter squabbling over property. Sharon had held out for the house on the lake – impractically, as Wilson thought – surrendering the Nashville residence to Pax, who'd later sold it. Reaching for the phone to call the hospital one more time, he wished again she hadn't done that.

His game of telephone tag with Central State went on for a couple more hours, unpromisingly. When the phone finally rang back around two-thirty, it was his wife.

'Not interrupting, I hope,' she said. 'Is it busy?'

'Not so you'd notice,' he said. 'It's been pretty quiet.'

'Well, we need a gallon of milk,' she said, 'and cornmeal. Would you stop on the way home?'

'I'll do it,' Wilson said, scribbling on the pad. 'Lisa driving you crazy today?' Their daughter was four years old, and frantic.

'How should I describe it?' she said, and laughed. 'This time next year she'll be in school . . . I'll miss her, though.'

'That's the spirit,' Wilson said. The light on his phone began to flash and Mrs Veech called down the hall, 'It's that Dr Meagrum!'

'I've got to take this call,' Wilson said. 'I'll be home on time, I think . . .' He pushed the button.

Dr Meagrum seemed to be already *in medias res*. '– there's an issue of doctor–patient confidentiality here, Mr uh, Wilson. I don't know who could have sent you that form but they did so without my authorization.'

'Did they?' Wilson said, catching his breath. 'As you may know, I represent Mr Morgan's ex-wife, and given the circumstances of the case, it seems to me appropriate that *both* of us should have been informed.'

'I can't agree with you there,' Dr Meagrum snapped.

'All due respect to your point of view,' Wilson said, trying to collect himself. The conversation had taken an adversarial turn too soon. 'I take it that Mr Morgan *has*, in fact, been released from your, ah, custodial care.'

'My records show that Mr Morgan has been responding favourably to a course of medication and was transferred to outpatient status two days ago.'

'I see,' Wilson said. 'What medication, may I ask?'

'I'm sorry, but that's confidential.'

'And what assurance do we have that he will actually *take* this medication?'

'He's in our outpatient program now, and we'll be monitoring him on a bi-weekly basis.'

'Bi-weekly, you say. That's *every two weeks?*' Wilson creaked back in his chair, gazing up at the join of his bookcase and the ceiling. 'Dr Meagrum, I would like you to consider' – he paused, thinking over the jargon as if fumbling for a key – 'consider returning Mr Morgan to *inpatient status*. Temporarily, shall we say. In the interests of the safety of his ex-wife and family.'

'Our file shows that any such step would be contraindicated,' the doctor said. 'Not in the patient's best interests.'

A white flash of light, something like heat lightning, burst over Wilson's mental horizon, obscuring his view of the bookcases. He found he was clenching the receiver in a strangle grip and talking much louder than before. 'Sir, you are describing a *piece of paper* to me, and I am talking to you about a man who has threatened to kill his wife, not once but many times –'

Dr Meagrum harrumphed. 'Yes, someone with this type of pathology might make such a threat, but I wouldn't suggest that you take it too seriously . . .'

'He came to her house with a thirty-nought-six rifle,' Wilson said. 'A *loaded* rifle – I'm now referring to the police report. They found him and the gun and they found her barricaded in an upstairs bedroom. With her two children, I should say. The boy is six now, Dr Meagrum, and the little girl is seven. Your *outpatient* has threatened to kill them too.'

Dr Meagrum resorted to the imperial 'we': 'We have no record that this patient is violent. We see no reason to alter the treatment program at this time.'

With a mighty effort, Wilson established a greater degree of control over his voice. 'Very well,' he said frostily. 'I do sincerely hope you'll see no reason to regret the course you've taken.'

By dumb luck his next call caught Judge Oldfield in his chambers, between cases, on the fly.

'I'm asking the impossible now,' Wilson said. 'Let's have him picked up. An APB. Lock him up and have a look at him. Just for a day or so.'

'You're right,' Oldfield said. 'That's impossible. I couldn't do it if I wanted to. This is Williamson County. We haven't got a police state here.'

'It's a free country, isn't it,' Wilson said. 'Well, I had to ask.'

'I wonder if you did, at that,' Oldfield said. 'You're acting mighty worked up about this, old son. Don't you think you might be making a little much of it all? He's been out two days already, so you say, and what happened? Nothing. The lady didn't even

know until you called her. Simmer down some, think it over. Go
home early. It's Friday, after all.'

'All right,' Wilson said. 'Might give it a try.'

'You get me that injunction and I'll pass it on to the sheriff
direct,' Oldfield said. 'I can't do any more than that.'

'I know,' Wilson said. 'Not until something happens. Well, I
appreciate it.'

He hung up and dialed Sharon Morgan at the office but she
was gone, gone for the weekend, had left half an hour before to
pick up the children from school. He plopped down the phone
and tried, forcibly, to relax. Try it. Judge Oldfield was no fool,
after all. Wilson picked up the pencil with a fleeting idea of listing
off what he was thinking, feeling, but that was a ridiculous
notion; probably that was how they spent their time at Central
State. Possibly nothing would happen anyway. Possibly. He
looked up Sharon's home number and dialed it, but there was
no answer, though it rang twenty times.

In ten minutes he had scratched out the requisite injunction
and handed it to Mrs Veech with instructions to type it and walk
it over to the courthouse when she was done. After she had gone
out, he sat doing nothing but covering the phone, which didn't
ring. The jingle of Mrs Veech's return moved him to at least
pretend to work. But he'd had it with the will for the day, though
it still wasn't quite finished. He scraped his agenda toward him
across the desk and ran his pencil point down item by item. There
were two boundary disputes and a zoning complaint. A piece of
frivolous litigation to do with somebody's unleashed dog. There
was a murder case where the defendant would plead, draw two-
to-ten and count himself lucky. A foregone conclusion, Wilson
thought in his present skeptical mood, though matters had not yet
reached that stage. At the foot of the list was a patent case that
would make him and his client rich if he could win it. This one
was the most remote, no court date even set for it yet, but at the
same time the most intriguing, as much for its intricacy as its
promise. He swiveled and dug in the cabinet for the file.

At four he called Sharon Morgan at the lake and got no answer.
For another half hour he studied the patent case, though he was

losing interest at an exponential rate. When he next called there was still no answer, and he was out of the chair and snatching his coat down from its peg before he even knew he meant to leave. On the highway bound for Keyhole Lake he began to feel a little foolish. He'd been presuming, counting the time from three o'clock, when school let out. It was not more than an hour from Nashville to the lake house, but he hadn't considered that she might have stopped to shop on the way, or taken the children to a movie or simply for a drive. Now it appeared to him that his every move that day had been an error. It was unlike him to have lost his temper with that doctor. Patience had always been his strength; he left it to his opponents to make mistakes in anger. Then too, that last call to Judge Oldfield was something he'd have to live down, and on top of all that he had wasted the day, and would need to come back in Saturday morning to recover the lost time.

All foolishness, and yet the thought did not comfort him. He drove carefully, a hair under the speed limit, sighting through the windshield across the burn mark on his knuckle. For no reason he could think of, he let the car roll past the Morgan mailbox and coast to a stop on the shoulder, where he got softly out. There was a little lip to climb before he could see down the driveway to the steeply pitched roof of the A-frame house and the blue lake distantly visible out past it. It was cooler here; the weather was turning, or else it was a chill coming off the water.

Below him, the drive was matted with fallen leaves. A staining fall of sunset light came slanting through the tree trunks on either side as the wind rose and combed the red leaves back, bringing a few more falling from the branches. Except for the wind it was utterly still; only across the lake the dogs in Jackson's kennel were barking, their voices echoing off the flat expanse of the water. But probably they were barking all the time. That was not the problem. What was wrong was that the passenger door of Sharon's orange Volkswagen had been left hanging open, sticking out stiffly like a broken arm. The car was pulled around parallel to the back porch, and over its roof he saw that the sliding glass door to the house had been left open too.

He walked to the dangling door and stopped. Just past the edge of the drive, not more than three yards from him, there lay a child's blue tennis shoe, a Ked, with maple leaves spread around it like the prints of a large hand. Some twenty paces farther on he found the second shoe and then the little boy, barefoot, lying face down in a pile of sloppily raked leaves. Wilson thought that his name had been Billy, but he couldn't be quite certain of it, which bothered him unreasonably. The child had been shot in the base of the neck; the entry wound was rather small. Beyond the leaf pile a wide swath of dun lawn swept down to the lake shore where a canoe, tethered to a little dock, rocked softly on the water.

A strip of almost total darkness fit into the gap of the glass door. The porch floor moaned as Wilson crossed it, and glancing down he saw a brass shell casing caught in a crack between two boards. He bent to pick it up, then stopped himself and put both hands in his pockets. Through the door was a large living room with no ceiling, only the peaked roof and the rafters. At this time of day it was very dim within and it took Wilson's eyes a moment to adjust. The daughter (he was almost sure her name was Jill) was sprawled on a high-backed wicker chair as if flung there by some strong force. There was a single wound in her chest. Her mouth was open slightly and her eyes showed a little white. Wilson thought it more than likely that Pax had shot her from a standing position on the porch.

It took him only a quarter turn of his head to locate Sharon's body at the far end of the long room, lying across a wide flight of steps that rose to the kitchen and dining area. Pax might well have shot her from the doorway; he was a marksman, the proof was plain, and efficient with his shells. Wilson crossed the room to the steps and paused. He couldn't tell just where she'd been hit, though she'd bled very heavily. She lay crooked, twisted over at the waist, the fingers of one hand folded over the overhang of a step. Her hair had fallen full over her face, and Wilson was grateful for that, but her position looked so uncomfortable that he was tempted to turn and straighten her. His hands were still jammed in his pockets, however, and he left them there.

He went up the steps almost on tiptoe, careful to avoid bloodying his shoes, and made a turn to the left that brought

him up against the metal kitchen cabinets. His breath was coming
very short, each intake arrested as though by a punch in the
midsection. He was aware of the tick of his wristwatch, and that
was all. There was a telephone on the kitchen counter, and
presently he detached a paper towel from a roll neatly suspended
beneath the line of cabinets, wrapped it around the receiver and
called the sheriff's office.

At the opposite end of the kitchen, a smaller set of sliding doors
opened onto a deck overlooking the lawn and the lake. With the
help of another paper towel, he slid back the door and went out
and sat on a bench to wait. The lake's surface had a painful
metallic glitter, with the sunset colours spreading across it like
corrosion. He had left his sunglasses in the car, and being in no
mood to retrieve them, he simply shut his eyes. In Korea, where
the Army had sent him, he had *seen some action,* as they say, but
afterward he had thought very little about what he had seen. In
some quietly ticking corner of his mind a speculation was going
forward as to how the bodies had come to be positioned as they
were, and now it came to him that after they were all inside the
house the boy must have missed his shoes and gone back to the
car – He opened his eyes with a jerk and looked up. A solitary,
premature firely detached itself from the treetops on one side of
the yard and floated dreamily across and into the treetops on the
other.

It was twilight by the time he had parked his car behind the
square, and for some reason he bypassed his office and walked on
down Main Street as far as Saint Paul's Episcopal Church. More
leaves had carpeted the white stone steps, and Wilson stood
looking at them, one hand curved around a spear of the iron
fence, and then turned back. The sidewalk was empty but for
him, and he could hear the dry leaves crisping under his every
footfall.

The street lights were coming on by the time he had returned
to the square. The windows of his office were dark, but he could
hear the telephone ringing as he came up the steps. Mrs Veech
had, of course, locked up before she left, and while he was
searching out his key the phone stopped ringing. He went inside

and pressed the light switch. Again the phone began to jangle, and he reached across Mrs Veech's typewriter to pick it up.

'Mr Wilson? It's Sam Trimble here. I had your paper to serve on Paxton Morgan?'

'Yes,' Wilson said.

The deputy cleared his throat. 'I thought you might like to know we picked him up. He'd gone straight back to his own house, you know, like they do.'

'Yes,' Wilson said again.

'We got him cold, if it's any comfort,' Trimble said. 'The gun still warm and blood on his shoes.'

'That's all right,' Wilson said. 'He'll plead insanity.'

He was not often here at night, and the overhead fixture was harsh and bright, bouncing blurred reflections from the flat black of the window panes, making his inner office look too much like a cell. But if he used only the desk lamp, the shadows reached toward him so. And yet he was still afraid to go home! He shouldn't have said what he had to Trimble, though at the moment he could hardly bring himself to feel regret for it. And he was late by now; he'd better call.

'Daddy, you're late,' Lisa said.

'That's right, kiddo,' Wilson said. 'Where's your mother?'

'She's outside,' Lisa said. 'We were both of us. I'll go call her.'

'No, you don't need to,' Wilson said. 'Just tell her I'll be home shortly. Say I still have to stop by the store, though.' Hanging up, he glanced at his watch. A fine evening like this, his wife would certainly spend outdoors, not bothering to watch the evening news.

Flushed with relief, he pictured their long curving yard, thick with fireflies, as it would be now, green pinpoints flashing and hovering in the dark. The lights of the house glowed warm behind the calm silhouettes of his wife and his daughter, and inside, the kitchen steamed with the scent of supper waiting. Upstairs, beside his bedside lamp, lay the copy of *War and Peace* he'd been rereading this fall; at a half hour or so a night, it would last him to Christmas or longer. He thought now of Prince Andrey lying wounded on the battlefield, looking up into the reaches of the sky, that radical change in his perspective.

Still, he was not quite ready to leave. He picked up his pencil and tapped the butt of the dried eraser on the pad. At home, tonight or tomorrow or whenever he finally had to tell the story there, then the murders would be absolutely realized and the alternative of their somehow not having happened would be permanently shut off. Above, the fluorescent fixture made a sort of whining sound; Wilson thought that he could feel it in his teeth.

He turned the pencil over in his hand and set the point on the pad, but there was nothing much to write. The yellow paper was down at the bottom of a long pale shaft, stroked with faint parallel lines which signified nothing. If he could note down all the ingredients of the episode, then they could be comprehended, wrapped in a parcel of law and so managed. Wilson was a believer in due process. Without meaning to, he had become a bystander in this case.

It was only dizziness because he had skipped lunch, undoubtedly, and when he remembered that, the pad came floating back up toward him and the desk flattened and held still. There were some scratch marks on the paper, as if during his vertigo he had been trying unsuccessfully to draw a picture. Now he wondered if he had *known* what would happen, and if he had *known*, what then? He had left no legitimate measure untried but still he could picture himself crossing the lip above the lake house with a gun in his own hand, seeing the Volkswagen door still closed, the glass door of the house pulled to and Pax Morgan outlined against the glimmer of the lake like a paper silhouette.

The pencil slipped from his fingers and hit the desk with a clacking report that broke the fantasy. Pax was alive and the others were dead. His freedom was better protected than their safety – that would be one way of putting it. Simple. It was time to go home. Wilson turned off the desk lamp, stood up and pulled his coat down from the hat rack. Safer and better to have no freedom maybe, but no, you wouldn't say that. The humming stopped when he flicked the light switch by the door. No, you wouldn't say that, would you? In the dark of the hall he could not see his way; he went toward the vague light of the front window with one hand on the wall. No, you wouldn't, but what would you say?

7 14 1525 27 40.   18

Other titles available from Robinson Publishing

Honour the Dead (hardback)   Steven Saylor   **£16.99 [   ]**
Based on a string of horrifying crimes that took place more than a century ago, *Honour the Dead* vividly evokes a fledgling American South in the aftermath of the civil war. This enthralling Texas-based historical thriller is an exciting new departure from Steven Saylor's internationally popular series of Roman detective stories.

At End of Day (hardback)   George V. Higgins   **£17.99 [   ]**
Based around the true story of two gangsters and their unusual relationship with the city's top FBI men, *At End of Day* is packed with characters displaying a broad range of human nature illustrating the power of corruption and greed. A last novel by a rich and complex literary talent.

The Friends of Eddie Coyle   George V. Higgins   **£6.99 [   ]**
This fast-paced, dialogue-driven story established George V. Higgins as the unrivalled chronicler of American low-life. Made into a classic film of the same name starring Robert Mitchum, *The Friends of Eddie Coyle* has previously been chosen as one of the top 50 post-war American novels.

The Crimes of Charlotte Brontë   James Tully   **£7.99 [   ]**
The story of the lives of the Brontë family is as haunting and tragic as their novels: three sisters and an alcoholic brother shut in the bleak and claustrophobic parsonage at Haworth. Noted criminologist James Tully became fascinated by the inconsistencies of their lives and deaths and decided to tell the story in the form of a novel.

Robinson books are available from all good bookshops or direct from the publisher. Just tick the titles you want and fill in the form below.

TBS Direct
Colchester Road, Frating Green, Colchester, Essex CO7 7DW
Tel: +44 (0) 1206 255777
Fax: +44 (0) 1206 255914
Email: sales@tbs-ltd.co.uk

UK/BFPO customers please allow £1.00 for p&p for the first book, plus 50p for the second, plus 30p for each additional book up to a maximum charge of £3.00.

Overseas customers (inc. Ireland), please allow £2.00 for the first book, plus £1.00 for the second, plus 50p for each additional book.

Please send me the titles ticked above.

NAME (Block letters) . . . .

ADDRESS . . . .

. . . .

POSTCODE . . . .

I enclose a cheque/PO (payable to TBS Direct) for . . . .

I wish to pay by Switch/Credit card

Number . . . .

Card Expiry Date . . . .

Switch Issue Number . . . .